Praise for When Darkness Descends
(The Relevation Trilogy: Book I)

"A fresh and intriguing fantasy...the author introduces an array of memorable characters... fantasy aficionados will...find themselves engrossed in the story from beginning to end."

'Get it'. Kirkus Reviews

"G. W. Lücke's *When Darkness Descends* is an engrossing addition to the high fantasy catalogue. Lücke's characters have a vivid energy; the land and people of Enthilen are illuminated with care and detail, and the plot runs at a tight, satisfying pace."

Indi Reader (Approved)

"Lücke's strength lies undoubtedly in his ability to build worlds with immense depth. With intriguing plotlines and continuously evolving character arcs, the story keeps the readers engaged and anticipating the next sequence of events."

US Review of Books (Recommended)

"The exquisitely created fantasy world of Enthilen, and a horde of twists and turns as Tom and Grin are put against a set of formidable enemies keep the pages flying. Lücke strikes a perfect balance between stunning worldbuilding and layered narrative as his hero struggles against powerful enemies while on a journey of self-discovery. Lücke is a writer to watch for."

The Prairies Book Review

"With dynamic characters, interesting histories, and compelling drama, *When Darkness Descends* is a new fantasy that is sure to suck readers in. Engrossing and immersive, Lücke's epic fantasy is filled with charming creatures and mesmerising landscapes. With a dramatic, irresistibly exciting cliff-hanger as its finale, readers will be locked to the page and left wanting more."

Book Review Directory

"In the engrossing fantasy novel *When Darkness Descends*, a young man seeks revenge in a mythical world."

Foreword Clarion Reviews

AT THE END OF EVERYTHING

The Relevation Trilogy:
Book II

G. W. LÜCKE

With Distinction Publishing

Published in Australia by With Distinction Consultants
PO Box 97, St Marys, Tasmania 7215
https://withdistinctionconsultants.wordpress.com/
First published in Australia in 2021

Book website: https://relevationtrilogy.com
Author Facebook page: https://www.facebook.com/GWLucke/
Maps produced under commercial licence by G. W. Lücke
using Inkarnate software https://inkarnate.com/
Cover design, typesetting: WorkingType Studio

 A catalogue record for this
work is available from the
National Library of Australia

National Library of Australia Cataloguing-in-Publication Entry:
Creator: Lücke, G. W., author
Title: *At the End of Everything. The Relevation Trilogy: Book II.*
ISBN: 978-0-6488207-2-7 (Paperback)
ISBN: 978-0-6488207-3-4 (ePub)
BISAC Codes: FIC009020 FICTION/Fantasy/Epic;
FIC009100 FICTION/Fantasy/Action and Adventure

For Mum, who taught me to never give up

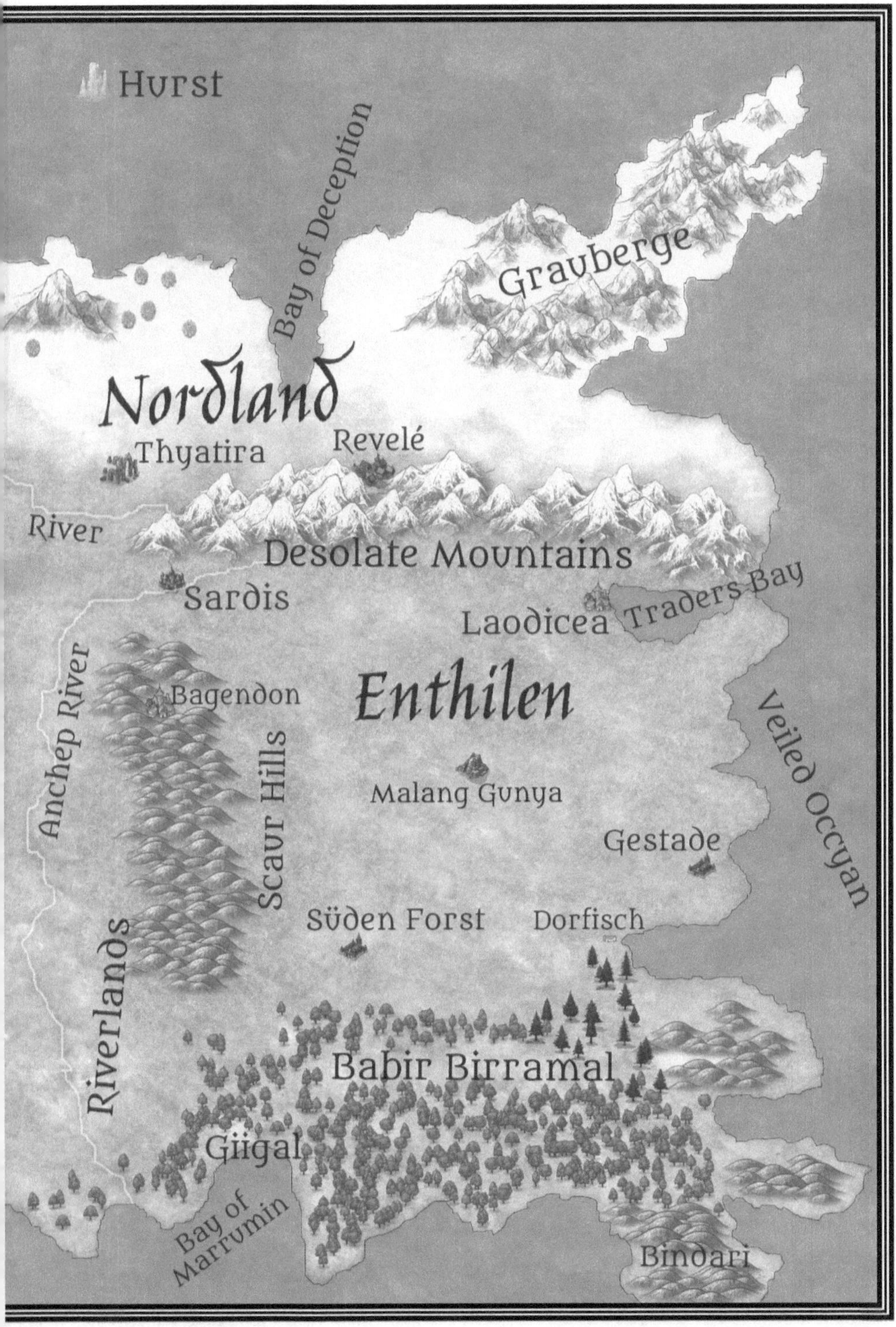
Hurst
Bay of Deception
Grauberge
Nordland
Thyatira
Revelé
River
Desolate Mountains
Sardis
Laodicea
Traders Bay
Anchep River
Bagendon
Enthilen
Veiled Occyan
Scaur Hills
Malang Gunya
Gestade
Süden Forst
Dorfisch
Riverlands
Babir Birramal
Giigal
Bay of Marrumin
Bindari

ENTHILEN

N

DESOLATE

THE FEIGN

SARDIS

ANCHEP RIVER

SLUMSTADT

RĀRIAN FALLS

GRŌZ WÜSTE

RIVERLANDS ESCARPMENT

BAGENDON

BREADELBANE

SCAUR HILLS

MOULDEWERP DWELL

RIVERLANDS

SÜDEN FORST

GERMALIAN CAMP

FLÜSSE

ERSTÜRMEN CAMP

FARMERS' FORT

ANCHEP DELTA

GIIGAL

BAY OF MARRUMIN

MOUNTAINS

LEVIATHAN STATUE

DETRANTÉ   LOKAN

TRADERS BAY

LAODICEA

VEILED OCCYAN

SAND BĕČE

ABROLOUS ISLES

BAY OF FIRES

MALANG GUNYA

DAMBAY PLAINS   GESTADE

DORFISCH

BRAMBLE ISLAND

RUFOUS

GRIN'S MILBI

BABIR BIRRAMAL
(GRŌZ FORST)

DALMAN

BINDARI

GADHANG

Rel`e*va"tion n. [L. *relevatio*, fr. *relevare*.]
A raising or lifting up.

Then I saw in the right hand of him who sat on the throne a scroll
with writing on both sides and sealed with seven seals. And I saw a
mighty angel proclaiming in a loud voice, "Who is worthy to break
the seals and open the scroll?"
(Revelation 5: 1 — 2).

~ What has gone before ~

My dear friend, hello. We've met before. Do you remember? I'm the tremor in the darkest corner of your mind, directing wayward thoughts down paths that lead to frightening places. Well, frightening for some. I believe the spire of greatness is built on foundations made from the sacrifices of the weak. Survival of the fittest, and all that.

I've been here from the very beginning, watching over this story. I have a vested interest in the outcome, after all. The Erstürmen call me Volerdie (*Voler-die*). I have other names. Quite a few, actually. You only need to remember Volerdie, the Divine Creator, for now. A long, long time ago, I ruled Ostamp, the world of the Erstürmen, Dobunni and many others, sitting on the throne of the dead in the city of Pergamos. But I abandoned Ostamp when an opportunity arose to spread my influence further. You'll learn more about that as the story progresses.

Anyway, enough of the introductions, it's time to remind you about what happened in the first part of our story. I'll start with Malphas; I know him best. His journey began at seventeen yarles of age when he murdered his father, King Alaric, and became King of Enthilen. Malphas called himself Oldaric back then. He killed his father because he wanted to be the one to rediscover the lost city of Pergamos. But King Oldaric floundered for the next thirty-three yarles, his ambition of discovery enslaved by the desire to retain the throne. When Oldaric spurned Erstürmen tradition and refused to abdicate at fifty yarles of age, his eldest son, Ewald, took the crown by force and banished him from the royal city of Sardis. The humiliation was the encouragement Oldaric needed to resume his search for Pergamos and all the treasures I had left behind when I fled Ostamp for another world.

During his wandering, Oldaric reinvented himself as Malphas, the Worshipful Master, and his ambition grew. Malphas wants me to return to Ostamp and lead the Erstürmen into an everlasting paradise. It's a noble ambition, although the methods used to achieve it may be questioned by some. And, of course, Malphas being Malphas, he wants to rule by my side in paradise. Every grand ambition has an element of selfishness to it.

What does Malphas need to fulfil his aspiration? You'll find out soon. For now, all you have to remember is that Malphas can't succeed without Tom Anderson, the young man who travelled from Earth to Ostamp (Enthilen, to be precise) using the eyes of lost souls. (Tom was tricked into using the eyes by a draughoul sent to Earth by Malphas).

Poor Tom, his life riddled with guilt because he failed to stop his grandmother from being murdered. But now he's in Enthilen, and he's convinced his grandmother's murderer is here too. Is this his chance to seek justice and redemption? A stranger in a strange land, Tom yearns to find his grandmother's killer and return home to Earth. But Malphas sent one of his tainted grells, Eroberung, to capture Tom. How did Malphas know that Tom had arrived in Enthilen? Do you remember the glowing eye sockets of the beast that crowns the throne of the dead? *My throne.* They were like a signal light to a ship, telling Malphas that someone had used the eyes of lost souls (also called the 'dark eyes') to travel between worlds. Almost certainly, Tom Anderson.

Eroberung nearly caught Tom at Süden Forst, but the young man proved surprisingly resilient — and he had help. One of those giant stone-grells, Grin, befriended Tom and became his guide. Then Dobunni rebels Jacob and Thaly got involved. Together, the four companions thwarted Eroberung's pursuit by escaping into the Scaur Hills, only to find themselves captured by mouldewerps. Strange little creatures those. Dwarrow is the cunning one. He knows more than he'll ever tell you, and he knew about the young man from another world. Dwarrow revealed some of his secrets to Tom and helped him understand why he'd been brought to Enthilen. The little werp also saved Grin's life, and Tom, Grin, Dwarrow, Jacob and Thaly all travelled to Bagendon, the Dobunni stronghold in the Scaur Hills. During the Pledge Feste, a mix of hope, stupidity and drunkenness saw Tom pledge allegiance to the Dobunni rebels. I wonder if he'll regret that one day?

While Tom sought redemption and a path home, other events played out across Enthilen and beyond. To you, they may have seemed like sideshows. Interesting, tangential sub-plots to colour-in the black and white sketch of Ostamp. But every act you saw will affect what happens to Tom in the end. To whether or not Malphas realises his ambition, and I, Volerdie, return to Ostamp. So, my friend, these 'sideshows' are too important to dismiss.

Leaving Tom for a moment, we turn our attention to Prince Adalwolf and that drunken fool King Ewald who lorded over Enthilen — a failing kingdom ripe for a rebellion of sorts, a temptation irresistible to Malphas. While Malphas needs Tom to realise his ambition, he also needs Adalwolf. Why? The following pages will reveal the answer. Suffice to say that when Prince Adalwolf is crowned king, he becomes an asset to Malphas. You see, Malphas' powers of influence over the Erstürmen are still limited. For Adalwolf to become king, Malphas had to dispose of King Ewald and eliminate Ewald's brothers (Prince Hadufuns, Prince Gerulf and Prince Widald) lest they challenge for the throne. As usual, Malphas relied on his tainted grells, Ende and Hunger, to complete this gruesome task.

Malphas hardly flinched at the murder of his four sons, but it's all in the name of discovering paradise. The end justifies the means, doesn't it?

What about Grinnian stone-grell? Grin. Tom's loyal and trusting friend. He stood by Tom under the most trying of circumstances. How long will his resolve last? By following Tom, Grin is estranged from his family and his beloved forest of Babir Birramal. He's due to be initiated soon, and the young stone-grell will have extra burdens to bear.

And then there's Athalee of Bagendon. Thaly. The brave Dobunni warrior now also snared in the tangled web surrounding Tom. Her parents abandoned her as a baby, and she's been proving herself to the Dobunni rebels ever since. What happens if the rebels are wiped from the face of Enthilen? Who does she turn to then? At the moment, she's adopted Tom as her charge to protect him from shared enemies. The companionship of the Dobunni rebellion still lives in her heart.

What about Caeli, the clichéd 'princess locked in a tower' in Sardis' Sunrise Keep? Like many parts of this tale, Caeli's story is not all as it seems. Did her flirtatious innocence distract you from things of much greater importance? If so, you may consider reading the first parts of her story again. She's a key that opens the most important doors, especially for young Tom. And she's not immune to sacrificing others to achieve higher goals. Her guard and friend, Jürgen, died to save Tom because of Caeli's intervention.

Jurelle Stansfield, the Traitor General, is also an essential part of this story. He turned his back on the Dobunni rebels to fight for King Ewald because he loved Princess Genevea, Ewald's sister. Leading Erstürmen soldiers in the Riverlands War, Jurelle was captured by the Germalians. They had much to tell him before releasing him back to the Erstürmen.

Their words will define the rest of Jurelle's journey until his last breath. But at the moment, all he cares about is rescuing his family from Sardis, where Ewald's death has caused an upheaval in the balance of power and duplicitous men like Hunfrid, Rostard, and Anselm are ready to cling to authority by whatever means necessary.

I imagine you're also wondering about Rosalie's part in this tale? The apprentice metalsmith living in Sardis' fifth circle. She grows more distant from her family each day, and her life is about to take a most disturbing turn. How might her story affect Tom? Well, you had a hint the last time you saw her. But the hint won't materialise until much later.

After Tom pledged allegiance to the Dobunni rebels, they enlisted him in a rebel plot to assassinate King Ewald and Prince Adalwolf in the inner circle of Sardis. The plot failed, and Tom managed to escape the clutches of Eroberung once again thanks to Princess Caeli and Dwarrow, the little werp guiding Tom through a secret passage out of the royal city and to safety.

Reunited with Grin and Thaly, Tom rode to war in Laodicea, where the Dobunni army led by Jacob, Thaly's closest friend, had marched to fight against a barbarian invasion. Tom also believed that his grandmother's murderer would be found in Laodicea. But Malphas finally captured Tom, and the most bizarre ritual played out atop Hansen's Bluff overlooking Laodicea, where Prince Adalwolf attempted to steal Tom's soul using the dark eyes.

At the end of the first part of our story, it appeared that Grin and Thaly had rescued Tom, while Jacob paid for the intervention with his life. Now, Tom, Grin and Thaly will face the most significant challenges of their young lives. Not all of them will overcome these challenges.

~ Prologue ~

Sunlight poured into the ruined monastery through crumbling archways perched high in the Desolate Mountains above the town of Revelé. Hál turned from the light and tilted her head back as a draughoul servant lifted a wooden cup to her lips and trickled cold water into her mouth. The chain of the silver lemniscate hanging around Hál's neck pinched her skin, and sunlight refracting through gemstones embedded in the weighty jewel sent a rainbow of colours dancing across the monastery walls. The shimmering kaleidoscope reminded her of the burden and treasure she'd borne for a generation.

The draughoul removed the cup and stood beside Hál's stone pedestal.

"Thank you, Pida," said Hál. "The season of storms does not usually bring such warm days."

"The cycle of seasons forever changes."

"Yes, you're right. Did I ever tell you the story of my ancestor, Lycious?"

"I cannot remember it."

"Then it's a nice day for a story." Hál nestled the stump of her legless torso into the silky white cushion sitting atop the pedestal and closed her eyes, reaching inside her mind for ancient memories borrowed from many others, but that now belonged to her.

"Long ago, before the stone-grells arrived, even before mouldewerps spread across the Dambay Plains, pilgrims and explorers from distant shores wandered the forests and mountains of the land the Erstürmen call Enthilen. Some sought treasure, others knowledge. The pilgrim Lycious desired both, her quest driven by whispers of the lost city of Pergamos where once ruled Volerdie, a man some believed to be a god and Divine Creator of everything in our world.

"Lycious' journey began in her homeland, far from the shores of Enthilen, where she spent her youth pursuing knowledge of the lost city until one story consumed her entire being; the fall of Pergamos and the flight of Volerdie from the world he created. She learned that a cataclysmic event destroyed Pergamos, where buildings tumbled, and paved streets buckled underfoot, wiping the city and most of its people from living memory. Those left alive claimed Volerdie himself ruined the city in a fit of jealousy. Bitter envy of another world whose beauty he coveted above all else. Amid the chaos of Volerdie's Wrath, the Divine Creator disappeared, but Lycious believed the lost city's ruins now lay hidden under the soil, housing a wealth of treasures. No greater legacy was the written word of the Divine Creator, *Da Und Sepcarture* — the First Scripture, for it contained Volerdie's Lore and many secrets.

"In the town of Maline in the land of Oder, Lycious stumbled across an ancient library in a dusty basement under the town's watchtower. On a damp, decaying shelf, she discovered a text of fragile pages bound together with frayed string. With obeisant fingers, Lycious turned to the first page. A map scratched onto the parchment in faded black ink showed a land across the ocean west of Oder. In the middle of vast plains, someone had marked a cross beside the words *Pergamos, Throne of the Creator.*

"Lycious stole the book, gathered supplies and began a pilgrimage to find Pergamos. In a canoe, she travelled alone for seven seasons, paddling from one island to the next until finally reaching the eastern shore of Enthilen. Dehydrated and famished, Lycious stumbled onto a freshwater pool, luminously clear and nestled at the foot of limestone cliffs. Drinking from its store, the pond replenished her strength and will, encouraging her to continue the journey. With the moons and stars as guides, she travelled south-west until reaching the place where the map showed Pergamos once stood. But there, she found only dirt and rocks.

"Undeterred, Lycious dug. For six days, using bare hands and sharpened sticks, she burrowed into the loam soil of the plains until blood dripped from swollen fingers and calloused palms screamed with every thrust. Exhausted and ready to abandon hope, her arms jolted when the digging stick hit a large, flat stone. She gouged at the soil around the rock until she'd uncovered all its edges. This is it, she told herself. This is the way in.

"Prising a thick branch under one edge of the stone, Lycious dislodged it from its resting place, exposing blackness and emptiness below. She pushed the rock aside and cast a firebrand into the darkness. It landed on the floor of a chamber right under her feet. She jumped into the void and collected the torch, sweeping its flames through dark corners that hadn't seen the light for generations, revealing a labyrinth of snaking passages lined with statues and pillars. Forgotten rooms and halls full of the trappings of a civilisation long gone, now basked in rare illumination. Pergamos unveiled by the flames.

"Lycious searched day and night, unable to tell one from the other in the underworld. She discarded numerous treasures, looking for the one thing that had plagued her thoughts for so long; the First Scripture. Finally, her persistence reaped its reward. Behind two colossal oak doors encased in metal, which squealed as she squeezed her slight frame between them, Lycious found a cavernous, sumptuous hall. At its centre, a throne of gruesome contortions haunted the darkness, desiccated bodies entwined to support the authority of the Divine Creator.

She examined every surface of the throne, casting the light from the firebrand into every shadow and prising her fingers into each crevice until something gave way. Her heart skipped as she opened a secret compartment and withdrew a scroll tied with cured human skin and sealed with seven wax seals.

"Holding the parchment to the torchlight revealed words scrawled in blood on both sides. Not a drop of saliva lined Lycious' dry mouth. She gasped for air, forcing it into her lungs as disjointed thoughts raced through her mind. Was she worthy to break the seals? Would Volerdie strike her down?

"Lycious refused to abandon the journey at the moment of her most significant discovery. She broke the seven seals and cut the cured skin, reverently unfurling the sacred document. With no doubt in her mind, she'd discovered *Da Und Sepcarture*, the First Scripture. Although the language was a vestige of another age, Lycious had studied antediluvian languages in her homeland. Days and nights blended into one as she read the text over and over, her attention always returning to a single passage: *Let the marked take the dark eyes from the throned beast and hold tightly. Unto them, eternal life may be granted.*

"Her mind erupted in wild thoughts. What treasure immortality would be! I must be one of the marked. One of Volerdie's chosen, she believed. She again sought the throne, but the eye sockets of the beast's head sitting atop the backrest were empty. Lycious searched all the rooms and passages for days without success before deciding the dark eyes had been stolen and hidden in the lands surrounding Pergamos.

"Taking the scripture, Lycious began a new pilgrimage to find the eyes. She searched for the rest of her life until old and nagging bones pleaded for an end. Eventually, a debilitating paranoia crippled her mind. A consuming terror that someone would steal the First Scripture and uncover its secrets before she did. One day, hiding in a cave above the shore of a wild ocean, a piercing shriek came from the clouds, and she rushed out to find a snow-white griffin flying overhead. Without thinking, she ran onto the beach to revel in the wonder of the mysterious creature. The griffin swooped down, grabbing Lycious in its talons and carrying her to a nest on a pinnacle of rock surrounded by perilous seas."

"Hurst?"

"Yes, Pida. The griffin had carried her to Hurst, the lonely stone tower in the Nordargen Sea. Lycious thought the creature would tear her asunder, but something drew it away. Alone again, she refused to accept the griffin's nest as her grave and found the top of a stairway carved into the rock on which the nest lay. Cautiously, she descended the stair."

Hál opened her eyes and faced her servant.

"Does the story end there?" asked Pida.

"Oh, no. That is only the beginning."

* * * *

"I found it, brother," Oldaric crowed. "I found the First Scripture. I scoured these lands for yarles and now it's mine."

"The scripture! What does it reveal?" Widukind leaned forward, almost toppling from his stool into the campfire burning atop the grey soil of The Feign. In the far distance, a faint light flickered like a star, marking the location of the royal city of Sardis.

Oldaric smiled at the eagerness plastered all over his younger brother's face. "It has many secrets, dear brother. *Countless* secrets." He drew a knife from his belt and held it above the fire, twisting the blade in his hand as firelight bounced off its keen edge and disappeared into the night. Flashing a wicked grin, he plunged the knife into his own chest.

Widukind gasped.

Oldaric cackled like a drunk witch, the bone handle of the knife protruding from his ribcage dancing along with the mirth.

"Take it," said Oldaric.

"What?"

"Pull the dagger from my flesh."

With a trembling hand, Widukind reached across and yanked the knife from Oldaric's chest. Eyes wide, he examined the clean, bloodless blade.

Oldaric knew Widukind idolised him. He hoped this new magic would fuel the adoration. "Eternal life, Widu. I've become immortal."

"How is this possible?"

"Like most of our kin, you forget Erstürmen history. Generations ago, our ancestors christened this land Enthilen and lived at peace under the watchful eye of our Divine Creator in the city of Pergamos. But, when the city fell and Volerdie fled, the scattering of ancestors still alive abandoned Enthilen and almost expunged Pergamos from all memory. The machinations of Erstürmen kings then consumed our time and distracted our attention from the only ambition of any importance." Oldaric took a charred tree branch from the ground, swivelled on his seat and stoked the fire. The glowing amber hue illuminated the stunned expression on Widukind's face as flames licked the dampness from the night.

Oldaric lingered, feeding the silent anticipation before continuing, "My banishment from Sardis by the myopic Ewald six yarles ago was a sign from the Divine Creator. Volerdie freed my thoughts and time, so I could complete his bidding. In Laodicea's library, I found a text recounting the story of Lycious, a fortuitous thief who stumbled on a scroll of considerable importance. Presented as no more than an apologue, the story still had a truthfulness I couldn't shake. From the description, I guessed what the scroll might be. The author of Lycious' tale claimed she was last seen travelling through Detranté to Nordland. I followed in Lycious' footsteps, walking until the bleak northland met the sea. Yet, I found nothing. No trace of her journey. No person that knew of her existence. I was about to turn back when I remembered Hurst, the tall, rocky outcrop in the Nordargen Sea where once griffins nested and the Erstürmen kings of old hid their treasure. Maybe Lycious also hid a treasure there? I had to find out, dear brother, plundering a boat from a wild Nordman to travel through the waves. Thirst and hunger almost defeated me until, finally, I saw a stone spire jutting from the horizon and ocean swell crashing onto jagged rocks. I'd found Hurst."

Oldaric threw the branch into the fire and reached under his stool for a silver goblet half-full of meduz. He took a swig and wiped his mouth. Still examining the knife, as if blood would soon seep from its blade, Widukind's eyes yearned with devoted curiosity. Oldaric knew then, he'd captured his younger brother's fascination.

"Over rocks and through crumbling passages, I searched until I discovered a stone door hidden within a wall and sealed from the inside. With toil and torment, I broke the seal, revealing a room that surely hadn't been visited for generations. A tombstone rested in a corner with one word scratched onto its surface: *Lycious*. It appeared she'd prepared her own grave and buried herself alive. I opened the lid of the stone coffin and found a skeleton inside clutching a threadbare scroll. After prising the document from bony fingers, I cast my eyes over the bloodied text, convinced I'd found the First Scripture. King Giltbert died right on top of it, the fool's skeleton and armour scattered across the crest of the pinnacle, likely the remains of a griffin banquet. If he had more wits, he could have escaped the beast's talons and found immortality instead of death."

"I still don't understand how you discovered eternal life, brother."

"You don't *discover* eternal life, Widu. You *earn* it. Remember how our father used to tell us the eyes of lost souls were a door to eternity?"

"That's only a metaphor. The dark eyes don't exist."

Oldaric reached into his coat pocket and withdrew a clenched fist, holding it towards the firelight. He beamed and spread his fingers, revealing the dark eyes sitting in his palm.

"They're real." Widukind's mouth hung open, the knife dropping from his hand into the dirt.

"After studying the First Scripture, I began my search for Volerdie's throne — the throne of the dead — and for the eyes of lost souls. In one of Lycious' pockets, I found a crude map. Before it disintegrated in my hands, I saw where she'd marked the location of Pergamos. The Erstürmen settlers led by King Faramund didn't find it, hidden under the foul temples of those pagan grells. Even when our father, Alaric, routed the last stone-grell from Malang Gunya, he was unaware the heathen city stood atop Pergamos, the one place he longed to find. It's a tragedy he died before he could begin the search. And he was so close, Widukind. So close."

Oldaric took another sip of meduz. "It fell on me to brave the atrocities of Malang Gunya and discover the entrance to Pergamos, deep under the soil of the Dambay Plains. Searching every corner of every underground room, I found a grand hall worthy of a throne, but it contained only the dais on which a throne might sit. As I stumbled in the dark, something hidden under a pile of rubble glinted in my torchlight. I swept away the dirt and uncovered the eyes of lost souls. The First Scripture explains their use, and the lore did not fail me, brother. I've used the eyes and to me has been bestowed the greatest gift of all."

Widukind sucked in nervous breaths, gasping for every detail of the revelations laid out before him. "Can I read the scripture, Oldaric?"

"It's written in a language you'll not understand. I spent yarles learning to interpret its meaning. There's no need for you to do the same. I can guide you." Oldaric placed the dark eyes back in his pocket. "Why do the Erstürmen revere the marked?"

"Because we believe a birthmark is a portent to a long life."

"Our mother was overjoyed when you were born with a naevus on your leg. Now she had two sons with birthmarks. She must have understood their true worth. Volerdie has marked us, Widukind. Chosen *us* for a special purpose. The First Scripture describes the significance of these marks. When a marked child is born in our world, another child with the same mark is born in Volerdie's adopted world at exactly the same time. The world to which the Creator absconded when Pergamos fell. This child is your birth twin. They won't look like you, but you will always share the same mark. It is the soul of your birth twin that you must capture with the dark eyes. It's their life you must end if you wish to become immortal."

"How is it possible to find my twin if they live in another world?"

"Clench the eyes, one in each hand, and you'll be transported to the world where Volerdie fled. I've been there. It's a vile and desperate place ruled by machines. You won't want to linger long. Through fortitude and cunning, you must find your birth twin. Then, with the dark eyes grasped tightly in your right hand, hold your fist against their heart. They'll twist and scream, but you must remain strong. Keep the eyes next to their chest. When their soul is taken, trapped within the dark eyes, only then will you be able to return home, bringing with you the gift of immortality."

Widukind buried his face in tremulous hands. "Oldaric, you're making my head spin."

Oldaric dug his fingers into Widukind's shoulder. "Steel yourself, little brother. There's more to reveal. About the young Prince Adalwolf and another child, and the blood connection linking us all."

~ Chapter 1 ~

Thaly twisted in mid-air and plunged feet first into the pool of reflection at the base of Hansen's Bluff in Laodicea. Grin landed flat on his back beside her, clutching Tom to his chest, shielding their injured friend from the impact of the fall. The shock of the cold water snatched the air from Thaly's lungs, but also sent a surge of energy through her body. She kicked upwards, breaking the surface and swimming over to Grin, who struggled to hold his head above water. The giant stone-grell raised his arms high, fighting to keep a limp Tom from going under.

"I can take him!" yelled Thaly.

Grin lowered Tom to the surface of the lake as Thaly flipped onto her back and looped her forearms under Tom's armpits, resting his body on her chest. She kicked with all her strength, pushing to the shore as the chop foamed over her face.

Lurking at the edge of the lake, a hunched umbra beckoned to her. "Over here! Give me y'hand."

Thaly didn't have time to be cautious, sinking under Tom's weight. She freed one of her arms and thrust a hand out to the wiry figure who dragged her and Tom ashore. Diving back into the lake, she swam to Grin, who had almost disappeared amid the froth and bubble of his thrashing arms. Thaly ducked under the water and tried to pull the drowning giant up, but he sank like a sack of stones. She broke the surface, stealing a mouthful of air as the tip of a wooden pole smacked into the water beside her. Grin's bald head emerged from the depths in a last gasp for air, and Thaly groped blindly, grabbing his hand and wrapping it around the pole. Treading water, she held her breath, hoping Grin would grasp the lifesaver and pull himself to shore. She relaxed when his fingers tensed and he reached one enormous hand in front of the other along the pole.

The hunched stranger teetered on the embankment, straining to anchor the length of timber by lying over its end. He managed to hold on long enough for Thaly and Grin to drag themselves onto dry land.

On hands and knees, Grin's drooped shoulders shuddered as wracking coughs spewed water from his mouth. He caught his breath and glanced at Tom. "Is he alive?"

A shallow breath inflated Tom's chest, answering Grin's question.

Thaly nodded. "We need to get him to safety."

"I gotta ship," said the sinewy rescuer. "Well, she ain't mine. I'm the skullard to Cap'n Adcock, so I runs things and all. Me name's Whibly."

Two grell shadows hurtled down the stairs cut into the limestone of Hansen's Bluff, their flaming torches bouncing light across the night sky.

"Seems like them coloured grells are after ya. Must have stirred up a hornet's nest of trouble on the bluff. I seen it through me lookin' glass. Why'd they have this fella tied to a cross?" asked Whibly, pointing at Tom.

Thaly ignored the question and stared at the top of the bluff. Jacob Seamaster, her trainer and friend, would jump soon, and she needed to be ready to rescue him from the lake.

Whibly continued nattering like an annoying fly hovering beside her ear. "Leastways, I don't want to be stuck here when them grells arrive." He gathered a bulging sack, the contents banging and clanging together as he heaved it over his hunched shoulder. "I'm headin' back to the docks. Y'comin'? We'll be ready to drop oars soon enough."

Grin picked up Tom and stood. "There is nowhere to hide in Laodicea, Thaly. This ship may offer a chance to escape."

Thaly clenched her jaw. "We can't leave without..." Where's Jacob? He should have jumped by now.

Cradling Tom in the crux of one enormous arm, Grin placed his other hand on her shoulder and shook his head. "We need to go. Jacob did not survive. I saw it."

She tried to swallow the painful lump in her throat. "I'll wait here in case he jumps. I have to wait."

"This ain't no time to be debatin'," said Whibly. "Them coloured grells are almost at the bottom of the stairs."

Tom's young, unmoving face with eyes pressed closed did nothing to ease Thaly's hurt. Why's he so important? she asked herself. Why did Jacob have to die for him?

Her panting breaths formed clouds of white amid the cold night air. She clutched at the empty scabbard hanging from her belt, remembering she'd dropped her sword on top of Hansen's Bluff when Krieg's arrow sliced across her arm. Grin had also lost his weapons, but Thaly had a knife tucked into the side of her boot if Whibly turned on them. And something else pressed into her thigh, jammed into the sodden front pocket of her pants; two glass baubles of obsidian black with a lick of flame in the centre. She'd taken them from Adalwolf during their fight, guessing they were important. They might even be the eyes of lost souls Grin and Jacob had spoken about. Could she use them to steal some-one's soul?

Thaly snapped at Grin, "Dammit. Alright, let's go."

They chased Whibly, who scuttled along the cobbled streets of Laodicea like a crab across wet sand. Although his spine was twisted, such that his right shoulder blade stuck out well above his left, nimble feet skipped across the pavers, eyes darting into every corner of the besieged city. And he talked the entire time.

"Our ship's the *Vulking*. Merchant vessel she is. We was tryin' to leave before the war started. Got stranded on the docks. Lucky for us, them barbarians ain't interested in simple traders. When their ships landed, they swarmed into the streets like flies after rottin' meat. We should be able to get out to sea now, no problems. Cap'n Adcock will see y'right. Don't worry 'bout that."

Thaly knew they couldn't stay in Laodicea. And this wasn't the time to mourn the loss of Jacob. The tainted grells would find them. Those monstrosities with red, black or pale skin. They would take Tom back to her enemies and finish whatever they'd started on Hansen's Bluff. And it seemed the barbarian raiders were determined to tear the city apart. With all other paths of escape cut off, travelling out of Traders Bay on a ship might be something her pursuers wouldn't expect. She needed to accept she was leaving Jacob behind.

*   *   *   *

Sword drawn, Master of the Southern Vale, Lady Lily LáDown, led Dealhia Rossingbird and two dozen Dobunni soldiers in a chaotic retreat from the Docklands. The barbarians had taken charge of the quarter, setting buildings alight with raging fires that spat flames into the streets like mythical dragons. Embers rained down on the beaten citizens of Laodicea, ashen black and burning timber shattering against cobblestones in a hail of sparks as walls fell like dominoes. Panic had gripped the city's residents. They packed shoulder-to-shoulder around Lily, the crowd staggering as one to the refuge of the Southern Vale.

The clang of duelling swords rang in Lily's ears as she pushed forward, ducking every time the hideous wail of flaming lumps of tar launched from barbarian mangonels whistled overhead before exploding into another home. Turning briefly against the fleeing tide, she tossed her shield away, sheathed her sword and grabbed the forearm of an injured Dobunni soldier, pulling her close to avoid being trampled. Together they brushed past a wild stone-grell who headed for the Docklands carrying a half-naked young man who looked to have seen no more than sixteen harvest seasons.

Why's the grell running *towards* danger? Lily thought.

On the Southern Vale's north-eastern boundary, she helped the injured soldier through the defence line established by the Dobunni rebels from Bagendon and handed her to a healer. While the line offered respite, it wouldn't hold for long once the barbarians arrived in number. The remainder of the Bagendon force held the south wall against the barbarian army encamped outside Laodicea. Soon, Lily expected Hunger's militia to make a push from the King's Quarter, squeezing the Southern Vale like an over-ripe grape under a giant black boot.

She rushed into the Master's Hall in the centre of the Southern Vale, seeking the counsel of Field Commander Kenelm, who paced around a crowded meeting room in the centre of the hall.

"How are our defences holding, Commander?"

"They're strained to breaking point, Master Lily. Even with the help of the Bagendon rebels, the south wall won't hold. We'll be overrun soon."

"Who's the leader of the rebels?"

Decked in chainmail from shoulder to knee, a short man with long blonde hair stepped forward. "For the moment, Master Lily, I am."

"You look too young to lead an army. What's your name?"

"Prime Lieutenant Maxton Nash. Our Field Commander, Jacob Seamaster, led a scouting party into the King's Quarter, but they were ambushed. No more than a dozen escaped. Jacob wasn't among them. Another leader, Edith Astley, fell in battle when we fought our way through the sieging barbarians and into the Southern Vale."

A weary Lily bent forward and braced her palms atop a table. The leather straps fixing the metal breastplate over her shirt tightened, threatening to squeeze the air from her lungs. Fighting wars and planning military strategies were as foreign to her as the barbarians attacking Laodicea. Hair drenched in sweat clung to her neck. She tried to shake it off as she absorbed the battle formations represented by little wooden markers placed over a map of the city. The people around the table expected her to lead. War allowed no time for doubt.

"We have to hold the south wall and the north-east defence at all costs." She turned to Maxton. "Where's Ryder?"

"He led a group to Sardis to assassinate King Ewald and Prince Adalwolf."

"A misguided folly. Ewald's already dead. The Erstürmen claim Dobunni rebels ambushed the king. I don't believe a word of it..." As Lily spoke, a clay pot full of burning pitch smashed through a window of the meeting room, setting tapestries and furniture alight. Soldiers rushed to quell the flames while Lily held steadfast and barked her orders. "Field Commander Kenelm, continue your defence of the south wall." The lanky commander nodded and marched from the room. Lily stood tall, placing her hand on Maxton's shoulder. "Lieutenant, do you know this city?"

"I was raised in the Terraces."

"Good. I need half of your army defending our boundary with the Docklands and scouts watching the King's Quarter in case the black grell's militia attack. Can you do that?"

"Yes, Master Lily."

"Hold the lines for as long as you can. We need time to plan our escape from Laodicea." Lily turned from Maxton and shouted above the crowd, "Dealhia, are you still with me?"

Dealhia's sturdy frame waddled into the light of the wavering candles melted into a chandelier hanging above the battle table. Dressed in the leather armour of the Dockland's Guard over a billowing floral shirt, and a skullcap balanced on unruly auburn hair, she looked as out of place as Lily felt.

"I'm here," said Dealhia.

"I need your counsel a moment longer."

Lily marched from the meeting room, stepping over the injured fighters strewn across the main hallway, and led Dealhia to her private quarters within the Master's Hall. She opened the door, and Dealhia gasped as they entered the room.

"How's the patient, Audie?" asked Lily.

"He's slowly recovering."

Lily's personal healer, Audie, glided around a heavily bandaged man lying on Lily's bed and lifted a loose dressing to apply a poultice to a festering wound. The sweet, medicinal aroma of honey mixed with meduz and animal fat wafted into Lily's nostrils.

"Who is he?" Dealhia hovered over the scarred face partially hidden beneath bandages.

"Prince Hadufuns Heine," said Lily. "The only one of Oldaric's sons to yet live."

"He wasn't murdered with the others?"

Lily slumped into a padded chair in the corner of the room, letting her arms fall outside the ornate armrests of wrought iron covered in plated silver. She'd slept here before, watching over Hadufuns during the first nights of his recovery. Guarding him in case his attackers came to finish the task. She would give anything to fall asleep now and wash away the exhaustion, dread and ceaseless doubts shadowing her thoughts. Behind her mask of bravery and decisiveness, a younger woman havered alone in a world of second guesses.

Lily scratched a fleck of silver from the armrest and rolled it around in slender fingers trembling with liability. "On the night of the assassination, I went to Widald's house with plans to broker a truce between the Erstürmen and Dobunni, desperately hoping we could face the barbarians together. His wife told me he was at work. As my guards and I approached the Master's Hall in the King's Quarter, we saw tainted grells and an old man dressed in a hooded robe leave the building. We held back in the shadows, then searched the hall for Widald. One of my guards found them in a back room. The bodies of three brothers lying together in a lifeless heap, or so we thought until Hadufuns gasped a breath. We brought him back here and placed him under Audie's care. She's the best healer I have." Lily paused when screams filtered in from outside, but her emotions had dulled to the sounds of war. "We cremated the bodies of Widald and Gerulf, spreading the news that *all* of the king's brothers had been murdered. There's no need for anyone to know the truth yet."

"Why save an Erstürmen royal?" asked Dealhia. "Should Adalwolf fall, Hadufuns will be crowned king and could rally our enemy against us."

"He's not in a fit state to rally anybody, and from what I know of the Wandering Prince, he has no ambition for power. Yet, he might serve other purposes to our advantage. Whatever the ends, we should keep him close and alive."

The patient rolled onto his side and grimaced. The petite Audie, her black hair covered by a white toque fixing a short, translucent veil in place, rested the back of her hand on the prince's forehead, but he brushed her off.

"Can you speak, Hadufuns?" asked Dealhia.

"I can talk and I'm not deaf. I hear your plans to gain something from my life. They will come to naught. You should have let me die with my brothers. I'm no use to you or anyone."

"At the least, your counsel may assist us," said Lily. "Barbarians camp outside our south wall. More of them have raised the Docklands. The black grell, Hunger, is the new Master of the King's Quarter, and his militia will soon test our flank. We're being pushed on all sides. Do you see a way out?"

"The old man you saw leaving the Master's Hall was the exiled King Oldaric, my father."

"He murdered his own sons?" said Dealhia, her mouth staying agape.

"Though our veins share the same blood, Oldaric won't hesitate at the letting should it bring him closer to the Divine Creator."

"Oldaric is the Worshipful Master the tainted grells speak of," said Lily. "The one who now calls himself Malphas. You've been repeating his name in your nightmares since we brought you here."

"What purpose does all this serve?" asked Dealhia.

"The return of Volerdie to Enthilen," said Hadufuns. "My father has an all-consuming desire to resurrect the Divine Creator's kingdom and rule by his side in an eternal paradise. One long-prophesied by Erstürmen curates, if you have a mind to believe them. Malphas certainly does, and he's willing to destroy this world to see the prophecy fulfilled. Laodicea will burn. If you stay here, you'll burn with it."

"A rightful claim to the Erstürmen throne could complicate his plans," said Dealhia. "That's why he tried to kill you and your brothers."

"My guess, as well," said Lily, "and why I expect Malphas was behind the death of Ewald. Yet, Adalwolf still lives."

"For now," said Hadufuns. "Adalwolf will be proclaimed king, and Malphas will convince him to lead his subjects to Pergamos where once Volerdie reigned. When I was a child, my father talked endlessly about the rebirth of the lost city. The transformation of Enthilen to what it once was."

"Where is this city?" asked Lily.

"The stone-grells built Malang Gunya over its ruins."

"Once Adalwolf leads the Erstürmen to Pergamos, then what?" asked Dealhia.

Hadufuns winced, and Audie, her pale skin flushed like a pink rose, turned to Lily. "He needs to rest now. He's still frail."

Lily sighed. She would like nothing better than to drift away in this chair. Let her mind wander back to the Abrolous Isles, where she had lived a simpler life. But such luxuries were for another time and other people. She lifted herself from the chair and nodded to Dealhia, and together they returned to the meeting room to plan the escape from Laodicea.

* * * *

Carnage littered the docks along Traders Bay. The barbarians ransacked and burned every building, hoarding whatever treasures they could find and tossing broken furniture, bedding and crockery into the water. Carrying Tom, Grin lumbered after Whibly, who dashed among the plunderers' discard piles like a red-backed skink chasing beetles. Without missing a step, the seafarer scooped down and snatched a gold necklace from the salt-soaked timbers of the wharf, dropping the jewel into the pocket of his waistcoat before glancing over his shoulder.

"Wait up!" Thaly yelled from behind Grin.

Whibly halted. Grin joined him, balancing his young friend up against his chest. Foam dribbled from the corner of Tom's mouth, down his pallid cheek and onto a scarred chest that barely rose with each breath.

As Grin waited, Thaly ripped a piece off the hem of her wet tunic and tied the cloth around the gaping wound on her forearm inflicted by Krieg's arrow.

"She needs to hurry," Whibly said to Grin. "The longer we stay here, the more chance these barbarians forget about tearin' the Docklands apart and come for us. Or them coloured grells catch up." He dropped the sack and rubbed his shoulder.

Grin wondered which of tainted grells, barbarians or merchant seafarers he should fear the most. He'd give anything to escape the menacing chaos of Laodicea and return to the solace of Babir Birramal, his forest home.

Whibly shook his head, slung the sack over his hunched shoulder and scampered off.

Thaly secured the cloth around her arm and ran up to Grin.

"Keep going?" he asked.

She nodded, and they continued chasing Whibly. He led them along the wharf to an old ship, its pointed front adorned with the carving of a faceless beast's open mouth, rows of barbed teeth waiting to catch unsuspecting prey. On the deck, the crew dashed about like panicked roaches, dousing flames with buckets of water. A short, plump man with a bald crown ringed by wisps of tangled black hair stood on a raised platform at the ship's rear and screamed orders.

Captain Adcock, thought Grin.

"Put it out, ya lazy slugs! Fill the buckets to the brim." The captain sneered when Whibly led Grin and Thaly up a plank of timber and onto the deck. "Where the hell you been, Whibly? I can't be herdin' these maggots all by meself. That's a skullard's job."

"I've got treasures for ya, Cap'n." Whibly dumped the sack on the deck, silver goblets and engraved platters spilling at Adcock's feet.

"At least ya ain't been wastin' time in the tavern." Adcock glanced over Whibly's shoulder, and a faint scowl breached the space where his thin moustache knitted with a platted beard. "Who's that?"

Whibly turned to Grin and Thaly and smiled, then faced Adcock. "They're passengers in need of help. We got room for 'em, ain't we?"

"We don't want more cargo," said Adcock. "We got enough worries thinkin' on how to escape these barbarians."

Although Grin had felt uneasy as soon as he stepped onto the *Vulking*, his hopes sank when Adcock dismissed Whibly's plea.

But the skullard persisted. "They been through a lot, Cap'n. Poor sods. I seen 'em on the bluff through me lookin' glass. There were strange things happ'n up there. The boy's hurt real bad. He was tied to a cross while this other fella, I coulda sworn he was the young Erstürmen prince from what I seen from paintings and all, he was...well, I don't rightly know what he was tryin' to do. Looked like he wanted to kill the boy. And them coloured grells, they were there. Not only the red one, three of 'em. Then..." Whibly leaned towards Grin and whispered, "I don't know ya names."

Grin hesitated, considering a formal greeting, then thought it unlikely to be appreciated given current circumstances. "Grin and Thaly," he said.

Whibly turned back to his captain. "Yeah, Grin and Thaly. They jumped off the cliff with the boy and landed in that lake, Felsie. Y'know the one. At the bottom of the Terraces. They'd rescued him. 'Cept the coloured grells didn't want to let 'em go. They come scamperin' down the stairs lookin' for blood."

"And ya thought it was a good idea to lead those demons here?" said Adcock. "I don't need tainted grells chasin' me rudder."

"I'm pretty sure we lost 'em, Cap'n. I was dodgin' all over the place. Stickin' to crowded alleys and the like. We lost 'em. I'll wager a season's purse on it."

Adcock shook his head.

Whibly grabbed his captain's arm and led him out of earshot.

Grin swayed unsteadily on the pitching vessel, still clutching Tom's limp, half-naked body to his chest.

Thaly leaned into his ear and whispered, "Do you notice anything about the crew?"

Grin had never seen a ship. He'd never been outside Babir Birramal until Tom Anderson, the birraman, arrived. What should he expect to notice? Around him, gaunt, skinny men dressed in soiled shirts and coats rushed about extinguishing fires, packed crates into the stomach of the vessel, or threaded ropes through pulleys. With the veil of night lifted by the rusting glow of fires consuming the docks, Grin counted nearly forty crew, although the *Vulking* looked too small to house that many. A strengthening easterly breeze washed over his face, bringing with it a stiff odour of unwashed skin and matted dreads of hair. Scents of men stewed in cramped, dank quarters. Men he had no reason to trust.

"No women," said Thaly, answering her own question. "I don't see a single woman on this ship."

"Is that unusual?" asked Grin.

"I don't know. But I don't like it."

Whibly finished talking to the captain and trotted over to his hopeful passengers. "Yur three lucky sods, that's for sure. I managed to bend Cap'n Adcock's arm if y'know what I mean. Convinced him to give ya safe passage. We're headin' for Bramble Island, off the east coast of Enthilen. Coloured grells ain't gonna find us there. I knew the Cap'n would see y'right. Sit yurselves down somewhere. We should be headin' off soon."

Whibly left and busied himself with the duties of a skullard, barking orders to other crew members.

"We cannot go back into Laodicea," Grin said to Thaly. "If we are to

27

escape Malphas and the tainted grells, this seems like our best chance."
He led her to the side of the ship, keeping out of the crew's way, and
they slumped to the floor, resting their backs against the outer railings
of chain threaded through timber posts that ringed the *Vulking's* deck.
The swinging chain was the only thing stopping anyone from tumbling
overboard.

Grin lay Tom at his feet, reminding himself to ask Whibly for blankets or clothes to cover his friend. The two diagonal scars on Tom's
chest marked him as a Dobunni rebel, and Grin wondered if rebels
would be welcome on merchant ships. Rebels or wild stone-grells.

* * * *

In the king's private residence on the second floor of the Master's
Hall in the King's Quarter of Laodicea, Malphas sat in a chair padded
with wool and covered in stitched, royal blue cotton, rubbing his thigh
through the skirt of his white robes to soothe the ache of old bones. In
the corner of the room on the floor, Prince Adalwolf Heine slouched
on an array of cushions, his head resting in his mother's lap. Romilda
caressed her son's black curls, damp from feverish sweat.

She's making him weaker, thought Malphas, leeching the strength he
needs to finish the task.

The meeting with Tom Anderson on Hansen's Bluff hadn't gone as
Malphas intended. Adalwolf had failed at the critical moment, and his
birth twin still lived. He must do; otherwise, Adalwolf would also be
dead because he and Tom Anderson were joined by a lifeforce only the
eyes of lost souls could decouple.

Another opportunity would come to steal the Anderson boy's soul,
thought Malphas, after Adalwolf's ascension to the throne. He stopped
rubbing his legs and traced the thumb of his left hand over the scar

on his right palm. The wound testified to his mastery of the dark eyes, reminding him of the trials he'd endured to discover paradise and reach the brink of an eternal reign.

"Volerdie wrote the First Scripture in his own blood," said Malphas, trying to capture Adalwolf's attention. "Knowledge of the scripture's existence almost disappeared from memory when Pergamos fell. Until, one day, a worthless thief stumbled on the parchment."

Adalwolf pushed his mother's hand away from petting his brow. "Why didn't Volerdie take the First Scripture with him when he abandoned Pergamos?"

Malphas smiled. "Isn't it obvious? He wanted us to find the scripture so we could follow his lore. When Ewald banished me from Sardis, I spent season after season searching for the text, convinced its revered words would explain Enthilen's future. On the beach where brave King Giltbert made his last stand, I escaped the brutish Nordmen now plaguing the lands once ruled by our ancestors, paddling a boat through the waves and as far out to sea as I could manage. Volerdie's guiding hand led me to the pinnacle of Hurst."

"Did you see a griffin?" asked Adalwolf, eyes wide.

"No, son. I fear the griffin will never be seen in these lands again. Hurst was a lonely and desolate place when the currents took me there. Do you know it once housed all the jewels in the Erstürmen Kingdom? Long before Giltbert's time. There were countless griffins in those days, and the Erstürmen kings and princes of old would ride the beasts on the wind to raid faraway lands. I searched through the maze of rooms within Hurst's solid bedrock, eventually stumbling upon a sealed chamber. With cunning and persistence, I cracked the seal and found inside a thief's lair. There, locked away from our world, was the First Scripture. I was destined to find it, and I'm the only one alive who can read its words."

Malphas rested his elbows on the chair's timber armrests, leaned forward, and nestled his chin onto the back of clasped hands, never taking his eyes from Adalwolf. "The First Scripture explains how to rescue Volerdie from his misbegotten conquest and have him rule over us once more. I shared this knowledge with your uncle long ago, but he betrayed me. I know you won't do the same."

"What plans do you have for our son?" asked Romilda, clutching Adalwolf's limp hand like a starving peasant guarding a mouthful of food.

Malphas turned his attention to the queen who would soon become Queen Mother, her continued existence needed only to legitimise Adalwolf's rule in the eyes of the Erstürmen people. "That Adalwolf is my son must remain a secret among only us," he said. "Given Ewald had no heir, and Dobunni assassins killed the king's brothers, Widald's eldest son is next in line for the throne."

"Helmut," said Romilda. "Do we know where he is?"

No, thought Malphas. Widald's family had disappeared before he could deal with them. "It doesn't matter where he is. Everyone believes Adalwolf is the rightful heir, and we must continue the ruse at all costs. The coronation will be held tomorrow evening."

"So soon?" asked Romilda, her face framed with worry. "There's no time to make the necessary arrangements."

"I began the preparations for this day yarles ago. The new King Adalwolf will bring hope to a frightened people, rallying his loyal subjects. During the coronation, we will announce the march to Pergamos and the resurrection of Volerdie's lost kingdom. The ash of Laodicea will float away on the wind, and Sardis will shrink to nothing more than a watchtower over our western border. In Pergamos, King Adalwolf will reign. Those savage grells desecrated a sacred place. We'll tear down what remains of their ruined city and rebuild the grand metropolis where Volerdie once ruled."

Adalwolf sat up, his fawn shirt hanging loose over frail shoulders, the bewildered look that had adorned his face for days still refusing to fade amid the candlelight. "What about the dark eyes? The rebel girl stole them. They could be sitting at the bottom of the pool of reflection."

"They're not," said Malphas. "I sent my draughouls to search for them, but the eyes of lost souls are not close by. Their momentary disappearance is unfortunate, but I'm confident the rebel will give them to the boy, and we'll find him again. In fact, I believe he'll bring the eyes to us. He has no other way of returning home." A knock on the door interrupted Malphas, and he called out, "Enter."

Krieg lumbered into the room, ducking below the door lintel, blood splattered across the black pauldrons and rerebraces covering his shoulders and upper arms. Lumps of flesh clung to the spikes of Krieg's flail as it dangled in his hand, and the unsettling stench of battle, a concoction of blood, sweat, smoke and oil, turned Malphas' stomach.

The red grell dropped to his knees before Malphas and bowed his head. "The Docklands have fallen, Worshipful Master. The Southern Vale will soon follow."

"Excellent, Krieg. When the sun rises, have the barbarians withdraw and await further orders. Queen Romilda will send messengers to announce that Adalwolf, the king in waiting, has demanded an end to the attack. All those who wish to thank him for this brave act and pledge fealty to the new king should attend his coronation tomorrow eve in the square of the King's Quarter. After the coronation, when the crown sits on Adalwolf's head, the barbarians can continue to dismantle the homes of the disloyal. What news of the boy?"

"The wild grell took him to the docks, but the crowds foiled our pursuit."

"Search every ship in the bay. If any of them depart, have the barbarians hunt them down, but make sure the boy isn't harmed. Our mission would have been much easier if Eroberung hadn't failed so miserably." Malphas waved Krieg away and faced Adalwolf. "Weakness is no mantle for a king. I've tasked Ende with your edification. She'll strengthen your body and mind and teach you to embrace pain with honour."

"Don't hurt him," said Romilda, wrapping her arms around the boy.

Malphas cinched his robes with a tasselled blue cord and rose to his feet. "He must endure to lead. Your only concern now, Queen Mother, is to prepare for the coronation." He reached a hand to Adalwolf, helping the boy off the floor. "It's time for you to see your new throne, my son. The draughouls had it hidden in a cave under the Desolate Mountains. I never discovered how it got there or who stole it from its rightful place in Pergamos. Regardless, it's up to us to return it. You and me."

The look on Adalwolf's face changed from bewilderment to curiosity, and Malphas knew the young man had taken another step towards the abyss.

~ Chapter 2 ~

Inside the throne room adjacent to the inner courtyard of Sardis, Hunfrid sat alone on Ewald's dark-timber throne and scratched the stubble on his chin as he pondered coming days. King Ewald and Eroberung, the white grell, were dead. Hunfrid ruled Sardis, at least until Adalwolf returned to the royal city and claimed the throne, or another monstrous tainted grell marched through the needle. Steward of Sardis for eight days, Hunfrid had entrenched his authority by ordering the newly-formed Steward's Shield to remove all evidence of Ewald's reign. The Shield had spread outwards through each of Sardis' seven circles to demand loyalty to the Steward, threatening execution or expulsion to those refusing to bend the knee.

Hunfrid stood, clasped his hands behind the back of his burgundy silk robe, ambled down the steps of the throne platform and past the baroque porcelain vases sitting atop granite pedestals lining the four walls. Each delicate vase contained the ashes of a fallen king, prince or other Erstürmen noble, the paintings on their gleaming surfaces telling stories about the people entombed within. Hunfrid hoped one day, his vase might grace a pedestal.

He paused at an empty plinth overlooked by a painting of King Giltbert sitting astride a white undred and hacking at a horde of barbarians with his battle axe. The huge undred, almost twice the size of a regular horse, towered above the carnage, barbarian blood splattered across its coat and a screaming invader impaled on the end of its curved horn.

According to legend, a griffin stole Giltbert away before the battle ended. His body was never recovered, so there was no corpse for the ancient burning ceremony. No ash to fill the ceremonial vase that would otherwise rest atop the plinth.

An empty memorial may also be Ewald's fate, thought Hunfrid. It seemed nobody in Sardis knew the whereabouts of the king's corpse. Not that Hunfrid cared. The less people remembered of Ewald, the better.

The oak door to the throne room creaked open, and in walked Conrad, Hunfrid's nephew and new Umbo of the Steward's Shield. The clatter of his polished silver armour echoed around the empty room as the gaunt young man marched up the aisle. He'd protested at his promotion to Umbo, claiming to prefer life as a regular Shield.

That's why he's the right choice, thought Hunfrid. No ambitions. He shook himself from his daydream and gestured for Conrad to speak.

"General Jurelle has disappeared without a trace, and, it appears, what's left of his family has gone with him."

"His son?"

"Jürgen's body vanished from the leichenhalle."

Hunfrid screwed up his face, picturing a maggot-riddled corpse lying on the floor beside him. "Stolen most likely. Such was a father's love, he was willing to carry the bloated corpse of his son through every one of the seven circles of Sardis." He dispelled the image from his mind and turned to Conrad. "We still have the head, correct?"

"Yes, Master Hunfrid."

"Then put it on a skewer and hang it outside the gate to the second circle with the other vermin. The traitor Jurelle may think twice before entering the inner circle again."

"Shall I dispatch a search party?"

"There's little point. The General has nowhere to go. The Dobunni rebels won't take him back. He'll wander these lands until misery and shame crush his spirit. Let's hope his equally treacherous wife dies in wretchedness at his side."

"What shall we do with Princess Caeli? She's been in the dungeon for five moons."

Hunfrid sighed as his hand reached down to rest on the growing roll of fat clinging to his stomach. "Conrad, it seems we're surrounded by traitors. Who would've expected, all this time, she hid a secret passage right under our nose?"

"Why didn't she escape?"

"A simple mind bereft of common sense, no doubt. Princess Caeli suffered as Ewald's concubine for yarles, enough misery to drive anybody far from here. Yet, it seems duty to the kingdom imprisoned her. It's a lesson for all of us, Conrad. Blind loyalty brings no reward." Hunfrid returned to the throne, pulling his robes across his knees as he sat. "I've appointed Rostard as Master of Executions. Princess Caeli will be our first offering. To send a message to the inner circle citizens that no misstep will go unpunished regardless of ancestry or past loyalties. Anselm will be next if he doesn't yield to my demands. His knowledge of the scripture verses is more valuable than ever given current circumstances, but we must be certain of his loyalty. Tell Rostard to begin the torture to sway the curate's mind."

A Steward's Shield entered the throne room and bowed before Hunfrid and Conrad.

"What progress on the secret passage?" asked Hunfrid.

"We're still being thwarted by the locked steel door, Master," said the soldier. "We've tried every key in the inner circle. None can open the door. And the battering ram is hardly making a mark."

"Keep trying. We need to know where the passage leads. And make sure it remains guarded. We don't want someone sneaking in from the other side. If you fail to breach the door, I'll consider blocking the passage off completely."

Hunfrid waved Conrad and the soldier away and retreated back into his mind, digging swollen fingers into the padded armrests of the timber throne as though a usurper threatened to pull it out from under him. Soon, somebody would come to end his rule, but who would it be? And would a profession of loyalty to this new master keep the axe from Hunfrid's neck?

He searched inside his robe until fingering a newly acquired and unusual trinket recovered from Eroberung's corpse. Hunfrid brought the treasure into the light and held it close to his eye, studying the goat's head with long, twisted horns etched onto the upper surface of a finely crafted, gold pentagram no larger than the palm of his hand. A conical lower surface tapered to a fine, sharp point, and he'd discovered if he balanced the pentagram on this point, it would spin of its own accord, turning like a wagon wheel at full speed. Moreover, he believed blood stained one of the five points of the pentagram and, unexplainably, when the star stopped spinning, the bloodstained point always faced in the same direction — towards Laodicea. He didn't have the knowledge to unravel the mystery of the five-pointed star, but he expected Anselm did.

*   *   *   *

Chained upright on a damp, crumbling dungeon wall beneath the kirika of the inner circle of Sardis, Princess Caeli's head lolled to one side, wrists aching from holding her weight. Her mind tried to dull the pain by escaping to a land from one of her favourite books where trees grew as tall as castle keeps, and gold and crimson flowers covered emerald meadows rolling on forever to the horizon. She ran across one of the fields, butterflies and bumblebees drunk on nectar swirling around her bare feet, and weebills and fantails flitting among the leaves of swaying branches. Above the crest of a hill, cirrus clouds soared like giant eagles across a sapphire sky.

Breaking the mirage, a statuesque man appeared atop the ridge. As Caeli got closer, the outline of a soldier in gleaming silver armour blinded her, a red banner with the sigil of a yellow griffin fluttering above his head.

Jürgen? Jürgen, is that you?

Caeli bolted towards the soldier, but the grass beneath her feet turned to mire, and puddles formed deep pools, drenching and staining the hem of her floral gown with stinking mud. She pulled her dress up past bare thighs to reveal gorging leeches feasting through holes incised in pale skin. Caeli yanked and twisted the parasites off her legs until blood streamed down filthy shins and decorated the mud with a crimson garnish.

Jürgen! Jürgen help me!

The shining soldier didn't come to her rescue. He vanished, and she sank further into the mire.

A bilious cough from across the room shattered Caeli's dream. Chained to the opposite wall, Anselm, Ewald's curate and scholar of Volerdie's Lore, hung limp and crestfallen. He hacked up another mouthful of phlegm and spat into the dirt and vermin excrement covering the squalid flagstone floor. Anselm hadn't been in the dungeon long, not even a full day, Caeli guessed. A small, slight man without a hint of fat under his skin, it appeared he had continued to refuse Hunfrid's demands for fealty, and she wondered how long he would last. How long both of them would draw breath before the executioner stilled their hearts.

"Princess Caeli. Princess."

Caeli strained to catch the hoarse whispers of the curate amid the ringing in her ears. She shook her head, flicking blood-matted hair from her jaw.

"Is it true there's a secret passage in your room?"

"What?"

"A secret passage. A way for us to escape."

"I'm not going to torment myself with false hopes, Anselm. Death will find me before freedom, though the waiting is a torture I don't have the strength to endure."

"All this time, Caeli, you could have fled Ewald. Why didn't you? We all know what he did to you in that keep."

"Regardless of the king's warped desires, I had a duty to my kingdom. To serve the needs of the Erstürmen people and deliver another heir should Adalwolf fall before his time. I'm sorry I couldn't fulfil the promise."

"You were the kingdom's most loyal servant. A loyalty to be honoured, not punished. I doubt the Steward of Sardis or King Adalwolf will foster such devotion."

"I think you're right, Anselm. We stand at the end of all we've once known and loved. At the end of everything." Above Caeli's head, footsteps echoed through the kirika. "I hope they're coming for me," she said. "To finish it."

"Don't wish that upon yourself, Princess."

"Doesn't death bring us closer to our Creator?"

"Only when darkness descends and Volerdie returns will the path to paradise be revealed. If you die before then, your soul will linger in purgatory until..."

"There's no paradise, Anselm," said Caeli, as a key turned in the lock of the dungeon door.

* * * *

Sombre and pensive, Rosalie Barron sat with her family in their koken around a dining table beside the fireplace, picking at scraps of fermented cabbage and stale bread. The last jar of preserves sat empty in the centre of the table, its glass as opaque as the family's future. Her father, Yonna, had closed the smithy. It appeared no-one in the fifth circle of Sardis or beyond could afford his wares.

Although six moons had passed, Rosalie kept replaying in her mind the moment she saw Harris Snape and the other prisoners being led to execution. The procession marked the death of a promised future with Harris, working metal and building a life together outside Sardis' oppressive confines. While nothing had replaced that dream, recurring visions of a lost young man shackled to the end of a chain filled her head.

Rosalie's stomach grumbled as her father took the last piece of bread from the table.

"The Steward's Shield spoke to me today," said Yonna, his jaw labouring on the stale crust.

Heady stroked her husband's forearm. "What did they want?"

"A pledge of fealty to Steward Hunfrid."

"Is the king dead, Papa?"

"Yes, Nettie. Killed by Dobunni rebels."

"I hate the Dobunni."

"They're filthy scum trying to destroy our kingdom and our lives," said Petas.

"How do *you* know?" Rosalie snapped at her brother.

"Why else are our lives so miserable?"

"Lots of people hated King Ewald. Anyone could have killed him. You don't know it was the rebels."

"It's the word of the Steward and I believe it," said Petas, pushing his chair back from the table and folding his arms.

"We blame the rebels for everything that goes wrong. Maybe…"

"What? Why do you care so much about the rebels?"

"Shut up, Petas. Stop being such a child." Rosalie cowered under Yonna's glare and shrank in her chair.

"We're in dire straits because some of us lost our way," said Yonna. "Refused to attend chapel. Ignored the lessons of the curate and the scripture. The Divine Creator is displeased."

Not this again, thought Rosalie. She shuffled her chair back from the table, stood and walked to the doorway, hoping to escape another inquisition. "I'm going to hammer metal."

"Sit, Rosalie," said Yonna.

Back turned to her family, Rosalie halted a step before entering the hall leading to the smithy. She knew what came next. She'd overheard her father and mother talking last eve.

"You can't work in the smithy again. It's time to end the fantasy. Women can't be metalsmiths."

Rosalie gritted her teeth and spun around. "I've done it for seasons. You never complained before, you were always happy for the help. I'm a better metalsmith than most men. I could be as good as you."

Heady stood and reached across to fuss with Rosalie's hair, brushing it from her shoulders. "You should find a husband. Start a family."

"I'm not ready for that."

"What happened to the scrap-metal merchant?" asked Petas. "What was his name?"

"Mind your own business," said Rosalie. "I don't need a husband."

"You'll do as you're told," said Yonna, half-standing to a threatening crouch.

Rosalie rested her hand atop her bruised shoulder, where the hammer had landed when Yonna threw her to the floor. She'd never feared her father before; she had no reason to, but since the argument in the smithy, she saw him in a different light — one exposing something volatile and dangerous.

Heady motioned for Yonna to sit, still holding her eyes on Rosalie. "We all have to marry, whether you want to or not. Women have a duty to the kingdom and the Creator to worship his creation by bearing children."

Nettie's shoulders drooped. "Do I have to find a husband?"

"Not yet, Nettie," said Heady. "One day."

"I don't want to marry Tully Scrungeface."

"That's not his real name."

Yonna sank back into his chair and plunged his fork into a piece of cabbage. "We've more important things to worry about, like where our next meal is coming from."

"You could make coins," said Heady. "When Adalwolf is crowned, all the coins with Ewald's image will be destroyed and replaced with new coins honouring King Adalwolf."

"I'm not feeling well." Allum pushed his plate away and rested his head on the worn timber dining table.

"You haven't eaten anything. What's wrong with you?" Heady placed the back of her hand on Allum's forehead. "Your skin's burning, and your neck's swollen."

"Many people are falling ill, not only children. They're calling it The Ravage."

"Don't wish that on our son, Yonna."

Rosalie crossed her arms and leaned against the door jamb. "Isn't the curate demanding the sick be sacrificed to appease the Creator? He claims it will end the sickness and break the curse afflicting us."

"That shouldn't be taken literally, Rosalie. Allum just needs to go to bed." Heady grabbed a damp cloth from the washtub and rubbed it over Allum's forehead while Yonna chewed the inside of his lip, his eyes drifting away with unknown thoughts.

Rosalie flinched when Nettie scratched the prongs of her fork across the top of the table. "Tully reckons sick people should sit between two roaring fires in a puddle of their own waste," said the little girl.

"We're not making your brother wallow in filth and then burn him alive," said Heady, pulling Allum up from the chair. "By Volerdie's mercy, I hope it isn't The Ravage. We can't afford a decent healer."

The walls of the cramped koken closed in around Rosalie, the malodour of a struggling family wafting from the frayed seams of once premium cloth. She hadn't washed her own shirts or pants in days, water now too precious to waste on such extravagances. Soon, a splash to clean the dirt from her blemished face would also be forbidden.

"It seems we've already descended into darkness," said Rosalie. "Isn't paradise fun?"

An enraged Yonna sprang from his chair. Heady blocked his path as Rosalie darted across the koken and ran from the house.

*   *   *   *

Jurelle Stansfield tugged on the reins of his grey stallion, Sphinux, stopping in a secluded valley at the base of the Scaur Hills, halfway between Sardis and the Rārian Falls. He waited for his wife, Genevea, to catch up, riding a bay mare with their daughter, Saskia, sitting in the saddle behind her. They'd managed to get out of Sardis in the moments of chaos as power shifted hands. But once Genevea and Saskia were safely hidden, Jurelle had to go back. To get his son.

He squinted into the morning sunlight as he turned to Genevea. "Will this do?"

She forced a smile. "This is one of the places we used to meet before Ewald discovered our affair," she said.

"It's why I chose it. Somehow, it seems fitting."

Genevea nodded.

Jurelle climbed down from his saddle. Behind him, slung over Sphinux's back, a long bundle wrapped in red cloth adorned with the sigil of a golden griffin hung limp. The Stansfield family banner covered the headless, bloated body of his son, Jürgen. As Jurelle heaved the corpse from his horse, the reek of decay made his stomach turn, accentuating the injustice he felt.

Genevea dismounted and walked over to him. "Let me help you."

He brushed her off. "I can carry him."

Saskia began to sob as Genevea lifted her down from the horse.

"I w-w-want to say goodbye," said Saskia, stumbling over to the tied bundle hanging low in the crux of Jurelle's arms and tugging at the cloth. "Take the cover off."

"You can't look at him, sweetheart," said Genevea.

"I want to."

"You can't, poppy," said Jurelle. "He's not...he's not all here."

The pained, confused look on his daughter's innocent face cut Jurelle's heart worse than any dagger. Genevea pulled Saskia away as he walked into a cluster of boulders hiding an alcove of grass ringed with shrubs. Several similar alcoves dotted the northern edge of the Scaur Hills, the region having been mined to build Sardis' walls. He lay Jürgen underneath a cutting in a boulder towering above his head. Genevea and Saskia stood at his side.

"We can cover the entrance with rocks," said Jurelle. "Make a burial chamber for him."

"No!" cried Saskia, dropping to her knees on the dewy grass.

Genevea winced, an almost imperceptible ache dulling the brightness of emerald eyes and causing a twitch at the corner of her mouth. Jurelle knew she fought with everything she had to stay strong for Saskia. He needed to do the same.

Kneeling, he reached around his neck, planning to take off Jürgen's griffin amulet and lay it with the body, but Genevea tugged his hand away from the top of his tunic.

"No," she said. "Jürgen would want it to stay in the family. To stay with us."

Jurelle nodded, stood and collected a rock from a nearby scree slope, laying it on the ground under the edge of the boulder overhang. The beginning of a wall and a tomb. Genevea followed his lead while Saskia sat on her knees with her legs tucked under her buttocks, still sobbing. The little girl picked at blades of grass and threw them into the air until they fell around her like green snowflakes.

What future awaited her? wondered Jurelle. Every rock he carried weighed heavier in his hands, jagged edges nicking and scraping his fingers, his body being worn down one skin flake at a time.

Saskia eventually dragged herself to her feet and collected stones to fill the gaps between the larger rocks. As dark clouds drifted across the midday sun, Jurelle laid the last rock to seal the tomb. He shivered from the breeze that fanned the beads of sweat clinging to his forehead. Genevea must have noticed, retrieving hooded woollen cloaks and a waterskin from the horses' saddlebags. Now almost the middle of the storm season, the days grew colder and shorter, and the long dark would soon envelop Enthilen. The family huddled together and shared a drink to toast Jürgen's memory.

"We should say something," said Genevea.

The mocking shadow of the Scaur Hills passed over Jurelle's face. The rocky slopes were his home once when he led the Dobunni in their rebellion against the Erstürmen invaders. He pictured the rebels watching him, sniggering at the Traitor General, hoping he would choke on the bitter taste of retribution for his betrayal. For conspiring with the enemy.

This isn't about you, Jurelle. It's about your son.

He clasped his hands out front and let them hang relaxed at his waist before bowing his head. "Jürgen. Young and brave. Loyal to the end. He died trying to protect his princess as duty demanded of him, and only a band of thugs could end his watch. A life taken too soon...*ahhh*, I don't know what to say. I shouldn't have gone to the Riverlands to fight Ewald's war. I should have stayed in Sardis. Gotten all of you out a lot sooner. Then Jürgen would still be alive."

"It's alright to cry," said Genevea, resting her hand on Jurelle's shoulder.

He wrapped his arms around his wife. Saskia snuck in between their waists and hugged her parents. They cried in each other's arms until the hurt had been expunged, at least for a moment.

~ Chapter 3 ~

"The barbarians have halted their attack, Cap'n. Seems they're withdrawin'."

Thaly craned her neck as Whibly called down from a platform perched high atop a pole at the rear of the *Vulking*, still moored at the wharves in Laodicea. The skullard must be able to see everything from up there, she thought. Tightening the bloodstained cloth on her forearm that covered the wound from Krieg's arrow, she hunkered close to Grin, who leaned against the outer railings, legs outstretched, Tom's head resting in his lap.

"This is our chance," said Adcock, "we should take it. Best we get outta here before them barbarians return to their ships. Drop oars, boys! Take her to the Leviathan."

Crew members took their positions on crude wooden seats next to long oars threaded through oarports, twenty on each side of the ship. Thaly had never been to sea, but she knew the parts of a boat had unusual names, remembering oarports from a story Jacob had told her while on one of their scouting missions. Starboard and port, helm and foredeck, they all referred to a part of the ship, although Thaly couldn't recall which part, the seafaring world as foreign to her as any other place outside Enthilen.

A young, gangling man, little more than a skeleton with skin, scampered along the jetty and untied all the ropes holding the ship in place before jumping back on board. Then, a rotund, bare-chested man with blue and white tattoos covering his entire body began drumming on a hollowed section of tree trunk with a bone the size of his arm. The black swirls decorating the surface of the bone reminded Thaly of the unfurling fronds of shimmer ferns. At the rear of the ship, Captain Adcock clutched a spoked timber wheel with tense hands. After pushing the boat from the dock, the oarsmen kept time with the drummer, and the *Vulking* lurched from its mooring, beginning a deft and low-key navigation among the empty barbarian ships spread across the bay.

As they moved out into the water, Thaly recalled her days in Süden Forst's dungeon with Jacob, prisoners of the Erstürmen. 'Save your energy and wait for the opportunity to escape,' he'd told her. The enigmatic depths of blue-green below the ship's hull beckoned to Thaly, and she pictured herself diving into the rippling ocean. But Grin can't swim, she thought, and Tom's almost dead, so we're trapped here for now.

She brushed strands of straw-coloured hair from Tom's face and caressed his feverish forehead, his shallow breaths keeping time with a metal pulley banging against the side of the rocking ship. After the ordeal on Hansen's Bluff, he looked a lot younger than sixteen harvest seasons. More fragile. Pupils quivering behind closed eyelids hid secrets she needed to discover. She should be angry with him. Jacob died for this stupid boy. For this 'birraman' as Grin had called him. Yet, Tom had helped her and Jacob escape Süden Forst's dungeon, and pledged allegiance to the Dobunni rebels before walking into the inner circle of Sardis to confront the Erstürmen king. Thaly and Tom were members of a companionship. They had a duty to protect each other, even during what may be the final days of Dobunni culture.

The *Vulking* glided out of Traders Bay, past the blackened façades of buildings on the Docklands' foreshore. Emerging through the smoke haze hanging above the waterline, a store's front window advertised in letters of garnet and teal: *Seamaster Cloth Merchants. Finest fabrics in all Laodicea.* Inside, flames consumed the gutted emporium, its shell casting a broken shadow on the surface of the bay. Thaly bit the inside of her bottom lip and thumped the salty deck of the *Vulking* with her fist, forcing her gaze east towards the open ocean.

*   *   *   *

By late morning, Laodicea had faded into the distance and silver gulls squawked above Grin, their white and grey bodies hovering on the breeze, suspended between the dark water and smoke-filled sky. He closed his eyes and pictured his forest home of Babir Birramal. With the onset of guma, the storm season, the garnet leaves of guyang shrubs would be abandoning the tips of twigs to spiral down to moss-covered ground shaded by colossal panalope trees. Thirsty forest creatures would be visiting the stream near his milbi shelter, flinching from the biting chill of the churning swell as it stung their lapping tongues.

Grin imagined his father, Frennan, now alone in the milbi on the edge of Babir Birramal, striding among the yurali bushes and collecting berries to dry and store for the long dark. Imagined him wandering too close to the Dambay Plains, hoping to find his lost son. Imagined Erstürmen soldiers capturing the old grell and selling him into slavery while his son rode the ocean waves to who knew where?

Would Frennan be proud of what Grin had become? A killer.

After the tribal war between the stone- and weald-grells that saw the latter abandon Malang Gunya, the elders decreed that grells should never again instigate conflict. They should never attack, only defend. Grin hadn't killed anyone before. Not until the ambush in Laodicea.

There, a murderous fury possessed his body and controlled the slashing blade, cutting down soldier after soldier without pause or second thought. An entity foreign to all he knew or thought he believed in, took hold of his will and squeezed until every last drop of vengeance escaped.

Had Grin honoured the elders' decree? When desperation cornered him again, would the monster of Laodicea return? He opened his eyes and rubbed his hands across his skin as if washing away a taint.

Whibly climbed down from his vantage point and scuttled over to Grin and Thaly. "How's the boy?" he asked.

"Alive, although weak," replied Grin.

"We ain't got no healer on board and nothin' much to heal with, but I knows where we can find one when we get to Bramble Island. In the meantime, see if he'll take this." Whibly fossicked inside the front pocket of his woollen waistcoat, retrieving a vial of viscid, hickory-coloured liquid no larger than his little finger.

Grin took the vial from Whibly, removed the cork and sniffed, his head jerking back with the stinging smell.

"Yeah, it smells horrible. Still, I seen many a drunken oarsmen come right to after takin' just one sip of that stuff."

"What is it?" Apparently unconvinced by Grin's assessment, Thaly leaned across and also inhaled, then threw her head to the side and dry-retched.

Whibly smiled. "Black hornet excreta. Giant wasps use it to glue the mud of their nests together. Y'have to squeeze their belly to get it and hope they don't sting ya. Only the mad and desperate collect it. Cost me some pretty coin, that did."

"I have heard of it," said Grin. He lifted Tom's head from his lap and prised open his friend's mouth, pouring a drop of the concoction onto his tongue.

"A little bit...a little bit...is all y'need. When he wakes, give him water straight up." Whibly snatched the vial from Grin and limped to his captain's side.

* * * *

Adalwolf marched towards Tom, holding his right fist out at arms-length, eyes vacant and unblinking like a bewitched, undead soldier. Tainted grells surrounded the two young men, resembling three humungous stone statues, one painted red, the other black and the last one a sickly, pale yellow. Adalwolf's fist punched Tom's chest. Fire exploded from Tom's groin and shot up the centre of his body, scorching his lungs and cooking his brain like a raw egg thrown into boiling water. The agony turned to numbness and pitch-black engulfed him, so dark he couldn't see his hand touching the tip of his nose. A speck of light appeared in the far distance, blinking and shimmering as it grew larger with painful lethargy. The light morphed into the shape of a head, at first blank and indistinguishable, then taking a familiar form. A bulbous nose and calloused skin. Dull, grey eyes masked by drooping eyelids. Twisted ears. The face of Malphas.

Tom waited for his tormentor to smile. Expected it. Malphas had come to gloat over his inevitable victory. Yet, the smile never came. Instead, Malphas looked anxiously into Tom's eyes, reached up and pressed the fingers of his right hand onto Tom's chin, pulling his mouth open. Malphas' left hand levitated before Tom's face, the tip of his index finger dripping blood. Tom tried to turn away, but couldn't move. The finger pushed between Tom's lips and a drop of blood landed on his tongue.

Tom bolted upright in a fit of coughing, lashing out blindly, trying to fight off the horror plaguing his mind.

"Stop fighting," said a woman's calm, assertive voice.

Tom focussed. *Thaly. Thaly's here.*

She propped her hand against his naked back and forced water into his mouth, but he spat it back out.

"What's this foul taste?" he asked.

"Drink some water. It should help," said Thaly.

Tom took another sip, washing away the vicious aftertaste lining his mouth, then clutched Grin's giant arm to steady himself. *Grin's here, too.*

"How are you feeling?" Grin's smile resembled a grimace.

"My body aches all over like I ran head-first into a brick wall. Where... where did you come from?"

"You don't remember?" asked Thaly.

"I remember us riding into the King's Quarter. Then the horses fell. I blacked out and woke up tied to a cross. I remember Adalwolf and the old man, Malphas...and more tainted grells."

"We were there," said Thaly, "on Hansen's Bluff, hiding behind the bushes preparing to rescue you."

"You saved me?" Tom steadied himself against a railing as the bow of the ship pitched in a wave. *Ship?* "Where are we?"

"The ship is called the *Vulking*," said Grin. "It is taking us from Laodicea to safety."

"Is Jacob here?"

Thaly withdrew her supporting hand from Tom's back and turned away.

"Jacob is dead," said Grin. "He sacrificed his life to save all of us."

A sharp stone sank to the bottom of Tom's stomach. "I'm sorry. Thaly, I'm so sorry."

She didn't turn back to face him.

"What was Adalwolf trying to do?" asked Grin.

"I don't know. He punched me in the chest, and the pain..." He began to shiver. Grin removed his giant tunic, the colour of warm buttermilk, and wrapped it around Tom. The crosses and circles scarring the grell's chest took Tom back to Süden Forst and the torture Grin had experienced in the outpost's dungeon. A peril Tom had saved his friend from, but now, undoubtedly, a debt long repaid.

The sky above the *Vulking* blurred, and Tom fell into Grin's arms and closed his eyes.

* * * *

A stiff north-easterly breeze stirred up Traders Bay, wiping the tears from Thaly's cheeks as she leaned over the railing to watch the *Vulking* cut through the white caps.

Whibly pointed past the rear of the boat and called out, "We got company, Cap'n."

Captain Adcock turned from the wheel. "Barbarians in pursuit. Why can't they leave well enough alone? Seems we'll have to call up our pod sooner than we wanted. Give the order, Whibly."

Whibly yelled to the drummer, who stopped his beats and blew a mighty breath into the mouthpiece on the end of a long, curved cylinder. Thaly leaned further over the railing, tracing the path of a shiny brass tube, no thicker than her finger, that extended down the side of the ship and disappeared underwater. Straining her ears, she imagined the sound of a high-pitched whistle floating up from the ocean depths.

In a flurry of activity, the forty oarsmen raised their oars and fixed them in place. Five men scurried to the front of the ship, the bow remembered Thaly, seizing ropes and harnesses and casting them into the water. The drummer launched more prodigious breaths into the tube and everyone on deck stopped and waited.

She turned to Grin, who still nursed Tom's sleeping head in his lap. "Do you know what's happening?"

"I have never been on a ship, Thaly. I have never been this close to so much water. I am doing my best not to think about it."

The foaming white tops of breaking waves yielded no clues. Thaly shuddered with quiet apprehension at the mercy of unseen currents waiting to drown her. The barbarian pursuers gained on the *Vulking*, the ominous silhouette of their twin-hulled ship growing with each passing moment.

Grin lay Tom on the deck and joined Thaly in her vigil for an explanation. The drummer sprang to his feet, pointed to the ocean and yelled. Exploding from the water, a gigantic beast flung itself into the air, twisted onto its back and smashed into the surf with a mighty splash, dousing Thaly and Grin.

"A huge yawarrang!" cried Grin, water streaming off his bald head and down over the black tattoo on his chin and cheeks; the facial crest of muwin, the ground spider.

"It's a whale," said Thaly, smiling. "That's Jacob's sigil. It's a sign, Grin. It's a sign he's watching over us."

Grin's gleaming lilac eyes smiled back at her as another three black and white whales burst from the surface. At the tip of the bow, the crew lowered harnesses into the water, and a sequence of clicks, whistles and wailing sounds emitted by the drummer down the brass tube appeared to guide the whales into position.

Everything proceeded with expert precision until the *Vulking* pitched violently from a rogue wave and ropes coiled off the deck and into the water. A hulking man dressed in a thick leather tunic and chaps jumped from a platform fixed to the front of the ship and grabbed one of the unwieldy ropes, throwing it across his leg until it bit into the leather and pinned his body to the deck. He screamed at another crew member who took the strain and tied the rope to a cleat. More men rushed about the bow, checking the position of the four whales and adjusting harnesses by tensioning or loosening ropes through a series of pullies.

Thaly almost toppled into the water, trying to watch the whales swim into position, threading their giant bodies through harness loops. When they were all harnessed to the front of the ship, they towed it forward at a steady clip. Thaly realised the crew must have done this many times and, in a corner of her grieving mind, she uncovered another story Jacob had told her about ships pulled by pods of giant whales travelling vast oceans, and the brave whale crews who drove them. A skill passed on through generations of seafarers.

"The harnessed whales will pull the ship," said Thaly.

"I have no knowledge of this," said Grin. "No stories passed from my ancestors."

"Jacob told me. Every ship travelling the Veiled Occyan has its own pod of whales that only respond to the whistles coming from that vessel. Their reward is meals of squid, shrimp and crawfish caught by the crew. The large man up front in the leather tunic, he must be the whale-master."

The whale-master turned to the drummer and raised his arm. Another piercing whistle dove down the brass tube and into the ocean. Thaly and Grin fell sideways onto the deck as the *Vulking* lurched forward and raced across the surface of Traders Bay.

*   *   *   *

"We got the fastest whales in all the Veiled Occyan," Whibly boasted as he stood beside Grin and Thaly, holding tight to the top chain-rail of the *Vulking's* deck.

Grin believed the skullard's word. The barbarian ship had faded into the distance, and the crew around Grin busied themselves with a likely familiar routine. He wanted to relax, but restlessness at the back of his mind kept his emotions on edge.

"Things'll quieten down once we reach the open ocean," said Whibly. "Crew won't be so busy then."

Tom still slept at Grin's feet, wrapped up in a blanket Whibly had found in the hold. Grin welcomed the return of his tunic to ward off the chill of the ocean breeze. His spirits lifted further at the sight of land up ahead to the east, illuminated by the afternoon sun. Separated by a narrow body of water, two rocky fingers on opposite hands almost touched, their enlarged tips taller than the surrounding land. To Grin's keen eyes, there appeared to be a bridge over the water connecting the tips.

"The headlands to Traders Bay are comin' up," said Whibly. "This y'first time through the heads?"

"Yes," said Grin.

"Then yur in for a *real* treat."

"Is that a bridge?" asked Thaly, pointing to the headlands.

"Kinda. It's the Leviathan. We'll be sailin' right under her belly."

"I have never heard of this," said Grin.

"It's an enormous statue, built by the Erstürmen. Supposed to represent a monstrous sea creature. I ain't never seen a live one and I don't want to."

As the *Vulking* approached the headlands to Traders Bay, the Leviathan statue filled the horizon. A tail resembling a nest of flailing serpents rested on one peninsula, and on the other rose a colossal, menacing head with a frill of spines emerging from the back of its skull. The Leviathan connected the headlands by the arch of its spine, and Grin pictured himself crossing from one peninsula to the other by clambering over the bumpy plates that ran the length of its back.

The *Vulking* cruised under the massive archway, the imbricated scales of the beast's stomach shadowing everyone onboard. If such a creature truly existed, Grin thought, a grell would look like nothing more than a fly on its skin.

Dwarfed by the Leviathan, a statue of a man dressed in simple robes and a skirt stood beside the tip of the monster's tail. The man's head had been knocked off and lay in pieces at the statue's base, covered in weedy vines.

"Who's that?" Thaly asked Whibly.

"Marduk, the guardian of the ocean."

"I know the name," said Thaly. "The Dobunni christened him the God of Envy. He who should be consulted when jealousy dominates your thoughts."

"The Dobunni didn't build that statue," said Whibly. "No-one knows who built it. It's been there longer than any seafarer can remember. Cap'n Adcock says Marduk was a traveller who disappeared from this world and ended up in a strange, distant place where people believed he was a god. When he returned home, he claimed to have been blessed with eternal life and demanded to be worshipped until the end of days. The worship didn't last, and Marduk disappeared once more, never to be seen again."

The Leviathan shrank into the west as the *Vulking* entered the endless horizons of the Veiled Occyan. Clouds masked the sun's warmth, and Grin's apprehension grew until a knot twisted in the pit of his stomach. He was leaving Enthilen for the first time and faced a frightening unknown. Focussed on escaping the barbarian pursuit and navigating through the treacherous heads of Trader's Bay, the *Vulking's* crew had ignored their new passengers. But now, with the threat passed, they began to take an uncomfortable interest in Grin and Thaly, muttering barely disguised insults laced with fetid breath.

Sitting on the deck beside Thaly, he leaned across and whispered in her ear, "Our welcome may be wearing thin."

"I don't want to think about it," she said. "All I want is for this journey to be over and my feet back on dry land. What will we do after we get to Bramble Island?"

"When Tom is well enough, I would like to take him back to Babir Birramal. He will be safer among the stone-grells. At the next garrabari, I will be initiated and instructed in our most important lore and can consult with the grell elders. They may know the best path for Tom. And when the first flower blooms on giagan, the sacred panalope tree, I will join my kin on the homage march to Malang Gunya to pay my respects to those who fell defending our home."

"I wish my future was as clear," said Thaly. "Laodicea is in ruins and I fear the same for Bagendon. All the rebels fought for could soon turn to ash."

"Do you miss Emelin and Dayna?"

"Part of me misses them less than it should. So much has already been lost. I sometimes wonder if I have the strength to continue to fight. It seems easier to give up."

"Never give up on your heart, Thaly. What does it tell you?"

"Avenge Jacob's death. Protect Tom. Do whatever I can to stop Malphas and his poisoned grells getting their hands on him again." Thaly turned to Grin with an expectant and pleading look. "I could come to the forest. We could all go together. It would be nice to wander among the trees, surrounded by birdsong and flowery perfume."

"You are always welcome among the stone-grells, Athalee…ah, I do not know your family name."

"I've taken Emelin's family name; Wallace."

"That is not your birth name?"

"It's the name I've taken." Thaly pulled her knees to her chest and averted her eyes.

Grin stopped probing. He knew little about Thaly, and she remained guarded, despite what they'd been through, keeping a shield between herself and those around her. The young woman held the world at bay, but she risked missing all its beauty and joy. Grin had grown up embracing the wonders of life. Surrounding yourself with a wall meant casting a shadow over every ray of light. A wall was no different from the lid of a tomb. Both ended a life worth living.

~ Chapter 4 ~

"Take the knife from your throat," said Audie. "I didn't save your life only for you to throw it away."

Sitting up in bed, pillows propped behind his back, Hadufuns' kept his arm raised and rested the blade of the cold knife against his skin. Audie stood in the doorway of Master Lily's private quarters in the Southern Vale of Laodicea, her right hand on her hip and her left holding a new poultice. The healer had done everything to keep Hadufuns alive, but his mind pressured him to disregard her efforts as a king dismisses the opinion of a slave.

Hadufuns measured each breath, the apparent control trying to deceive floundering thoughts. "You've wasted your time, Audie. I'm sorry I've stopped you from healing others with lives more worthy." He pressed the keen blade harder on his skin, feeling droplets of blood trickling down his throat and onto his bare chest.

Audie sighed, stepped into the room and placed the copper pot with the poultice on the table beside Hadufuns' bed. The sweet smell of crushed flower petals mixed with crystallised nectar wafted past his nose, one of Audie's favoured potions. She removed her toque and short veil, adjusting the needle running through a hairpin that fixed her black hair up into a bun, and leaned against the side of Hadufun's bed.

"Who am I to judge the worth of a life?" she asked. "Even a lowly peasant may alter the course of a kingdom. You'll never know how important your life may become. Let fate set the bounds to your future, not the desperate act of an impetuous fool."

"I'm on the brink, Audie. I can't seem to pull myself back. This war will soon engulf us and all will be lost. Better the distraction of my misery ends now." Hadufuns flexed his arm, expecting Audie to lunge at him and drag his hand from his throat. Instead, she sat at the end of his bed, rested her dainty hands in the middle of her pleated cotton skirt, and sought his gaze. He couldn't turn away, her equanimity suppressing his thoughts of hopelessness.

"The barbarians have withdrawn from Laodicea," said Audie. "Prince Adalwolf ordered the retreat. He'll be crowned this eve in the square of the King's Quarter. Masters Lily and Dealhia say this is our chance to escape, while there is a lull in the fighting. Now is the time for leaders, not martyrs."

The tremble in Hadufuns arm stilled. He lowered his hand and placed the knife on the bedside table, feeling childish and foolish at the resurgent longing to end the torment of untameable emotions.

Audie glanced at the knife. "Where did you get that?"

"It was among my clothes. I have a sheath stitched inside the shaft of my boot."

"That's an elaborate hiding place."

"The knife was a gift. From my wife."

"Where is she now?"

Hadufuns turned from Audie as the ebbing moans of the injured lying in the hallway filtered into the room.

"Sorry," said Audie, "I didn't mean to intrude."

"Her name was Godeliva. The broadhead of my arrow killed her."

Audie stood, stepped across to the window and flung open the curtains, letting shards of sunlight in through timber shutters left ajar. Hadufuns waited, expecting to have turned Audie's kindness into repugnance at a man who murdered his wife.

She stood at the window, looking out. "Why did you go to the Master's Hall in the King's Quarter seventeen moons ago? The night you and your brothers were attacked."

"I saw an opportunity to rescue a failing kingdom. To end my wandering and help build a better future for Enthilen. I knew it could be a trap."

"Yet, you went anyway. You cared for something other than yourself, risking your life in the process." Audie faced Hadufuns. "That doesn't sound like the actions of a heartless killer."

A single tear trickled down Hadufuns' cheek. "It was an accident. I didn't mean to kill my wife."

"When you're healed, you'll have another chance to atone for the past. The young King Adalwolf will need guiding hands around him."

"My father won't let me anywhere near Adalwolf. Once Malphas finds out I'm alive, he'll hunt me down lest I become a threat to the throne."

"Does this Malphas have such a desire for power?"

"There's more to it than personal ambition. My father has always sought the return of Volerdie to Enthilen and unveiling the path to paradise. Although leading our people to a better life is a noble aim, I fear his mind's been corrupted by a singular desire to be achieved at any cost. Adalwolf's ascension serves this purpose. Though I don't know how."

Audie stepped from the window, took the poultice from the bedside table, lifted a corner of the soiled bandage on Hadufuns' chest and smeared the sweet concoction of petals and nectar over his wound. He flinched when the cold paste met gaping flesh. Audie took a deep breath.

Hadufuns knew she would attempt to distract his pain with a story, as she'd done on previous occasions.

"I grew up in a small village far across the ocean. Life was simple. Our cares centred around food, shelter and family. The ambitions of rulers rarely infiltrated our world. I became the village healer. Dreamed of falling in love. Having children. Then the Oderans, you call them barbarians, raided our village, murdered my family and stole me away. They imprisoned me for seasons, forcing me to heal their wounded. One day, two yarles ago, we docked in Traders Bay, and my captors let me ashore to purchase medicines. Fate intervened, and my path crossed with Lady Lily LáDown, who didn't need words to understand my distress. Lily's guards dispatched my escort and saved me. Although she offered freedom, I had nowhere to go, so I asked to be her healer." Audie finished applying the poultice and sat on the bed next to Hadufuns, her round face decorated with a tireless smile. "Although a Dobunni saved me, I've saved the lives of their enemies. People like you."

"I'm not your enemy, Audie."

"One day, you might be. Or one day, you may be my saviour. I can't foresee the future and I have no right to diminish its options. The Erstürmen aren't evil, although they may fall under its spell, like all of us. Who will break the spell and expose the false promises of those with wicked plans? Who will lead the Erstürmen on a different path?"

Eyes half closed, Hadufuns drifted with the gentle cadence of Audie's words. "How can you be so skilled as to heal the body and the mind?" he asked.

Audie leaned in and brushed her thin lips against his ear. "I cannot heal your body if your mind is ill, and your mind, I cannot mend if you let your body wither and weaken. I must heal both. One is connected to the other."

Audie gathered her toque and veil, stood and marched to the door. "I'll leave the knife beside your bed. If you decide to use it, don't make a mess of the bed linen. No-one has the time to clean it. We're all too busy saving lives."

*   *   *   *

In the Master's Hall of the Southern Vale, the sounds of battle subsided, replaced by wails and sobs as the injured lay dying and the dispossessed broken. The cries of the refugees packed into the hall like bees in a hive tugged at Lily's emotions, urging her to deliver salvation. She joined Dealhia and Maxton at the map table, familiarising herself with the landscape between Laodicea and Gestade. She couldn't remember the last time she'd slept or removed her armour, or didn't have a hand reaching for a sword. Although the barbarian attack had begun only two moons ago, it felt like they'd been fighting for yarles.

"The messenger from the King's Quarter claimed Adalwolf has called the truce and will enforce it, but I have my doubts," said Lily. "Once the coronation is complete, the attack will resume. We must prepare to leave Laodicea immediately."

"The barbarians wait for us outside the gate, Master Lily," said Maxton. "We have to go right past them."

"We'll escape tonight when most eyes are turned to the coronation. Put our best fighters on the flank nearest the barbarian camp. If they attack, we'll be ready, though we can't engage in a prolonged battle. Our aim is to flee the city as quickly as possible and head for Gestade. The road is flat and straight, and should be easy travelling."

"They may pursue us," said Maxton.

"They may. Yet, the barbarians are nothing more than thieves seeking riches. They'll know refugees of war carry few treasures. The Terraces are where most of Laodicea's wealth resides, and that quarter of the city remains largely untouched. They won't pursue us when the jewel of Laodicea is yet to be plundered."

The frown on Maxton's face told Lily he wasn't convinced. The plan might be folly, but she had few choices. An escape offered hope. The crumbling Laodicea offered none.

"What remains of our army will escort you from Laodicea, but we'll return to Bagendon when you're safely on the coast road," said Maxton.

"I understand," said Lily. "I know you worry about an attack on your home. You're right to."

"Adalwolf will expect a pledge of fealty from the Dobunni of Laodicea," said Dealhia.

"I'd rather die than pledge," snapped Lily.

"What if this buys us more time? A proclamation of loyalty, however false, may stem the attack for another day or so, allowing us to save more people. Adalwolf may end the fighting altogether."

"Do you believe that, Dealhia? I don't trust Adalwolf or Malphas. If we send a delegation, they'll likely be slaughtered before the crown is placed on the boy's head. There will be no reprieve for your people or mine."

"What about Hadufuns?"

"He's our key into Gestade. If Malphas finds out he's alive..." Lily locked eyes with Maxton.

"I won't tell anyone," he said, before placing his finger on a map of Laodicea city. "What about the caves leading from the Terraces into hidden valleys in the Desolate Mountains?"

"It'll take too long to get all our people through those caves. And Lord Sleame won't open the gates of the Terraces to a horde of refugees."

"War has taken our lives and our trust," said Dealhia.

Smoke from burning buildings stung Lily's nostrils, and a fist of anger clenched in her stomach. "What did you expect? Did you think this would come to a peaceful end? You heard what Hadufuns said. Adalwolf will turn his back on Laodicea *and* Sardis, and follow his new master to resurrect Pergamos. Our city will be nothing but ruins. If you stay here, the rubble will be your grave. The Dobunni of the Southern Vale are leaving at nightfall. You're welcome to follow."

Lily stormed from the room and into the hallway, stepping over prostrate bodies weeping blood onto the timber floor. Audie darted among the injured, dispensing pragmatism and comfort in equal measure, and whatever medicines she still possessed. Three other healers assisted Audie, but they wouldn't be enough. Most of the desperate people seeking refuge in the Master's Hall would die here.

Lily escaped the claustrophobia of the hall and stood on the front porch, overlooking a smouldering city. She'd been too harsh on Dealhia. Both of them needed friends now more than ever, and both would have to lead the refugees to Gestade. The Docklanders wouldn't abandon Laodicea without their master. Lily feared some of the Dobunni from the Southern Vale would also refuse to leave. Laodicea, *Bethesda*, had been home to the Dobunni for over a thousand yarles. She would be the first master to urge her people to forsake their heritage.

*   *   *   *

At sunset, spectres of grey sea fog blew in off the ocean, floating through the streets of Laodicea like a fright of ghosts risen from the bodies of the dead piled against the walls of the city. The living residents shuffled into the square in front of the Master's Hall in the King's Quarter to wait for the coronation of King Adalwolf. Despite the carnage of war, enough had survived to pack the square cheek-by-jowl with weary bodies. Most were Erstürmen citizens from the King's Quarter who'd accepted Ewald's reign had come to an end, and Adalwolf would be their new king. Around a hundred came from the other quarters of Laodicea, perhaps believing a pledge of allegiance to King Adalwolf would bring peace.

At the behest of Malphas, leaders of the barbarian tribes from the lands of Oder, Setux and Morund also attended the coronation. While they wouldn't pledge loyalty to the king, they'd promised not to attack the new monarch or his subjects residing in the King's Quarter. However, their assault on the rest of Laodicea would continue after Adalwolf was crowned.

The barbarian chiefs drew fearful looks from the people of Enthilen. Tall, brawny men and women with crude, abstract designs painted on their naked torsos in garnet, teal and sable, spoke of faraway lands with odd customs and alien cultures. Circlets of tanned serpent skin stretched around bare thighs and upper arms, and crowns of teeth, bone and sweeping feathers longer than an arm enhanced the foreboding aura surrounding the chiefs. Reputably, these raiders from strange lands could cripple renowned kingdoms on a whim. The Erstürmen had experienced their might first hand and offered no quarrel with such a conclusion.

Even taller than the barbarians, and head and shoulders above the rest of the crowd, stood twenty armoured grell soldiers, each carrying a long broadsword, hooked along the top edge. A grilled, black helmet covered the giants' scarred faces and bald heads, with a spiked pauldron strapped to one shoulder and thick, studded-leather gauntlets covering both hands. Below naked chests, black plackarts protected their stomachs and greaves shadowed bare feet. Malphas had christened the grell soldiers the Rephaim, and they answered only to him or his sergeant, Krieg.

As the daylight dimmed, grell slaves lit torches around the square, the firebrands projecting white halos amid the fog. Simultaneously, soldiers in the King's Shield unfurled dozens of black banners of inferior cloth and crooked seams, the best that could be produced at short notice, depicting a crimson, two-headed serpent coiled upwards into an incomplete circle. There was no characteristic murmur among the crowd. Most stood silent with bowed heads like mourners. An uncertain future lay before them, draped in hope as ephemeral as the strands of sea fog.

*   *   *   *

Inside the king's private room in the Master's Hall of the King's Quarter, Romilda fussed over her son, Adalwolf, while three tainted grells and another man, Lothar, loitered in the background, projecting an intensity that filled her with unease. The pale grell, Ende, had her sickly gaze fixated on Adalwolf.

She's always watching my son, thought Romilda. Always judging him.

This evening, Adalwolf would be crowned King of Enthilen, then he'd have the authority to dismiss the scrutiny of tainted grells. The coronation wasn't in the inner circle of Sardis as Romilda had hoped, and much of the pomp and ceremony would be missing, but Adalwolf would be king. The only thing that mattered.

She walked around her son, who stood as stiff as cold steel in the middle of the room. "Adalwolf, straighten your robes," she said, tugging at an alabaster gown, golden thread stitched into every seam, attempting to flatten the creases bunching up near his waist. She pulled the gown across the silver breastplate embossed with the sigil of the two-headed serpent. Underneath the breastplate, a linen robe of bright yellow and pitch black, tied at the waist with a crimson fabric girdle patterned with pentagrams, stretched almost to her son's ankles. The alabaster gown complemented Adalwolf's dark, curly hair and lightened his often-brooding face.

He looks so handsome, she thought.

"The gown is too long for me," he said.

"I'll pin up the hem."

"No. This'll do. Stop fussing." Adalwolf waved his arm, attempting to push her away.

Romilda wouldn't be dismissed so easily. "Your hair needs a brush. You bathed, didn't you? We can't have the new king smelling like a poor man's chamber pot. Let's splash this fragrance on you." Reaching for a bottle of lavender essence from the top of the dresser, she sprinkled two drops of the scent behind Adalwolf's ears, then turned her attention to other parts of his attire. "Are you sure these boots have been polished?"

"Yes."

She pulled a handkerchief from the sleeve of her black dress and dabbed it on the corners of Adalwolf's mouth. "Let me clean you up."

"Leave it!" Adalwolf snarled and smacked her across the arm. "I've had enough of your incessant fretting. Never touch your king without permission."

Romilda froze, stunned. The red grell, Krieg, and the black grell, Hunger, their bald heads pressed to the ceiling, began to menace her thoughts. The stooped Ende leaned on her sparth like a crutch, a faint smile flickering across her scarred face.

These monsters and their horrid master are abducting my son, thought Romilda. She retreated into the corner, resolving to steel herself for a long battle. She hadn't spent the last sixteen yarles culturing her son's love and devotion to let it be stolen from her without resistance.

A King's Shield clattered into the room, his entire body covered in silver armour, polished for the ceremony. He removed his spangenhelm and bowed his head. "All is in readiness, your majesty. The throne awaits."

Throne? thought Romilda. Is that what you call it? The gruesome cathedra, fashioned by the imagination of a deranged madman. Her son deserved something grander and less grotesque.

Lothar stepped forward, scratching his greying beard with his left hand and holding a book with a black cover in his right. Romilda had met him seven yarles ago when he studied under Anselm, Ewald's curate in the inner circle. When Lothar completed his studies, Ewald sent him to Süden Forst at Anselm's request because Lothar had shown certain disagreeable tendencies born from an unlimited adjuration for Volerdie. Lothar had practised his depraved worship in Süden Forst for three yarles before Malphas appointed him curate of Adalwolf's court. The new royal curate had taken the title of 'Hoch-Vater'; high-father of Enthilen. Romilda wondered how Anselm would receive the news. Such a title was reserved for the most esteemed curate in the entire kingdom, and Anselm had used it on numerous occasions.

"The Worshipful Master has asked me to begin the proceedings, majesty," said Lothar. "With your permission, of course."

Adalwolf turned to Romilda. The movement looked instinctive, and she smiled. He still needs me, she thought.

He dismissed her just as quickly and said to Lothar, "Permission granted."

Lothar bowed and followed the soldier out of the room, the Hoch-Vater's sangria robes trailing across the polished floorboards. Everyone went deathly quiet, except for Adalwolf tapping the toes of his boots on the floor. Romilda thought about scolding him, then bit her tongue. Fawning or nagging wouldn't win back her son. She needed a better strategy.

* * * *

Lothar stood at the front terrace to the Master's Hall of the King's Quarter, overlooking the main square now packed with citizens here to witness the coronation of King Adalwolf. The blurred shape of a single crescent moon appeared through the fog masking the night sky, floating above the cliffs of Hansen's Bluff. Lothar clutched in his right hand, *Polus Sepcarture* — the scripture verses, the book the Erstürmen believed to be the correct interpretation of the First Scripture. The Heilig-jün lined up behind him, twenty-four old men dressed in simple white robes cinched with black corded belts, and a wreath of twigs crowning each head. Lothar's assistants offered unconditional service to the Divine Creator, and Lothar had made it clear to Malphas he wouldn't consider the position of Adalwolf's curate unless accompanied by the Heilig-jün.

Beside Lothar, a herald stepped forward and unrolled a parchment. The burgeoning crowd stilled as the herald cleared her throat and read aloud, "All those assembled, hear my word. Bear witness to the rise of King Adalwolf the Redeemer and the beginning of his glorious reign. Answer his call to worship and sacrifice. To prostrate our bodies, offering our souls to Volerdie, the Divine Creator. Accept Adalwolf as Volerdie's agent in Enthilen until darkness descends amid the daylight and bathes true believers in the waters of eternal paradise."

The herald stood to one side. Lothar stepped off the terrace and strode along a path lined with onlookers who parted like the ocean ceding to a ship's bow. The Heilig-jün followed, and together they marched to a large, timber platform in the middle of the square. Lothar trotted up the steps and planted his feet on the deck while the Heilig-jün encircled the platform and bowed their heads, each clutching a copy of the scripture verses at their waist.

Surveying the crowd, Lothar gathered the hem of his robes and turned full circle, smiling at the expectant faces in need of a shepherd. He opened the scripture verses and read aloud from the first page, "He who strays from my word will be lost. He who forgets my lore will find in the darkness death, not paradise. There can be no ruler of all the lands unless in Pergamos that ruler resides. No order shall be followed unless from Pergamos the order comes. Abandon your towns and cities of desperate faith. Worship only in my halls, bowing only before my throne. For those that embrace me, I will embrace. Those that lay before me will rejoice in my comfort."

Lothar shut the book with a theatrical clap, holding it aloft in his right hand. "The Erstürmen have lost their way. Sardis and Laodicea are not our homes. We didn't march from the north seeking the destitution of these foul cities. We have fallen into poverty and depravity because of this mistake. Weak leaders and their complicit lambs have failed the faithful. Our bellies are empty, and our minds filled with the nonsense of past rulers. King Adalwolf offers new hope and new faith. King Adalwolf offers us a chance for redemption. To Pergamos he will march, and we will follow him. In Pergamos he will reign, and we will praise him. And when darkness descends, and Volerdie returns, it will be King Adalwolf the Redeemer that walks beside the Divine Creator, leading us all into paradise!"

The King's Shield standing among the crowd cheered and thumped their breastplates with clenched right fists. "Hail, King Adalwolf! Hail the King!" Others followed suit, the damp sea fog clinging to their hair and faces, droplets of moisture trickling down their cheeks like a stream of joyful tears.

Lothar waited for the commotion to subside before continuing, "The decisiveness of King Adalwolf saved the King's Quarter from the rebel attack on Laodicea. Our new king foresaw that the Dobunni rebels would march to Laodicea and try to overrun the city. It was his wise counsel that arranged for our barbarian friends to come to our aid. Yet, the fate of Laodicea or Sardis does not concern us now. We must come together to resurrect Volerdie's lost capital. To rebuild his glorious halls and shining steeples. To fashion a city fit for a king and his Creator."

He pointed at the Master's Hall, where two trumpeters stood on the balcony and blasted a musical proclamation announcing the beginning of the royal procession. From the main door came a troop of twelve King's Shield, covered head-to-toe in polished silver armour, their breastplates embossed with the sigil of the two-headed serpent. They marched into the square and surrounded the platform, interspersing between the Heilig-jün and smacking the cobblestones with the blunt end of their halberds as they stared into the crowd.

Next came two grell slaves carrying a stretcher draped in blue and black cloth on which lay King Ewald's naked corpse. Some in the crowd gasped. It wasn't normal Erstürmen custom to display a dead king's body at his successor's coronation.

But this was no ordinary coronation, thought Lothar. The Worshipful Master had demanded the exhibition of Ewald's corpse to quell the rumours the king wasn't dead, and Adalwolf had no legitimate claim to the throne.

The grell slaves placed the stretcher on a pyre of logs in front of the platform, stood to one side and bowed their heads. Lothar leaned over the dead king and winced at the clumsy attempt to sew Ewald's head back onto his torso. He stepped back when Romilda, dressed in a flowing black dress with a wimple and veil covering her hair and face, shuffled along the path to the corpse. A flicker of sorrow punctured Lothar's emotions. Sympathy for a queen mourning the passing of her husband while celebrating the rise of her son.

The Queen Mother paused at the unlit pyre and lifted her veil. No tears sullied her cheeks, her breath calm and measured. She placed the back of her hand against Ewald's frost-white cheek in a final act of affection, then climbed the steps to the top of the platform to take a seat behind Lothar.

Out of the Master's Hall thumped Krieg and Hunger, dressed in the armour of the Rephaim, their giant sabatons pounding the timber steps of the porch like hammers driving in nails. Lothar had counselled against including the tainted grells in the ceremony. Still, Malphas believed a public acknowledgement of the grell's authority would convince Adalwolf's subjects of their value and loyalty. Yet, the eyes of the people lining the procession route grew wild with terror as the tainted grells passed and marched up the steps of the platform, taking their oversized seats beside Romilda.

Trumpets sounded from the hall balcony and the crowd craned towards the main door. Four armoured grells, the pole bearers to the king's throne, trudged outside with arms hanging stiff and low. They paused on the terrace before raising the poles onto their shoulders. The backrest to the throne smacked into one of the terrace's roof beams, and King Adalwolf almost toppled from his royal seat, ducking his head to avoid the obstruction.

It looked awkward and foolish, thought Lothar, hoping it wasn't an omen of the reign to come.

* * * *

Adalwolf lorded over his subjects as the grell throne-bearers paraded along the path to the platform. As murmurs rippled through the crowd, he wondered what they were thinking. A boy king too young to take the throne? An unremorseful son basking in pageantry while his father's body rots? They were probably awestruck at the sight of Volerdie's throne, the throne of the dead. Adalwolf may be the first king to sit on this throne since Volerdie himself.

As the throne passed through the crowd, those closest turned mortified faces away. Ignorant, thought Adalwolf, caressing one of the petrified human arms forming the throne's armrests. At the end of the armrests, fingers like claws clutched two stone balls, while desiccated calves and feet formed the throne's four legs. Atop the backrest, the head of a wild beast resembling a horned wolf glowered, teeth bared, with empty eye sockets swallowing the light.

Malphas had told him the eyes of lost souls belonged to the wild beast. The empty sockets reminded Adalwolf of his failure on Hansen's Bluff when the rebel girl stole the dark eyes. But he would get them back. Then he would take Tom Anderson's soul and live for all eternity as Enthilen's immortal monarch.

The crowd nearest the platform dropped to their knees as Adalwolf approached. Fear, excitement and adulation congealed inside his mind to mould a sense of entitlement, sweeping away the timidity that had festered in Sardis. The shyness born from Ewald's drunken assaults. Now, with Ewald dead, Adalwolf would accept his birthright. The past anxiety of ascension began to dissolve like the sea fog veiling the crowd, replaced with a growing ambition for control.

The Rephaim throne-bearers carried Adalwolf up the platform steps and lowered the throne to the floor in front of his mother and the tainted grells. The Rephaim retreated to the rear of the podium when Lothar stepped forward. Following Erstürmen custom, the Hoch-Vater would introduce the new king to his people. He looked at Adalwolf, and the soon to be crowned king nodded his permission.

Lothar raised his arms, holding the scripture verses in one hand as he spoke, "When Pergamos fell, the First Scripture was lost, but its lessons are contained in this book — the word of Volerdie. Those who listen to his word will understand the significance of this moment. For it is written," Lothar opened the book, "...in the tumult of my absence, a king shall rise and his reign will promise eternity. In Pergamos he will rule as I once did, and all who follow him will know grandeur and prosperity. Seated on the throne of the dead, he will judge his subjects, delivering mercy or punishment, and through the greatest sacrifice, he will bring forth the darkness and open the way for my return."

Lothar shut the book and pointed at Ewald's body. "Here lies a failed king. A *feeble* king. Unknowing and blind. He couldn't see the traitors in his midst. Dobunni assassins and their sympathisers infested his kingdom. Murdered his brothers. Lay in wait for him as he secretly fled Sardis like a rodent fleeing a fire. The Dobunni flushed him, and these traitors will pay for the murder of Enthilen's ruler. But have no sympathy for Ewald, for he deserves none. Have no compassion for his reign because it saw the Erstürmen fall into destitution. On this eve, we burn his memory to ash."

Lothar waved his hand. A grell slave stepped forward and poured serpent oil over Ewald's body.

Adalwolf frowned, his thoughts caught by surprise. Although Malphas had told him what to expect during the ceremony, he didn't tell him about this: the dead king's cremation. That would usually be done in private.

Lothar took a flaming torch from the platform's edge, walked over to Adalwolf and smiled as he handed him the firebrand. Adalwolf's legs twitched as the Hoch-Vater yelled to the crowd, "Cast the flame into your father's corrupted soul. Let all those assembled bear witness that your law is now the law of Enthilen."

What? thought Adalwolf. He can't expect me to...to do that? He clenched the wooden stave of the torch, hoping it might dissolve in his hand. Behind him, his mother sobbed. The expectant eyes of the crowd chilled his blood as an inescapable pantomime began to play out around him.

Get it over with, he thought.

Adalwolf stood and stumbled to the edge of the platform, almost tripping on the hem of his alabaster robes. He held the torch aloft, its flames wavering with the quiver of his arm, then cast the firebrand onto Ewald's corpse. The fire spread quickly with the oil, exploding amid plumes of acrid black smoke. Someone in the crowd yelled, "The king is dead! Bring forth the crown!" and the demand spread through the congregation.

Adalwolf returned to the throne of the dead. From the main door of the Master's Hall, a hunched figure draped in a white, hooded robe shuffled down the steps like a parched horse staggering to water. The masquerade of Malphas, the frail old man. Adalwolf laughed aloud at the subterfuge. Or was his mind giddy with the madness of sitting on a throne made from dead people while a headless king burned before him?

In his outstretched arms, Malphas carried a burgundy cushion cradling the coiled skeleton of a snake, head poised to strike with an open mouth and bared fangs.

Ewald's crown, thought Adalwolf. Now *his* crown.

Malphas ascended the platform, and Lothar nodded, taking the serpent crown from the cushion. The sly old man then shuffled to a chair directly behind Adalwolf.

Lothar stood facing Adalwolf and held the crown aloft. "With this crown, I proclaim you King Adalwolf the Redeemer, King of all Enthilen and her peoples, King of all Erstürmen and their allies, vessel of Volerdie and the deliverer of his justice in this world. Let the will of our Divine Creator empty the souls of all who fail to honour our king."

Trumpets blared from the balcony as Lothar placed the crown on Adalwolf's head. The crowd cheered, and Adalwolf grimaced a forced smile, heart palpitations shuddering through his chest. His reign had begun.

"Bring forth the pledges!" Lothar bellowed.

People stepped from the crowd and formed a queue leading to the platform. The herald stood at the head of the line and announced each pledge waiting to honour the new king. "Your majesty, I offer you General Badulf Wolfhart, a veteran of the Riverlands War and newly appointed Umbo of the King's Shield."

General Badulf climbed the steps, dropped to both knees before Adalwolf and bowed his head. "I pledge my fealty to you, sire, utterly and eternally, and swear to protect your life at all costs until Volerdie takes my soul."

Adalwolf pulled his robes over his knees as the easterly wind whipped up a thickening fog. Badulf remained bent and motionless at his feet, and Adalwolf pictured the sagging old man polishing his boots with his tongue.

"We lost the Riverlands War," said Adalwolf.

"Yes, majesty," muttered Badulf.

"Weren't you the Field Commander of that campaign?"

"Well, yes, majesty, but it was the traitor Jurelle who led us straight into an ambush, turning the tide of the war against us."

"My father sent General Jurelle to the front. Are you saying King Ewald made a mistake?"

Badulf mumbled a response that Adalwolf couldn't make out. "What did you say, General?"

"No, majesty. We were simply outnumbered."

"Outnumbered and outwitted. I thought about having you executed, but my advisors assure me you're the best choice for Umbo. I hope they're not mistaken." Adalwolf turned to Lothar for direction.

The Hoch-Vater leaned down and whispered into Adalwolf's ear, "Accept his pledge and bid him rise."

Adalwolf nodded. "Rise, General Badulf. I accept your pledge."

The night wore on. Adalwolf became cold and bored as pledges from different factions made their way to the platform to bow before him; Erstürmen nobles from the King's Quarter and Sardis, masters of the grell slaves, the Field Commander from the Erstürmen outpost near Detranté, and administrators from Laodicea and surrounding towns.

At the back of the line trudged a despondent figure, stooped over from carrying a wooden chest larger than his own torso. When he reached Adalwolf, he dropped to his knees and opened the trunk, coins, gold and gems spilling out onto the platform.

The herald announced his arrival. "Your majesty, I offer you Lord Sleame Excelis, Master of the Terraces of Laodicea."

"Your majesty, on behalf of the Terraces, I pledge fealty and offer all the treasures our people can gather."

Adalwolf coveted the treasure and went to dismiss the master when Malphas' whispered to him from behind the throne, "They have more."

Adalwolf sat up straight and pulled his robes in tight. "You insult me with this pittance, Sleame. I know the terrace-dwellers hide more treasure in their caves. I demand all of it if you wish to garner my protection."

Sleame trembled at Adalwolf's feet. "B-b-but majesty, we'll have nothing to buy food or clothing."

Adalwolf leaned forward, spitting venom. "You'd be well advised never to question my demands lest you wish to face the executioner's axe." He relaxed back into his throne. "You're fortunate I'm a virtuous king. I'll give you one more chance to honour my request."

Sleame bowed his head lower. "I wish only to serve, sire. Your bidding will be done."

The Master of the Terraces departed. Adalwolf turned to Hunger sitting behind him. "Raid the Terraces and bring everything you find to me. Kill anyone who stands in your way, starting with this *Lord* Sleame."

He looked to Malphas for affirmation. The old man who claimed to be his father smiled underneath the crumpled white hood.

* * * *

Lily ran her fingers over the toppled stone wall of a house in the centre of the Southern Vale, crumbling mortar clinging to her fingertips. Silhouetted in the foggy night, thin pillars of stone resembled a family of giant ghosts reaching into the sky, searching for the roof that once sheltered them. Inside the building, a lone table stood with plates and utensils set neatly at four place-settings in readiness for the evening meal. On a fragment of wall, coats hung from metal spikes driven into the stone. Nothing moved inside other than the mist skirting the empty and roofless rooms, shrouding every crevice with morbid dampness.

Who lived here? she wondered. Were they still alive?

Barbarian mangonels had done their damage, but the machines of war were silent now. Lily guessed the respite would be brief, resuming soon after Adalwolf's coronation. This lull offered the best opportunity to escape.

"We're ready," said Dealhia.

Lily turned to her friend and nodded. In silence, they plodded towards the south gate, leading thousands of refugees from the Docklands and Southern Vale; a throng of terrified, confused, angry faces, each one leaving their home behind. Some, Lily thought, who likely had never stepped outside the walls of Laodicea. Mothers and fathers carried children. Brothers and sisters heaved bags of grain or flour, or bundles of clothes and blankets over their shoulders. Soldiers with grim expressions clutched weapons as if swords and halberds were more precious than food or water. Few rode horses, preferring instead to load the beasts with supplies, keepsakes or injured loved ones.

Amid the crowd, a covered wagon transported Hadufuns and Audie.

How much food could that wagon carry? thought Lily. How many children? Without the wagon, though, she would have to leave the Erstürmen prince behind. And without him, her chances of gaining refuge at Gestade were substantially dimmed. Everyone followed her now. Trusted her. War leaves no time for self-doubt.

A knot twisted in Lily's stomach as she led the refugees through the Southern Vale's south gate and towards the tents of the sieging barbarian army. Shouts rang out from the enemy camp, followed by a hail of arrows that swished and cut through the night like a soar of falcons diving from the sky.

"Shields!" yelled Lily.

Those with shields, raised them above their heads.

Thock. Thock. Thock. Arrows embedded in wood. But the shields were too sparse, and dozens of refugees dropped to the road with arrow shafts and ornate fletching jutting from their chests, shoulders or backs. Lily spun around to check on Dealhia, who huddled near the ground with her husband and five children.

"Keep moving!" Lily cried into the crowd as more arrows came. Although she didn't want to fight the barbarians, she may not have a choice. As she gathered Dobunni soldiers around her, a hurna wailed across the night sky. The aerial barrage ended, and shadows in the distance rushed into formation.

"What's happening?" asked Dealhia.

"It seems the barbarians are preparing for another assault on Laodicea." She clasped Dealhia's hand. "Now is the time to bid a final farewell to our home."

~ Chapter 5 ~

Jurelle crouched behind a thorny blemmel bush, spying on two soldiers standing outside a circular guardhouse perched atop the zig-zag road that led down the face of the Riverlands Escarpment beside the Rārian Falls. The soldiers wore the basic armour of men-at-arms, not the polished silver of the King's Shield. More voices came from inside the guardhouse's whitewashed walls, its glassless window shining bright orange from a blazing fire.

Where the soldiers' allegiances lay, Jurelle could only guess. Loyal to Adalwolf, Ewald or Hunfrid, it mattered little. He needed to deal with them. They were a barrier threatening to stop him from reaching the Grōz Wüste and delivering his family into the arms of their new saviours. The darkness, and the mist pooling in the valley between the northern Scaur Hills and the Desolate Mountains' western edge, should keep him hidden. He hoped to take out the soldiers one by one.

Jurelle snuck back to Genevea and Saskia, who hid in the shadows of a grove of bullom trees. Massive trunks with bark resembling gnarled swords lain one on top of the other supported twisting, knotted branches that reached out into the mist until their tips disappeared in the night. Beyond the edge of the canopy of swarming leaves, Sphinux and Genevea's horse, which Saskia had named Crinkle, grazed on the dewy grass.

The gloom shadowing Genevea's face accentuated her apprehension, strands of long, tawny hair, wet from sporadic drizzle, clinging to her cheeks. Jurelle plucked a hair from the corner of her mouth as if picking the most delicate of flowers.

"I can't tell how many," he said. "Five or six."

"They might leave," said Genevea. "We could wait until morning."

"New guards will come. Whoever's in charge of Sardis now won't want Enthilen's western border to go unwatched, and the longer we wait, the more chance we'll encounter stragglers from the Erstürmen army that fought in the Riverlands."

"Aren't you in charge of that army, Dada?" asked Saskia.

Jurelle forced a smile and placed his hand on top of his little girl's head. "I was, once, poppy. But now...now all I have to worry about is you and Mama."

"What are you going to do?" asked Genevea.

Jurelle's stomach churned at the thought of more death. "I'll do what I have to. Stay here with Saskia. If I don't return by sunrise, go into the Scaur Hills and seek out the rebels. Tell them everything. Beg them to take you in."

"An Erstürmen princess and her daughter won't be welcome in Bagendon."

"You have as much chance there as anywhere else."

Jurelle knelt and took the griffin amulet from around his neck. He spread the chain wide and lifted it over Saskia's head, letting the jewel fall to her chest. She held the griffin to her face, turning it over in smooth, innocent fingers.

"Can you look after this for me, poppy?"

"This is Jürgen's."

"It belongs to our family. It travelled with our ancestors across the oceans a long time ago. We brought it to Enthilen, and now I want you to take it with you. Keep it safe."

Saskia looked up to her mother, tears welling in her eyes.

"I'll help you look after it," said Genevea. Jurelle stood, and Genevea pulled him into an embrace. "Come back to us. I can't do this without you."

He kissed his wife on the cheek, turned away and walked over to the horses. Undoing the belt holding his sword and scabbard from around his waist, he tied it to Sphinux's saddle. He wouldn't use the sword, a knife was a better weapon for quiet, hand-to-hand combat, and Genevea needed something to protect herself with. Jurelle took a length of rope from Sphinux's saddlebag, nodded to Genevea, then trotted off into the darkness.

The ends of branchlets reached out and tugged at the frayed wool of Jurelle's hooded cloak as he dodged between trees and bushes, cursing the twigs crunching under his boots and the occasional slosh of an errant foot in a puddle. The suffocating mist created a stillness that amplified his every move. As he neared the guardhouse, he crouched low and crept around to the back of the building. The two guards were still outside, smoking and leaning against the wall, their halberds propped up beside them. One of the guards flicked the smouldering stub of his rolled bunbili weed into the forest. It sailed across the night like a falling star. He said something to his partner then disappeared into the guardhouse.

Jurelle's opportunity had come sooner than he expected. He picked up a stone and threw it into a clump of bushes near the front of the guardhouse. The remaining guard's head jerked up. He stubbed out his smoke, collected his halberd, pointed it into the night and walked to the bushes where the stone had landed. Jurelle left his hiding place and snuck up behind the soldier, pausing when the guard began searching the foliage with the tip of the halberd's blade.

Blood pounding in his temples, Jurelle tiptoed up to the soldier, placed a knife at his throat and whispered into his ear, "Make a sound and I'll slit your throat. Release the halberd and drop to your knees."

The guard complied. From his pocket, Jurelle took a piece of cloth and shoved it in the guard's mouth, tying another piece securely around the back of his head. He cut a length of rope, hogtied the man's hands and feet together, and then ducked behind the bushes.

Another soldier appeared outside and called out, "Yute? Where y'gone?"

The bound guard muffled a reply. Jurelle crouched lower as the second guard gathered his halberd and walked towards him, peering into the darkness. "Ya over 'ere?"

The guard on the ground didn't stay quiet, rolling and groaning, and attracting the attention of his companion.

"What da..."

Before the second guard could finish his sentence, Jurelle sprang from the bushes behind him and slashed a knife across his windpipe. The soldier stood in place, a muted gurgle marking his final breath, then fell to the ground beside his bound companion. Jurelle considered killing the first guard, but decided against it, hoping one life could be spared this night. He raced up to the guardhouse and peered inside the window. In the middle of the sparse, single room, four more soldiers sat around a table, eating cured meat and drinking meduz. It seemed they didn't expect any trouble, their breastplates and spangenhelms hanging from hooks driven into the wall. A fire roared in the hearth, smoke escaping up a chimney built into the wall. Swords and halberds rested in a timber rack beside the door.

Jurelle couldn't tackle all of the soldiers at once; he needed a plan to single them out. As he turned from the window and pressed his back against the whitewashed wall, a tingling crawled across his skin when a shapeless shadow passed close by.

Was that a deer? thought Jurelle. A wild dog?

The shadow floated around to the front of the guardhouse then disappeared.

Murmurs from the soldiers inside turned to cries.

"What y'doin'?"

"Get away. We don't want yur kind 'ere."

"What are ya...no, don't...*ahhhh.*"

Screams blistered the night. A soldier ran from the door and into the mist, his whole body on fire. He wailed the most awful, painful howl Jurelle had ever heard, throwing himself onto the ground and rolling atop the dew trying to put the fire out. Jurelle stepped in front of the window, confronted with an entire building set aflame. One man still sat on his chair, seemingly melted in place, flames licking his calves and thighs. The other two, also on fire, staggered around the room, bouncing from the walls and clattering into the cindered furniture. In the middle of the carnage stood a slender, hunched, withered woman untouched by flame. She looked straight at Jurelle and he froze.

"I've come for you, General Jurelle," she said.

Jurelle wanted to turn away. To run back into the forest. Back to his family. Grab the horses and gallop down the face of the escarpment, fleeing this failing land. But his legs wouldn't move. The woman glided out of the burning room, through the door and around to the window to stand right beside him. He knew now, she was a draughoul.

"What...what did you do in there?" he asked.

"Oil and fire. Now you must come with me."

"I'm not going..."

"They are waiting for you. At the edge of the never-ending sands."

"Who are you?"

"A guide sent by the Germalians. I will take you to them."

"I need to get my family," he said.

"Meet me on the road at the top of the escarpment."

* * * *

Jurelle, Genevea, and Saskia walked Sphinux and Crinkle slowly down the narrow switchbacks etched into the face of the Riverlands Escarpment, following the draughoul who claimed to be leading them to the Germalians. The roar of the Rārian Falls beside them drowned out any sound, the cascading Anchep River drenching their bodies with sheets of mist and spray that coasted across the jagged, moss-covered boulders of the cliff-face. Jurelle thought it sounded like a vast herd of stampeding tufted goliaths thundering over the Dambay Plains, a migration he hadn't experienced in more than forty yarles.

The horses' hooves slipped and skidded on the narrow path. Random stones worked loose, abandoning the roadway and careering over the cliff down into the darkness below. At the bottom of the escarpment, a ring of embers glowed orange where the timber-shingled roof of the second guardhouse would have sheltered a circular wall. Tendrils of smoke wafted up and into Jurelle's nose. It seemed the draughoul had dispatched those soldiers also.

As a dull morning light crept down the face of the escarpment, they passed the smouldering guardhouse. Charred bodies with arms and legs melted into hideous contortions lay outside the doorway. Saskia turned her head away and sobbed. Jurelle wondered how she would cope with the next leg of the journey.

The draughoul led them along a stone path atop the dam wall at the base of the Rārian Falls. The wall held back the Anchep River, creating an immense artificial lake consuming the bottom of the falls. Above the dam slipway, they crossed a wooden suspension bridge that swayed with the stagger of nervous horses. The Anchep River continued its journey below them, falling again into a sheer gorge and rushing south to the Riverlands before emptying into the vast ocean of Gadhang.

Leaving the dam wall, the group headed west, following a track weaving through clumps of sludge grass with flower spikes dispersing winged seeds like flutters of butterflies spiralling above Jurelle's chest. The dry, grey soil that cracked under the horses' hooves was soon replaced by shifting, vermillion sand. The quiet and the warming sun now breaching the top of the escarpment made Jurelle sleepy, and he slumped forward in the saddle, fighting to keep his eyes open.

He jerked upright when Saskia cried out behind him, "What's that?"

Trotting down the face of a steep dune came a woman riding a gangly beast, curtains of red sand sliding under the creature's broad feet.

Jurelle turned to his daughter. "It's called a kamel."

Peeking from behind her mother's back, Saskia screwed up her face. "It's ugly."

"Hush," said Genevea.

"General Jurelle Stansfield," called the woman as she approached. Delicate, tan dress-cloth billowed behind her, wrapping around her trim torso like a flag around a pole. "We were never entirely sure you would come."

"Where else have I to go?"

"Quite," said the smiling woman, the glisten of her pearl-white teeth contrasted against skin as dark as a moonless night. Locks of raven hair poked through gaps in a turban of rolled cotton encircling her head. "This must be Princess Genevea and the little Princess Saskia."

"I'm not a princess," said Saskia.

The woman faced Jurelle. "And your son?"

He shook his head.

The woman stiffened in her saddle. "My condolences to all of you. I am Zenais, a senator of the Germalian Conventus in Portum. I imagine

General Jurelle has already told you all about us, from what little he knows."

"Thank you," said Genevea. "Thank you for sheltering us."

"Ordinarily, we wouldn't offer refuge to the Erstürmen or those who have served them, but these are not ordinary times. And...well, some in your family are not ordinary Erstürmen." Zenais moved her kamel alongside Genevea's horse. "Would you like to ride with me, Saskia? My kamel's name is Predance."

Saskia inhaled, then coughed. "It stinks."

"Stop it," said Genevea.

"It's alright," said Zenais, "you get used to the smell." She looked down at the draughoul. "Thank you, Fullō. Your service will long be remembered. I would ask one more favour."

"Lead the man back," said Fullō.

"You've already guessed."

Genevea turned to Jurelle and narrowed her eyes. "What's she talking about?"

Jurelle winced. He'd made a pledge to the Germalians when they captured him during the Riverlands War and routed his army — a promise in exchange for freedom and a future. Genevea would have to understand.

"I must return to Enthilen," he said. "To complete one more task."

"We've just escaped! Why would you go back?"

"Jurelle has made a promise to us," said Zenais.

Genevea's face flushed an angry rouge. "We don't want your charity if it means my husband has to risk his life again. I'm done with that. I had to bury my only son less than two moons ago." She moved Crinkle next to Sphinux and reached across for Jurelle's hand. "We don't need these people. Now we're here, we could travel south to the Riverlands. Find a plot of land and start a farm. Change our names. No-one will ever know who we once were."

Jurelle's heart thudded against his ribcage, wanting to break free and go with Genevea and Saskia far over the red sand dunes. But his conscience wouldn't allow it. "I have to go back, Genevea. You know I do. To resolve the one thing that has fed my guilt for eighteen yarles."

"Jurelle's success in this matter is paramount to the future of all the peoples of Enthilen," said Zenais.

"Why do you care about Enthilen?" asked Genevea.

"Because the disease growing there will spread across the sand like a slider serpent, poisoning all in its path. Germalia will not be spared from the madness inflicting your homeland."

Jurelle sought his wife's eyes. "I'll keep safe and return before you know I'm gone."

"Fullō will guide him," said Zenais.

"I know a secret path," said Fullō. "Through the waterfall and underground. No good for a horse."

Zenais leaned forward and tugged on the headstall of her kamel's bridle. "The 2nd/43rd Battlement is waiting, Princess Genevea, on the other side of this sand dune. You and Saskia will come with us while General Jurelle completes his mission. There's little time to waste."

Jurelle squeezed his wife's hand. "Go with Zenais. It's our best chance. I'll be following close behind."

Saskia crossed her arms and glared at him. "You're leaving us."

"If there was another way, poppy, I'd take it. We'll be a family again soon enough and live out our days in peace in a shining city on the edge of the sea."

~ Chapter 6 ~

Tom had been drifting in and out of sleep for two days, continuing his recovery from the trauma on Hansen's Bluff. Whenever he woke, Thaly and Grin were always at his side, keeping him warm and fed. The crew of the *Vulking* didn't offer any quarters for shelter, leaving the three companions to sleep on the deck. Whibly gave Tom a filthy cotton shirt that was probably white once, and a leather waistcoat to match the pants he'd been wearing since Jacob and Thaly's camp in the Scaur Hills. Although the leather pants were scuffed and torn about the knees and bottom, they kept him warm and dry.

Captain Adcock didn't speak to his passengers, yet rarely took his eyes from Tom. The captain's bulky, admiral-blue coat, with triangular buttons resembling the teeth of a ravenous carnivore, reinforced his authority as he barked orders from the helm. A bulging waist pressing against a beige undershirt suggested the captain didn't want for sustenance, unlike those under his command.

On the morning of the third day since leaving Laodicea, Tom opened his sleepy eyes to storm clouds brewing above the ship and Thaly adjusting a pillow made from a folded blanket under his head. An almost sweet, fruity smell like squashed grapes came from her wounded arm.

Tom sat up. "Your arm, Thaly. The bandage is soaked."

She dismissed his concern with a shrug of the shoulders. "You're finally awake. You've been sleeping for ages. How are you feeling?"

"I'm getting better. You need to change the bandage on your arm. The wound will get...." Tom searched for the word in Erstürmen, but couldn't recall an equivalent for the English word *infected*.

"Get what?"

"Dirty. Turn red and sore and weep pus."

"I think that's already happening." Thaly unwrapped the strip of cloth from around her forearm, the fabric sticking to the oozing blood and greenish pus seeping from the gash in her flesh.

"You should clean it with seawater. The salt will do it good. Then you can..." Tom reached into his pants pocket and embraced the familiar, clean cotton of the white handkerchief, embroidered by his grandmother with his initials: T. A. He remembered the last thing his mother said to him before leaving the house; 'Phone me...if you're going to be late.' Should he hand over the only tangible evidence he had of home? Wrapped up in the handkerchief was the key Dwarrow had given Tom when they first talked inside Dwarrow's dwell in the Scaur Hills. It seemed such a long time ago. The key had unlocked Tom's shackles in Sardis and saved him from Eroberung. According to Dwarrow, it would open many other things.

Thaly's doleful brown eyes waited patiently as Tom unwrapped the key, leaving it in his pocket, and pulled out the handkerchief. "Then you can wrap this around it," he said, handing her the white cloth. "It's clean."

Thaly rubbed her fingers over the embroidered letters. "This is something you cherish. I've seen you clutching it when you're worried. I can't take it." She tried to hand it back.

"You need to cover the wound with a fresh bandage. Please, Thaly."

Thaly nodded. "Alright. I'll keep it safe and return it to you when my wound is healed."

"Tom! You are awake." Grin strode over the deck with a beaming smile on his face. "I have been sitting at the bow, watching the whales. They are amazing creatures. I have never seen an animal so big."

"How much longer until we reach the island?" asked Tom.

"They won't say," said Thaly. "I can't wait to get there, though."

"We're safe here, aren't we?"

Grin sat beside Tom and whispered, "We need to be cautious."

"Once we get to Bramble Island, we can make our escape," said Thaly.

"Where will we go?" asked Tom.

"I want to go home, Tom. Back to Babir Birramal. You understand?"

"Yes, Grin."

"Thaly also wants to visit the forest."

"We'll need a boat," said Tom.

"I've been told Bramble Island is well known among fishers," said Thaly. "There's bound to be someone there who'll take us to the mainland."

Back to Enthilen and back to Malphas, thought Tom. "Malphas killed my grandmother," he said, reaffirming the fact in his mind.

"Are you sure?" asked Grin.

"I recognised his face. We found Nanna's killer. Now I have to bring him to justice."

"Maybe you cannot, Tom. It might be time for you to move on."

"No. I can't move on." As soon as the words left his lips, Tom flinched at the hurt on Grin's face. "I'm sorry, Grin. I've always trusted your advice. I want to trust it now. Yet this tearing of my insides won't relent."

"Are you sure killing Malphas will end it?" asked Thaly.

"What if we do not have to kill him?" said Grin. "He could be imprisoned until the end of days."

"By who?" asked Tom.

"The weald-grells of Giigal could watch over him."

"With tainted grells and who knows what else at his command, we're not getting anywhere near Malphas," said Thaly.

Tom's mind churned, wondering how he could deliver justice to Malphas, avoid endangering his friends, and find a way home. To do any of these things, he needed answers, and Princess Caeli told him he'd find answers in the graveyard of the grells. Bindari. He faced Grin. "You're going to be initiated soon, aren't you?"

"Yes," said Grin, "at the next garrabari. If I can return home in time. Why?"

"Initiated grells know the location of Bindari. Dwarrow told me. When you're initiated, you'll know how to find it. The elders will tell you, and you can tell me."

"I am not sure I can do that."

"You have to," said Tom, raising his voice in demand. "I need answers. Caeli told me I would find them in Bindari. I think someone's there who can make sense of all this."

Grin shook his head and turned away.

Thaly fixed her unblinking gaze on Tom. "This was never just about you, Tom Anderson. This was always about *us*. Grin is trying to stop wild grells being wiped from the face of Enthilen. I'm fighting for a lost homeland and to avenge Jacob's death. We all have needs."

Tom didn't shy from Thaly's glare. "Caeli gave me a new purpose."

"You're placing a lot of faith in the word of an Erstürmen princess. You need answers, but so do I. I want comfort that Jacob's life wasn't lost in vain. I need to know everything you know. About Malphas, the tainted grells, and what happened on Hansen's Bluff."

"I'm not sure..."

Snap!

Something above Tom's head cracked as a violent gust of wind blew across the *Vulking's* bow. A flailing rope slapped into the deck's railing, and Whibly yelled, "Duck!" Another rope, weighed down by a metal pulley, swung across the deck. All the crew crouched and covered their heads except one; the gangling young man. Foiled by slow reflexes, the metal pulley smacked into the man's face, knocking him over the railings and into the ocean.

"Man overboard!" cried Whibly, scurrying to the side of the ship.

"Who is it?" asked Adcock.

"It's Scootle, Cap'n."

"No loss. Let the ocean take him. We'll get another deck boy soon enough. One with better ship sense."

"I can get a rope to him, Cap'n," said a panicked Whibly.

"I said leave it, skullard. Back to ya post."

Whibly sneered at the captain, a fleeting moment of dissent before the skullard gained control of his emotions.

Tom turned to face the shimmering fear in Grin and Thaly's eyes. "We'll get out of this," he said, trying to sound confident.

The three companions sat in silence until mid-morning, although the clouds had become so thick overhead, it felt more like dusk. Tom dwelled on how easily Captain Adcock had dismissed Scootle. How effortlessly a life had been brushed away like an annoying bug.

Grin yawned and stretched his giant arms above his head, then faced Tom. "What would you call these black and white whales in your language? Do you have a name for them in English?"

Your language. English.

Grin was a dutiful student, always keen to learn new words, but now his enthusiasm accidentally exposed one of Tom's secrets.

Thaly glared at Tom. She'd caught the misstep.

Grin frowned with regret. "Sorry. I have said too much."

It doesn't matter, thought Tom. *It's time she knew.* "Do you know what the eyes of lost souls are, Thaly?" asked Tom. "The dark eyes?"

"Jacob told us they can be used to steal a person's soul. Some believe they can make you immortal."

"Adalwolf has them. He showed me. They were in his fist when he punched my chest. Malphas wanted him to steal my soul."

"Why you?"

"It seems Adalwolf and I were born at the same time in different worlds."

"Different worlds?"

"I'm a traveller, Thaly. A birraman. I speak a different language and come from another world. Not across the oceans, but from across the skies."

"Across the skies? How is that possible?"

"The eyes of lost souls brought me here. I remember only fragments of what Malphas said on Hansen's Bluff. Something about Adalwolf and I sharing the same mark, and the chance for Adalwolf to live a life eternal."

"What mark do you share with the prince?" asked Grin.

"I don't know."

Thaly loosened splinters from the ship's deck with broken fingernails. "So, Malphas wants Adalwolf to become immortal. What advantage does he gain from that?"

Tom's thoughts drifted with the ocean breeze, nausea and weakness starting to overwhelm him again. At the helm, Captain Adcock struck a lodestone against the metal needle of the ship's compass and checked their course.

Grin's resonate voice floated on the breeze. "Our land could never endure an Erstürmen king who is immortal. While Adalwolf has the dark eyes, it appears that is the threat we are all facing."

"He doesn't have the eyes," said Thaly.

Tom's thoughts were wrenched away from Adcock and narrowed to a pin point as Thaly reached inside the front pocket of her pants. She pulled out the eyes of lost souls, the flaming pupils casting light from inside the obsidian across the palm of her hand.

"Where did you get those?" said Tom.

"When I was fighting the stupid prince on Hansen's Bluff. He dropped them on the ground, and I scooped them up. I don't think anybody saw."

A brooding suspicion darkened Tom's mind. "Give them to me."

Thaly jerked her hand back. "Why do you want them? Do you want to live forever?"

"No…but they're mine. The eyes were given to me. Stolen from me by Eroberung. They could be my only chance of getting home."

"Are you in a hurry to leave us?"

Tom growled, "The eyes of lost souls brought me here and they'll get me home again. I'm sure of it."

"How are they going to do that?"

Thaly juggled the balls of black glass in her right hand. The clink of the eyes knocking together pecked at Tom's brain like they were mocking him.

"If you hold one in each hand, you'll disappear from this world and end up in another. My world most probably." *Damn. I shouldn't have said that.*

"Are you sure?" asked Thaly.

"No…but…"

"Do you mean hold them like this?" She placed one of the eyes in her left palm. "Nothing seems to be happening."

"Don't! If you close your hands it'll happen. Don't do it. Give them to me." Tom jumped up and pushed Thaly into the side railings. Her shoulder smacked against a timber post, jolting the dark eyes from her hands. The eyes bounced onto the deck and rolled towards the consuming ocean until Grin swooped down and snatched them up as Whibly approached.

"What's the commotion here?" said the skullard, pulling Tom off Thaly.

Tom faced Whibly. "Everything's fine," said Tom.

Whibly grasped Tom's chin and turned his face side-to-side. "Well, there's a lot more colour to y'cheeks. Seems you've recovered enough for a meetin' with the Cap'n. He wanted to know when ya were feelin' better. I'll go get him."

Whibly hobbled off. Grin gave the eyes to Tom, who stuffed them in his pants pocket.

Thaly stood tall, rubbing her shoulder and glaring at Tom. "Don't *ever* attack me again."

Before Tom could respond, Captain Adcock marched towards him. "Whibly said ya were livelier. I can see a brightness in yur eyes at least. What's say we hasten yur recovery with a meal in my cabin?"

Tom couldn't think about food. He wanted to apologise to Thaly, but he didn't want to explain anything to Adcock. "I'm not hungry," he said.

"Really?" queried Adcock. "Ya haven't eaten much since we left Laodicea."

"We gratefully accept your offer of a meal," said Grin.

"Not so fast, grell. I need to talk to the boy alone. Whibly'll sort you and the girl out."

Adcock grabbed Tom's upper arm and lead him away.

"My friends will be alright?" asked Tom.

"Sure, they will," said Adcock. "Ya worry too much. Anyone ever tell ya that?" He took Tom to his quarters at the back of the ship and shut the door behind them.

* * * *

Grin stepped towards Adcock's cabin as Tom disappeared behind a door.

The barrel-chested drummer blocked his path, pointing a curved blade at Grin's throat and sneering, "Ya ain't goin' nowhere, slave."

Thaly drew the knife from her boot and held it at arms-length, her back pressed up against the top chain-rail. "Leave him alone."

"This one's feisty," said another crew member. "It's gonna take some strong men to 'andle these two."

At least a dozen crew crowded in around Thaly and Grin. Even if he unleashed the killer that had appeared in Laodicea, Grin didn't think he could fight his way out of this. Swinging her arm from left to right, Thaly slashed the air with her knife, not knowing which attacker would come first.

Whibly pushed through the crowd. "Put y'weapons down. No...no need for any of this. You heard the Cap'n. I'll find some rations for 'em... just a couple of mouthfuls...and settle 'em back down again."

The big, hulking whale-master towered over Whibly. "Mind y'business, cripple. Adcock ain't here to protect ya, and we've lost Scootle. Unless y'want to be next, y'better scuttle back under y'rock."

Thaly lunged at the whale-master. The knife skidded off the top of his leather chaps, and she tumbled forward into the arms of another crew member who wrenched the knife from her hand.

"Let go of me!" yelled Thaly.

"That ain't likely," said the whale-master. "Out on the lonely ocean, we need comfort. And y'got a comfortable look about ya. Let's get these two below deck."

As the crew dragged Thaly into their quarters, Grin simmered. He smacked the blade from his throat and threw a punch that cannoned into the drummer's face. The drummer's head jerked back, and the snap of a breaking neck shattered the tension a moment before he collapsed onto the deck.

Whibly's mouth dropped open. "Holy Marduk."

Anger screaming inside his mind, Grin flailed his arms like the branches of a panalope tree lashed by a windstorm, throwing crew members into the railings. But a thick rope dropped down over his head and torso, and drew tight, pulling his arms into his sides.

Almost as tall as Grin, the whale-master raised himself onto his toes and whispered in Grin's ear, "I can tame a half-dozen whales. What makes y'think I can't handle a little grell like you?"

~ Chapter 7 ~

Pulling the hem of her ragged dress up to her knees, Seronan disembarked the serf-wagon, then trudged bare-footed into the stables adjacent to the Master's Hall in the King's Quarter of Laodicea. The smell and heat hit her first. Sixty sweaty, dirty grell slaves crammed into a building designed to house no more than half-a-dozen horses. Then the murmur of oppression fouled her ears. The dull, moaning sorrow she'd grown so used to. Aching bones, bruised muscles and failed lives.

Pushing her way through the crowd of slaves that squashed against the timber walls, Seronan stumbled, steadying herself by clutching the arm of her young friend, Myan, who limped along beside her. Of course, she would never call him Myan within earshot of the overseer, Henruld, or any other Erstürmen. Grell slaves were forced to abandon their birth names in favour of a label chosen by their overseer. Henruld liked to use animal names for his slaves. He called Myan, Flea, and Seronan, Wortle, because he said she resembled a cross between a worm and a beetle.

Seronan and Myan found a corner of the stable with enough room for them to sit, and slumped down onto claggy straw bound in clumps by wet manure.

Despite their exhaustion, Myan's voice bubbled with energy. "We're marching to Malang Gunya."

"What?"

"Malang Gunya. I overheard Master Henruld talking. King Adalwolf is going to rule from the old city."

"The Erstürmen will not rebuild our home, Flea."

"Then why..."

"They will destroy what remains and build on the ruins."

Myan's excitement abated, and he pressed his fingers into the scar running the length of his forearm, a legacy of a beating by Henruld. Seronan knew her friend always rubbed the old wound when he felt confused or threatened.

"Why go there at all?" asked Myan. "What purpose will that serve?"

"Hoi! Keep da noise down else y'get no meal," yelled Henruld from outside the stables.

Sad, thought Seronan, that her mouth still salivated at the mention of the evening portion; a lukewarm stew made from offal, potato skins and straw. Henruld mistakenly called it a meal.

Myan whispered, "I've never seen my true home and now we march to destroy it?"

"I am surprised you care about a place you have never seen."

He winced, and the glimmer in his lilac eyes faded. "Malang Gunya is the spiritual home of all stone-grells. Even ones born into slavery like me."

"The home of stone-grells *and* weald-grells."

"Yes, sorry, Wortle. And weald-grells."

"Even when I was free, I never visited Malang Gunya. Females have always been forbidden to undertake the homage march. Once, my mother told me a story about another city, an ancient city lying beneath the flagstones of Malang Gunya. She said my great, great grandmother fell down a hole one day and discovered a whole room full of treasures."

The gleam returned to Myan's eyes. "We could find treasure. Then we'll buy our freedom."

"I doubt we can find enough treasure for that." Seronan leaned forward and grimaced, a fiery twinge shooting down her side. "I saw Henruld's new master today. Hunger, the black grell, beat me for taking too long to load crates into the king's wagons. What has turned these tainted grells into such as that? What did they endure to become a willing servant of our oppressors?"

"Come get y'meal!" yelled Henruld.

Like a herd of goats waiting their turn at a single feed trough, Seronan and Myan queued with the other emaciated slaves for the only meal of the day. Even the sick and injured found a reserve of energy to make sure they didn't miss out on the meagre portion dished up by the overseer. Once bound in slavery, grells rarely survived more than a handful of harvest seasons. Seronan and Myan had persisted much longer than that, serving a kindly Widald, the former and now deceased Master of the King's Quarter.

Seronan shuffled along the line, grabbed a wooden bowl from the table and held it towards Henruld, arms stretched and head bowed. The overseer sloshed a single ladle full into her bowl and waited.

"Thank you, kind master," she muttered, then limped back into the suffocating stable, clutching the bowl to her chest. She plonked down beside Myan.

He emptied his bowl in one gulp, not letting a drop of watery stew soil his hessian top, then licked the bowl clean. "Not like we used to get at Master Widald's. That was real food. This tastes like dirty water."

"You should make it last, Flea."

"The straw always sticks in the back of my throat. I need to wash it down with something." He peered into Seronan's bowl. "You still have a couple of mouthfuls left."

She hovered her face over the bowl like a wary den mother. "I am taking my time. I want to keep the broth for later."

Myan threw his empty bowl into the straw, rested his back against the wall, and stared up at the rafters. "Grell soldiers carrying notched broadswords and wearing armour and helmets guarded the road today. One of them told me the new king wants to build a grell army. The Rephaim. Who would've thought the Erstürmen would arm grell slaves? I'm thinking of asking Master Henruld about it. I can fight."

"*I am* thinking of asking," said Seronan.

"What?"

"I have told you before, if you want to speak like a free grell, you must say each word. Never shorten them."

"I still don't understand why grells speak like that."

"*Do not* understand. When the Erstürmen drove the last stone-grells from Malang Gunya and forced us to use their language, the elders decided we would poison our mouths with every one of their foul words to remind us of our suffering. The words are the fuel keeping the fire of resistance burning."

"It sounds depressing."

"We should never feel comfortable in the world the Erstürmen have created for us. If we do, we will lose the will to fight. Why do you want to join the Rephaim?"

Myan shrugged, then yawned. "It has got to be better than this. The guard told me they get real beds to sleep in, and two meals a day."

"It is one thing to suffer the repression of a slave without quarrel. It is another thing entirely to fight for your oppressors. If you join this army, Flea, you will be asked to kill other grells. Do you think you can slaughter your own kin?" Seronan lowered her voice to a faint whisper, "What is going to happen when the wild grells march to Malang Gunya, like they do at every first flower of giagan, the sacred panalope tree, and find the king tearing the city apart? Do you think they will welcome each other with open arms?"

Seronan shook her head. Myan had already fallen asleep, his snores louder than the murmur from the other slaves still finishing their meal. More grells crowded in around her, sitting in the hay or on cold stones. The thought of grell pilgrims confronted by the Erstürmen army in Malang Gunya began to nip at her mind. One false step could see the end of many lives and the vanishing of stone-grells and weald-grells from Enthilen forever.

*   *   *   *

Adalwolf stood at a window of the Master's Hall in the King's Quarter, facing the Terraces, and breathed in the smell of victory. The scent of conquest. Smoke, tar, blood and ash. Although the King's Quarter remained untouched, the barbarians had resumed their attack on the rest of Laodicea.

It's more a dismantling than an attack, thought Adalwolf. Few citizens remained to resist the onslaught. To his surprise, the terrace-dwellers mounted a defence, even managing to resist raids by Hunger and his militia. Lord Sleame must have warned his citizens that all their riches would be plundered. The barbarians pounded the white cliffs of Hansen's Bluff with boulders fired from their mangonels. Chunks of fallen rock tumbled into Felsie, sending geysers of milky froth shooting into the air above the lake, while terrace defenders sheltered behind barricades of wood and stone, trying to hold out for as long as possible. Adalwolf pictured Sleame and his lackeys ferrying treasure out through the caves and tunnels leading into the Desolate Mountains in a futile attempt to avoid the inevitable.

King Ewald had always feared the barbarians, but Adalwolf felt safe inside the Master's Hall. Although, he'd be happier when the barbarians left Enthilen and returned the land to its rightful king. He stepped from the window and squatted on a wooden stool, sitting at his father's feet. Malphas slouched atop the throne of the dead like it was his favourite evening chair. The same seat Adalwolf had claimed during his coronation. The throne of the dead had been Volerdie's seat of power, but now it was the king's throne. *His throne.* Right?

Dressed in bulky robes of royal blue and black, the traditional colours of the Heine Empire, he began to feel like a king. Strangers bowed to him. Called him 'sire' and 'majesty'. Thumped their right fist against their chest and yelled, 'Hail, King Adalwolf!' He felt like a king everywhere except in the presence of this old man who claimed to be his father. This Worshipful Master. This Malphas.

Adalwolf pondered his ascent to the position of king. *Position*, not power. He hadn't gained power yet. It seemed Malphas wanted to keep that from him. But why did the old man put Adalwolf in this position at all? What might Malphas gain from it? He claimed Adalwolf would become immortal and rule for an eternity if he used the dark eyes to steal Tom Anderson's soul. That would extinguish any chance of Malphas taking the throne for himself, wouldn't it?

Lothar paced around the room, his sangria gown sweeping the dusty floorboards as if cleaning away the filth of any unbelievers. Always full of pious energy, the Hoch-Vater had a devout zeal that made Adalwolf uncomfortable. To what ends would Lothar go in his worship of the Divine Creator?

"Preparations for the march to Pergamos are well advanced, Worshipful Master."

"Thank you, Lothar." Malphas pushed Adalwolf's knee with his foot. "I think the new king should spend time overseeing the work. Walk among your people, Adalwolf. Take Hunger with you and a cohort of King's Shield, or better yet, the Rephaim. Convince the people of the promised majesty of Pergamos."

"Are we abandoning Laodicea, Fa...Worshipful Master?" asked Adalwolf.

"Not entirely. Appoint Hunger, Steward of the city. While much is in ruins, the King's Quarter still stands and we need a trading port. Hunger can organise commerce with merchants, and Krieg has arranged for our barbarian friends to raid the ships refusing to enter Traders Bay, and to share the spoils with us."

"What about Sardis?" asked Lothar.

"Let Hunfrid believe he's in charge of the city for now. Krieg will pay him a visit when we leave for Pergamos, to retrieve a treasure Eroberung had. Hunfrid may be able to enlighten us on the ornament's whereabouts. Adalwolf, you will order General Badulf to travel to the Erstürmen outposts and secure a pledge of fealty to the new king. When Pergamos is rebuilt, we'll be the envy of all, and envious eyes are tempestuous and foolhardy. We need to be ready for any challenge."

"When will I have a proper court?" Adalwolf asked with a flash of boldness. "Ewald appointed a Master of Executions, a curate, a soothsayer."

Malphas leaned forward and fingered the ratty, grey beard growing like a tail at the point of his chin. "You only need us, Adalwolf. I will guide you. Lothar will be your voice when you're unable to speak for yourself; *The Proclaimant of the King*. When Krieg has finished training the Rephaim, you'll have bodyguards more loyal and deadly than any King's Shield. And Ende will continue your tuition."

Adalwolf baulked at the mention of the pale grell. She stood in the corner of the room, her shadow dulling the white serpent crown resting on a burgundy cushion atop a side table.

"Thousands of Dobunni and their miscreants fled the city during the coronation, taking the coast road to Gestade," said Lothar.

"Let them go. When Badulf visits Gestade, he can order Field

Commander Hartmut to dispense with any refugees lingering near the outpost." Malphas dismissed Lothar with a wave of his hand.

The Hoch-Vater bowed to Malphas, then strode from the room, leaving Adalwolf alone with his father and Ende.

"There are certain things only you and I should discuss, Adalwolf. The eyes of lost souls. Tom Anderson. Our *relationship*. We must keep these things secret."

He didn't want to, but Adalwolf looked at Ende and couldn't look away.

"Don't worry about Ende," said Malphas. "She's my most trusted confidant. She'll take my secrets to her grave."

"What about the other tainted grells and my mother? She heard you speak..."

"Your mother is no threat to us," snapped Malphas. "More than anything, she desires your rule. Stories of dark eyes and scriptures will vanish among the jumble of her mind, swamped by the singular blinding love a mother has for her son. And Hunger and Krieg would slaughter their own offspring should I order it. Their loyalty to me is unbounded."

"Do you think Tom Anderson is still alive?"

Malphas growled and shook his head. "Are you completely witless? He must be alive because *you* are alive."

Adalwolf had tried, but failed to grasp everything his father said. Malphas reached inside his white cloak, withdrew a parchment and beckoned Adalwolf over.

After unrolling the parchment, Malphas pointed to a drawing of a sun between two orbiting spheres painted as eyes. "I copied this illustration from the First Scripture. It represents the eyes of lost souls melding two life forces across two worlds sharing the same sun. You and the boy are connected as the dark eyes are connected by the sun's rays in this drawing. When he dies, you die."

Adalwolf's mouth dropped open. He grabbed the throne's backrest to steady himself.

Malphas continued, "*Unless*...unless both of you occupy the same world at the same time, and one of you captures the other's soul using the dark eyes. Then the victor will live forever, and the soulless body of the vanquished will become a draughoul and wander the land until they waste away into dust and shattered bones."

Adalwolf's temples pounded in concert with his heart. "We...we can't let him die before his time. Before I'm ready to..."

"No. You're right. If he dies before we find him, our plans will come to naught. Alas, we can control only so much. That rebel bitch stole the eyes, yet she won't understand their significance. Her weakness will surrender the eyes to the boy, and he'll bring them to us. If he doesn't, or if he dallies in this task, I'll think of a way to encourage him. When Krieg finds the blood compass, we can track the boy's whereabouts. Your blood will lead us to Tom Anderson, and he'll have nowhere to hide."

~ Chapter 8 ~

Tom teetered on a three-legged stool inside Captain Adcock's quarters, his knees knocking against a low table covered in maps and charts, a plate of food scraps, and a mug of meduz. A brass lantern hanging from the low ceiling swung with the rocking ship, illuminating the mess on the table, and the coats, shirts and bags that dangled from hooks driven into the back wall. Adcock sat opposite Tom, chewing salted pork and picking at his teeth. He swivelled his chair and pulled another map from the top drawer of a dresser, checking his teeth in the mirror. A padlocked chest wrought with timber and metal straps sat beside the dresser.

I bet that chest contains treasure, thought Tom. I wonder if Dwarrow's key opens the lock? Forget about treasure, and focus.

"Oh, forgive me rudeness," said Adcock. "Would ya like somethin' to eat?" He held a sliver of cured meat towards Tom, who shook his head. "We also got barnacles, scraped from the side of the ship, no less. Sounds horrible, but they're surprisingly tasty if cooked right. What 'bout somethin' to drink? Meduz? Or water if ya want to keep a clear head."

"No thanks."

"Suit yurself." Adcock shoved more food into his mouth and studied his maps.

Tom sat in silence, his jittery bare feet tapping up and down on the cabin's floorboards.

"Don't worry 'bout yur friends," said Adcock. "Whibly'll take care of 'em. I bet they're all sittin' in the mess eatin' a nice meal. Merchant seafarers are a hungry lot. You should eat somethin', too...Tom, is that right? That ya name?"

"Yes."

"You'll see yur friends again long before we land at Bramble Island next eve. I thought, given yur injuries, ya might want to sleep in a real bed tonight. I'll be at the helm most likely anyway."

Tom screwed up his nose, almost tasting the reek from the captain's soiled, unmade bunk in the corner of the room. *You've already left us on the deck for three days. Why so concerned now?*

"You've been through a testin' time by all accounts. Did the black hornet juice make ya feel better?"

"It tasted awful."

"That's true of most things that are good for ya." Adcock leaned back in his chair and clasped his hands behind his head. "Now, why don't ya tell me a bit 'bout yurself."

Resting his hands on his knees to stop them hitting the underside of the table, Tom recounted his faux story about being a goat herder from the Desolate Mountains.

An attentive Captain Adcock remained curious. "Why were ya in Laodicea? Didn't ya know war was comin?"

Tom's nerves vanished, replaced by a flush of defiance. "Why were *you* in Laodicea?"

"Ha! There's pluck in ya yet. Yur right, though. We were fools to be trapped in Traders Bay when the barbarians came. Me crew was scattered all across the city. Couldn't get the idiots on deck quick enough. Lucky for us and lucky for you, we finally got things together. Though

the barbarians weren't happy to let us go. They sent a ship after us. Do
ya know anythin' 'bout that?"

Tom shook his head.

"Never mind." Adcock leaned forward and shuffled parchments
around his desk. "Have ya seen a map of these lands before, Tom?"

"No." Tom clenched his buttocks, sore from sitting on the hard stool.
Although he was worried about Grin and Thaly, despite Adcock's reassur-
ances, he was curious, too. The map might show the location of Bindari.

"We're 'bout here now..." Adcock pointed with a dirty yellow finger
to a spot on the map, "...south of Laodicea and headin' down the east
coast of Enthilen, or so the Erstürmen call it. Others got different names
for this place. Look, here's Gestade, the coastal outpost. We trade there
sometimes. Field Commander Hartmut runs a tight ship. Well, tighter
than this one." The captain sniggered. Tom failed to see the humour.

"Not far from Gestade is Dorfisch. Most villagers there are fishers. Excellent sea slug if you've got the stomach for it. We're headin' to
Bramble Island, part of the Abrolous Archipelago..."

As Adcock spoke, Tom searched the map for familiar places. He found
Sardis, inland west of Laodicea and perched on an island surrounded
by the Anchep River. The Scaur Hills lay south of Sardis, yet the map
didn't mark the location of Bagendon or the mouldewerp dwell. Tom
might know things the captain didn't. Babir Birramal, Grōz Forst on
the map, covered much of the southern half of Enthilen, with Süden
Forst guarding the forest's northern edge. In the middle of the Dambay
Plains was a dot with the name *Grell City*.

"Malang Gunya," Tom muttered to himself.

Grōz Wüste covered almost the entire area west of the Riverlands, with
a region called Germalia located along the west coast. East of Enthilen,
across the Veiled Occyan, were unfamiliar lands, but no Bindari.

Tom pointed to a region called Setux. "Who lives here?"

"That's where the barbarians come from. Well, see, the Erstürmen and Dobunni call 'em barbarians. That's the name they give people they're afraid of and don't understand. If they learned more 'bout their culture, they wouldn't keep losin' fights. The barbarians come from different tribes dependin' on current alliances, which can change on a whim. They spend more time fightin' each other than raidin' together. The fact the red grell got 'em *all* together says somethin' 'bout his skills of persuasion. Some of the raiders that attacked Laodicea are Setuxons, others Oderans. There were even tribes from lands not marked on this map. The so-called civilised folk consider 'em bloodthirsty fiends, but they're only wanderers lookin' for treasure. A bit like merchant seafarers, I guess."

Adcock took another swig of meduz. "I've been to Setux. Didn't linger long. They're an unruly mob. I've even circumnavigated all of Enthilen and neighbourin' lands. Ostamp, the Erstürmen call it all. Ya can't land here." Adcock pointed to an unnamed peninsula on the south-eastern edge of Grōz Forst. "Too many cliffs shrouded in fog, and the bays are littered with boulders the size of a house hidden less than an arm's length below the surface. The weald-grells live further along the coast, here at Giigal. I don't trade with 'em. They ain't got anythin' I'm interested in. I've been to Germalia. Now that's a strange place. Women rule those lands. Men are nothin' more than servants."

As Captain Adcock spun his tales, Tom began to relax, keen to learn more about the new world he'd entered. "Where's your home?"

"The city of Ephesus, on the Nordland side of the Afonwee River. If ya pass through Detranté or travel 'round the north coast, you'll come to me homelands. The Erstürmen aren't fond of Nordmen. A long time ago, me ancestors routed their kingdom and sent 'em packin'. But we're not warmongers. I haven't been back home since last harvest season." He pushed his chair from the table and stood up, the top of his bald head brushing against the low ceiling. "If ya want to become rich, Tom, don't take on the life of a merchant. We do little more than scrape by. After I've paid me crew, I'm usually left with only a pittance. That's why it's important to keep yur eyes open for other ways to make coin." Adcock flashed a crooked smile.

"You let that man drown," said Tom, tensing up again.

"Scootle? Whibly warned him, but his wits were dim. He would have died another way soon enough." Adcock rested his palms on the table and leaned in towards Tom, his fetid breath punctuating every word. "Scootle's life weren't much fun, bein' at the bottom of the peckin' order and all. He was often a victim of the achin' loneliness that plagues seafarin' crews if ya know what I mean. He's better off at the bottom of the ocean."

"I'd like to return to my friends." Tom stood up, turned his back on Adcock and stepped across to the door. He grasped the handle and pushed. The door wouldn't budge. The captain must have locked it.

"Don't be hasty, Tom. We should talk more. Why don't ya tell me 'bout yur adventures in Laodicea?"

Tom squeezed his hand around the doorknob, his bloodless knuckles white with unease. "There's nothing to tell."

"Oh, I think there is. The scars on y'chest mark ya as a Dobunni rebel, but y'don't sound like a Dobunni, and ya just told me y'spend most of y'time herdin' goats in The Feign, not fightin' any rebellion. And there's those strange scars on ya hands. I ain't never seen any like those before. Whibly saw ya on Hansen's Bluff, spreadeagled on a cross. Was that Prince Adalwolf — well, King Adalwolf now, I imagine — was he up there with ya?"

"I don't know what you're talking about." Tom kept his left hand on the doorknob and put his right hand in his pants pocket, wrapping his fingers around the eyes of lost souls. They were his again, for what good it might do. He thought about trying Dwarrow's key to unlock the door, but didn't want to reveal his treasure to Adcock. Any treasure.

"I trust Whibly's eye. His body might be lame, but he ain't as slow-witted as old Scootle was. Me skullard saved you and yur friends from drownin'. If it wasn't for him, you'd all be dead by now. Look at me, Tom."

Tom pulled his hand out of his pocket, then turned from the door as Captain Adcock's stout body filled the room. "What interest might a king have in a goat herder? Whibly said Adalwolf was tryin' to kill ya. I wonder what the new monarch would pay for another chance at that?"

Tom spun back to the door and pounded on the timber. "Grin! Thaly! Help!"

"They can't help ya. This is between you and me. I can make ya talk if I want to. That would be unpleasant for both of us. I'd rather we deal with this like honourable men."

Tom faced the captain and clenched his jaw, preparing for a fight.

Adcock kept talking. "A merchant's life is a hard one. Any extra coin I can scrounge is a blessin'. I'm thinkin' yur worth more coin alive than dead."

Someone thumped on the outside of the door, making Tom jump.

"Storm's on us, Cap'n!"

Adcock grabbed the front of Tom's waistcoat. Tom squirmed and fought, clutching at Adcock's arms, trying to break the hold. But his strength hadn't recovered from Adalwolf's assault on Hansen's Bluff, and the captain managed to drag him across the room, throw him on the floor and tie his wrists around the foot of the bed.

"Best ya stay here for now. Try to keep out of harm should things get rough. I don't want me precious cargo damaged." Adcock marched from the room and locked the door behind him.

Damn. I should have tried Dwarrow's key. I should have found a weapon.

Could've stabbed the bastard. Tom yanked on the rope binding his wrists. The fibres bit into his skin, and the bed didn't move. *Probably bolted to the wall. You'll get out of this, Tom. Find Grin and Thaly and...and...think of something.*

* * * *

Thaly never thought she'd be so thankful to see a storm. The men had gone, rushing back on deck to prepare the *Vulking* for the coming torrent. Men? *Monsters.* Monsters whose lecherous shadows still haunted the sleeping quarters. Eyes open or shut, Thaly couldn't make the nightmare disappear. She still flinched at the groping clutch of salacious hands. Still recoiled at the nauseating stench of grimy, sweating bodies. Still gagged at the smutty drool dribbling onto her cheeks.

Although Jacob's training had prepared her for certain types of battles, maybe he thought she wasn't ready to confront the worst of it? The lowest ebb this world could reach. An agony far worse than the stab of any blade. How could he ever prepare her for it? How could anyone?

As she poked her fingers through the holes of the shredded tunic that still clung to her quaking body, tiny slices of skin trapped under the edge of her fingernails worked loose against the fabric. She sank into the thin mattress of the bed, wondering if the monsters' faces would torment her for the rest of her life. From a tear in the mattress cover, she pulled out a single feather and held it aloft, hoping a giant bird would appear to claim it and carry her from this awful, awful place.

Thaly pressed her eye against a hole in the wall to the outside world, searching...longing for escape. Dark clouds churned above the *Vulking.* Lightning flashed in the distance, and thunder chased it. Rain began to slap the deck boards, the wind wailing through a ship that creaked and groaned around her as if the waterlogged timber was alive, still a tree growing in the forest. A wave smacked into the *Vulking*, jolting the ship sideways and knocking Thaly's face against the wall. She thrust an arm out to brace herself.

The voice of Captain Adcock vociferated against the howling wind. "Release the whales! Drop the sea anchor!"

Thaly held her breath as another bolt of lightning lit the broody sky, and the thunder clapped sooner and louder. The storm settled right above the *Vulking*, bringing pummelling waves and sheets of rain as the sky and ocean joined in a terrifying cacophony. The ship pitched down and to the left, throwing Thaly off the bunk and onto the floor. She landed on her back, splashing into shallow water that sloshed around her bare legs and arms. It seemed the *Vulking* was already sinking.

Was that the best she could hope for? When the storm calmed, the monsters would be back. Better the floating sewer sink to the bottom, rats and all.

Thaly clutched onto the side of a bed and pulled herself up into a sitting position. Then she noticed Grin lying naked and face down on the floor against the opposite wall.

Oh, Grin. What have they done to you?

A violent lurch threw Grin's limp body across the room like an empty hand puppet. Plates and cups bounced off his giant frame and skidded onto the grubby floor. He reached up and pulled a blanket down around his shoulders like a cloak, to ward off the danger penetrating his world. As he tried to sit up, the storm threw him back down again, his head smacking against the floor. Loyal, strong Grin, reduced to nothing more than a discarded rag.

Thaly couldn't bear it. All this pain. Hers and Grin's. All this horrendous, deplorable suffering.

The boat pitched again, throwing her across the room and into a wall.

As she tried to stand, her legs buckled under her. Grabbing the edge of a bunk, she fought to stay on her feet.

Damn the monsters, she thought. She needed to get out of here. She needed to get Grin out of here.

*　　*　　*　　*

Inside Adcock's quarters, Tom twisted his hands one way then the other, trying to loosen the rope, but it bit tighter into his skin. In desperation, he fumbled around in his pocket and pulled out the eyes of lost souls.

I know it's pointless, but...

He managed to grasp one in each hand and clench his fists, slamming his eyes shut, hoping it would make a difference. It didn't; when he opened them again, nothing had changed.

Fuck! Fuck! Fuck!

A strange and unusual fury coursed through his muscles. Swivelling his legs around and bracing them against the bunk, he jerked his arms backwards. The leg of the bed worked loose and he yanked again, the timber breaking free and slipping out from between his arms. Staggering to his feet, he dropped the dark eyes back into his pocket and brought the knot in the rope up to his mouth, biting at the rough fibre with manic incisions. It loosened enough for him to undo the knot and free his hands.

Outside the window in the ship's stern, a sheet of cloth resembling a parachute made by patchwork quilters dragged in the water. *Sea anchor.* Tom had seen one before. Next to the sea anchor, a whale breached the surface of the wild ocean. It raised its black head above the water in the lull between waves and locked eyes with Tom as the stern dipped low, filling his mind with an eerie calm.

A wave broke the illusion, the floor of Adcock's quarters pulled out from under Tom's feet as his head smacked into the ceiling.

*   *   *   *

"Grin," said Thaly. "Please. We have to get out of here."

Although Grin's clouded eyes found Thaly's face, she wondered if he saw her. She placed a hand on his shoulder to keep him sitting upright against the wall, and with her free hand, tugged a pair of large pants up his legs.

Yes, stupid, she thought. They were going to die soon. But she would have a final dignity if it took every last ounce of her energy.

Grin stirred, lifted his buttocks off the floor and pulled the pants over his genitals. Thaly tied the cord at the front, wincing at the trickle of blood seeping out from under her friend. Her *friend*.

She couldn't see her own pants among the debris that floated on the water rising slowly up the walls. But she still had on her shredded tunic. It would have to do. She couldn't stay in this room any longer.

"We'll drown if we stay in here," Thaly said to Grin. "We might have a chance if we find something to cling to. Something that will float."

Grin didn't speak. Didn't even look at her. Yet he pushed himself off the floor, and together they tumbled up the steps leading to the deck.

As they emerged outside, the *Vulking* rolled in the waves, tossing crew members against the railings. A couple fell overboard into the ravenous ocean.

Good riddance, thought Thaly.

"Leave 'em!" Adcock screamed against the tempest. "Drop the oars!"

The waves swelled, lightning streaked across the sky, and thunder roared overhead. Thaly and Grin wrapped their arms around each other, trying to keep their feet.

Crack!

A rope snapped and a tangle of patchwork fabric flew across the top of the ocean. The *Vulking* spun side-on to the breakers, and a colossal wave, as tall as the tallest tree Thaly had ever seen, loomed over her and Grin. She took Grin's hand and forced him to grasp the edge of an empty barrel pressed up against the railing. She placed her hand over his, a moment before they were tossed overboard as the ship rolled down the face of the wave.

*   *   *   *

Tom bounced around Adcock's quarters like a rubber ball thrown into a closed circle of boulders. A metal rod smashed through one of the outer walls, and water gushed into the room as the ship listed heavily to one side. Disoriented, he panicked, pushing against the flooding seawater and trying to reach the exit created by the metal rod. Outside, men screamed, the howling wind failing to drown out their terror.

Tom tried to concentrate. *I can't fight against the water pouring into the room. Wait until the waterline is above the hole in the wall, then try to swim through it.* He counted his breaths as water filled the room, up above Adcock's bunk, then consuming the top of the table and the chest of drawers. *Eighty-five, eighty-six, eighty-seven...*

With the hole submerged and the waterline at his chin, he took one last gasp of the remaining air and swam through the exit, kicking up towards a dull light and emerging to a surface littered with carnage and debris, and the nightmarish wails of the shipwrecked crew. Tom latched onto a piece of the broken ship. Another giant wave came, lifting him high above the devastation and into the acrimonious skies. Time stopped briefly, before he plummeted back down into the wreckage.

~ Chapter 9 ~

In the secret passage leading to the top of the Sunrise Keep in Sardis, a steel-capped battering ram made from the trunk of a panalope tree thudded against a so-far impenetrable metal door. The arms of the four soldiers carrying the battering ram shook violently with every assault, and their puffed-up faces flared ruby as they struggled with the demanding weight. The sergeant-at-arms shook his head and ordered the soldiers to rest.

They lowered the battering ram to the floor and followed the sergeant back up the tight passageway while another two soldiers guarded the door. Amid the noise of the farewell, it appeared the guards didn't hear the click of a tumbler moving in the door lock.

A wet black nose poked around the edge of the ajar steel door and sniffed the air. With the necessary information collected, the probing proboscis snuck back and its owner whispered to his companions in a language rarely heard in Sardis. The door creaked open and seven small, furry mouldewerps hurried into the passageway. The two guards had only enough time to look down to their knees before stone-tipped spears, thrust upwards, pierced their windpipes and ended their lives with a bloody gurgle.

The tallest of the seven mouldewerps, a satchel slung over his bare shoulder and a dozen pouches dangling from a twine belt holding up tiny britches, beckoned the others to follow him. They scampered up the narrow passage, staying behind the retreating sergeant and his soldiers until reaching the entrance into the room atop the keep. Emerging from the darkness, the werps surprised another two guards and dispatched them as quickly and as easily as the first. A heated discussion ensued regarding what to do next until the tall one stumbled on a book slipped underneath a cabinet. He dropped to his knees, seized the book with a clawed hand, turned to the first page and inhaled deeply.

The mouldewerp shut the book, got to his feet and tottered through the keep door, loitering at the top of the spiral staircase and muttering to himself in Erstürmen, "The scent of the princess still lingers on the stairs."

When the words cooled from another animated conversation, two of the seven werps returned to the dark of the secret passageway and stood guard. The remaining four followed the nose of their taller companion and rushed down the staircase of the Sunrise Keep.

*   *   *   *

In the smothering damp of Sardis' dungeon, Caeli faced an empty wall opposite her. Anselm had been gone for ages and she wondered if he would return. The dungeon echoed with her weakening breaths and the skitter-scatter of rats as they darted across the stone floor. Sometimes they stopped to nibble at her toes, and she had to squirm and yell to scare them off. Yet, the rodents always returned, hungrier than before. She imagined them eating her alive from the feet upwards, but she wouldn't be here that long. The gaoler had already come to announce her execution, scheduled for tomorrow.

She accepted her death as the reckoning for an awful transgression. Punishment for sacrificing Jürgen's life to save Tom Anderson. She hoped her father was right, that Tom must be protected to avoid plunging Enthilen into chaos. Otherwise, Jürgen died for nothing.

Caeli squeezed her buttock cheeks together, the edges of a concealed silver tausen, a gift from Tom, pressing into her skin. Demanding to use the chamber pot in private, she'd managed to hide the coin from the guards. Extract and re-insert, and squeeze tight in case it slipped out.

Keeping the coin was stupid and desperate, she thought. But it was the only thing left reminding her of happier times, long ago, shared with people who loved her. The silver tausen invoked memories of her father, and she planned to take the coin to her grave.

A scuffle and muted cry from outside the prison door interrupted Caeli's thoughts. "They've come for me," she whispered to herself.

A key turned in the lock, but it wasn't the gaoler or Rostard, the Master of Executions, entering the dungeon. Instead, into the dull light waddled a welcome face.

Despite her aching bones, Caeli beamed. "Dwarrow. You found my scent."

"Never any doubt, Princess. Easy to find. Very easy. I could have smelled you all the way from the Scaur Hills."

"What would I have ever done without you over these countless seasons? You're a true friend."

Dwarrow's salmon-coloured face blushed underneath a crown of spiky black fur. "No time for pleasantries. No time at all. We must get you out of here."

"Where to?"

"We've secured the secret passage for now."

Caeli bit her lip. "I'm not sure, Dwarrow. I have a debt to pay. If I don't pay it now, it will catch up to me eventually."

"You've done more than most to serve your kingdom, Princess. It's time to think of yourself for a change."

Dwarrow whistled, and another mouldewerp trotted through the door. They appeared to argue for a while in Werpish, a language Caeli knew she'd never master, until the second werp crouched and Dwarrow climbed onto her shoulders. He balanced there, unlocking the shackles around Caeli's wrists with one of his special keys. She fell to the floor, her legs buckling underneath her.

Dwarrow climbed down from his companion's shoulders, unlocked the bands around Caeli's ankles, then placed his hand on her back. "Are you able to stand, Princess?"

"I'll be fine." As she tried to stand again, her legs failed a second time.

Dwarrow and the other werp helped Caeli to her feet. She rested her hand on Dwarrow's furry shoulder to steady herself. "I've never been down that passage. Not one step. I was always too scared someone would find it. Or me, thinking I was trying to escape. It'll be strange to finally use it."

"We have to go, Princess. The kingdom you once loved is no more. There's nothing here worth your loyalty."

"You're right. It will be so nice to feel the grass beneath my feet again." Gingerly, with the help of the werps, Caeli followed Dwarrow through the shadowed corridors of Sardis' inner circle towards freedom.

* * * *

Next to Sardis' dungeon, Anselm sat alone inside the torture chamber, a small, claustrophobic room with a single candle burning in the corner illuminating dozens of implements hanging neatly on the walls in their own specific spot, marked by an outline painted in red. Anselm didn't know what the implements did, having never been inside the chamber before. He tried not to imagine as he regarded head-shaped clamps, hinged cages with spikes inside, rolling pins with rows and rows of barbs embedded in the cylinder, and an assortment of hooks, chains and whips. And then there were the things he could barely see. Tiny screws and clamps that might fit a thumb or a tongue.

The books surprised him the most. Six shelves of them, each shelf longer than his arm-span. It seemed torturers were methodical, tidy and well-read. He wondered what macabre notations the books contained. Had somebody actually taken quill and ink to painstakingly document the atrocities of this place?

Beads of sweat pooled under his thin cotton shirt, squeezed out by the smother of the room. How had King Ewald's curate been reduced to this? he wondered. Service to Volerdie and Erstürmen royalty deserved better treatment.

Tied to the rigid metal seat for at least half a day, his buttocks and back ached for release. He wondered if the waiting was part of the torture. Why he'd been left alone for so long. Yet, the quiet isolation gave him time to think on a path to freedom. He knew Rostard, previously Ewald's soothsayer, had now been appointed the Master of Executions, and one of his duties would be to extract a pledge of fealty from Anselm for Steward Hunfrid, using whatever means. Anselm knew other things about Rostard he would happily exploit to circumvent his punishment or gain an advantage.

Behind him, the door creaked open and he turned his head, the ropes binding his wrists to the armrests cutting into his skin. In walked tall, lanky Rostard, dressed in new, embroidered finery — a white, long-sleeved shirt with ruffled cuffs and collar, a red vest with gold buttons, and a black cape. He looked nothing like a torturer and every bit like a nervy, twitchy mantis, the soothsayer's mind probably filled right now with inexplicable visions.

The time had come to turn foe into friend, thought Anselm. "I never saw Hunfrid clothed in such fine fabric when he was Master of Executions."

"Times are changing," said Rostard, strolling around to the front of Anselm's chair and sitting on a flat bench adorned with ropes and winches, the hem of his cape brushing against long thighs dressed in canary-yellow leggings.

"Indeed," said Anselm. "And as the royal soothsayer, you would have seen these changes coming from afar, deep in the night, as your mind flittered around its varicoloured world. Do you prefer soothsayer or executioner?"

"You assume I had a choice in the matter."

"All of us have choices, Rostard. You've chosen to pledge your loyalty to the Steward and a boy king who may have stolen the throne."

Rostard flinched like a man who knew more than he'd ever admit, and took from the wall one of the apparatuses of torture; an iron mask with an internal protuberance that appeared to be designed to force and keep the mouth open.

"Do you know how to use it?" asked Anselm.

Rostard placed the mask on the bench. "No. The whole idea sickens me."

"Then why are you here?"

"Succumb to the new order or die. I've chosen the former. It appears you've chosen the latter."

"If King Adalwolf is confirmed the legitimate king, I will bow before him. Currently, all we have is Hunfrid's word, twisted by his desire to rule Sardis."

"You'll be dead before Adalwolf returns to Sardis."

"There's a reason Hunfrid hasn't executed me yet." Anselm shifted the chair to face Rostard front on, using his bound ankles to yank the chair legs across the stone floor. "Why did you never marry, Rostard?"

"I'm wed to the service of my king. I have no time for other pleasures."

"One of the labours of a curate is to share the joys and burdens of parishioners. Provide counsel in times of confusion and certainty in times of doubt. Those who attended my chapel often confided in me. Revealed secrets never spoken to anyone else."

Rostard's eyes narrowed and his spindly fingers traced the joints and rivets in the iron mask sitting beside him. Underneath his pretty red vest, Anselm swore he could count the soothsayer's racing heartbeats.

"Secrets or lies, how can one tell the difference?" said Rostard. "In your pious world, the promise of the future atones for the transgressions of the past. It's noble and convenient."

"More than one confidant shared the same secret. Whispers of private, forbidden liaisons."

"The inner circle is a cesspit of gossip. It's been that way since our birth inside these walls over forty yarles ago."

"You and I know that in the Erstürmen culture, certain desires are… discouraged. Subject to shame and punishment."

Rostard stood and unhooked a whip from the wall. "Shall we start with this?"

His eyes betray him, thought Anselm. *He doesn't want to inflict pain; he wants something else.* "Hunfrid makes his plans, yet he's no ruler of Enthilen. His reign will end soon and we could end with it. But a shared desire might forge a bond between us that secures our future."

Rostard swallowed so hard the Adam's apple of his taut neck bobbed up and down like a dancing, male scorn-jay. The hand holding the whip went limp and he crouched before Anselm, tracing his tongue over thin lips.

"What do you want?" he asked.

"To seal a pact," Anselm whispered so that Rostard had to lean closer to catch his words. With free fingers, he stretched across and caressed the back of Rostard's hand. "We seal the pact in your chambers and then plan our survival when Hunfrid falls."

Rostard's eyes widened. He leaned forward and nearly toppled over, thrusting his lips upon Anselm's in an awkward, slovenly embrace.

Anselm kissed back before turning his head away. "Wait. Not here. A guard might come through the door."

Rostard withdrew, pulled a knife from his belt and began cutting the ropes around Anselm's wrists with the vigour and innocence of a young man about to lose his virginity.

"When we're done, you'll need to beat me," said Anselm. "To make it look convincing when I next face Hunfrid."

*   *   *   *

In the throne room of Sardis, Hunfrid cradled an ornate, delicate vase in his lap, feeling the weight of the ashes entombed in the porcelain. A living, breathing person, reduced to nothing more than a pile of dust. Rolling the vase over, careful not to dislodge its lid, he absorbed the intricate decorations on the vase's surface depicting scenes from Slumstadt, the shantytown outside Sardis' main wall that he'd never visited, and hoped he never would.

The paintings reflected what little he knew of Brynlee's life. Typically, a peasant would never be afforded the honour of cremation and tribute with their own purposely commissioned vase, instead being thrown into an unmarked hole in the ground. But Hunfrid was the Steward of Sardis. He made the rules now, and he decided who should be celebrated and who should be scorned.

He'd met Brynlee when she entered the inner circle padlocked to a rusty chain that still glinted under the bright blue sky. While the other prisoners trudged across the cobblestones, she glided, her beguiling blue eyes begging for deliverance and ensnaring the Master of Executions. Right then, he hatched a plan to save her, personally conducting each execution. When Brynlee came forth, Hunfrid tempered his blow, injuring the white-haired beauty enough for her to collapse on the stones yet still live. He pronounced her dead and escorted her body to the leichenhalle to rest with the other corpses.

That evening, Hunfrid secreted Brynlee to his private quarters, saving her from the death pit. He tended her wounds for days, falling further in love with every caress and every cleanse. However, King Ewald found out about Hunfrid's illegitimate companion. To save her life a second time, Hunfrid convinced the king to embed Brynlee among the Dobunni rebels as a spy for the Erstürmen. The plan improved Hunfrid's standing within the inner circle when information from Brynlee thwarted a Dobunni assault on the King's Shield.

Hunfrid never abandoned hope his lover would one day return to his arms. When she did, it wasn't as he planned. Eroberung, the white grell, interfered and changed the course of events. Nevertheless, as a chance for love died, an opportunity for ascension emerged. The trappings of power had fallen into Hunfrid's lap to replace the loved one he longed for.

The door to the throne room opened, and two soldiers dragged a beaten Anselm across the floor, tossing the curate at the foot of the stairs to the throne platform.

Hunfrid woke from his daydream. "Leave us alone."

The black boots of the guards slapped the tiled floor as they marched out. Anselm pressed his face against the mosaic pattern embedded in one of the tiles, staining the depiction of King Ewald's coronation with blood dripping from his nose.

"Lift your head, Anselm. There's an easy way out of this. Pledge loyalty to me and the torture ends."

Anselm raised himself up onto his elbows, then collapsed back to the floor, the bloodied tiles muffling his reply. "Adalwolf?"

"When...if Adalwolf returns, past allegiances will likely count for nothing. All of us will be expected to pledge fealty to the new king, but I'm Steward of Sardis until then. Those remaining in the royal city owe me their loyalty."

"You're a traitor to our kingdom."

Hunfrid cocked his head. "Did you call *me* a traitor? Ewald begat treachery. If I wasn't sitting on this throne, someone else would be. Ask yourself, would you rather bow to a tainted grell?"

Anselm clambered onto his knees. Hunfrid placed Brynlee's vase on a pedestal beside the throne, stood up, walked down the stairs and hooked his hand around the underside of Anselm's elbow, guiding the curate to his feet. He retrieved a chair from the side of the room and encouraged Anselm to sit.

Hunfrid sat opposite, on the steps of the throne platform, to look Anselm in the eye. "We're old friends, you and me. Both of us born in the inner circle. Both in Ewald's service since his coronation."

"However, only I remained loyal to the king."

"What good is loyalty without reward? Do you think Ewald gave fair recompense for your nearly twenty yarles of dedicated service? Our world is churning, Anselm. Currents drag us in different directions and try to snatch the future from our hands. Sometimes, my friend, I feel like I'm drowning. You must feel it too. Don't you want to hold your head above water a little longer?"

"You speak in riddles, Hunfrid. I would respect a more direct approach."

"Adalwolf will be crowned king, yet he doesn't rule Enthilen. Our fate belongs to the tainted grells and their so-called Worshipful Master. It's true I was caught in their web. Helped them gain power. But I'm forever wary of the traitor's knife moving closer to my back."

Anselm rubbed his hands across his bloody shirt. "Who is this master you speak of?"

"Gerulf never offered a name, but we could work it out. Once we know our enemy, only then can we defeat him." Hunfrid pulled his emerald robes over his knees, feeling a sudden chill breach the throne room. "Either way, I don't trust the new order. The new king. Blind faith led to Gerulf's downfall, not Dobunni assassins as we've been led to believe. We must be wiser, my friend. We must stay one step ahead of the usurpers lest they crush us with covetous hooves."

"Why should I trust you, *friend*? How quickly you embraced the title of Steward in Ewald's absence. How quickly you grasped power when the throne sat empty."

"Rumours are spreading through the circles of Sardis. They say King Adalwolf will not return to the royal city. That he will rule from Pergamos. Scores of our citizens are already preparing to leave."

"Pergamos? The lost city had almost disappeared from memory until the exiled charlatan Oldaric stumbled onto it. He came to me to boast of his discovery. To urge me to convince the faithful to settle there. The only picture I could sketch from his ramblings was one of empty halls and crumbling ruins. Roots and worms reside in that failed dominion. King Adalwolf inherits an empty shell."

"Careful, Anselm. You border on heresy. Impious, too, is the ascent of Adalwolf and his master to the exalted position once held by our Divine Creator. They appear to offer themselves as deities to the Erstürmen. This is an abomination."

Anselm's face creased as if a harrowing concentration caused him pain. "Is there any chance this Worshipful Master you speak of is Oldaric?"

Hunfrid shook his head, unconvinced. "He's not been seen in Enthilen for more than twelve yarles."

"No-one else I know is so blinded by the myth of Pergamos. What is it you want from me, Hunfrid? You haven't kept me alive for no reason."

Hunfrid paused and thought again whether he should reveal his treasure to Anselm. Although he had tried in vain to decipher the mystery himself, it appeared beyond him. "I need help understanding something I found. No more than a trinket, I imagine, though it may have value I can't see. Will you help an old friend and not betray his trust?"

"Show me this *trinket*."

From inside his robes, Hunfrid retrieved the gold pentagram.

Anselm's eyes lit up. "Where did you get this?"

"Eroberung had it. Do you know what it is?"

Anselm took the pentagram from Hunfrid and brushed his fingers over the etched surface, lingering on the blood staining one point of the five-pointed star. He turned it over in his hand, studying the intricate patterns carved into the metal, then stood, held the pentagram between his thumb and forefinger such that opposing star points dug into his skin, and placed the object on his stool. Balanced on the tip of the conical under-surface, the pentagram spun rapidly of its own accord before coming to a complete halt, still in perfect balance.

"That is strange," said Hunfrid. "When previously it stopped spinning, the bloodstained tip always pointed in the direction of Laodicea. Now it seems to be pointing further south, towards Gestade. What do you make of this, Anselm?"

The curate crouched beside the stool, his knees pressing against his chest. "This is a blood compass. One of the seven treasures from the throne of the dead. From what I've read, the compass can be used to find your birth twin should you have one."

"Such tales come from lost times. What relevance do they have now?"

"It is believed those marked at birth have a twin, born at the same time and carrying the same birthmark — a naevus. Born, not in this world, but into the world to which Volerdie fled. Should your birth twin manage to travel to our world or you to theirs, the compass will find them if you stain one of its points with your blood."

"Whose blood stains the compass now? Eroberung's?"

"No. Volerdie's failed progeny do not have birth twins. Only we, his exalted creation, are bestowed that honour. Yet, only a few of us are marked and even less share the same mark lasting until our death. Most curates say the marks are ancestral. More likely to occur in certain families than others."

"Then Erstürmen blood is on this compass," said Hunfrid.

"Erstürmen, Dobunni, Nordman. I don't know. However, it seems clear to me whoever's blood stains the compass, their birth twin has managed to travel to this world, and they are currently somewhere south-east of here."

* * * *

Rosalie had been spending more time away from home. She didn't feel comfortable there anymore. Allum's sickness had worsened and her father grew increasingly desperate to help his son. She worried Yonna would try something dangerous — a pontifical abomination preached by the curate that would end Allum's life. Heady didn't have the strength to stop it, and Rosalie didn't have the will as she drifted from her family with meek resistance.

On this chilly, cloudy morning, she wandered previously unexplored streets, approaching the entrance to Sardis' fourth circle. She'd never been past its gates, but times were changing in the royal city. Neighbours from the fifth circle had told her the Steward's Shield weren't bothering to check the insignias branded into residents' skin. Citizens from the fifth to seventh circles, and even from Slumstadt, could now wander into the fourth and third circles without challenge.

As Rosalie strolled up to the open gate, she pulled the sleeve of her coat down over the sword and hammer seared into her forearm, identifying her as a resident of the fifth circle and, therefore, not authorised to enter the smaller circles without permission. Guards stood relaxed on either side of the entrance talking among themselves. A gaggle of young children raced up behind Rosalie, nearly knocking her over, and bolted through the gate like they were entering a fair. The guards didn't baulk. Trying not to look suspicious, she followed the children into the fourth circle.

As soon as she passed the gate, her mouth dropped open. Laid out before her were the finest houses she'd ever seen, two and three stories high with porticos guarded by tall, white columns, and balconies shadowing walls covered in climbing ivy. Most houses had turrets with pointed roofs dressed in tangerine clay tiles and multiple chimney stacks, meaning more than one room had a fire. A handful of homes had glass windows. Opaque, rough, sometimes cracked, but real glass, unlike the timber louvres covering the fifth circle's windows.

Rosalie knew the houses belonged to the wealthy merchants who called the fourth circle home, owners of stalls and shops throughout Sardis selling all manner of items. Given the palatial dwellings, she expected the streets to be full of refined ladies and gentlemen strolling pristine, leafy pavements, sampling the wares of renowned traders. Or market squares lined with lofty statues of famous Sardisians watching over trimmed gardens and crystal fountains. Instead, the streets were almost empty. Waste piled up against shop walls, and sewer rats bustled along the thoroughfares, hoarding treasured refuse. A compost of fallen leaves, food scraps and excrement choked gutters and drains, filling the air with an insulting, caustic odour.

Her brown, shin-high boots echoed on the cobblestones as she walked past row after row of closed shops, stopping to read notices pinned to one of the doors. *Printed notices*, not hand-written. Something she'd heard of yet never seen before.

Hunfrid Announced Steward of Sardis by Royal Appointment.

King Adalwolf to be Crowned in Laodicea.

Dobunni Rebels Defeated.

The Ravage Spreads.

Volerdie's Damnation is Upon Us.

Rosalie turned from the door and walked into a market square where a crowd gathered. As she passed through the gathering, she glanced at any bare forearms. Although some residents had two overlapping coins branded into their skin, the insignia of residents of the fourth circle, many did not. She shied away from the pale, sickly-looking citizens with hacking coughs and took her place at the edge of the crowd.

A young man stood on a wooden crate in the square's centre, waving a black book around in his left hand and prophesying loudly. "We suffer because Volerdie is angry with us. Too few follow the scriptures. Too few listen to the curate's words. I have the scripture verses here in my hand."

"How did you get that?" yelled someone in the crowd. "You're not a curate."

"I've been permitted to interpret the scriptures while the curate recovers from his illness, and I have read, my fellow Erstürmen, I have read that a crippling sickness will befall any who loiter in failed cities. A sickness that will end the lives of all, believer and non-believer. Only in Volerdie's halls will atonement be found. Only in the ancient city of Pergamos can we halt The Ravage."

The crowd grew larger, the man seemingly energised by the burgeoning congregation. "I know you've heard the rumours. When King Adalwolf is crowned, he won't return to Sardis. He'll march to Pergamos and we must follow him."

Some in the crowd became restless. A family near Rosalie turned their backs and walked off as the young man continued his oration, "When Adalwolf resurrects Volerdie's kingdom in Pergamos, darkness will descend amid the daylight, heralding the return of the Divine Creator. Only then can paradise be found!"

Rosalie scuffed her leather boot against a worn flagstone. She'd heard this sort of prophecy before and didn't want to listen to it again, leaving the crowd and heading to the gate into the third circle.

Inside the third circle, houses more elaborate than those in the fourth circle lined the streets. Cobbled paths meandered through manicured courtyards surrounded by wrought iron, palisade fences, leading to entrances lined with granite columns supporting slate roofs. Outside the houses, servants and grell slaves packed furniture and tea chests into covered wagons. It appeared the masters and administrators who resided in the third circle were preparing to leave the city.

Ambling along the streets, free of waste and vermin, she dreamed of life inside a mansion, marvelling at the detailed metalwork adorning the fences; hundreds of stakes sharpened to a point and lined up perfectly in almost endless replication. Even her father would struggle to master such skill. Enormous gardens, like caged forests, bristled with birdlife. The destitution of Sardis wrought by royal upheaval and The Ravage hadn't permeated the third circle yet.

It would soon, though. Rosalie expecting The Ravage to follow the citizens of Sardis wherever they fled. Maybe she could move into one of the empty manors and batten the doors and windows against the sieging illness?

She arrived at the gates to the second circle, once the home of the King's Shield. A cohort of Steward's Shield guarded the entrance, cloaks of emerald green pinned to the pauldrons of their silver armour, marking their allegiance to Hunfrid. The guards seemed to be allowing only military commanders or Shield soldiers to pass through the gates.

Rosalie wouldn't test their mettle. She crept closer though, attracted by the macabre display of severed, preserved heads hanging from the wall beside the gates — a warning to traitors and criminals. A long, metal spike had been rammed horizontally through the ears of four heads, piercing the skulls and squashing the vanquished together like chunks of meat on a skewer. Chains at either end of the spike held the heads high above the ground. They bounced against the wall as a strong breeze whipped across the stones.

Rosalie lingered by the heads, searching the closed faces of the damned. A woman with brown hair like hers, an older man with grey stubble, a young man with a strong jaw. She stopped at the last face and squinted, wavering over the prominent nose, dark hair and crooked ears. Despite the tortured expression, the face had a familiarity born from intimacy.

She swayed on her feet, her mind drifting away to the banks of the Anchep River. There she sat on soft, vermillion sand and engraved words in the silt with fingers lightened by the tenderness of new love.

Is it him? she wondered. Harris Snape. Did it matter? Her future was elsewhere now.

~ Chapter 10 ~

Thaly clung to an empty barrel, strands of long, dark hair tangling like seaweed over her cheeks as her head bobbed above the surface of a calm sea. Slumped over the other end of the barrel lay Grin, shrunken and dazed, and seemingly having only enough strength to force one breath to follow the other. If he slipped, she wouldn't be able to save him from this fathomless monster beneath them.

The violent storm had passed, leaving behind complete destruction. Surrounding the two survivors floated the shattered remnants of the *Vulking*. Splintered timber, torn cloth, ropes, and crates, all draped in mist and drizzle. At times, faint cries for help drifted through the fog, yet Thaly never responded, fearful of attracting unwanted company. A fear more pressing than her desire to find Tom should he still be alive. Circumstance trumped friendship. Pain surpassed care.

Grin hadn't spoken since they were flung from the ship. Since the attack. Thaly wondered if he ever would after what happened to them on the *Vulking*. A wave of dread had doused the usual sparkle of his lilac eyes and crushed his beaming smile. A wound lay open that would burn and sting whenever it was exposed to the light. Thaly's burned now, threatening to explode into a blinding fury.

The lost, confused-looking Grin mirrored Thaly's feelings, but she didn't have time for pity. One of them had to find the strength to fight, or they'd both die. It appeared a broken Grin had nothing left. It was up to her.

They'd been drifting...well, Thaly couldn't tell how long because the dull, grey fog masked the sky. Her muscles screamed in agony, fixed in place as she tried to prise her fingers underneath the metal strap holding the staves of the barrel together. Something nibbled at her bare feet as if the ocean wanted to tug her into the depths. She slipped from the lifesaver, then pulled herself up again, digging broken fingernails into the sodden timber to avoid the ocean's grasp.

Grin lifted his head from the barrel. "I am exhausted, Thaly. I do not know how much longer I can hold on. If I sink into the ocean, do not try to save me and risk your own life."

"We'll get out of this," she said. "Somehow."

"Those men...they..." started Grin.

"Try not to think about it."

"I cannot *stop* thinking about it. I hear their voices. Feel their...we need to..."

"Not now," snapped Thaly. Although she felt the agony wracking Grin's face, she had to suppress her own pain; otherwise, they wouldn't survive this.

Through the droplets of dew that dripped, dripped into her eyes, a shape appeared in the distance, crouched above the waterline. As the shape drifted closer, it took a familiar form. Thaly clenched her jaw and reached for a splinter of timber floating nearby.

"Yur alive! Thank Marduk and all the gods of the Veiled Occyan."

At the sound of Whibly's voice, Thaly kicked her legs under the water, pushing the barrel further away.

"Hey! No need for that. I'm here to save ya."

Thaly's kicks turned into nothing more than dabs at the water as fatigue took hold amid an ocean too vast to offer any chance of escape.

Whibly dunked a broken oar into the water, his makeshift raft of flotsam, strapped together with torn cloth and rope, coursing towards Grin and Thaly. It butted up against their barrel with a thud.

"I thought I was the only one. I heard people yellin'. When I tried to find 'em in the fog, there was nothin' there. Think it was sirens tryin' to trick me. Here, grab hold of the oar, I gots room for all of us. Seems like I'm savin' yur life again." Whibly splashed the oar next to Grin, who didn't move.

Thaly sneered at the skullard. "We'd rather die than accept your help."

Whibly flinched. "I tried to stop 'em. I did. It's just...things like that happen at sea."

"Things like that," mumbled Thaly. Inside, she growled — a hot, fiery snarl sending a jolt of energy through her muscles. She pushed off the barrel, reached for Whibly's raft and heaved herself onboard.

"That's it," said Whibly. "Yur almost..."

"ARRGGHH!" Thaly lunged at the bent, pitiful man, thrusting the point of the splintered timber up under his chin until it drew blood.

Whibly raised his arms in surrender, pleading through a mouth almost forced closed by the press of Thaly's primitive weapon.

"Hang on," he said. "No need for that. Ya won't get out of this alone. I know the currents in these waters like the back of me hand. I can get us all to safety."

Thaly knew they would die without Whibly's help. The anger inside her wavered, but didn't diminish as she pulled the timber away. "One misstep, and I'll throw you into the ocean without a thought or a scrap of guilt."

Whibly lowered his hands. "Course, I understand."

Thaly helped Grin onto the raft, then faced Whibly. "Did you see Tom?"

"I ain't seen the boy since the Cap'n locked him in his chambers. He would've been trapped there when the storm hit. Drowned like a ship rat, most likely. Poor sod. What's so special 'bout him, anyways?"

Thaly ignored the question.

Whibly persisted. "I thought the boy might be valuable, after what I seen on the bluff and all. Thought Prince Adalwolf might offer us a reward. It was only business. Don't take it personal. When I sees an opportunity to make some coin, I don't always think it through. It's all over now, anyways. The *Vulking's* gone. We're alone out here, but we can reach land if we share the rowin'. I knows how to use the currents, and I knows which way to go. Head for the risin' sun."

"I can't see any sun," said Thaly.

"It'll clear soon enough. Mark my words."

"You're a liar. Why should we trust you?"

"Yur a Dobunni rebel, ain't ya? And Grin's a big, strong grell. I should be scared of you."

Grin doesn't look like a strong grell anymore, thought Thaly. He looks like a lost child. She sat in the middle of the raft, planting herself between Whibly and Grin, who had retreated to a corner.

"Do you have food and water?" she asked Whibly.

"One full waterskin. If we go cautious with it, the water'll last until we reach land. No food, though."

Thaly pointed to a crate floating past the raft. "What's in these crates?"

"We sold most of our wares in Laodicea. Not that we had much to sell. Some'll have food in 'em. Not sure which ones."

Grin stirred, reaching out and pulling a crate to the raft. He glared at Whibly before punching his fist through the timber, smashing the crate open like a bird's egg. The skullard got the message, his face wide-eyed and fearful. Grin searched inside the container and found nothing.

"We could be lookin' in crates all day." Whibly fished inside one of the pockets of his soaked pants. "I got a length of line here and a hook.

And..." He crawled to the opposite corner of the raft, pulled something from a bundle of clothes and unwrapped it.

Thaly gagged.

"I know. Poor sod," said Whibly, holding a severed arm above his head as if offering it to one of the gods of the sky. "But we can use the flesh as bait. There's plenty of fish between here and Bramble Island."

"We're not going to Bramble Island," said Thaly. "We're going home, to Enthilen."

Whibly rubbed his chin, then looked at Thaly and then Grin. "Long way to row," he mumbled. "Sure. Enthilen. We can go there. We'll have to head for the settin' sun and follow different currents."

Is this the moment, wondered Thaly, where she would abandon Tom? She stood, the makeshift raft tilting and swaying under her feet, its edges close enough for her to topple overboard, and placed her hands on either side of her mouth.

"Tom!"

Still sitting in the corner, Grin yelled through the veils of mist with his booming voice, "TOM!"

The three survivors waited in silence. Whibly rested the severed arm in his lap.

"Tom!"

"TOM!"

"Ain't no use..." started Whibly, then stopped when Thaly glared at him.

Teeth chattering and goose-bumps covering her skin, she sat, leaned forward and wrapped her arms around bare knees.

Waiting, silence, nothing.

Whibly was probably right, thought Thaly. Tom had drowned. If they stayed to look for him, they'd die out here as well.

"I ain't got a spare tunic, but I got some trousers," said Whibly. He wrapped up his gruesome trophy, then pulled a pair of pants from the clothes pile and held them towards Thaly.

She snatched the pants. "Start rowing. When you get tired, we'll bind your wrists and ankles. One mistake, and we push you overboard."

Whibly nodded, knelt at the side of the raft and plunged the oar into the water.

~ Chapter 11 ~

Melinda rowed the elongated coracle past the breakers and into smooth water off the coast of Bramble Island, relishing the freedom of the open ocean. Her Da, Jameus, had agreed to let her go fishing alone. Usually, he'd say she was too young to go by herself, but not today. Today he couldn't resist her pestering.

Under clear blue skies, she headed out to the reef where Da always caught the biggest fish. Whitecaps marked the reef's location, a dozen or so oar strokes ahead. The calm waters were in stark contrast to the wild storm that struck three moons ago. Melinda and Jameus had spent much of the past two days cleaning up the mess from the storm and securing their beach shack so it wouldn't collapse on top of them.

When Melinda reached the reef, she stowed the oars and tossed an anchor over the side of the boat. Then she grabbed a fishing pole made from a stallart sapling she'd felled near her home village of Dorfisch on the east coast of Enthilen. She missed home, having been on Bramble Island with her Da for all of the harvest season and nearly half of the storm season. Now, with crates full of salted, dried and smoked fish, they would be heading home in a couple of days.

She baited the hook with a piece of squid, tossed the line into the water and waited for the first nibble, tracing the horizon with her eyes and relaxing into one of the numerous daydreams that entertained her during these long fishing trips. The sun warmed her face, and she almost drifted off to sleep until a tug on the hook bent her fishing pole down towards the water. She sat up and began to reel in the catch, the pole arching with the strain.

It's a big fish, she thought.

Melinda steadied her balance, but the coracle tipped to the side and she fell forward, almost losing her grip on the pole. Undeterred, she regained her feet and reeled the colossal sea monster closer to the boat, screaming with excitement and delight when a large silverback trevaleigh sprang from the water, fighting against the hook in its mouth.

"Da will be impressed," she said to herself, the silverback being one of the most prized catches in the waters surrounding Bramble Island.

With a final effort, Melinda hoisted the fishing pole skyward and yanked the fish from the ocean, landing it right in the middle of the coracle. She danced in place, her ruby curls bouncing across her forehead with the jig, gave herself a clap and bashed the trevaleigh on the head with a wooden club. Balancing the limp fish in her right hand, she placed it up against her left arm. From tip to tail, the trevaleigh measured from her shoulder to past her fingertips.

Not a bad catch at all, she thought. If the fish were biting, she might catch more. She re-baited the hook and cast the line into the ocean, the sinker disappearing under reflected sunlight, and sat in the middle of the coracle.

The lazy day ambled on, the midday sun burning Melinda's face as she drifted from one daydream to the next. She worried she might drown from the sweat trickling down her chest and back underneath the thick leather tunic Da made her wear when fishing.

'Easier to clean fish guts from oiled leather, lil darlin,' she could hear him say.

The fish had stopped biting and she thought about heading back to shore until a mysterious object floated closer to the boat.

Looks like a pile of rags on driftwood, she thought. Probably washed out to sea by the storm or from a shipwreck...*whoa*! The rags moved.

Melinda's mouth turned dry. She reeled in the line, stowed the fishing pole on the floor of the boat, pulled up the anchor, grabbed the oars and began rowing back to the island.

As the oars splashed in the water, a face appeared among the bundle of rags, pleading in a faint, feeble voice, "Help me."

Is that a person? Melinda stopped rowing and called out, "Hello?"

"Help," came the delicate plea again. "Need...water."

Melinda sat in the coracle, thinking. Can't just abandon it, her, him, whatever. Da wouldn't like that. He'd row over there to see if he could help. She yanked on the oars and glided towards the driftwood. As she got closer, the bundle of rags took the form of a young man lying prostrate on a piece of timber.

"What're y'doing out here without a boat?" she asked.

"Water...please."

Melinda retrieved a waterskin from the floor of her boat and tossed it to the stranger.

He pulled himself up, wincing and groaning like every one of his muscles ached, and emptied the contents of the waterskin in two gulps.

"Thank you," he said.

Melinda waited for the young man to get his bearings before peppering him with more questions. "Who are you?"

"My name's Tom. I'm a goat herder..."

"There aren't any goats out here. This ain't a meadow, y'know." She flashed a smile to reassure Tom. "My name's Melinda. I'm a fisher, like my Da."

"I was on a ship. It sank in the storm. I've been floating..."

"For days, I'd reckon. By the looks of ya. No offence or nothin'. That

145

storm was a bad one, alright. My Da said anyone caught in that would be prayin' to the sea gods to be sittin' at home in front of a nice warm fire nestlin' a lovely bowl of stewed fish on their lap. What was the name of y'ship?"

"The *Vulking*, but it wasn't my ship. It was supposed to take us to safety."

"Us?"

"My friends and I. You haven't seen a wild grell or a young woman with long, dark hair, have you? They were on the ship with me when it sank."

"I've only seen you. A bit of rubbish washed up on the beach. Rope, nets and stuff, but no grells or dead women." Melinda caught herself. She probably shouldn't have said *dead women*.

The young man, Tom, sat in silence for a while, clutching at something in his pants pocket. She wondered what he was thinking about. *He's probably delirious from lack of food and water.* She could offer him raw fish after she gutted the trevaleigh.

"Are you alright?" she asked.

"Do you have any food?"

"I caught a silver trevaleigh — a *real* big one. I could gut it and pull the flesh off its bones. Raw fish ain't that nice, though. We have other food in our shelter, on the beach. My Da and I, we've preserved enough fish to feed us for a couple of seasons. We might even sell some at the market in Gestade. Do y'want me to take ya ashore?"

Tom nodded.

Melinda pulled up the oars and grabbed a rope from the floor of the boat. "I'll throw ya a rope. Y'can pull yourself over and jump in my boat. It'll carry two. I'm supposed to be fishin', but my Da won't mind I caught somethin' unusual."

Tom held back, looking at her with suspicion. "Where are you from?" he asked.

"Dorfisch. Have ya heard of it?"

"No…well, yes."

"Which is it? Yes or no?"

"I only heard of it recently. I don't know much…"

"It's a small fishin' village on the east coast of Enthilen. About a day's walk south of Gestade. We don't live right in the village. Our shack's in the dunes a bit further south. Da ain't got much time for noisy or nosy neighbours."

"Are you Erstürmen or Dobunni?"

"Neither. My Da says our family came from a place called Germalia. It's way over the other side of the world. He says our ancestors fled from per-se…per-se…per-se-cu-tion."

"What about your mother?"

Melinda dropped her chin, focussing on the motionless silverback in the bottom of the boat. "She died."

"Sorry. I didn't mean…"

Melinda snapped, "Do y'want to come with me or not?"

"Yes. Thank you. Throw me the rope."

Melinda tossed a rope onto the driftwood, and she and Tom heaved together until his lifesaving piece of flotsam and the little coracle were abreast and secured together. Tom struggled with his balance as he stumbled into the boat, Melinda helping him aboard.

"Won't take us long to get ashore," she said. "I'm stronger than I look. That's what my Da always says." She gathered the rope, seized the oars and started rowing.

"It's only you and your father on the island, right? No-one else?"

"Yep, only us. Well, on this part of the island. Not sure who else might be here. It's a big place, Bramble Island. We come here every harvest season to fish. The best spots near our home in Dorfisch have been fished out. Too many greedy people with fishin' poles, my Da says."

The coracle rode the breakers into shore. Melinda jumped into the shallow surf and started to drag the boat onto the sand. Tom tried to follow her, but he stumbled and toppled over the vessel's edge into the water. Kneeling in the surf, waves crashing into his back, he looked miserable and exhausted.

She pulled the coracle onto the sand and ran back into the surf, offering Tom her hand. "Come on. I'll help you. It'll take a while before y'get your land legs back."

Tom clutched Melinda's hand and she hoisted him upright onto unsteady legs. As they passed the boat, she grabbed the silverback trevaleigh in one hand and held onto Tom with the other. They walked together along the beach, Melinda trying to keep her castaway from tumbling over. When she spotted her shack, she released his hand and sprinted ahead.

"Da! Da! Come see what I caught!"

Her father appeared from inside the simple hut, his massive frame and round belly almost filling the doorway, and a warm, kind smile plastered across his cherry-red face. She never tired of seeing her father smile. It made her want to smile, too. Shoulder-length wisps of his wavy, ginger-brown hair fluttered in the breeze, reminding Melinda where her red hair came from. Streaks of fish guts and blood covered Da's leather apron, but fish intestines weren't going to stop her from racing up to his cosy belly and giving it a big hug.

"Da, I caught a silverback! Look here — it's *huuuuge*. And, and, I found Tom. He's a goat herder. I said there ain't any goats in the ocean and he got caught in the storm and lost his friends and his boat sank and he has no food, but I saved him and..."

"*Whoa*, hold on there, li'l darlin'. Too much noise for me ears to make any sense of. What's all this about goats?"

Melinda ran back to Tom and grabbed the front of his waistcoat, pulling him to her father. "Da, this is Tom. I rescued him from the ocean. He was on a driftwood raft..."

"Alright, not so fast. Me mind ain't as quick as it used to be." Jameus sized-up the young man before him. "I imagine you've looked and felt a lot better than y'do now, son. Where y'from?"

"The Feign," said Tom. "The Desolate Mountains."

Jameus screwed up his face. "Not my piece of dried fish, if y'know what I mean. Too cold and windy up there for the likes of Mel and me. I'm Jameus."

Tom held out a hand towards Melinda's Da.

What's that for? she wondered. And look at the scar on his palm. How'd he get that?

"Are you offerin' me an empty hand so I can put somethin' in it?" asked Jameus.

Tom blushed and dropped his hand.

Jameus laughed and smothered the young man in a bear hug. Melinda beamed.

"Shipwrecked, hey," said Jameus. "That would've been an ordeal. Quite an ordeal indeed. What were y'doin' out in the storm anyways?"

"We escaped from Laodicea after it was attacked by barbarians."

"I knew them fleet of ships we heard about in the Bay of Fires was an ill omen. We been here almost a season and a half. Had no idea there was any attack."

"We were trapped in the city. The skullard of the *Vulking* rescued us and said his captain would take us to safety. Turned out he was lying. Have you seen a wild grell or young woman come ashore — a Dobunni rebel?"

"Most grells I know are slaves."

"We've got a grell," said Melinda.

Jameus frowned at her. "Annian's not our slave." He faced Tom. "She keeps our house if y'know what I mean, son. I pay her with warm lodgin' and food, and a li'l coin if I can spare it. I can't raise a young girl all by meself y'understand. Mel's mother passed before Mel could walk. Annian's very old. I'm plannin' to release her from our service when we get back home."

"No, Da! You can't do that. Who's gonna tell me stories at bedtime?"

"She can't look after us forever, li'l darlin', and yur almost old enough to look after y'self. Annian was already old when I rescued her from that nasty piece of work overseer. He used to beat his slaves every day 'til most of 'em dropped dead. It's nearly time for Annian to find her final restin' place."

Melinda pouted, thinking about how to change Da's mind.

"Well, enough chit chat," said Jameus. "You must be famished, son. We've got dried fish, smoked fish or salted fish."

"Or fresh fish." Melinda smiled, holding her prized catch under her father's nose.

Jameus ruffled her hair. "Ya, nice, fresh fish. We might be able to scrounge other morsels too."

Melinda's stomach grumbled. She raced inside to find the scaling knife.

*　*　*　*

Tom sat under a shelter made of tree branches, driftwood and fern fronds, his stomach gurgling from a feed of fried fish and a platter of fruit Melinda called bunya bread; wedges of pulpy, juicy, yellow flesh with a pale-green skin that reminded him of rockmelon. Jameus and Melinda lay nearby on a reed mat, having an afternoon nap. The big man with wispy red hair and a straggly, unkept beard snored loudly. The little girl with the freckled face talked to herself in her sleep. Tom wondered if she ever stopped talking.

She couldn't be more than ten or eleven years old, he thought. Jameus and Melinda appeared friendly and trustworthy. Not likely to sell him for coin or try to steal his soul.

The pair of fishers had made makeshift walls and shelves out of wooden crates, most filled with preserved fish ready to be transported back to the mainland. Outside the hut, a boat bobbed idly in a sheltered bay. Although less than a third of the size of the *Vulking*, like the larger ship, the boat had no masts for sails, not even a single pole at the stern to climb and keep watch as Whibly had done on the *Vulking*.

Although Tom tried to rest in the warm afternoon sun, his swirling mind wouldn't let him sleep. He snatched at his pocket and wrapped his hand around the hard, smooth surface of the dark eyes. Still safe.

Is that all you care about, Tom?

Stepping outside, he plodded along the beach, his bare feet sinking into the wet sand, in a muted attempt to look for Grin and Thaly. They could have been washed ashore.

Or still out there floating in the ocean. Or worse yet, lying on the seabed.

He dug his fingernails into the scars on his palms, recalling the fight with Thaly over the eyes of lost souls. That might be the last time he saw her. And Grin. Now Grin was gone, Tom may never discover the location of Bindari where Princess Caeli said he'd find all the answers he desired.

Why'd the stupid grell have to go and die?

Collapsing onto his haunches, a cruel, destructive anger filled his mind. He smacked his forehead, again and again, screaming thoughts pounding his brain. *You're a selfish arsehole! Arsehole! Arsehole! Selfish — fucking — arsehole! Worthless piece of shit. Worthless. You should have died instead of Grin and Thaly.*

His head hummed from the rain of blows. But the punishing energy abated as quickly as it had arisen. *Stop it, Tom. Stand up and start looking for them. Focus on the now.*

He dragged himself onto weary legs and trudged further along the beach. The setting sun shimmered low over the ocean horizon, the curve of the sun's bottom seeming to touch the waves. He thought back to the maps strewn over the table inside Adcock's quarters. Bramble Island was off the east coast of Enthilen. To get back to the mainland, he needed to travel west, across the ocean. Jameus and Melinda could take him to Dorfisch, but after that? He'd work it out. Grin and Thaly couldn't help anymore. He was on his own.

He'd found Nanna's killer — Malphas. Now he had to find Bindari; the grell graveyard, the gorge running east-west, the light that never goes out and the door only he could open. Whoever's behind the door will have the answers he needs. They'll know how to defeat Malphas. They'll be able to tell him how he can return home. Won't they?

Yes, Tom.

He came to a spit of land covered in a dense thicket of twisting, climbing vines draped over stunted trees and guarded by a crowd of jagged rocks poking up out of the sand. Past the point of the spit, another beach curved southward and disappeared into the horizon. He clenched his jaw and began to climb over the rocks. Their sharp, lacerating edges tore at the skin on his hands, crevices and cracks swallowing his feet and holding his legs firm such that he had to yank them forward over one rock at a time. Each new obstacle appeared more enormous than the last until, immediately before reaching the vines, a wall of stone loomed over him. Stretching above his head, he wriggled his fingers into a fissure and heaved, searching for a supporting ledge with his left foot. He found one, then another to rest his right foot. He scaled the wall; fissure, ledge, crevice and crack becoming his friends, helping him reach the safe, sandy soil above, covered in greenery.

The beach on the other side of the spit appeared through the tangle of vines, branches and undergrowth. He grabbed a branch of deadwood and hacked at the vegetation, trying to make a path, but the blunt instrument couldn't conquer the botanical ramble. So, he tossed the deadwood away and began to crawl, down on his elbows, stomach and knees, slithering underneath the snaring vines like a famished serpent pursuing its quarry.

He clambered through the vegetation and walked onto the neighbouring beach that stretched into the distance, ending at a hill covered in parakeet-green grass. The colour reminded him of his pet budgerigar, Miss Priss. This beach was more exposed than the one where Jameus and Melinda had their hut. Waves taller than Tom pounded a rocky ledge a stone's throw from the sand before rolling gently to shore. Mounds of seaweed tumbled in the surf and littered the beach all the way to parakeet hill, filling the air with a rotten-egg smell.

Halfway along the beach, an assortment of flotsam had washed ashore: broken crates, ropes and nets, fabric and splintered timber. And something else, rolling and billowing in the gentler surf, masked by the settling dusk light. Tom pooled his energy and broke into a trot, heading to the beached mystery.

Looks like a person. Too small for a grell. Thaly?

Trying to run, he stumbled and careered across the sand like a drunken sailor who'd never stepped off a boat, falling face-first into a pile of stinking seaweed. He picked himself up and staggered forward again. The sky grew darker and the tide pulled the person back out to sea.

Run, you idiot.

Tom raced up to the body, then stopped. Even in the low light, he recognised the admiral blue coat with the triangular buttons. Captain Adcock's coat. He crept over to Adcock, who lay face down on the sand, waves lapping at his leggings. When he reached the captain, he pushed on Adcock's shoulder with his bloodied and bruised foot, but the deadweight stuck fast to the sand. Tom knelt, squirmed his arms underneath Adcock's chest and waist and heaved, rolling the cast-away face up. No sign of life. Tom crouched there; satisfied justice had been served.

Then, something unnerving happened. Adcock breathed. Feeble. Rattling down into the depths of his throat. But a breath nonetheless. Then another one.

Shit. He's alive.

Tom stood and checked the beach. Although it appeared empty, he couldn't see much in the failing light. He turned back to Adcock, lying on the sand, shallow breaths inflating the chest under his sodden white shirt. Tom could leave the captain to the whims of the ocean tide, but Jameus or Melinda might find him. They might *save* him. That wouldn't do. He thought about rolling the body back into the surf, but it would likely wash ashore again.

Adcock groaned and Tom almost jumped out of his skin. There was only one thing to do. He walked into the surf and grabbed Adcock's legs, turning the body side-on to the ocean. Positioning himself land-side of the captain, on the upper slope of the beach, he knelt in the sand and thrust his arms under Adcock's back. Adcock groaned louder. Tom stiffened his shoulders, dug his feet into the sand and pushed, rolling the body closer to the water. Adcock flailed an arm. Tom gritted his teeth and pushed harder.

Facedown. Faceup. Once more. Facedown again.

Facedown in a shallow pool, Adcock fought to hold his head above water. Tom crawled up beside him, and with every ounce of strength remaining, knitted his hands together at the back of Adcock's skull and pushed the captain's face into the surf. Adcock's arms thrashed to the side like the flippers of a beached whale.

Do it. Do it. Do it.

Adcock squirmed under Tom's grip. Splashing, gasping, grabbing.

Tom held tight, his body throbbing with so much adrenaline he swore he could feel the blood gushing through his arteries.

And power. Power over life and death.

He gritted his teeth, but then, into his mind flashed an image of the Bad Man straddling Nanna's recumbent body, slashing at her arms with a knife. The Bad Man turned to look at little Tommy cowering under the bed, and Tom saw his own face beneath the crumpled hood of a killer.

No. No. Stop. Stop this. Stop it!

Tom released his grip, and Adcock pushed his torso up out of the water, gasping for air. Frightened little Tommy crawled backwards, away from the surf and onto dry sand. Salt water spluttered and gurgled out of Adcock's mouth as he dragged himself onto the beach and collapsed. Tom sat there, watching the captain sucking air into his lungs, and started to count the breaths. How many more before Adcock died or regained his strength?

Dusk turned into night. A dark night with only one moon; the quarter moon of Bargan. A waxing crescent that would grow larger in the coming days. Stronger. Tom felt inside the front pocket of his pants to check on the eyes of lost souls. It had become reflex now, like a regular, nervous twitch. He didn't find what he expected. One of the eyes was missing.

Damn it.

He searched inside his other pockets, finding Dwarrow's key and nothing else. He dug his fingers through the sand, razing a circle around where he sat. Not there. Crawled back towards Adcock, running his hands over every patch of wet sand until he reached the edge of the surf where the captain's body lay. And there it was, lying beside Adcock's waist, the flaming pupil of the dark eye being rocked gently back and forth by the lapping waves.

Get it and get out of here.

Tom slunk over to Adcock and reached for the dark eye with his right hand. He must have briefly turned away because he didn't see it coming. A thick, sodden mitt with grappling fingers latched onto Tom's throat, pinching and squeezing like the talon of an eagle. Tom grabbed Adcock's wrist and tried to pull the hand away, but the captain dug deeper, forcing his fingernails under Tom's skin.

Can't breathe.

Tom dropped the dark eye and groped about behind his back, stretching his arm until his shoulder ached. Adcock growled like a bear, trying to roll on top of Tom.

Found something.

Tom clutched a piece of driftwood and swung it across his body, smacking it into Adcock's face. A pulpy thud like the sound of a tomato hitting a wall disrupted the monotony of the lapping waves. Adcock's hand went limp and fell from Tom's throat. Tom retrieved the dark eye and pushed back up onto dry sand. Keeping still and quiet, he waited for another breath to come from the shipwrecked captain. Nothing came.

I've killed him.

~ Chapter 12 ~

Emelin led Dayna and five other Dobunni rebels through the maze of boulders and stunted shrubs covering the northern half of the Scaur Hills. Dark clouds brushing the top of the hills masked the midday sun and mirrored their mood. They'd failed to rescue any Dobunni prisoners from the deeping pits, the barred, muddy holes the Erstürmen called a gaol sitting empty and unguarded. Hiding among the suffocating poverty of Slumstadt for four days, the rebels had waited for word about their leader, Ryder, and the attempted assassination of King Ewald and Prince Adalwolf, eventually learning of the assassins' execution and the flight of the royal family from Sardis right into an ambush. Word also spread through the shantytown that barbarians had overrun Laodicea and routed the Dobunni army. Some in Slumstadt blamed the rebels for all the upheaval, claiming the Dobunni ambushed the king and provoked the barbarian attack by marching their army east. Emelin knew the rumours weren't true, but truth rarely prospered amid conflict and desperation. For Dobunni rebels, Slumstadt had become even more dangerous and unruly, and she needed to get her group back to the safety of Bagendon.

As she trudged over scree that sank and shifted under leather boots with worn soles, her thoughts turned to home and family. She longed for news about her adopted daughter, Thaly, and Jacob, the Dobunni army leader, hoping they'd return to Bagendon with the other survivors of the Laodicea campaign. Pragmatism told her it was a vain hope. The future for Bagendon looked similarly bleak now its defences had been so weakened.

How could they protect the settlement from an Erstürmen attack? she wondered. For it would come. Soon. Whoever took power in the vacuum created by Ewald's death would seek an early, decisive victory to demonstrate their authority. And Bagendon was a sitting duck. An easy target for anyone wishing to make a statement.

Emelin's birth daughter, Dayna, walked beside her, the grey cotton scarf around Dayna's neck bouncing with her gait. The blossoming young woman looked so much like her father, Emelin had to catch herself sometimes, thinking her husband, Thane, had returned from the grave. While Dayna had Thane's blonde hair and dimples, she hadn't inherited his broodiness or suspicions about the world. At fifteen harvest seasons old, Dayna's innocence made her vulnerable. She wouldn't survive an assault on Bagendon. With Thaly's whereabouts unknown, Emelin had only one family responsibility now; protect Dayna. But how? As a Dobunni leader, Emelin would never consider fleeing Bagendon. It was the last home, the only home the Dobunni had. However, Dayna could go. Find a safer place and fulfil the promise of her life.

Lost in her thoughts, senses dulled to the surroundings, Emelin forgot to keep watch. To stay on guard. A masked stranger walked right into her path. She jerked her head up and reached for a weapon.

The stranger raised the palm of his gloved hand. "That isn't necessary. I'm not here to attack you."

Emelin clutched the grip of her sword, assessing the ambusher. Two scabbards hung from his belt, one holding a short sword, the other a long knife. He wore a stiff, broad-brimmed hat pulled low over brown eyes, and a mask of black cloth covering the bridge of his nose to below his chin.

She sensed the nervous energy of the rebel group. Dayna stepped up beside her and, instinctively, Emelin reached across and pushed her back.

"Who are you?" Emelin asked the stranger.

"Someone who is seeking one of your own."

"You're either bold or stupid to confront a band of rebel soldiers alone. We could easily strike you down or take you prisoner."

The man lowered his hand. "Neither is necessary. I offer no threat to you or any other Dobunni. Instead, I seek your help. I'm looking for a young woman. A rebel soldier called Athalee. Do you know her? I was told I may find her in your...camp."

Emelin flinched at the mention of her adopted daughter. "What do you want with this *Athalee*?" she asked, determined to give nothing away.

"I have a message for her."

"Give it to us and we'll see she gets it."

The man's brown eyes smiled. "So, you do know her?"

"I may have seen her in camp from time to time."

"I must deliver the message in person. It could save Athalee's life."

"Thaly went to Laodicea to fight the barbarians," said Dayna.

Emelin scolded her daughter. "Hush. Give nothing more to this man."

The stranger relaxed and rested his hands on his belt. "Laodicea has fallen and Sardis is bereft a king. A new ruler rises and his influence will spread. Bagendon will not escape the purging of the unbelievers from Enthilen."

Emelin narrowed her eyes. "What do you know of Bagendon?"

"The Erstürmen have always known about your town in the hills. Only because of Ewald's laziness is it still standing. Mark my word, the new master of these lands won't be so lax. Your defences cannot hold against an attack even if your defeated army arrives back from Laodicea in time."

"You seem to know a lot about the plans of the Erstürmen. You might be one of them, hiding your face to mask your treachery."

"I'm here only for information on Athalee's whereabouts. Since you can't help me, I will seek out what remains of your army." The masked stranger tipped his hat and vanished into the maze of boulders and shrubs scattered across the Scaur Hills.

Emelin removed her hand from her sword.

"Who was that?" asked Dayna.

"His voice sounded familiar, but I can't place it."

"Is Thaly in trouble?"

Yes, no, I don't know, thought Emelin. Thaly may never return from Laodicea. If she did, trouble would come for all of them eventually.

*   *   *   *

Stinging rain pelted Emelin, Dayna and Payton, Jacob Seamaster's lufu, as they huddled beside the eastern gate of Bagendon, waiting for the army from Laodicea to return home. They didn't speak, the splatter of raindrops on their hooded, oiled cloaks drowning out nervous conversations. Other families crowded around the gates, standing ankle-deep in mud, their faces full of worry or hope.

Adrenaline pulsed through Emelin's body as the lead group of returning fighters appeared from between two boulders, barely visible through the walls of water bucketing down onto the Scaur Hills. Banners hung sodden and flaccid. Soldiers stumbled and limped through the sludge sucking at their boots, and horses slogged with bowed heads, their saddles draped with the injured. Maxton Nash, not Jacob Seamaster, led the remnants of the rebel army through the gate, riding beneath a banner with the sigil of a burrowing merlet, a small, flightless bird, common on the Dambay Plains, that his family had adopted as their crest.

Tugging the hood of her cloak down over her brow, Emelin stepped into the path of Maxton's horse and grasped its bridle, yelling through the rain, "Where's Jacob?"

"He fell," said Maxton.

"Athalee?"

Maxton shook his head and urged his horse forward. Emelin refused to let the matter end there. She returned to Dayna's side to search every face coming through the gates. Payton had gone, apparently accepting his lover, his lufu Jacob, wouldn't be coming home. Welcoming parties oscillated between expectant and crestfallen as they waited for the returning warriors to shuffle past. Occasionally, a joyful reunion lightened the dour air that had settled over the town.

The battle for Laodicea had reduced the rebel army from five thousand to a couple of hundred. Eventually, the last soldier lumbered home. She wasn't Athalee.

Emelin clutched Dayna's hand; now, it seemed, her only daughter. "Go home, Dayna. I have to go to the longhouse." Dayna's shoulders slumped underneath her sopping, sage-green cloak. She might be crying. Emelin couldn't tell in the rain. "Go home. I'll be there shortly."

Dayna released Emelin's hand and walked off without a word. Emelin followed Maxton to the longhouse. She knew he'd go there, having no immediate family to greet him, his parents and three sisters taken by a merciless disease inflicting Bagendon. In Slumstadt, they were calling it The Ravage.

Maxton dismounted outside the longhouse and tied his horse to the hitching post, not bothering to take the weary beast to the stables. Emelin joined him under the thatched eaves of the meeting hall that provided respite from the stinging rain.

"Don't you want to rest?" she asked.

"I'll rest inside," said Maxton.

"I didn't see Edith among the returning warriors."

"She fell as we fought our way into the Southern Vale."

Emelin nodded and guided Maxton through the door. Alfred sat alone at one of the tables, drinking meduz. A short man, hunched and withered, he appeared to be shrinking in his seat as tired old bones crumbled beneath loose, leathery skin covered in sour wrinkles. Alfred and Emelin were now the only remaining members of the leadership council.

Maxton and Emelin hung their cloaks on iron pegs driven into one of the timber columns supporting the rafters and stood beside the fire roaring in the pit dug in the centre of the longhouse to dry their clothes.

Alfred shuffled up to Emelin. "We need to choose a new leader."

"In due course," said Emelin. "Ryder's boots are still warm. And Jacob's." She draped her wet hair over the front of her shoulders and turned to Maxton. "What happened?"

Maxton removed his leather gauntlets, threw them on a table and hovered his hands near the flames. "Jacob led a scouting party into the King's Quarter, aiming for the Terraces. There were thousands of barbarians outside the south wall blocking the gate into the Southern Vale. I thought we might be able to establish archer cover from the terrace balconies and march our army through the King's Quarter and the centre of Laodicea to reach the vale. It was a stupid idea. The Erstürmen ambushed the scouting party. Only a dozen scouts returned. Jacob...they hung his severed head from the tympanum above the west gate."

"Thaly went with Jacob," said Emelin.

Maxton nodded. "She didn't return and I didn't see any evidence...I don't know what became of her. She rode with that boy, Tom, and the wild grell."

"Tom Anderson? The one who went with Ryder to Sardis?"

"Yes."

"How did he escape the royal city when all other rebels failed?" asked Alfred.

Maxton shrugged.

"It seems he wasn't to be trusted after all," said Alfred.

Emelin swallowed hard, trying to control her emotions. If Athalee died in battle against the Erstürmen, it would have been as she wanted. However, the warrior's aspiration of a glorious end was less appealing when the warrior was your adopted daughter.

Maxton buried his face in tired hands and groaned through his fingers. "I'm sorry, Emelin. I couldn't protect her."

She placed a hand on his forearm. "Don't blame yourself."

"Now's not the time for self-pity," said Alfred. "Our war has not ended."

"A masked stranger confronted us in the hills today," said Emelin. "He believed the new rulers of Enthilen will not let Bagendon rest as Ewald did. An attack appears imminent."

Alfred stepped in front of Emelin, the light of the longhouse fire turning the sheen of his bald head amber. "I've been saying the same for seasons. We must flee these hills, now."

Emelin growled, "I refuse to flee my home. The Erstürmen have taken everything from us. They expelled us from Iglund and the Dambay Plains. Destroyed Laodicea. Bagendon is all we have left. If I stand here alone at the parapets, then I will stand."

"Bickering will undermine morale further," said Maxton. "We need to prepare the town's defences and appoint a new leadership council and a new leader."

Alfred crossed his arms. "I'm the most experienced. I should be the new leader."

"That decision is not yours to make," said Emelin. "We ask for nominations, then the people will choose the leader."

"Haste...haste is required." Maxton rocked on unsteady legs, the exhaustion of past days catching up with him.

"I agree," said Emelin. "It'll take three or four moons to prepare the battlements and arm every able-bodied man, woman and child. Only then should we hold an election. In the meantime, we'll double our patrols. We have no idea what will come for us. Let's be prepared for anything."

* * * *

The rain eased as Emelin sloshed along the silent, muddy streets of Bagendon to her cabin. The paths would remain quiet for a long time. The Dobunni had lost over four thousand fighters in the battle for Laodicea. No more than two thousand trained soldiers remained in Bagendon. Two thousand soldiers and a thousand residents if that, less than a third of its regular population. Many citizens had already fled the town, fearful of an attack. Bagendon had become a ghost waiting to descend into the void.

She opened the front door of her cabin and stepped into a dark, cold room. Dayna slouched at the dining table, her head lying on folded arms resting on the tabletop.

"You should be in bed," said Emelin, removing her cloak and hanging it on a hook behind the door. Taking a candle from the mantlepiece, she held the wick against a glowing ember in the smouldering fire. From the lit candle, she dripped wax onto a ceramic plate in the middle of the table, pushed the bottom of the candle in place, then sat opposite Dayna.

"Did Thaly fight bravely?" asked Dayna, lifting her head.

Emelin tried to smile. "I'm sure she did."

"We should have gone with her instead of wasting our time in Slumstadt. I could have protected her. You could have..."

"There's nothing we could have done, Dayna. Maxton said the barbarian forces were overwhelming."

"That masked stranger seemed to care more about her than you do."

"What? Don't be ridiculous."

"He's out there looking for her. You're sitting here doing nothing."

"I have to prepare to defend our home."

"What's left to defend?"

Emelin stood and stepped across to the fireplace, hovering her hands above the dying coals in a futile attempt to warm herself. "The stranger can search all he wants. He won't..." Behind her back, Dayna pushed her chair from the table, the legs scraping on the timber floor.

"He won't find her. Is that what you were going to say?"

Emelin stiffened at the anger in Dayna's voice. In despairing times, blame spread like a plague of locusts through a wheatfield. Dayna should be more forgiving, but she was still young. Naïve. Emelin clutched the front edge of the stone mantlepiece, thinking she might topple into the fire. Her chest heaved with searching breaths, then she released the mantle and faced her only child.

"We have to accept that Thaly may not come home."

Dayna's glare pierced the candlelight. "Why don't you say it?"

Emelin's legs buckled and she flailed an arm onto the mantlepiece.

"Mother. Say it!"

A scolding hurt fired Emelin's cheeks. "Dead! Is that what you want me to say? Thaly's dead." She lurched towards Dayna and swept her arm across the table, hurling the candle into the wall. It fluttered out, sending the room back into darkness. Emelin knelt on the floor and clutched at the hem of her daughter's tunic, sobbing. "Thaly's dead. I should have gone to Laodicea. I should have protected her. I failed and now she's dead."

Dayna sat rigid and quiet as a dull throb spread through Emelin's body. Mother and daughter searched for comfort in the cold room until Emelin's knees ached, and the rain began again.

She lifted her head to find her daughter's eyes. "You should go. Leave Bagendon."

"Alone?" asked Dayna.

Emelin sat up and rested her hands atop Dayna's thighs. "The Erstürmen will come for us. We can't defend the town against them. You'll be safer elsewhere — a chance to live. Find a lover. Marry, even. Have children, if you want them. Anything's better than sitting here waiting to die."

"You will stay, though," said Dayna. "You'll stay to defend our home until your last breath."

Emelin nodded.

"Then, so will I. Now Thaly's gone, you're all I have left. I'm not leaving you."

Emelin rested her head on Dayna's lap, and they held each other and sobbed until the rain stopped.

~ Chapter 13 ~

Dwarrow sniffed the cold air. "I've never smelled anything like this, Princess."

Princess Caeli hid with Dwarrow and six other mouldewerps in the shadows of a conifer forest covering the southern edge of The Feign, perched on a ridge overlooking the main road connecting Laodicea and Sardis. Below them, a snaking procession slithered along the road, the Erstürmen royal party at its head and surrounded by the King's Shield. Adalwolf sat atop a throne carried on the shoulders of four grell pole bearers. His summited position acted as a beacon to his followers, thousands of civilians and soldiers forming the spine of the serpent as they walked behind him.

Although it had been four days since the mouldewerps rescued Caeli from Sardis' dungeon, adrenaline still rushed through her veins when she thought about the dash out of the inner circle of Sardis and down the passage that she'd kept secret for twelve yarles. Dwarrow had comforted her the entire way, supplying herbs and potions to try to mend her body. But guilt over Jürgen's death still harried her thoughts, and she hoped for an opportunity to honour his sacrifice. A chance to demonstrate her own commitment to a better future for Enthilen that would serve as her atonement.

Once outside the secret cave, Caeli and the werps had rested in an abandoned dwell at the foot of the Desolate Mountains to prepare for a long journey ahead, although she didn't know where the journey would lead. She'd even begun to enjoy werp food. At least, she had a new appreciation for it.

Lying on her stomach on a bed of brown pine needles, Dwarrow standing beside her, she peered over the lip of the ridge to get a better view of the procession. "Where do you think they're going, Dwarrow?"

"I would have guessed Sardis, Princess, but it appears they're travelling south."

As Dwarrow spoke, the head of the procession turned at the juncture where the Laodicea–Sardis road met the main track south, taking travellers into the Dambay Plains to Malang Gunya. Although Caeli had never been to the grell city, she'd read a story about King Alaric's conquest of Malang Gunya and how he'd died from his battle wounds.

"Look, Dwarrow, they have grell soldiers. Who is that leading them?"

"It's the red grell. Krieg."

A band of nearly fifty armoured grells riding black undreds towered above the other pilgrims, led by Krieg on a giant chestnut stallion. The dark red sheen of the horse's coat matched the tainted skin of its master so closely that they appeared from a distance to be a single creature. Nervous tingles spread across Caeli's skin; her mind mesmerised by Krieg's hulking frame and the sight of so many undreds in one place, the gathering of curved horns protruding from the beasts' foreheads resembling a moving forest of spears.

Dwarrow's chattery voice broke the sorcerous beguilement. "Giants armed for killing and led by a tainted grell. This is a most disturbing development, Princess. Most disturbing. If the Erstürmen manage to build a grell army, they'll be unassailable."

Adalwolf passed right below Caeli, wearing the white serpent crown she'd seen gracing Ewald's head so many times. The prince must have been crowned in Laodicea, she thought, recalling the shy, odd boy who'd visited her room in Sardis at night to stand at the door and peer in through the barred hole. If she was awake, she'd try to talk to him, but he always scuttled away. One of the night guards told her Adalwolf would sometimes come and watch her sleep. Knowing she belonged to Ewald, the prince seemed to be torn between terror and infatuation.

Caeli pulled the hood of a furred cloak over her forehead to shade her eyes, the garment snatched from her room before the hasty escape from Sardis. "King Adalwolf sits on a strange-looking throne," she said.

"A devilish stench fills the air," said Dwarrow. "Look closely, do you see shapes drifting in the shadows? They'll be hard to spot in this bright sunlight. Most likely hiding along the edges of the road in the dense verge."

"Yes, I think so. I count twelve. They seem to be following the throne, almost like they're bound to it."

"It's as I feared. King Adalwolf sits upon the throne of the dead. What you see following it are draughouls, desperate to be near the trappings of Volerdie's power. It explains why we didn't see any in the secret cave. The emergence of the throne must have lured them out of hiding."

"Draughouls. My father told me scary stories about them when I was a child. I've never understood if they were alive or dead."

"Their souls are forever trapped within the dark eyes and their soulless bodies linger, slowly decaying until bone turns to dust. Some draughouls are thousands of yarles old. I hope they'll be released from their pitiful existence one day."

"How?" asked Caeli.

"The draughouls will be freed when the spell cast by the eyes of lost souls is broken. The eyes need to be cleansed of evil, though I don't know how."

"The throne of the dead. The eyes of lost souls. Dwarrow, it seems our world is becoming much darker."

"Now the throne has been found, there's only one place in Enthilen where it belongs — Pergamos, Volerdie's ruined city that lies beneath Malang Gunya."

The tail of the King's Shield surrounding Adalwolf turned south, followed by two palanquins carried by grell slaves. Queen Romilda sat inside the first palanquin, waving to a family of peasants standing by the side of the road. The drawn curtains of the second palanquin shielded the occupant from scrutiny. An old female grell mounted on a pale horse rode beside the closed litter, followed by a chariot pulled by two lumbering undreds and carrying a grey-haired man dressed in sangria robes.

As the end of the royal party followed the King's Shield into the Dambay Plains, Krieg and the armoured grells broke from the group and galloped west towards Sardis.

"My thoughts are dire, Princess. I see no good in any of this. King Adalwolf sits on the throne of the dead and keeps the company of tainted grells. No doubt their master is lurking in the crowd. The assembly of elders foresaw this. They've urged me to forge new and binding unions among those who might oppose this diabolical uprising. I've been appointed to a vital ambassadorial role, tasked with brokering an alliance between the mouldewerps and the stone- and weald-grells. This could be the most important of my many important dealings."

"The grells hunted you once, didn't they?" asked Caeli.

"The perils of the present demand that the transgressions of the past are forgiven. Otherwise, the cultures of Enthilen and beyond won't be able to resist the coming tide, and all we love will be lost." Dwarrow brushed his wet nose across the back of Caeli's hand. "We've been friends for countless seasons, Princess. My assigned task is daunting for someone so small. Would you be so generous as to share this burden?"

Caeli rolled onto her side and smiled at Dwarrow. "You're my best friend. My only friend. I'll help in whatever way I can. *Assistant to the Ambassador*. It has a nice ring to it."

"Excellent, Princess. Very excellent. We'll travel south to Babir Birramal. I plan to attend the grells' garrabari and make my presentation to their leaders."

"South it is!" Caeli rolled onto her back and clapped her hands.

"*Sssh*," said Dwarrow, "we don't want to attract any attention."

Caeli whispered, "Sorry, Ambassador. After we've completed our duties, I want to find my father."

"You're going to risk it?"

Yes, thought Caeli. Free from the Sunrise Keep, she was now a threat to her father's safety. Those pursuing him could use her to flush him out or torture her until she revealed his location. The keep may have been her prison, but it also protected her and her father from schemes more heinous than Ewald could conjure. Duty and fear had imprisoned Caeli like King Ewald never could. But now, after many yarles apart, she needed to see her father again. To find out if he still loved her.

"Where is your father?" asked Dwarrow, breaking Caeli's concentration.

"I promised him I wouldn't tell, not even my closest of friends. I may have already given too much away."

"I understand." Dwarrow clutched his walking stick. "We have a long road ahead of us, Princess, and we'll need a mount since...since..."

"Since what, Dwarrow?"

"How selfish of me. I haven't thought of my grell friend, Grin, since we last parted, or of the young man, Tom Anderson. I wonder where they are now? They foolishly rushed to war. That never ends well."

Caeli placed her hand inside a pocket of her ratty dress and brushed her fingers over the coin Tom had given her. "I hope Tom's safe and on his way to the answers he seeks."

"Well, he's alive at least," said Dwarrow. "We can be sure of that."

Caeli knew Tom was alive. How did Dwarrow know?

The little werp smiled at her and tapped the end of his nose with a claw. "Time to go, Princess. We can't be watching royal parades all day long."

Dwarrow led Caeli and the six werps from the ridge and deeper into the conifer forest. Tall, straight trees with fissured bark and needle-thin, pointed leaves, crowded together like soldiers in formation and blocked out the sun. At ground level, dead needles blanketed the forest floor, smothering any chance for understorey except the mushrooms that grew in patches, pushing the needles up in tell-tale mounds. Two of the werps collected the mushrooms as they walked and placed them carefully in their packs.

Caeli felt like they'd been hiking for ages. Her inflamed feet ached with every step, covered in pointed dress shoes she'd grabbed in the dash from Sardis. She wished she'd taken more time to find a decent pair of walking shoes. Not that she ever needed such a thing in her prison keep. Above the tree canopy, dark clouds gathered to mask the sun. Caeli guessed it was late afternoon when the group came upon a clearing where the carpet of brown needle-leaves gave way to lush, green grass.

"I have to rest, Dwarrow." She flopped to the ground and pulled the fur-lined cloak around her to ward off a chill breeze.

"Well, Princess, it's lucky we've reached our first destination," said Dwarrow.

One of the werps whistled while the others stood in a circle looking out into the forest. Too tired to ask, Caeli lay on her back, drifting away with the clouds above her.

Looks like rain, she thought. She'd almost fallen asleep when a snort breached the stillness. She bolted upright, expecting danger. Instead, a striking riderless mare strolled into the clearing, her near-white coat studded with patches of mottled grey. The horse trotted up to Caeli and nuzzled against her shoulder.

"I think you've been chosen, Princess," said Dwarrow.

"What? Is she...mine?"

"For now."

Caeli stood, the aches melting from her body, and stroked the horse's neck. "What shall I call her?"

"Her name's Casfern."

"Casfern. She's beautiful. It'll be a challenge to ride her without a saddle and in a dress. And to keep you on board, also. I haven't ridden since I was a child."

"You won't have to worry about me, Princess. I have my own mount." Dwarrow unshouldered his satchel and retrieved a slim, pointed, flat piece of wood decorated with dot paintings of splayed lizards and tied to the end of a thin rope.

"What's that?" asked Caeli.

"It's called a bullroarer. Though, I'm not sure why. I've never called up a bull with it." Dwarrow let the bullroarer out to the end of the rope and swung it above his head, around and around, twirling fast and furious until a dull roar echoed through the trees. The werp's feet almost lifted from the ground as he spun wildly atop the grass. Caeli had to put her hand over her face to mask a giggle.

Dwarrow staggered to a halt, nearly toppling over in dizzying disorientation. From the shadows of the forest, a growl responded to the bullroarer's call. Dwarrow steadied himself and pointed his nose at the sound, sniffing the air. The guttural rumbling grew louder. Caeli thought it resembled the contented growl of a dog enjoying a well-chewed bone.

The werps stood at the edges of the clearing, waiting for the creature to appear. A low branch on a conifer tree rustled when something pushed it aside. Out from the shadows sauntered the largest lizard Caeli had ever seen, its massive body lurching from side to side as it swaggered to Dwarrow.

"It's a dragon," exclaimed Caeli.

Dwarrow shook his head. "No. No. No. There are no dragons in these lands. None at all. This is my trusted steed, Xaviary. She's carried me on many long journeys."

Almost as tall as a horse, Xaviary's smooth back reached well above Dwarrow's head. The other werps tried to lift him up onto the lizard, but he ushered them away and waited for Xaviary to swing her long, thick tail around until the appendage formed a ramp. He scampered up onto her back and sat behind the short frills decorating the nape of her neck. The werp rubbed the lizard's scaly head and offered a handful of slitherweed, which she gratefully accepted.

"My friends will leave us here, Princess. They'll return to our dwell to tell the elders all we've seen. You and I must make haste. We should stay off the road and travel through the grassland plains of Dambay. My visit to the mouldewerps' ancestral home will be filled with both joy and sadness."

Caeli pulled off her uncomfortable shoes and tossed them into the forest. The werps helped her mount Casfern. Straddling the horse's back, the torn skirt of her dress flapped against her bare, bruised legs.

"I'm not dressed for riding, but it'll have to do. Lead on, Ambassador."

"Follow my nose, Princess!"

Dwarrow turned Xaviary south, and Caeli trotted after him, clutching Casfern's mane, feeling like she would fall at any moment.

* * * *

Sitting in her palanquin, the landscape of Enthilen passed by Romilda through the open, cream curtains as the royal party turned south towards the middle of the Dambay Plains and the promise of Pergamos. Although she hadn't travelled outside of Sardis for yarles, she remembered to employ the regal wave and well-practised smile as the procession passed through the villages west of Laodicea. Standing beside the dirt road, some of the townsfolk cheered the royal party, but most stood bemused and silent. A few showed outright defiance, turning their backs to the royal procession. The silent accusations made Romilda squirm.

In between the towns, farming families had watched the procession with dull eyes. Around them, fields lay cropless and sterile, eddies of dust spiralling up into the sky, fertility scattered on the wind. Occasionally, restless souls tossed meagre possessions into carts and baskets and joined the march.

Would their prospects improve within the bosom of Pergamos? she wondered. Would her son build a kingdom of ambition and prosperity or succumb to the same paranoia that had crippled Ewald?

Up ahead, Adalwolf sat stiff and awkward on the throne of the dead, failing to acknowledge the people lining the road. The gold stitching in his mahogany robe glinted in the sunlight, the blinding white of the serpent crown contrasted against his black hair.

Although he looks like a king, Romilda thought, he's not acting like one. Adalwolf needed to restore hope to the people of Enthilen. She would have to speak to him about that.

As dark clouds drifted across the face of the sun, the grell slaves carrying her palanquin navigated rough ground, jolting her mind to other thoughts. Behind her, in the second palanquin, travelled Oldaric. The exiled king. Her lover. Once. Although he'd remained calm in recent days, she knew blind ambition simmered below the surface, occasionally exploding in cruel anger. The new persona of Malphas would likely do nothing to quell this ambition despite assurances he only wanted to guide King Adalwolf in his duties.

Something lurked in the shadows of Malphas' mind. An unspoken desire. Romilda knew she'd never uncover the truth from Malphas himself, yet there was another she might interrogate. The Hoch-Vater, Lothar. Whatever plans Malphas had, they would be connected to the First Scripture; Volerdie's Lore. Malphas claimed his utmost desire was to see Volerdie rule over Enthilen once more and lead the faithful into paradise. But how would this happen? What labours needed to be completed to persuade the Divine Creator to return to his creation, and what role would her son play in fulfilling this yearning? Romilda knew an awful thing happened on Hansen's Bluff. A dreadful thing involving this other boy, Tom Anderson. When she asked Adalwolf about it, he withdrew from her. Became fearful and evasive. She wondered if he understood much more than she did.

Lothar might uncover Malphas' plans. The Hoch-Vater could find meaning in the scripture verses. He might even cast his eyes over the First Scripture itself if Romilda could discover where Malphas hid it. That's where the answers to her questions lay. She needed to cultivate a relationship with the Hoch-Vater — the newly appointed Proclaimant of the King. She needed to discover his desires and exploit them to protect her son.

* * * *

The closed black curtains of Malphas' palanquin flapped against a strong easterly breeze. Low, thick clouds trapped the air, unusually warm for the middle of the storm season, and Malphas sweated inside the covered litter, his aged body jostled by the loping grells who bore his weight. He felt under his seat, searching for the locked box containing the First

Scripture to reassure himself it was safe. He smiled when it dawned on him that the throne and scripture would rest in the grand hall of Pergamos together, likely for the first time since the raid by Lycious. And when he retrieved the eyes of lost souls, the blessed triumvirate would be complete, a perfect setting for the second coming of Volerdie.

First, though, was the matter of the boy. Tom Anderson had been more problematic than Malphas had anticipated, and, after the misstep on the bluff, the boy had forewarning of what to expect when they met again. Malphas had to alter his plans, ordering Krieg to visit Sardis to find the blood compass. With the compass in hand, Malphas could renew his search for the boy. Tom Anderson couldn't be too far away. Probably with his allies, the wild grell and rebel girl. All of them would pay for disrupting the ritual on Hansen's Bluff and threatening the ascent of true believers into paradise.

Malphas had ordered Krieg to test the battle skills of the Rephaim by routing the Dobunni rebels from the Scaur Hills. Tom Anderson had scars on his chest, marking his allegiance to the rebels. Malphas couldn't risk the Dobunni sheltering the boy. Better to eradicate the threat.

Krieg would also arrange for the citizens remaining in Sardis to abandon the city and march to Pergamos. The Rephaim and King's Shield would maintain a garrison around the inner circle to watch the kingdom's western border. The new royal city would be in the centre of the Dambay Plains, where it should have been all along.

Malphas leaned forward and pulled the curtains apart, gesturing to Ende, riding beside the palanquin on her perlino mare, to come closer.

"This is a momentous occasion, Ende. Finally, we return to our first home."

"Yes, Worshipful Master. A wonderful occasion."

"Pergamos will rise from the ruins of Malang Gunya. Did I ever tell you what happened to the grell capital?"

177

"No, Master."

"A sickness came upon the savages. One sent by Volerdie himself to punish the heathens for daring to build their foul monuments on top of the sacred city. When my father and I arrived with the Erstürmen liberators, the few wild grells still alive were feeble and wretched. It took little effort to cleanse the land of their filth. When I became king, I considered pulling Malang Gunya apart stone by stone and building an Erstürmen city on those plains. My subjects wouldn't listen. They feared the sickness that had afflicted the grells, believing the land around the city to be cursed. If only I'd been more forceful, I could have discovered Pergamos sooner. Instead, I had to travel a much longer journey during my exile. But I reached the destination nonetheless. One has to be fatalistic about these things, Ende. I took the path Volerdie chose for me. I have no right to question his reasoning."

"The wild grells will march to Pergamos soon, Master. To honour the fallen."

"Yes, that's right. When Malang Gunya fell, it was the beginning of the end for the wild grells. I've always wondered why they want to relive the defeat. It's good fortune for us, though. We can finally finish what my ancestors began by taming the savage beasts until their only joy is found in my service."

* * * *

Behind the thousands of citizens following King Adalwolf to a new future, Seronan toiled with the other grell slaves, forming the tail of the processional serpent. Her aching body stooped low, bent over from the wicker basket full of clothes and bedding strapped to her back, such that she was no taller than the Erstürmen overseers guarding her. Myan walked beside her, seemingly content with the fate circumstance had bestowed on him, likely because it was all he knew. Myan's father and mother had also been slaves, his birth the result of a secret and forbidden relationship that ended with their execution and the discovery of the newborn. Myan would have been killed too if Seronan hadn't intervened. She pleaded with Master Widald to save the infant grell, vowing to raise the baby as her own. Widald took pity on Myan and agreed to Seronan's request. She knew such pity would never be granted by her current masters.

Myan shifted the weight of the timber-panelled chest thudding into his back with every step. "What an honour it is, don't you think?"

"What are you talking about, Flea?"

"Who would have thought *all* Master Henruld's slaves would be requested to serve King Adalwolf? Our master must have impressed the king's advisors."

"I doubt it will improve our lives," said Seronan. "It is surprising the young king allows grell slaves anywhere near him. What if we were to rise up in a bloody rebellion?"

Myan jerked his head around to where Henruld marched behind them, then glared at Seronan. "*Sssh.* You shouldn't say such things. We'll be executed for talk like that. Maybe the new king better appreciates our service?"

"I fear my service will not last much longer. My feet burn with cuts and blisters, and this basket on my back grows heavier with each step. I hope I live long enough to see my ancestors' home. It is ironic, though."

"What is?"

"If I were a free grell, I would never be allowed to march to Malang Gunya. The males forbid females to go. They claim it is much too dangerous. Only as a slave will I have the chance to pay my respects to those who died trying to protect our home."

"Do you miss Babir Birramal?"

"Yes...and no. Sometimes, I lament my decision to live on the edge of the forest with my husband. To put my only child in such danger. But we refused to hide with the other weald-grells in Giigal. We wanted to protect the forest from Erstürmen incursions like our stone-grell brothers. Why should they bear all the burden? Our ambition was our downfall. My husband and child died at the end of an Erstürmen halberd. My friends and I were enslaved. Then, my life ended, and my survival began."

"Hoi, Wortle!" Henruld stormed up to Myan and Seronan. "Less talkin' and more walkin'. I got plenty other slaves if I need t'leave yur corpses by da side of da road."

"Yes, Master," replied Myan, staring at the ground.

Seronan followed suit, but inside her soul, a rebellious fire smouldered, waiting for a gust of wind to fan the flames once more. Her secondment into royal service offered an opportunity she may never experience again. A chance to put a chink in the armour of this new Erstürmen Kingdom. Her thoughts turned to plans of insurrection.

~ Chapter 14 ~

In Rostard's private quarters in the inner circle of Sardis, Anselm lay awake in his lover's bed while the soothsayer snored beside him, drawing wheezing breaths through a hawkish nose and thin lips the colour of peach-skin. The curate smiled at his own reflection in the mirror attached to the underside of the tester above him, wondering what other scenes of seduction the looking glass had borne witness to. Atop a chest of drawers beside the bed sat a glass vial, no bigger than Anselm's thumb, with a drop of glistening blue liquid inside. *Embruisia*, Rostard had called the liquid temptation. 'Cerulean honey.' Anselm had heard of it. A mind-altering substance injected under the skin using nothing more than a sewing needle.

Rostard had professed his devotion to embruisia, attempting to captivate Anselm with descriptions of the visions the cerulean honey invoked. He even declared his soothsaying would not be possible without it. Anselm wasn't convinced, abstaining from this particular temptation, despite succumbing to other desires. Although strategic pleasures offering personal advantage should never be discounted, Anselm still believed solemnity and sobriety were the hallmarks of a curate's life.

And he'd been able to return to that life after helping Hunfrid interpret the blood compass and pledging begrudging fealty to the Steward. Freed from the horrid dungeon, he could move about the inner circle and recommence his sermons in the kirika, praising the forgiveness of Volerdie. He could also return to his study of the scripture verses, examining the text for more information about the blood compass. The appearance of the compass with a blood-stained point meant someone in Enthilen was almost certainly searching for their birth twin. A twin who had somehow travelled from Volerdie's adopted world. But who was the pursuer, and who was the pursued? And what ultimate purpose drove the pursuit? In answer to these questions, Anselm's thoughts always returned to the exiled King Oldaric.

Rostard snorted, rolled onto his back and opened his eyes. He lay there, getting his bearings, and Anselm let fantasies of tall, spidery men binding his naked body with webs drift into his mind. Having both seen forty harvest seasons, he and Rostard were the same age, yet had never previously shared much in common, underscored by the tension usually existing between soothsayers and curates competing for the king's favour. Often, each offered different paths for their monarch to navigate the future. Over the past four moons, Rostard's lust had become infatuation, and Anselm understood the danger of courting the soothsayer and sharing his bed, even behind locked doors. But the liaisons served other purposes beyond satiating sexual desires.

"I saw him," said Rostard in an unusually hoarse voice.

"Dreaming of other men," teased Anselm, tracing his index finger along Rostard's neck.

"More a nightmare than a dream. A portent of war is coming to Sardis. Krieg, the red grell."

"Who will attack the royal city? The Dobunni rebels are on their knees."

"Not an attack on us," said Rostard, "but a battle nonetheless. Krieg will be the new ruler of Sardis."

Anselm sat up, propping his back with pillows resting against the headboard. "What of Hunfrid's future? Did the giests offer any guidance on the fate of the Steward?"

"He will have to bow before Krieg or die."

"And anyone standing by his side will die with him." Anselm paused, tussling Rostard's scraggly, dark hair, then offered a baited hook. "Hunfrid has a new infatuation."

Rostard faced him, eyebrows raised.

"Nothing more than a tin star," he lied, "but of special significance for any scholar of the scripture verses. My guess is Krieg is hunting this treasure for his Worshipful Master."

"The one you think is Oldaric?"

"I'm almost certain. Something tells me Hunfrid will not relinquish the treasure willingly. He seeks to profit from its value even if it means risking his life. We can use this infatuation against him. Find the treasure and deliver it to Oldaric's servant. Demonstrate our loyalty to the new order and dispose of Hunfrid in the one motion."

"Your resistance to this new order seems to have lessened," said Rostard.

"There is writing on the wall, my lover. We only have to read it."

Anselm threw back the duck-down quilt and swung his feet onto a floor rug made from the hide of a tufted goliath, curling his toes in among the fur. He stood and walked across to a fire smouldering in a massive stone hearth. If the relative opulence of Rostard's private quarters were any guide, it seemed soothsayers were more valued in the royal court than pious curates.

Strange, thought Anselm, the most devoted servants of Volerdie should willingly accept their austere bequests.

"If this *star* is valuable," said Rostard, "Hunfrid would keep it well hidden."

Anselm shivered and moved his naked body closer to the fire. "He never lets that vase out of his sight. The one containing the ashes of his dead, pet jezebel. I'll wager he's buried the treasure among her refuse." The quilt ruffled behind him, and bare feet pattered the tiled floor as Rostard approached. The lustful soothsayer stood behind Anselm and wafted warm breaths on the back of his neck.

"What can we do?" whispered Rostard.

Anselm smiled to himself. "Distract him with your visions of the red grell. If Hunfrid thinks Krieg will soon arrive in Sardis, he'll turn his attention to reinforcing the loyalty of the Steward's Shield. Building a wall of fealty around him to ward off any usurpers. Power is Hunfrid's most coveted possession. With his mind focussed on that, he may briefly forget about the other treasures he hides. Then, the time will come when Brynlee's ashes sit unguarded. And we will pounce."

Rostard's erection pressed into the small of Anselm's naked back. The curate breathed deeply and turned to embrace his fervent lover.

* * * *

"Leave him!" yelled Nettie.

"It's for the best," said Yonna. "We've tried everything."

"No. Don't take him. Keep him home."

Inside their koken in Sardis' fifth circle, Rosalie saw Nettie clench her jaw as the little girl grabbed at her twin brother, trying to pull him away from Yonna. Allum hung limp and quiet in his father's arms, the boy's legs dangling to the floor.

Yonna stumbled over to the doorway, trying to get outside. "I have to take him to the curate. That's our only chance to save his soul."

"He'll kill him!" yelled Petas, jumping from his chair.

"Quiet," said Heady. "The neighbours."

"No, no, no, no, NOOOOOOO!" Nettie snatched at Allum's ankle, clinging to her sibling like ice to frozen ground.

Rosalie sat at the dining table, grinding her teeth. "Allum needs a healer, not a curate."

"We can't afford a healer," said Heady.

"The smithy's full of tools. Sell them."

"Who'd buy them?" asked Yonna. "The curate offers his service for free."

"His *service*," growled Rosalie. "That's a pleasant way of putting it."

"If Allum dies without the curate's blessing, his soul won't enter paradise when Volerdie returns."

"Only you, Father, would consider the sacrifice of your own son a blessing."

Heady stood over the cooking pot, stirring broth with a wooden spoon. "We've tried everything, Rosalie. Onions, herbs, vinegar. Nothing works. If we don't appease the Divine Creator, The Ravage will spread further and consume all of us."

"Damn the Creator," said Rosalie.

Yonna peeled Nettie's hand from Allum's ankle and pushed through the door. The little girl dropped to the dirt floor of the koken, sobbing.

"Let's eat," said Heady. "It'll distract our thoughts. Nettie, get up, sweetheart."

Rosalie stood and clutched the back of the chair. "Do something, Mother. Stop hovering over that infernal, empty cooking pot and do something!"

Heady froze but didn't face her family. "I can't, Rosalie. You know I can't."

"Then, I will." Rosalie stormed from the kitchen and raced into the smithy. She took a rusty old sword from the pile of scrap metal, its weight dragging her arm below her waist. She didn't know how to wield a sword; she never had reason to. But she'd worked on them enough times, forging and honing the blades to razor sharpness, and knew the damage a sword could do to a body. To her father.

Rosalie lifted the sword to her side and pushed through the smithy door into the street. In the distance, Yonna staggered towards the kirika, struggling with Allum's weight. She marched after him, holding the sword across her body, trying not to look threatening in case somebody stopped her. The scattered residents wandering the fifth circle's streets shrank away or scurried past, wanting to avoid any confrontation.

Rosalie bore down on her father and yelled out, "Yonna Barron."

He stopped and faced her. "What are you doing with that sword, Rosalie?"

"Give Allum to me."

"Are you going to strike your own father?"

"If I have to. Let Allum go."

"Please, Rosalie. Leave the sword and go home." Yonna turned his back.

Rosalie stepped towards him and raised the weapon, ready to swing it down onto her father's shoulder.

"Hoi!" came a yell from behind her.

She kept the sword raised and didn't turn to the voice. Adrenaline swamped every sense when a Steward's Shield stepped between her and Yonna. The soldier didn't look much older than Rosalie, his face bright but stern. The top edge of a triangular shield strapped to his back poked out above his pauldrons, and he held a halberd with both hands diagonally across his filthy, dented breastplate.

"What's goin' on here?" asked the soldier.

Rosalie steeled herself. "This is between my father and me."

"Ya could do some damage with dat rusty sword. Put it down, now."

Yonna approached the young soldier. "She's on her way home, sir.

There's no trouble here. I'm the smithy, Yonna Barron. My daughter was showing me the sword she hoped to work on, that's all."

The soldier relaxed his grip on the halberd and smirked. "A woman forgin' metal. Now I heard everythin'."

Rosalie pressed her hand against the quillon block of the sword. "My brother's ill. He needs a healer. Our family can't afford one, and my father thinks the enchantments of a curate will save my brother's soul before he's sacrificed on the altar."

The soldier swung the halberd vertically and clacked the blunt end on the cobbled street. "Sounds to me like yur father's makin' a wise decision. Best ya go home. Cook him a nice meal or somethin'."

Yonna's eyes pleaded with Rosalie. "Go home, Rosalie."

She pushed the leather soles of her boots into the stones, making a point in her mind. "Not without Allum."

"Do what ya father says," said the soldier.

No, thought Rosalie. Not anymore.

Yonna lay Allum on the ground, faced the soldier and rested his hand on his gauntlet. "I can sort this out, sir. You don't need to trouble your-self any longer."

"Get yur hands off me," snarled the soldier. "It's an offence to touch a Steward's Shield."

Yonna withdrew his hand and raised it in deference.

Rosalie stood over Allum. "I'm taking him back home."

"Leave da boy," said the soldier. "If he's got Da Ravage, he has to be taken to da curate."

She turned to the young man who'd raised his halberd again, letting her eyes drift over his armour. She'd seen the Shield armour before, helping her father make suits of it, and knew how the thin, light metal fitted together and where its weak points were.

Yonna stepped towards Rosalie, and she pushed him back with her free hand. At the same time, the young soldier thrust the point of his halberd at her stomach. She dodged the blade, lifted the rusty sword above her head and swung it down, aiming for the folds of the gorget. It smacked into the metal, knocking the soldier sideways.

"No!" Yonna yelled.

It was too late. The soldier staggered across the cobblestones, bent over, one hand at his neck. Rosalie bashed the sword into his spangen-helm, and he fell to the ground, screaming. She stood frozen, entranced with fear. The sword slipped from her hands and clattered against the cobblestones as Yonna crouched over the Steward's Shield.

"What have you done, Rosalie?" he asked. "What have you done?" He stood and grasped her shoulders. "Get out of here. You have to get out of here. Run! Now!"

Yonna's urgency broke the entrancement. As the soldier writhed on the ground in agony, Rosalie turned for home, forcing her legs to move as fast as they could. But it felt like they were sinking in thick, sticky mud, and the harder she pushed forward, the further she sank. The breath of a monster hungered at her neck. Soon, the mud would hold her fast, and the beast would devour her.

More soldiers trotted along the street past Rosalie, drawn by the screams of their injured companion. It wouldn't be long before Sardis' most famous metalsmith, Yonna Barron, would have to explain himself and beg for mercy for his wayward daughter.

Somehow, Rosalie made it home. She headed straight for her bedroom and began throwing clothes and metal trinkets into an old sack.

Nettie trudged into the room, her worn linen kirtle still covered in dirt from the koken floor. "You didn't bring Allum back."

A breathless Rosalie ignored her sister.

Nettie sat on her bed. "What are you doing?"

"I have to leave home," bit Rosalie.

"Why?"

"I've done something stupid."

Heady's gaunt frame blocked the bedroom doorway. "What happened, Rosalie?"

"She's leaving," said Nettie, her tremulous voice betraying her sadness.

Heady's eyes widened. "What? Why?"

"I struck a Steward's Shield with a sword," said Rosalie. "I think he's badly injured."

Heady stepped into the room and slumped onto Nettie's bed, her face riven with shock. "Volerdie's mercy," she said.

"They'll come for me. Papa told the soldier our name. He'll tell his friends. Everybody knows Yonna Barron the smithy."

"They'll come for all of us," said Heady. "Nettie, start packing. We're all leaving."

"No," said Rosalie, "I'm going alone. If you help me escape, you'll definitely be punished. Executed most likely. If you say I acted alone, that you condemn my actions and beg for mercy, they might leave you be."

From the koken came a vicious, hacking cough. Heady turned her head to the sound. "Petas?" Another cough, this one more brutal.

"Have mercy," said Heady as she stood and walked out to the koken.

Nettie sat on Rosalie's bed, sobbing. "Please s-s-stay, Rosalie. What w-w-will I do without you?"

Rosalie shoved a scarf in her sack, placed the bag on the floor, sat with her little sister and pulled her close. "Be strong. Grow into a courageous, determined woman and stay true to everything you believe in. Everything you know is right." She pulled a necklace of fine, interlocking bronze circlets with rose-coloured glass set in a spiral at the front over her head and handed it to Nettie. "Take this. To remind you of your big sister."

Rosalie released Nettie, collected the sack and, without saying goodbye to Heady or Petas, strode down the hall, through the smithy and out into the streets of Sardis.

*   *   *   *

Rosalie took her first step across the tall bridge that traversed the Anchep River, walking shoulder-to-shoulder with the daily stream of peasants she'd often watched from the Sardis side of the riverbank. The communal tide ebbed and flowed across the lacquered deck to or from whatever business filled their insignificant lives. Slumstadt lay on the other side of the river, the sprawling, pulsing shantytown full of poverty and shattered dreams. A maze of streets wound in tortuous paths, and rickety shacks leaned roof against roof. If one fell, it seemed all others would follow, collapsing one after the other in a crushing, catastrophic cascade.

Slumstadt was the perfect place for Rosalie to hide. The Steward's Shield would never think to look for her in there. Who in their right mind would flee the fifth circle of Sardis into the destitution of Slumstadt? Rosalie decided she wasn't in her right mind, but nobody in Slumstadt knew who she was, and she expected most didn't care. She could fade into the background without so much as raising an eyebrow of curiosity.

Rosalie left the main road after crossing the bridge and stepped onto a muddy path, its edges marked by rivulets of excrement. She gagged at the stench of the shantytown, the smothering poverty threatening to suffocate her. Clenching her jaw, she heaved the sack of clothes and trinkets over her other shoulder and lumbered through the rows and rows of dilapidated shacks built from rags and driftwood washed down the Anchep River. Light rain pattered her hair. She needed to find shelter — any shelter she could.

~ Chapter 15 ~

In the vastness of the Veiled Occyan, the isolation of the raft offered no comfort for Grin. He'd been travelling with Thaly and Whibly for four days without sight of land. Their fresh water had run out, and he was sick of eating raw fish. When he wasn't rowing, he curled up in a corner and endured a muddle of dreams and nightmares that wrested his thoughts back and forth between two worlds. One he loved — the sanctity of the forest, the beauty of living creatures, his culture and kin — and a foreign world he began to hate.

Hate. Grin never expected that word to dominate his life. There was so much he never expected when he left his home in Babir Birramal with the birraman, Tom Anderson. He recalled his father's warning about Tom, '...his path will lead to tragedy. If you follow it with him, you will follow it to your end.'

The naïve, innocent Grin had dismissed the warning. But he was dead now. That stone-grell died on the *Vulking*. Ebullience and innocence had been replaced by timidity and hate, and an overwhelming loss of hope. He began to understand how a wild grell could be tainted. How their will could be bent to follow the designs of something inherently malicious. Filled with hate and with no promise of a better future, a grell might be capable of anything — a piece of malleable clay ready for their master to mould his monster.

The splash of the oar in the water pulled Grin from his wallow. Thaly knelt at the side of the raft, her shoulders hunched and back bent, pushing determinedly for home. Although Grin knew she hurt like he did, the emotional armour protecting her from the bitter world had thickened such, he wondered if anything could get through. They hadn't spoken much since the shipwreck. Not here. Not in front of Whibly. But Grin needed to, soon, lest the hurt consumed both of them.

The skullard sat at the front of the raft, his hands bound behind his back, peering into the distance. Then, without warning, he clambered to his feet.

"Land!" cried Whibly.

Although Grin scanned the eastern horizon, the famed keenness of grell eyesight eluded him. Or else, Whibly was lying.

"Land. I see it," said Whibly. "Thaly, can y'see it?"

She stopped rowing, and her shoulders slumped with the release of a burden. "Yes, I see it."

Grin searched again for his home, and there, in the far distance, what he hoped was the east coast of Enthilen shimmered above the waterline, bathed in brilliant light from the rising sun. He rubbed a swollen tongue along the inside of his incisors, then across parched lips, blackened by the tattoo ink of muwin. Part of him had expected to never see land again.

Whibly turned his back and thrust his bound hands at Thaly. "Untie me. I can help y'land the raft."

"I don't need your help," said Thaly.

"Aw, be fair now. I guided y'here, didn't I? Found the currents. Helped ya row. I ain't no threat. Please."

Thaly ignored Whibly, thrust the broken oar into the water and increased her stroke rate. The skullard spun around and pushed his foot into Grin's ankle. "We've reached land. Take this rope off me wrists."

Grin dismissed Whibly, prised a splinter from the sodden timber and picked at the fish flesh lodged between his teeth.

Whibly stared at him, his face twisting in deformed grimaces. "I don't think I can hold on 'til we reach land." He pointed his finger at his buttocks. "Y'know what I mean. I've been tryin' to hold on. Believe me, I have. But it's comin' and I ain't gonna stop it. If ya untie me, it'll make things a lot easier."

Grin shook his head, and Whibly's face sagged. The skullard sighed and lay on the raft, resting his head on the bundle of clothes in the corner.

Grin crawled over to Thaly. "Let me row. I have rested long enough."

Thaly nodded and handed the oar to Grin.

From that moment, the three survivors travelled in silence until midday. Grin navigated the raft through the breakers and pulled it up onto a sandy beach covered in shells crunching under his bare feet. Thaly tried to stand and fell sideways off the raft and into the shallows. She pulled herself up and staggered onto the beach.

"We need to find fresh water," said Grin.

Whibly stumbled out of the surf, his wrists still bound. "By my reckonin', we ain't too far from Gestade. Could get there tomorrow eve. The coast road must be nearby. Walk inland a bit, then we follow it south."

"We?" asked Grin, raising his eyebrows.

"I'm weak from hunger and thirst. I can't survive by meself. Don't leave me here to die."

"Keep him with us, Grin. We could sell him to a slave-master."

As Thaly spoke, Whibly's face oscillated between pleased and displeased.

"If you stay," said Grin, "your wrists remain bound."

"Thank you, Grin. Thank you, Thaly. I won't be any trouble. I promise. I can find the road for ya."

Thaly collapsed onto the beach. She sat there, running her fingers over the soaked white handkerchief tied around her forearm — the bandage from Tom covering the arrow wound inflicted by Krieg on Hansen's Bluff. Grin sat beside her, and Whibly limped into the sand dunes lining the beach, checking for a path inland or somewhere to relieve himself. The days trapped on the raft had no noticeable adverse effects on the skullard, his crab-like shuffle looking entirely at home on the beach.

Finally, Grin and Thaly were alone.

"Does your arrow wound still hurt?" asked Grin.

She faced him, her brown eyes looking more doleful than he'd ever seen them. "We're home. That's all that matters."

"You have other wounds, too. Ones we share."

Thaly returned her gaze to the ocean.

"When I close my eyes, I still see those men," said Grin. "Six of them had to hold me down. I hear their grunts and sniggers. Feel them violating me. 'Worthless slave,' they kept saying. That is all I was to them. I never knew such filthy, careless evil existed. When they..."

Thaly whispered in a wavering voice, "They raped us."

"There is a word for it? Such horror is so well known it has a name?" Grin clutched at the sand with his fingers, wondering what other terrors might be waiting for him in the shadows of an unknown world. "Do these things happen among the Dobunni?"

"I've heard stories. The perpetrators are often punished. Sometimes severely."

"I wanted to kill them. Every last one of them. I wanted to tear the crew apart. I am sorry, Thaly, I should have protected you."

Thaly stiffened. "You're not my keeper. I can protect myself."

Grin flinched, tears welling in his eyes.

Thaly faced him. "Is that what your culture demands of you?"

"Female stone-grells are precious. There are so few wild grells, and our numbers dwindle with every passing season that those who can bear young are the most valued members of our community. It is my responsibility to protect them with my life. I am sorry I projected that responsibility onto you."

Thaly shook her head. "No, I'm sorry. I spoke without thinking. We should have protected each other."

"My thoughts are so filled with hate. Do you not feel the same?"

"It hurts to feel. I want to block it out."

"If I lock away the pain and anger, I fear it will destroy me."

"Emelin once told me that some scars last a lifetime. But these marks, these memories, however foul, remind us of our strength. We were hurt, and we survived."

Grin let the sand run through his fingers. "In this survival, all I see is the end of a life worth living."

* * * *

Thaly wondered if she could offer Grin the support he needed and whether he could do the same for her. Despite their shared pain, both struggled with the emotional trauma of the assault. Right now, Thaly needed Emelin more than ever.

They sat in silence for a while, then trudged up the beach, the shifting white sand squeaking under Thaly's bare feet and tugging on her calves. Trails through the succulent groundcover made the going easier. Past the dunes, the vegetation changed to low, gnarled shrubs, tortured by the salty wind. A path lined with rocks led to a shack hidden in a swale. A roof of dry thatched shrubs sat over four walls of weathered grey timber. Whibly fossicked around inside the hut, and Thaly poked her head through the open door.

"There's grains and cured meat here," said Whibly, "and I found a well out the back."

Grin ducked his head under the door lintel and peered into the empty shack. "We could stay here until the owners return."

"I want to press on," said Thaly. "To Gestade. Tom might be there."

"We should take only a portion of the food and refill our empty water-skin," said Grin.

"Whibly has coin. I heard it jiggling around in his pants. We'll leave a payment."

Despite the skullard's protests, Grin took three coins from Whibly's pocket and left them near the fireplace. They filled a sack with rolled oats and dried, salted meat, and walked out of the shack into the late afternoon sun.

After shuffling along narrow, sandy paths through dense heath and sparse woodland, the three castaways came to a wide dirt road.

"Ain't no doubt this is the coast road," said Whibly. "It connects Laodicea with Gestade. If y'follow it past the Erstürmen outpost, it'll take ya south to Grōz Forst. Sorry, Grin, I meant Babir Birramal." Whibly turned and peered north, up the road. "Looks like we got company. I hope they ain't Erstürmen soldiers or anythin' to do with them tainted grells."

Thaly and Grin turned at the same time. On the road north, a group of people in the far distance moved towards them. Hundreds, maybe thousands of people.

"We shall wait here until they arrive," said Grin.

"What if they try to kill us?" said Whibly.

"You are right. It is better to be cautious. Thaly and I will hide in the bushes. You can talk to the strangers when they come. If you strike trouble, I am sure you will think of a way out of it."

"That ain't fair."

"Not much in this world is fair anymore." A flicker of a smile lit Grin's face before he continued, "We will wait together."

As the strangers approached, Thaly's spirits lifted at the sight of Dobunni rebels dressed in chainmail coifs walking among a throng of civilians in dirty clothes. A handful of people rode horses, but most staggered forward on unsteady legs, carrying sacks or bundles of clothes and blankets slung over their shoulders. The sullen whine of children floated on the ocean breeze amid the jangle of harnesses connecting weary horses to laden wagons.

A tall, elegant woman with greying hair led the group, but the sword hanging from her belt didn't sit comfortably. A short, plump woman with auburn curls walked by her side, a young boy clutching the leg of her pants.

The tall woman approached holding her hands out front and above her head, palms facing inwards, preparing for a formal grell greeting where the new acquaintances would rest the tips of their fingers on each other's cheeks. However, Grin stepped back and turned his face away.

Thaly winced, Grin's discomfort accentuating her own. He doesn't want to be touched, she thought. Leave him alone. She stepped in front of the woman. "I am Athalee, a Dobunni rebel from Bagendon. My companion is Grinnian stone-grell. Grin. Oh, and Whibly, the skullard of the *Vulking*."

The woman smiled with warm blue eyes. "I am Lady Lily LáDown, the Master of the Southern Vale of Laodicea, though that quarter of the city is no more. My companion is Dealhia Rossingbird, Master of the Docklands. We are leading refugees of war to Gestade."

"Grin and I rode with the Dobunni army to Laodicea to defend the city against the barbarians," said Thaly. "We escaped on a merchant ship that was wrecked in a storm. Can you spare any water or food? We have a little, but not enough. And we're famished from days at sea eating nothing more than raw fish."

Lily gestured to a soldier standing beside her who trotted off to a wagon. Dealhia walked on with five children in tow.

"Your face is familiar," Lily said to Thaly. "Have we met?"

Thaly shrugged and averted her gaze.

"Never mind," said Lily. "You're welcome among us. There's a handful of rebel soldiers in our group, plus those Dobunni that called the Southern Vale home. The rest of your army returned to Bagendon."

"Have you met any other shipwreck survivors?" asked Grin. "We are missing our friend, a young man called Tom Anderson."

"You're the first I've met. Others in our group may have seen your friend. Don't give up hope."

Thaly lifted her head. "Why are you abandoning your home? Fleeing from battle."

"Death is the only reward for those who fight battles they can't win, and suicide is not in my nature. I have to keep my people safe. That's more important to me than fighting an enemy I can't defeat. You're wounded."

Thaly wrapped her hand around Tom's handkerchief, covering the wound on her arm.

"We have healers with us," said Lily. "When you've had food and water, seek one of them out. They may be able to ease your suffering. You might also find fresh clothes and weapons. Why is the skullard tied?"

"The ship's crew turned on us before the storm hit," said Thaly. "The captain took our friend, and we were..." She swallowed hard, fighting with everything to control her emotions and steel her thoughts. "Whibly helped us reach land, but we don't know if we can trust him."

"Y'can trust me for sures," said Whibly. "I ain't gonna hurt no-one."

Lily pointed to a passing wagon. "Put him in there. We can decide what to do with him when we reach Gestade." She started to walk off, calling back over her shoulder. "We also have Erstürmen with us. Those who refused to pledge loyalty to Adalwolf. Don't stick a knife in their throats. I've promised them a safe passage."

Grin lifted Whibly into a wagon carrying wounded Dobunni soldiers who agreed to keep an eye on him. The soldier sent by Lady Lily returned with food and guided Thaly and Grin to a wagon carrying spare clothes and weapons. Thaly changed out of her torn tunic into a fawn shirt, a soiled brown coat with no buttons on the front, a pair of belted, canvas pants, and weathered boots. Grin found a canvas tunic large enough to fit a grell and a strip of fabric he used as a belt to cinch around his waist. He handed Thaly a sheathed short sword and kept a knife for himself.

They made a wet mash of cold oats in a wooden bowl, then walked together shovelling congealed lumps into their mouths with their fingers and washing it down with bitter water. Thaly felt self-conscious, eating in front of the thousands of refugees who trudged along the coast road to Gestade. They all looked so hungry.

"You should see a healer, Thaly," said Grin. "Your arm needs tending."

"I doubt a healer can help me."

"We cannot seem to help each other."

No, thought Thaly, it seems not. But we're trying. "Will you still go home to Babir Birramal?"

"Yes. If we follow this road past Gestade, we will arrive at the northern edge of the forest." Grin bowed his head and went silent.

"You feel guilty. About abandoning Tom."

Grin nodded.

Thaly sighed. "Where would we start looking? Should we search the coast in case he made it ashore? Do we find a boat and row into the waves hoping we might stumble on his weary body?"

"I will never give up on Tom, but you are right, there is little we can do, and both of us need to heal. The forest is the only place I can do that."

"When you go back to the forest, you'll be initiated?"

"The stone-grell elders guarding the edge of Babir Birramal have chosen this cycle as my time. All of my family will be at the garrabari. My father, Frennan, and my mother, Mirrian, and little sister, Hannian, will come from Giigal. If I miss the ceremony, I may not be selected again for many cycles, if ever."

"Tom told me you had an older brother?"

"Yes. His name was Merran."

"Why do you introduce yourself as first born?"

"The grell formal greeting is complicated. It is a tremendous honour to be first born, and the honour passes to younger children should the older child die. The hierarchy of the greeting applies only to the living. If Merran was alive, I would introduce myself as second born."

"Sorry, I didn't mean to intrude."

"Your interest is no intrusion. Hanni, my younger sister, introduces herself as first daughter because it is a greater honour to be known as first daughter than second born. If a grell introduces himself as third son, you know he has two older brothers and at least one older sister; otherwise, he would introduce himself as third born. Do you understand?"

Thaly nodded, trying to hide the fact she was more confused than ever. But she was glad to have shepherded their thoughts to more pleasant things. "I'm looking forward to seeing your home."

"I would be honoured if you came to the garrabari with me."

"Is it allowed?"

Grin smiled for the first time since the storm. "It is now."

~ Chapter 16 ~

It had been two days since Tom found Captain Adcock washed up on a beach at Bramble Island. Two days since he *killed* Adcock. He'd never killed anybody before. Why would he have? Sure, he'd cut the arm of one of the drunk rebels who accosted Dwarrow back in Bagendon. That was self-defence, like his altercation with Adcock.

It was self-defence, wasn't it?

Tom had replayed the event over and over in his head. Pictured himself pushing Adcock's face into the surf. The shipwrecked captain gasping for air and flailing his arms. The dull thud of driftwood hitting flesh and bone.

He understood now what Thaly had told him in Bagendon about how she felt after cutting down one of Grin's torturers in Süden Forst. As if a creature had taken over her body who could kill on a whim. Tom had met that creature, and it terrified him. But he had to come to terms with it. Eventually, he decided Adcock deserved his end. Taking a life didn't make Tom feel strong or powerful or satisfied. Only empty. He hadn't spoken to Jameus or Melinda about it. What would he say? Better to forget it happened.

Standing on the shore at Bramble Island, sporadic raindrops started concentric rings floating outwards on the calm sea, and Tom began to count the rings then caught himself. He distracted his mind with memories of summer beach holidays with his family when rain clouds filled the warm sky, and showers wet his head as he stood neck-deep in salt water, immersed in the soothing magic of a tranquil ocean during rain. He wanted to strip off and recreate the experience, but a wintry breeze reminded him of the cold.

Rubbing his chin, his hand brushed over a thickening growth of facial hair.

When did that happen?

Tom hadn't studied his reflection since arriving in Enthilen, not even in the tall mirror Princess Caeli hid her secrets behind.

I'll have to start shaving. Somehow.

He reached inside his pocket and pulled out the eyes of lost souls, rolling them around in his hand to feel their smooth surface and a dull cold that assuaged the rawness of his scarred palms. He flinched, remembering how the eyes burned into his skin when he travelled from Earth to Enthilen. Adalwolf's vacant stare atop the windswept peak of Hansen's Bluff flashed into his mind, the prince's fist trembling as he clenched the dark eyes and punched Tom in the chest, and the shock that coursed through Tom's body like a jolt of electricity.

My heart almost burst.

"Did Nanna feel that?" Tom muttered to himself. He closed his eyes, picturing his grandmother lying on the bedroom floor. The Bad Man pressed down on her, pushing his fist against her chest as her body convulsed beneath him.

I saw the Bad Man's face. Malphas. In my bedroom. On Hansen's Bluff.

Tom recalled what Malphas had said to him on the bluff. 'Born at the same time...with the same mark.' He'd wondered about this 'mark' until he remembered Nanna had a birthmark on her right calf, shaped like a pear. A mark she was born with. Little Tommy saw it sometimes when Nanna sat on his bed reading stories, her nightie riding up to her knees. At the time, the mark gave him comfort. He didn't need to be embarrassed by his own birthmark — the naevus shaped like a crescent moon on his shoulder-blade. Nanna said the marks were special.

If this is my mark, then Adalwolf has it too. A crescent moon on his shoulder. That means Malphas must have a birthmark like Nanna's on his calf. And when two people are born in different worlds sharing the same birthmark...

"What are those?"

Tom started and dropped the eyes back into his pocket, trying to look nonchalant. Melinda had snuck up on him amid the daydreams. "Nothing," he said. "Trinkets."

Melinda shrugged. "Don't tell me then. Da says we'll be ready to leave soon. Will ya go and see your family when we get to the mainland?"

Tom replied, without thinking, "No. They're in another world...I mean, they're a long way away."

"Da says the Desolate Mountains are like another world."

Tom relaxed. "It isn't that bad a place if you like goats."

"We had a pet goat once. Her name was Briddle-flower, after the pink flowers growing in the sand dunes near our home. I called her Briddy. We ate her."

Tom nodded and returned to searching the horizon.

"Don't worry. Your friends might be alive. Strange things happen at sea, Da always says. Not sure why. Nothin' strange has ever happened to me. Though findin' you was strange, so maybe Da's right. I can be your new friend if y'like."

"I'd like that," said Tom, smiling at the boisterous, red-haired girl. "I need all the friends I can get."

"Well, since we're friends, can y'help me with one more job before we head home? Da has asked me to collect fuzzy sugar nuts."

"Fuzzy what?"

"Sugar nuts. They're delicious. We can take 'em home with us."

Melinda slung a satchel over her shoulder and led Tom from the beach into dense forest near the shoreline. They pushed their way through twisting vines with white flowers, and ferns with broad, shamrock-green leaves wider than Tom's chest and bending in half with their weight. A sandy path took them to a clearing ringed by tall, straight trees with sweeping pinnate leaves bunched at the top of the tree and growing straight out from the smooth trunk like the canopy of an umbrella.

Melinda stood under one of the trees and pointed up. "See where the bases of the leaves connect to the trunk?"

Above Tom, a cluster of brown, furry lumps resembling a dozen hairy coconuts, each about the size of a human head, nestled around the trunk immediately below the leaves.

"I'm not climbing the tree if that's what you think," he said, crossing his arms.

"We don't need to. All you've got to do is knock 'em down with a stone." Melinda unshouldered her satchel, opened the flap and tipped a pile of stones onto the ground. "I can't throw very high. Da usually does this. He told me to ask you."

"What exactly do you want me to do?"

"Knock the fuzzy sugar nuts off the tree by throwin' stones at them. They ain't stuck on too hard. A direct hit will do it. They're the crunchiest nuts you'll ever taste. Inside, they have a sweet juice like milk and cream and honey all mixed together."

Tom's mouth salivated at the thought. He hadn't had anything resembling the sweetness of honey since arriving in Enthilen. He picked up a stone, took aim at one of the nuts, drew his arm back and threw. The stone sailed above the tree canopy, missing the cluster of nuts, and fell back to earth.

"That was close," said Melinda, kindly, because the throw wasn't close at all. "Try again."

Tom took another stone and threw. This one fell short of the mark, cannoning into the tree trunk.

"One too high. One too low. The next one will be spot on." Melinda handed Tom another stone.

He aimed carefully this time, and the stone smacked right into a fuzzy sugar nut.

Melinda clapped her hands. "Got it!"

However, the nut didn't fall. Tom began to wonder why until the nut unfurled itself to reveal a white face with big eyes glaring at him and Melinda. The face opened its mouth, baring long, glistening canines, and rangy arms and legs stretched out to the side. To Tom, the creature resembled a cat-sized monkey.

"Uh oh," said Melinda. "Looks like you've made 'em mad."

Tom turned to her, confused. "You told me these were…"

A deafening howl, the closest thing to a roaring engine Tom had heard in this new world, drowned out his words and appeared to shake every leaf in the jungle. More of the 'fuzzy nuts' unfurled and snarled at Tom and the curly-haired trickster standing beside him.

"We probably should go," said Melinda. "Howlin' gaffes don't like to be disturbed."

"Howling gaffes?"

Melinda giggled and pointed as the gaffes began shinning down the tree trunk. "Oops, here they come."

"What will they do?" asked Tom. He didn't have to wait long for an answer. A howling gaffe swung out from the trunk, positioned its genitals right above Tom and released its bladder. A golden shower rained down around him.

Tom covered the top of his head with his forearms. "Bloody hell. It's pissing on me!"

Melinda began to laugh. "They'll do that. Among other things."

"You knew this was going to happen, didn't you?"

Another gaffe stopped mid-trunk and hovered its bottom over an open hand. Tom couldn't see what it was doing and guessed too late. The howling gaffe defecated in its hand, clenched its fist, and threw the poo missile right at Tom, almost hitting him in the face.

"Did that monkey throw shit at me?"

Melinda couldn't contain herself, clutching her stomach and doubling over with laughter such that Tom thought her head might fall off. More gaffes descended the tree, howling in an agitated caterwaul as urine and faeces bombarded Tom and Melinda.

She stumbled to the edge of the clearing, still laughing.

"You set me up," said Tom.

"Run like you're chasin' goats!" she yelled between the guffaws and disappeared into the jungle.

Tom followed her, leaving behind the wailing howls and the flying waste. The pair burst onto the beach, and Melinda fell onto the sand, still holding her stomach and laughing, tears streaming down her freckled face.

Tom joined her, trying hard not to smile. "You tricked me."

Melinda struggled for composure. "Fuzzy...fuzzy...sugar nuts. I...I... made that...made that bit up. Didn't think you'd believe me. That was funnier than when I got the howlin' gaffes to throw poop at Da. He weren't too pleased about it neither."

Tom lay beside Melinda and laughed with her until a conch rang out across the beach.

Melinda jumped up. "That's Da! We're ready to go. Come on, Tom Anderson. I'll race you."

206

*   *   *   *

Jameus and Melinda's boat, Binalong, sat low in the water with the weight of three passengers and twelve crates of dried, salted and smoked fish. With the supplies stored, and the beach-shelter left empty and alone to face the next storm, Jameus threaded two oars through the oarports and began rowing, his cheeks turning beetroot purple from the strain. Although he was a big, hulking man, Tom still marvelled at Jameus' strength to move the laden boat through the shallows and into deeper water. Melinda sat at the stern and waved goodbye to Bramble Island.

"Why don't these boats have sails?" asked Tom, settling onto a bench seat near the front of the boat.

"What's a sail?" asked Melinda.

"It's a big piece of cloth tied to a mast, li'l darlin," said Jameus. "Some boats have 'em. Winds can be fickle though, especially round 'ere, and there's a more reliable method of travellin' over long distances."

Jameus rowed for a short while, then stopped where the seafloor dropped away sharply, the boat bobbing, insignificant, above the vast ocean depths. Tom pictured Grin and Thaly lying on the bottom of the ocean, their lives wasted because of him.

"I want to do it," Melinda cried to her father.

"*Alright.* You're gettin' bossier with every passin' moon." Jameus stowed the oars.

Melinda pursed her lips to the mouthpiece of a horn that extended down the boat's starboard side and into the water. She blew until her cheeks ballooned, and Tom thought her freckles might start popping off her face. He strained his ears for a sound, catching the faintest of whistles. Melinda beamed with pride at her trumpeting, and the three passengers sat in the boat in silence, the gentle lap of the waves massaging the oiled timber.

Nothing happened, so they waited a little longer. Melinda's smile faded. Still nothing. They waited some more. Jameus drummed his thick, bulbous fingers on the side of the boat, and Tom started to count the nails fixing metal straps to the edges of the wooden crates jammed together across the floor.

Melinda tapped her feet on the seat. "She's takin' her time, Da. Shall I blow again?"

"Wait a moment, li'l darlin', it's been a while since we needed her, but she knows we're overdue to leave. She'll be feedin' nearby, no doubt."

Melinda fidgeted, picking at the threads of her worn, salty shirt. With exaggerated breaths, she glanced at Jameus on every exhale. "I definitely think I need to..."

Before she could finish her sentence, an enormous grey whale exploded from the surface, breached next to the boat, and drenched the three seafarers with seawater. Tom clutched onto the sides as the waves from the whale splash threatened to tip them overboard.

Melinda screamed with delight. "There she is! Ahoy there, Freckles!" She turned to Tom. "I call her Freckles on account of all her spots. Like the ones I have on me face."

Freckles swam to the front of the boat, and Jameus threw buckets of shrimp overboard, the whale swallowing the treat in a single mouthful. Jameus prepared a harness, similar to what Tom had seen on the *Vulking*, then dove into the water beside Freckles. Together, the fisher and the grey whale swam, dipped and pirouetted in an aquatic dance that saw the harness looped over the whale's head and secured between her eyes and front fins.

"I'm gonna be the whale-master this time." Melinda grabbed the reins of the harness and strapped herself into a wooden seat perched at the tip of the bow.

A soaking Jameus pulled himself onboard and rolled his eyes at his daughter. "Ya know what happened last time. Y'were pulled overboard."

"I can do it, Da. Freckles don't need much drivin'. She knows how to get home."

"Remember, we need to stop along the way so she can feed. I'll have to remove the harness..."

"I *knowww*. Whales like Freckles feed-on-the-bottom-of-the-ocean. If we don't set her free, we'll be dragged under and end up spendin' the rest of our days in the court of the squid king. Blow the whistle, Da! Let's head for home."

Jameus blew into the tube, and the boat careered ahead, Tom losing his balance and toppling onto a crate of fish.

"Yeeha!" Melinda cried, with the wind in her curls and a gleam of mischief in her eyes.

* * * *

The three passengers travelled for two days before the mainland of Enthilen appeared in the distance. The boat was surprisingly comfortable, a raised section at the rear padded with thick woollen blankets where two passengers at a time could lie flat and sleep. Tom enjoyed the company of his new companions, warming to Melinda's lust for life and Jameus' forgiving nature. Importantly, Jameus didn't ask too many questions, seeming to accept for the time being the young man from The Feign was in his care. Yet, despite the excellent company, Tom longed for a meal other than preserved fish.

With Enthilen looming on the horizon, he tried to put the past behind him and focus on his next objective; find Bindari. He wondered about Annian, the old grell who Jameus had said was ready to find her final resting place.

Could this be Bindari? Would she tell him how to get there?

It hurt to dismiss the fate of Grin and Thaly so readily, but what else could he do? If they were alive, they'd be better off without him. Safer away from Malphas' searching glare and the relentless pursuit of tainted grells. Although Tom hoped they were alive, he had to shoulder this burden without their help.

Close to the coast, Jameus set Freckles free and rowed the boat into a pretty cove with pearl-white sand and granite boulders covered in orange and red lichen. The water sparkled sapphire blue in the mid-morning sun, schools of fish swimming under the boat as it pulled into shore. Jameus threw the anchor overboard and jumped into the water with a length of rope resting on his shoulder. He tied the rope onto one of the boulders and fetched a raft from the beach, which he pulled up alongside the boat. Tom and Melinda handed crates of preserved fish to the large man, and he stacked them onto the raft before hauling it to shore. After three more trips, and with the hold empty, the two helpers boarded the raft, and Jameus took them to dry land. They loaded a handful of crates onto a cart, which all three lugged along a rough track through the dunes, the sand squeaking under their feet.

They soon came to a modest shack nestled among a ring of tall sand dunes and shaded by stunted trees that reminded Tom of melaleucas. Smoke wafted from a stone chimney poking through layers of thatch covering the pitched roof. Strewn across the front veranda, a mess of empty crates, fishing gear, crab pots, ropes and other flotsam and jetsam almost hid an old grell who sat on a stool peeling a yam.

"Annian!" cried Melinda. She dropped the cart's pull-bar and sprinted to the porch.

The grell stopped peeling and held out welcoming arms, catching the young girl in a giant hug. Annian sat Melinda on her lap, face-to-face, and the reunited friends placed the ends of their fingers on each other's cheeks in a formal grell greeting.

Annian broke from Melinda's gaze and smiled at Jameus. "Welcome home. Fishing good?"

"It was Annian. It was. Plenty to keep us goin' durin' the long dark. Let me introduce..."

"Wait," said Tom, stopping Jameus mid-sentence.

Tom strode over to Annian and tripped on the front of the porch, almost falling on top of Melinda. He composed himself and placed his hands on the old grell's cheeks, her skin still warm from Melinda's embrace. All the emotions of life were etched onto Annian's weathered face, framed by thinning grey hair, and her sparkling turquoise eyes advertised to the world her heritage as a weald-grell.

Tom studied the faded facial tattoo that resembled a swan floating on a lake and waited for Annian to reciprocate the formal greeting by cupping his cheeks. She remained motionless, glaring at him over the top of Melinda's head.

Undeterred, Tom began his introduction. "Greetings. I am Tom Anderson. Son of Bert and Elaine Anderson, herders of goats from The Feign in the foothills of the Desolate Mountains."

Annian raised her eyebrows. Melinda squirmed, then jumped onto the porch.

Tom waited for Annian's response. *Have I offended her?* He removed his hands from her cheeks. "I'm honoured to make your acquaintance. I'm close friends with Grinnian stone-grell, protector of Babir Birramal and son of Frennan and...and..."

Annian rolled her eyes and looked at Jameus. "Who this fool?"

A bellowing laugh exploded from the crusty seafarer. "A shipwrecked fool no less. Melinda saved him from being shark food."

"Hey," cried Melinda. "Tom's no fool. He's my friend."

Annian smiled. "If friend of yours, little one, I tolerate him."

Tom's shoulders slumped. He'd made better first impressions.

"Help with crates." Annian got up from her stool, her hunched, fading body bent over such that she was no taller than Tom. As she lifted one of the crates, wiry muscles bulged under tanned skin.

Tom tried again to make friends. "Let me do that."

"No need," she said. "Not ready to crumble into soil yet."

"Sorry about the attempted greeting. I was only trying…"

Annian straightened her back and glared at Tom. "Too old for pretence. If kind, I see it. If not, I see that too. Be who you are, no more, no less."

Melinda placed her arm around Annian's waist. "Da says Anni doesn't waste smiles on fools."

Tom worried he would never see a smile from Annian.

By sunset, the crates of preserved fish had been stacked in a storeroom behind the cabin. Tom joined the family as they sat down for the evening meal, which, thankfully, included a vegetable mash and soup as well as preserved fish. Inside the small, neat shack, Jameus' bed had been squeezed into the main room, alongside the cooking area and dining table, while Annian and Melinda shared a second room. There were no bathroom facilities, and Tom didn't expect any. He'd grown accustomed to depositing his waste outside in a well-dug hole and cleaning himself with washrags.

"Have y' thought any more 'bout when you'll leave us, Annian?" asked Jameus.

"No, Da!"

"Hush, child. Don't make it harder than it already is."

Annian put her arm around Melinda's shoulder and pulled her close. "You and me, best friends. I know you since baby. We share many seasons. You and me always friends, no matter time, place, together or alone. Our friendship last longer than oldest tree in oldest forest ever grown."

"Forever?" asked Melinda.

"Forever."

"I'm going to miss you."

"And I miss you. Means we share something special. Would you rather not miss me?"

Melinda shrugged.

"Nobody escapes end of life. A sacred time for grells. Sometimes happen quickly, unexpected. Other times, see end coming from long way off. When life nears end, a place beckons where we return to soil that gives all life. A place where we are honoured and remembered on giant pillars of stone."

"Will y'take your totems?" asked Melinda.

"I must. No-one to pass them to."

"I can look after them. I'll keep 'em safe, and then, then I can write my own story on a new one, and when I have a baby daughter, I can pass them on to her."

"That is too much to ask, Melinda," said Jameus.

"But...but...Da, I'll treat them like my own special treasure."

"Where is this final resting place?" asked Tom, hoping his nonchalance might slip under Annian's guard.

The old weald-grell sat back in her chair, crossed her arms and looked sideways at him. "Only grells can know."

Tom persisted because he had to. "I need to find a place called Bindari. Is that where you're going?"

Annian remained silent, got up from the table and cleared away the dishes.

Tom's eyes followed her around the room. "It is Bindari, isn't it? The grell graveyard. That's where you're going to die?"

"Don't say that!" Melinda sprang from her seat, glared at Tom and ran into her bedroom.

Tom focussed on Annian's back as she washed the plates, but he still noticed Jameus' glower out of the corner of his eye.

"Let it be, son," said Jameus. "Let it be."

~ Chapter 17 ~

Hadufuns lay in the back of a canopied wagon travelling among the refugees of Laodicea to Gestade. Audie had made him a bed from woollen blankets and treated his face and chest wounds every day, satisfied the injuries were healing as well as could be expected. The bones of his broken left forearm appeared to be knitting together, Audie having strapped the arm and tied the strap around the back of Hadufuns' neck, so his forearm rested across his stomach. Audie's skill meant he could soon take care of himself. He should feel blessed at having recovered from injuries that would have killed most people, but the idea of spending less time with Audie soured his thoughts.

The journey along the coast road to Gestade, now in its eighth day, had been painfully slow, every rut in the road seeming to jolt the wagon sideways and causing Hadufuns to flinch and moan. Although the chatter among the refugees walking close to the wagon helped distract his mind, his thoughts inevitably turned to the coming days. He knew Lily LáDown had asked her best healer to tend his wounds because she wanted him to convince Field Commander Hartmut to shelter the refugees of Laodicea. Hadufuns and the commander were friends when they lived together in the inner circle of Sardis. A young, ambitious Hartmut grew into a loyal and honourable leader. Lily had chosen her destination wisely. If any

Field Commander of an Erstürmen outpost was going to provide protection for a motley band of war refugees, it would be Hartmut.

Audie sat on the bench seat beside the wagon driver. As the saunter of the horses rocked the wagon from side to side, Hadufuns' mind drifted with the hypnotic beauty of Audie's gently swaying ponytail. Trying to stay awake, he sat up and spun himself around until his head was at the front of the wagon tray, and spoke through the parted flaps of the canopy, "What do you see, Audie?"

"We're almost at Gestade. There are high stone walls taller than six men standing on each other's shoulders, and ramparts topped with banners of the two-headed snake and another creature."

"That would be a mongoose, Hartmut Adelmund's family sigil," said Hadufuns.

"Surrounding the base of the wall is a sprawling town of neat timber houses and green fields."

"Gestade was always the jewel among the Erstürmen outposts. Hartmut would have it no other way."

With night setting in, and the moons of Seena and Bargan rising in the sky, Audie left the bench seat and ducked back under the canopy with Hadufuns. "We're in town now. It's well past sunset, yet the market square is still crowded with people. Oil-fired lanterns light up every stall. I haven't seen so much food for...well, a long time. Clothes, utensils, tools, weapons; it's all here. The townsfolk seem curious about their uninvited guests, yet no-one has tried to turn us away. I feel like we've left Enthilen and entered another world."

"Soldiers, ma'am," said the wagon driver.

Audie poked her head outside. "Soldiers on horseback with the armour of the King's Shield and carrying black banners with the red serpent. They appear to be escorting us."

"Hartmut will listen to our pleas," said Hadufuns. "Whether he accepts them is another thing entirely."

Audie turned and smiled at him. "That's where you come in. Your wounds are healing well. I imagine you'll be keen to visit the Field Commander as soon as possible."

"I sometimes wonder, Audie, if Lady Lily gave you one chore above all others. Soften me up, so I cede to her wishes and beg Hartmut to give everyone refuge."

"If I knead your aching muscles until sunrise, will that make you soft enough?"

"It's worth trying."

Audie tossed a cloth onto Hadufuns' bare chest. "Why don't you start without me? I'm going to set up the infirmary."

As she went to leave the wagon, Hadufuns grabbed her arm. "Wait. Tell Lily, if the need arises, I'll do whatever I can to help. I'm hoping she can convince Hartmut to harbour the refugees without my intervention. If Malphas finds out I'm alive..."

"Do you still have that exquisite knife?"

Hadufuns nodded and released his grip on Audie's arm. "There's no risk. Not in your company. Gloomy thoughts are swept away."

Audie frowned. "*Hmm.* I'm not able to accept your contentment as my burden. I have too many other responsibilities."

Hadufuns clasped Audie's hand. "I'm sorry, I didn't mean... You're right, the burden is all mine. I'm still saddened at the thought of sharing less of your company."

"I'll always be close by. If you seek me out, I'm sure I could find a spare moment for us to walk together or sit under the moons and talk."

"I'd like that, but..."

"But what?"

Hadufuns shook his head and released her hand. "Nothing. Don't let me delay you further."

Audie smiled and climbed down from the wagon as it came to a stop, leaving Hadufuns alone with his thoughts. To help the refugees, he would almost certainly have to announce his presence to Hartmut and his lieutenants. Even if they swore to secrecy, he expected word of his survival to spread quickly throughout Enthilen. 'The Wandering Prince still wanders. He wasn't killed in Laodicea after all.' Eventually, Malphas would hear the news, and the hunt would begin to bring down the Wandering Prince forever so he couldn't challenge for the throne.

*　*　*　*

The refugees from Laodicea settled outside the walls of Gestade, and a field of campfires sprang up to fight the cold and dark, dotting the landscape like amber stars. People erected tents and lean-tos, moved wagons into circles, or threw packs and bedding onto dishevelled piles and collapsed to the ground, exhausted. Word filtered through the camp that Field Commander Hartmut would meet with Masters Lily and Dealhia in the morning. The refugees could rest and hope until then.

Thaly sat alone on fallow soil, her knees pulled up to her chest, beside a campfire encircled by wagons. The hem of her buttonless brown coat extended to her ankles, and the cuffs swallowed all but the tips of her fingers, keeping the cold of the storm season at bay. Grin had abandoned her for now, determined to meet every refugee to ask about Tom. Thaly didn't have the strength to join him, focussing instead on trying to overcome the trauma of the *Vulking*. The rape. Internalising the torment, hoping she could squeeze it out of existence.

Thaly knew things like that happened. Heard about them in whispered conversations among her friends in Bagendon. Be wary of drunk men. Lustful men. Ones seeking control. Although she'd managed to avoid the threat until now, there was no escape from the *Vulking*. Nothing she could have done differently.

Or was there? Would Jacob or Emelin have saved her and Grin? Would they have found a way out?

Whibly's voice drifted on the sea-breeze into the circle of wagons, the skullard regaling an audience with tall tales of seafaring adventures. Thaly could have killed him on the raft, but a speck of pity for Captain Adcock's lapdog stayed her hand. For some strange reason, she missed being adrift. There, she had a clear purpose — one oar stroke after another. Chase the setting sun and head for home. Now, only an uncertain future glimmered on the horizon.

She thought of Bagendon, picturing the timber cottage where she grew up, with its shingled roof and stone chimney, Emelin and Dayna at the dining table eating their morning porridge, warmth filling the room from a roaring fire. Closing her eyes, Thaly saw herself sitting between her adoptive mother and sister.

Dayna leaned across and wrapped her arm around Thaly's shoulder. 'So, you like Ebba. Why did you choose her?'

'Stop teasing your sister,' said Emelin.

Dayna smiled. 'Ebba's cute. If I liked women, I'd pick her too.'

Jacob appeared at the door and beckoned Thaly to follow him. Time for another lesson. She walked outside and drew her sword.

He shook his head. 'No sparring. Today we consider our purpose for being.'

What was that purpose?

'Banish the Erstürmen from Enthilen and take back our home.'

Thaly swept the dreams from her mind. Although Jacob had instilled in her the ambition of a rebel warrior, what did such ambition matter now? Laodicea lay in ruins and the rebel army in tatters. And the fighter inside her had been shaken beyond all comprehension. Could the warrior Thaly rise again?

Lost in her thoughts, she barely noticed an older woman come and sit on the ground within the circle of light cast by the campfire.

Thaly started when Master Lily spoke,

"Fire burns before me

Its coals scorch my feet

And I see souls torn and twisted

By flames that offer no warmth

Only the pain of hearts contorted

I withdraw

My life aborted

To a place inside my brain

That the fire cannot claim

And slowly go insane."

A sombre hum drifted in the firelight as the two women sat in silence until Lily spoke again, "My husband wrote that poem, on a parchment he left on the mantelpiece the day he took his own life and those of our three children."

Embarrassed by the wallow of her own hurt, Thaly averted her eyes and whispered to the ground, "How did you recover?"

"Truth is, Athalee, I've never recovered. Sometimes, I feel his thoughts of hopelessness invade my mind, and the battle to overcome them continues. But I fight to serve my people. I can't abandon them in their time of need." Lily threw a log onto the fire, and sparks escaped into the night sky. "You say we haven't met, and I believe you. Yet your face is familiar. I've seen its features before. Olive skin, high cheekbones, dark brown eyes, a proud, strong jaw. It's the face of a leader I once knew."

"I don't know what you're talking about."

"The resemblance is compelling. Who are your parents?"

"My parents abandoned me when I was a baby. The rebels at Bagendon adopted me. Emelin Wallace is my mother now. I don't have a father."

"Why did your parents leave you?"

"I don't know," snapped Thaly. "How could I?"

"Of course. I apologise for the intrusion. Will you return to Bagendon?"

"You expect something of me that you dismissed. I should protect my home while you abandoned yours."

Lily dropped her head, strands of grey hair slinking down the front of her shoulders. "It wasn't an easy decision."

"Why didn't you lead the refugees to Bagendon? What's left of our army could have provided an escort."

"I considered it."

Thaly wanted to be angry. Yet, she understood Lily's decision and accepted it. "You expect Bagendon to fall, don't you? You wouldn't lead the refugees there because you know it's not safe."

"We have a new king. He'll want to entrench his power. Affirm the devotion of his subjects with an easy victory. Yes, I believe Bagendon will be attacked, and it won't be able to resist. There's less chance the Erstürmen will attack one of their own outposts. Hence my decision to bring the refugees here."

Thaly hugged her knees closer to her chest.

"What happened on the *Vulking*?" asked Lily. "You said the crew turned on you."

"I don't want to talk about it."

"One of the rebel soldiers told me Jacob Seamaster was your trainer. It must have hurt when you lost Jacob. Then, on top of that..."

"I will endure. I have to." Thaly set her jaw, grinding her teeth together.

"Don't be ashamed to show your pain. It gives others permission to help. Few can endure the challenges of life alone."

"What about you? Can a leader ever show weakness?"

Lily sighed. "There's a difference between sharing pain and showing weakness, but yes, I sometimes hide my hurt lest it weakens those around me. Let my doubts and suffering escape only during private moments. Yet, I'm learning a true leader doesn't hold themselves apart from their followers. That respect can be gained by showing people you're flesh and blood like them."

Lily stood. Free of her armour and weapons, dressed in a plain gown with a furred hood, she could have been any one of the many women Thaly had seen marching from Laodicea.

"Should I return to Bagendon?" Thaly asked Lily.

"Do you want to?"

"I miss my mother and sister. They won't leave the town if the Erstürmen attack. I should be there, standing beside them."

"There's little to be gained in sacrificing another Dobunni life to the invaders. I have a feeling that you, Athalee, have a lot more to offer this world than simply a target for Erstürmen bowmen." Lily hugged her chest and shivered. "Whatever happened on that ship, don't let it define you. Become the person you were always destined to be." She turned and walked off into the restless night.

Thaly sat by the fire a little longer, then stood and searched among the wagons for bedding and a place to sleep. In the back of a wagon, she stumbled across a copper tub, the kind used for bathing. The tub's owners agreed to let Thaly bathe, even being kind enough to bring her warm water from the fire and donating their last cake of soap.

With the tub full, Thaly stripped naked and squeezed into the bath, her knees pressing up to her chin. Despite the confinement, she clutched the soap and lathered it over her body, rubbing the congealed lump of tallow, quicklime and ash onto every fleck of skin, raking salt crystals across the dirt clogging her pores.

Thaly hadn't bathed properly since Bagendon, and tonight she scrubbed with a fervour impelled by a desire to remove more than the visible filth.

*   *   *   *

Grin had been searching for Tom all night, stopping everyone he came across and asking if they'd seen a young man — brown hair to his shoulders, short and slight, satin-grey eyes, no more than sixteen harvest seasons old. Although he didn't expect to find his friend, he needed something to distract his mind from the trauma of past days. Part of him wanted to stay with Thaly, but she had closed herself off. Shut down and turned inwards, and built the wall surrounding her even higher.

And the forest called to Grin. Told him the journey that began with Tom in Babir Birramal many moons ago had now ended.

With the morning sun warming his back, he strode up to the main gate of Gestade.

A young guard blocked Grin's path, clutching a halberd across his chest. "No refugees inside da gate."

"I am looking for a friend," said Grin. "A young man. The survivor of a shipwreck."

"He ain't in here." The guard peered at Grin, tilting his head to the side. "Yur a wild grell, ain't ya? Dat paintin' on y'face is bold, not faded like da ones da slaves have. Where ya from?"

"Babir Birramal."

The young soldier looked blankly at Grin.

"Grōz Forst," said Grin.

The soldier nodded. "What's da name of dat city you grells built on da plains?"

"Do you mean Malang Gunya?"

"Dat's da one. I heard King Adalwolf's leadin' a pilgrimage dere. He plans to pull it down."

The soldier's words stabbed at Grin like a knife prising between the bones of his ribcage. "Malang Gunya is our home."

The guard flashed a smug grin. "It used to be *our* home. King Adalwolf's found da lost city of Pergamos underneath da plains. He's goin' to rebuild da city. You heathens desecrated a sacred place."

The ache in Grin's chest started to burn. A feverish, resentful cinder that had smouldered inside wild grells for generations now burst into a wildfire roaring across his flesh. Hate came with a rush like a wolf pack chasing down prey. Hate that had lain dormant for seasons, awoken on the *Vulking*.

He growled at the soldier. Cavernous, guttural, primal. Giant hands swollen with rage, Grin wrenched the halberd from the young guard and snapped the handle like a twig. The soldier's skin turned whiter than ice, his terrified eyes as wide as his mouth. *Fear.* The fire inside Grin wanted to feed on it. Hungered for it. He thrust a hand out and wrapped it around the soldier's helmet, crushing the metal like a stone crushes the shell of a nut. The helmet ground against the soldier's skull and blood trickled down his cheeks. Grin sneered, preparing for the final clench.

"Stop!" came a woman's voice from behind him. "Stop that."

The plea doused the fire inside Grin like a burst of rain, and he stepped back from the soldier. A woman pushed between them. Grin recognised her. Dealhia Rossingbird, one of the leaders of the refugees.

She shoved Grin in the stomach, "Get back. We don't want this," then turned her attention to the distraught soldier who had removed his crushed spangenhelm. Dealhia took a cloth from her dress and dabbed at the blood on his face. "We have healers. Good ones. I'll take you there."

Two more soldiers marched towards Grin. In silence, he turned and walked off.

Dealhia intervened again, calling out to the soldiers, "Your friend's alright. Only a misunderstanding. No harm done."

Grin walked on, dreading to look back. Nobody came for him, and he disappeared among the throng of refugees as well as any giant stone-grell could.

He wandered about the camp until midday, wondering what was happening to him. Wondering how so much hate could have hidden inside him for so long. Tom Anderson disappeared from his thoughts, and he began to dwell on the new threat to his kin. Soon, stone- and weald-grells would march to Malang Gunya to honour those who fell trying to protect the city during the Erstürmen invasion. He planned to join the marchers for the first time after being initiated at the next garrabari. However, if the Erstürmen settled Malang Gunya, they wouldn't welcome grell mourners. And if the invaders dismantled the remains of the city, wild grells would find it hard to control their anger. Grin now understood that better than he ever imagined. Confrontation appeared unavoidable. Someone had to warn the wild grells: his father and mother, and all those who would march. The homage to Malang Gunya must be stopped.

He found Thaly slouching against a wagon wheel and chewing a piece of dried meat. He slumped down beside her, elbows resting on thighs, cradling his head in his palms. She offered him food, but he wasn't hungry.

"I guess you didn't find Tom," she said.

Grin shook his head. "So much is going wrong, Thaly. I attacked an Erstürmen guard."

Thaly sat up straight and glared at him. "What? Why did you do that?"

"He told me King Adalwolf is leading his followers to Malang Gunya to finish what his ancestors began and build a new city on the ruins of my home. A demon possessed me, and I could not control my anger."

"Is the guard dead?"

"He would have been. I would have killed him if Dealhia Rossingbird, the woman we met on the coast road, had not intervened. She saved him and me."

"Thank goodness. We can't jeopardise the refugees' chances of gaining asylum."

"We need to go. To Babir Birramal. I have to warn my father and stop the wild grells from marching into a massacre."

Thaly nodded. "You can run. I'll need a horse."

"We do not have a horse."

A flicker of determination lit Thaly's eyes. "I bet Whibly has coin stashed away."

Grin sighed and heaved himself from the ground, then helped Thaly to her feet. They searched among the refugees until stumbling upon the skullard, free of his bonds, playing knucklebones for coin with injured Dobunni soldiers.

Whibly sat cross-legged in the dirt, coins piled high next to his shins. "Right, me hearties, call for last coin. I'm wagerin' on three bellies. Throw for three bellies. Hey up!" He tossed four knucklebones into a smoothed patch of dirt bordered by a crudely drawn circle. The soldiers sitting around the circle leaned in expectantly to watch the bones fall. Three of the four knucklebones landed with their convex side facing up.

Whibly whelped with delight, "Three bellies!" and pulled another pile of coin to his shins. "Who wants to goes again?" The soldiers around him grumbled and walked off. "If y'leave, ya can't ever gets yur coin back."

"Whibly," said Grin.

"Well, if it ain't me old shipmates. Come to tie me up again, have ya?" Whibly's rogue smile vanished under Thaly's steely glare.

"We have a proposition for you," said Thaly. "We need coin to buy a horse, and you have piles sitting there at your feet."

"Why should I give ya any of me coin? I won this on fair wager."

"I'm a Dobunni rebel. I have pledge scars on my chest to prove it. What do you think those soldiers would do to you if I told them what happened to us on the *Vulking*?"

"Don't tells 'em 'bout that, Thaly. They're only just gettin' to like me. I'm sorry 'bout what happened, truly I am. None of it was right."

"I'm offering you a chance for redemption. Give us enough coin to buy a strong horse, and I won't tell anyone about your part in our torment."

"I ain't gonna win an argument with ya, am I?"

"It seems you've already won plenty."

"Alright. How much do y'need?"

Whibly smiled as he handed over enough coin to pay for a horse and some food.

Thaly held Whibly's eye. "Use the guilt you feel to help others face the challenges of this world."

*   *   *   *

Lily sat with Dealhia in the map room of the Command Hall of Gestade, adjacent to the private office of Field Commander Hartmut. Prince Hadufuns waited alone in the hallway, dressed in plain clothes covered by a grey cloak with a broad cowl pulled low over his face. The guards outside the Command Hall didn't blink as Hadufuns passed them, giving Lily confidence he wasn't recognised. The prince wanted to see if Hartmut would agree to Lily and Dealhia's request without having to reveal himself.

A clean, uncluttered desk sat in the centre of the meticulously organised map room, with books, maps, armour, vases, ornaments and other paraphernalia arranged in perfect rows on shelves or in display cases. Tapestries made by local craftspeople hung from the stone walls, as did the traditional red and black Erstürmen banner of the double-headed serpent.

Hadufuns had told Lily that Hartmut was a short, thin man. This stature belied his reputation as a mighty leader, loyal to the Erstürmen culture and proud his outpost was considered the finest in all Enthilen. The soldiers under his command called him 'The Mongoose' after the Adelmund family sigil; small but ferocious. Hadufuns said Hartmut's military standing had profited from the many barbarian raids he'd repelled along this part of Enthilen's coast.

Lily already had a picture in her mind of a tightly forged bundle of determination and protocol, unlikely to yield to poorly constructed arguments. And Dealhia had told her about the shipwrecked wild grell attacking an Erstürmen guard. If news of the assault had reached Hartmut's ears, this would likely be a short meeting, Lily having to seek asylum elsewhere.

She rubbed sweaty palms on the woven fabric of the padded chair and stood to admire a tapestry hanging on the wall depicting civilians and soldiers working together to maintain the township surrounding Gestade's walls. In the town pond, a white swan and black swan swam together, the ripples on the surface created by their movement merging to form a single circle of companionship. She started when the door to Hartmut's private office opened, and out strode a tall, lean man with a neatly-trimmed, tawny beard. He nodded and squeezed into a chair on the other side of the map table, his armour clanking against the chair's armrests, balancing his spangenhelm on his lap. A shorter, clean-shaven man followed, dressed in a supple, black leather tunic with gold stitching at the seams and cinched by a black belt adorned with silver buckles. Lily guessed this was Hartmut. He smiled at her, and her palms began to sweat again.

"Greetings. I'm Field Commander Hartmut Adelmund. This is my lieutenant, Roben," said Hartmut, pointing to the tall man.

Dealhia stood. "Field Commander Hartmut, with immense gratitude, we've come to thank you for accepting the refugees of Laodicea into your outpost."

"I haven't accepted anybody yet. Eight thousand people turn up at my gate uninvited. What else might I have done?" He waved his hand, motioning for Dealhia and Lily to sit.

"I'm Dealhia Rossingbird, Master of the Docklands of Laodicea before it was burned to the ground by savages. My colleague is Lady Lily LáDown, Master of the Southern Vale."

Lily and Dealhia returned to their chairs, both ladies sitting awkwardly under billowing layers of fine dress fabric, worn to create a good impression on their possible hosts.

Hartmut sat in the chair opposite Lily, his tunic riding up over cream trousers, a chiselled jaw and cheekbones set like a granite statue. "I've heard of both of you. Widald was a close friend, and I still mourn his passing. He spoke highly of you."

Lily flashed a sideways glance at Dealhia. Widald had never mentioned his admiration for the pair.

Dealhia continued, "Then you would know we are honest and loyal people. True of word. To seek refuge in times of calamity asks much of the citizens of Gestade. But I wish to speak of what we can offer in return for your hospitality. There are strong fighters among us. Skilled labourers and craftspeople. Farmers to work the fields. Fishers to harvest the coast. Blacksmiths to make arms…"

Hartmut raised his palm. "You've made your point, Master Dealhia.

229

Yet, the Dobunni and Erstürmen are sworn enemies. How do you think we'll fare keeping order among the people?"

Lily pressed the bunched midriff of her rosewood dress into her body and leaned forward in her chair. "We harbour Erstürmen, also. The Dobunni and Erstürmen lived side by side in Laodicea before it was routed by the barbarians. With strong leadership and proper counsel, we can exist and work together."

"The truce in Laodicea was always a tenuous one," said Hartmut.

Roben hovered his spangenhelm a finger-width above the map table, then let it fall from his hands with a bang. "If we spare any more stores, our supplies will exhaust during the long dark. We can't feed your refugees, lest our own people starve."

Hartmut pressed the tips of his fingers into his temples, then stood, clasped his hands behind his back and faced one of the tapestries on the wall depicting the coronation of King Faramund. "A messenger came from Laodicea today. General Badulf Wolfhart will be visiting all the outposts to seek our dedication and unrestrained loyalty to King Adalwolf. The General will arrive here soon enough, and he won't look kindly on your refugees or those who harbour them."

"You have a reputation as an honourable man, Commander Hartmut," said Lily. "Would an honourable man want to be responsible for a massacre? We have trained soldiers among the refugees, including Erstürmen soldiers. If you bring them behind the walls of Gestade, they could help you defend the outpost."

Hartmut turned to Lily, his eyebrows raised above glistening grey eyes. "Are you suggesting we establish our own fiefdom, Lady Lily?"

"We all know King Ewald wasn't loved by the people, but he was the rightful king. There are rumours Adalwolf is a servant to tainted grells and their master."

At the mention of tainted grells, Hartmut looked at Roben and nodded.

"We have similar information," said Roben. "One of our scouts met a man in a Slumstadt inn claiming to be the driver of the king's wagon. The driver was drunk, yes, but he swore the truth that tainted grells and an old man ambushed Ewald's wagon, not Dobunni rebels. It was the last time Ewald was seen alive."

"I saw these grells leaving the Master's Hall in the King's Quarter right before we found the bodies of Prince Widald and Prince Gerulf," said Lily.

"Aren't you forgetting someone?" asked Hartmut.

Before Lily could answer, the door opened and in walked Hadufuns. He pulled the cowl from his face, the scar on his chin still showing through a shortly-cropped beard.

Hartmut's eyes widened. He strode across the room, dropped to one knee and bowed his head. "Prince Hadufuns."

Roben stood and did the same.

"There's no need for that," said Hadufuns.

Roben returned to his seat, and Hartmut rose, standing before Hadufuns. "This is a welcome surprise, your highness. First, you are lost in the wilderness, feared never to return, and when you finally reappear, Dobunni assassins stab you in the back."

"It wasn't a Dobunni knife that pierced my flesh, Commander. My wounds were inflicted by the servants of a man who now calls himself Malphas. Once, he was my father, the exiled King Oldaric."

"Oldaric?" said Hartmut.

"He's behind it all. The murder of Ewald. The death of my brothers. The ascension of Adalwolf to the throne. If you called Widald a friend, you should seek revenge on those who ended his life, not bend the knee to a usurper king and his maniacal puppeteer. They'll ask for your fealty and offer only death in return."

"What is your counsel, Prince Hadufuns?" asked Roben.

"I owe my life to Lady Lily LáDown and her healer. A Dobunni saved me from certain death, and her word and that of her colleague, Master Dealhia, is beyond reproach in my eyes. If they offer you support, that is what they'll deliver. If they say their people will fight for Gestade, they'll fight until their last breath. My advice, Commander Hartmut, is to prepare for a battle. Bring the refugees under your banner, bolster your provisions and secure your defences. Forget Erstürmen loyalties of the past and forge new allegiances."

"I've always been loyal to the Erstürmen Kingdom," said Hartmut.

"This new kingdom deserves no loyalty," said Hadufuns.

"You ask for much, Prince Hadufuns, but since it is you who asks, I will carefully consider your words."

"You're right to put the welfare of your own people above all others," Lily said to Hartmut. "I would do the same thing. We understand our numbers stretch your supplies. I've already arranged for work parties to harvest food from surrounding forests and the nearby ocean. Merchants are busy preserving what we've collected. This can be added to your stores. Healers work day and night to mend wounded soldiers, preparing them to defend your walls."

Hartmut nodded. "You and your friends present a convincing argument, Lady..."

"Call me Lily."

Hartmut's eyes sparkled as Lily smiled. He paused, letting an awkward silence descend upon the room.

"Krieg led the barbarians who attacked Laodicea," said Hadufuns. "Hunger's sword sliced open my chest. Now they sit at King Adalwolf's side. These new rulers are more of a threat to Erstürmen culture than any I've known. If it's our culture you wish to defend, Field Commander Hartmut, then tainted grells and usurper kings are your true enemy."

"If you order it, Prince Hadufuns, I'll accept the refugees into our care," said Hartmut.

Lily turned expectantly to Hadufuns. This is what she'd hoped for, but Hadufuns failed her. "I won't order it. I want you to accept the decision as your own. To willingly offer refuge because it is the noble thing to do, not because it has been imposed on you by a higher authority."

"As you wish. I will consider the proposal and make my own judgement. There is a lot to contemplate, and I will take my time. Poor judgements are often made in haste. In the meantime, I won't stop the refugees from sheltering outside our gate."

A crestfallen Lily fought to stop the flicker of hope inside her from extinguishing. Without Hadufuns' order, there was no certainty for the refugees, but she refused to believe all nobility had been erased from Enthilen.

*　*　*　*

A backpack full of supplies lying at his feet, Hadufuns sat on the cot inside his private tent and scratched out a letter on a scrap of parchment with quill and ink.

Dearest Audie

There has been no more wonderous joy in my life than to feel the caress of your caring hand and have my troubled thoughts soothed by your luminous smile. Your lightness lifted my spirits to heights never known. It is only because of you I could continue on. In welcome dreams, we walk together, hand in hand. I will always cherish those dreams.

But I cannot share your company any longer, lest I risk your life. Soon, my presence among the refugees will be exposed. The spies of my enemy never rest, and their pursuit will be relentless. When I am found, those who stand beside me will face certain death. That is a burden I can never bear.

Beautiful Audie, I must say farewell. You should forget we shared these moments. Wipe my name from your lips and my memory from your thoughts if ever I found a place there. But know I'll always hold your hand to my chest so you can feel the virtue in my heart,

Your Prince.

~ Chapter 18 ~

I t was a clear morning, a glorious morning, thought Emelin, though she had no mind to enjoy it. Recent storms had passed, ceding to a radiant blue sky. Such contrasts were characteristic of the storm season. She scouted the nearby hills outside the north gate of Bagendon, clambering over rocks and along steep trails to check on the town's defences. Over the past four days, Bagendon's residents had worked tirelessly to build traps designed to slow an advancing army. Boulders had been rolled onto paths and wedged in place by timber beams to block access points. Almost invisible tripwires had been stretched across narrow passages between sheer rockfaces. When triggered, the wires would pull braces out from under thatched panels holding piles of stones in place, sending murderous avalanches onto unsuspecting attackers. Barbed metal spikes, their tips poisoned with the orange fruit of earala bushes, had been jammed into shallow channels dug into the dirt. The spikes would pierce the leather soles belonging to the boots of careless soldiers. Although they wouldn't die from the poison, it would incapacitate them for days.

The traps set in the hills around the town meant a rapid escape from Bagendon was nigh impossible. Combined with the already rugged terrain, the barriers would slow an advancing army, but also anyone wishing to flee.

Standing on a ridge looking south, Emelin gazed over Bagendon's north wall and into the town. Most of the empty houses had been dismantled, their timber beams turned into sharpened palisades surrounding Bagendon's four walls.

So many lost homes now, she thought. So many Dobunni families already wiped from existence. Yet, even with only a third of its regular population, Bagendon didn't have enough supplies to see out a long siege. If the Erstürmen tried to starve them, the rebels would have to attack, but they needed to elect a leader first. And today, that choice would be made.

A gentle breeze raised the hairs on Emelin's forearms as people carrying banners began to congregate in the town square. Each person, a representative of every surviving family still living in Bagendon, clutched a banner stitched with their unique family sigil: a boulder lion, leaven grass, an anvil, the watchtower of Al Mōr Sŭrl, the Anchep River, a stolid flower, a tufted goliath, among others. The banners numbered fewer than Emelin could remember seeing. She recalled the election of Ryder as Dobunni leader when thousands of people gathered and banners masked the sky, and the election of Jurelle, a time of immense hope that now seemed so distant. She sighed, then trotted down the face of the ridge towards the north gate.

In the town square, Emelin took her place beside the three other candidates for leader of the Dobunni rebels: Alfred Harrington, Maxton Nash and Maida Astley. Maxton and Maida had joined the leadership council two days ago, cast with the hopefulness of youth to lead the Dobunni to a brighter future. Emelin wished she shared their hope. Dayna stood among the crowd gathered in the square, holding the staff of the Wallace family banner with the sigil of two stalks of grain bordering a wooden bowl. Emelin's sigil.

The candidates spaced themselves in a single line facing the crowd as the Elagear, the election overseer, stepped forward and rang a handbell. "Gather 'round. Gather 'round." She stilled the bell and waited for the crowd to settle before continuing, "We assemble today to elect a new leader of the Dobunni rebels. Each of the candidates come from the leadership council, and only one can be the leader of that council and the Dobunni people of Bagendon." She faced the candidates. "As I speak your name, come forward. Emelin Wallace."

Emelin stepped into an empty circle of rocks, her head bowed and hands clasped at her waist.

"Maxton Nash," said the Elagear.

Maxton stood near Emelin inside his own rock circle. She nodded and smiled at the young man with flowing blonde hair and jade-green eyes. Soldiers returning from Laodicea had told her Maxton acquitted himself well despite the defeat. Embraced the role of Field Commander when Jacob fell. She expected many of the soldiers' families to vote for Maxton, and she'd be happy if he became the leader of the rebels.

"Alfred Harrington."

Alfred strode forward, dressed in his finest silk robes, looking younger than Emelin ever remembered seeing him. She smiled to herself, wondering who in the crowd would fall for the ruse. Nobody in Bagendon knew how old Alfred was, and neither could they recall a time when he wasn't around. He'd been a candidate for leader during the election of Ryder and Jurelle. Although his experience was well respected among some Dobunni families, Emelin expected his age to work against him.

"Maida Astley."

Young, innocent Maida, thought Emelin, only two harvest seasons older than Dayna. The Dobunni had more sense than to throw Maida into the den of leadership, didn't they?

The Elagear continued, "Each family representative will take their banner and stake it in the ground in front of the candidate they are voting for, within the circle of rocks marking the voting space for that candidate. The person attracting the most banners will be chosen as leader." She stood aside and waited.

Alfred's brother stepped forward, carrying the sigil of Al Mōr Sŭrl, and thrust the staff's sharp end into the mud of Alfred's voting circle. Likely, Alfred had urged his sibling to go first to create an impression of preference. Emelin couldn't help but admire the old man's cunning. Maida's mother then placed the banner of the emerald raven inside her daughter's voting circle. Recognising the moment, Dayna jostled her way to the front of the crowd and marched up to Emelin, placing their family banner near her feet.

Emelin's heart warmed, not at the vote, but at Dayna's acknowledgement. They'd reconciled somewhat after their argument four nights ago, yet Dayna remained distant and unsettled. Emelin needed to talk to her daughter. Before the end.

Dayna nodded and returned to the crowd.

Poor Maxton, thought Emelin, he has no family to support him. Her worry disappeared when a wounded soldier placed his family banner beside Maxton. One vote each.

The voting continued as the sun rose above Bagendon. Maxton attracted many votes; his leadership potential clearly recognised. Alfred had far fewer and Maida even less. Emelin was surrounded by banners such that she could hardly see the crowd between the flapping rect-angles of cotton. The choice would be between her and Maxton. She wouldn't begrudge the young soldier his victory should it come, cele-brating with the rest of his supporters.

Voting ended, and the Elagear stepped forward and began counting the banners and checking each sigil to ensure no duplicates had snuck in. She dismissed Alfred and Maida, Alfred downcast as he trudged off, and tallied the flags surrounding Emelin and Maxton again. The vote was close.

After a second count, the Elagear faced the crowd. "At the tally of votes, I declare Emelin Wallace the new leader of the Dobunni rebels."

A muted cheer broke through the sombre crowd. Emelin smiled and nodded to the Dobunni families. She should feel grateful. She *was* grateful, though she knew there was little to cheer about. Her reign as leader could be the shortest in all Dobunni history. With a rejuvenated enemy waiting in the shadows to strike, now wasn't the time for apprehension. The Dobunni rebels looked to her to lead them in the fight of their lives, and she wouldn't shirk the responsibility.

Maxton gave her a hug of congratulations, as did Maida. Even Alfred managed to appear humble in defeat, taking Emelin's hand and squeezing. He looked her in the eye and forced a fragile smile, but didn't say anything. He didn't need to. They both knew the immensity of the challenge before them.

Other Dobunni families came to congratulate Emelin. She acknowledged their well-wishes, all the time scanning the crowd for Dayna. But her daughter had disappeared. Emelin knew she had one crucial thing to do before the final preparation of Bagendon's defences.

*   *   *   *

Emelin walked along the main street of Bagendon, past boarded-up shop fronts and empty market stalls. Some shops had been abandoned; others turned into small fortresses to protect against looters. The crowd from the election had dispersed, the main street and town square falling quiet again.

As she approached the soldier training ground, a middle-aged man and woman, and four children, emerged from a neat timber house, carrying clothes, blankets, food, weapons and tools. She knew they were leaving Bagendon and wondered if she should try to convince them otherwise. Guilt hit her hard then. Only four nights ago, she'd encouraged Dayna to leave. How could she deny this family the same opportunity? The man tipped his hat as she passed, and she smiled in acknowledgement. Let the family have their chance at a new life.

Dayna sat alone on a tree stump at the end of the main street, head downcast, boot heels drawing patterns in the mud.

She looked up as Emelin approached. "Are you the new leader?"

Emelin nodded.

"I knew you would be," said Dayna. "You're the best choice."

Emelin sat with her daughter, both facing a chasm of uncertainty.

Dayna broke the silence. "This is where I last spoke to Thaly. Before we left for Sardis and she went with Jacob to Laodicea."

"Do you miss her?" asked Emelin.

"When she became a scout, she spent a lot of time away from home. I always expected her to return. Now, it seems she'll never come home. Do *you* miss her?"

"Yes. Although, I'm not sure..." Emelin trailed off.

"Not sure about what?" asked Dayna.

"If Thaly came home and I lost her again, I'm not sure I could take it."

"Do you love her more than me?"

Emelin sighed and flung her arm around Dayna's shoulder. "Of course not. That's a stupid question."

"What about Papa?"

"You look so much like your father, with his wavy blonde hair and delicate nose. I remember how excited he was when you were born. I mean, he loved Thaly as much as I did, but you were his flesh and blood. His only flesh and blood. There was a special place in Thane's heart for you, Dayna."

"He would get angry, though?"

"Yes, he brooded. Left to the quiet of his own thoughts, he would dwell on things. Mull them over again and again until the torment plagued his mind. You were only five harvest seasons old when he died, his patrol ambushed by the Erstürmen near Breadelbane. Your father was a reluctant warrior, despite his name. Easy pickings for Erstürmen soldiers."

"Some say he was a hero."

"Yes, he was a hero." Emelin remembered something her mother told her a long time ago. 'A past glorified signals a future abandoned.' She pulled her daughter close, fighting back tears. There was no future for Dayna. Emelin had lived a life; it seemed Dayna would not. Although she was brave and willing like her father, she wasn't a warrior.

"What will come for us?" asked Dayna.

"I don't know," said Emelin before kissing her daughter's hair.

~ Chapter 19 ~

Inside the throne room of the inner circle of Sardis, Hunfrid's emotions careered from self-pity and loathing to staunch determination. He ruled the royal city, his Shield holding sway inside the inner and second circles, yet, Sardis had become a shadow of itself. Citizens abandoned the city's seven circles in droves, marching for Pergamos and the promise of a new life as subjects of a boy king. Time and opportunity played on Hunfrid's mind, and how best to stitch his authority into the fabric of the kingdom before usurpers came to unravel the tapestry of his rule. He pondered the balance of submission and resistance that would placate the new authority, yet still see him cling to a thread of power.

Rostard strode into the throne room like a mountain elk. "Steward Hunfrid. The red grell is here."

A lump set in Hunfrid's throat. The wait for the usurper hadn't been long. "How far away?"

"They've entered the main gate."

"They?"

"Krieg leads forty-eight armoured grell soldiers riding undreds."

Hunfrid rubbed his fingers across his clammy forehead. "Grell soldiers?"

"I believe these are the Rephaim we've heard about."

"Your rendezvous with giests failed to foresee this event, Rostard."

Hunfrid's suspicious thoughts narrowed. "Or else you *were* forewarned and failed to tell me."

Rostard stopped at the foot of the throne platform and began fidgeting with the frills on the right cuff of his shirt. "I've been distracted by the executions. The giests have not visited me in a dozen moons."

A shout came from the guards outside the throne room, followed by a clatter of armour against stone. Hunfrid stood, adrenaline gushing through his body. The oak door to the throne room groaned under its own weight and in strode Krieg and his guard. Hunfrid and Rostard gasped in unison at the sight of the armoured Rephaim, their enormous frames filling the doorway as they marched behind their leader. A grilled helmet crowned with a deadly spike covered Krieg's face, his broad shoulders and bulging upper arms capped by pauldrons and rerebraces shadowing a naked and pockmarked blood-red torso. As he marched down the centre of the throne hall, his sabatons smacked the tiles like claps of thunder.

The end is nigh, thought Hunfrid. War has come to Sardis. He shuffled down the steps of the throne platform while the Rephaim lined up along the walls of the room, standing to attention like a well-drilled military unit.

Hunfrid and Krieg reached the bottom step at the same time. The Steward of Sardis bowed his head and dropped to one knee before the red demon. "Welcome, Vater Krieg."

"Both knees," said Krieg.

Hunfrid almost looked up, an instinct that could have killed him, then thought wiser of it, kneeling on both knees as quickly as his weary bones would allow. Submission had trumped resistance in the blink of an eye. The tainted grell held out a gauntleted hand. Hunfrid pressed his forehead against the cold steel, his deferent bow lingering, eyes transfixed on the black, pointed sabatons covering Krieg's feet. He inhaled a faint smell of fresh blood rent with metal before standing and retreating to allow Rostard to demonstrate his compliance.

"Welcome to Sardis, Vater Krieg," said Rostard, dropping to his knees.

Krieg waved him away and faced Hunfrid, his rasping breaths lacing droplets of spit through the grill of his helmet. "King Adalwolf sends greetings to the Steward of Sardis."

"Thank you, Vater," replied Hunfrid.

"The circles of the city are like graveyards. Where are Adalwolf's loyal subjects?"

"Some have followed the king to Pergamos. The Ravage has taken others, but...but many remain, eager to return the royal city to its former glory."

"This is the royal city no longer. King Adalwolf cares only for a watch on our western border."

"And w-w-we will watch," said Rostard.

"Who is this stammering fool?" asked Krieg.

"This is Rostard, Master of Executions. He was Ewald's soothsayer. Now, he and I desire nothing more than to serve King Adalwolf," said Hunfrid.

"Serve you will. My Rephaim need lodging and food. Can your *executioner* accommodate them?"

"Yes, Vater," said Rostard. "If they can follow me." He led the Rephaim out of the throne room, leaving Hunfrid alone with the red grell.

Krieg scaled the steps of the throne platform two at a time, then lowered himself onto Ewald's old throne, the dark timber creaking under the bulk of the red colossus. He removed his helmet, looking for a place to rest it, and Hunfrid scuttled up the steps and took the vase containing Brynlee's ashes from the pedestal beside the throne, clutching the cold porcelain to his chest. Krieg placed his helmet atop the pedestal and cast his black eyes at Hunfrid, who squirmed like a worm pressed against a rock with the blunt edge of a knife. He traced the web of scars on Krieg's chin and cheeks with his eyes, trying to imagine what the grell's facial tattoo would have looked like.

Krieg broke the uncomfortable silence. "Who was here when my brother, Eroberung, fell?"

"He was slain by the traitor, Jurelle Stansfield. Ryder, the rebel leader, and one of his lackeys were here also. With bravery, the white grell dispatched them before his end."

"Who disposed of Eroberung's body?"

Hunfrid shook his head. "I don't know, Vater. Soldiers, most likely. Burned his body as is the Erstürmen tradition for any with noble blood."

Krieg leaned forward, his gauntleted hands clutching the throne's armrests. "Where were you when all this transpired?"

"In my quarters, unaware the madman Jurelle had unleashed his fury. I only heard about it after the event." The vase of ashes nearly slipped from Hunfrid's grasp. He rested a hand underneath it to stop it from falling.

The stumble drew Krieg's attention. "Which noble graces the inside of that vase?" he asked, pointing at Hunfrid's chest.

"Nobody important. A woman of the inner circle."

Krieg removed his gauntlets, placing them on his lap, and held out his left hand, palm up. "Give the vase to me."

Hunfrid paused, and his mind screamed. *No.*

Krieg waited, his huge red hand unwavering and demanding. Hunfrid swallowed hard and placed the vase onto Krieg's left palm. The grell balanced it there before wrapping his right hand around the neck of the vase, encircling the entire circumference with his fingers.

Holding the vase close to his chest, he peered over its lid at Hunfrid. "Why were simple foot soldiers left to honour the body of the revered white grell? Should that not be the purview of the new Steward?"

"They acted without my order or knowledge."

"You must have punished them severely."

"I would have, Vater, but they abandoned the city before I...."

Krieg scowled. His fingers tightened around the neck of the vase, and Hunfrid thought he heard the porcelain crack. "This puts me in an awkward situation. I have been tasked by King Adalwolf to find a special item. A treasure belonging to the king — a spinning pentagram of engraved gold, last in Eroberung's possession. Have you found such an item?"

Hunfrid couldn't take his eyes from Brynlee's vase. "No, I haven't seen it. What is its value?"

"Only the king can appreciate its true value. I cannot return to him until I have found it. Whoever keeps it from me will suffer a painful end." Krieg held the vase up to his face, studying the images of Slumstadt painted on its surface.

What would he know of those pictures? thought Hunfrid. How could he appreciate the beauty of the person who lived that life? He shifted on nervous feet and focussed his eyes on the wall behind the throne, trying to keep his emotions in check.

Krieg lowered the vase and held it towards Hunfrid. As he went to take it, the red grell leaned forward and spat a fiery breath. "I suggest, *Steward*, that you, and you alone, find the pentagram. Mention this to no-one else. When it is found, bring it to me in the king's private quarters. I do not wish to see you otherwise."

"Yes, Vater." With shaking hands, Hunfrid took the vase and stumbled from the throne room, his thoughts reeling. It was foolish to lie to a tainted grell, but lie he had. There was no going back. He knew the pentagram had value beyond his comprehension. Anselm had confirmed it. A worth that could be key to gaining favour with King Adalwolf and the Worshipful Master without the intervention of the red grell.

Adalwolf will rule from Pergamos, thought Hunfrid, meaning the old royal city still needs a leader. And the blood compass could be the bargaining piece securing Hunfrid's rightful position as Steward of Sardis. He must be the one to deliver it to the new king.

*   *   *   *

Anselm hid in the royal garderobe of the throne room of Sardis, surrounded by luxurious, elegant cloaks of every colour he could imagine, made from the finest silks, linens and wools. A handful had collars and hems stitched with spotted white and black fur belonging to long-dead animals he couldn't name. The cloaks hung limp, waiting for the next king or prince to choose a favoured garment to adorn the royal shoulders.

Anselm wondered if Krieg would ever step inside the garderobe to seek such attire. Not likely, he thought, despite the red grell now settling himself into Ewald's throne. Hunfrid stood on the throne platform shaking like a half-drowned kitten while Krieg toyed with the Steward's most valued possession, the vase containing Brynlee's ashes. If only the red grell suspected what Anselm had convinced himself he knew. That the vase contained the treasure Krieg sought. The 'spinning pentagram'. The blood compass.

Krieg returned the vase to Hunfrid, who cradled it like a baby as he marched from the room. Peeking through a gap in the door to the garderobe, Anselm's palms began to sweat. Instinctively, he went to wipe them on a robe of royal blue and black, the Heine family colours, then withdrew.

A certain level of respect should be maintained, he thought, lest the whole of Enthilen descends into savagery.

Shallow breaths almost keeping pace with a thumping heart, Anselm's mind turned to Rostard. His lover had nearly given him away, stealing a glance towards the garderobe as he announced Krieg's arrival to Hunfrid. Of course, Anselm knew long before Hunfrid of the red grell's visit to Sardis, the forewarning of certain events being a fringe benefit of bedding a soothsayer. And Anselm expected Krieg would come straight here to the throne room and supplant Hunfrid's expanding backside on Ewald's old throne.

Now, what to do next? Anselm could have approached Krieg less surreptitiously, in a manner befitting the royal curate. But he needed to be sure of the red grell's demands. That the grell sought the blood compass. No other way out, he could wait inside the garderobe until Krieg left the throne room, but time was of the essence. Who knew what schemes brewed inside Hunfrid's mind? There was only one logical course of action.

Anselm turned to the royal blue and black robe, smeared his sweaty hands over the front of it, then stepped into the throne room and strode towards Krieg.

"Vater," said Anselm, trying to keep his voice steady and confident.

"Who are you?" asked Krieg, turning in his chair. "Why were you hiding in the dark?"

"I am Anselm, curate of the inner circle during Ewald's reign." He walked to the front of the throne platform and dropped to both knees.

"A scholar of *Polus Sepcarture*, how admirable. Were you spying on us?"

"I was cleaning lint from the royal robes."

"Does the inner circle not have servants for such tasks?"

"Attending to traditional responsibilities has been abandoned during these times of terrible upheaval." Anselm raised his head and didn't waver from the soulless black eyes staring back at him. "I believe there is nothing more important than keeping faith with the oldest of traditions. Ensuring Erstürmen lore is carried out following Volerdie's wishes as conveyed through the scripture verses." He took a deep breath to calm his nerves. "I couldn't help but overhear you mention the blood compass."

Krieg rested his elbow atop the leather skirt covering his upper thigh and placed his chin on the knuckles of a giant red fist. "You know of this?"

"The scripture verses have various passages speaking of the purpose of the compass. It comes from the throne of the dead, does it not? I may be the only person in Sardis who understands its true value." Anselm stood, not waiting for Krieg's permission. "I know you've tasked Hunfrid with its recovery, but he is witless in these matters and not to be trusted with such a sacred relic. Maybe I could be of assistance?"

Krieg leaned back into the throne, and Anselm swore the red grell actually smiled before speaking. "I gather you expect a reward for such loyal service?"

Anselm pulled his sangria robes in tight. "It's reward enough to know I've aided our beloved King Adalwolf, but if his majesty's kindness should stretch a little further?"

*   *   *   *

A forlorn Rosalie sat on the dirt floor of one of Slumstadt's countless hovels. Zaria sat opposite her, a blind old man with expressionless eyes that stared at nothing, and wild wisps of grey hair growing in patches like untamed weeds. He spoke in random, disconnected fragments of sentences, often engaging in unresolved arguments with unseen antagonists. His granddaughter, Tilly, had found Rosalie sleeping on the banks of the Anchep River two moons ago. A kind young girl, though sometimes ill-tempered, she had refused to leave Rosalie's side until the new arrival to Slumstadt had accepted her offer of shelter.

'It's not safe on the riverbank,' Tilly had said. 'Too many bad people. Come home with me.'

Rosalie paid for her first nights of lodging with dry bread and salty, fermented radish she'd bought with unfinished jewellery taken from Yonna's smithy. There were no beds in the hovel. Zaria slept on a wicker mat, and Rosalie and Tilly on clothes and rags spread across the floor, their three bodies filling almost the entire inside of the shelter. They kept warm around a fire pit dug in the centre of the small space, smoke escaping through holes in the poorly stitched, fading canvas tied over a driftwood frame.

Despite its shortcomings, Rosalie appreciated the shelter. She knew she couldn't return home lest she put all her family in danger, but the pressing misery of Slumstadt began to wear her down, the intense murmur at night often punctured with screams and the relentless moaning and coughing from the sick. The Ravage had spread through Slumstadt like ink on blotting paper, taking the elderly and children first, struck down by chills and burning fever, and severe stomach pains that, for most, ended in death. And here was Rosalie, sharing a tiny shelter with an old man and a child. It wouldn't be long before The Ravage opened the canvas flap and marched in to claim her.

To cope with the malaise caused by the spreading disease, the deeping pits had become a prison for the dead or dying, corpses piled high in mass graves. Every evening, acrid black smoke blanketed Slumstadt, the fires fuelled by serpent oil poured onto pale, flaccid bodies. The wails of those still breathing echoed through the shantytown as they were burned alive, the dreadful stench of scorched flesh wafting down every muddy street.

Word of King Adalwolf's march to Pergamos seeped through the town. The hopeful and courageous collected their meagre possessions, strapped them to their backs and began the long walk to a better life. Although Rosalie thought about joining them, it would only return her to the oppression of Erstürmen rule. While her assault on the Steward's Shield meant she had to escape Sardis, she'd been longing to flee a life that had become increasingly foreign, even if that meant never seeing her family again. So, the daughter of Sardis' most renowned metalsmith had resigned herself to a dirt floor surrounded by indigence.

Tilly stepped into the hovel, and Zaria woke from his trance. "Ravage! Here. Flee. Out, out, out of my way. Fools and death. Out of my way."

"It's only me, Ompa," said Tilly. Cradling something in her arms, she turned to Rosalie. "Look. I have taters."

"Where did you get those?" asked Rosalie.

Tilly ignored her and sat beside the smouldering fire. "We could roast 'em."

"You stole them, didn't you?"

"Ella!" yelled Zaria. "She's here...not that...wear this, stop it...come back."

"Tilly?" pressed Rosalie.

Tilly shrugged. "We're hungry. What else can I do?"

"You'll get caught one day, and they'll throw you into the pits with the dead."

"No, they won't. The Steward's Shield never come into Slumstadt."

"Empty the dead!" yelled Zaria. "Who's there?"

"It's me, Ompa. Tilly."

Zaria groped for the walking cane he used to help lift himself up — a fancy piece of polished cedar with a gold handle cast as the head of an eagle. Rosalie doubted the handle was solid gold, more likely gold plated. Nevertheless, the walking cane was the most expensive thing in the shelter and possibly the most expensive thing on their street. How had a blind man managed to hold onto the treasure for so long?

Zaria dug the end of the cane into the dirt, stood on shaky legs and stumbled outside. It seemed he only left the hovel to relieve himself.

Give thanks for small mercies, thought Rosalie. "Do you ever think of leaving Slumstadt?" she asked Tilly.

"Since the king killed Mama and Dada, I'm the only one to look after Ompa. He can't go anywhere, so I can't."

"If we could find a cart for him..."

"We've got no coin for a cart, and where would we go?"

"Laodicea?"

"They had a war in Laodicea, didn't you hear?"

"It might be over now. There're other places. The Feign. Lokan. The Riverlands."

"I never heard of any of them places. This is the only home I've ever had." Tilly used a blunt, rusty knife to make a nest among glowing embers and placed three potatoes inside. Zaria staggered back into the hovel, his pants still around his ankles. He fell onto his wicker mat and began snoring. Rosalie held her breath, grabbed his pants and pulled them up over his genitals.

"I'm going for a walk," she said to Tilly.

"Won't you wait for the taters?"

"I'm not hungry."

"I know that's a lie," said Tilly.

"I have to get out for a while."

Rosalie wandered the streets of Slumstadt all afternoon, brushing past beggars and keeping her distance from anyone who coughed or spluttered. Despite The Ravage and the march to Pergamos thinning the population, a crush of people still lined the narrow lanes of Slumstadt, squashing together and fighting for every snatch of space they could wrestle from their neighbours. The community bickered and fought their way to a restless understanding of how life should be.

The town sprawled like a maze, and Rosalie had to concentrate lest she got lost or stumbled into a wretched dead end where skeletons draped in flaps of skin looked at her with thoughtless hunger. She ambled past an open tent where a dozen children sat on the ground in rows, facing a woman spelling out words on a piece of slate with white chalk. Aspiration fought to overcome impoverishment. Rosalie watched for a while, the children's laughter reminding her hope still blossomed in barren fields.

Early evening, she came upon a strangely quiet street with houses crowded eave to eave lining both sides. Real houses with doors and windows, not the small, miserable hovels filling the rest of Slumstadt. Slime seeped through a hole in her left boot as she trudged up the muddy alley and peered into the front yard of every house. From one yard came a tall young man with clean, brown skin and curly blonde locks, dressed in a fine horsehair coat over a soiled cream shirt and black trousers.

She wondered how he could afford the coat, then waved him away as he approached. "I don't have any coin."

"I ain't beggin'," he said. "I ain't seen you up this street before."

Rosalie hugged her arms across her chest, a thin tunic doing little to ward off the night chills, and continued walking.

"Don't run off," said the man. "I ain't gonna hurt you. What's y'name?"

Her nerves twitched like the antennae of a wasp as he persisted in following her up the street that climbed a middling hill overlooking the rest of Slumstadt.

"Me friends call me Snick. You lookin' to escape Slumstadt for a while?"

Rosalie stopped and turned to Snick. "Do you have a cart?"

"I could get one for the right coin. You thinkin' of marchin' to Pergamos?"

"You ask a lot of questions."

"I like to get to know people."

"I don't have enough coin for a cart or anything else for that matter."

"I can help you relieve the pain. Won't cost nothin'."

Everything costs something, she thought, then replied to Snick, "I'm not in any pain."

"Everyone in Slumstadt's sufferin'. If The Ravage ain't got 'em, hunger has. Or some other affliction. Misery and death pave these streets, but it dain't need to be that way. Wouldn't y'like to escape, even for a moment?"

Yes, thought Rosalie, she was desperate to do that.

Snick reached inside the fancy horsehair coat that hung low past his knees. "I dain't normally do this, and the mage would kill me if he found out, but..." He held something towards Rosalie in the palm of his hand. The glass of a small vial glinted under the light of the quarter and half-moons, translucent blue liquid shimmering inside.

"Embruisia," said Snick. "Cerulean honey. It'll take you wherever y'want to go. I can give you a taste for nothin'. You won't get a better offer in Slumstadt."

Bile rose in the back of Rosalie's throat, and her skin crawled, beads of sweat forming on her chest despite the cold night air. Had The Ravage finally found her? She began to sway, her legs weakening.

Snick reached inside another pocket and pulled out a tin, something Rosalie's father could have made in a morning of metalsmithing. He took off the lid, exposing a neat row of sewing needles. "It's only a little jab. Real easy. Dain't hurt none. Dip the needle into the embruisia and..."

Rosalie shook her head and resumed walking. "Not interested."

From near the top of the hill, another man with a pale, shaved head and neat black beard marched down the street towards Rosalie.

Snick placed the vial and tin back inside his pocket and leaned into her ear. "That's Elmbray. The mage."

"Snick. What are you doing?"

"Nothin', sir. Just talkin' to this lovely young lady."

Elmbray swept his ivory robes up out of the mud and approached Rosalie. "I hope he's not bothering you. He has a habit of being a pest."

"I'm leaving," said Rosalie.

"Don't let Snick scare you off. The residents here are quite neighbourly." Elmbray placed his hand on Rosalie's shoulder, his arresting green eyes showing concern. "You look hungry, my dear. Would you like something to eat? My place is only seven doors up."

"I never realised there were actual houses in Slumstadt."

"Oh yes, this is the old neighbourhood. These homes were built back in the time of King Faramund, long before the plague of Slumstadt descended upon us. Houses on the hill were prized for their views of the then pristine Anchep River." Elmbray moved his hand to the small of Rosalie's back, a comforting yet uncomfortable touch. "Your face, my dear, it's so gaunt and barren. You don't have The Ravage, do you?"

Rosalie shook her head.

"Good. Can't have that in my house. However, I do have nice hot soup on the range. Fresh vegetables and barley, and slices of spiced sausage. You sure you wouldn't like a bowl?"

The grumble of Rosalie's stomach echoed along the empty street. "I don't have any coin," she whispered.

"Then you're a true citizen of Slumstadt," said Elmbray. "I'm not after coin. Your company will be payment enough. It gets lonely with only Snick to talk to." Elmbray brushed his ruby lips across Rosalie's ear and whispered, "He's not well educated like you and I. Simple but harmless." Elmbray withdrew. "Don't you have somewhere to be, Snick?"

Snick nodded, "Yes, sir," and walked back down the street.

"I should go home, too," said Rosalie.

"Is Slumstadt really your home?" asked Elmbray. "You don't look like you've been here long. There's still a flicker of life left in those amber eyes of yours."

"I came from the fifth circle."

"Sardis?" Elmbray grabbed her bare forearm and twisted it around to check the branding scar. "My goodness, you're telling the truth." He released her arm. "We *are* honoured to have such a guest on our humble street. And from one of the better circles. Your family must be crafters?"

"My father is a metalsmith."

"Not Yonna Barron?"

Rosalie nodded.

Elmbray's eyes lit up like the sun through malachite. "He's the best metalsmith in all Sardis. Well, that settles it. You must come with me. I have an example of your father's work on my front porch. A gorgeous brass lantern. You have to see it."

Rosalie wanted to resist. The hairs on the back of her neck told her to be wary. But hunger and exhaustion had worn her defences, and the usual fire in her stomach hadn't been fed properly in days. Elmbray placed his hand on her back again, guiding her up the street.

"I can't believe we have a famous Sardisian walking up our little street alone and starving. And to think Snick was your introduction to the neighbourhood. How unfortunate. What did you say your name was, my dear?"

"Rosalie," she said.

"Rosalie Barron. Daughter of Yonna Barron. I am blessed indeed."

Elmbray led Rosalie to a two-storey, timber-panelled house with neatly trimmed hedges at waist height bordering a porch covered in climbing ivy. She followed him up the stairs to a black door with a barred peep-hole in the centre. Beside the door hung a brass lantern of exquisite workmanship; finely-crafted metal, forged, shaped and cut into intricate patterns of stars, moons, trees and birds. Inside the lantern, a blue flame cast a cerulean glow across the stone pavers.

Her father *could* have made the lantern, thought Rosalie.

She paused, waiting for Elmbray to tell her the story of its purchase, but he ignored the lantern and quickly unlocked the door, ushering her inside. They entered a hall lined with dark timber, and floorboards covered in rugs woven with scenes of naked, cavorting pixies dancing across fields of crocus flowers. Off the hall, Elmbray led her into a bright room with a three-tiered chandelier of twenty-four lit candles hanging from the ceiling. A couch stitched with floral designs sat in the middle of the room. Next to the couch, a fire roared in the hearth under a granite mantlepiece.

"Sit, please," said Elmbray, waving his hand at the couch. "I have bread, too. Sourdough. I bake it myself. It's my mother's recipe."

He disappeared, and Rosalie sank into the couch. Although she tried to keep her guard up, the warm and cosy room was better than anything she'd seen in the firth circle. She missed the comforts of home, though she didn't like to admit it. A part of her hoped Elmbray would ask if she wanted to sleep on the couch. Or better yet, a spare bed with a straw and feather mattress, and a down quilt and pillow.

He returned almost immediately with a tray carrying a porcelain bowl and a silver platter of crusty bread. "Smell this," he said. "Beautiful, fresh vegetables. Mind the spiced sausage though, it has a real kick to it." Elmbray placed the tray on a low table in front of the couch and sat beside Rosalie.

"You're not eating?" she asked.

"Oh, no. I had my supper a while back. The soup's still warm, though." He handed her the bowl of soup. "Tuck in. I'll wager this is the first decent meal you've had since the fifth circle."

Rosalie took the bowl, careful the metal spoon resting on the side didn't fall into the soup. "Truth is, we didn't have anything this good in the fifth circle. Not recently, at least."

"My, my, the fortunes of Sardis have gone downhill something terrible. I blame the Dobunni rebels myself. If the king didn't have to expend so much effort quashing their silly rebellion, he'd have more time for his subjects. Of course, Ewald's gone now. I wonder how the new monarch will fare?"

Rosalie tried not to slurp the delicious soup. Spoonful after spoonful passed her lips and excited her tongue, spreading warmth as it slid down her throat and into her stomach. She placed the bowl of soup back on the table and took a piece of fresh bread, trying to catch crumbs with her spare hand as she chewed.

"Are you really a mage?" she asked.

Elmbray leaned back in the couch, his ivory robes falling open to reveal burgundy trousers of fine silk or linen. "Is that what Snick told you? The poor fool thinks magic happens around every corner, but he's always a blink too late to see it. People spend way too much time bewitched by the promise of divine enchantment and not enough time in wonder of the real magic all around them. That happens every day. Like the dip and whirl of a flock of crested merrets as they fly in perfect synchrony over the rushing waters of the Anchep River. Or the hum and flicker of fire-beetles dancing across the bark of a syphus tree in the pale moonlight. No, Rosalie, I'm no magician, but I'm always seeking ways to enhance the beauty of life."

With the warm fire and a full stomach, Rosalie's eyelids grew heavy. She went to stand up, but Elmbray placed his hand on her knee, gently pushing back down. "I have dessert, too. Alpine erdberries all the way from the Desolate Mountains, covered in whipped cream. The most wonderous dessert you've ever tried."

"Thank you for the soup," said Rosalie, "and the bread. But I should be going."

"I can't have you wandering the desperate streets of Slumstadt this time of night. I have a spare bed upstairs. You should sleep there, but first..." Elmbray reached into his robes and pulled out a vial of blue syrup. The same sort Snick had shown her earlier. He held it up to the candlelight, and it glittered like an azure gemstone. "We call it *swirling*. The swirl is the only way to truly escape the shackles of Slumstadt."

Rosalie knew she should leave. She was a fighter. Smart, resourceful, strong. Every sinew in her body tightened, ready for her to spring out the door. Yet, something stopped her muscles from firing. They wouldn't work like she wanted. Maybe, she didn't want it enough?

Elmbray uncorked the vial and dipped the point of a grooved needle into the viscous, blue liquid. The embruisia glistened in the candlelight, clinging to the needle tip like cerulean honey, as Snick described.

Before Rosalie could react, Elmbray clutched her wrist and plunged the needle into her arm. She cried aloud, yanking her arm free, then half-stood before tumbling backwards into the couch. It hit her almost immediately and without warning. *The swirl.* Her head flopped to the side, saliva flooding her tongue as her mind exploded in colour and movement. She pulled a rug from the couch and wrapped it around her body like a cocoon, waiting to be turned into a beautiful butterfly.

She could almost see the beaming smile on her face as her mind flew away. Swirled. It floated above the couch, out the door of Elmbray's house, and into the night sky among a boundless arena of twinkling stars. The reek of Slumstadt disappeared, replaced by the perfume of a thousand flowers. She escaped the shantytown, swirling above the impoverished and broken. Above the horrid smoke billowing from the deeping pits. Above the walls of the seven concentric circles of Sardis and then down into its innermost sanctum.

Through barred gates and a corridor so narrow she could touch opposing walls with the back of her hands, she swirled. Past armoured guards standing to attention like radiant silver statues, and into a grand room with polished mahogany floors swept by the feet of a hundred dancers. She saw herself in the centre of the dancefloor, dressed like a princess in satin and lace, a flowing red gown brushing the floorboards like a twirling broom. A tiara clung to her long brown hair, threatening to topple with every dip.

A stranger with a kind smile and satin-grey eyes grasped her waist and swung her in a giddy arc. She tilted her head back and laughed. Laughed at the madness and wonder of it all.

On a stage raised above the dance floor, a naked, faceless woman smashed a fired sword between hammer and anvil. Sparks flew from the sword, a fountain of incandescence cascading down to her feet and shrivelling to nothing more than black specks. The sheen of the metal-smith's pale skin radiated across the stage and bathed the dancers in magical light.

Rosalie's mind broke free of her handsome dance partner and swirled to the stage. Stepping onto the platform, she held her arms wide, ready to embrace the faceless stranger. As Rosalie approached, the metal-smith turned, and the featureless skin of her face tore open, a tongue like a serpent springing from her mouth and lashing Rosalie across the cheek. She reeled, falling backwards off the stage and into an abyss of endless black.

~ Chapter 20 ~

Malang Gunya sprawled across the Dambay Plains like an immense stone forest. Intersected by a grid of paved streets, many of the original sandstone buildings still stood, a testament to the masonry skills of stone-grells. A rectangular green space filled the city's centre, housing an arboretum full of the rich diversity of plants found throughout Enthilen. Previously tended by the now expulsed grells, the arboretum had grown into a wild and uncivilised strangle.

Four precincts, once devoted to education, healing, culture, and the study of nature, bordered the arboretum. Buildings three stories high guarded each precinct, their archways and balconies framed by massive stone columns secured with capitals and pedestals sculpted into the faces of wild beasts. Two generations ago, the open, airy rooms inside each building would have been filled with the sonance of profound thought. Now, only the arguments of rats and crows bounced from the walls and landed, unresolved, among the waste and debris covering the flagstone floors.

An amphitheatre dominated the culture precinct, with twenty-four tiers of seating that reached for the sky, giving any audience commanding views of important ceremonies and performances. Dozens of stories high, a massive stepped pyramid towered above the nature precinct, crowned by a lookout the grells had used to survey their country and wonder at the moons and stars. The lookout oversaw all the lands surrounding Malang Gunya, a patchwork of fields bordered by stone walls and thorny hedges still bearing luscious, purple berries.

Sculptures of plants and animals the grells had worshipped for providing food and medicine lined the city's thoroughfares, interspersed among modest living quarters. Now roofless and empty, rows and rows of homes stood in disrepair, overgrown by weeds and desecrated by vandals and looters. Rubble clogged the dry irrigation channels snaking through the settlement, designed to bring water from the nearby River Milawa. Graffiti and careless destruction dishonoured what remained of Malang Gunya, the once white sandstone now tanned with age and neglect.

Amid the ghostly shells, in one of the buildings in the education precinct, a murmur of activity still hummed. Here, the Erstürmen had established an outpost, home to thirty-six disenchanted soldiers assigned to the second least desirable posting in Enthilen, dethroned only by the garrison at Detranté. The soldiers at Malang Gunya rarely saw anyone else. Their busiest time came during the long dark when wild stone- and weald-grells from Babir Birramal marched to the city. In yarles past, the soldiers would have used this opportunity to capture slaves or kill for amusement. Now, this effort offered them little reward, and they had accepted a truce of indifference, letting grells honour their fallen without harassment.

*　*　*　*

Perched high on the throne of the dead, Adalwolf spied the top of the pyramid that travellers used to mark the location of Malang Gunya. As the procession moved closer, the magnitude and majesty of the grell city revealed itself. He'd been told by Malphas that Malang Gunya was a blight on the landscape. Nothing more than a handful of awkwardly laid rocks, as if a child had tried to build a castle of sand amid an incoming tide.

However, nothing could be further from the truth, thought Adalwolf. Despite falling into disrepair, Malang Gunya looked like a grand city fit for a king.

The royal procession had left Laodicea eight days ago. As it snaked through the countryside, more and more pilgrims joined the throng. The King's Shield told Adalwolf the pilgrimage had swelled to more than fifty thousand people, emptying towns along the processional route already decimated by famine and disease. It appeared the townsfolk were willing to abandon what they knew and place their faith in what they hoped for. A new king brought renewed belief. All these people, these subjects were following him. He was the beacon to which they rallied, not Malphas or tainted grells.

Adalwolf wondered where all the people would live and how they'd feed themselves. Malphas wanted the irrigation channels cleared to reinstate water flows from the River Milawa, and ordered Adalwolf to send the old and very young into the fields to prepare the soil for planting. Although not much could be sown during the storm season, the earth could be tilled, and garden beds prepared, ready for the growing season. The stores the pilgrims had brought with them would need to be supplemented through hunting and other means.

As the head of the royal procession approached the city's outskirts, a band of soldiers stood under an archway that Adalwolf assumed marked the entrance to Malang Gunya from the north. Only one man sat on a horse, Adalwolf guessing this was Field Commander Folcher. Malphas had referred to Folcher as a 'geriatric fool' because of the commander's ignorance of the sacred ground on which he stood and because the soldiers at Malang Gunya now tolerated the pagan rituals of the grells.

Folcher walked his horse over to Adalwolf. At the same time, Lothar urged his undred-driven chariot past the grell throne-bearers and up to the commander. Pulling to a stop, the Hoch-Vater released his right hand from the reins and thumped his chest.

"Hail, King Adalwolf," said Lothar.

"Hail the king," replied Folcher with less enthusiasm than Adalwolf had grown accustomed to. He ordered the throne-bearers to stop beside the commander.

"Welcome to Malang Gunya, sire," Folcher said to Adalwolf.

"The king will have your office and private quarters," said Lothar. "His court will have what remains. The best available."

Folcher turned his horse to face Lothar. "And you are?"

Lothar steadied his undreds, tied the reins to a hitch poking through the tanned black leather stretched over the chariot's metal frame, stepped down and marched up to the Field Commander. "I'm the Proclaimant of the King. Hoch-Vater of Enthilen. Our majesty's voice and protector."

Folcher rolled his eyes. "My soldiers can guard the king."

"That won't be necessary," replied Lothar. "The king has his own private guard. Make sure all Erstürmen soldiers are assigned the best housing. The remainder of this rabble can sort themselves out. A work detail will be established at sunrise. We cannot delay in removing the stain from this landscape and resurrecting the glory of our Divine Creator."

* * * *

Adalwolf strutted around Folcher's quarters, a modest room in one of

Malang Gunya's grander halls with a single, canopied bed in the corner, a desk and chest of drawers, a washbasin and full bath, and its own fireplace.

The quarters will suffice, for now, Adalwolf thought, *but he'd need a grander residence soon enough.* He faced his mother, who stood in the doorway. "What a city I will rule over, Mother. Did you see the magnificent halls? Towering arches and spires piercing the clouds. Sure, they're crumbling, but we can rebuild them. Rekindle a lost glory."

"Yes, son, but..."

"And what a ruler I'll be. My subjects adore me. Along the roadsides they stood, waving and calling my name. Dropping to their knees as I passed. Praising me. *Worshipping* me. My Shield told me fifty thousand pilgrims have come. Imagine, fifty thousand subjects willing to build their lives at my command." He grasped Romilda's shoulders, noticing he must have grown taller in recent days because now he could look her directly in the eye. "I'll be a ruler for the ages, Mother, like you always hoped for. The most celebrated Erstürmen king that has ever lived."

Malphas pushed past Romilda and Adalwolf and walked into the room. "The grell city is even more of an abomination than I remembered. We must dismantle it without delay."

Adalwolf turned to his father. "I disagree. We should keep some of these buildings. They are worthy of my kingdom. I want to rule in a grand hall."

"The grandest halls lie beneath our feet," said Malphas, "in Pergamos. To resurrect the Divine Creator's kingdom, we must first destroy the grell city."

"I don't want to destroy Malang Gunya. Who cares who built the halls? As long as the people can worship their king, that's all we need to concern ourselves with. The pyramid will be the perfect place for me to hold public court." Adalwolf looked to his mother for support, but she stood motionless, a pale shade of terror painted on her face. He understood then; he'd overstepped the mark, the excitement of the arrival filling him with perilous bravado.

"Leave us," Malphas said to Romilda.

She disappeared into the hall, and Malphas shut the door and turned the key in the lock. A knot twisted in Adalwolf's chest and tightened as Malphas ambled over to him, grabbed Adalwolf's chin and squeezed. "*Never* question me again. Understand, *boy*, that I rule Enthilen. And when Volerdie returns, I will rule at his side for eternity. You are king only because of me."

Adalwolf yanked his face away and slunk into a corner. "I thought you wanted *me* to be an immortal king."

Malphas' fury subsided. "Yes, you'll be an immortal king, but one who follows the commands of his Divine Creator and Worshipful Master."

A knock at the door broke the tension.

Malphas unlocked and opened the door.

Lothar entered the room and bowed. "I await your orders, Worshipful Master."

"At sunrise, we begin pulling this aberration apart, stone by pitiful stone. Don't waste the rubble, though. We'll build an enormous wall around Pergamos to keep the savages at bay. Begin preparing the labourers. All those who aren't working the fields."

"Yes, Worshipful Master."

Lothar left, and Malphas faced Adalwolf. "I have something to show you."

He led Adalwolf from the quarters and into the streets of Malang Gunya. Around them, thousands of pilgrims unpacked their possessions and began searching for a place to stay. A fight broke out among a group of men over one of the few houses with a roof. As Adalwolf passed, the men stopped fighting, turned to him and thumped their chests, hailing the new monarch.

Do any of them wonder about the old man leading the king? Adalwolf thought.

Malphas stopped at a hole in the ground, guarded by four soldiers, near the base of the enormous stepped pyramid towering over the city. A temple had been built beside the pyramid with marble columns encircling a floor painted with scenes of grells undertaking daily life. Exposed to the elements, the paintings had faded and peeled off the flagstones.

Adalwolf walked between the columns to get a closer look. "What is this place?" he called back to Malphas.

Malphas marched over to him and scowled. "A temple of heathen worship. They call it the calendar of life. When the grell pilgrims arrive from Grōz Forst, we'll turn it into a theatre of demise." He yanked on Adalwolf's arm and dragged him back to the hole where a rope ladder descended into the dark below. "You go first."

Adalwolf glanced at the guards who ignored him, staring into the surrounds and waiting for an invisible threat to materialise. He removed his cumbersome outer robe, folded it, and laid it on the pyramid's first step. Turning his back to the hole, he knelt and poked his foot into thin air, searching for the first rung of the ladder. Bracing himself on the edge of a cracked paver, he lowered his body into the darkness, carefully stepping his feet down to find each new rung until he could grasp the rope to steady his balance. In twenty-four steps, he reached solid ground into a circle of light cast by two flaming torches bracketed to the wall.

Malphas soon joined him.

"Where are we?" Adalwolf asked.

"Volerdie's Kingdom," said Malphas as he took one of the firebrands and led Adalwolf into a dark room. "This is one of the smaller halls connecting to a passageway."

They stumbled past chunks of broken stone lying on the floor, over fine dirt that covered Adalwolf's shoes in a cloud of white dust, and through a side doorway leading into a long corridor twisting away into the darkness.

Partway along the corridor, Malphas stopped at double oak doors towering over his head. "You'll have to help me push," he said to Adalwolf. They pressed their shoulders against one of the doors and tried to find purchase as their feet slid on the dust-covered stone floor. With a final heave, the bottom of the door scraped across the ground, leaving a gap they could squeeze through.

On the other side of the door, Malphas swept the torch across the darkness, exposing a massive chamber lined with pedestals, a handful still crowned with ancient busts of people long forgotten. Square stone columns, thicker than the trunk of a panalope tree, rose up to a roof that remained hidden from the torchlight. At one end of the hall, far from the door, sat an empty platform with six steps leading to the top of the dais.

Malphas led Adalwolf to the platform. "This is where we must put Volerdie's throne. I found the throne hidden in a dank cave under the Desolate Mountains, surrounded by those pitiful draughouls. Likely, they stole it from here yarles ago."

"This...this is the throne room?" said Adalwolf.

"The throne *hall* of Pergamos. Your hall, until Volerdie returns."

A deep, threatening growl drifted through an archway at the side of the room. Adalwolf spun around, looking to his feet for a chunk of stone he could use as a weapon. Malphas appeared at ease and walked over to the growl. Into the half-light crept two monstrous hounds with wiry, grey fur and sepia fangs dripping with saliva. Instead of eyes, they had only shallow depressions covered with wrinkled black skin.

Malphas walked right up to the hounds, the saddle of their backs taller than his waist, and ran his fingers through their fur. "Sterben. Zusteller. You still remember me." The beasts turned their twitching black snouts to Adalwolf and sniffed the air. "They know your scent is strange," said Malphas.

Adalwolf's fear clawed at the inside of his ribcage, urging him to flee. "W-w-what are they?"

"Weregrims. Descendants of Volerdie's hounds. If I wasn't here, they would have torn you apart by now. I discovered them down here long ago when I first explored the endless tunnels and caves adjoining Pergamos. The weregrims must have survived by hunting rodents and the other creatures that misfortunately stumbled into their lair."

"Can they see?" asked Adalwolf.

"They have no need for eyes in the darkness, but their sense of smell is unparalleled."

"Are there more?"

"Yes, dozens. I've only tamed these two for now. I managed to block off the tunnel entrance where I found the others." Malphas pulled a piece of torn cloth from his white robes and held it aloft. "Do you remember?"

Adalwolf reached inside his mind, drawing a blank.

"When you fought the rebel girl on Hansen's Bluff, the one who helped rescue Tom Anderson, you ripped a piece of her tunic. I kept it. Now the boy has allies, we need to stop them from disrupting our plans any further." Malphas took a dagger from his belt and rubbed the torn cloth across the noses of the hounds, simultaneously jabbing the tip of the blade into their flesh. They whelped and growled, pain and anger forged as one, the torment forever tied to the scent filling their nostrils.

"Wherever the rebel girl is, my weregrims will find her. It appears they shun the daylight, but tonight, I'll release them to begin the hunt." Malphas turned from the hounds, sheathed his dagger and placed his arm around Adalwolf's shoulder, leading him out of the throne hall.

"This evening, Ende will continue your tuition. I hope you're taking heed of her words. You'll not find a better teacher."

Adalwolf flinched, hoping Malphas didn't notice. He wanted to master a ruler's skills, yet Ende's lessons were moments to endure, not embrace.

*   *   *   *

"Master Henruld says I'm strong enough to train for the grell army."

Seronan looked up from her bowl of broth and into the eyes of her naïve companion, Myan. They were crammed into a single, roofless room of one of the old stone-grell houses with the other eighteen slaves in Henruld's cohort. Not enough space to lie flat, the grells rested their backs against each other or the wall.

Seronan's spirits had lifted as she walked into Malang Gunya. Even as ruins, the city looked more beautiful and sacred than she could ever have imagined. Like Myan, she tried to convince herself the Erstürmen masters would rejuvenate the city, not pull it apart, but she knew the hope was frail, and she needed to shake it from her mind.

"I was in the king's private quarters today," she said to Myan.

"What's he like?" asked Myan.

"I think boldness and fear wrestle for dominance in his mind. He is like a timid child when the old man appears. The Worshipful Master. This master appears to be the true ruler of Enthilen."

"The king will grow strong. It takes time."

"Why do you hope for a different future under King Adalwolf?"

"Already, we have new opportunities. You serve the royal court. I may be a grell soldier."

Seronan shook her head. "When we walked into this city, I wept at its majesty. I was home for the first time. Even though I am a weald-grell,

Malang Gunya is home to all of us. Our ancestors built and shared this place before the tribal war that split us apart. In my mind, I see the streets brimming with life. Water flowing through the irrigation channels. Food in the fields. Learning and culture, and love of the natural world. Do you not want to see that again, Flea? Do you not hope one day Malang Gunya will return to the care of free grells?"

Myan bowed his head, and Seronan leaned forward and placed her hand over his. "Why do you want to fight for those who wish to destroy our home?"

His voice came as a rasping whisper, "What else can I do? We can't defeat the Erstürmen. They're too strong. Why is it such a disgrace I choose to fight for them? To try to make something better of my life?"

Seronan removed her hand and leaned back against the wall. "You are right, Flea. We cannot fight them. Not openly, at least. But we could weaken them. Chisel at the rock of their kingdom until a fissure appears. I have access to the king's court. That is a gift we could exploit. If you have such a desire to become an Erstürmen warrior, then the resistance could use you to infiltrate the army."

Myan's lilac eyes grew wide. "Resistance? What resistance?"

Seronan pulled him close. "Hush. Lower your voice. I have been speaking to the other slaves. We can no longer stand idle and watch all we love torn asunder. When the wild grells from Babir Birramal arrive, they will not submit to the Erstürmen destruction. They will fight, and we must help them."

Myan shook his head. "I can't do that. I won't do that."

"Are you such a coward?"

Myan withdrew and fell silent.

"I am sorry, Flea. It is hard to be brave in the face of oppression. I understand. But we must try." She clutched Myan's forearm. "How many wild grells do you think still exist?"

He faced her and shrugged.

"When I attended the last garrabari, there were no more than a thousand weald-grells and stone-grells combined. That was many harvest seasons ago. Still, I expect hundreds to undertake the homage march to Malang Gunya. Imagine if the Erstürmen wipe out hundreds of grells in a single day. It could mark the end of wild stone-grells forever. Yes, the weald-grells would still persist in Giigal, but for how long? Do we wish that the only grells remaining in Enthilen are either slaves or soldiers?"

"No," said Myan.

"Then help me. I cannot do this alone."

Myan went quiet again as more slaves pushed in around him and Seronan. She had spoken to some of them. Began to learn who could be trusted and who to be wary of. The resistance she spoke of built slowly, and she worried that not enough would answer her call by the time the wild grells marched into Malang Gunya.

* * * *

Ende's footsteps shuffled towards Adalwolf, and her rancid breath wafted across his face as she stopped and hovered before him. He tried not to squirm, knowing this pantomime was designed to make him feel uncomfortable. His knees ached, pressed into the cold flagstone floor of Folcher's quarters, and his naked body shivered with bleak unease, droplets of cold sweat seeping under his blindfold and stinging his eyes. The threatening squeal of Ende's sparth dragging along the floor echoed around the room, Adalwolf trying to shift his thoughts to other, more pleasant, things.

Ende's voice broke his concentration. "The fear in you must be exorcised. A leader must be emotionless." It felt like a strand of her hair brushed across Adalwolf's forehead before she sucked in another breath.

"I know you are afraid. I can smell it. But there is another emotion you are trying to hide from me. Love. Is that not so? Love and fear. Two strong emotions that will be hard to expunge. I know who you fear. Who is it you love?"

Adalwolf had played this game with Ende before. She would ask a question, and his answer would yield a consequence, often unpleasant, sometimes distinctly so. He hadn't learned what answers he should give to avoid the most painful consequences. But answer he must as no response always resulted in agony.

Adalwolf steeled his nerves. "M-m-myself..."

"Only yourself?"

"Yes."

"A lie."

Adalwolf tensed before searing pain uncoiled across the small of his back. He stifled a scream as warm blood trickled down the crack in his buttocks. The cut from Ende's sparth wouldn't be deep. The pale grell inflicted her punishments with devastating precision. Nonetheless, the agony was enfeebling.

"What of your mother? Do you not love her?"

Adalwolf fought the ache and calmed his breathing, his ears straining to capture another sound in the room. Faint, subservient, desperate sobbing that moved from his left and stopped right in front of him.

"Do you love your mother?" Ende pressed.

Thoughts bounced around Adalwolf's head, trying to grasp an acceptable answer. "My mother is always dragging me down. She wants to weaken me, so I turn to her for protection."

"Weakness is a transgression against our Divine Creator. Love *is* weakness. We must banish all trace of it." A hand rested on Adalwolf's shoulder. "There is lust in you also. The lust of a young man."

"No," Adalwolf lied, hoping to keep the secret.

"Yes. I sense it. I have guessed it."

"There is no-one...*ahhh!*" Adalwolf shrieked when the sparth nicked his chest.

"You lusted after *her*. Ewald's concubine."

No. No. How could Ende or Malphas possibly know about his desire for Princess Caeli? Did his mother betray him?

"Were you jealous of the failed King Ewald?" asked Ende. "He could quell his lust among her welcoming flesh whenever he chose. You were forced to crave her from afar. Sometimes the hunger overwhelmed you. In the black night, like a thieving rodent, you ascended the spiral stair to steal a glimpse of her seductive charm lying naked under a thin bedsheet. Demanding from her guards a vow of silence lest the king uncover your secret."

Someone had betrayed him, thought Adalwolf. Told Ende all of his secrets. The pale grell knew even more than Romilda. The blindfold clinging to Adalwolf's face began to smother him, damp from tears and sweat that failed to escape the tightly bound cloth.

"Fear. Love. Lust. Emotions only for a failing heart. Weakness that must be banished. Stand, King Adalwolf."

Adalwolf stumbled to his feet, naked and vulnerable, before steadying his balance. Someone, Ende, grabbed his shoulders and twisted him around. The sobbing became louder.

"Mother?" whispered Adalwolf.

"Silence," snapped Ende, placing something smooth into Adalwolf's right hand. "Grasp the handle of the sparth with both hands and raise the blade high over your head. In your mind, I want you to see her: the temptress, Princess Caeli. I want you to see her kneeling before you, begging for your love. Promising to fulfil all of your desires."

Adalwolf groped in the darkness for a steady grip on the weapon. The sobbing grew louder, punctuated by laboured breaths that sounded like they were coming from below his waist. He tried to do as Ende commanded, picturing Princess Caeli kneeling before him, head bowed, her long auburn hair brushing the floor. But his mother's face fractured his vision. She smiled at him. Caressed his forehead and dissolved rambling thoughts with comforting susurrations. He raised the weapon as high as he could, his quivering bottom hand level with his forehead.

"Wait." Ende adjusted the position of the sparth. "Now we are ready, your majesty. Thrust down with all of your strength. Sever the whore's head cleanly from her body and smile when the skull lands with a dull thud on the floor of this pagan hall."

Adalwolf wanted to scream. Whoever knelt before him was going to die. He was going to kill them. He'd never killed anyone before. He'd seen enough death witnessing Ewald's executions to last a lifetime.

Ende's breath caressed the back of Adalwolf's neck. He clutched the sparth tighter and swung it towards the floor.

~ Chapter 21 ~

Tom had shared the little shack among the dunes south of Dorfisch with Jameus, Melinda and Annian for four days. The storm season had turned bitterly cold with short days and long, bleak nights punctuated by occasional snowfall. To ward off inevitable questions from his hosts, Tom had spun a web of lies, telling Jameus and Melinda his parents were dead, killed by wild men of the north, and he'd abandoned his home in The Feign to look for work in Laodicea. When war erupted, merchant seafarers offered an escape for him and his friends, then the storm took his friends and now he had nowhere to go. These lies didn't explain the Dobunni pledge scars on his chest he tried to keep hidden or his desire to find Bindari, a longing that had forced a wedge between him and Annian. The old grell bristled whenever Tom mentioned the grell graveyard, and as the days passed, he became increasingly worried he would never uncover the secret of its location.

Despite the uncomfortable relationship with Annian, Tom managed to relax in his new surroundings. While only eleven harvest seasons old, Melinda proved the perfect foil for his anxiety. They developed a strong friendship, spending days fishing, beachcombing and exploring the trails leading to the road that ran the full length of Enthilen's east coast, linking Laodicea with Gestade and Babir Birramal.

Tom reconnected with the nature of Enthilen, calming his nerves by exploring rock pools to spot mussels, anemones and crabs, sitting alone among dense, prickly heath to wait for a passing thrush or wren, or staring out into the waves, hoping to see Freckles the whale.

Jameus had given Tom a thick coat lined with rabbit fur to wear over his cotton shirt and waistcoat, sturdy leather pants soaked in fish oil, and boots made from goatskin. The burly fisher also built Annian a small cart so she could carry supplies on her upcoming journey. Made from the light, flexible wood of the supallow tree, the cart had a flat tray with short sideboards, two large, spoked wheels higher than Tom's waist, and a t-shaped pull-bar. Melinda's despondence grew as work on the cart progressed, her usual cheerful demeanour disrupted by attention-seeking tantrums. Annian whispered soothing incantations into her ear after each outburst, and it appeared the young girl grew to accept her family would soon become smaller.

Tom understood how Melinda felt. He'd lost his friends and family from Earth, not knowing if he would see them again, and now his new friends — Grin, Thaly and Dwarrow — had also gone. Although he had thought about making a home for himself inside the shack with Jameus and Melinda, he knew, one day, a tainted grell would come calling, placing everyone's lives in danger.

*   *   *   *

Melinda woke to a frosty morning and rubbed the sleep from her eyes. Next to her, Annian's bed lay empty. Annian's probably making breakfast, she thought. On cue, the warm, comforting aroma of freshly baked bread wafted into Melinda's nostrils. She jumped out of bed, pulled on her pants and short tunic, and walked into the next room. The breakfast table was set, neat and tidy, with everything in its right place and a bunch of dried flowers sitting in a clay vase in the centre. A soup bubbled in the cast iron pot hanging over the smouldering fire, and a brown loaf sat in the bread oven at the back of the fireplace.

Tom was still asleep on the floor, but Annian and Jameus weren't in the shack. Melinda wandered outside and stood on the porch, stretching her arms towards the white sand and welcoming the sound of crashing waves in between yawns. Jameus worked at the chopping block, splitting logs for the fire. Melinda smiled and waved at him, then began looking for Annian, until...

The cart's gone. "*Daaaaaa!* The cart's gone!" She jumped off the porch and raced barefoot to the narrow path leading to the coast road.

"Da! Ya stupid big oaf. Annian's gone." Melinda sprinted along the path after her best friend, but caught a tree root with her foot, falling hard into the sand. Grabbing a rock, she spun around to face her antagonist. With blow after blow after blow, Melinda smashed the tree root into a wet mash before flinging the rock into the bushes. She tried to resume the pursuit, but her ankle twisted, and she collapsed again to the ground. Jameus lumbered up to her, dropped to his knees and held her tight.

Salt was such a familiar taste to Melinda, yet the salty tears streaming down her face gave her no comfort. She withdrew from her father and tried to scowl at him. "Wh-wh-why didn't yu-you stop her?"

"It's better this way. Annian didn't want to say goodbye. It was too hard for her."

Melinda clenched her fists and thumped her father's chest. "Stupid... big...oaf. Stupid..." She wrapped her arms around his neck and squeezed. "We could go after her."

"That's not a good idea. Annian wanted to take this last journey alone."

Melinda whispered in her father's ear, "You won't leave me, will you?"

"I'll never leave ya, lil' darlin. Never."

Over her father's shoulder, Melinda saw Tom on the porch, staring at the path.

But he's going to leave, she thought.

*   *   *   *

"Are ya sure ya want to do this?" asked Jameus. "Annian won't be pleased if y'find her."

"I have to go." Tom shoved supplies into a backpack he'd borrowed from Jameus. Annian's departure had caught him off guard, and he needed to begin the pursuit. "You've been so kind and generous. I hope I can repay you one day."

"Hurry up and go." Melinda sat at the table with her arms crossed.

"Why are ya so desperate to get to Bindari?" asked Jameus.

"Princess Caeli told me…" Tom stopped himself, cautious of giving too much away.

"You met a princess?" Melinda's quivering bottom lip stilled.

"In Sardis," said Tom.

Melinda uncrossed her arms and sat forward in the chair. "What did she look like?"

"She had the kindest smile I've ever seen."

"Y'been to Sardis, too? What were y'doin' there?" asked Jameus.

"It's a long story."

"Did you see the king or a prince?" asked Melinda.

"No, only a princess."

"Da says the royal city has seven circles. Seven circles of sin. The one right in the middle is the worst one. Did ya go right to the middle?"

Tom averted his eyes and checked his pack. "Kind of. I don't want to talk…"

"Then don't. You're a curmudgle, Tom Anderson."

Full of bread, dried fish, two waterskins, a flint for lighting fires and a woollen blanket, Tom's backpack bounced on his shoulders as he jogged along the sandy path to the east-coast road, following the wheel marks from Annian's cart. Tom had bid Jameus farewell and thanked the fisher for all he'd done. Melinda ran alongside Tom, planning to accompany him until they reached the main road before returning home.

"Ya ain't still mad at me for the fuzzy sugar nuts?" she asked.

Tom laughed. "No. It was a good joke."

"I reckon we'll catch Annian, and I can convince her to come back home."

"Don't get your hopes up. The disappointment will only hurt more."

"Do *you* ever get your hopes up? Ya often seem so gloomy."

Tom stopped and faced his young friend. "I'm scared to hope for too much. It feels like I'm setting myself up to fail."

"That's plain dumb. Ya gotta have hope. If it doesn't work out, hope for somethin' else."

"You're right, Mel. I should stop worrying so much."

"It ain't all bad. Ya taught me how to count."

Tom laughed aloud. "I'm an expert at counting. I'm glad it finally came in useful."

By mid-morning, Tom and Melinda reached the coast road. The dense, heathy coastal vegetation had changed to short-cropped, flaxen coloured grass growing below widely spaced trees with fissured bark and spreading, drooping branches sweeping the sandy soil. The wheel marks from Annian's cart had disappeared, and Tom stood at the intersection of the path and road undecided whether to travel north or south.

"South," said Melinda. "She told me she was goin' south into the forest."

Tom smiled at Melinda, a heaviness filling his legs such that he almost changed his mind. "I'm going to miss you, Mel."

Melinda scuffed her boots on the road and sulked. "I s'pose I'll miss you. No, yes, *yes*, I will. I'll miss you."

Tom bent down and hugged the young girl.

"If y'find Anni, tell her I miss her already, and it's not too late to change her mind."

"I will."

"Be careful, Tom Anderson. My Da says it's a dangerous world out there." Melinda released Tom and walked back down the path, waving to him as she went.

He waved back and turned south. *Annian's a bent-over old grell pulling a laden cart. It won't take me long to catch her.* The coast road of crushed stone and packed dirt was flat and smooth, and wide enough for two carts travelling side-by-side. Tom tried to focus on reaching Annian, but he worried about other travellers using the road and who they might serve. He expected any moment to hear the clomp of horses' hooves or marching soldiers, or the deathly thud of tainted grells. As he jogged south, stands of thin, pencil pines with needle-like leaves and pointy tops dusted with snow, grew thick along both sides of a narrowing road. Despite the cold, Tom tied the thick coat around his waist, his trot raising a sweat that dampened his shirt. There were no wheel marks on the road, and clouds brewed overhead, darkening the sky. By late afternoon, navigation became difficult, and his thoughts at the intersection seemed like famous last words. He'd kept a good pace, but still no sign of Annian.

He left the road to the east and made a camp beside a fallen tree, a short distance from the verge, planning to regain his strength and resume the pursuit tomorrow. Resting alone with his thoughts, a pang of anxiety tested for weakness, trying to puncture his rambling mind with nagging, prising, depressing thorns that could wedge themselves in his conscience and not let him be. *What if I don't find Annian? Or Erstürmen soldiers catch me? Or Malphas. Will I ever avenge Nanna's death? Or find my way home? This is stupid. I should give up. Give up, Tom. Give up. Much easier to give up.*

Not wanting to light a fire for fear of attracting attention, he pulled his coat on and buttoned it up to his neck. He swallowed a mouthful of dried fish, then wrapped the blanket around his shoulders, slumped against a tree trunk and settled into a restless night drifting in and out of sleep, dreams mashing with conscious thought.

Too soon, the handful of birds braving the chill morning announced the sunrise. Tom collected his pack and tried to warm his weary body by swinging his arms around in arcs and lifting his knees to his chest. While the coast road provided the most straightforward passage, he wanted to avoid unwelcome company, so he hiked through the pine woodland bordering the roadway's eastern side, keeping the road in sight to avoid getting lost. Occasional clusters of white and brown mushrooms poked through the snow at the base of the pencil pines, but Tom didn't pick any of the fungi, not knowing which ones he could eat. He walked the entire morning without seeing another soul. Even the wildlife remained elusive, likely hunkering down against the cold air.

With the sun overhead, he stopped and ate a piece of stale bread before continuing his journey, keeping the road on his right-hand side, walking between it and the coast. Although he set a good pace due south, by mid-afternoon, Tom realised he hadn't seen the road for a long time. He changed direction and travelled what he thought was west, trying to find the road again, but thick clouds obscured the sun, and he became disoriented.

The road didn't appear, and Tom anxiously pinched at the straps of his backpack, counting as he went. The light in the forest dimmed with the waning sun. He panicked. Confused, he doubled-back on his own tracks, walking in circles. The sun set. He was lost.

Shit. Shit. Shit.

Frustrated, he picked up a fallen branch and bashed it against the funnelled bark of an old, dead tree. The branch snapped in two, and the sound echoed through the wood such that anyone close would hear. Feeling exposed and stupid, he sought shelter beside a rock with a slight overhang and cuddled up to its cold, moss-covered face. Another day passed, and the old grell still eluded him.

*　*　*　*

Tom woke during the night to the smell of cooked food floating on the breeze. He stumbled around in the dark until managing to climb the boulder that was his shelter. Perched up high, he squinted into the dark woodland. *There* — a faint, red-orange glow between the trees and the distinct aroma of cooked mushrooms. He slid down the rockface and gathered his backpack, racing towards the burning embers. The outline of a cart with two large wheels emerged from the darkness. *Annian's cart*. He'd found her. He stopped a short distance away and weighed up his options.

Don't go blundering into her camp. She doesn't want to tell me about Bindari or lead me there. But I could follow her. She's an old grell. How hard could it be?

As Tom wrestled with his mind, his eyelids grew heavy, and he rested his back against a tree trunk. He'd wait until sunrise before making the final decision. He planned to sit and watch for signs of movement, but exhaustion won, and he fell asleep.

When he woke again, Annian was gone. He rushed into her camp and placed his hand on the cold, damp coals of her campfire. At the perimeter of the campsite, the forest opened, exposing an ill-defined path, and on the ground, faint wheel marks had compacted the velvety black dirt. Tom resumed his pursuit.

By mid-morning, he followed a faint creaking sound, like the hub of a wheel rubbing against an axle. If it was Annian, she maintained a steady pace, and he had to draw on all his reserves of energy to keep up. The almost empty pack hanging loosely on his shoulders reminded him he had only one or two days of supplies left. There'd be no time to hunt or collect food because he might lose her again. He'd have to approach the old grell after all; otherwise, he'd starve.

With the sun at its highest point in the sky, the cart's squeaky wheel went silent. Tom ran, straining his ears for any sound other than twigs snapping under his feet. At a dogleg in the track, a dense stand of trees blocked his view of the path ahead. He rounded the corner, and there, a few steps away, was the back of Annian's cart. In front of the cart, the old grell hunched over the ground, a furred cloak pulled high on her shoulders.

He'd stumbled too close to avoid detection. "A-A-Annian?"

Behind him, a twig snapped, and before he could turn around, something smacked into the back of his legs, and a sting shot up his calves.

"Ow!" He spun around to find Annian standing there holding a stick.

"Did not expect stubbornness to bring you this far," she said. "You have connection with nature, but weak. Will die in two or three more moons." Annian lowered her weapon and went to collect her cloak, pulling it off a tree stump. "I know why you follow me. You are persistent, but not welcome."

"I have to find Bindari," said Tom. "It's my only hope. I know you're going there."

"Why want this place so bad?"

"Princess Caeli of Sardis told me Bindari is where I'll find the answers to my questions. How to deliver justice to my grandmother's killer and then return home." Tom grimaced. He'd betrayed Caeli's trust.

"You believe her?"

"I have to. I don't have another option."

"Go home to Feign."

"I'm not from The Feign. I'm a birraman, Annian."

"Birraman? Not heard that word for long time."

"Frennan stone-grell told me a dark-skinned birraman walked among the first ancestors. She taught them new words and culture and carried with her two glass eyes." Tom reached into the pocket of his waistcoat and pulled out the eyes of lost souls.

Annian stepped back. "Keep away. My soul belongs under stone pillar, not stolen by trickery. You cursed to bear this burden."

"I feel cursed. I feel it more each day. Can't you see why I need help? I never wanted to be a birraman. If I could throw these stupid eyes away, I would. All I want to do is deliver justice and go home."

Annian lifted the pull-bar of her cart and walked off.

Tom followed. "There's a gorge in Bindari always filled with mist. I think somebody lives there, at the bottom of the gorge, behind a door only I can open. Somebody who can make sense of everything."

"Never heard of this place. Princess lied."

"Let me find out for myself. Help me reach Bindari."

"No. Go back to Melinda and Jameus. Leave me be."

Annian walked off, and Tom stood alone in the forest, thoughts of giving up harassing him again. It *would* be easier. To give up. Everything else was so much harder. Following Annian. Finding Bindari. Bringing justice to Malphas. Keeping safe from tainted grells or whoever else might be chasing him. Returning home. All of it was hard. Too hard.

~ Chapter 22 ~

Caeli lolled from side-to-side with Casfern's gentle walk, following Dwarrow perched atop the giant lizard Xaviary. The trip across the Dambay Plains had been slow. Seven days had passed since they saw the royal procession, and they still had days to travel to reach the forest of Babir Birramal. Dwarrow told Caeli they would arrive at their destination on the first day of the stone-grell garrabari. She didn't ask how he knew when that was, expecting he wouldn't tell her. The mouldewerp always chose carefully which pages he would reveal from the endless book of knowledge resting inside his head.

Dwarrow's dawdling during the journey had frustrated Caeli. He spent an enormous amount of time exploring old dwells and reacquainting himself with the mouldewerps' ancestral homes, or foraging for food and water. Across the plains, pyramids of stones, no taller than Caeli's shin, marked watering points. Underneath the rocks, holes the width of Caeli's wrist had been drilled into the limestone bedrock exposing the water table below. After dismantling the pyramids, Dwarrow would take a wooden cup tied to the end of a long string and drop it into the well to collect the water.

'Too precious for bathing,' he'd said when she asked. She'd have to put up with the mouldy smell wafting from her dress for a while longer.

Evening settled over the Dambay Plains. With Seena at half- and the larger Bargan at three-quarters full, the night was bright and the travelling comfortable, but they would have to make camp soon. Dwarrow led Caeli towards a winking glow in the distance. As they got closer, the light morphed into the flames of a crackling campfire, and the aroma of roasted meat beckoned the weary travellers.

Despite her hunger and exhaustion, Caeli remained cautious. "We should look elsewhere, Dwarrow. We don't know whose camp this is."

"I'll scout ahead, Princess. Pleasant company is a welcome thing on the plains at night, and we can share the fire."

Dwarrow trotted off with Xaviary, leaving Caeli alone in the dark with Casfern. Above her, an immense, silent ocean of stars stretched across the sky from one horizon to the other. She imagined the glimmering eyes of millions of angels keeping watch on all of creation. The vastness of the sky and the land below it still took her breath away. The small window cut into the wall of her prison keep had been her only view of the world for nearly twenty yarles. That tiny slice could never do justice to the beauty and majesty of the landscape she called home.

Dwarrow returned sooner than she expected. "It's a lone traveller and his horse," he said. "I don't smell any threat. In fact, his smell is familiar, but I can't quite place it. He seems harmless enough, and his fire is warm, and there's a brace of hares roasting over the coals. We could at least ask to share his company?"

Caeli smiled. "I trust your nose, Dwarrow."

"Then let's follow it."

Dwarrow and Caeli walked their mounts towards the fire, then dismounted under cover of darkness. Dwarrow left Xaviary to wander while Caeli knocked a peg into the ground and tethered Casfern to it. Together, they crept into the amber circle of light cast by the campfire.

"That is strange," said Dwarrow. "Our traveller seems to have abandoned his camp and taken the hares with him. How discourteous. Never mind, we can still use the fire."

"I'm not sure about this, Dwarrow."

"Nonsense. My nose doesn't smell any trouble, and my nose is never wrong. Well, seldom wrong." Dwarrow sat beside the fire and pulled a jar of something from his satchel.

Caeli joined him, screwing up her nose and wishing the traveller had left the roast hare behind. "Fermented slugs?" she asked.

"What? No, how preposterous," said Dwarrow, struggling to get the lid off the jar. "They're rootworms preserved in a brine of pig's blood."

"Oh. That's much better."

Dwarrow tilted his head to the stars, his long, animated proboscis swaying with the flames of the fire. "*Hmmm.* I think our traveller may have returned."

As he spoke, a man walked into the firelight holding a short sword. Caeli recognised the man's face and stifled a gasp, dropping her head to the ground to avoid his stare.

"This camp is occupied," said the man, standing steady and assured, as if he knew he had the measure of the new arrivals.

"You can lower your sword," said Dwarrow. "We're no threat to you. No threat at all. We were going to ask permission to share your camp, then you disappeared and took the hares with you."

"I'm not your provider."

"We could trade. I have a jar of lovely rootworms here."

"Sounds tempting. I'll stick with the hare." The man sheathed his sword and sat beside the fire, opposite Dwarrow. Caeli could feel him staring at her, but she kept her head down. "If you're going to share my camp, I'd appreciate an introduction," he said.

"I'm Dwarrow. A mouldewerp, in case you've never seen one before and think I'm a talking sheep. This is my Ambassadorial Assistant," said Dwarrow, tilting his head at Caeli.

"Does your assistant have a name?"

"I've given you my name; how about you share yours?" said Dwarrow.

The man paused, seemingly reluctant to comply.

Caeli knew she couldn't hide. Couldn't escape what had happened. A sorrowful ache began to well inside her.

"I know who you are," she said, lifting her head. "General Jurelle Stansfield."

Jurelle didn't take his eyes from her. "Princess Caeli. I thought you looked familiar, though I've seen you only a handful of times. But my son died protecting your life. I could never forget that."

A lump set in Caeli's throat. Of course, Jurelle wouldn't forget she was to blame for Jürgen's death. "I'm sorry," she said. "Please, forgive me."

They were the only words she could utter before twenty days and nights of agony came crashing down on her. She wept, tears turning the clear night into a blur of misery, and pulled her knees into her chest to try to quell the guilt shuddering through her body. Dwarrow placed a comforting, clawed hand on her shoulder while Jurelle sat in silent judgement, allowing time for the regret to punish her a little longer.

As her weeping subsided, Jurelle stung her again. "Did you love him?" he asked.

How could she answer? thought Caeli. The truth was so much more complicated than she had the words to explain.

"Do you think you understand what love is, General Jurelle?" asked Dwarrow.

"You can dispense with the formalities. I'm no longer an Erstürmen General."

Caeli lifted her chin from her knees and faced Jurelle. "If I did love Jürgen, would it make it easier for you to accept his death?"

"I want to know his life had a purpose."

"He was brave, kind and honourable. Isn't that enough? I could offer Jürgen friendship, but it would have been cruel to pretend to offer him more." But she *had* done that, hadn't she? Flirted with Jürgen to achieve her ambition. Jurelle didn't need to know. "I belonged to Ewald. If I was still in Sardis, I'd be dead by now. Whatever path men took to snatch the power they so desperately long for, my life was never going to be part of it. It would have been more callous to offer Jürgen a false hope, don't you think?"

Beneath his tunic, Jurelle's muscular chest lifted and fell with a sigh. "Life is full of strange happenstances. I find myself sharing a campfire with the one person in Enthilen who can explain why my son died. Why *he* died, and she still lives, freed from her prison and the royal city. If I gain nothing else from this journey, I will have an answer to my question, and you'll not leave until an answer is provided."

"Well," said Dwarrow, "things are getting tense. I always find deep breaths can help calm the nerves. General Jurelle, I think you're too harsh on the princess. I'm sure she'd deliver the answer you seek if she could. All we wish is to have a nice meal, some rest and then be on our way."

The corner of Jurelle's upper lip flared like a snarl. "I retrieved my son's bloated, headless corpse from the leichenhalle in Sardis before those madmen desecrated his body further. Pinned a guard to the wall with my sword at his throat until he told me the body had been found outside Princess Caeli's door in a pool of blood. I know that's where he died, but I don't know why. We buried him at the foot of the Scaur Hills behind an unmarked pile of rocks. When his family passes, he'll be forgotten. But I remember him now. I'm holding those memories close to try to suppress the anger and suffering that wracks every waking moment. What hurts more than anything is knowing those memories are incomplete. It seems he cared for you, Caeli, enough to give his life. Did you care for him?"

"Jürgen cared for his duty," said Caeli. "Cared for honour and loyalty. Yes, I cared for him. As a friend. However, I exploited the friendship for another end that saw Jürgen die."

Even in the sombre light of the fire, Caeli could see Jurelle's face burning red as he shouted at her, "What was that end, dammit!?"

She stilled the ache in her stomach and clenched her jaw. "To protect Enthilen from descending into eternal chaos. Jürgen died to save the life of a young man called Tom Anderson. He..."

Dwarrow cleared his throat and shook his head. Although Caeli understood the werp didn't want her to say any more, she had to unburden herself before it consumed her.

"Tom is a traveller from another world. King Adalwolf's birth twin. Do you understand what that means?" she asked Jurelle.

Jurelle calmed his heaving chest, peeled off a piece of roasted hare and threw it into his mouth, chewing and speaking at the same time. "Vaguely. If one of the twins kills the other, he'll become immortal? At least that's what the Erstürmen believe."

"It's true. If King Adalwolf takes the life of Tom Anderson using the eyes of lost souls, then Adalwolf will live forever."

"An immortal Erstürmen king. That's all Enthilen needs. How does the exiled King Oldaric come into this?"

Caeli glanced at Dwarrow. Jurelle appeared to know more than he was letting on.

Dwarrow poked the coals with the end of his walking stick. "Oldaric now calls himself Malphas. He is the master of the tainted grells and, I fear, the master of Enthilen. Malphas is the one pursuing Tom Anderson. The one who wants Adalwolf to capture Tom's soul and become immortal. I don't know why. There most certainly is a reason, and I expect the reason is not something Adalwolf is privy to or would welcome. The young king has likely been blinded by the lure of eternal power, but he won't rule for eternity. My guess is, he'll hardly rule at all. Malphas wants Adalwolf for something more than a puppet. The elders have spoken to me about this. They are sure the endless reign will not have Adalwolf as its monarch."

"Can you kill an immortal?" asked Jurelle.

"Yes, indeed," said Dwarrow. "One immortal can take the life of another."

"My father knows why Malphas is doing all this," said Caeli. "He's never told me, but he knows."

"Your father disappeared a long time ago," said Jurelle.

Caeli perked up. "I'm going to find him after we've spoken to the grells. You should come with me, General. Then both of us can learn more about the threat hanging over Enthilen and work together on stopping its spread."

As Caeli spoke, the wind changed direction, and Dwarrow's face sprang to life, his nostrils flaring and his long nose bending back on itself. "Oh my, this isn't good," he said. "Not good at all. That smell's not familiar, but it's a wicked smell nonetheless. And it's close. How did it get so close without me realising?"

Jurelle jumped to his feet and drew his sword. "Seems whatever it is, it was travelling into the wind. The wind change caught it by surprise."

"Sneaking upwind to mask their scent. Very clever."

"There's more than one?" asked Jurelle.

"At least two different smells, but the same creatures."

"Do you know what they are, Dwarrow?" asked Caeli, scanning the darkness beyond the campfire.

"I sense a bind of raw, intense power corrupted by unfathomable hate."

A growl burst from the shadows surrounding the camp. Caeli sprang to her feet and grabbed the unburned end of a branch from the fire, the flames from its burning end extinguishing as soon as she lifted it into the air, leaving only the smouldering tip to serve as a weapon. Dwarrow stood, clutching his walking stick diagonally across his furred chest.

Jurelle raised his sword as a black shape half the size of a horse leapt over the fire and snapped at his shoulder. He swung into nothingness, almost toppling over with the effort. The creature landed at the fringe of the fire's glow and faced the startled travellers, bared canines as long as Caeli's hand dripping with saliva and malice. A thick, blocky head that looked too big for the sleek body, swayed from side to side as the creature gauged its quarry. The head had no eyes, only depressions of black, wrinkled skin that masked any light still flickering amid the savagery.

With hackles raised, the huge, dog-like creature flung itself at Jurelle's chest. He ducked under its body and thrust upwards, tossing the animal into the air. At the same time, a howl splintered the night, and another beast hurtled from the shadows, opened its massive jaws and latched onto Dwarrow in a single, terrifying bite.

Caeli screamed, "No! No!" Instinctively, she thrust the smouldering tip of her branch into the fleshy cavity where the eye should have been. The creature tossed its head as if shooing a fly. It clenched its jaws, and Caeli thought she heard the crunch of bones. She dropped the branch and grabbed a rock from the edge of the campfire, ignoring the heat of the stone blistering her skin, and lunged at the monster that still held a limp Dwarrow in its mouth, smashing the rock into the creature's skull. Fear or reflex made it relax its hold, and Dwarrow dropped to the ground. Caeli screamed and snarled, and bashed the rock into its head again. The monster staggered sideways, but she didn't relent, pressing in on the beast. Thrashing, crushing, pulverising. Again, again, again until blood flowed down the back of her burned hands and along her forearms.

Exhausted, she dropped the rock and backed away. The devilish hound still stood, growling and snapping at her. Its muscles tensed, and she knew it would lunge for her again, but she couldn't resist this time, no energy left to protect her life or Dwarrow's. Collapsing to her knees, she waited.

The hound leapt for her. At the same time, an even larger shadow sprang from the darkness and knocked the attacker to the ground. Xaviary thrashed her tail like a giant, scaly whip, smacking the hound across the head and neck. It yelped a cry of pain or surprise and cowered away. Xaviary showed no mercy, picking the creature up in her massive jaws and crushing its ribcage like the heel of a boot squashes a spider.

Jurelle still fought the other hound, his sword having left only nicks and scratches in the beast's hide. The two combatants had reached a standoff, the creature waiting tense and wary, Jurelle unwilling to advance. The hound's chest expanded with a single, massive breath as it lowered itself to its haunches and vaulted at Jurelle's head. The General held his sword back until the last moment, then thrust it forward like a lance as feverish jaws threatened to rip into his face. The tip of the blade disappeared down the hound's throat, and it wailed and gnashed in horrifying, contorted agony.

Caeli threw her hands over her face, peering out between trembling fingers. Jurelle withdrew his sword, and the hound stumbled sideways, tripping over its legs and falling into the campfire. It squealed as the flames ignited across its wiry fur.

Caeli removed her hands and crawled over to her friend, who lay motionless on the ground. "Dwarrow? Please. Please. Please. Dwarrow?"

The little werp opened his eyes and moaned. "Am I still in one piece, Princess?"

Caeli rested her bloodied hand on his chest, sobbing.

"We need to check for wounds," said Jurelle, kneeling beside Dwarrow and running his hands across the werp's body. "I can't see any puncture marks, but there will be bruising. It seems mouldewerps are not easy to kill. Your friend is fortunate."

"Apparently, we're not very appetising," said Dwarrow, trying to sit up. "This demon-wolf probably had one bite and couldn't stomach another morsel."

"Lay back down," said Caeli. "You need to rest."

"I'll be alright, Princess. Thank goodness for Xaviary. That's not the first time she's saved my life."

"What were those things?" Caeli asked Jurelle.

"I've never seen anything like them. Blind hounds with black souls. They must track by scent alone."

"Which makes them even more dangerous," said Dwarrow.

Xaviary disappeared into the night, and Jurelle pointed at her retreating tail. "Should I be worried about that giant lizard?"

"Xaviary?" said Dwarrow. "She wouldn't hurt a fly. Well, unless it was attacking me."

"I'll take your word on that," said Jurelle. "Both of you need to rest. I'll keep watch for the remainder of the night. There might be more hounds waiting in the darkness."

Caeli laid with her friend and closed her eyes, but her mind raced, and she couldn't sleep. Time passed slowly, Caeli expecting at any moment to hear a growl announcing another attack. Nothing came for her except the morning sun and a family of grass robins hopping and darting between spiky clumps of growth and the occasional shrub, searching for an elusive worm that dared poke its head from the soil to greet the dawn.

She sat up and checked Dwarrow, who slept soundly and apparently without discomfort. Otherwise, the campsite was empty, Jurelle having disappeared with his horse. Next to the cold firepit lay pieces of cooked hare and a note. Caeli unfolded the note.

It appears Jürgen died for a worthy cause. This puts my mind at ease. I couldn't share your company any longer as I have a quest of my own to fulfil. I wish you safe travels and a speedy journey.

Jurelle.

~ Chapter 23 ~

On the fringes of Babir Birramal, less than half-a-days walk from the Dambay Plains, Thaly followed Grin stalking an evening meal. Dusk settled on the forest, and the animals of the night began to wake from their daytime slumber. Grin had made a throwing stick, a 'birrang' he called it, by whittling a piece of wood into a curve shape as long as his forearm. He told her they could use it to hunt wilay. Thaly was too embarrassed to admit she didn't know what a wilay was. She'd never taken much notice of the forest, even though she and Jacob had used it for cover when scouting the comings and goings at the Erstürmen outpost of Süden Forst. But, with Grin as her guide, the world of Babir Birramal began to open up before her.

'Nature is a language,' Grin had said. Another language for Thaly to learn.

On entering the forest, her stone-grell friend transformed. The giant tower of muscle had always stood out among the Dobunni and Erstürmen. Now, he blended into the woods so well she sometimes lost sight of him, even when she knew he was only a handful of paces ahead. Amid the dense groves of shrubs and massive trunks of panalope trees, four of Thaly's arm-spans in circumference, Grin became another unobtrusive creature wandering through this colossal living organism.

As night enveloped dusk, Thaly's ears pricked to the sound of claws scratching on tree bark before she spotted a cat-like shadow strolling along a horizontal tree branch.

"Wilay," Grin whispered into her ear while pulling the birrang from his belt.

As the wilay sat and turned towards him, he drew his arm back and launched the throwing stick at the target. Simultaneously, the wilay sprang from the branch, and the birrang clattered harmlessly into unoccupied wood.

"Out of practice," said Thaly.

Grin turned to her, lighting up the darkness with the broadest smile she'd ever seen from him. "I was close. I think the forest wanted to keep her for a while longer. Hard to catch wilay." He collected the birrang from the leaf- and moss-covered forest floor. "It is too dark for hunting now, Thaly. There will be food stored in our milbi. If my father is cooking, we may arrive in time for the evening meal."

"Are you nervous about seeing your father again?" asked Thaly.

"Yes. He did not want me to follow Tom Anderson. I disobeyed him. He may be angry. I hope he will welcome us nonetheless."

Grin led Thaly further into Babir Birramal. After selling the saddle and bridle to a nearby stable, she'd freed her horse, allowing him to search for a herd of his own. He was better off on the plains than in a dark, dense forest. She could have sold the horse. The extra coin would have come in handy. But she'd grown tired of living things being shackled and imprisoned to serve the desires of others.

With the two moons poking through the canopy of trees, they approached a dome of rock, almost the same size as Thaly's cottage in Bagendon. Under the moonlight shadows, the surface of the stone looked smooth and dark grey.

This must be Grin's milbi, she thought.

He strode ahead of her and stopped a step outside the rock shelter. She held back, not knowing what to expect. Would Grin's father, Frennan, come out to greet them? Did Grin have to knock? In the dark, Thaly couldn't see a door.

Grin stood motionless as if hypnotised by the smooth stone wall before him. She was about to say something when he stepped forward and disappeared through the rock.

What the...? thought Thaly. Should she go up to the milbi? Wait here?

The night grew darker, and the forest closed in around her. She began to long for the open, rocky vistas of the Scaur Hills. Her home. She started when a *mopoke mopoke* call came from the treetops. 'That is the gugug owl,' she remembered Grin telling her. Other sounds filled her ears. Forest animals scuttling through the litter. A baying howl in the distance. A swoop and crash among the canopy. She'd never been in the forest alone. Always with Jacob, and always with a campfire to keep the wild at bay.

Thaly unsheathed her short sword, hoping Grin wouldn't take too long to return.

He appeared from the milbi, looking concerned as he walked over to her. "My father is not here, and his pack and other supplies have gone. I expect he has already left for the garrabari. Inside the milbi, there is food and two beds. We will sleep here tonight and leave tomorrow."

"Are you sure I'm allowed to attend your sacred ceremony?" asked Thaly.

"I will not leave you here alone, even inside the milbi. The stone- and weald-grell leaders will understand. It is getting cold. Let us go inside."

Thaly sheathed her sword and followed Grin to the wall of the stone shelter. "I can't see a door," she said.

"You must clear your mind and think only of this moment." Grin moved his hand forward, and it disappeared into the stone.

Thaly gasped. "Do you expect me to walk through solid rock?"

Grin smiled. "No. The door is hidden, but it is here. The fact you cannot see it is a testament to the masonry skills of stone-grells. We have made these doors, so the Erstürmen invaders find it almost impossible to enter our homes."

"Clear my mind..." Thaly's voice trailed off.

"Yes. When we first arrived, I could not find the door. My mind has been full of suffering and anger. Those who attacked us on the *Vulking* are still punishing me. The Erstürmen invaders again threaten my ancestral home. I had to put all that aside to see the door. You must do the same. Forget about the loss of Jacob and what happened on the ship. Dismiss your worries about Emelin, Dayna and Tom. Focus on the now. Unless you wish to sleep under the stars tonight."

Thaly nodded. "Alright. I'll try. Clear my mind and focus on now."

Grin turned from her and stepped through the wall. No, thought Thaly, he didn't step *through the wall*, he entered via the door. And she would do the same.

She faced the smooth stone, shivering beneath the ill-fitting coat that failed to keep the night air at bay, and trying to clear her mind of all the stabbing thoughts that had plagued her in recent days. Images of the pale grell hovering above Jacob with her sparth raised. The lecherous seafarers. Bagendon set aflame.

Lock all the thoughts in a box, at least for a moment, and free her mind of the torment. *Focus on the now.*

In the darkness, shadows of things moved across the stone surface. Lines and shapes formed pictures. Birds flying. Snakes slithering. Antelope walking through fields. And trees growing. Every creature came together into a single design creating a door.

Thaly walked into the milbi.

Grin stood inside, already changing into a patchwork, skirted animal-skin tunic. Sitting on a stone table, a rock the size of Thaly's hand shone brightly, illuminating the circular room. A puff of warm air caressed her face, but there didn't appear to be a fire or fireplace in the milbi. She hovered her hand above a flat stone near the end of a cot, the stone's gentle warmth making her skin tingle.

"Guyang walang," said Grin. "The firestone. And the light comes from the sacred giba stone."

Thaly nodded, trying to absorb everything around her; the strange yet familiar. Rows of clay pots, dried herbs and fruits, and bulging sacks sat on shelves embedded into the wall. Above the firestone, wooden cooking utensils hung from hooks, and spears and tools rested neatly against a timber rack holding spare clothes. Two cylindrical rocks resembling chairs sat on the floor beside a stone table, in between two single beds of animal skins stretched over wooden frames.

"The stonework is amazing. How do you do it?" asked Thaly.

"When the first ancestors travelled to Enthilen, they brought with them special tools of hard metal. Hammers and chisels that can flake any rock. Long-handled tools with thick axe-heads that can split the hardest stone. And other, secret implements. We used these tools to build Malang Gunya and every milbi on the edge of Babir Birramal. The metal does not exist in Enthilen, and we cannot make new tools that will do the same job."

Thaly found Grin's home neat and comforting. Nothing looked out of place, except for one thing; a pile of strange objects, neatly stacked on a shelf. She walked over to the items and began looking through them: a small box made of a material she'd never seen before, part of which opened when she pushed on one of the square buttons; a thin, button-less shirt with writing on the front and the faces of three men; pants cut off at the knee, and a pair of brightly-coloured, soft shoes.

She picked up a book with a patchwork-leather cover the colour of bruised skin and held it aloft. "What is this?"

"Tom called it the blue book. It is written in Erstürmen and English, the language Tom speaks. Those are his things," said Grin, pointing to the neat stack. "Objects he brought with him from the other world. The one he called Earth."

Thaly opened the book to the front page where a picture had been drawn of two circles painted as eyes, each on opposite sides of a sun whose rays reached out to touch them. There were words underneath the picture, but she couldn't read them. She couldn't read anything.

"Can you read this book?" she asked Grin.

"I can read most of the Erstürmen. And Tom had been teaching me some of the English words."

"Do you know what this design means?" She showed Grin the picture.

He shrugged. "I think they are the eyes of lost souls connected by the rays of the sun."

Thaly closed the blue book and placed it back on the shelf. Everything about Tom Anderson was strange.

Grin searched through the shelves of preserved food. "We have dried meat and grains. I could make soup?"

Thaly smiled. "A nice warm soup would be lovely. Your father won't return tonight?"

"No. The garrabari is held in a secret location called Dalman, far inside Babir Birramal. From here, it is three to four days of difficult walking. The walk is much harder now my father is older. I am sure he has left already."

If the walk was challenging for a grell, thought Thaly, how much harder would it be for her?

"Do not worry about the garrabari," said Grin. "You will be my guest. We have much to tell the leaders about what we have seen. About the changes coming to our world."

"Will there be females at the ceremony?"

"Yes. Weald- and stone-grells will come from Giigal, including Mirrian, my mother, and Hannian, my sister. I have not seen them for such a long time."

Thaly sat on the bed, the tiredness of past days overwhelming her.

"Rest while I prepare the meal," said Grin.

She forced a smile and sank back into the thick animal furs covering the bed, not sure which dead animal she lay upon. Now inside, the piercing thoughts returned. They'd escaped from their locked box and threatened to torment her for the rest of the night. She closed her eyes and tried to drift away with the tempting smell coming from the firestone.

* * * *

Savouring the moments before sunrise, Grin sat alone in the forest, reconnecting with the only home he'd ever known and the nature he loved. Brown, trident-shaped leaves spiralled down from the panalope trees, reminding him that everything alive would one day return to the soil from which it came. A campfire smouldered nearby, tendrils of smoke diffusing into the damp morning air, creating a thin, delicate haze that wrapped itself around the roots and lower trunks of trees. Nothing stirred in the forest. No hoots of owls or croaks of frogs or the rustle of dead leaves as creatures scurried across the forest floor. Not even a waft of breeze disturbed the stillness.

Grin had a restless sleep inside the milbi, waking in the early morning and deciding to sit among the trees and prepare for the garrabari while Thaly still slept. He took a softstone and rubbed it against a piece of granite, creating a powder of orange-yellow, the colour reminding him of honey. At the garrabari, he'd mix the powder with water to make a paste to smear across the dancers' naked bodies. In his mind, he could see the performers stamping their feet and swinging their arms above their heads. He hummed a tune, a favourite among the female singers from Giigal.

A puff of smoke on the opposite side of the campfire swirled and twisted as if dancing to his song. A breeze must have navigated its way around the panalope trunks, he thought, until a scattering of leaves and twigs stirred above the soil. Grin put down his softstone, pulled his crossed legs in under his animal-skin tunic, and leaned forward. The ground beneath the leaves throbbed as if the soil had a heartbeat. A small, tight whirlwind, a bulbin, sprang up, collecting litter from the forest floor and suspending it in a column that resembled a tree trunk; a moving, shifting pillar of life reaching into the darkness above.

Grin wanted to run into the milbi to wake Thaly up. Show her what magic the forest had revealed, but he was frozen in place and struck mute. The bulbin stopped spinning, yet the forest litter remained suspended in mid-air, still and focussed. Inside Grin's mind, a gentle, almost imperceptible voice spoke to him.

You are damaged.

Grin replied with his thoughts, 'Yes.'

Anger grows inside you.

'I do not want it. Though I feel it more each day.'

The suspension of leaves and twigs shimmered and spun, moving over the forest floor and encircling Grin until he sat in the calm eye of an ancient storm. Around him flew the detritus of the forest, blacking out everything beyond. Its voice became louder in his mind.

Anger will consume you. The forest can heal.

'Will you show me?'

No. You must find your own path.

'Where does it lead?'

Pain. Anguish. An act of honour. The end of everything in a strange land. And his return.

'What are you talking about? What strange land? Who returns?'

You are damaged. The forest can heal.

The suspension of litter fell to the ground, leaving a circle of debris around Grin.

'Are you there? Are you there? Come back.'

"Grin," came a woman's voice. "Grin."

Grin opened his eyes to the sunrise and Thaly standing over him. "I was visited by a forest spirit," he said. "Guwindharr. It spoke to me."

"What did it say?"

"I think it gave me a warning, but it made no sense."

Thaly shrugged. "I've never seen a forest spirit, so I can't help you."

Grin searched among the forest litter surrounding him, thinking the guwindharr may have left a clue.

"Ah," he said, cupping his hand over the ground. Gently, he curled his fingers into a cage, lifted his hand and held it towards Thaly.

"What is it?" she asked.

Grin opened his fingers to reveal a plump spider sitting in his palm. "This is muwin, the ground spider. It is my crest."

"That's the thing you have tattooed on your face?"

Grin smiled. "Yes. I am bound to care for it. Would you like to hold it?"

Thaly took a step back. "Not fond of spiders."

"It will not hurt you."

Thaly frowned. She held her hand open, and Grin tipped muwin onto her palm, the spider's legs dangling off the side.

"Muwin is gentle," said Grin. "Although, if you step on it, it will sting you."

"*Now* you tell me." Thaly tilted her head down and examined the black hairy spider sitting quietly on her palm. "I'd like to put it back now." She crouched, tipped her hand sideways and let muwin fall gently to the ground. It scurried away, disappearing under the litter once more.

"I have packed everything we need to take to Dalman," said Grin. "Food, water, bedding, coloured powders."

"I'm ready to go when you are," said Thaly.

Grin stood, and they returned to the milbi to collect the laden packs. He wondered about the reception he would receive at the garrabari. Gone from his home for so long, following the path of a birraman against his father's wishes. He went to convince the grell leaders, the Mulugan, not to allow the homage march to Malang Gunya. A march that had occurred during every ngurung-ginya, the season of the long dark, since before he was born.

Would the threat of an attack from the Erstürmen be enough to convince the pilgrims not to march?

And he brought with him a stranger — a Dobunni rebel. He had never heard of anyone other than weald- or stone-grells attending the garrabari. How would the leaders respond to Thaly's presence, and would Grin's actions jeopardise his chance for initiation into the most sacred secrets of grell culture?

~ Chapter 24 ~

Anselm stood with Rostard, waiting outside the doors to the throne room of Sardis. Two monstrous Rephaim guarded the entrance, the grell soldiers decked in black armour of leather and spiked metal, with a grilled helmet covering their faces. They each held a hooked broadsword resting on their shoulder as if facing an imminent battle. Anselm wondered what they had traded away to find themselves in the service of Krieg and his master.

It was significant, thought Anselm, the Rephaim rather than the Steward's Shield guarded the throne room. Hunfrid's time may have already passed.

Rostard fidgeted beside him, twirling the tasselled ends of a silver cord tied around his waist that cinched a purple silk robe. Anselm wanted to tell him to stop. To badger him. Had their blossoming relationship already come to this? Each getting on the other's nerves with their ceaseless quirks.

They'd been summoned by Krieg, and now the red grell made them wait like naughty children preparing to face an unyielding father. Anselm had yet to retrieve the blood compass from Hunfrid, and he was nervous about admitting his failure to Krieg. The Steward never let the damn vase out of his sight. A surreptitious theft of the compass seemed impossible.

Anselm began to tap his polished white shoes on the tiled floor, and Rostard glared at him. Yes, thought Anselm, their relationship had already come to this.

The doors to the throne room swung open, saving the pair from descending into a quarrel over nervous twitches. Another Rephaim carried out a beaten and groggy Hunfrid, the Steward hanging limp in the grell's arms. Anselm and Rostard looked at each other simultaneously.

"Close your mouth, Rostard," snapped Anselm. "And steel yourself."

One of the guards at the door waved them inside. They walked into the room and down the centre aisle, approaching the throne platform like lambs creeping up to a caged wolf. Shards of smashed porcelain and a scattering of ashes lay at the base of the throne platform. Atop the podium, Krieg lounged on the throne, cradling the blood compass in his giant red hand. The gold pentagram glinted in the light cast by the dozens of candles placed in tiered chandeliers hanging from the ceiling. The red grell had found the treasure without Anselm's help, and he wondered how that might change his future.

When they reached the platform's bottom step, Anselm and Rostard dropped to their knees and bowed their heads, being careful to avoid the broken porcelain.

"I am flattered by your reverence," said Krieg. "You may stand."

Rostard and Anselm glanced at each other, then stood.

"Thank you, Vater," said Anselm.

Krieg held the pentagram aloft, opposing star points pressing into his thumb and index finger. "Hidden in the vase, as you suggested, Anselm."

Anselm searched his memory. Did he suggest that? He had told Rostard he thought Hunfrid hid the compass in the vase containing Brynlee's ashes, yet he couldn't remember telling Krieg. Had he been double-crossed? He desperately wanted to turn and confront the soothsayer. He'd see the lie in his lover's eyes.

The compass disappeared inside Krieg's fist. "It spins no longer," said the grell. "The blood must be too old for it to work."

"What of Hunfrid?" quivered Rostard.

Krieg sneered. "He will be hung from a saltire outside Sardis to face the judgement of his subjects. You need not concern yourself with him. We have other matters to attend to, such as the destruction of Bagendon. Delivering the final blow to wipe the Dobunni filth from the face of Enthilen. My Rephaim are aching to be tested in battle. We march for the Scaur Hills tomorrow."

Seizing an opportunity before Rostard thought of it, Anselm stepped forward. "May I ask, who will rule Sardis in your absence?"

"While we are slaughtering the Dobunni, you, Anselm, will act as Steward of Sardis."

Anselm dropped to one knee and bowed his head. "Thank you, Vater. I will serve you until darkness descends amid the daylight and Volerdie leads us into paradise."

"You display more respect than your superior, Lothar."

Superior? thought Anselm, but feared lifting his head to seek an explanation. Krieg accommodated him nonetheless.

"Lothar is calling himself Hoch-Vater of Enthilen," said the red grell. "Did you know?"

The revelation made Anselm's face burn crimson as if it had been slapped. He fought to still his anger. "No, Vater," he whispered to the floor.

"And you have been curate of the inner circle for yarles. How vexing. Nevertheless, personal ambition can distract us from completing Volerdie's labours. And I have one such labour for you to undertake while we are gone. I am leaving behind four of my Rephaim. I want you to send them through Slumstadt and burn the den of poverty to the ground. Any peasants escaping can march to Pergamos to help rebuild the lost city and honour the glory of King Adalwolf the Redeemer."

Behind Anselm, Rostard shuffled on anxious feet. Still fuming about Lothar's presumption, Anselm stood beside Rostard, catching a nervy glance from his lover.

Rostard stepped forward. "I look forward to assisting Anselm in his duties, Vater Krieg."

Krieg flashed a brutal smile that jumped out from his scarred face like the lashing claw of a bear. "I have other plans for you, Rostard. As reward for your service, I am appointing you Field Commander of the King's Shield. You will lead them into battle against the Dobunni while I command the Rephaim."

Rostard's long, spindly arms began to tremble, and his legs wobbled so much, Anselm thought they would give way. He looked across to Anselm as if seeking an intervention from the curate that would change Krieg's mind, but Anselm continued to fix his eyes straight ahead, fighting to keep an expressionless face that revealed nothing.

"Is there a problem, Rostard?" asked Krieg.

"It's...it's just, I was the king's soothsayer, then Master of Executions. I've never fought in a battle. There must be better choices."

"The key to being a successful commander is simple. Surround yourself with good lieutenants and loyal men, and the battle is already won. You have lasted this long, which means you are no fool. I know you will not fail me. Prepare the forces tonight, ready to march in the morning."

Anselm checked his emotions. His lover, the soothsayer, would never survive in battle. He could hardly hold a quill steady, let alone a sword. It appeared the affair with Rostard would soon end. Yet, it had been fruitful for Anselm. He had risen to the position of Steward, at least with Krieg absent from Sardis. His inability to recover the compass apparently hadn't disadvantaged him.

A shard of porcelain crunched under Anselm's white shoes, reminding him what had become of the previous Steward. Now he must plan to avoid a similar fate and prepare for his reclamation of the position of Hoch-Vater, the high father of Enthilen. Lothar's presumption could not go unchallenged.

*   *   *   *

The peasants of Slumstadt sauntered past Hunfrid, gawking at the deposed Steward of Sardis, his wrists and ankles now bound and nailed to a saltire placed at the edge of the market square. A few people spat into his open wounds or threw stones that landed with a thud against numb flesh. Others hurled abuse and then ran, apparently worried a loyal Steward's Shield might spring from obscurity to accost them. But there was no loyalty left for Hunfrid. No shield to protect his broken body. The threat of a tainted grell had managed to quell any devotion the soldiers or citizens of Sardis or Slumstadt may have had for their Steward. Although Hunfrid had accepted his ascension would be brief, such expectation failed to dull the ache of the fall. Now, he simply waited for death to end the humiliation.

The banner of the two-headed serpent flew beside the saltire so onlookers would know King Adalwolf had ordained Hunfrid's execution. *Adalwolf* was the ruler of Sardis, and Krieg his regent. Any challenge to this power would be dealt with harshly.

As evening fell, the peasants abandoned Hunfrid's torment and vacated the markets, trudging over the Anchep Bridge to disappear into the mud and waste of the shantytown. Hunfrid drew what would likely be his last breaths and closed swollen eyes, trying to conjure up more pleasant thoughts. He pictured Brynlee's tempting smile and wondered if love could be resurrected when he joined her in the afterlife.

Would Volerdie find a place for both of them in paradise? Did such a paradise exist in the absence of the Divine Creator watching over

Ostamp? Did it exist at all? The Erstürmen believed the souls of the dead waited in limbo, unable to enter paradise until Volerdie returned to Ostamp. Hunfrid wondered how long the wait would be.

A burning discomfort flashed across his chest, and he forced his eyes open. A young girl in a threadbare, sullied dress wandered up to the saltire and placed an empty crate near his bound feet. She clambered onto the makeshift step ladder and pulled a rag from her dress. With attentive care, the girl wiped dried blood from his chin, then fetched a waterskin tied to her waist and placed the opening at Hunfrid's lips, gently squeezing the receptacle. His throat constricted with the dribble of water, an explosive cough jolting him out of his stupor.

Hunfrid focussed on the little girl's face, his distant, raspy voice barely audible even to his own ears. "Don't bother, child. The end is almost upon me. Go home to your parents."

"My parents are dead. Now it's only Ompa and me. And Rosalie."

"What happened to your parents?"

A grimaced smile flashed across the girl's muddy face. "Don't you remember?"

"Should I?"

"Darius was my papa. Mama said he was a good man. Her name was Ella."

A vision emerged through the cloud of Hunfrid's crucifixion, clear and stark like a fiery sun in the dry, midday heat. A pale, innocent face framed by knotted blonde hair. A tiny hand barely able to grip the handle of the knife as she hacked at the rope. Strands of fibre unravelling before the crack echoed through the inner circle of Sardis. Time froze, a lance suspended in mid-air, poised to rip this little girl's world apart.

"Every day, Mama told me she loved me..."

"Stop," pleaded Hunfrid. "Stop. I remember now. I remember."

"Do you remember my name?"

Hunfrid combed his memory, finding only the energy to shake his lolling head.

"Tilda. My mama and papa called me Tilly. And you are Hunfrid, Master of Ex...Exe...Ex-e-cu-tions. You gave me a knife and told me to cut the rope that...that..."

Hunfrid squeezed his eyes closed, tears or blood trickling down his cheeks. Tilly wiped them from his face with her rag.

"Why are you doing this?" he asked. "Why not seek your revenge?"

Tilly ignored his question and fingered the leather pouch hanging from Hunfrid's belt. "What's this?"

Hunfrid's dying heart laboured with longing beats. "A handful of ash. A memory of a promise. She lived in these streets once, like you. I tried to save her. I thought I'd found love, but I'm a fool, Tilly. A fool who deserves to die."

"No-one *deserves* to die." Tilly dabbed Hunfrid's cheeks. "You don't have to be scared, Master Hunfrid. My papa said there's a special place we go when we die. Where the moons are bright, the sun is always warm, and the squishy grass tickles your feet. Everyone there is kind. Nobody's scared. Ever."

"Your papa was a wise man. My father told me we must serve Volerdie in life and in death, for all eternity. Only then would we find paradise. He was a fool, like me." Hunfrid calmed another hacking cough before facing the little girl again. "I won't ask for your forgiveness, Tilly. Instead, I request a promise."

"A promise?"

"To make the most of your life. Not to spite me, but in spite of me. Live it for your mama and papa."

Tilly nodded and climbed off the crate. "I have to get back to Ompa. He can't look after himself. Goodbye, Master Hunfrid."

Tilly disappeared over the bridge, and Hunfrid closed his eyes again.

No visions of better times came to him, only silent, wretched darkness swallowing the last flicker of hope. His heart stuttered, and his breath caught in his throat. He realised his soul was about to enter the void to wait for paradise to be unveiled, or to discover that the existence of paradise had been the greatest lie ever perpetrated.

* * * *

Her head pounding, Rosalie crouched over the muddy ground of the Slumstadt markets and unfolded a piece of torn cloth, laying out two jars of pickled corums, strips of salted meat and a bag of wild rice. She'd stolen the food from a neighbour, surprised they had managed to get their hands on so much. She could...should share it with Tilly and Zaria, or not have stolen it in the first place, but she needed...wanted coin. For more embruisia. The first taste from Elmbray was free. Rosalie had to pay for the second and third, handing over all her clothes except the tatty dress and worn boots she now wore. The descent into craving dependence frightened her. But not enough. She needed the cerulean honey. The sticky blue syrup clung to every corner of her mind, the magic swirl all she had to relive her family's love and escape the destitution of Slumstadt.

And she deserved to escape, didn't she? Yes, she deserved it.

Her headache subsided as the crowd thinned, only a handful of stolid faces still lingering around the empty market stalls. Stallholders rarely braved the Slumstadt markets at night. Less competition, Rosalie thought, more chance to sell her wares. A resident of the inner circles of Sardis might even brave the threatening desperation of the markets to look for a bargain. After all, poverty could be entertaining for the wealthy.

A soldier marched into the market square dressed in blood-red armour of a type she'd never seen before. It seemed nobody in Slumstadt knew who ruled Sardis now. News of the Steward's punishment had raced down every muddy street. At the edge of the market square, Hunfrid hung loose and lifeless, spread-eagled on a saltire. Some said King Adalwolf occupied the inner circle, the stories of his march to Pergamos no more than wild fantasies. Rosalie couldn't care less about the machinations of rulers. Her thoughts were now simple. More coin. More embruisia.

The soldier stopped at Rosalie's display and removed his spangenhelm, running his fingers through long, black hair. "How much for the rice and meat?"

"I got corums too," said Rosalie. "Pickled."

"Not interested in the corums. How much for the rest?"

"Five coin."

"Too much. Two coin for both."

"I can get more than that." Rosalie bit her tongue. She shouldn't argue. The soldier could take what he wanted and leave her with nothing. How dare she try to barter with him?

He tucked the spangenhelm up under his arm. "Alright. Three coin. No more."

Three coin would buy one vial of embruisia. One vial of quality cerulean honey. "Deal," said Rosalie.

The red soldier fossicked inside a pouch tied to his wrist, then tossed three coins onto the cloth and collected the meat and rice. Rosalie snatched the coins and shoved them into her right boot, the good one without any holes, the cold metal pressing against bare, calloused feet. She would wait until she sold the corums. They'd get another two coin, for sure.

"Corums! Two jars of pickled corums. Only two coin."

People that probably had coin walked past, avoiding eye contact. The famished stood around a fire pit warming thin hands and staring at her food with unblinking eyes.

"Corums. Two jars. Only one coin. One coin for both!"

Potential customers shied away. Goosebumps spread across Rosalie's skin, underneath her cotton dress. She gave up and tossed the jars of corums and the cloth into the sack, her mind filled with the taste of embruisia. She stood, rested the bag over her shoulder and marched to see Elmbray.

As Rosalie trudged up the muddy alley to Elmbray's house, a patch of blue emerged from the shadows, the flame flickering inside the lantern hanging on the wall of his porch. The lantern her father had supposedly made. As the blue light grew brighter, her mind craved like a fish breaching the waterline and gasping for air. Elmbray had embruisia, and she wanted it.

She sprang onto the porch and knocked on the door. The wooden panel behind the steel bars embedded in the centre of the door slid across, and Snick smiled at her.

"Rosalie. You lookin' to swirl?"

Rosalie nodded. Snick disappeared, then reappeared shortly after. "You'll have to wait 'ere a bit. We got another visitor to sort out first."

He slid the wooden panel closed, leaving Rosalie on the porch alone. She studied the intricate designs cut out of the lantern's metal cylinder that cast bird- and tree-shaped silhouettes on the walls, picturing how she might create such a delicate item in the smithy. A moth fluttered in and circled around the flickering blue flame, sprinkling powder from its fawn wings like fairy dust. It misjudged its flight, stuttering through a hole in the metal and flying too close to the flame. The blue fire caught the edge of its wing, and the moth burned to death as Rosalie watched.

She started when the door to Elmbray's house opened, and out walked a tall, thin man with a hawkish nose protruding from the front edge of the cowl covering his head. She backed into the corner, but the man didn't turn to acknowledge her, striding down the steps and out the gate.

Dressed in black robes, Elmbray stepped out of the doorway. "Rosalie. What a pleasure to see you again, and so soon. Come in, child. Come in. It's been a busy night."

Rosalie followed Elmbray through the timber-panelled entrance hall and into the bright room with the chandelier, comfortable couch and roaring fire. Snick stood beside the fireplace, leaning on the granite mantlepiece and grinning like a cat with a belly full of mice.

"I need embruisia," said Rosalie as she slung off her sack and slumped onto the couch.

"Straight to the point," said Elmbray as he sat on the armrest. He leaned towards her conspiratorially and whispered in her ear, "That was Rostard, King Ewald's old soothsayer."

Rosalie scrunched her face. "Who?"

Elmbray leaned back. "The man who just left. He's been a patron of mine for many yarles. You won't tell anyone, will you? He likes his privacy."

"I don't know anybody who would care."

Elmbray smiled. "Quite. Hunfrid made him Master of Executions, but now, one of those awful tainted grells has arrived and ordered Rostard to lead the soldiers to war. Poor thing. He's beside himself."

"Lucky embruisia wipes all your worries away," said Snick.

Elmbray turned to his pet. "What else was I going to tell Rosalie?"

"Barrons left Sardis."

Elmbray spun back to Rosalie, his eyes wide. "That's right. Did you hear? Yonna Barron has closed the smithy for good and taken his family to Pergamos."

The couch swallowed Rosalie as she recalled the suffering and loss she'd felt when first abandoning her family. At her most desperate, she'd considered returning to the fifth circle, hoping she wouldn't be discovered by the Shield. That wasn't an option now. Her father and mother had left her here to rot. Who could blame them?

"Everyone?" she whispered to Elmbray.

He shrugged. "Sorry, I don't know any more." He placed a comforting hand on her shoulder. "How are you, my dear? You look..."

Rosalie tried to conjure up familiar faces. Picture her family in her mind. Nothing came except blank shapes fading into the distance. Her family had escaped Sardis. She wanted to do the same, and she knew only one way. Embruisia.

"I've got three coin," she said to Elmbray.

"Why don't you relax. Wine? Meduz?"

"I don't drink."

Elmbray studied Rosalie's face as if he'd decided to take on the role of doting mother now her real one had fled. "How old are you, Rosalie?"

"What?"

"How old? How many harvest seasons have you seen?"

"Eighteen. Why's this important?"

"You look tired. Tragedy hides at the bottom of the furrows ploughed across your face. Youth stolen and age thrust upon you with no mercy, and now your family has gone."

"Why do you care? Can I have my embruisia?"

Elmbray shook his head and turned to Snick. "Get some water."

The little rat slunk off, then returned with a crystal glass filled with water. *Crystal.* Rosalie gulped the water down, the dryness in her mouth absorbing the liquid like a sponge.

"I've got three coin," she repeated. "One vial for three coin."

Elmbray sighed. "The price has gone up. It's five coin now."

"What? It was three coin only two days ago."

"Embruisia is getting harder to come by. The soil doesn't offer the bounty it once did, and my growers are abandoning their fields, leaving crops to die."

"Please. I need it." Rosalie yanked off her muddy right boot and pulled out the coins. "Three coin. Here. Take it. Please."

Elmbray sat beside her, placing his hand on her knee below the torn hem of her dress. "We can work something out."

She leaned forward, opened the drawstring on the sack and took out the corums. "Three coin and two jars of pickled corums."

"Rosalie."

"Ain't had pickled corums for ages," said Snick.

"Alright." Elmbray nodded to Snick, who pulled a glass vial from his pocket, half-full of cerulean honey.

Another thumping headache attacked Rosalie like a throng of soldiers with hob-nailed boots marching across her forehead. "Is that all?" she snapped.

Elmbray shrugged. "I'll give you a new needle as well."

Rosalie jumped from the couch, snatched the vial and needle from Snick, threw him the coin and corums, and raced out the door dragging her sack behind her.

The hovel's too far away, she thought, go to the river. She trotted down to the banks of the Anchep River and searched for a hole she could crawl into. People in Slumstadt without shacks lived here. An excavation dug into the sandy banks of the river. A pit for the lowest of the low. Rosalie knew many of the homeless drowned in the flood surges of the growing season, the churning waters cleansing Slumstadt's weeping sores.

She found an empty hole, fell onto her back and fumbled for the vial, pulling the cork out of the top with trembling fingers. Holding the needle between her thumb and forefinger, she dipped it into the blue syrup, twisting the metal so that more embruisia adhered to its surface.

She pulled out the needle and plunged it straight into her wrist. The swirl began immediately.

Rosalie beamed and rubbed her body into the sand, making a bed, and floated into the arms of her family. A child again, she sat on her mother's knee as Heady ran her fingers through Rosalie's long hair and whispered professions of love in her ear. Yonna walked into the koken, still wearing his apron from the smithy. Rosalie broke from her mother's embrace and swirled across the room, jumping into her father's arms. As he spun her around, the apartment walls sparkled with jasper, chrysolite and jacinth, gems embedded into every stone. Rosalie giggled like a child. Chased Petas and Allum around the dining table, overflowing with a cornucopia of food. Hid with Nettie under a down quilt, telling each other stories about magical lands in faraway places. The sun cast luminescent beams through the bedroom window, warming joyous faces.

But a dark cloud came. Snaked across the sun like an army escaped from Volerdie's dungeon. The swirl ended, and the headache and nausea resumed much too soon.

~ Chapter 25 ~

In the refugee camp outside Gestade, Lily sat alone as a gentle rain pattered onto the canvas tarpaulin above her head. Shallow pools formed in the mud outside her shelter, the water still clean and clear, and untainted by the stirring of the sediment. Two white feathers, ends curled up, floated on the surface of a pond with the gentlest of touches. A breeze caught the vanes, and the feathers twirled together like lovers in a dance.

Around Lily, the refugee camp bustled with activity, people securing the supplies from Laodicea, gathering, preserving and storing food, and sharpening weapons. All had been ordered to give the impression they would make a valuable contribution to Gestade's future while Field Commander Hartmut continued to deliberate on whether he would accept the refugees indefinitely. Lily found the waiting unbearable, almost as bad as watching for the barbarian ships to arrive in Traders Bay. And the disappearance of Hadufuns had made the situation worse. It seemed the Wandering Prince had resumed his travels, and she couldn't rely on him to plead the refugees' case if Hartmut decided against providing shelter.

Her adrenaline raced when the Field Commander marched towards her looking purposeful, his lips pressed together in a flat, unyielding line. But even from this distance, his grey eyes smiled. Hartmut stopped at the puddle with the feather dancers and made a point of stepping over it before reaching the edge of Lily's shelter. He stood there, still in the rain, and nodded a hello.

"Get undercover, Commander. You're shivering from the cold," she said.

"Thank you, Master Lily." Hartmut stepped under the tarpaulin and removed his coat.

"Please, call me Lily. Drape your coat over the chair and sit with me a while if you have time."

The Field Commander turned the chair to face Lily and sat. "I like we can dispense with formalities. Call me Hartmut. The camp is busy, despite the rain."

"We're doing all we can to prove to you our worth."

"Your worth was never in doubt. It's Gestade's capacity to honour that worth that's plagued my mind the last six days."

"Have you reached a decision?"

Hartmut rested his hands in his lap and inhaled. "A tortured conscience would follow me to the grave if I turned you away. We'll have to make the best of things. Together."

Lily wanted to jump from her chair and wrap her arms around him. "Thank you, Commander...Hartmut. Thank you. I knew we made the right decision coming here. You're a man of honour. I'm glad some still exist."

Hartmut surveyed the bustling camp. "Others would consider me a fool. How will I care for all these people?"

"We. How will *we* care. You're not alone in this responsibility. Dealhia and I can share the burden. We've already organised work and hunting parties, placed lookouts in a perimeter around the outpost and gathered enough food to reach the end of the long dark."

Hartmut laughed. "It seems I've been made obsolete."

Lily leaned forward and placed her hand over the top of his. "We need you now, Hartmut, more than ever." She withdrew when a soldier strode over to the shelter and interrupted their meeting.

"Field Commander Hartmut, General Badulf Wolfhart approaches along the coast road with an escort of more than twenty King's Shield."

Hartmut turned in his seat to face the soldier. "He comes to seek a pledge of loyalty to the new king. Gather a dozen riders. We'll go out to meet him."

The soldier nodded, and Hartmut faced Lily.

"I'll come with you," she said.

Hartmut raised his eyebrows. "It might be dangerous."

"I've faced danger before. I'm not about to shy away now."

He nodded. "It would be a good idea to present a united front. Show Badulf we're committed to working together to protect innocent people."

"He won't like it."

"He won't like any of this," said Hartmut. "Neither will King Adalwolf or his master."

* * * *

Lily and Hartmut rode out front of twelve horsemen from Gestade, under banners with the two-headed serpent, and the sigil of a white mongoose on a cobalt-blue background. The banners hung low and flaccid, soaked by the rain that had gathered strength since they left the camp. On the edge of Gestade's agricultural lands, as they rounded a bend in the road, twenty-four Erstürmen cavalry emerged through the sheets of rain led by, Lily assumed, General Badulf riding under a banner with the sigil of the snow-wolf. As they got closer, the riders from Gestade and Laodicea tugged on the reins of their mounts, and the horses slowed to a walk before standing, face-to-face, in the middle of a road lined with dense thickets masking the fallow fields resting on the other side.

The leader of the visitors came forward. "Field Commander Hartmut."

"General Badulf," said Hartmut, touching his forehead below his spangenhelm in a sign of respect.

"No need to organise a welcome party. I know my way to Gestade's main gate."

"It's been a long time, General. You were only a sergeant-at-arms when last you visited, if my memory serves me correctly."

"Your memory is sound. And you were nothing more than a guard. The Erstürmen military has been kind to both of us. So kind, King Adalwolf has now appointed me Umbo of his Shield."

Lily moved her horse beside Hartmut, who glanced at her and then back to Badulf. "This is Lady Lily LáDown, Master of the Southern Vale in Laodicea," said Hartmut.

Badulf smirked behind the rain dripping off the end of his crooked nose. "No Southern Vale left to be master of, from what I've seen. All has been turned to rubble and ash. If Master Lily and her cowardly refugees had stayed to fight instead of fleeing Laodicea, they might have saved the quarter."

Lily bristled. "It was hardly a fair fight. Swamped by barbarians..."

Hartmut cleared his throat, interrupting her. "We've agreed to provide the refugees with shelter for as long as they need it."

Badulf sat up straight in his saddle, a worn, haggard face setting stern. "The decision isn't yours to make. King Adalwolf will decide the fate of the Laodicea refugees."

"Are you sure it's Adalwolf ruling Enthilen now?"

"He was crowned in the Master's Square of the King's Quarter of Laodicea. I attended the ceremony myself."

"I've heard tainted grells, among others, shared the coronation stage with the king. Is an Erstürmen General of such high esteem as yourself content with taking orders from tainted grells and their master?"

"I take my orders from the king and no-one else."

Pushing through the thickets along the side of the road, stepped a group of six fighters with Dealhia out front, dressed in the leather armour of the Dockland's Guard. Hartmut spun in his saddle to face Lily, his eyes wide. She shrugged. Although she knew Dealhia had taken soldiers to watch the road, she had no idea they were here.

The King's Shield around Badulf shifted nervously in their saddles, yanking their horses around to face a potential new threat.

"Is this an ambush, Commander Hartmut?" asked Badulf. "Do you have more of these renegades hiding in the bushes to spring a trap on us?"

"I can assure you I had no idea they were nearby," said Hartmut. "This is no more than coincidence."

"A plea to coincidence is used too often to mask deliberate treachery. First, you welcome me with a Dobunni traitor riding by your side, then you tell me you'll shelter their refugees. Now, a band of thugs appears from the roadside brandishing weapons."

"We're not here to cause trouble," said Dealhia. "We were guarding the road and decided to announce our presence only to support Field Commander Hartmut and Master Lily. The Erstürmen, Dobunni and Docklanders stand as one in this part of Enthilen. Should your presence threaten any of them, you threaten us all, and you will face the consequences."

Hartmut's face turned red, and steam rose from a body warmed by supple black leather. Lily glared at Dealhia, trying to encourage her friend to hold her tongue lest the situation got out of hand.

Badulf swung his horse around to face Dealhia. "You dare challenge a messenger of the king?" Soldiers behind him unhitched crossbows from their saddles and loaded bolts faster than Lily had seen it done before. Others drew swords.

Hartmut raised his hand in deference. "There's no need for that, General Badulf. As you said, King Adalwolf will make his decision about the fate of the refugees. I ask you to return to him with *my* decision. I've composed a letter explaining my reasons." Hartmut reached inside his coat.

"You're more a weasel than a mongoose," sneered Badulf. "I won't deliver your letter. My task is to secure your fealty to the new king. If I return with anything less, I will be executed. You must pledge loyalty and duty to King Adalwolf and complete his bidding when he decides on how to dispose of the traitors you house."

Hartmut withdrew an empty hand from his coat. "I won't pledge fealty to a usurper king. Ewald was assassinated before his time of succession by the same tainted grells now standing beside Adalwolf. And I know the exiled Oldaric hides in the shadows, twisting the thoughts of the boy king. I will serve neither a usurper nor a puppet."

Behind Lily, Hartmut's soldiers drew their swords, the scrape of blades against the scabbards' metal lockets a signal for her adrenaline to begin racing again. Yannus, Dealhia's eldest son, cocked and loaded his crossbow. Other Docklands soldiers did the same. Lily reached to her belt, forgetting she had no weapon.

Dealhia turned her back to Badulf and spoke to her guard, "Lower your weapons. This is not the time for battle."

The rain fell harder, and lightning breached the sky over the nearby ocean. A clap of thunder soon followed, spooking the horses. Everything around Lily became a blur. Shapes weaved through the raindrops. Men yelled. Horses neighed. A bolt from a crossbow whooshed past her ear, striking the neck of a soldier sitting behind her. She couldn't tell if the bolt came from Badulf's men or if it was a mistaken, trigger-happy shot from a Docklands Guard. It didn't matter. Nothing would hold back the deluge now.

The twang of taut bowstrings let free filled the air, bolts flying in all directions. Lily ducked down in her saddle, trying to make herself smaller.

Hartmut raised his sword as if drawing lightning from the sky, looking ready to charge at Badulf. Instead, he screamed for calm. "Hold your fire!"

The firing stopped, and the rain eased. Still crouched in the saddle, Lily pressed her face into the mane of her horse.

Badulf confronted Hartmut. "Since when do the Erstürmen fire on their own? I've lost three men."

"Enthilen is not the land it once was," said Hartmut. "The land we grew up in. It's not too late to reject the false future promised by Adalwolf and Oldaric, and join us at Gestade."

"Do you think you can withstand the forces of the new king? He's building an army of grells. I've seen them — the Rephaim. One day, their numbers will reach into the thousands, then they'll be unstoppable. Adalwolf will be unstoppable."

"We'll stand for as long as we can," said Hartmut. "Better to live a noble life, however short, than die from regret."

The rain pattered onto Badulf's armour as he sat in silence, seemingly weighing up decisions in his mind.

Hartmut tried to direct his decision making. "If you continue with this assault, General, you and your men will die here. There are thousands of refugees who will see to your end. And if you return to Adalwolf without our fealty, you will be executed by order of the king. It would seem to me if you wish to live, your only choice is to join us and help defend Gestade against the usurpers."

Badulf shook his head, scowled, turned his horse and led his men back up the road.

Lily sat up. As the sound of galloping hooves receded, something else floated through the softening rain — a mournful sobbing from the side of the road. There, Yannus knelt with his mother's head resting in his lap, a crossbow bolt sticking from her chest, piercing the inadequate protection of the leather breastplate.

Lily's world crumbled. "Dealhia?" She jumped from her horse and ran to the roadside, dropping to her knees. "Dealhia?"

Yannus shook his head, tears streaming down his cheeks, fighting for space amid the raindrops.

"No," said Lily. "Dammit. Dammit. No." She uncinched the strap from under Dealhia's chin and removed the leather skullcap that never sat properly, then ran her fingers through her friend's thick auburn mane, tangling hairs around her fingertips. "Wake up, Dealhia. Please wake up."

But Dealhia's once rosy face had already gone pale.

Lily crawled around in the mud, slapping her hands in turbid puddles that gushed sprays of frustration and heartache. "Stupid, stupid, stupid." She glared at Yannus, "Why'd you come here? Why? You should have stayed away. You should have...," then slumped forward and dropped her head onto Dealhia's chest, kicking her legs out at the road.

Lily lay there crying until Hartmut came, sat beside her and pulled her into his embrace.

* * * *

Whibly staggered to a cluster of bushes on the fringe of the refugee camp at Gestade, glanced back over his humped shoulder to check the coast was clear, then yanked his penis from his pants. He teetered in place, rocked by all the meduz fed to him by his new Dobunni friends, and sang a seafarer's ditty while attempting to spell-out his name in the sandy soil with an uncontrollable stream of urine.

"Seeee the maidens, sittin' fairrrr

On the...*ugh*...siren rocks down therrrre

Seee the boatmen st-stand and starrrrree

At the maidens' gold-en hairrrr

A wistful...*belch*...mourn...drifts through the airrr

Careful lads don't..."

Whibly stopped short as something sharp pressed into his twisted spine, and a hot breath lingered on the back of his neck. He smiled to himself and announced to his assailant, "No point robbin' me. I lost all me coin to them damn rebels. Go ask 'em yurself. Ain't got a single one left."

"I've already spoken to your rebel friends. It's not coin I'm after."

"I don't have anythin' else to give ya. Look at me, I'm all bent outta shape. I'm no use to anyone."

The attacker pressed the tip of his sword harder into Whibly's skin. Whibly released his shrunken manhood and let it dangle precariously outside his trousers, still dribbling, as he raised his hands in surrender.

"One of the soldiers told me he's seen you in the company of a wild grell and a rebel woman with dark hair and olive skin."

Beads of nervous sweat formed on Whibly's brow, and the meduz threatened to bubble up into his throat.

"Was the woman's name Athalee? Thaly?" asked the stranger.

Whibly didn't know how to answer. This accoster might have heard about what happened to Thaly and Grin on the *Vulking* and was looking to enact revenge. He panicked.

"I ain't had nothin'...*hic*...nothin' to do with nothin'. I didn't hurt no-one."

"Was Thaly hurt?"

Damn it, thought Whibly, don't give too much away. Yet, even when sober, he knew his wits weren't the sharpest, and he couldn't help

329

engaging his mouth when it would have been better to keep it shut. Bile burned the back of his throat, and nausea threatened. He swallowed hard, fighting to get the right words out of his mouth.

"I tried to stop it. Thaly and Grin were me friends. Sort of. I saved 'em from the lake *and* the ocean. They're alive 'cause of me." He doubled over, projectiles of vomit exploding from his mouth, covering the urine traces with chunks of rabbit stew. He staggered upright and continued arguing his case, "They would...*ugh*...would have died. I saved 'em. They...tied me up...no good reason."

"They were last seen in your company. Where are they now?"

Another thought passed through Whibly's mind. This stranger could be hunting Thaly. He steeled himself, sucking in as much courage as possible, and spun around to face the assailant. In the blink of an eye, the tip of a short sword pressed at his throat. Whibly again raised his hands in deference, bleary eyes trying to focus on a tall, masked man with a broad-brimmed hat pulled low over his brow. A cold ocean breeze whisked through Whibly's open trousers, accentuating his vulnerability.

"Right...right...alright. Keep y'sword at bay. I got friends, y'know. They'll seek my revenge."

"I'll make a note to be wary of your friends," said the masked stranger. "You have nothing to fear from me if you're truthful."

"How do I know ya ain't gonna hurt Thaly? She don't need more hu..."

"I only want to help her." The stranger moved the tip of his sword up under Whibly's chin.

Lie, thought Whibly, and that's the end of your seafaring days. Any days.

"Grin and Thaly took most of me coin to buy a horse. I overheard them talkin' 'bout goin' back to the forest. Though I don't knows why anyone would want to go there."

"To Babir Birramal?"

"Yeah, somewhere like that. I think the grell was homesick."

The masked stranger lowered his sword and pulled a pouch of coins from his belt, tossing the bag to Whibly. "You were cheated by the rebels. They set up the game of knucklebones so you would lose."

"I knew it!"

~ Chapter 26 ~

Romilda sat still and quiet in one of Pergamos' oppressive underground rooms now turned into a temporary dining hall, a translucent black veil covering her face. While the slash extending from her forehead to chin would heal eventually, it would leave a terrible scar. Yes, her son was blindfolded when he swung the sparth, but she was still shocked he could do such a thing regardless of who knelt before him. Too quickly, she'd become a helpless spectator to Adalwolf's corruption. Hideous tainted grells, slaves to the murmurs of their deranged master, cast a foul shadow over Enthilen. Adalwolf had to drag himself out of the shadows and end this insanity before it consumed him.

Her eyes flicked across the faces present in the dining hall as if she'd spoken the thoughts aloud, and everyone now expected her to explain herself. Yet, nobody acknowledged her presence. The Queen Mother was of little importance in the grand scheme of things. Malphas let her live only to legitimise the new kingdom. On this evening, he'd called for a feast to celebrate the return of the Erstürmen to Pergamos. Carpenters had built temporary stairs so the king's court could descend into the dining room with ease. Slaves had worked day and night to pile dirt and rubble for extraction, clean the pedestals lining the walls, prepare the capitals for the adornment of new treasures, and scrub the white marble cornices carved with scenes of worshipping crowds lying prostrate before the Divine Creator.

Adalwolf sat at the head of a long table, flanked by Ende and Malphas to his left and right, facing each other. Next to Ende sat Romilda and Field Commander Folcher, sitting opposite Lothar and Folcher's lieutenant, Strentan. A handful of King's Shield stood guard near the stairs, and grell slaves scurried around the table, delivering a banquet of gastronomic delicacies including grueber, cured pork encased in the stomach lining of a boulder lion.

Romilda marvelled at how the giant grells managed to flit among the guests, nimble and unobtrusive. Ewald would never have allowed grells into the inner circle of Sardis except to kill them.

When one of the slaves put a plate of food beside Romilda, she clasped the back of the servant's hand. "What is your name, dear?"

The slave bowed her head and whispered deferentially, "Wortle, majesty."

"Wor-tle. Was that name given to you by your overseer?"

"Yes, majesty."

"You seem nervous. Don't be. I mean no harm. Do you remember your grell name?"

Wortle avoided eye contact and fidgeted with her dress, looking like she wanted to be anywhere else except here.

Romilda persisted. "You must have had one. I can still see the outline of your facial tattoo. You were a wild grell once, and you had another name. You may speak it."

Wortle turned her head away from the table and mumbled, "Seronan."

"What, dear? I can barely hear you."

"Seronan, majesty."

"It's a beautiful name. Such a pity it's been resigned to a cruel silence. Come closer, dear." Romilda pulled on Seronan's wrist, dragging the slave down to her chair, then leaned into her ear. "I saw you hide food in your dress. Don't let anyone else catch you stealing. They'll be less forgiving than me."

Seronan bowed, pulled her hand free of Romilda's grip and scuttled away. Romilda returned her attention to the conversation around the table.

"What shall we do when the wild grells arrive?" asked Adalwolf.

Malphas spoke through a mouthful of food, "They are untamed heathens, sire, but we can break their will. What do you consider to be a suitable course of action?"

Adalwolf leaned back in his chair, eyes wide, seemingly as taken aback by Malphas' acquiescence to his opinion as Romilda was. She guessed the charade was for the benefit of Folcher and Strentan. Adalwolf wiped crumbs from the corner of his mouth, and she noticed the first signs of facial hair on his upper lip. Her boy was becoming a man.

"I say we kill them," said Adalwolf. "Wipe them from the face of our land. Already we have enough slaves to rebuild Pergamos and fight in our army."

"Complete annihilation?" asked Malphas.

Adalwolf nodded and smiled, appearing content with his decisiveness.

"Is that a little hasty, sire? We could be more selective."

Adalwolf frowned, and Romilda sensed him trying to decipher Malphas' intent.

The old man didn't bother to wait for a response. "I would advise giving the grells a chance to pledge loyalty to the king. If they refuse, we may still be able to capture and tame the strong ones. The old and the weak, we can dispose of. Once Krieg has destroyed the rebel stronghold of Bagendon, he'll return to Pergamos with the Rephaim. It will be the ultimate test of loyalty to pit our grell army against their own kin."

Folcher cut a slice of grueber with his long knife and tossed the portion into his mouth. "Wouldn't it be a hollow victory to defeat the wild grells?" he asked. "They're not warlike and have no real weapons or armour. A bigger challenge would come from picking daisies on the plains."

Strentan placed his hand over his face, trying to mask a guffaw.

Malphas' eyes burned with bristling intensity. He grabbed Seronan's forearm as she filled his tankard, almost spilling the pitcher of meduz over the table.

"People say the grells are pitiful, of no threat and no worth," said Malphas. "When I see ones like this slave, I agree. Look at her. Too old to breed and too weak to fight, but she makes the perfect slave. Smart enough to follow orders and knows when to keep her tongue."

Romilda's skin crawled as Malphas smiled at Seronan and released her, then continued with his lecture. "The strong ones, though, they're a different story. They can be a threat, no doubt. We *could* nullify the threat by wiping out all wild grells or...*or*, my dear Field Commander, learning how to bend their simmering anger to our advantage." Malphas grabbed a chunk of pickled goat's brain and stuffed it into his mouth, pieces of the creamy cerebrum spraying across the table as he spoke, "The grells are a resource never used to full advantage. When I took an interest in them, told others of my plan to train them to fight, I was ridiculed. But I've proved everyone wrong. My Rephaim grow stronger by the day. I was told I couldn't take grells into my closest confidence. Wrong again. Ende here is my most trusted and faithful servant. I've now gifted her to King Adalwolf so he may benefit from the same devoted loyalty."

Malphas leaned down the table towards Folcher, crushing a loaf of bread under his chest. "There's a beautiful irony here, Commander. I've managed to subvert the grells' will so they offer unconditional loyalty to the same power seeking to crush them." He cackled and sat back in his chair.

Folcher's lips pursed and warped as if the contortions would help his brain decipher the machinations playing out around the table. Even to Romilda, critical pieces of the puzzle remained missing. She smiled at Lothar through her black, diaphanous veil, but the Hoch-Vater didn't acknowledge her gesture of friendship.

He'll see me, she thought, when the time's right.

"How goes the destruction of the city, Field Commander?" asked Adalwolf.

"Well, sire, many buildings have been turned to rubble, and we've begun the foundations of the city's wall. My men have overseen..."

As Folcher spoke, a draughoul floated past a side doorway of the dining hall. Malphas excused himself from the table and walked into the corridor after the ghostly creature. They disappeared from Romilda's view, and she took the opportunity to engage Lothar, who sat directly opposite her.

"Where will we build the kirika, Hoch-Vater?" she asked.

Lothar leaned back in his chair and brushed crumbs from his sangria robes. "Right in the centre of Pergamos. I've identified a location near that monstrous pyramid."

"Will you be conducting the sermons?"

"If the Worshipful Master requests it."

"I look forward to hearing them."

Lothar's eyes didn't meet Romilda's. Instead, he stared across the table, straight past her and into nothingness as if wishing the conversation would end.

She persisted in trying to gain his attention. "I always enjoyed Anselm's sermons in Sardis. They were so insightful and uplifting. However, I imagine they'll pale in comparison to yours. I heard so much about your homilies from those who visited Süden Forst."

Lothar locked eyes with Romilda and nodded. Finally, he'd noticed her.

Malphas re-joined the table as Folcher addressed Adalwolf. "You are fortunate, King Adalwolf, to have your grandfather, the *banished* king, act as an advisor. King Ewald came to a sad and untimely end. You must miss your father."

"What is there to miss?" interrupted Malphas. "Ewald was weak and his kingdom an embarrassment."

"At least he didn't overstay his welcome." Folcher took another swig of meduz, fuelling his bravado, and picked up a hind quarter of roasted hare, lunging his rotting teeth into the flesh. Through gristled chews, he pushed the old man further, appearing to enjoy the taunts. "This name you've taken, Oldaric, this *Malphas*, where does that come from?"

"The scripture," spat Lothar. "If you attended chapel, you'd be well aware of the provenance of the name."

"Our outpost never had a chapel, and King Ewald didn't bother to send us a curate. This is the most attention we've received since establishing the outpost nearly fifty yarles ago. Of course, Oldaric here," Folcher pointed the chewed hare bone at Malphas, "has visited us regularly over the yarles. Appearing and disappearing at will. I never understood any of it. And now this change of name. I mean, what are you trying to hide, Oldaric?"

This is it, thought Romilda. Folcher has pushed things too far, and he won't see the next sunrise. She couldn't take her eyes from Malphas, picturing a spitting pot of gruel boiling up inside of him.

But the Worshipful Master remained composed, tugging his white robes out from under his buttocks. "I'm not trying to hide anything," said Malphas. "I'm honouring the Divine Creator. You would be well advised to do the same. Instead, you've remained ignorant of your surroundings since first setting foot in this sacred place."

"One outpost is much the same as another," said Folcher. "Why's this one so special? Never believed all that Pergamos nonsense anyway."

"Volerdie's Damnation will punish your lack of piety," said Lothar.

Folcher shrugged. "How old must you be now, Oldaric? I mean, you were banished nearly twenty yarles ago when you reached fifty harvest seasons, the age of succession. You don't seem to have aged much."

"The Divine Creator has blessed me with a youthful disposition," replied Malphas.

"Not like poor Romilda here," said Folcher. "She's aged something terrible and now is so ashamed she has to hide behind a veil."

"Silence!" Adalwolf thumped his hand on the table, and Romilda's heart jumped into her mouth. "Persist with these insults, Commander Folcher, and I'll have you executed."

"Sorry, sire, it wasn't clear to me that you were the one giving the orders."

As Folcher spoke, the floor of the hall began to shake, and fragments of plaster and marble splattered onto the table. Cracks spread across the scenes of worship painted on the ceiling, and the grell slaves beside Romilda ran from the room, not waiting to be dismissed. A lump of plaster landed on Malphas' balding head. It would have knocked out most men, but appeared to have no effect on the Worshipful Master. Plates rattled across the table, and pedestals swayed in place, dancing to the thunderous rumbling.

Adalwolf staggered to his feet, and Romilda yelled at him, "We must go. Now!" She sprang from her chair and bolted for the staircase leading to the surface. The King's Shield had already abandoned their guard. At the foot of the stairs, she turned to check on Adalwolf, who followed close behind with Malphas, Lothar and Ende beside him. Folcher moved last, grabbing another quarter of roast hare for his trouble. As the Field Commander and Strentan raced for the stairs, a marble slab broke from the ceiling and crashed down onto them. Romilda gasped and ran up the stairs, reaching the surface as the shaking stopped. Adalwolf arrived, and she clutched his hand, peering back down the staircase where the prostrate and lifeless bodies of Folcher and Strentan lay, barely visible under the rubble.

Pity them and not Malphas, she thought.

The Worshipful Master and his lackeys joined Romilda and Adalwolf.

"Volerdie must have grown tired of Folcher's impertinence," said Malphas. "One less execution we need to concern ourselves with. We should avoid the halls of Pergamos until we're confident Volerdie is no longer angry. If you can release your mother's hand, Adalwolf, we need to meet in private."

Even in the moonlight, Romilda noticed the fear in Adalwolf's eyes. Although he had the face of a man, he still had a boy's soul. He released her hand and followed Malphas, Ende in tow.

Lothar spoke, as if to himself, "I must retreat to my quarters and beseech Volerdie for his forgiveness."

Romilda stood alone as Pergamos' new residents stumbled among the debris strewn across the streets. She ordered soldiers to remove Folcher and Strentan's bodies. Nearby, Seronan cleared chunks of stone from a fallen wall pinning two other grell slaves.

They'll die soon enough, thought Romilda, one way or the other. Confirming her thought, Seronan dropped to her knees beside the broken bodies and buried her face in giant hands. Romilda walked over to her.

"Are you alright, Seronan?"

Seronan looked up through tear-filled eyes. "I could not save them."

"Don't blame yourself. None of us can escape Volerdie's Wrath. I'll make sure the bodies are cremated."

"They should be buried in Bindari."

"What is that?"

"The grell graveyard." Seronan stood. "But there is no-one to take them there."

Romilda reached out for Seronan's hand. The slave withdrew and cast nervous eyes up and down the street.

"Don't be frightened," said Romilda. "Ser-o-nan. I like that name. It has a musical tone to it."

"I am forbidden to use it."

"How long have you been a slave?"

"For as long as I can remember, majesty. My master, Henruld, arranged for me to serve King Adalwolf and his court."

"You could be called to worse duties. Will you walk with me a while?"

Seronan cast a longing glance at the bodies of the slaves still trapped under the rubble, then joined Romilda as they ambled through the chaos of the cracked streets.

"Your ancestors built a wondrous city here," said Romilda. "It's a shame to see it torn apart. It seems the Erstürmen have a habit of destroying things of beauty. I was locked in the inner circle of Sardis for so long, I didn't realise how desperate everything had become out here, in the real world. But I saw it all when we marched from Laodicea. The hunger on the faces of the people, the scorched land of Enthilen, the brutality of slavery."

Seronan remained silent, staring at her feet as they picked their way through the rubble.

Romilda stopped and faced her. "Lift your head, Seronan."

The grell looked up, and Romilda raised her veil. Seronan stifled a gasp.

"Hideous isn't it? My son inflicted this wound. Our king. Should a son treat his mother so?"

"No."

"No." Romilda lowered the veil. "Yet, what can I do? What can any of us do to change the future? You want your freedom. I want to save my

340

son and his kingdom. It seems that, on its own, yearning is not enough. We need a plan and the courage to enact it."

Seronan shuddered either from fear or the bracing night air.

"You don't trust me, do you?" said Romilda. "I don't blame you. I had glorious hopes for my son. An alliance with the Dobunni forged by marriage. Lasting peace in Enthilen and Adalwolf hailed as the king for all cultures. I see no chance for that now. No path other than war and destruction."

"The wild grells..." whispered Seronan.

"What was that, dear?"

Under the ragged, thin dress overseers outfitted all their female slaves in, Romilda could see the tremble of Seronan's chest as the slave's heart thumped wildly. The encounter reminded her of attempting to pet a wild doe, skittish and wary, expecting a hunter's arrow would soon whoosh through the trees and pierce her flesh. If Romilda was to gain Seronan's confidence, she needed to be gentle.

"You have my permission to speak freely. Despite being only the Queen Mother, I still have more authority than any overseer. You mentioned the wild grells?"

Seronan nodded. "They will march to Malang...to Pergamos soon, majesty."

"*Hmmm.* Malphas wishes to see the grells destroyed or enslaved, or forced to fight in this horrid army of his. What if we could save them? Even if only a few? The last thing I desire is the end of your culture. If we work together, we could stop the slaughter."

"How?"

"Let me think about it. I know where to find you." Romilda dismissed Seronan and turned her attention to Lothar.

* * * *

Romilda waited in the dark, quiet street outside Lothar's quarters, the knuckles of her left hand resting pensively against a timber door carved with scenes of the inner circle of Sardis. The men under Folcher's command had refurbished over a dozen grell buildings, decorating them with reminders of home. This relatively modest sandstone dwelling had housed Folcher's sergeant-at-arms.

Murmurs intersected with slapping sounds seeped through the closed door and into the street. Beads of sweat gathered underneath Romilda's translucent veil as she pondered her next move. How would Lothar, Hoch-Vater of Enthilen, receive her? And how might she deceive him? She waited for a moment of silence, then knocked on the door.

"Enter," came Lothar's voice.

Romilda opened the door and stepped inside, shutting it behind her. Her eyes adjusted to the dim torchlight before she caught her breath. Lothar knelt, naked, at the foot of his bed, his lean, muscular back slashed with bleeding wounds that sent rivulets of blood seeping down into the crack of his buttocks. In his right hand, he held a whip with a bone handle and twelve strands of thin cord, each knotted at the end. Muscles quivering under taut, pale skin, he didn't face her, continuing to stare at a tapestry of Volerdie sitting on the throne of the dead, which hung on the wall.

She took a single step towards Lothar. "I apologise for the interruption, Hoch-Vater."

"What do you want?"

"I was hoping to seek your counsel. It seems we may have experienced the punishment of Volerdie's Wrath in the dining hall. I'm worried we could displease the Divine Creator further."

"You've listened to your curate. Only true believers would understand the significance of the event."

"I attended kirika in Sardis almost every day."

Lothar continued to stare at the tapestry as though speaking to Volerdie himself, not Romilda. "I accepted the vision of the Worshipful Master to resurrect Pergamos. However, the event in the dining room gives me pause. It was clearly a sign from Volerdie. A whisper of his wrath, warning us against blasphemy. If we don't heed the warning, a more grievous punishment will befall us. It is why I had to come here to offer my own chastisement to subdue the Divine Creator's anger."

"The Worshipful Master may be, unknowingly, placing all of us in danger." Romilda removed her coat and hung it from a hook on the back of the door. She took another three steps into the room, the hem of her gossamer-like nightgown caressing her thighs.

"I hope Malphas is taking you into his confidence," she said. "Anselm told me your knowledge of the scripture verses is unparalleled."

Waves of resentment splashed across Lothar's face. "The Worshipful Master speaks to me only to issue orders."

"That must be hard to deal with, a man of your theological standing. Anselm considers you the most enlightened curate in all of Enthilen."

"Did he say that?" asked Lothar.

She smiled under her veil. "Yes. During private counselling."

"Anselm was my teacher, before Ewald sent me to Süden Forst."

"Such a waste of your talents to be banished to that decaying outpost. I could speak to Malphas on your behalf. He and I were lovers once when I was still Ewald's wife."

Lothar turned his head slowly to face Romilda, his eyes sharp and piercing. "He succumbed to the enticement of forbidden flesh?"

"He was Oldaric back then. No more than an exiled king. Now...now he has grand ambitions no-one could ever guess."

"I have guessed," whispered Lothar.

Romilda opened her mouth and ran her tongue over dry, cracked lips. "Only a true scholar of the scripture verses could make such a discovery."

"The scripture verses contain only a part of the knowledge. There is another..." Lothar stopped, apparently deciding he'd divulged enough to his visitor.

Romilda stepped in front of his naked, hairless chest, lifted her nightgown to the top of her thighs and knelt before him. Reaching a hand out, she gently traced her fingers over the sinews of his right shoulder, feeling his body shudder under her touch.

Here was a man, she thought, who had refused to succumb to the temptations of this world. Who refused to let his body become flaccid and weak. But he must have secret desires. A longing buried deep in his loins that she could reveal.

And she needed to satiate her own carnal appetite. Ewald had shown little interest in her for yarles. Now, he was dead, leaving Adalwolf as the only man left in her life. For the first time since her wedding twenty-four yarles ago, Romilda was free of Ewald. She could have suitors who weren't frightened their lust would lead to a meeting with the executioner's axe. And the zealot Lothar was fit, lean and alluring.

"Go on, Hoch-Vater," she whispered, moving her hand down to his muscular chest. He trembled again, and she wondered if he'd ever been touched by a woman other than his mother. Touched by anyone.

Lothar placed the bloodied whip on the floor beside him. "*Da Und Sepcarture* directs the master's actions, but only he is permitted to read it."

"The First Scripture must be such a temptation to you, a man who has devoted his life to the service of Volerdie. To have the Divine Creator's word, written in his own blood, within your grasp only to be denied the opportunity to study it. I can't imagine the affront. What right does Malphas have to keep Volerdie's Lore hidden from you? You're the one who's taken the sacred vows of a curate."

"You approach blasphemy, Queen Mother."

Romilda placed her finger on Lothar's lips. With her other hand, she pulled at the ties securing the top of her nightgown over her shoulders. The ties came loose, and the gown fell to her waist, exposing her naked breasts. Lothar's eyes widened, and she placed her hand over his chest to feel the thumping beat of his heart, then slowly, gently, moved her hand down across his tense stomach and prised apart his thighs to grasp the swelling erection betraying his suppressed desire.

Lothar moaned and grimaced as if the touch caused him pain. "I've seen it," he whispered. "The First Scripture. Malphas has been careless."

Romilda caressed her palm up and down the shaft of his penis. "It appears this is Volerdie's desire. To reveal the scripture to you. To give you permission to begin your interpretation. If this isn't so, wouldn't the Divine Creator have struck you down by now?"

"Yes."

"His message is clear. Learn the lessons of *Da Und Sepcarture*. Learn Volerdie's teachings and guide the Erstürmen to the promised paradise when darkness descends."

"The language...the language is difficult," stammered Lothar. "Foreign."

"You're a scholar of Volerdie's Lore. You'll find a way to decipher its meaning. Volerdie wants you to be his voice. To fill your soul with all the pleasures of this world. Together we can discover the ambitions of the failed King Oldaric, lest Volerdie's Wrath destroys all of us before the door to paradise is opened."

Romilda shuffled back, removed her veil, opened her mouth and bent down to Lothar's swollen phallus.

* * * *

Seronan and Myan crouched in a dead-end alley near their quarters in

Malang Gunya as other slaves from their cohort cleared rubble from the streets. They had only a brief moment before Henruld would notice their absence, but Seronan couldn't wait to tell Myan of her conversation with the Queen Mother.

"Our kin will soon gather at the edge of Babir Birramal and prepare to march," she said. "We do not have much time to form a plan for their protection."

"What can we possibly do?" asked Myan.

"I have spoken with the Queen Mother. She may be able to help us. She does not want to see the wild grells slaughtered."

"The Queen Mother?"

"*Sssh.* Keep your voice down."

"It's a trap to see if you fall in, and then punish you for the mistake."

Seronan shook her head. "I do not believe so. I spoke carefully. She gave much more away than I did. The Queen Mother longs for her son to preside over a peaceful kingdom."

"Are you sure you can trust her?"

"I do not know. I feel hopeful and desperate."

Myan didn't look convinced.

Seronan continued, "I will deal with the Queen Mother. You need to focus on securing as many recruits as possible."

"Recruits for what?"

"Protecting the wild grells from any attack. Now you have been accepted to train for the Rephaim, you can access weapons and other grell soldiers. We could have a whole company at our disposal. How many of you are there now?"

"More than one hundred. But they train us in small groups. We're rarely together all at once. The Erstürmen masters say our commander, Krieg, will soon arrive back in Malang Gunya. They're planning a display so we can impress him with our progress."

"You need to convince as many grell soldiers as possible to fight for their kin."

"I don't know. The masters watch us so closely."

"Then whisper," hissed Seronan. "Hide in dark corners. Pass notes between each other, then destroy them. At least try, Myan."

Seronan took a risk using his proper name, Myan, instead of his slave name, Flea. But breaking such rules seemed trivial, given they were plotting rebellion. She realised then she had reached the point of no return.

"The wild grells have no hope without us," said Seronan. "Even if the Queen Mother is true to her word."

"I fear being exposed as a traitor."

"Overcome the fear. We have so little to lose. Now is the time to risk everything. I am thinking about a plan to help assassins reach the Worshipful Master."

"Assassins?" said Myan.

"I watch the movements of the royal court every day. The Worshipful Master is our oppressor and the true ruler of Enthilen. If we could remove him from power..."

"What about poison?"

"Slaves taste every meal immediately before serving. I would be willing to die if I knew the poison would also reach Malphas, but I cannot be sure I will be the one asked to do the tasting."

Myan covered his face in his hands. "Too much is happening around me. Malphas, the Queen Mother, assassins, begging grell soldiers to protect the pilgrims. So many ways for our masters to catch us and punish us. So many ways for them to trip us up."

Seronan placed her hand on his shoulder. "You are strong, Myan. We are strong. That is why the Erstürmen made us slaves. Soon, we must demonstrate we are stronger than them. The time is long past for us to rise up and find our justice."

*   *   *   *

"Hold out your hand," said Malphas.

Adalwolf held his right hand out, palm facing up, and gritted his teeth to try to stop the hand from shaking. In front of him, Malphas fumbled inside his robes while Ende stood in the corner, stooped over, clutching her sparth and staring into blank space, seemingly mesmerised by every speck of dust floating around inside Adalwolf's private quarters.

Late at night, Adalwolf's eyes drifted in and out of focus, the stresses of recent days depleting his energy which had been stretched between the brutal tutoring of Ende, the demands of Malphas, the pleading susurrations of his mother, and the theological disdain of Lothar. Adalwolf's ascent to the royal throne had yet to yield its rewards, although he enjoyed walking among the people who showed him loyalty and respect. Sometimes he stopped to talk to them, asking about their hopes and plans for a future in Pergamos. Soon, he would feel like a proper king, and he would have...

"*Arrgh!*" Adalwolf yanked his hand away, blood now seeping from a wound in the middle of his palm. "What did you do?"

Malphas held up a gold pentagram, one tip of the five-pointed star dripping with Adalwolf's sizzling, hissing blood. "Krieg found the treasure I sought. A draughoul delivered it during our feast."

"The blood compass?" asked Adalwolf, clutching at his hand.

"Yes. Now we can set our bearings on the whereabouts of the Anderson boy."

"My blood appears to be boiling."

"It's bonding with the metal. A bond that will last for days." Malphas walked over to a low table beside the open fire in Adalwolf's room and set the compass down, the point of its conical underside balanced on the dark timber. He released his fingers, and the compass spun, fast and

348

furious, like a cart wheel racing downhill, the reflection of the flames from the fire bouncing off its etched gold surface and prancing across the walls of the room. The compass kept spinning, and Malphas frowned until eventually, it started to slow, then stopped, pointing south-east.

"He's further away than I hoped," said Malphas. "The compass spun quite rapidly. It slows down the closer he gets."

"What is south-east of here?" asked Adalwolf.

"More of that infernal forest." Malphas paused and rubbed his chin. "And then the ocean."

"What if he boards a ship and travels far across the seas?"

"He won't. I have a feeling he'll walk right into Pergamos."

"Should we send scouts to find him?"

"This is the only blood compass left from the throne of the dead. The other four are missing, probably destroyed. I can't risk losing it again. However, you're right; we should send scouts. They may well stumble across him. I will gather the draughouls."

~ Chapter 27 ~

Tom hadn't given up. Yet. After finding Annian, he'd shuffled along behind her for another two days. Whenever she stopped for a rest, he'd camp nearby, trying not to fall asleep in case she disappeared again. He'd eaten all of his food and drunk all his water. Beneath the rabbit-fur coat Jameus had made him, Tom could feel his body wasting away. His feet and legs ached from walking, and his mind often wandered in disjointed thoughts, longing to return home to a simpler life. That wouldn't happen, though. Not unless he got answers. Not unless he reached Bindari.

As the sun waned, Annian rested the pull-bar of her cart on the ground, unhitched the harness from around her shoulders and began to set up camp among a grove of densely packed trees, collecting kindling for a fire. Two dozen steps away, Tom unshouldered his pack and slumped against a tree stump, setting himself to keep watch over her.

As she'd done the previous two nights, Annian took two sticks from the cart, one round, as long as her forearm, and as thick as her middle finger, the other a rectangle of hands length, thicker than the first with a bowl and notch cut into the wood. She placed the rectangle on the ground and gathered a handful of dry, dead grass that she piled beside the notch. Taking the long, round stick between flat palms, she placed its tip inside the bowl, stood the stick on its end and began to rub vigorously.

It twirled between palms gyrating against each other, and smoke rose from the bowl as the friction of the two pieces of wood rubbing together created hot dust that spilled into the pile of dry grass. She rubbed until enough of the hot dust had collected on top of the grass, then knelt and blew on the pile to feed air into the smoulder. It caught alight, and she moved the pile of now burning grass underneath her tepee of kindling.

To Tom, the whole process had a familiarity he had difficulty explaining. He vaguely recalled people back on Earth starting fires this way, although he wasn't sure where he'd seen it done or by whom.

Annian stood and warmed her hands over the growing fire. She was dressed in a knee-length, patchwork tunic, stitched together from animal skins as any free, wild grell would wear. Her attire reminded Tom of the tunic Grin had made him when he first arrived in Enthilen. The one Thaly said made Tom look like a grell child. He'd give anything to be tucked away safe and sound in Grin's milbi again. Even for one night.

He nestled his buttocks into the damp soil and fought to keep his eyes open, expecting Annian to eat her meal and then fall asleep. Instead, she surprised him, strolling over to where he sat.

"Hungry?" she asked.

"Yes, I'm starving," said Tom.

"Help make fish stew."

Tom nodded and collected his pack. They walked in silence back to Annian's camp, gathering more firewood along the way, then nestled in around the welcome fire. Annian prepared fish stew seasoned with mushrooms and herbs. Tom shivered, each exhale from his pursed mouth a white ghost drifting into the night.

"Aren't you cold?" he asked Annian.

She shrugged. "Grells cope with different seasons. Even old slaves. Yet bones ache more now. I have wilay-skin cloak. Thick fur. You want?"

"No. I'll be alright."

"Stubborn man. We almost at Babir Birramal."

"I need to go to Bindari," said Tom.

"Enough food only for one day. You have more?"

"My pack's empty other than a scrap of dried fish."

"A story instead." Annian swished water around her bowl, swallowing the last vestiges of the stew.

"What?"

"You tell story. Eat my food, swap for story. About family."

Annian waited in silence as thoughts swirled around Tom's mind in a vortex of turmoil. Secrets and burdens. He had plenty to choose from.

"I miss my mother," he said.

"You say she die?"

"That was a lie, Annian. Back in the hut, everything I told you about my past was a lie. Who would believe I'd used the eyes of lost souls to travel here from another world?"

"I believe now. Why miss mother?"

"I'm closest to her. She's been my best friend for most of my childhood. Some nights, I'd sit on her bed and talk forever about things happening in my life. She'd always listen. When I was younger, my mother had to work, and my grandmother helped raise me. I miss her too. She told me bedtime stories every night."

"What kind?"

"You wouldn't like them. My favourite author was Dr Seuss. He wrote silly rhymes."

"Rhymes?"

Tom scratched the dirt with a stick, wrestling with his imagination, then sat up straight and inhaled.

"And by the fire I sit, cradling stew in my lap

The smell of dried fish, hits my cold face like a slap

An old grell I did chase, and in the end, I caught

But it seems to me now, that the chase was for naught."

Annian cupped her hands together and smiled. "Very clever."

"My grandmother was killed when I was young. Right in front of me."

"By who?"

"Someone from this world. I think I found the killer in Laodicea. I'll know for sure when I see his mark."

Annian fixed her unblinking gaze on Tom, and all his defences withered. "The dark eyes brought me here from another world, but they won't take me home. And my grandmother's killer wants to kill me. Well, he wants King Adalwolf to kill me. I think it's got something to do with eternal life, though I can't be sure. When I reach Bindari, I'll find the answers I seek and be able to make sense out of all this. At the moment, it's all I've got to keep hold of. I've lost my friends, my family and my home. The promise of Bindari is the only reason I can still put one foot in front of the other."

*   *   *   *

The next morning, Tom woke to find Annian still in camp. They shared a meagre breakfast of cold yam mash, then Annian packed her things, and Tom resigned himself to another day walking behind her, hoping he wouldn't get lost. However, the old grell surprised him again.

"Cart heavy," said Annian. "You help pull it?"

Despite the promise of an extra burden, Tom's legs lightened at the thought. "Yes. Yes, I can."

Annian smiled. "Good. We walk together for while."

She discarded the harness, throwing it onto the cart tray, then she and Tom picked up the t-bar together and pulled the cart behind them. They soon trudged shoulder-to-shoulder along a narrow path between the conifer trees where the brown, dead pine needles thinned and rocks and bare soil poked out through the groundcover. Tom almost didn't notice when the first large, broad tree appeared with far-reaching branches and trident-shaped leaves the size of his chest turning brown with the cold.

"Now in Babir Birramal," said Annian.

Tom had returned to where it all started. *How far away is Grin's milbi?* he wondered.

The air felt warmer in the bosom of the forest, thick moss covering the ground and tassels of lichen clinging to tree branches swaying in a gentle breeze that carried familiar scents. Large, squawking birds, black with yellow patches in their tail feathers, careered overhead, looking like they would crash into a tree trunk before long. Grin would call them 'bilirr'. To Tom, they resembled black cockatoos.

The wonder of the forest soon dissipated when Tom thought Annian may now dismiss him. They'd reached Babir Birramal. No need for her to guide him any further.

"Do you want me to leave now?" he asked.

"No. Walk together while longer."

Tom sighed in relief. It seemed his persistence may have paid off. He tried to keep Annian talking, familiar and comfortable with her stilted vocabulary, a legacy of being taught basic Erstürmen by her overseer.

"Your facial crest is faded," he said. "I can't tell what it is."

"Dhundhu. Black swan."

"Did you think about returning to the wild grells?"

"No. Jameus offer freedom, but I owe him debt. And I love Melinda. Only leave when time to die."

"Are you afraid of dying?" As soon as the words left his lips, Tom screwed up his face. *That was a callous and stupid question.*

Annian didn't miss a step, marching forward with her head bowed, her long, grey hair dangling almost to her waist and threatening to tangle around the cart's pull-bar.

"No fear death. I leave mark. Others remember me."

"I tried to kill myself once."

Annian stopped, forcing Tom to do the same, and glared at him. "Why?"

"The future scared me. I thought the only way to stop worrying was to end it. I failed, of course. I can't even get that right."

"Foolish to think. More foolish to do. No failure if life continue. Future frightening or hopeful. Depends on," Annian tapped her temple with her finger, "inside head."

"How you manage your thoughts?" guessed Tom.

"Words, pictures inside head. Must tend like garden."

"My mum always said no-one can foresee the future. Who knows what might be around the corner? What you might achieve in life? Sometimes, though, it doesn't help. I feel like I'm floating in limbo, trapped between the child I used to be and the man I should be."

"Nothing good come easy. Welcome challenge. When challenge over-come, rewards follow. Enjoy simple things. Walk with friend. Blue sky. Forest scent after rain. Live for journey and leave mark, so others follow."

"What mark did you leave?"

"Mark left on young girl and her father, and now on you. I will be remembered."

Yes, thought Tom, *I'll remember Annian.*

By early afternoon, Annian couldn't continue, and they decided to rest until the next morning. Even though he had a flint, Annian taught Tom how to light a fire using the fire sticks, and together they made a thin soup and sat quietly enjoying the sounds of the forest. High in the canopy, a warbler trilled, and the breeze rustled dry leaves as he rested his back against a panalope tree and nestled his bottom into spongy, lime-coloured moss wedged between the tree's roots. Closing his eyes, he drifted off to sleep in the afternoon sun.

The onset of a dream ended abruptly with the ping of metal on metal and the whinny of a horse. Voices drifted through the trees, and Tom forced his eyes open.

Someone's close by. We need to hide.

Annian snored, lying asleep under her possum-skin cloak. He crawled over and shook her shoulder. "Wake up."

She jolted awake as three dishevelled soldiers dressed in filthy, dented armour, their eyes glowering with hunger and desperation, walked their horses into the camp. Tom recognised the Erstürmen symbol of the curled, two-headed snake embossed into the breastplates. Bloodstained saddlebags hung flaccid and unbuckled over the backsides of the gaunt and neglected horses, stinking black mud caked on their legs almost to the shoulder. Tom's stomach churned at the smell following the soldiers into camp, guessing they'd been living rough for many days.

"Whoa. What 'ave we 'ere?" The tallest soldier jerked the reins of his mount until the feeble horse stopped. Tom thought the beast may topple over.

"Boy and his grandma by da looks," said the second soldier, his mouth masked by a matted beard.

Tall Soldier dismounted, tethered his horse to a low hanging branch and walked over to the waning fire, warming his bony hands. "I think she's a grell," he said. "Look at her face. Low brow, slanty eyes, and she's got one of them ugly face tattoos."

Tom tried to think on his feet. "She's my slave."

"How come y'let her keep da tattoo?" asked Bearded Soldier.

"Didn't make her any prettier," said Tall Soldier, his companions laughing along with the apparent joke.

The third soldier, short and stocky, leaned forward in his saddle. "Looks like she couldn't hold a broom upright. You lost out 'ere, boy? Where y'headin? Dese are old paths."

"I'm taking my slave back to her forest home," said Tom.

"Why bother?" asked Tall Soldier. "Why not work her 'til she drops?"

"I have more respect for those in my service."

Bearded Soldier dismounted, tethered his horse and walked across to Annian's cart. "Let's see what you've got 'ere. Smoked fish. Haven't had dat in ages. We'll be keepin' dat."

I'm not going to miss it, thought Tom.

"I like da look of dat fur rug," said Short Soldier. "Dat would keep me nice and warm durin' dese bleak nights."

"I saw it first." Tall Soldier stepped over to Annian and yanked the cloak off her legs.

"No, y'didn't." Short Soldier dismounted and confronted his companion.

Bearded Soldier intervened. "Settle down. Settle down. Let's get da old bag to cook us some food. Ya don't mind us borrowin' yur slave for a while, do ya boy?"

"We don't have much food left," said Tom.

Bearded Soldier held a whole smoked fish aloft. "Dere's a bit 'ere. Enough for all three of us, I wager. At least more dan we had in a while."

"Dat's cos yur the worst hunter dis side of Süden Forst." Short Soldier laughed to himself.

Bearded Soldier ignored his companion and continued to rifle through Annian's belongings. Tom held his breath when the soldier unwrapped her family totems and raised one of the taper-candle shaped stones above his head, examining the swirl of white on pale-green softstone that glimmered under a waning sun. Tom remembered the totems inside Grin's milbi and Frennan's words about them. 'They are precious.'

"What are dese?" asked Bearded Soldier to no-one in particular. "Dey might be worth some coin."

357

"They're worthless," said Tom, hoping the soldiers would lose interest.

Tall Soldier marched over to his companion and snatched the totem from his hand. "I know what dey are. I seen other grells with 'em. Somethin' to do with family history. Is dat right, grell?"

Annian stayed silent, head bowed.

"Grell, I asked you a question." Tall Soldier raised his arm and flung the totem at Annian, striking her in the chest. She flinched, yet didn't cry out, gathering the totem from the ground and clutching it to her body.

"Dere are a lot of dem totems 'ere. We might be rich," said Bearded Soldier.

"Take the totems and leave us alone." As soon as he said it, Tom hated himself for dismissing Annian's valued possessions.

Tall Soldier placed his hand on the hilt of his sword and hovered over Tom. "We ain't goin' nowhere, boy. Not till we've had a feed."

"Where y'from?" Short Soldier asked Tom.

"Dorfisch."

"No wonder y'smell like rotten fish."

The soldiers laughed, took most of the supplies from the cart and placed the bounty in their saddlebags. As dusk settled on the forest, they stoked the fire and forced Annian to cook a meal for them with what little food remained, scoffing it down as soon as it was ready.

"Somethin' ain't right here," said Tall Soldier through a mouthful of fish stew. "How does a boy get a slave?"

"And one so old," said Bearded Soldier.

"I inherited her when my parents died," said Tom. "She has served our family for yarles. She's an excellent cook."

"I don't think much of dis stew." Tall Soldier tipped the remnants of his stew over the ground.

"Have ya tried grell?" asked Short Soldier.

"What?"

"Roasted grell. I've tried it. Not half bad."

"She'd be as tough as old boots," said Bearded Soldier.

"Not if we cook her long enough. Boil chunks of her flesh slowly in a pot. I got a pouch of seasonin' in me saddlebag. Seven Spices. From da Docklands. We'd be doing her a favour. She's gonna drop dead soon. Let's be merciful and end her misery now and fill our stomachs at da same time."

"We could eat her and keep da boy as our serf," said Tall Soldier.

"Yeah, he might come in handy," said Bearded Soldier.

"Ya ain't thinkin' of runnin' are ya, boy?" Tall Soldier brandished a knife and flashed a cruel smile at Tom.

From somewhere in the pit of his stomach, Tom drew forth a burst of defiant courage. "I'm not afraid of you. I've faced more menacing threats than you three idiots. I've been hunted by tainted grells, had vile princes try to rip my soul from my chest, and greedy merchants lock me in cabins to sell me for coin. Yet, here I am. They couldn't break me, and neither can you."

"Brave talk. But yur a coward, I reckon." Short Soldier stood, drew his sword and swung it at Tom. Annian lunged sideways, throwing her body in front of the blade. It cut into the animal-skin tunic covering her chest.

"No!" Tom picked up a rock and stood, ready to throw.

The other soldiers jumped to their feet and drew their weapons. Before they could deal another blow, a throwing knife whished through the night air and pierced the throat of the tall soldier who slumped to the ground.

Tom didn't stop to think. He swooped down and snatched the sword dropped by Tall Soldier. *Disarm* came Thaly's voice inside his head. He clenched his jaw and swung the sword at Short Soldier's bare hand, slashing across his knuckles. Short Soldier cried out and dropped his sword.

Shield breastplate has a gap under the arm. Tom feigned to strike Short Soldier in the head. As the soldier raised his arm to ward off the blow, Tom changed his sword's trajectory, thrusting it into the soldier's unprotected side. Metal crunched on bone as the blade slipped through a gap in the ribcage, sliding into the soldier halfway up the sword's fuller. Tom released his grip and staggered backwards.

Another knife whistled through the air and embedded in a tree trunk next to Bearded Soldier. He dropped his sword and stammered at the invisible threat hiding among the trees, "Alright, alright. I ain't goin' to hurt no-one."

"Leave your horses, supplies and weapons," came a man's voice. "Take only the clothes on your back and run. If I see you again, I'll kill you."

Bearded Soldier turned and scampered into the forest. Tall Soldier and Short Soldier lay beside each other, dead or dying, their blood spilling over the spongy moss.

Tom knelt by Annian's side, checking her injury.

"Cut not deep," she whispered.

"She's courageous," said a man, stepping into the light of the campfire. "You both are." He placed his foot on Short Soldier and drew the sword from his side, the man groaning with the pain, then plunged the blade into the soldier's neck. He died with a muted gurgle.

"The other one's already dead," said the man as he pulled back the hood of his cloak to reveal a weathered, unshaven face with a scarred chin. One arm hung loosely by his side.

"You saved our lives," said Tom. "Is your arm hurt?"

The man glanced absently at his left arm. "It was broken a while back. I expect the bones haven't knitted properly yet. Fortunately, these fools left a spare knife in one of their saddlebags, and I can throw with either hand. Is your slave wounded?"

"She's not my slave," said Tom.

Annian sat up. "Still here for while yet. Thank you." She pointed to her chest. "Annian weald-grell." Then at Tom. "Tom Anderson."

Tom flinched when Annian mentioned his name, but the stranger didn't react like he'd heard it before. *Why would he?*

"My name is Hadufuns Heine."

Tom knew the name. The Dobunni rebels had spoken about the murder of Ewald's brothers. *All* his brothers. "Hadufuns Heine is dead."

The man smiled. "I was left for dead, no doubt. The Dobunni saved me, such is the irony."

Tom relaxed at the mention of the Dobunni. "You really are Ewald's brother?"

"The last one left, it seems."

I was supposed to help assassinate Ewald, thought Tom. *And your nephew, Adalwolf. Now Adalwolf wants to kill me. I don't know if I can trust you.*

Annian didn't appear to have such reservations. "Join us," she said, waving her hand at the dying fire. "No food to share, but fire still warm."

Hadufuns took off his dirty, brown cloak to reveal equally tatty clothes underneath. Garb hardly befitting a prince. He crouched and unshouldered a backpack, pulling out a dead possum. "One of my snares caught this. We can skin her and cook the meat."

Tom took the sword the Bearded Soldier had dropped, and Annian glared at him. *He's Ewald's brother,* thought Tom. *He might have been sent to find me.* He placed the sword beside Annian's cloak and began to roll the short soldier's dead body away from the fire. *Another one dead. First Adcock, now this stranger. Why does it make me feel so ill?*

Hadufuns removed the knife from Tall Soldier's throat and dragged him from the campsite and into a thicket of shrubs.

"This trail not well known," Annian said to Hadufuns.

"I've travelled it before when seeking solitude. I spotted these soldiers a while back. Most likely renegades from Süden Forst. I heard Field Commander Theodoar has abandoned his charge, and the outpost has been taken over by impoverished militants loyal to no-one."

"The soldiers were Erstürmen, and you're an Erstürmen prince," said Tom.

"They were about to kill you. I have no obligation to murderers. Enough innocent blood has already been spilled in recent days. You *are* innocent, aren't you?"

Yes. No, thought Tom. He ignored Hadufuns' question, and they sat beside the fire while Annian skinned the possum.

"Where come from?" she asked Hadufuns.

"I escaped the attack on Laodicea and travelled to Gestade with other war refugees."

"You didn't happen to cross paths with a wild grell called Grin or a Dobunni rebel called Athalee?" asked Tom, thinking, hoping his friends may have reached the mainland.

"There were grells and rebels among the refugees. I didn't ask their names."

"Why leave Gestade?" asked Annian.

"The new ruler of Enthilen, Malphas, wants me dead."

Malphas, thought Tom. The old man on Hansen's Bluff. Nanna's murderer. He longed to blurt out — *Malphas wants me dead, too* — but kept his mouth shut, wary of Hadufuns' allegiances.

Hadufuns continued, "Soon, Malphas will send his hunters to find me. It's not safe to share my company, and I won't dally here much longer lest I put your lives in more danger."

"Old paths hard to find," said Annian.

"Those soldiers found them easy enough."

After a meal of possum, the three travellers talked into the night. Hadufuns spoke about the fall of Laodicea and the rise of Malphas and King Adalwolf. Tom didn't reveal he already knew some of the story, or talk about his encounter with Adalwolf and Malphas on Hansen's Bluff.

"If what you say is true, it seems the rule of Adalwolf and his master will be an enduring blight on this land," said Tom. "Why not challenge for the throne?"

"Enthilen needs a leader to unite all its cultures. Erstürmen, Dobunni and grells. I'm not that leader. Replacing one Erstürmen king with another will continue to drive a wedge between us. And Malphas will not relinquish power so easily."

"Malphas old man. Easy to defeat?" queried Annian.

"There's something about him I don't understand. He's old, but he hasn't aged as he should. His strength seems undiminished by time, and he keeps his secrets close."

Tom sensed Hadufuns wrestling with his thoughts, confusion and torment etched on the prince's face. He knew the signs of self-doubt and depression. It made him want to reach out and reassure Hadufuns he wasn't the only one plagued by the shadow of Malphas. But it would require divulging all his secrets, and he wasn't ready for that yet.

Hadufuns got to his feet and yawned. "I'll make a bed nearby. If you have further trouble, I'll hear your calls for help."

* * * *

The next morning, Tom woke to find four fresh rabbit carcasses stacked beside the smouldering fire. Hadufuns' snares had produced a fine bounty, and they'd eat well for a couple of days. Annian still slept, the rigours of the journey taking their toll. He slipped out from under the possum-skin cloak he and Annian shared to keep warm, and stumbled bleary-eyed out into the silent, frost-covered forest to collect firewood. Ice crunched under his shoes as he pulled his coat up high around his neck.

No dawn chorus greeted him, and Tom shivered. *Too damn cold even for the birds.* He wandered around the outskirts of the camp, piling deadwood into the crux of his elbows, and thought about turning back when he came across Hadufuns' camp bed; two blankets tied in a roll with a leather strap. A walking stick leaned against the roll, and a short sword lay across a backpack.

Hadufuns must be close by, thought Tom. "Hadufuns?" No reply. The rising sun peeked through a gap in the trees and started to thaw a wedge of frosty ground. Wisps of mist curled up to the forest canopy, hanging like frozen ghosts above the prickly yuri shrubs and fallen, rotting tree trunks.

Tom called again. "Hadufuns?"

Maybe he's with Annian? As he turned from the bedroll, a glint of sunlight bouncing off metal near the base of a panalope tree caught his eye. He edged over to the tree, and there, resting up against its trunk, was Prince Hadufuns, his body slouched, chin resting on his chest. Tom stepped around the tree trunk and dropped the bundle of kindling.

Hadufuns' pale, lifeless face stared blankly at the ground. Blood, still warm, ebbed from a gash across his throat, and the prince's right hand dangled limply by his side, fingers cradling the handle of a knife. Tom dropped to his knees and shook Hadufuns' shoulder, causing the body to topple to the ground. He felt for a pulse, but found nothing, so he knelt there, not knowing what to do or think, mesmerised by the blood that dripped, dripped, dripped onto a patch of white, frosty grass. A thought jumped into his head. *Don't touch the blood! Stupid little boy.*

Tom took Hadufuns' knife, wiped the blade clean on the top of his pants and studied the ornate handle carved from bone or ivory that fit neatly into his palm. Etched near the heel of the blade was a picture of a wolf's head, howling to the moon. Tom ran the knife across his finger and flinched as the razor-sharp blade sliced his skin and blood seeped into his palm. It wouldn't take much to end it. A quick slash and it would all be over.

Hadufuns looks so peaceful.

No need to worry anymore about finding Bindari. About confronting Malphas or Adalwolf, or how to get home. No need to feel guilty about failing to save Nanna. Or losing Grin and Thaly. Or killing Adcock. All the anxiety would end.

Don't think about it. Do it.

Tom removed his coat, laid it on the ground and pulled the right sleeve of his shirt up to his elbow, exposing a bare forearm.

He spoke to himself in English, "*Lengthways. Cut lengthways, not across. If you want to do it properly, cut along your wrist and arm. It'll all be over. All this worry. All this fear. Malphas is going to find you. You can't bring him to justice. You were stupid to think you could. You're never going home. End it. Lengthways. Do it. Just fucking do it.*"

Tom put the edge of the blade against his skin and pressed down.

~ Chapter 28 ~

In the vertraúlich of Sardis' kirika, Anselm cinched the beaded white cord around his sangria robes, the official attire for curates of the highest order, as he prepared to address his parishioners. Lothar may be calling himself Hoch-Vater of Enthilen, but as curate of the inner circle of Sardis, Anselm still considered himself the prime theological authority in Enthilen. A power he would refuse to surrender under any circumstances.

The levit, a young boy employed to assist the curate in daily tasks, polished Anselm's pointed white shoes with animal fat until the leather shone like a pearl. Anselm peeked through the curtains of the vertraúlich into an almost empty nave. Less than a third of his usual congregation warmed the chapel benches. It seemed the remainder had already left for Pergamos. His mind nagged him to do the same. The once royal city of Sardis was dying, and curate to a middling garrison sounded particularly unappealing. He may be Steward for the time being, but when Krieg returned, Anselm would begin preparations to travel to Pergamos and challenge Lothar's misbegotten authority.

Anselm's thoughts turned to the grell soldiers he'd sent to Slumstadt to burn the pit of destitution to the ground before the next sunrise. He doubted the citizens remaining in Sardis would miss the shantytown. It had always been the royal city's abscess, and it should have been lanced long ago.

And what of Rostard? thought Anselm. Did his lover have any chance of surviving the attack on the Dobunni rebels in the Scaur Hills, and would he join Anselm in a pilgrimage to Pergamos? The affair had been fleeting, and his attachment to Rostard no stronger than a cotton thread. If the soothsayer returned, Anselm had few qualms about breaking the thread.

He waved the levit away, picked up a copy of the scripture verses from a lectern, and pushed through the gap in the curtains. The congregation stood, each one holding a lit candle balanced on a chamberstick, and bowed their heads as Anselm strode over to the pulpit and smacked the scripture verses down onto the lustrous timber. He need not open the holy book. He'd memorised every word.

Wavering on bandy legs, he cleared his throat and proclaimed to his diminished flock, "Let darkness descend."

"And engulf us all," they replied in unison.

"For in the darkness, Volerdie will reveal his paradise. Sit, please."

The congregation sat, and Anselm placed his hand on the black cover of the scripture verses. He stood in silence, contemplating his next words, wondering whose authority he championed by uttering them and if any word he spoke mattered. It *would* matter, he decided, if the congregation read them with him.

Anselm turned his head and cried out, "Boy!"

The levit appeared from behind the curtains and stood with his hands clasped in front, head bowed.

"Bring out twelve copies of the scripture verses," said Anselm.

The boy's head jerked up, his eyes wide. Anselm thought he mouthed the word 'why'.

"Hurry now," said Anselm. "The padlock on the bureau is open."

The levit scuttled back through the curtains. The congregation stared at Anselm, clearly unsure what came next. Every Erstürmen man, woman and child knew it was forbidden for anyone except curates to access the scripture verses. To read the verses. Execution would be the punishment for such a transgression.

However, times are changing, thought Anselm, and blasphemous supplanters in Pergamos threaten the very foundation of Volerdie's authority.

The levit pushed back through the curtains balancing a dozen books in his arms, piled up to his chin. He almost tripped on the altar as he carried the books to Anselm.

"Put them on the edge of the stage," said the curate.

The boy crouched and stacked the twelve copies of the scripture verses before returning to his sanctuary behind the curtains.

"Take a copy to share among you," Anselm said to the congregation.

Some of them gasped and sat open-mouthed. Others turned to their companions with confused looks. None dared to be the first to stand.

"Volerdie's authority is vested in me, and I give you his permission to read his words. No-one will punish you. I've been appointed Steward of Sardis, at least temporarily, by order of King Adalwolf. Come to the stage and collect a copy of the scripture verses."

The bravest among them stood — a young woman no older than sixteen harvest seasons with radiant blond hair and inquisitive eyes. Anselm thought she resembled a divine spirit. She placed her candle on the pew, then crept to the stage like a blind thief searching for a path to the most precious of jewels. When the young woman placed her quivering hand on the first copy of the verses, she looked again at Anselm, and he nodded to her and smiled. She smiled back, clutched the book to her chest and returned to her seat.

The other parishioners followed her lead until everyone in the congregation could read the forbidden words.

"We begin on page twenty-four, verse seven:twelve." Anselm waited for the rustle of turning pages to settle before continuing, "And Volerdie wrote, *Beware the supplanter of my authority. The duplicitous changelings of Volerdie's Lore who claim to act in my name, yet seek reward only for themselves. For there are none I despise more than such creatures; none who deserve more to wither under the fury of my judgement. Let all who face these usurpers rise up against them. For paradise will never be revealed while they covet my throne. Wrest them from that seat of power, and prepare to bask in the glory of my return.*"

*   *   *   *

"Watch out!"

Rosalie started, still unaccustomed to Zaria's outbursts. Tilly didn't flinch, the little girl tending the fire inside the Slumstadt hovel and humming to herself.

She turned and smiled at Rosalie. "Does your head hurt again?"

Rosalie pulled her fingers from her throbbing temples, examining the tips as if they were covered in blood. An aching, craving mind needed another swirl. Now.

"You should stop goin'," said Tilly.

"Going where?" asked Rosalie.

"I've seen you. Walkin' up the street where the fine houses are."

"Did you follow me?" snapped Rosalie. She didn't need anyone watching over her. Judging her.

Tilly ignored Rosalie's question, wrapped a rag around her bare hand to stop it getting burned, then took a rusty metal pot from the fire and scooched over to her grandfather. "I have soup, Ompa."

Zaria sat up, using the fancy cane to lever his body into a sitting position.

Tilly tipped watery soup into a wooden cup and blew over the top

369

to cool it. "Careful, it's hot," she said, lifting the cup carefully to Zaria's lips as he groped blindly with his mouth to find the cup's edge.

The old man's slurps screaked inside Rosalie's mind like a wailing cat.

"Are you happy here?" asked Tilly.

It took a while for Rosalie to realise the question was directed at her. "Is anybody happy in Slumstadt?"

"You're always tryin' to escape with that blue stuff. I seen others usin' it. Stumblin' along the streets in a dream or lyin' in the mud with silly grins on their face like someone gave them a bag of coin. My friend Robbie says it's poison. His big brother says it's magic. Maybe I should try some?"

"No," said Rosalie. "Don't do that."

"Why not? You do it."

"I'm not used to this life. It's…"

"Worse than the life you had in Sardis?"

"Yes. Do you understand?"

"When the soldiers took me right into the middle of Sardis, I saw all the fancy houses and pretty women wearin' beautiful dresses. Sometimes I dream about them. I wish I could make the dreams come whenever I wanted."

Zaria knocked the wooden cup out of Tilly's hands and yelled, "Fire coming, burning alive, fire coming…"

"Ompa!" cried Tilly. "Stop that. I'm so tired…" She mopped her grandfather's brow with the sleeve of her filthy dress. "There's no fire. There's nothin' here." She picked the cup off the floor, tipped in more soup and held it up to Zaria's lips. He shook his head and collapsed back onto the wicker mat he used for a bed.

Rosalie became mesmerised by Zaria's cane with the flawless, polished wood and the golden handle. It must be worth something, and she had no coin. Nothing to buy another vial of embruisia. A thought set in her mind. A horrible, desperate thought. Was she willing to steal an old man's only possession from people who'd provided her food and shelter? He wouldn't need it for much longer. He'd be dead soon, and Tilly wouldn't have a use for it.

"We need more water, Tilly," said Rosalie, "and I'm too tired to go to the river."

Tilly put the rusty pot of anaemic soup beside the fire. "I guess I'll have to go. Will you watch the soup for me?"

Rosalie nodded. The little girl gathered an empty waterskin and ducked out of the canvas flap that served as the hovel's door. Zaria lay on his sleeping mat, already snoring and mumbling to himself, his wrinkled, blotched hand clutching the shaft of the walking cane lying across his chest. Rosalie crawled over to him and sat near the cane, resting her hand at its tip. Zaria snorted and shifted his body. She watched the canvas flap in case Tilly returned.

She won't be back for a while, thought Rosalie. Get it done.

Rosalie wrapped the quaking fingers of her left hand around the bottom of the cane and tried to pull it free, but it wouldn't give. With her right hand, she began peeling Zaria's fingers from the wood; his middle finger, thumb, index finger. She yanked again.

As the cane fell loose onto the ground, Zaria bolted upright, turned his blind, milky eyes to Rosalie and said, "Get out now. While you still can."

Head pounding, she grabbed the walking cane, burst through the canvas flap and sprinted down the dirty street.

With the cane tucked under her dress, Rosalie trotted up towards Elmbray's house as the sun set over Slumstadt, not having the will to try selling the treasure in the market. Instead, she would trade it for embruisia. She'd almost reached the porch with the flickering blue light when Snick appeared from a side street.

"Hey, Rosalie. Lookin' t'swirl?"

"Is Elmbray home?" she asked.

"Nah, he's gone away for a while. What y'got there?" Snick's eyes lingered on the heel of the polished timber poking out from under the torn hem of Rosalie's dress.

"When's he getting home?" she asked.

"Dain't know. Dain't matter though, I've got what y'need. He gave me his best stuff before he left."

Ignoring the pangs of regret, she pulled the walking cane out. "Trade?"

"Let's have a look." Snick snatched the treasure from her, turning it around in his hands as if appraising a rare antique. "This handle gold?"

"Yes," lied Rosalie.

He picked at the eagle's head with a long, cracked fingernail and examined the flake of gold adhering to the tip of his finger. "You ain't tryin' to short me, are ya? I dain't think this is real gold."

"Gold-plated then. It's definitely gold-plated."

"*Hmmm.*" Snick turned the walking cane around and around in his hands, looking down it lengthways like he was checking the straightness of an arrow.

Rosalie's patience abandoned her. "For goodness sake, do you want it or not?"

"One swirl," he said.

"What!?"

"Enough for one swirl."

She dug her thumbs in around the base of her skull as another headache worsened.

"Take it or leave it," said Snick, holding the walking stick towards Rosalie.

"Alright," she said.

He opened his horsehair coat, slipped the cane under his belt and pulled a bottle of embruisia from an inside pocket. Rosalie had never seen so much embruisia at once, and she thought about snatching the bottle and running for her life, but didn't have the energy, and the wiry Snick looked fast and unyielding. He unscrewed the bottle's cap, took an empty vial from another pocket and carefully tipped three drops of cerulean honey into it, then popped a cork on top, handing the vial to Rosalie.

"Need a new needle?" he asked.

Rosalie shook her head. "I've got one."

Snick smiled, and Rosalie felt like a thousand spiders had covered her naked body, skittering and scuttling across bare, fragile skin. She clutched the vial and marched down the street, away from Snick and the lure of the blue light. Impatient to reach the river, Rosalie slumped in the mud beside the stump of a dead tree, pulled the cork from the vial and fumbled around in the cuff of her dress where she'd stuck a needle. Scraping the needle around the bottom of the glass, twirling the blue honey like a caterpillar spinning a cocoon, she encased the metal tip with every last drop of embruisia. Hand shaking, she stabbed at her wrist, forcing the needle and sticky blue under her skin, closed her eyes and waited, ready to embrace the swirl.

Nothing happened.

Rosalie opened her eyes and examined the tip of the needle, thinking the embruisia may still be there. A drop of glistening blue clung to the metal, hopefully enough to make a difference. She stabbed again, deeper this time, grimacing at the sting.

Nothing.

No. No. No.

She stabbed again, and blood started to trickle down her arm. Blood mixed with cerulean honey — red, black and blue.

Still nothing.

Rosalie screamed, "Damn. Damn. DAMN!" Her head thumped, louder and heavier than ever before. She tossed the vial into the mud in disgust. A knot set in her chest, and she vomited a stream of blood across her legs, thick and ebony, with the reek of an open sewer.

It'll pass, it'll pass. Wait it out.

Clasping her blood-soaked knees to her chest, she closed her eyes, fell onto the ground and curled up like a baby.

Despite the throbbing ache, she must have slept or passed out. When she opened her eyes again, the full moon of Bargan and the three-quarter moon of Seena illuminated the street so brightly, it seemed a new dawn would arrive imminently. A haze hung in the night like a fine mist, motionless and silent. She breathed in and almost gagged on the ashen, stinging smell of smoke.

Sitting up, she looked back to Elmbray's house. In the distance, a tall, blocky shape charged across the street carrying a flaming torch and disappeared into someone's yard. Screams filled Rosalie's head, and she thought she might be having a bad swirl. The blocky shape appeared again, taking the form of a massive, hulking grell with dried black mud caked all over its naked body. The giant ran onto the porch of a house and touched the firebrand to the timber wall. It caught alight like wood soaked in oil.

The grell ran back onto the street the same time Snick ambled out from one of his hiding places, unaware of what was happening around him. With the grell arsonist upon him, he spun around to meet a flailing torch that smacked into his horsehair coat, sending glowing cinders shooting into the night and setting a fire in the fabric. It exploded like dry kindling.

Rosalie thrust her hands over her ears to block out Snick's baleful, horrifying wails. He ran for a moment, like a giant rushlight, then dropped to the ground, writhing in the mud to extinguish the flames.

The grell stepped over his victim and made a path straight towards Rosalie.

Get up, get up.

She half-stood and stumbled away, focussed on making her legs move one after the other as the smoke swirled around her, down the hill overlooking Slumstadt, towards the amber glow of sunrise. But it wasn't sunrise. Rosalie stopped and caught her breath. Before her, Slumstadt burned. A colossal curtain of flame reached into the night, plumes of acrid black smoke funnelling across the faces of the moons. Hundreds of hovels had been set alight like a city of bonfires, endless rows of flaming shacks collapsing onto each other, feeding the ravenous fire as fear feeds a monster.

Amid the thousands of petrified citizens crashing and stampeding through the labyrinth of streets, two more monstrous grells fought against the crowd, one throwing buckets of oil onto canvas and skins while the other set the oil aflame.

Tilly's down there.

Rosalie ran, faster than she thought she could, down the slope and into the shantytown. Her holey boots slipped on the mud, and she tumbled backwards, crashing to the ground. She got up and started running again, her torso leaning ahead of her legs, trying to keep her balance while sprinting forward. As she reached the first row of hovels, the heat from the flames scalded her face. Rosalie took off her cotton dress and draped it over her head and shoulders, leaving only delicate undergarments to protect the rest of her body from the furious fire. With everything alight, finding the right hovel would be nigh impossible. But she had to. Tilly and Zaria might still be there. She pushed into the street against a crush of people running the other way, fleeing the flames like vermin jumping a burning ship. Some of the people were on fire, stumbling into canvas walls that exploded in flame. The horror closed in around Rosalie. A screaming, jostling, chaotic madness of desperation and awful, painful death.

She fought against the crowd and drove herself forward, passing burning hovel after burning hovel until she reached a street corner she recognised. Every shelter was aflame except one, hers. She rushed inside to find Tilly trying to get her grandfather on his feet.

Rosalie grabbed Tilly's arm. "We have to get out of here."

"I'm not leavin' Ompa. Someone stole his cane."

"Forget about the cane. We have to go."

The little girl screamed, "Not without Ompa!"

"I stole it," said Rosalie.

Tilly started to cry. "Why'd you do that?"

Rosalie crouched, slung Zaria's arm over her shoulder and tried to lift the old man. Despite him being nothing more than skin and bones, he felt heavy, and she dropped to her knees. "I'm sorry, Tilly. I can't do it."

"Move, Ompa," pleaded Tilly, pulling at his shirt. But her grandfather lay back onto the ground and rolled away.

Rosalie thought she heard him say something in the hushed, quiet tones of a man who knew he was about to die. *Leave me be.* She clenched her jaw, stood and grabbed Tilly's arm, lifting the little girl to her feet. "I'm not going to let you die here."

"Let me go!" Tilly turned and pummelled Rosalie's stomach with tiny fists. "Why'd you come here? Things got worse when you arrived. Leave Ompa and me alone. Leave us alone!" She pulled away from Rosalie, knelt and kissed her grandfather on the forehead.

Rosalie waited to allow a last act of affection. Then she bent down, wrapped her arm around Tilly's waist, and heaved the little girl up, dragging her kicking and screaming out of the hovel and back into the chaotic streets.

Rosalie ran with the crowd now, pushing and fighting her way to the river, the only safe place in this demonic inferno. Tilly's resistance diminished, and the sobbing little girl found her own feet and ran beside Rosalie, both of them wheezing and coughing from the fumes of blazing poverty. Rosalie wondered which of the smoke or the oppressive heat that drowned her near-naked body in sweat would kill her first.

They fell over the lip of a steep embankment and tumbled down to the edge of the Anchep River. Crowds had gathered in the water, fighting against the current rushing past their waists like a forest of saplings trying to stay grounded amid a flood. A burning man jumped down the embankment and flung himself into the water head first.

A cleansing before the end, thought Rosalie, unmoved by the trauma. She grabbed Tilly's hand and dragged her into the river.

Tilly pulled back. "I can't swim."

"Would you rather drown or burn?" snapped Rosalie. She picked up the little girl and clutched her to her chest, wading deeper into the water. They turned to watch Slumstadt groan and blister. Many of the hovels had already collapsed, lying one over the other like sooty charcoal blankets surrounded by dying fountains of flame.

"Goodbye, Ompa!" yelled Tilly.

Goodbye, Ompa, thought Rosalie. Goodbye, Slumstadt. Goodbye... everything.

"We'll find somewhere else," said Rosalie. "I promise. We'll find a better place to live."

Tilly wrapped her arms around Rosalie's neck, and Rosalie kissed her on the cheek.

"I promise," said Rosalie. "We're not giving up."

~ Chapter 29 ~

Emelin, Alfred and Maxton stood behind the parapets of Bagendon's northern wall, surrounded by the threatening night. In front of them, campfires burned among the hills like a field of fiery daisies, each one warming a cohort of Erstürmen soldiers. The enemy numbered close to three thousand with over forty armed grells among the attackers, led by Krieg, the tainted red grell.

Had the grells formed an alliance with the Erstürmen? wondered Emelin. The thought seemed preposterous. Maxton had seen Krieg leading the barbarians in the attack on Laodicea. It appeared the tainted grell had an intimidating capacity to gather forces for war.

Lined up along the top of the north wall, a Bagendon force of less than one thousand stood transfixed; weary or injured soldiers from the Laodicea campaign, old men and women hardly able to stand upright let alone fight, and children, some decked in suits of chainmail with hems dragging on the ground. The thought of children fighting monsters to protect the promise of their future cut deeply into Emelin's sensibilities. She accepted the mantle of leader, even though she felt like a farmer pushing lambs into the butcher's holding pen.

Behind the north wall, Dayna stood among an anxious crowd with her sword drawn as if the enemy had already breached the gate. Emelin sensed her young daughter's naïve mind oscillating between bravado and dread, her pale eyes darting among her companions who stood shoulder-to-shoulder beside her. Dayna had never experienced the madness and chaos of battle. The reek of gushing blood as it pooled on the ground. The agonising screams of the fallen. The terror of savage eyes with no glint of mercy. Naivety was Dayna's shield. Soon, it would be shattered into a hundred pieces.

Alfred paced back and forth across the top of the wall. "Our weapons are poor. I've seen some holding no more than sharpened sticks. And most have no armour. Tunics and leggings won't stop the slash of a sword. We should have fled when we had the chance."

Emelin tensed. "They would have hunted us like dogs. Behind these walls, we might at least hold them off."

Alfred stopped pacing and searched the night. "When will they come?"

"A desire to hasten the embrace of death destroys all hope." She glanced at Alfred, then back to the field of fires laying siege to Bagendon. "Grell soldiers. Who would have thought?"

"Why are they fighting for the Erstürmen?" asked Maxton.

"With Krieg in command, it appears the Erstürmen are fighting for the grells. Tainted grells. The world we once knew died with Ewald. Although his son sits on the throne, we face something other than the Erstürmen Kingdom. Something new and wholly depraved."

A soldier raced up the steps and interrupted Emelin. "You're wanted at the south gate. We have visitors."

She nodded at Maxton and Alfred, they'd keep watch during her absence, and followed the soldier through the centre of an empty town, every resident either armed and waiting at a wall or cowering inside their home. As they reached the south gate, the moonlight revealed a welcome surprise — a cluster of small shadows holding spears that rose above their heads. Two or three dozen mouldewerps. More than she'd ever seen.

"Do any of them speak Erstürmen?" Emelin whispered to the soldier.

"One does. He seems to be their leader."

Emelin approached, hands held out front. "Welcome. I am Emelin Wallace, leader of the Dobunni in Bagendon."

A werp stepped forward. "I am Wirrikow, son of Dwarrow."

"I know Dwarrow. I didn't realise he had any children."

"He gave birth to me before his change," said Wirrikow.

"Gave birth...before...?"

Wirrikow didn't offer an explanation to gratify Emelin's confusion, and she had more important things on her mind. "I'm sorry we don't have time for formal greetings, and my question may seem odd, but why are you here?"

"You have an army on your doorstep," said Wirrikow. "On *our* doorstep. We're here to help defend our home. Our weapons are basic, but the elders would not have you stand alone."

Emelin dropped to her knees and hugged Wirrikow. "Thank you. Your presence here means a lot."

She stood and led the werps to the top of the north wall, amid murmurs of surprise and confusion among the other defenders of Bagendon, and together they continued their watch over the enemy. Bargan and Seena drifted down to the horizon, Seena the first to disappear behind a ridgeline. Darkness descended on the town as a hurna blared across the Scaur Hills from the enemy camp. Burning torches bobbed in the night, gathering together in rectangular formations of one-to-two hundred each and marching to the north wall.

"They're so confident of victory they announce their attack, then advertise their positions with lit torches," said Alfred.

"They want us to see the end coming," said Emelin. "They want us to give up before they even reach the gate."

"They're not targeting the gate," said Maxton. "They're coming for the wall first."

Emelin squeezed the handle of her halberd as cracks and booms echoed through the hills. The Erstürmen had sprung some of the Dobunni traps, sending boulders rolling and tumbling onto unsuspecting attackers. Cheers rang out from atop Bagendon's walls, almost masking the screams of those trapped beneath the rubble.

Some of the firebrands went dim, but not enough, thought Emelin. They're still coming.

Out of the darkness lurched a dozen grell slaves carrying limp Erstürmen soldiers likely killed or maimed by the Dobunni traps. The grells threw the bodies against the sharpened ends of the timber palisade defence that ringed Bagendon's walls.

Emelin looked on in horror. "What are they doing?"

"Making stepladders from the corpses," said Maxton.

Enemy soldiers began to clamber over the bodies, and Emelin raised and lowered her hand, signalling Dobunni archers who sent volleys of arrows into the Erstürmen ranks. More torches fell, but the assault spurred the enemy onwards. The grell slaves ripped palisade logs from the ground creating a space for soldiers to funnel through. They raced to the base of the north wall and hoisted ladders against the timber merlons. For the first time, Emelin faced her foe up close. Erstürmen soldiers clad in leather armour scurried up the rungs, breaching the parapet despite the rain of Dobunni arrows.

"Push the ladders back!" she screamed. However, hooks on the top rungs gripped the wall like the talons of an eagle.

Another ladder smacked into the wall, and then another. The assault distracted Emelin's attention.

"Battering ram!" yelled Maxton beside her. A tree trunk encased in metal and carried by six grell slaves lurched towards the north gate.

"Aim for the battering ram!" Emelin screamed to her archers.

Arrows flew from behind the parapets, felling two of the grell slaves. Their demise brought forth a more hideous spectacle. Armoured giants lumbered through the ranks of Erstürmen soldiers, the tallest and broadest of them leading the way, his dark red skin glinting in the torchlight. An arrow struck his shoulder in the gap between the edge of his pauldron and bare neck. He looked at the projectile with disdain before breaking off the end like a twig stuck in his clothes.

Wish we had time to poison *all* the arrows, thought Emelin.

Two grell soldiers replaced the fallen slaves, carrying the battering ram to the gate.

"Heave!" came a call from the enemy.

The north wall under Emelin's feet shook as the metal end of the battering ram slammed into the timber gate. Grell soldiers formed a shield wall above the war machine and began to chant a rhythm to keep the battering ram in time.

"Thrum. Heave. Smash. Thrum. Heave. Smash."

She turned away to look for Dayna on the other side of the gate. Breaking dawn accentuated every flinch coming from her daughter's body, reacting to the *thud, thud, thud* of the battering ram smashing into the north gate. Dayna's sword fell from her trembling hand onto the ground. As she bent over to pick it up, Emelin wanted to call out. *Flee! Run!* Run for the south gate, into the maze of the Scaur Hills and never look back.

Alfred yelled in Emelin's ear, "We need to...," but his words were cut short when a lance hurtled through the air and split open his chest. He tumbled over the parapets the same time the timber of the north gate shattered in a terrifying crash. The gate swung open, the rebel fighters inside ducking to avoid a hail of splinters. The monstrous grell soldiers came first, pouring inside the walls like a flood, their oiled muscles glinting in the torchlight, heads masked by menacing grilled helmets blacker than the night. They bolted towards Dayna and the other defenders.

"Sheer!" yelled Emelin, and from the side of the gate, a massive timber log swung across the entrance, knocking the first line of grells flying. It swung back again, but the enemy was ready for it now, falling onto their chests to duck beneath the swaying threat.

As the grells regained their feet and rushed forward, a dozen werps dropped from the top of the north wall, their spears thrust downwards, and embedded stone blades into grell necks and shoulders. The raining assault caused a moment of chaos among the enemy, and Emelin almost cheered aloud. Her mind screamed to the ground forces, *attack now!* This was the time for the defenders to advance while the enemy was disorientated. But she couldn't give the order. Her daughter stood in the front line of fighters, and she couldn't give the order.

Maxton didn't hesitate. He rushed down the stairs and into the throng of confused fighters, slashing his sword into grell chests above the plackart strapped to their stomachs. To Emelin's surprise, Maxton felled two of the giants. Hope is not lost, she thought, until the enemy regrouped and met the Dobunni. Swords, axes and halberds clashed in a frantic clanging of metal. Erstürmen soldiers from the King's Shield surrounded Maxton, swinging their halberds and slicing at his body. His sword fell to the ground, and he collapsed.

Krieg came, towering over everyone, even the other grells, a red and black monster sucking all the light around him into a bottomless abyss. He swung his spiked mace into Maxton's chainmail coif like a farmer attacking a head of wheat with a sickle. The blow pulled the air from Emelin's chest, and she turned away. When she looked back, Krieg was on the move, and for some reason, some inexplicable reason, he marched straight for Dayna, her sword held aloft like a candle against a howling wind.

"No!" Emelin cried, sprinting down the steps with her halberd held at the ready. She reached the ground as Dayna swung her sword, nicking

Krieg's bare stomach. The blood hardly showed against his garnet skin. Emelin pictured a cruel grin behind the grill of Krieg's helmet as he clutched the tip of Dayna's sword and wrenched it from her grasp with his gauntleted hand.

Emelin raced to her daughter, who had dropped to her knees in a cowering surrender. Krieg whirled the mace above his head, preparing to end Dayna's life, when something fell from the sky and landed on his shoulders, knocking him off balance.

Wirrikow bounced from Krieg's back and rolled along the ground among trampling feet. The werp's bravery stung Emelin into action. She leapt into battle, planting herself between Krieg and Dayna, and thrust her halberd at the red grell. He dodged the blade and swung his mace simultaneously, cleaving the halberd's timber handle in two. She screamed, the force of the impact yanking her left shoulder from its socket.

Dayna clutched at Emelin's waist like a child hoping a mother's love could protect her from the red monster. With her right arm, Emelin pulled her daughter up off the ground. They would face Krieg standing. Defiant and proud. Yielding only to death.

~ Chapter 30 ~

Grin navigated the fields of tightly packed, razor-sharp rocks hidden beneath blankets of moss and lichen surrounding Dalman, leading Thaly to the site of the garrabari, a clearing in dense forest that could accommodate a gathering of hundreds of grells. They climbed down a steep ravine, then up the other side using tree roots that stuck out from the crumbling soil as handrails, and rockfaces as footholds to lever themselves up. A rock worked loose under Grin's bare feet, and he yelled a warning to Thaly as it tumbled down towards her. She covered her head and ducked, the rock skirting past her and into the soggy depths below.

As Grin scrambled over the lip of the ravine, Dalman emerged through a single line of trees, the clearing already crowded with stone- and weald-grells encircling a campfire shadowed by the boulder of Marradir, as large as any milbi. On the face of the rock, the stone- and weald-grells had etched the wording of the truce that had kept the peace since the tribal war many generations past. Dangal shelters made of branches lashed together with twine and covered with thatches of sedges, bundled sticks and panalope leaves, dotted the outskirts of the clearing. Grin hadn't seen such a throng of grells since he was a child, estimating almost six hundred had arrived for the garrabari. He waited for Thaly to reach the top of the ravine, and together they walked into the crowd.

At the edge of the gathering, Hannian, Grin's little sister, played among a grove of bilawi trees, clinging to the thin trunks and swinging her body around in a giddy arc. A beaming smile suggested she enjoyed the dizziness of it all, but she stopped dead, and the smile dropped from her face like a stone when she caught sight of Grin. She released her hand from the tree trunk and ran faster than he'd ever seen her run, straight into Grin's arms.

He swept her up and kissed the top of Hanni's brown hair. "Look how much you have grown."

Hanni's smile returned. "In two days, I will have my own facial crest. I knew you would be here to see it." She wrapped her arms around his neck.

"I wonder what the elders have chosen for you?"

"A lodle, they swim all around Giigal. Or a bibidya swooping down to catch its prey, or, or a giant spear fern or..."

Grin laughed at Hanni's excitement. "Any one of those would be a magnificent facial crest and worth the honour of your protection." He swung her up onto his shoulders, and she clutched the top of his bald head to steady herself.

Above the murmur of the crowd, Grin recognised his mother's voice shouting in Grellian, "Nginha ngurambang marunbunmilgirridyu!" Mirrian reverted to Erstürmen and raced towards him, yelling to anyone within earshot, "Grin is here!"

She rushed up to Grin and placed the tips of her fingers on his cheeks, covering the legs of muwin, the ground spider tattooed across his face. He did the same, tracing his fingers over Mirrian's crest of the tubular, fringed petals of the panalope flower. His legs almost gave way amid the loving embrace of a family reunited.

Mirrian repeated in Grellian, "Yamandhu marang? Yamandhu marang?"

Are you well?

386

He withdrew his fingers from her cheeks and smiled. "Yes, Mother. I am well."

She hugged him tightly. "We thought you were dead. Your father did not know where you were. Then a Dobunni scout came to the milbi and told him you were safe in their camp. Frennan could not go there. He is too old to make that journey. Then the Dobunni went to war in Laodicea. Your father feared you might go with them to fight the Erstürmen."

Yes, he'd gone to war, thought Grin, but his mother didn't need to know that yet. The time would come to speak of his adventures. Waiting in the background, Frennan stood in stilled silence, Grin's father momentarily estranged from his family. Shafts of morning sun breached the forest canopy and bathed Frennan in a circle of light. Grin released his mother and swung Hanni off his shoulders, placing her back on forest soil.

She danced around him, unable to control her excitement. "I knew you would come home. I knew it."

He caressed her hair again and then walked to his father. When Grin reached him, Frennan attempted a formal greeting, but the attempt crumbled like parched soil, the tips of fingers sliding down tear-drenched cheeks.

Frennan hugged Grin close and whispered in his ear, "I thought you may not return."

Grin let the embrace linger. "You understand I had to leave?"

Frennan nodded. "You wanted to protect the birraman. I should have been proud, but my fear disallowed pride. The lonely days of worry and guilt have accentuated my shame."

"A decision made with an honest heart is the right decision no matter the outcome."

Frennan withdrew and looked to Thaly, who stood in the shadows of the trees. "She is not the birraman," he said.

Grin had almost forgotten about his travelling partner. About his friend. He beckoned for her to join him and his family. She walked across the sacred ground of Dalman, cautious and respectful, glancing at all the grell faces that turned to her with suspicion and judgement in their eyes.

They would understand, Grin tried to convince himself.

She stood, smiling, and he introduced her to his family. "This is Athalee Wallace, a Dobunni rebel from Bagendon. She prefers to be called Thaly."

In turn, Thaly engaged in an awkward, yet kind, formal greeting with Frennan, Mirrian and Hanni.

"Where have you travelled from?" asked Mirrian.

"Gestade," said Grin. "I bring disturbing news. Prince Adalwolf is now king, and he marches with many pilgrims to Malang Gunya. They plan to destroy what remains of our home and build a new city on top of the rubble."

Frennan shook his head. "It is hard to imagine worse news."

"The homage march to honour the fallen cannot go ahead. We will be walking into a massacre."

"Such decisions are for the Mulugan to make," said Frennan. "Nothing has stopped the march before."

"They'll be countless Erstürmen there," said Thaly. "Thousands and thousands of them."

"They may let the ceremonies proceed peacefully," said Mirrian. "We should not give up that hope."

"Where is the birraman?" asked Frennan.

Grin cast his eyes downwards. "He disappeared. In the ocean."

"The ocean?" said Hanni. "You were near the ocean?"

"We were *on* the ocean," said Grin.

Mirrian shivered. "How terrifying. It is bad enough being surrounded by all that water at Giigal."

Yes, terrifying, thought Grin, as Thaly glanced at him with a hurt that sullied her face. He turned to his father. "I have invited Thaly to participate in the garrabari. We have much to share with the decision-makers of the Mulugan. Things we have seen that threaten the future of all grells."

Frennan tensed. "The garrabari is sacred. For stone- and weald-grells only."

Thaly flinched, and Grin's shoulders slumped.

Frennan must have noticed. He softened his voice. "The time we now share is more dangerous than I can remember. Under such circumstances, old traditions must adapt. Mirrian and I will speak to the other members of the Mulugan. We will ask them to let Thaly join the ceremony."

Grin placed a protective arm around Thaly's shoulder. Other grells stepped forward to engage in formal greetings, and Grin made sure they acknowledged Thaly also. She nodded and smiled at every new face, and the atmosphere of suspicion began to thaw.

*   *   *   *

Caeli walked with Dwarrow, following a trail through the middle of Babir Birramal. They'd left Casfern and Xaviary to graze at the edge of the forest and had been hiking for four days. Dwarrow said they would reach Dalman today. Caeli hoped so. Her bare feet wouldn't suffer another day of marching over rough ground and through the dense forest. She shouldn't have tossed her dress shoes away back in The Feign.

They came to a clearing, and Dwarrow stepped onto a flat, innocent-looking patch of leaves and grass. Caeli followed him.

Snap!

A crack and a whoosh echoed through the trees, and the leaves and grass beneath Caeli's feet flew up, sweeping her and Dwarrow into the air. Something like a sack enveloped them, plunging the unsuspecting travellers into darkness and suspending them in mid-air.

Dwarrow rolled around inside the sack, flailing his arms, fighting against an unseen enemy. "We've been trapped, Princess. This is most disagreeable and completely uncalled for."

"Stop swinging your arms, Dwarrow," said Caeli. "You'll knock me out."

Dwarrow calmed his panting breaths. "The utter indignance of it."

"Who's setting traps out here?" asked Caeli.

"It's those blasted grells. I bet my dwell on it. Trying to stop anyone finding their sacred site."

"If we wait here, they'll come and collect us."

"Don't hold your breath, Princess. Grells never do anything in a hurry."

Caeli pushed at the sack around her. It smelled of leather and appeared to be made from the single skin of a giant animal. There were no seams for her to pick at. No holes for her to peep through. Whoever their captors were, they'd crafted an almost inescapable trap. A pinhead of sunlight filtered through the top of the sack where the drawstring had been pulled tight. If they wanted to escape, they would have to cut themselves free.

"Where's your knife, Dwarrow?"

"In my satchel. Let me get it out, and we can..." Dwarrow stopped short as voices in the distance became louder.

"Are they speaking Grellian?" asked Caeli.

"Yes, I think they are. It sounds primitive and barbaric, like the squeals of a wild pig caught in a snare." Dwarrow climbed on top of Caeli and began sniffing at the top of the sack. "The rancid smell is unmistakable," he said. "Definitely grells. I knew it."

"You're squashing my stomach."

"Sorry, Princess," whispered Dwarrow as he climbed off. "We should stay quiet until we know where this adventure is heading."

At least two voices approached the sack, then hands prodded through the animal hide, followed by an excited discussion. Someone released the rope holding her and Dwarrow in mid-air, and she braced herself to fall on the ground, but more hands grabbed the top of the sack and flung it sideways. Caeli and Dwarrow bumped around in the dark, knocking against each other as their captors carried them into the unknown. Although she strained her ears, trying to catch a familiar sound, whoever held the sack had fallen silent, and she heard only bird calls and twigs and leaves crunching beneath marching feet.

The stale air inside the sack soon became stifling. Dwarrow began to pant fast and shallow, and she worried the little werp might be suffocating. She was about to plead for release when the captors halted and dropped the sack on the ground.

"Ow," said Dwarrow. "A modicum of respect would be appreciated."

The drawstring opened, and sunlight streamed in, Caeli having to shade her eyes. The sack fell around them, and Dwarrow jumped to his feet, holding his staff across his body, ready to defend against any attackers.

Caeli almost laughed at the sight. Dozens, no, hundreds of wild grells surrounded her and Dwarrow, glaring at the new arrivals. A little werp would hardly stand a chance against a forest of giants.

Dwarrow lowered his staff and cleared his throat. "Hel-lo. Does-any-one-here-speak-Er-steer-men?"

"We all do," replied a stone-grell with a facial tattoo resembling the wings of a falcon.

"Thank goodness," said Dwarrow. "I'm too tired to bother with that gobbledegook you call a language."

Caeli got to her feet slowly, worried any sudden movement might be seen as a threat.

The grell with the falcon-wing tattoo took a step towards her. "Why are you intruding on our sacred ceremony? How did you find this place?"

"Intruding?" said Dwarrow. "We are doing no such thing. No such thing at all. It is the grells who intruded on us. And as far as finding you, well, there's such a rancorous fetor oozing from this part of the forest, an olfactorily-challenged snail could have found you."

Caeli rolled her eyes. "*Dwarrow*. Diplomacy, remember?"

"Sorry, Princess. I forgot myself. Briefly."

"Our scouts said you were skulking around in the forest before they captured you," said the grell. "What business do you have here? Mouldewerps never come into the forest, and none have been seen on the plain for generations."

"We weren't skulking," said Caeli. "We're on a diplomatic mission. Let me introduce Ambassador Dwarrow of the mouldewerps of western Enthilen. I'm his assistant, Princess Caeli of Sardis."

"The world is becoming a strange place when mouldewerps and Erstürmen form an alliance."

"It's going to become a lot stranger," said Dwarrow. "A lot stranger, indeed. Mark my words." He climbed out of the sack and shuffled up to the grell, brushing his nose against the giant's shins. "Your smell is familiar. Who am I speaking with?"

"I am Frennan stone-grell. Third born of Brennian and Feyan. Protector..."

"Yes, yes, yes. Protector of Babir Birra...whatever you call this calamity of trees. Never had the nose for forests. Prefer a nice damp dwell underneath sweeping plains."

"Dwarrow?" someone called from the back of the crowd.

Dwarrow turned, and his small, salmon-coloured face exploded into a beaming smile. "Grin! Finally, you've returned. And not a moment too soon. Not a moment at all. I have many tasks requiring your attention. I can't do everything myself...*arrghhh*." Dwarrow yelled as Grin grabbed him and threw him into the air, catching him on the way back down. He threw him up again.

"I'm feeling ill," cried Dwarrow. "Air sickness."

Caeli laughed.

Grin held Dwarrow out in front. "Dwarrow, my old employer. I am glad I can still be of service. How did you get here? The location of this place is a secret known only to grells."

"There are no secrets from me," said Dwarrow. "None at all. Now put me down. I'm starting to get vertigo."

Back on his own two feet, Dwarrow tilted his head and sniffed the air. "There's another familiar smell here. A more charming perfume fighting its way through this grell *redolence*. Athalee? Athalee, is that you?"

A young woman with taut muscles shaping olive skin tiptoed through the crowd of grells. She looked awkward and unsure, much like Caeli felt. The woman crouched and smiled, hugging the bundle of fur and pink skin.

"Hello, Dwarrow," she said.

"Oh, Thaly, it is so wonderful to smell you again." He released the embrace. "And where is that boy? Involved in a clutter of mischief and trouble, no doubt."

Grin appeared to grimace, and Thaly's eyes glistened with welling tears.

"I failed to protect Tom," said Grin. "I let him down."

Thaly stood, glanced at Grin, then rested a comforting hand on his back.

Something happened, thought Caeli, and not only to Tom Anderson. Grin and Thaly's faces are etched with trauma.

"If you are an ambassador, you must bring news, offers or demands," said Frennan.

"Yes, yes, yes," said Dwarrow. "That can wait. We're famished. Do you have any pickled lizard?"

* * * *

Grin sat with Thaly as a shrewdness of grells gathered under the midday sun. The arrival of a mouldewerp and an Erstürmen princess had taken all the attention away from the Dobunni rebel. While some grells had questioned Thaly's presence at the garrabari, their opposition to guests had wavered under Dwarrow's unbending persistence. This certainly would be a garrabari long remembered in grell history. News had spread that Dwarrow, the ambassadorial mouldewerp, would be making a presentation to the group. A speech. Grin remembered his own speech made to the werps back in the Scaur Hills as he tried to save his life. Since then, so much had happened, the memory of those early days with Tom, Thaly and Jacob now fading. Grin's love for the world around him waned, not because he loved it any less, but because the future of this land seemed so dire. He ached at the confronting sadness of being in love with something he expected to lose.

And hate had risen up inside him more than once, fuelled by the assault on the *Vulking*. Hateful feelings frightened him more than the nightmares of the salacious faces of the ship's crew. He wondered how Thaly coped with it all. She still held things back, keeping her emotional distance from everyone.

Grin guessed the entire camp of six hundred grells had turned out to hear Dwarrow speak. Most had never seen a mouldewerp or a princess. He wondered about the meeting between Caeli and Tom. Why did an

Erstürmen princess help Tom escape Sardis and put her own life in danger?

The murmurs of the crowd died down as Princess Caeli lifted Dwarrow onto a tree stump overlooking Dalman to address the gathering. The werp blew his nose on the trident leaf of a panalope tree, and Grin cringed at the disrespectful act. Dwarrow probably knew what he was doing, and Grin couldn't help but smile inside at the werp's pluck.

"Dear stone-grells and weald-grells, my name is Gwuendā-hæ Dwinë D'elch. You can call me Dwarrow. Dwarrow the mouldewerp. I imagine most of you have never seen a mouldewerp since you hunted us to near extinction when you plundered our..."

"Dwarrow!" Caeli glared from the base of the tree stump, and Grin's smile broadened.

"Alright. Yes. I forgot. Diplomacy. My apologies, everyone. With Princess Caeli, I've travelled far across the Dambay Plains to seek your counsel. I represent my elders, and all werps still occupying these lands. It's fitting we meet during guma because, if my mission fails, a storm will break, bringing forth an endless torment for all of us. I come here seeking an alliance between the mouldewerps and grells. An alliance and a resistance to face the evil now marching into the heart of our home and our heritage."

Dwarrow conveyed the news of King Adalwolf's march to Malang Gunya, confirming what Grin had heard at Gestade. It should be easier now for him to convince the Mulugan to abandon the homage march. Some in the crowd gasped when Dwarrow spoke of the grell soldiers now fighting for the Erstürmen.

The werp continued, "...and so, you see, we face a grave challenge to protect ourselves from the rise of this new power. We cannot do it alone. An alliance of werps and grells is only the first step. We will need others to join our cause."

"What exactly is our cause?" asked Mirrian.

"To fight this malevolence until it crawls back into the cave from whence it came."

Caeli helped Dwarrow down from the tree stump.

Frennan stood. "None of us can see the future. Who was to know King Ewald would fall and his son claim the throne of the dead? Who could have foreseen the defeat of the Dobunni rebellion and the Erstürmen march to Malang Gunya? These are grave and serious threats. After the ceremonies, the Mulugan will decide what action we will take."

Grin began to doubt his own thoughts. At the end of the garrabari, he would be initiated and allowed to undertake his first homage march. Forgoing this privilege to avoid a slaughter was the correct decision, wasn't it? Or was it time for all grells to rise up and face the threat confronting the land they loved?

*   *   *   *

As evening fell on Dalman, Thaly stood on the fringe of the clearing away from the crowd gathering around a large bonfire. Unaccustomed to grell rituals, she didn't want to get in the way of important events or insult her hosts with her ignorance. Grin's family sat near the fire, cooking possum stew and laughing and talking in their own language. Hannian played a game with Grin, tapping him on the back of the shoulder, then trying to run to the rock of Marradir before he jumped to his feet and caught her. The game quickly descended into fits of laughter as Grin and his little sister wrestled each other to the ground.

Little? Hanni was likely half Thaly's age, yet still a head taller than the Dobunni rebel. The love and respect binding Grin's family together both warmed Thaly's heart and tore it asunder. She would give almost anything for a blood family of her own. One she could be proud of. One that loved her. Emelin and Dayna had done their best, but still, something was missing.

The full moons poked bone-coloured faces through the canopy of trees, and the fire waned. Thaly shared the meal with Grin's family, then Hanni sat with her on a log, appointing herself interpreter of the meaning behind each of the garrabari ceremonies. Thaly understood the honour being afforded to her. With Dwarrow and Princess Caeli, they would be the first outsiders to ever see a grell garrabari. The closer ties being forged between the cultures of Enthilen may be an unexpected consequence of Malphas' rise to power, thought Thaly, one he never anticipated.

The crowd stilled and the sharp clack of two flat stones being clapped together echoed through the forest, slow at first, then gaining momentum. Next to the stone clapper sat a female stone-grell blowing through a hollowed legbone painted in cobalt and ochre colours.

Hanni leaned across to Thaly. "That is the bone of the giant wombodon. My mother says it has been handed down from the first ancestors. The elder will recreate calls from the land through the hollow bone."

Thaly closed her eyes and listened, recognising the cry of a wild dog baying at the moon and the distinctive hoot of a wangi owl. She realised how much her knowledge of the natural world had grown, and now, surrounded by it all, she couldn't escape the immersion.

Wails from the wombodon bone faded, and dancers carrying stone-tipped spears walked into the ceremonial circle surrounding the fire. On one edge of the ring stood twelve male stone-grells, their naked bodies covered in red and black paint made from powdered stone mixed with water. Directly opposite them stood twelve male weald-grells decorated in blue and white.

"This dance tells the story of the tribal war that rent us apart long ago," said Hanni to Thaly. "The weald-grells were defeated, and they abandoned Malang Gunya and built the city of Giigal where I live now. Then the Erstürmen expelled the last stone-grells from Malang Gunya, chasing them all the way to Babir Birramal. Among the trees, stone- and weald-grells fought until the elders of both tribes signed the truce written on Marradir."

The clacking of the stones grew louder and females sitting around the circle started to chant and sing. The males began their dance, feigning thrusts with their spears, playing out the battle as their bodies heaved and sweated beside the smouldering fire in the middle of the circle. Thaly drifted with the sights and sounds, imagining a time long ago when only grells and werps lived in Enthilen, and a vast city rose up from the middle of the Dambay Plains.

The dance ended with the stone-grells prevailing and the weald-grells retreating from the circle. Elders from the two tribes came forward, placed painted stones at the base of Marradir, and re-enacted the sign- ing of the truce written on the face of the boulder.

"The painted stones are tokens of respect and remembrance to renew the vow of peace," said Hanni.

When the elders retreated, female grells entered the circle, their naked torsos painted with impressions of coloured hands, and ceremo- nial dresses made from mugi feathers and gunirr skins wrapped tight around their waists. Hanni explained to Thaly the female dancers performed the gathering dance, which depicted the collection of vital forest foods and the making of waterskins and baskets. The hunting dance came next, a handful of grells acting as prey and others as hunt- ers with spears held high or blunt arrows nocked.

After the ceremonial dances, the proceedings became more jovial and relaxed.

"We can dance now," said Hanni, offering Thaly a hand.

Thaly forced a smile. "You go. I'm feeling tired."

Hanni left to dance with her kin. Thaly smiled for real as Dwarrow and Grin joined the dancers, Dwarrow re-enacting the capture of a giant grell and his friends, and then saving them all from certain death. She thought about Tom, twisting his white handkerchief around her arm. The arrow wound had almost healed, and she didn't need the bandage anymore, but would keep it on her wrist nonetheless to remind her of a brief friendship that could have lasted much longer.

"Is your arm hurt?" asked Princess Caeli as she sat on the end of the log.

Thaly dismissed the princess, pretending to be engrossed in the dancing. "The wound has healed," she said.

"That's good. I've been listening to Grin's stories. It sounds like you've been on an amazing journey. I wish I could go on such an adventure."

"Be careful what you wish for."

"Grin said you're a rebel fighter from Bagendon."

"And you're an Erstürmen princess, which makes us sworn enemies."

"I always hoped for a life without enemies. I guess that was a naïve hope. Grin said that you saw whales. How amazing. What are they like? I always wanted to see one. Big and blue, and leaping from the water." Caeli threw her arms into the air like a young girl trying to catch falling leaves.

Thaly's expression hardened. The thought of the ocean and whales took her back to the *Vulking*.

"Sorry," said Caeli. "I act like a stupid child sometimes. It comes from being locked up. Everything outside is so wonderous because most of it I haven't seen for such a long time, or never seen at all. I shouldn't expect others to feel the same way."

"It's not that," said Thaly. "It's...forget it."

"After Dwarrow has finished his important dealings, I hope to see my father. I haven't seen him for so long. He left me to grow old, locked in a tower. A prisoner in service to the kingdom."

Thaly fought to keep her emotions subdued. To show no weakness to the enemy. She pressed her lips together in a straight line of hardened steel.

"Being a Dobunni can't be easy," said Caeli. "We stole your home, destroyed your lives and chased you into the hills. You're brave to fight back."

Thaly's line of steel cracked, and she faced the princess. "I didn't fight when I needed to the most."

Caeli slid along the log, closer to Thaly, and brushed her hand across Thaly's thigh. "Sometimes you can't fight. You want to with all your strength. You ache for it, but your will falters."

The disarming mix of naivety and worldliness characterising the princess' personality began to weaken Thaly's defences. Each time Caeli spoke, another layer of Thaly's armour peeled away, and she began to feel like a newborn, naked and defenceless, barely able to whisper, "You don't understand what I'm talking about."

"Feeling helpless and hopeless? I understand that. I understand what it's like when someone else controls you. When he's stronger than you. Has more power and authority. Resisting...fighting makes it worse. It hurts more. He's rougher. Hits you harder. It's easier to pretend you aren't there and let your body go limp. Drift off to another place. Give in. And you hate yourself for it. You hate yourself every waking moment."

Caeli looked up through the forest canopy covering the sacred site like a baldachin, staring at the glimmer of stars as if they were actors performing the story of her life. "Every time the key turns in the lock, you wonder if it's him. Back to punish you again. To twist your feelings so what should be pleasure is pain, what should be love is hate, and what should be a gentle caress is a slap in the face. Then something really cruel happens. You start to care for him. During the quiet moments when he sleeps beside you. A monster in your bed. You start to care, and you ask yourself why? Are you so desperate for love? To *be* loved? You wonder what real love is. An offer of affection from someone else fills you with dread. So, you push them away — those that care. You push them away, and every time you do, he's punishing you again. He's *controlling* you again. He's raping you — again."

Thaly's eyes welled, trembling lips catching the tears. "What did Grin tell you?"

Caeli didn't answer. She simply smiled and grasped Thaly's hand. "I'm not your enemy, Athalee of Bagendon. There's a pain in your eyes I've only seen before in a mirror. A suffering we will always share. Something that bonds us. And together, we can heal. Together we can grow stronger."

Thaly broke. The last layer of armour peeled off, and she fell into the warm embrace of a princess. And there, under the stars and full moons, Caeli held her tight while Thaly sobbed, every tear exorcising a shred of agony locked inside.

~ Chapter 31 ~

"Put knife down, Tom."

Did I say that?

Kneeling on the frost-covered ground, a warming calmness fought against the chill of despondency. Lines raised and red, like parallel naevi, marked Tom's right wrist and forearm. The exploratory cuts weren't deep, but they exposed a deadlier ambition.

How did that happen?

Annian stood over him, her wrinkled face, decorated with the weathered crest of dhundhu, looking stern. "Give me knife."

"Hadufuns," whispered Tom.

"Took own life. Could not save him. Give me knife."

Tom's left hand hung by his side with the bone handle of a knife dangling in its grasp. Droplets of blood trickled down the arresting blade that had been crafted with skill and care, the etchings on the keen surface showing a river of stars being swallowed by a howling wolf.

Where did this come from? I didn't have a knife.

In a daze, he handed it to Annian, and she shoved it under her belt.

"We go now," she said. "You help pull cart."

"Shouldn't we do something...for Hadufuns?"

Annian knelt, placed her hand on Hadufuns' forehead, whispered in

Grellian, and then faced Tom. "Nothing more to do. Forest will return him to the soil."

A bewildered Tom ambled after Annian back to their camp. She'd already packed the campsite and freed the soldiers' horses, giving the mistreated animals a final chance at a better life. Tom thought about tossing a sword onto the cart, but he couldn't bring himself to it. He didn't need to be carrying another lethal weapon at this particular time.

"What happened?" asked Annian. "Back there."

"Hadufuns gave up. Then I...I think I wanted to give up, too. It's all so hard. I'm sorry, Annian. You shouldn't have to deal with this."

"No giving up now. Help pull cart. We climb to Bindari."

Help? Bindari?

Tom and Annian picked up the pull-bar of the small cart. They trudged in silence all morning, Tom using the focussed monotony of counting his footsteps as a shield against another anxiety attack. An attempt to tame the seemingly unconquerable mental demons and convince himself the moment with Hadufuns was only a relapse, nothing more. He needed to be wary of them, but he could push on. He had to.

As the morning faded into midday, the cart weighed heavier, and Annian began to struggle. Tom guessed the sword swipe by the Erstürmen soldier had damaged her ribs more than she admitted. They rested under the shade of a panalope tree to drink and pick at the food left by Hadufuns.

Annian held a piece of cold rabbit towards Tom, who shook his head.

"Not hungry?" she asked.

"Why didn't you end it, Annian?"

"End what?"

"I mean, being a slave isn't much of a life. Why didn't you kill yourself?"

"Stupid question." Annian tossed the portion of rabbit into her mouth and chewed with worn, mustard-coloured teeth. "I never lose hope. Hadufuns lost hope. You cannot. You must walk different path and etch marks into stones for others to follow."

Leave your mark, thought Tom. "You said before, *we* would climb to Bindari."

"Yes. Together. Will anger miyans. That burden I accept."

"Who are the miyans?" asked Tom.

"Guardians of the graves."

The revelation lifted the sombre clouds drifting through Tom's mind. Annian would show him the way to Bindari, and he would find the answers he so desperately needed.

After eating, Annian fell asleep, resting her back against the tree trunk. Tom sat, counting her shallow breaths and watching the twitches of her face make her wrinkles skip. She woke mid-afternoon, keen to continue. They slogged further, dragging the cart behind them until, at sunset, the land started to slope upwards, and the trees thinned. Annian told Tom tonight's camp would be the last with the cart. They built a fire and made a feast from the remaining supplies, including two rabbits and mushrooms Annian had harvested from the forest. Suddenly famished, Tom wolfed down his share like it was his last meal.

Food would have to be rationed for the remainder of the journey, Annian estimating they had another day or two of hard walking. Tom thought it may take longer, the old grell's pace slowing as each day passed, and the grimaces on her face betraying her agony.

By the next morning, Annian's condition had deteriorated further. They abandoned the cart, and Tom fashioned her a walking stick from a tree branch. He gathered the last pieces of cold rabbit and Annian's totems from the cart and placed them in his backpack. The pair hobbled onwards, Annian leaning on Tom's shoulder when she needed support. There was no distinct trail to follow, only a line of grass flatter than the rest, but they walked ever upwards, through sparse trees and into endless vistas of tufted, wiry grassland, interspersed with patches of spongy moss and lichen. In shallow swales, their feet sank in boggy ground, the sucking mud slowing progress further.

Mist floated in from the east, shrouding the way ahead. When the fog thinned, glimpses of a cyan ocean appeared at the end of valleys set among rolling hills, and the smell of salt drifted in the air. A bracing wind whisked over the hilltops, droplets of dew clinging to the travellers' strained faces. No sound breached the stillness, other than the squelching mud as it engulfed every aching footfall.

The fog thickened, but Tom knew where to go now. Up. Always up. He led Annian along the face of a hill, keeping the steep side to his right and her on his left. As the sunlight dimmed, he pulled his coat up around his neck to deflect the cold. He assumed the sun had set, though he couldn't see the sky. When the steepness to his right flattened out, he picked up his pace, looking for shelter where they could rest the night. In the numbing tedium, he momentarily forgot about Annian, losing contact with his elderly companion. He stopped and waited on the faint path, expecting her to emerge from the fog, listing to one side as she leaned on her crutch. But she didn't appear.

"Annian!" The fog swallowed Tom's tired voice. He walked back down the path, following the muddy depressions. Through the rolling mist, a bundle appeared, lying on the ground and curled up in a ball. He raced over to a shivering Annian and knelt beside her.

"You have to get up," he said. "We need to find shelter."

Annian pulled her face from the mud. "Cannot make it. Let me be."

"We can't stay here. Walk a few more steps until we find somewhere warmer to rest."

"Save yourself, Tom. I cannot reach Bindari."

"I won't leave you here to die."

Annian rolled onto her back, desperate wheezes struggling to draw air into her lungs. She grasped Tom's hand. "Help one last time. Find plant. Dark green leaves with four prongs. Black stems. Only shrub growing here. Bring me leaves."

"Will they heal you?"

"Leaves are poisonous. Will ease passing."

"You want me to help you die?"

Annian nodded.

"How is that any different to what Hadufuns did? I can't help you commit suicide."

"I suffer. Cannot walk further. Bones...hurt. Will die in mud."

"I'll find shelter. I won't be long."

Tom jogged ahead, not too far lest he lose Annian again or get lost himself. He found a hollow under ancient, treeless roots offering protection from the wind and mizzly rain that had begun to fall. When he returned to Annian, she couldn't stand, even with his support. So, he carried her. It seemed she'd lost weight during the journey, her animal-skin tunic hanging more limply than Tom remembered, yet the body of a weald-grell was still heavy in his arms, and he stumbled only six paces before needing to rest. Nevertheless, he cradled Annian again and pushed forward. A few steps more. Rest. A couple more. Rest again.

Inside the hollow, Tom laid Annian on the ground as the night wrapped its chilling darkness around them. Her teeth rattled, an old and weary body shuddering from the cold. With no wood to make a fire, Tom pulled the blanket from his pack and draped it over his and Annian's chests. They cuddled together underneath the thick wool, Tom wishing he'd remembered to bring the possum-skin cloak.

Annian brushed her hand across his cheek and whispered, "Do not risk own life for mine, Tom Anderson."

"We make it to Bindari together or not at all," said Tom.

Too weak to continue the conversation, the pair fell asleep in each other's arms. When Tom opened his eyes, the fog had thinned, dispersed by a bright, burning sun. To the north, he could see all the way over Babir Birramal and into the Dambay Plains, imagining a speck of light glinting on the horizon that might come from a tall spire somewhere in the middle of the savannah. To the south, a vast ocean stretched on without end.

Gadhang, thought Tom, the ocean the first stone-grell settlers crossed long ago to land on the shores of Enthilen. He understood now why the grells chose Bindari as their final resting place. It appeared to be located right between their past and their future. The perfect place for ancestors to watch over their kin.

Bindari must be close. He shook Annian's shoulder. "Annian. Wake up and look at the view."

Her eyes closed, she responded only with shallow, gasping breaths.

Tom wrapped the blanket around her, picked her up, clenched his jaw and started walking. Every single step had to be winched from a well of agony, but he trudged on, refusing to surrender. Puddles of mud reached up to his knees, trying to suck him into the earth and bury him and Annian alive. Rivulets of water trickled off the slopes to his left, weaving their way through drifts of muddy snow and disappearing over the steep edge of the path an arm's length beyond his right foot. One slip and he'd crash and tumble with Annian into a treacherous valley forged by a rushing stream strewn with boulders.

So, he wouldn't slip or make a single misstep. He would push on, squelching, heaving and fighting through the mud.

Near sunset, Tom breached the crest of a grassy ridge and confronted an army. In the distance, rows and rows of enormous monoliths stood to attention across rolling, grass-covered hills. The scattered trunks of stone reached up into the strands of sea fog racing across their parade ground — a graveyard for giants.

Bindari.

He tried to lift his foot for another step, but the mud refused to yield. Despite the cold, he broke into a sweat, Annian's weight pressing down into the crux of his arms. He heaved her up and almost toppled backwards. Held in place, all he could do was stare at the grey monuments as if waiting for their magnetism to draw him closer. Then, a monolith moved.

Tom managed one more step before his legs gave up, and he and Annian toppled into the mud.

* * * *

Tom Anderson. Tom drifted towards the voice. *Tom Anderson.* He opened his eyes with a start. A giant hovered over him with grey skin the colour of granite, and a thick fur coat riding up past his cheeks. It took Tom a while to recognise the creature as a male stone-grell.

A miyan, he thought, guardian of Bindari.

Tom rubbed his face, feeling the biting cold of his exposed cheeks. "Were you calling me?"

The miyan didn't respond. Tom sat up, inadvertently resting his hand on a body lying beside him, wrapped in a shroud. He snatched his hand away. The miyan crouched over the body and pulled back the cerement to reveal Annian's still, peaceful face.

"She's dead," said Tom, matter-of-fact.

The miyan nodded and returned the covering.

"Who are you?" asked Tom.

The stone-grell miyan remained silent. Then, Tom remembered Annian had told him the miyans of Bindari took a vow of silence out of respect for the dead. He absorbed the features of the guardian's grey face, edges of a black tattoo reaching up above the fur collar of the coat and spreading across weathered, gaunt cheeks to lilac eyes. They were inside a shelter of sorts, rocks stacked into a wall at the back, and the doorless opening facing away from the ocean and the cold, south-easterly winds. There were none of the comforts Tom had seen in Grin's milbi, the miyans apparently living an austere existence with a bed cot in one corner of the shelter and a fire pit in the other.

"This is Bindari, isn't it?" he asked.

The miyan nodded again.

Tom reached for Annian's hand that poked out from under the shroud, and caressed her fingers. *We made it.* No tears. He'd come to terms with Annian's end as she had, relieved they'd reached her final resting place. Annian wouldn't have suffered any histrionics.

"Where are her totems?"

The stone-grell pulled Tom's backpack out from under the cot, opened the pack and retrieved the totems, laying them side-by-side next to her body in a perfectly straight line, equal distance apart. Tom recognised Annian's totem. He'd seen her etching words into its surface with a fine metal needle back at the fishing shack and during their journey. He picked up the totem and cradled it in his hand. All of the words were Grellian except for two right near the bottom — *Tom Anderson.*

"We have to bury her."

* * * *

Tom flexed his fingers against the frigid mid-morning air, cupping his hands over his mouth and blowing warm breaths into the scars on his palms. Plunan — the grell miyan had scratched his name on a rock when Tom asked — battled with the half-frozen ground using a blunt shovel made from timber and rusted metal. Tom crouched and scraped the mud from the side of the hole with a piece of flat board no bigger than his hand.

With the grave dug, they lowered Annian's shrouded body into the ground. Tom made the sign of the cross despite not being religious and never having attended church except for one wedding and a funeral. Nevertheless, he wanted to do something to acknowledge the end.

The grell miyan began to fill the hole.

"What about the totems?" asked Tom. "Won't they be buried with her?"

Plunan stopped digging and guided Tom to one of the stone monoliths, an elongated rectangle with a blunt top almost twice Tom's height. Rubbing his hand over the surface of the smooth stone like a blind person reading braille, Tom traced the words etched into the rockface. Plunan pointed to Annian's totems, then to the monolith and acted out writing something. Tom guessed Plunan would first transpose all of the stories from Annian's totems onto the face of the monolith before burying the totems alongside her.

The last shovel of mud fell into Annian's grave, and Tom turned his thoughts to the pressing reason he'd come to Bindari. To find answers. "There's a gorge here somewhere with a light at the bottom and a door. Do you know where it is?"

Plunan nodded, dropped his shovel and took Tom's hand. Strands of mist wafted across the hills and caressed the stone pillars like a doting lover as the miyan led Tom up a muddy path, over a rise and across a wooden suspension bridge spanning a fast-flowing brook littered with boulders crowned with ice. He pointed south and pushed Tom forward. As the path faded, an emptiness between two hills appeared, belching fog into the air like the steam from a pot of boiling water. Tom turned to thank Plunan, but the grell had already gone, disappearing among the giant grey stones dotted across the hills.

Tom walked on in silence as other miyans watched him from the crests of sodden hills, eyeing the stranger invading this sacred place.

He stayed on the path, such as it was, careful not to step on a gravesite, thinking such a heinous act would see him evicted from Bindari. A short distance from the stream, he found the gorge Princess Caeli had described; wide and sheer, running east-west, with thick fog filling it like a pail of milk. As he leaned over the edge trying to see the bottom, a rock slipped out from under his goat-skin boot and cascaded into the white depths, eventually thudding to a stop far below.

He crept along the edge of the gorge, searching for the first stair in the path leading to the bottom. His foot caught on the lip of a stone cut crudely into the wet and slippery bedrock. The mist thinned, revealing a pale light shining out from the dullness at the bottom of the gorge. The light that never went out.

Catching Tom off-guard, vertigo pounced, spinning the landscape around inside his head so much he had to plump onto his backside to quell the nausea. He dug his fingers into the cold ground. "Get hold of yourself. Can't turn back now."

He gathered what courage remained, and on sore and bruised feet, and tired legs that buckled with every step, he descended the stairs. Melting ice trickled across his hand as he held fast to the rock face on his left, avoiding the slimy green algae clinging to the tops of the steps. A slip now would mean certain death. The fog closed in again, and Tom lost track of his progress. He focussed all his attention on the next step in front of him and counted aloud, "81, 82, 83...177," until reaching the bottom of the gorge.

The ground sloped upwards, and the gorge narrowed as he walked due east to where he thought the light came from. Sometimes, he stumbled into a sheer wall on his left and then his right until the fog lifted again, revealing a lantern in the west-facing side of the gorge, hanging in an alcove protected from the weather. Next to the light, embedded in the rock, was a wooden door with rusted iron hinges and straps running perpendicular to the jamb. A metal handle and lock, once painted black but now chipped and corroded, kept the door shut.

Tom raced up to the door and thumped on the timber, the frantic thuds echoing around the gorge. He waited. Nobody answered. He knocked again. "Hello!" And waited. Grasping the door handle, he pulled, then leaned into the door and pushed. The door didn't budge.

Dwarrow's key.

From his waistcoat pocket, he took the key the little werp had given him so long ago, and inserted it into the lock, jiggling it around and twisting the bow. The tumblers didn't move. Not one bit. He tried again, turning the key the other way.

Nothing. Fuck it.

He plonked down on a lichen-covered rock, weary, dizzy, sad and alone.

The answers are behind that door. The way home is here. Don't give up now.

Tom jumped up and charged into the door with his shoulder, bouncing off the immovable object and falling into the mud. He lay there, fuming.

"Hello!? Answer me!"

That's not going to work. Think about it. Caeli said, 'To open the door, you must solve a puzzle. Only you will know the answer.' What did she mean by 'solve a puzzle'? Why am I the only one with the answer? What's unique about me? I'm not the only person to travel from Earth to Ostamp. There was the dark-skinned woman who visited the grells, and Malphas, he's been to Earth, I saw him in my bedroom. Malphas and Caeli speak English. Maybe the princess has visited Earth, too? Is it something to do with my family? Friends?

Of all the things he thought of, he realised someone else knew about them. Yet, despite the mental and physical exhaustion, a picture drifted into his mind of something that had consumed his thoughts for almost his entire childhood — the blue book. The one left in the hole at the bottom of the big redgum tree back home in Australia. The one Malphas admitted to writing.

Malphas knows about the book. Is there something unique about it only I could know?

In front of the door, like a doorstep, sat three flat stones, each the size of a dinner plate and shaped as perfect circles. The flat stones were clean, not covered in moss or lichen like the other rocks and no mud dirtying their surface. He stood and hovered over the stones, noticing a hairline gap between their outer circumference and the bedrock in which they were embedded. He pushed his toes onto the unsoiled, flat surface and shifted his weight forward, thinking the stone may sink into the ground. Nothing happened.

Of course, nothing's going to happen. It can't be that easy.

A pile of rocks, each one no bigger than Tom's little finger and cut square like tiny bricks, had been stacked adjacent to the circular stepping stones. He sat and counted the bricks. *24.* Three flat stones and 24 bricks. *8 per circle.*

He divided the bricks equally and placed them on the stones. Nothing happened.

"Think a bit more. What's unique to me? My age?" He placed 16 bricks on each of the three stones in turn. Nothing. He repeated the step and divided the remaining bricks evenly across the other two stones. Nothing.

"It must have something to do with the blue book. What do I know about it no-one else does?"

Page numbers.

When Tom found the book, the pages weren't numbered. He'd numbered the pages. Malphas likely wouldn't know how many pages there were, and Tom had memorised which story began and ended on which page. It's something he would do. Count and number the pages, and memorise the numbers.

"Five hundred and sixteen pages. 5-1-6. That's the total number of pages in the blue book." He placed 5 bricks on the first stone, 1 on the second and 6 on the third and stepped back. "This must be it." Nothing happened. "Use all the bricks." He added 5 + 1 + 6 and placed 12 bricks on the first stone, and 6 on the second and third stones. Nothing. He moved them around. Nothing.

Oh, for fuck's sake. He hurled a rock at the door, screaming in English, *"Fuckin open!"* He tried different combinations of numbers until his head ached, but the three stone circles never budged. Then he recalled something strange about the blue book. Something standing out from the rest, written in a different hand. The lemniscate on page 462, beside the word Revelé. *462.*

Tom placed 4-6-2 bricks on the three stones. Nothing. He tried 4-2-6, 6-2-4, 6-4-2, 2-6-4, 2-4-6. *Nothing, nothing, nothing, nothing, NOTHING!*

"Add them up, like before. 4 + 6 + 2 = 12." He placed 12 bricks on two stones and left the last one empty. Nothing. He moved them around. Nothing.

"It's more complex. You need three numbers. Think. Three numbers. Add 4 + 6 = 10 bricks on stone one. 4 + 2 = 6 bricks on stone two. 6 + 2 = 8 bricks on stone three." Tom waited. He almost gave up again when a squeal of stone rubbing on stone pierced the mist, and three circles sank into the ground. A click came from the door, and it swung open.

Got you, you bastard.

Jumping to his feet, he stood at the doorway, staring into the blackness beyond the jamb and calling out, "Hello?" Hopping over the doorstep, he stepped inside the door, the pale light from outside illuminating an entrance hall rendered in cracking clay. "Hello?" His heart beat so loud he doubted he'd hear a response. Under a door at the side of the hall seeped a red-orange glow. Overcoming his fear, he marched to the door and knocked. On creaking hinges, the door swung open.

Inside the dull room, a fire smouldered in a sooty fireplace with a stone hearth and chimney, warming a padded lounge chair upholstered with a worn paisley print. Discarded and disrespected, empty mugs and plates of half-eaten, mouldy food, littered the floor around the chair, and a literary carpet of books lay scattered and open, face down, their spines creased and flattened. Above the fire, dust-covered trinkets lined the sandstone mantlepiece, watched over by a crookedly hung painting, frayed at the edges and framed in splitting wood. Across the painted landscape, a young girl galloped her horse through an emerald meadow.

Tom crept towards the back of the chair, unable to see if anyone occupied the seat, as a rat scampered into the corner carrying a crumb of mouldy bread.

"Hello?" Stepping around the side of the chair, he grabbed the handle of the knife slipped under his belt. The knife Hadufuns had used to kill himself. The one Tom had taken from Annian's dead body. He didn't need the weapon because the chair sat empty.

A hiss spat out from behind him. "Have them, do you?"

Tom spun around. A draughoul blocked the doorway.

"Have them?" The draughoul drifted into the room and forced Tom into a corner.

Tom poked the knife at her. "Have what?"

"You know what. The *eyesss*. Show me."

"I don't have them."

"I feel them. Very close."

The draughoul grabbed Tom's arm. He squirmed under her crushing grip, but she held fast. With her free hand, she groped at his coat.

Won't be long before she finds them...

A faint plea came from the hallway. "Leave him, Mother."

The draughoul hissed, released her grip and stepped back.

"Let him be," said the voice, louder now.

The draughoul wailed and withdrew, retreating from the room and pushing past a man standing in the doorway, silhouetted by the daylight streaming in from outside. A man who resembled Malphas. Then the door slammed shut, and a key turned in the lock.

~ Chapter 32 ~

In the centre of Dalman, the grells had erected a shelter of de-furred animal skins stretched over a frame of supple tree branches covering the truce rock Marradir like a shield wall. A fire burned at one end, warming those who had been called to the most crucial meeting held in a generation. The Mulugan, an assembly of six stone-grells and six weald-grells, sat cross-legged on the damp ground beside the fire. While only the initiated could serve in the Mulugan, its members spanned different ages and genders. They were the principal decision-makers in grell culture, especially involving pronouncements affecting both stone- and weald-grells. Grin sat at the back of the shelter, unable to avoid the rippling disquiet spreading through the group. Yet to be initiated, he shouldn't be here, and neither should his companions; a Dobunni rebel, a mouldewerp and an Erstürmen princess. Inviting those outside the Mulugan to a meeting such as this was unknown in grell lore.

Extraordinary times, indeed, thought Grin.

Nannian, the balgabalgar for the meeting, held aloft the speaking stone — gari yala, an elongated oval of smooth granite slightly larger than her hand, to quiet the gathering. A well-respected stone-grell, Nannian had been a member of the Mulugan since her initiation many seasons ago.

"Welcome leaders and guests," she began. "Today's proceedings will

417

be conducted in the Erstürmen language for the sake of our visitors. The importance and urgency of this occasion should not be lost on any of us. For the first time in the memory of anyone here, we have gathered together grells, werps, Dobunni and Erstürmen. A meeting between all the main cultures of our homeland. I hope it will not be the last. The grave tidings we have heard can only be addressed by a united response. I have much to say, but first, I want to give others a voice. I declare the meeting open."

A shorter grell with turquoise eyes, the top of whose head would reach to Grin's shoulder, stood and raised his hand. Nannian gave him gari yala.

"I am Wyan weald-grell, a leader from Giigal. I have attended many of these meetings. While I am concerned an uninitiated grell has been granted an attendance, I am most angered by the invitation offered to our Erstürmen enemy. What if this princess is a spy, here to discover our weaknesses? Rumours are spreading throughout the camp."

Wyan returned gari yala to Nannian. "I accept your concerns, Wyan. However, the majority of the Mulugan voted to allow our guests. We are all bound by this decision."

Caeli stood and raised her hand, accepting gari yala from Nannian and cradling it in her palm. She traced her fingers over the decorations spiralling around the stone's surface. Grin didn't know Caeli well, holding his breath in anticipation of a fractured harmony.

She clutched the stone. "I could plead innocence and assurance, although I imagine some of you would still dismiss it as lies. I can't soothe all of your discomforts. The Erstürmen do not deserve such grace. Yet, I have chosen to be here in good faith and with hope. I have abandoned my kingdom and will serve it no longer, seeking only the solace of my kin. Before I ride to his embrace, I offer to share all I know among only you and keep all I learn to myself."

A sternness set on Wyan's face as Caeli passed gari yala to Frennan. "Now is not the time to cast doubt on the loyalties of our guests. They, too, could question our resolve. Tainted grells haunt our lands. Grell soldiers fight for our enemy. Could not the mouldewerps or Dobunni ask with honesty where *our* allegiances rest?"

Grin's cousin, the stone-grell Sunan, took gari yala. "I agree with Frennan. Now is the time for reflection and to consider the plight of all the cultures of Enthilen. What role can wild grells play in shaping the future? Are we so weak and easily corrupted, our prospects are only slavery or treachery?"

A weald-grell who Grin didn't know jumped to her feet. "We are enslaved not because we are weak, but because we are strong. Others may not suffer the same punishment and still endure."

"The slaves must rise up!" someone yelled.

Nannian raised her hand and seized gari yala from Sunan. "You cannot speak without the stone. There will be no more interruptions. Each will have their turn."

Wyan took the speaking stone. "What do we know of these tainted grells? Has anyone here seen them?"

Grin held up his hand. Wyan clenched his fist around gari yala, glaring at him, while murmurs spread through the group.

Someone said, "Let the uninitiated speak."

Wyan relented and handed gari yala to Grin.

"I have seen them," said Grin. "Been hunted by them. With my Dobunni friends, I confronted the tainted grells on a bluff above Laodicea. A female with sick, pale skin. A male with garnet skin like his body had been stained with poisoned blood, and another male with tainted skin of malevolent black. There is a white one also — Eroberung, who almost captured us in the Scaur Hills. The tainted grells fill me with fear and sorrow. Their crests have been stripped from their faces, the light in their eyes forever scarred. I cannot imagine the anguish they endured to exist in such a state, heartless and without spirit. I only hope they have not crossed a threshold from which there is no return. That they can be saved."

The gathering sat silent long after Grin finished speaking. Some rubbed their skin as if washing away a stain with coarse river sand. Dwarrow stood and tottered over to Grin, tapping him on the knee with his walking stick and holding out his clawed hand for gari yala.

"Please don't take offence at what I'm about to say," said Dwarrow. "It may surprise you that a werp knows anything about grells. But, you see, we know a lot. It's the only way we can avoid you."

Dwarrow smiled, but his attempted humour fell in the silent forest like a heavy, dead tree. He gripped gari yala tighter. "I understand you hunted us out of naivety, not malice, because you failed to appreciate this new land you had settled. My ancestors were there when your dugouts landed on our southern shores. As seasons passed, they watched you spread through the forest you call Babir Birramal, seeking open space where you could run and hunt. Then one day, you found it, the place you call the Dambay Plains. However, it wasn't an empty space. We were there, under the surface, living in our dwells as we had done for generations. To you, they probably resembled nothing more than a scattering of holes in the ground — the burrows of plains rodents. No doubt our language sounded like grunts and howls. There was no avenue for either of us to negotiate peace, and you were hungry.

"My elders now realise grells and werps should be enemies no longer, and we have nothing more to fear from you. That, indeed, we should be friends with much wisdom to share. It will be a long time before werps and grells again live together on the Dambay Plains. I hope I'm alive to see that day. Us, in our dwells, and you in your grand halls and towers.

"Now, we must come together to face a common foe. No culture has suffered more at the hands of the Erstürmen than the grells, not even the Dobunni. Your community, crushed by slavery. Desperate grells looking to escape the malaise have agreed to fight for the Erstürmen. Pity them and hope for them, don't lament their existence or punish your will for its frailties. When the Erstürmen come for the werps, what traits of ours might they exploit to further their stranglehold on Enthilen? Don't focus your anger on the grell soldiers or even the tainted grells. Focus it on the one monster who orchestrates this whole malfeasance."

"Who are you talking about?" one of the leaders shouted, then shrank under a stern look from Nannian.

"His name is Malphas," said Dwarrow, "and his presence swamps our lands, foul deeds following his every footprint. He is a cunning horror cloaked in the veil of a feeble old man, taking attributes like strength, loyalty and respect, and steering them to repellent outcomes. You are strong, so he uses your strength to build an army. You are loyal, so he preys on your loyalty to secure an allegiance. You are respectful and willing, so when your spirit is broken, he knows he can trust you with his closest confidence. You see, my friends, a trait is neither good nor bad; it just is. The context defines the outcome. My elders say I'm stubborn and belligerent, but it's my stubbornness that sees me here today, that saved Princess Caeli and Tom Anderson, and may one day save our home. Sometimes I'm embarrassed by my unwillingness to back down, and other times I'm amazed by it."

A female weald-grell took gari yala from Dwarrow. "I am Quenan weald-grell. Thank you for your candid words, Dwarrow. They bring me much comfort. However, I feel we are not being told all there is to know. That our new friends may be holding things back, or even our own kin are keeping secrets. I want to know more about this Tom Anderson."

Quenan waited. Grin glanced at Frennan and then at Thaly. Dwarrow bowed his head, and Caeli's eyes drifted off into the forest. Grin knew each of them held a part of Tom's story in their memory, but even together, they likely didn't understand the whole. Despite the significance of the occasion, only one was prepared to be the first to speak.

Frennan raised his hand and took gari yala. "Tom Anderson is a birraman."

A couple of leaders gasped. Frennan paused, then continued, "Grin saved him from drowning and brought him to our milbi at the edge of Babir Birramal."

"There has not been a birraman among us since the first ancestors," said Wyan, followed by further outbursts from other leaders.

Control of the meeting slipped from Nannian's grasp.

Frennan persisted. "He came with things we have never seen. Things from his world. A world like ours in some ways, but unlike ours in many others according to what he told us. And, he came with the eyes of lost souls."

"He is damned!"

"Curse him!"

Frennan raised gari yala above his head, trying to still the gathering. "We all know the lore. Grells must never touch the dark eyes. Grin and I were careful. Tom took the eyes when he left our milbi. Now others are hunting him. We should not get involved in these matters any further." Frennan sat, casting a determined look at Grin.

Grin took the speaking stone from his father. "There is no need to concern ourselves with Tom Anderson. I am almost certain he is dead."

"Not at all," blurted Dwarrow. "Not dead at all."

What? thought Grin. How does the werp know? Thaly stood at the fringe of the shelter, mouth agape, as Grin handed Dwarrow gari yala.

"Well, it seems I'll have to explain myself," said Dwarrow. "Tom Anderson and King Adalwolf share the same lifeforce. They are birth twins. While Adalwolf still lives, so does Tom. When Adalwolf dies, so does Tom. And vice versa. Unless one kills the other using the eyes of lost souls."

A burden fell from Grin's shoulders. Thaly must have felt it, too, as her body relaxed. Tom didn't die in the shipwreck. Somehow, he survived.

Thaly walked over to Grin and placed a comforting hand on his arm. "Tom's alive."

He nodded and smiled.

Thaly took the speaking stone from Dwarrow before facing the Mulugan. "You can't avoid it. All that is happening. To you, to the Dobunni, to our home. It's all in the plans of just one man. I saw Malphas on Hansen's Bluff, wielding the power of tainted grells with a wave of his hand. I believe he seeks to unleash a suffering on Enthilen that none will endure."

"We must kill Malphas."

"Attack the Erstürmen and end this."

"Grells do not attack. We only defend."

Nannian took gari yala. "Where is this Malphas?"

"Almost certainly in Malang Gunya with King Adalwolf," said Dwarrow, not waiting to be handed the stone.

Nannian let the lack the protocol pass. "Then it appears the desires of the grells and our new friends have converged. As with every first blossom of the sacred panalope tree, the grells will march to Malang Gunya. There is where the enemy resides. We must face them and crush this new invasion of our ancestral home."

Grin didn't know whether to cry or rejoice. Part of him wanted to convince the Mulugan not to march. To call it off and avoid a massacre. Another part of him wanted to fight. To confront Malphas again like he'd done on Hansen's Bluff, but this time to cut him down and end the terror, not flee from the old man's cruel taunts like they were arrows. In the end, he knew the decision wasn't his to make. The Mulugan would decide.

"With what shall we fight?" asked Sunan. "Wild stone-grells are few in number and our weapons basic. We have no armour and no army."

"The weald-grells must fight!" yelled a leader.

Wyan sprang to his feet. "The weald-grells at this garrabari will defend our kin, but we will not attack. Such aggression is what led to the tribal war. It is written on Marradir, and on Marradir we signed a pledge, weald- and stone-grell, never to show this aggression again. Once the anger in us is unleashed, it...it...we will not follow that path again. Those still in Giigal will stay there, safe and free."

"For how long?" asked Quenan.

Mirrian stood, clutching gari yala. "Let the females march."

"It is too dangerous," said Frennan.

Mirrian looked down at her ngubaan, who sat cross-legged on the ground. "I am too old to bear young. I spend my days in Giigal fretting over the safety of you and Grin. I want my life to have a purpose again. I want to fight for our home, like you."

Grin shook his head. This wasn't right. He never expected his mother to argue for the females to march. They'd not marched for many seasons and risked being slaughtered.

"If the females march, then all the weald-grells should too," said Sunan. "Why do they hide in their city? Why are they so weak?"

"Weak!?" Wyan loomed over Sunan. "It is the stone-grells who are slaves. The stone-grells who are tainted. I venture it is stone-grells marching in this new Erstürmen army. You are the ones who are weak. You are the ones who threaten our future."

"Weald-grells are slaves too," growled Sunan. "But you are too weak to be fighters. Small and cowardly..."

Wyan lunged at Sunan as she jumped to her feet. The other leaders stood, tensed.

Mirrian pushed between the combatants. "Stop it! If we fight among ourselves, then our enemies' victory is assured."

Quenan shouted over the din, "Abandon the march! Bring all the wild stone-grells to Giigal. If the Erstürmen come for us, we can make a stand there, together and strong."

Nannian held gari yala high above her head, resting her other hand on the face of Marradir. "Sit, everyone. The casting of aspersions must cease. Sit. Please. We witnessed this truce many seasons ago. It will stand at whatever cost."

The gathering calmed as Nannian's face showed a steely resolve. "Quenan asks us to abandon the march. There is no obligation for anyone to place their lives in danger. There never has been. Yet, I know most of you will not abandon the memory of our ancestors. Mirrian seeks permission for females to honour that memory. A long time ago, we agreed females should remain in the forest. That we could not risk their lives lest wild grells disappear from Enthilen forever. However, those days are gone. I cannot live to see Malang Gunya fall again. To have it despoiled by the enemy a second time and bear the burden of doing nothing. The males want to protect us, but what for? What for when all we love is being torn apart before our eyes. I will not sit and wait. I will not hide or slink back to the miraged safety of the weald-grell city. When the panalope flower blooms, I will march."

Wyan stood, holding out his hand for gari yala. The stone-grells near him tensed. Nannian handed Wyan the stone. "There is no higher honour among weald-grells than to honour the truce of Dalman," he said. "I will march."

Wyan gave the stone to Mirrian. "I will march," she said.

Grin stood, walked over to his mother and took gari yala. He looked into her eyes, never averting his gaze. "I came here to warn you not to march. But what future am I asking you to embrace? We can honour our ancestors and the land sustaining us in no greater way than to lay down our lives. I see that now. I will march."

Thaly stood beside Grin, her determined face set hard and a fire burning in brown eyes that had looked so sad since Jacob's death. The muscles of her arm tensed as she took the speaking stone from him and planted her feet firmly into the soil of Dalman.

"I will march," she said. "For my friend Jacob. For my family. For all the Dobunni."

In turn, every leader committed to march. The last to speak, Frennan, took gari yala. "It is settled. We march at the first flower. That has always been the custom and always will. Until the last grell fails to draw breath."

* * * *

Thaly had found a second home among the grells in their beautiful forest and a new friendship with an Erstürmen woman who, under different circumstances, she would consider an enemy. This was a storm season, guma the grells called it, Thaly would remember forever. A season where dark clouds rushed across the horizon, bringing change and upheaval, and hard, stinging rain that pelted the skin to remind you of your vulnerability. A season punctured by intermissions of vast, blue skies and the scents of nature cleansed by crystal air. This land, Enthilen, had changed forever, and she would change with it.

At dawn on the morning after the meeting of the Mulugan, Thaly held Hanni's hand as the young grell received her facial crest, the spear fern 'gama'. The fronds began at Hanni's chin and unfurled across her cheeks, tips pointing to resolute lilac eyes glimmering with innocence.

Mirrian tattooed her daughter using the fang of a cave python dipped in a special ink made from the sap of the panalope tree mixed with a black die extracted from the fruit of a plant known only to grell elders. As the fang pressed in and under Hanni's skin, the young grell squeezed her eyes tight and pressed her lips together, trying not to show the pain. Yet it writhed across her face such that Thaly flinched whenever Mirrian began a new part of the crest design. By mid-morning, the ordeal was over, and Hanni sprang to her feet, asking everyone how it looked.

"Is it fierce?" she asked Thaly.

Thaly smiled. "Fierce and beautiful. Like you."

She hugged Thaly, and they engaged in a formal goodbye, Thaly being especially careful not to press her fingers too hard on Hannian's newly tattooed cheeks. Hanni was too young to march and would return to Giigal. Little more than a child, and now she would be separated from both parents for the first time and, possibly, lose them forever. Thaly knew the ache, and she hated that Hanni might know it as well.

With the sun overhead, the grells began their walk to the ngulubul, a place on the edge of Babir Birramal where a giant panalope tree grew, and where they would wait for the first flower blossom to signal the beginning of the homage march. Grin had already left, taken with six other initiates by a group of elders further into the forest to a remote and secret location. There, over the next three days, Thaly had learned the young male and female grells would be instructed in the most sacred of ancestral lore. After their initiation, they would meet up with the other grells on the edge of Babir Birramal and join the march.

Without Grin or Hanni for company, Thaly walked with Caeli and Dwarrow, who acted like the closest of friends. She pressed Dwarrow further about the connection between Tom and Adalwolf, learning both had a chance at immortality if they killed the other using the dark eyes. She wondered if Tom understood this and whether he'd be seduced by the temptation of eternal life. The events that transpired on Hansen's Bluff now made more sense to her. Adalwolf was trying to kill Tom using the eyes of lost souls and become immortal. Why did Malphas desire such an outcome? Even Dwarrow could not explain that to Thaly, or he kept the explanation to himself.

On the afternoon of the third day since leaving Dalman, they arrived at the location of the ngulubul, the meeting place.

"This is where we must part ways again," Dwarrow said to Thaly.

"You're not marching with us?"

"I will meet you at Malang Gunya. First, I must return to the Scaur Hills to speak with the werp elders. The Mulugan gave me a special gift; a flake of stone from Marradir with a secret symbol etched onto its face. They call it 'gulba' — the peace stone. It signifies they have accepted the werps' offer of a truce. Now I must see if I can convince my kin to fight alongside the grells at Malang Gunya if it comes to that. When next we meet, I hope to have a wild, ravaging horde of werps at my disposal."

"I need to leave also," said Caeli. "How will I find Casfern?"

"No need to fret, Princess. Xaviary will be looking after her. We weren't far from here when we left them. I'll call them up." Dwarrow fished around in his backpack and pulled out a strange-looking implement. He must have sensed Thaly's bewilderment.

"It's a bullroarer," he said.

Thaly shrugged, still confused.

"You'll see." Dwarrow unwound the string from the bullroarer, raised himself up on the balls of his clawed feet, and spun the instrument over his head, nearly whacking the shins of a nearby grell who had to jump to avoid the whirling missile. After a lot of noise and commotion, Dwarrow ended the roarer's flight, wound the string around its smooth face, and stuffed it back inside his satchel.

"Who's Xaviary?" asked Thaly.

"So many questions," said Dwarrow. "Be patient." He tapped his foot on the ground and sniffed the air, his flexible nose twisting in all directions, then folded his arms and tapped his foot some more. Xaviary didn't appear. With a huff, he retrieved the bullroarer from the satchel and sent it on another flight. A pulsating hum reverberated among the trees as the werp swung the instrument so hard he knocked himself off balance and crashed onto the grass, the bullroarer colliding with his head.

"OW! Ow, ow ow."

Thaly and Caeli looked at each other, fighting hard not to laugh.

Dwarrow sprang to his feet, brushed himself off like nothing had happened, and inhaled. "I can't even smell her. Or Casfern. I wonder what's taking so long?"

Frennan approached the group. "What are you waiting for?"

"I'm *not* waiting for more silly questions." Dwarrow stiffened and raised his hand. "Stop. Stand still. Don't disturb the scents. I thought I smelled something." He sniffed again. "Wait. She's coming."

After further delay, Thaly almost gave up until an enormous lizard lumbered out of the trees, standing as tall as the spotted grey mare following it. Caeli ran to the horse, and the lizard sauntered straight up to Dwarrow, bent down and flicked its tongue across his face.

"*Errgh.* I wish she wouldn't do that," he said. "Her breath does not have a particularly pleasant bouquet."

"That is a ngambuny," said Frennan.

"No. No. No. It's not a *gambunny*. It's not a *dragon*. Her name's Xaviary."

The lizard swung her tail down, and Dwarrow used it as a ramp to climb onto her back. At this height, he could almost look Frennan directly in the eye. "We will meet again, my new grell friend, on the outskirts of Malang Gunya."

"I hope it is a time of celebration." The tone of Frennan's voice and his sombre face suggested he didn't believe in his own hope. He nodded at Dwarrow and walked off.

The werp clutched Xaviary's neck and leaned down towards Thaly. "I know you feel like you've abandoned Tom, but have faith we'll see him again, probably when we least expect." Dwarrow bid his goodbyes to Thaly and Caeli before turning his mount north towards the Scaur Hills.

Thaly strolled over to Caeli, who stood on the fringe of the gathering, feeding and brushing Casfern's flank. "I guess you're leaving today also?" said Thaly.

Caeli looked up. "Yes. I'm going to find my father. It's been so long since we've seen each other. Mirrian was kind enough to confirm my directions. Seven days of riding and walking, and I should be there. I hope I have enough supplies for the journey."

"Safe travels."

Thaly turned away, but Caeli reached for her arm. "You understand that just because someone is Erstürmen, they are not immoral. My ancestors were also refugees. Banished from our home by the Nordmen."

"But you came to conquer, not to make peace. The Dobunni would have taken you in. Provided shelter. Shared our knowledge and our home."

"You're right, Thaly. Conflict defines us. Dictates our culture. It seems an untethered patriarchy yields never-ending battles."

"Can't women hold positions of power?"

"Never. Men have always ruled. I'm of royal blood, yet my value rests only in my ability to give life to another man. Leadership is inherited, through family, by the first-born male of the king. If the king has no sons, then his eldest brother will take the throne and his sons after that. Adalwolf's ancestors have held the throne for generations."

"It sounds like a sad and desperate place for a woman. Dwarrow told me about your life. Locked away. Ewald's plaything. How did you survive?"

"I endured because I had a duty to my kingdom, and I needed to keep my father safe. Outside the keep prison, others could use me to get to him."

"I'm sorry you suffered for so long."

Caeli smiled. "Even from my barred window atop the Sunrise Keep, I could see the good in people. Every day I watched them help each other overcome the challenges of life. Erstürmen people. Men and women. There is good and bad in both. I can't give up on them. If we all give up, how will anything ever change?"

Caeli squeezed Thaly's hand and tried to let go, but Thaly pulled her in and kissed her on the lips. Caeli jerked her head back, big, round eyes flashing surprise.

A flush of embarrassment stung Thaly's face, and she withdrew, averting her gaze. "Sorry. Sorry. I'm a stupid idiot. I'm so sorry."

Caeli clasped Thaly's hand again and smiled. "Don't be sorry. It was an act of honest affection. I will cherish it always."

"I forgot to thank you," said Thaly.

"For what?"

"You helped Tom Anderson escape Sardis. He thought you had died."

Caeli winked. "I'm much harder to kill than that. But an honourable young man gave his life to protect Tom. An Erstürmen King's Shield. His death is a burden I will bear for the rest of my life."

"Do you think Tom made it to Bindari?" asked Thaly. "That's where you sent him, isn't it?"

"If he did, then I hope he finds the answers he seeks." Caeli finished brushing Casfern and checked the supplies in her pack. Thaly helped her mount the horse, the princess having to steady herself on Casfern's bare back.

"You need a saddle," said Thaly.

"I also need a pair of pants," said Caeli, smiling. "A torn skirt and ratty old cloak are not the best riding attire. I'll make do like we all must. At least the grells gave me a pair of moccasins to protect my feet." She grasped Casfern's reins, a makeshift harness made from weathered rope. "Farewell, Athalee of Bagendon. You have endured much. Don't let the suffering of the past destroy your future. Each day begins anew, and on one of those days, we'll meet again. When we do, we'll meet as friends."

Caeli pulled a cowl over her head and masked the bottom of her face with a handkerchief. She turned her horse and rode off into the forest.

Thaly stood alone until Caeli disappeared from view. It was only her and the grells now; one Dobunni rebel and a few hundred stone- and weald-grells preparing to march against the entire Erstürmen Kingdom and the demon Malphas.

~ Chapter 33 ~

Adalwolf stood at the bottom of the gigantic pyramid that dominated the skyline of Malang Gunya, counting the steps to the dais at the top where six fluted, granite columns with a roof of imbricated slate tiles crowned by a polished spire shimmered in the muted light of dawn. He still thought of this place as the grell city. It wasn't Pergamos yet, though he made sure never to use the name Malang Gunya in the presence of Malphas or his confidants.

After counting to one hundred and fifty steps, he gave up with at least that many more left to count. Partway up the steps, there was an entrance into the belly of the colossal monument. If he didn't reach the top, he could at least explore the chamber hidden there.

For once, Adalwolf was alone, Ende not shadowing him, Malphas not calling him to another audience. Guards stood at the base of the pyramid watching over the hole in the ground leading to the halls of Pergamos below. But they were *his* guards, the King's Shield, and he'd ordered them to stay put. Dressed in fawn pants and a light tunic, not the cumbersome robes of a king, he'd been planning this adventure ever since arriving in Malang Gunya, and he would make the journey to the top of the pyramid by himself.

Adalwolf tackled the first step, lifting his leg until his thigh was parallel to the ground. The steps were made for grells, not people, and the prospect of hundreds of such efforts made his muscles baulk. Nevertheless, he attacked the lower steps with zeal, bounding up one after the other like a mountain sheep desperate to reach a lush alpine meadow. Soon, sweat trickled down his chest underneath the tunic, the storm season yielding bright blue skies today and a morning sun that kissed his skin with a sting.

A quarter of the way up, he reached a balcony and the chamber entrance he'd seen from the ground. He stopped outside to mop the perspiration that dripped down his face and drenched the thickening facial hair on his upper lip. He'd have to sharpen his knife and start shaving, unless he wanted to cultivate a bushy, tousled beard like the one that had adorned his departed predecessor, Ewald.

Ambling into the chamber through a segmental arch wider than two arm-spans, Adalwolf welcomed the shade and the chance to rest. Pasture swallows burst from the shadows making him jump, their perches of dried mud clinging to the corners of the chamber atop shin-high piles of droppings. In the middle of the vast space, stood a single slab of square rock with a smooth, flat top, almost as tall as Adalwolf and larger than his bed.

An altar, once? he wondered, the rock now cracked and chipped, fragments of stone littering its base like lost children, and dangles of spiderwebs clinging to the lip of the dais. On the sides, the grells had carved pictures of themselves walking on the plains or rowing canoes across unknown waters.

Did they worship a god in this place? Several gods? He knew nothing about the wild grells, and now he expected a horde of them to arrive on his doorstep, Malphas demanding the king take charge of the encounter. If Adalwolf wanted to please his father and avoid further torment, he needed to decipher the best outcome of the grell's pilgrimage to Malang Gunya. At least, he knew that the pilgrims couldn't leave the city without paying a price.

Faded paintings of forests, rivers, plains and animals decorated the chamber walls, now covered with scrawls of graffiti denouncing all respect for grell culture. Ogee arches marked the entrance to dark passages, likely leading further into the bowels of the pyramid. Adalwolf had no intention of exploring the paths alone, not knowing where they went and picturing them filled with giant, vengeful ghosts looking to serve justice to the destroyers of their civilisation.

His body cooled in the shade of the chamber, and he shivered at the thought of grell spirits before resuming his exploration. The pyramid steepened the further he climbed, his thigh and calf muscles protesting with every step. Stiffness and pain would assault him in the coming days, the war wounds of a conquest of Malang Gunya's highest peak. As the city's streets shrank into insignificance, nauseating dizziness set upon him, and he turned his eyes to his feet and kept them there. A topple backwards would almost certainly mean crashing to the flagstones below.

Reaching the top, Adalwolf stepped onto a flat, circular platform ringed by the six, fluted stone columns with pedestals resembling the roots of trees, and capitals adorned with carvings of broad, trident-shaped leaves. A dozen men could squeeze onto the platform at once, possibly half a dozen adult grells. The mid-morning sun burst through a gap in the columns facing east, reminding him no walls around the platform would stop him from plummeting to his death from an errant footfall.

Under his feet, carved into a stone that appeared to be a cross-section from a single, massive boulder, was a circle with lines radiating outwards tipped with arrowheads pointing to different parts of the city and beyond. His eyes followed one of the arrows, leading to a collapsed building in the distance that may have been five or six stories high once. Tangled plants grew out of the rubble, now being cleared by Erstürmen pilgrims who resembled a plague of mice from this high up.

The largest arrow pointed south to Grōz Forst, which Adalwolf convinced himself he could see as a dark line on the horizon. Yet another arrow pointed due north to the Desolate Mountains. Defying vertigo, he stepped to the platform's edge and breathed in the spectacle at his feet. Here he was, in the centre of Enthilen. The centre of his kingdom. *His* kingdom. His subjects toiled below, clearing debris from irrigation channels that would soon run with water, erecting timber and stone barricades to defend against covetous enemies, laying the foundations of an enormous wall that would surround the city, and guiding oxen-drawn ploughs that furrowed the grey soil of the Dambay Plains.

What would Pergamos look like when the work was done? What majesty would he lord over? The halls underground were grand, no doubt, yet they paled in comparison to the shining metropolis he could build using the skeleton of Malang Gunya.

A mirage in the distance took form, breaking the spell of his daydream. Riders on the plain, thick-set and monstrous, galloped towards the city on dozens of horned beasts. The largest rider on a red horse led the group, his tainted skin like a blood-red sunrise heralding a new dawn. Krieg had returned to his master, reminding Adalwolf the new Erstürmen Kingdom was held together by threads woven with sinister malice that threatened to wrap him in a deathly shroud.

* * * *

Lothar marched through the oak doors and into the throne hall of Pergamos, summoned by the Worshipful Master. As he strode down the aisle, grell slaves clambering atop timber scaffolds plastered over the cracks and holes in the walls and ceiling to hide the evidence of Volerdie's Wrath. Others placed busts of Volerdie or his disciples onto pedestals or hung rewoven tapestries and refreshed paintings of the joy of life during Pergamos' glory days.

The clean-shaven, youthful face of the Divine Creator once again watched over his seat of power. Depictions of Volerdie were deliberately plain: a young, androgynous face that could be male or female; a medium nose and eyes with flecks of blue-green, brown and grey such that they could be one or another depending on the light; and straight hair draped across broad shoulders. The unremarkable illustrations meant many citizens could see their own face in the image of the Creator. For an older man with a thick, grey beard, such youthful apparitions held no relevance, and, anyway, Lothar considered the comparison of oneself to the Divine Creator as blasphemous.

He stopped mid-aisle as a grell slave pulled on a rope threaded through a pulley bolted to the ceiling, hoisting an enormous, tiered chandelier with nearly fifty candles up to the height of her chest. She took a metal flint striker and lit a wick soaked in oil, touching the flame to each candle and not flinching once at the fire scalding her knuckles. Lothar imagined the chandelier crashing to the floor in a streak of embers should the new residents of Pergamos invoke Volerdie's Wrath a second time. Though the Worshipful Master considered the threat of such an event to have passed, Lothar wasn't convinced.

Outside the double oak doors, across a wide passageway, the bustle and clatter of servants moving chests and furniture into nearby residences filtered into the throne hall. The royal court continued its recolonisation of the long-lost emptiness. Malphas, Adalwolf, Lothar, Romilda and the tainted grells would have their quarters here, the Rephaim housed further along the hall in larger rooms being outfitted as military barracks. Lothar wondered if Volerdie would have let a grell heathen grace his halls.

He reached the bottom step of the six leading to the summit of the throne platform. Atop the podium, Malphas lounged on the throne of the dead, his body draped over those now petrified and resembling part of the contortion. Ende stood behind her master as she often did, expressionless black eyes staring into space.

Lothar wondered what, if any, thoughts might pass through her head. Do grells dream? Part of him hoped for Ende's sake they didn't. Otherwise, he could think of nothing other than torturous visions of an unending procession of death.

Behind the platform, Malphas had chained his draughoul spies to the wall. Twelve of them wavered in a line, leaning achingly towards the throne of the dead. Malphas used their insatiable desire to be close to the trappings of Volerdie's power to his advantage. Time in the presence of Volerdie's treasures could be exchanged for service to the Worshipful Master as spies and messengers.

Lothar dropped to his knees before the bottom step and bowed his head waiting for his master's acknowledgement.

"What news do you have for me, Lothar?" asked Malphas.

"A victorious Krieg has returned, Worshipful Master. Bagendon has been burned to the ground."

"I would have expected nothing less. The burden I bear is considerably lessened by the devotion of faithful servants."

"There was Eroberung," said Lothar, feeling the regret of a fool as soon as the words left his mouth. It was unwise to remind the Worshipful Master of past disappointment.

"You can rise," said Malphas.

Lothar stood and lifted his face, fighting to keep a placid expression.

"Eroberung's failure is of little consequence," said Malphas, grasping the armrests of the throne and lifting himself to his feet. He paced across the platform in silence, hands clasped behind his back, then stopped dead and turned to Lothar. "Where is Adalwolf?"

"I've not seen him this morning, Master."

"*Hmmm.* Neither has Ende. Preparations for the cleansing of Pergamos of the wild grell heathens need to be taken seriously. I hope the boy hasn't absconded in his duty."

"I can find the king," said Lothar, eager to be released from Malphas' attention.

"No need. Adalwolf can't avoid his responsibilities for long. I mean, what choice does he have? What choice do any of us have? All of us share the burden of preparing Enthilen for the return of Volerdie and of demonstrating sufficient piety to enshrine our place in paradise." Malphas glanced at Ende, who stared straight ahead, holding herself upright against the handle of her sparth. "I'm dismissing the King's Shield from immediate royal duties," he said. "Now the Rephaim have returned, they'll be the new king's guard, watching over the halls and rooms of Pergamos and keeping us safe."

Lothar started as Malphas clapped his hands once and yelled to the slaves, "Leave us!"

The hall emptied in a handful of blinks. As the last slave left and closed the doors behind herself, Lothar's thoughts returned to the reason he may have been summoned. A reason soon to be revealed. He rolled up onto the balls of his feet, then back down to his heels over and over, trying to get the blood flowing into aching legs. Malphas tottered down the stairs and stood almost shoulder to shoulder with Lothar, looking at the main door behind Lothar's back. They waited there together in silence, Lothar finding his eyes always settling on Ende's pallid face despite his attempts to avoid her. Underneath his sangria robes, sweat trickled down his back, stinging the open wounds inflicted by the lash of repentance that marked the yearn for Volerdie's forgiveness.

The silence grew so terrifying in Lothar's mind he began to think about fleeing.

Malphas released the press. "Silence reveals a truth not found in the loudest proclamations of those pleading innocence. Don't you agree, Hoch-Vater?"

Lothar opened his parched mouth, but no sound escaped.

Malphas continued, "Those in my confidence, including you, know I possess *Da Und Sepcarture* — the First Scripture. Indeed, it was the promise of discovering the scripture's secrets that lured you here in the first place, was it not? That encouraged you to accept my offer to become Adalwolf's curate and the high father of Enthilen?"

"Yes, Worshipful Master. Though, I would have gladly served without such motivation." Lothar didn't dare turn his head. Nevertheless, he sensed Malphas smile.

"Indeed," said Malphas. "Few understand the First Scripture's value. My tainted grells have no interest in it, and Adalwolf and his mother are simpletons. I could place the scripture under their pillow, and they'd likely use it to wipe their royal backsides. But you, Hoch-Vater, you know the worth of such a document."

Lothar bowed his head and didn't respond lest a quivering voice betrayed him.

"Imagine the collective longing of all the curates in Erstürmen history that have forged their dreams into the singular hope of one day discovering the First Scripture. That convinced themselves the sacred parchment truly exists, rather than an aberration from a lost world. Imagine how they would feel to know I was the one to find it. Nothing more than a lowly, exiled king. How does it make *you* feel, Lothar?"

"I'm not sure what you mean, Worshipful Master."

"Your eyes must ache with the promise of reading Volerdie's words written in his own blood. To be so close to the will of the Divine Creator."

"I'm content serving the Creator in whatever way you deem appropriate."

"But it must play on your mind that I'm yet to show you the scripture. It must play on your mind something terrible." Malphas sidled closer until his breath pressed into Lothar's left ear, beating against the drum like a pulsing gale threatening to tear a flag from its mast. Ende stepped to the front of the throne platform and tapped the end of her sparth on the edge of the marble platform, making Lothar flinch. His mind screamed for him to avert his eyes from the face of death, but fear froze every muscle in his body.

Malphas sighed another ear-piercing breath. "Servants moving furniture into our new quarters, unpacking chests, cleaning up after Volerdie's Wrath. Amid all this chaos, a careful thief, a duplicitous confidant, may use the opportunity to secure access to that which he has no right. While the First Scripture was securely stored, I can't dismiss this constant nagging in the marrow of my bones that the chest in which it was housed had been moved to a place I did not request it."

"If you're worried about your capacity to secure the First Scripture, Worshipful Master, I could watch over it for you." A bold bluff, thought Lothar.

A muted laugh left Malphas' lips. "That won't be necessary, Lothar. No doubt, I worry for nothing. The burden of rule enhances one's paranoia. No, I've found another safe place for the scripture. Guarded by the descendants of Volerdie's hounds."

Malphas turned and climbed the stairs, one slow step at a time, pushing his hand into his upper thigh to lever himself up.

The pretence of the frail old man continued for the benefit of who? thought Lothar.

When Malphas reached Ende, he tangled his fingers in the strands of her long, wispy hair, twirling the ends around his fingertips like the caress of a lover.

"One day, Hoch-Vater, I'll show you the First Scripture. When

Volerdie deems you worthy of such a privilege. Until then, you must prepare with Adalwolf for the coming of the grell pilgrims."

Another silence filled the cavernous throne hall. Lothar waited to be dismissed, but Malphas stood with this back turned, engrossed in Ende's thinning mane. Finally, Lothar bowed to no-one other than the face of death, and scuttled from the room.

*   *   *   *

Romilda sat in her new underground quarters in Pergamos on a plush, high-backed chair, the cushion and backrest covered in royal blue velvet. Yet to be opened, chests lined the walls, waiting for servants to unpack and decorate the room with the possessions she'd sent for from Sardis. Even though the room had not been used for generations, once revived, the surroundings would match the quarters she shared with Ewald in the royal city.

A fireplace with a granite mantlepiece stood to the side of the room, it's hearth full of debris and the chimney almost certainly blocked with yarles of dust and dirt. Romilda pitied the servant who would be required to clamber down the chimney to get it functioning again. At least, she thought, it wouldn't be a grell slave. They were much too large to squeeze inside the brick column.

Her bed from Sardis dominated the room's centre, a dark timber frame with four posts carved as spirals supporting a railed tester from which hung black curtains that could enclose the entire mattress. Romilda smiled to herself. Such privacy was hardly necessary. She wouldn't share this bed with anyone unless a chance for another liaison with Lothar presented itself. Unlikely, she thought, expecting death to be the next companion to soil her sheets.

Seronan appeared at the doorway to Romilda's quarters, trying to look small and insignificant like she often did. Romilda smiled at the foolishness of a goliath who attempted to appear as a mouse. She knew a fire smouldered in the slave's belly — a determination that could be exploited.

"Come in," said Romilda.

Seronan entered, her crown brushing the underside of the door lintel. "I have come to clean your room, Queen Mother. Shall I change the chamber pot first?"

"Leave it for a while. Come, sit and talk with me. Your company is more desirable than a clean room."

Seronan went to sit on one of the tea chests, but Romilda stopped her. "Sit on my bed. It's much more comfortable."

Though smaller than the stone-grells, the weald-grell slave's frame still sank into the feather mattress as she sat on the edge of the bed beside Romilda, her eyes fixed and frozen like a doe under the claw of a lioness.

Romilda leaned across and whispered, "You can call me Romilda. Here in my chambers, when no-one else is listening."

Seronan nodded.

"When do you think the wild grells will arrive?"

"Soon, Queen...Romilda. They will wait for the first blossom of the panalope tree marking the beginning of the long dark. Then they will begin the march from Grōz Forst."

"It seems unusual to have a plant flowering when the days are so short and the nights long and bleak."

"It is a reason why the tree is so worshipped, being one of the few plants to radiate life and colour amid the dark."

Romilda leaned back in her chair, clutching in her hand the veil that usually covered her face. "I will speak to my son."

Seronan looked like she didn't know what Romilda meant.

"About the pilgrimage," continued Romilda. "I will convince him to let the wild grells alone. To let them remember their kin in peace and to leave this place unharmed. He still yearns for my comfort, despite what he did to me. Though he may be the king, he's a boy at heart. One that seeks his mother's counsel. Do you have children, Seronan?"

The slave shook her head. "She was killed."

"Oh. I'm sorry."

"Is it possible," asked Seronan, "to let the marchers remember in peace?"

Romilda smiled, feeling the tug of the scar on her cheek. "I imagine you wonder where the power lies in this court. Malphas has power; there's no doubt about that. However, his authority is not absolute. That's why he had to have Adalwolf crowned in Laodicea. Only the rightful king could lead the Erstürmen to the promise of Pergamos. The promise of a city lying in ruins. Although Malphas desires Pergamos' resurrection to suit his own ambitions, he needed my son to begin this journey. Yes, the Worshipful Master controls the tainted grells and this new abomination, the Rephaim, but he doesn't control the Erstürmen people. Some would still remember him as the exiled King Oldaric and expose him as a usurper, denouncing any claims to rule. He needed Adalwolf to lead the people here, but he needs my son for another purpose. One I will soon uncover with your help."

"H-h-how?" asked Seronan.

"Lothar, the Hoch-Vater, the Proclaimant of the King, as if that poor excuse for a curate could claim to speak for the King of Enthilen, has a weakness. I've tested it and found him wanting."

Seronan sat still and quiet. Romilda sensed her weighing implications in her mind. The grell slave was smart; her will unbroken. Romilda had spoken to Henruld the overseer about her, learning of an attentive disposition punctuated by moments of defiance. Wise, intense and desperate to protect her kin.

"No doubt you're wondering what it is I want from you, Seronan? In exchange for my plea to King Adalwolf to spare your beloved wild grells."

For the first time, Seronan stopped staring blankly at the wall and turned to Romilda, not a flicker of repulsion crossing her face.

She's not concerned about the hideous scar blighting my complexion, thought Romilda. She's looking deeper — into my soul.

"Yes, Romilda. I wonder what you will ask me to do."

Romilda sat forward, reached across to the bed and grasped Seronan's giant hand, gently but firmly. "Lothar's new quarters neighbour mine. The doors to these rooms have no locks. Malphas placed guards outside to watch them, but I've arranged for the guards to be temporarily assigned to other duties. Even as the lowly Queen Mother, I still wield some authority. I've asked them to fetch my son. He's climbing your wonderous pyramid this morning. It'll take them an age to find him, plenty of time for you to complete your task." Romilda leaned closer and whispered, "I want you to go into Lothar's quarters and begin your cleaning duties. And while you're cleaning, I need you to search."

"What for?"

"Do you know what a parchment is? Paper and writing?"

Seronan nodded.

"I'm seeking notes Lothar may have made. Writings of his. They won't be out in the open. They'll be hidden somewhere, almost certainly locked up."

"I cannot open a lock."

Romilda stood, stepped across to a chest of drawers, pulled open the top drawer and clutched a ring of keys. "The locked chests in our rooms come from the inner circle of Sardis. All the keys that are needed to open the locks are on this ring. Ewald made sure he had a copy of every key to every lock in the inner circle, and most keys open more than one lock. His paranoia had value, after all. If Lothar has locked his notes in a chest, a key on this ring will open it. Can you read, Seronan?"

Seronan cast her eyes to the floor.

"You can tell me," coaxed Romilda.

"It is forbidden for slaves to read."

"Yes, but you're smart. Despite the bondage and the beatings of your overseer, your mind refuses to yield to servitude. I see it."

"I can read."

Romilda stifled a smile. She'd chosen well. "Skim the parchments, as many as you can, and keep any with the words *First Scripture* or *Da Und Sepcarture*. Bring them to me immediately."

"There could be dozens of parchments."

"Bring all you can. We won't get another chance. When Lothar returns, I'll claim we were raided by thieves. I'll turn my room upside down to confirm the story. With the guards absent, brutal thugs took advantage and raided our quarters. There are many desperate people in Pergamos, enough to enhance the plausibility of such a ruse. Lothar will have no desire to draw attention to the theft; you can take my word on that."

Romilda stepped across to the bed, crouched before Seronan and lifted the slave's chin with the tips of her fingers. "Slap me."

Seronan's eyes grew so wide, it appeared they may burst from her face. She tried to look away, but Romilda firmed her grip. "You have large, strong hands, Seronan. I don't want you to hold back. Strike my face, so it bruises. Draw blood if you can. This horrid slash across my cheek will bleed if opened up." Romilda stood. "Get up, Seronan. Think of all the wild grells you will save. We need to convince Lothar thieves raided our rooms."

Seronan stood, her legs shaking so much, Romilda thought she may collapse back onto the bed.

"You know what to do," said Romilda. "You know what I want. Now strike me."

* * * *

Seronan double-checked the empty hall before opening the door to Lothar's room with a blood-smeared hand still stinging from the slap she'd delivered to Romilda's face. How strange this world had become that the Queen Mother of Enthilen would plead for a strike from a slave. She scurried inside and shut the door behind her, instinctively checking under Lothar's cot first, pulling out the sloshing chamber pot. The curate slept on a simple, single bed with a hardwood base and thin mattress, a much more modest arrangement than the other royal quarters. She placed the chamber pot up against the door. If someone opened the door from the outside, it would clatter into the pot and warn her.

Seronan went straight to a locked chest and pulled the keyring from the sack she used to carry dirty clothes to the washroom. Hesitating to ponder the wisdom of her actions, she did as Romilda suggested and thought about the safety of the wild grells. With Myan securing more than a handful of Rephaim as allies, it seemed Seronan's kin had a good chance of paying their respects in peace. Taking one of the dozens of keys, she placed the bit against the lock, but the key was too big. She took another, trying to match key and lock dimensions by eye.

No good, she thought. Try again. Hurry.

Another key, another failure. Try again. A match. Seronan turned the key, snapped the hasps open and lifted the lid to a box full of silver and gold plates, and goblets with etched designs of five-pointed stars and goat heads with curled horns.

Cursing, she shut the lid and locked the chest, turning her attention to the second of the six trunks in Lothar's room. This one contained

447

delicate, diaphanous garments that looked like they would crumble in Seronan's calloused hands that had begun to sweat with the pressing need to find her treasure.

As she locked the lid to the second chest, a shuffling came from the hallway outside. She turned to the door and waited for it to bang into the chamber pot. But the door stayed closed, and the shuffling disappeared.

The third chest yielded Seronan's reward of a box full of parchments. She almost reached in and grabbed as many as she could, picturing herself clutching the bundle to her chest and racing next door to Romilda's quarters. Instead, she held her nerve and began the search, her eyes darting across the words on the paper, trying to make sense of Lothar's flowing, cursive hand, repeating in her head what she needed to find as if it would make the fabled words appear.

First Scripture. Da Und Sepcarture. First Scripture. Da Und Sepcarture. First Scripture. Da Und Sepcarture.

Near the top of the pile, she found a parchment of crisp, white paper with fresh, bold ink. Adrenaline coursed through her body as she scanned every sentence until three words sprang from the page: *Da Und Sepcarture.* Not reading further, she stuffed the parchment under her slave rags up against her breasts and resumed the search.

She wasn't sure if she heard the shuffling again or it was merely fear causing the hairs on the back of her neck to tingle, but without hesitating, she stood up, dropped the keys into the chest and closed its lid. As she turned to the door, it opened and clattered into the chamber pot, almost spilling the contents across the flagstones.

"Sorry," she said. "I have left the chamber pot in the way."

She moved the pot, and the door swung open, Ende framed by the jamb. Wiping sweaty palms on the front of her tattered dress, simultaneously pressing the stolen parchment closer to her body, Seronan tried with every skerrick of concentration to appear innocent. "I am cleaning the room."

Ende stepped inside, dragging the end of her sparth along the stone floor. "Where are the guards?"

"I do not know."

"My master would not be happy that these rooms sit unprotected."

Seronan stood in front of the chest with the parchments, the padlock hanging open on the clasp, trying to block Ende's view. The pale grell leaned over the chamber pot, sniffed and frowned.

"Once I have made the bed, I will empty the pot," said Seronan.

"What are you doing in the corner? The bed is not there."

"I was dusting these old chests." Seronan needed to distract Ende's thoughts before the pale grell guessed what was going on. She bit her tongue and took the plunge. "How did you end up this way?"

Ende cocked her head to the side, apparently failing to understand the question, the split ends of her long, grey hair caressing her waist.

"To be such as you are," said Seronan. "How did a wild grell become a servant of death?"

Ende flashed an ugly smile. "Better to be a servant of death than a victim of it."

"We will all be a victim one day."

"Not all," said Ende. "There are some who can escape even my sparth."

"Do you not long for the life you had before?" asked Seronan.

"I have no memory of it. I could have been a slave, like you. Or one of those wild creatures still staining this land."

"Is that how you think of our kin, as blemishes on the land?"

"What other purpose might they serve?"

"Your master uses them as slaves and soldiers."

Ende stepped further into the room, walked over to the fireplace and traced a crooked finger along the edge of the mantle. "You have not cleaned here."

Seronan shuffled sideways, still trying to block Ende's view of the unlocked chest. "I was working my way to the mantle. These rooms have not been cleaned for generations. There is so much to prepare for the masters."

"Was Lothar here when you arrived?"

"No. I have not seen him today."

Ende stood in silent contemplation. Eventually, the pale grell heaved a sigh as if finally realising that being a servant of death was the most tremendous burden any creature could bear.

"I will find the guards and send them here."

Ende left the room, and Seronan almost fell onto Lothar's bed in relief. She left the door open, dropped to her haunches, raised the lid of the chest, retrieved the keys and placed them in the chamber pot. Clicking the padlock shut, she decided one parchment would have to do, her nerves not willing to risk a further delay.

She picked up the chamber pot and strode out of the room.

~ Chapter 34 ~

Tom sat in the paisley chair, shivering in front of the cold fireplace. The worn upholstery, riddled with dust and stains, reminded him of the chair his grandmother had in her bedroom when he was a toddler. He smiled at the memory of her sitting in the chair, a buzzing radiator warming her feet, knitting another jumper for her fast-growing grandson.

With no way of measuring time, Tom guessed he'd been locked in the room at the bottom of the gorge in Bindari for days. There were no windows, the only light coming from candles he'd lit using the metal flint from his pack. He'd long given up calling out. No-one responded. Sometimes, a faint shuffling came from the other side of the door, but whoever stood in the hallway never spoke. Meagre portions of food and water appeared at irregular intervals, coming through a serving hole in the wall, most often when he was asleep or drowsy such that he never saw who delivered the food. A chamber pot sat in the corner of the room, but it would be over-flowing soon enough, and he dreaded the thought of having to dispose of the contents.

Despite the deliveries, a famished Tom had resorted to tasting the food scraps lying on the floor after scraping off the green and white speckled mould that grew tiny trees like feathered bonsai. He'd scanned the books lying spread-eagled across the floorboards as if discarded by a reader who'd thrown them down in disgust, insulted by the words on the page. All the books were written in Erstürmen, and none provided clues to what he might expect from his hosts. Inside the front cover of one book about the city of Thyatira, someone had drawn a lemniscate, the symbol for infinity, hundreds of times, laying one on top of the other in a mad scribble. It reminded Tom of the blue book and the lemniscate on page 462 beside the word Revelé, the hint he'd used to crack the code to open the door to this bleak place.

Underneath the scrawled symbols, a couplet had been written in a neat hand.

Blood and bone

Destroy the throne

Tom had no idea what it meant. *Whose blood and bone? What throne?*

Nodding off to sleep in the chair, he started when the door lock clicked, sprang to his feet and spun around, expecting Malphas or the draughoul would charge through, screeching like harpies. Or Adalwolf would be there, demanding the dark eyes to steal Tom's soul.

Nobody came, and the door remained closed. He took Hadufuns' knife from his belt.

I need a weapon, and I'm not going to try to cut myself again, am I? Not now.

"I'm a friend of Caeli," he said, wondering if it mattered. His announcement yielded no comfort, silence the only housemate. The bone-handled knife tottered in his fingers as he shouldered his pack and stalked the closed door like a cat preparing to pounce on unfamiliar prey, assembling enough courage to try the caramel-coloured brass doorknob. It stuck as he twisted it in his hand and drew the door to him, thrusting the knife into the gap between the door and its jamb. The keen blade sliced nothing more than musty emptiness.

In a moment of impulsiveness, Tom flung the door open and rushed into the hall.

No-one here. The enemy must have fled in terror.

He crept along the dark passage towards a glow at the far end, a worn runner laid over decaying floorboards muffling his footfalls. From a doorway came the smell of cooked food and the sound of people talking and metal clinking on crockery. As he inched closer, the talking stopped, and he froze outside the open door, holding the knife at arms-length, waiting.

A voice wafted through the doorway. "Don't just stand there."

Hunger fuelled Tom's courage, and he walked into the room.

Momentarily blinded by the light cast from lanterns hanging from the ceiling, he stumbled into the corner of a table, knocking against a chair. His eyes adjusted to the light, revealing a man sitting at the far end of the table, the same man who'd locked him in the room with the paisley chair.

That's not Malphas, thought Tom. *Too young and not as much grey hair. But he looks like Malphas.*

A draughoul stood behind the man, holding a tray of food like a servant. He waved her away and continued eating in silence.

"Princess Caeli sent me," said Tom.

Mouth full, head bowed until his scraggly dreadlocked hair swept the table, the stranger spoke at his plate, "Are you going to stick me with that fancy knife of yours? Gut me like a pig? Put it down. It's of no use here."

"Princess Caeli sent me." Tom waved the knife at the stranger. *If you come at me, I'll stab you. Just try me.*

"Said that already. Isn't she dead yet?"

"No. Well, I don't know. She wasn't when…"

The man took a gulp from a silver tankard, letting frothy meduz

453

dribble down a black beard that looked like it hadn't been tended to in yarles. "She's probably dead by now."

Squawk!

Tom jumped when a large bird trotted across the floor, its head level with his waist. The man cut a piece of apple and held it above the bird's head. It reached up, opened its huge, bulbous bill and plucked the fruit from the man's gloved fingers.

Tom's mouth dropped open. "That bird looks like a dodo."

"That's because it is."

"But they're ex...never mind. Princess Caeli said I'd find answers here."

The man coughed up a piece of gristle, spitting it onto his plate. "That depends on the question." He shooed the bird away and took another gulp of meduz, Tom studying his grimy face for a sign of danger or comfort.

"I solved your puzzle. The one to open the door. How do you know about the blue book? About the pages in the book?"

"What book?"

"The book with the blue cover. It has stories about the Erstürmen in it. It translates English to Erstürmen. I used it to learn your language."

"Sounds fascinating."

Tom frowned, frustrated with the stranger's disobliging nature. "If you can't help me, is there someone here who can?"

"I'm not running a boarding house. Only ones here are me and her." The man pointed a chewed bone at the draughoul hovering in the corner.

Tom's neck tingled, imagining the draughoul drooling, her unbroken stare burning its way through his pockets, searching for the dark eyes. He pointed the knife at her.

"Oh, and Mr Prickles," said the stranger.

"What?"

"Mr Prickles. The dodo. He lives here too."

"Don't you want to know who I am?"

"You opened the door. I already know who you are."

"Then why'd you lock me in that room for days?"

The man sighed. "You can never be too careful. Mother wanted to join you."

"Who?"

The man poked his bone at the draughoul again. "My mother. She would have loved nothing better than to spend all that time locked up in a room with you and the dark eyes."

How does he know I've got the eyes? The draughoul knew.

"Who are you?" asked Tom.

The man took another drink, slurping loudly through pale, cracked lips. "Didn't the grells tell you? The miyans. What a morbid existence that is. Guarding the dead."

"They don't talk."

"Ah, that's right. I forgot. Been so long since *belch*...since...ah..."

Tom waited for the stranger to finish his thought. For a light of recognition to appear inside his foggy, evasive eyes.

"Oh, I remember. When I arrived in this forsaken place, they...they called me Murrigal. Broke their stupid vow of silence to say it. *Murrigal, Murrigal*, they cackled, like crows fighting over a carcass."

"How do you know Caeli?" Tom's arm ached, and he lowered the knife.

"I don't know her. Not anymore."

"I came here looking for answers."

"I don't have any *fucking* answers!" Murrigal yelled, finally looking Tom in the eye.

Tom jolted upright, taken aback not at the volume of Murrigal's voice, but because he'd sworn in English. He raised the knife again, and the draughoul, Murrigal's mother, began a stifled, moaning wail, clutching her arms across her chest and swaying her body back and forth.

Murrigal smelled the air like a hungry dog. "Got any food in your bag?"

Tom put the knife on the table and unshouldered his pack. He dug around the bottom, not expecting to find anything until his hand grasped a bony piece of dried fish wrapped in cloth that had escaped his hunger. He tossed the morsel to Murrigal, who rolled it around in the thin leather gloves covering his hands, sniffing every corner of the cloth, then unwrapped the fish and ate it in one gulp, bones and all, washing the treat down with more meduz. Murrigal banged his empty tankard on the table until the draughoul floated to his side and filled the cup.

"Long time since we've had fish, isn't it, Mother? Long time since a lot of things."

"You look like Malphas," said Tom.

Murrigal crushed the fish skeleton with his yellowed teeth. "Is that his name now? *Mal-phas.* What a conceited *arsehole.* Names himself after one of Volerdie's chosen. Who the *fuck* does he think he is?"

Despite sitting in the paisley chair for days, Tom still hadn't recovered from the journey from Dorfisch and his legs buckled under him. He draped his coat over the dining chair at the other end of the table to Murrigal and plonked himself down, fixing his gaze on the grouch. Mr Prickles waddled over and pecked at Tom's pants.

"I know who Malphas is," said Tom. "He's the murderer of my grandmother. I've come to Enthilen to seek justice for her. I'm come here to kill him."

A smile blossomed underneath Murrigal's crooked nose. He placed the knife and fork on the table, pushed his chair back and started laughing, wrapping his arms around his stomach as if his insides might explode. His mother rocked back and forth in the corner of the room, wailing an aching lament. Murrigal didn't seem to care; he laughed and laughed, a bitter taunting laugh, tears streaming down his pockmarked cheeks.

"You...you...are going...going to kill him? Kill Malphas? *Ha...ha... hahahaha...*"

Anger burned inside Tom as he glared at Murrigal. Fixed his gaze on him as if his eyes held the point of a sword at the tormentor's throat. He wanted to grab the knife with the wolf's head etched into the blade and plunge it into Murrigal's chest.

Murrigal finally controlled himself. "You can't kill him."

"I can. I'm a Dobunni rebel. A member of the companionship. I have brothers and sisters that will help me deliver justice. I'm a friend to stone-grells and mouldewerps. All of them will help me."

Murrigal shook his head. "You don't understand, Tom. You can't kill Malphas because he's immortal."

Tom's mind stopped dead. All the thoughts and plans swirling around in there disappeared in an instant. A rug had been pulled out from under every hope. The sole reason and purpose for being in Enthilen, his one chance to still his anxiety by delivering justice to Nanna's killer, had been stolen from him. What a fool he'd been. What a complete and utter fool. Why had it taken him so long to work out?

Malphas is immortal. He stole my grandmother's soul with the dark eyes. And when Adalwolf steals my soul, he'll be immortal, and I'll be a draughoul.

Tom sat back in his chair, broken and despondent. "Why am I here?"

"Malphas wants something from you," said Murrigal.

Tom reached into his pack again, pulled out the eyes of lost souls and placed them on the table.

The draughoul's wailing and moaning grew louder. "The eyes. The eyes. The eyes. My soul..."

"Malphas wants Adalwolf to kill me with these," said Tom, dismissively flicking his hand at the eyes, deciding they weren't in any danger here in this dank house at the bottom of the gorge. "He wants Adalwolf to become immortal and rule Enthilen forever."

Murrigal shook his head. "Oh, no. You haven't got that right. Yes, he wants Adalwolf to become immortal, but the prince won't rule for long."

"What do you mean?"

"When Adalwolf becomes immortal by taking your soul, Malphas will use him for the ultimate sacrifice. Do you know the story of Thiemo?"

Tom nodded.

"He was an immortal, sacrificed in the hopes of enticing Volerdie to return to Enthilen. You see, if Volerdie is to return, he needs an empty vessel that his soul can occupy. And a vessel who already has the gift of eternal life would be the perfect choice. Malphas seeks to sacrifice an immortal Adalwolf. When Adalwolf's soul withers, Volerdie's will grow. And then, Malphas hopes to rule by Volerdie's side for all eternity in the paradise he's always longed for. The paradise, the hope of which, keeps Erstürmen believers complicit. All Malphas needs to fulfil his ambition is you and the throne of the dead."

Tom retreated into his thoughts. *Throne of the dead? What's that? Does Adalwolf know any of this?* "How can you sacrifice an immortal?" he asked.

"One immortal can kill another. That's the only way, as far as I know. Malphas will place the immortal Adalwolf on the throne of the dead, and then he will kill him. When the time is right."

Tom's eyes narrowed. Murrigal guessed his next question.

"The time will be right when darkness descends amid the daylight. When the two moons of Seena and Bargan block the light of the sun."

"A solar eclipse," said Tom.

"Malphas must expect this event to happen soon. Otherwise, he wouldn't have bothered bringing you to Enthilen." Murrigal turned to the draughoul. "Stop your incessant moaning, Mother."

"Who took her soul?" asked Tom, thinking Murrigal may have done it himself.

"Oldaric...I mean, *Mal-phas* took her soul with those things." Murrigal pointed at the dark eyes before slurping another mouthful of meduz. "Practising he was. Practising...*belch* so he could make a clean kill when he found his birth twin."

"My grandmother."

Murrigal shrugged. "Tell me about Caeli. What's she like now?"

Tom gave the best description he could of the pudgy, child-like princess, having been with her only a short time, also telling Murrigal about Dwarrow and the secret passage, and about Jürgen and how he thought Caeli may have been in love. As Tom spoke, tears welled in Murrigal's eyes. Then something dawned on him he should have guessed ages ago.

"You're Caeli's father," said Tom.

Murrigal replied in a raspy whisper, "I miss her. Every day, I miss her."

"Did you give her that book — *Through the Looking Glass*? Did you teach her how to speak English? How do you even know my language?"

"You're clever, Tom. It's a pity you're marked for death. Eat something."

Murrigal pushed a plate of dry bread towards Tom. As he reached for a slice, the sleeve of his shirt rose up, exposing the red marks on his wrist.

Murrigal noticed it. "Tried to cut yourself."

Tom pulled his sleeve down and blushed.

"Maybe you should? If you die, then Adalwolf dies, as long as the dark eyes aren't involved. That would *fuck* up Malphas' plans. *Fuck 'em* up royally. Hell, I should kill you myself." Murrigal flashed a stained, cruel grin, staggered to his feet and reached for a knife. The dishevelled man dressed in clothes made from hessian sacks stepped over to Tom with malice growing tall and wild. It lasted only a moment before Murrigal relaxed and shrank away, dropping the knife on the floor. He took another swig of meduz, draining the entire cup, and clutched the back of his seat to stop himself from tumbling over. "I'm a monster, Tom. That's all I am — a drunken monster. I deserve to be locked in this place. Forever."

"Caeli said to tell you she misses you." Tom lied, wanting to catch Murrigal off guard.

Murrigal's withered body shook until the feet of the chair clattered against the floor. "How dare you...how dare..." He slumped back into his chair and buried his tear-strewn face in worn leather gloves. In an act of ghostly comfort, the draughoul floated up behind him and massaged her son's shoulders with her bony fingers. She tilted her head to the side and started singing into his ear.

Tom sat with mother and son, waiting for the songs to end. Around the dining table, empty shelves in mouldy cabinets gathered dust and cobwebs. Rising damp consumed the mortar setting the stones in the walls, drifts of flaked mud and straw piling into every corner. Above Tom's head, flames flickered in brass lanterns behind flower shapes cut into the metal. The warmth of their glow did nothing to ward off the chill seeping down his spine.

Murrigal finally broke the stillness. "Hand me the eyes, Tom."

Tom hesitated, fighting against indecision. Too tired to fight for long, he stood, walked to the opposite end of the table and gave Murrigal the eyes, hoping this man wouldn't steal them or use them against him.

The obsidian clinked together as Murrigal rolled the dark eyes around in his gloved left hand. "Who would think such power rests in these two small baubles? Such power. Death and eternal life. They can deliver both, even at the same time."

"Why can't I use the eyes to go home?" asked Tom.

"Oh, they'll take you home, but only when you capture your birth twin's soul. Adalwolf. If you don't, you can never return. You'll die here." Murrigal smacked the eyes onto the table.

Tom's heart sank into his stomach like a jagged stone. "Then I'm lost. I can't deliver the revenge I seek, and I don't want to kill Adalwolf, so I can't go home."

"Malphas will end your torment soon enough. All his will and thought will be focussed on this one thing. He'll be searching for you now, sending out his spies, using black magic. Don't worry, he won't find you here. This gorge keeps us hidden from malicious eyes. However, if you leave us, you will almost certainly die."

Then I'm a prisoner, thought Tom.

Murrigal's mother served him a cup of water, flavoured with flower petals floating at the top of the mug like tiny yellow rafts. He started to count the petals.

Murrigal's eyes grew wide, and he sat tall in his chair. "Wait. There might be another way. To foil Malphas. To save you and Adalwolf. There might be another way." He stood, walked to a doorway at the side of the dining room and stopped. "Go back along the hall. Behind one of the doors is a bed. Get some rest, Tom."

*   *   *   *

Despite Murrigal's pronouncement — *there might be another way* — playing in his head, Tom managed his first decent sleep since leaving Jameus and Melinda's shack. The adventure had drained so much of his energy, nothing remained to feed his fear. Likely, it also had something to do with being in a proper bed with a soft mattress and pillow. He refused to pull back the covers of the musty bed, fearing what he might find, but it was comfortable.

On waking in the pitch black of the bedroom, Tom lay recumbent on the woollen bedcover listening to the nothingness and thinking. Despite his grumpiness, Murrigal revealed so much, Tom's thoughts smashed inside his skull, ready to burst out and search for meaning. Although Murrigal *had* provided answers as Caeli promised, they weren't the answers Tom hoped for. Malphas was immortal because he must have killed his birth twin, Tom's Nanna, using the dark eyes to take Jean Anderson's soul and then return to Enthilen. Now Malphas wanted Adalwolf to become immortal by killing Tom, but only so he could sacrifice Adalwolf to pave the way for Volerdie's return. And Tom could only return home if he killed Adalwolf with the dark eyes.

He couldn't do that, could he? Adalwolf may be as much a victim in all this as Tom. The brutal irony of these revelations was that if he did kill Adalwolf with the eyes of lost souls, he would become immortal and only then could he confront Malphas and deliver the justice he longed for.

Tom got up and walked down the hall into an empty dining room. He took the side door and explored more windowless rooms, each one as dark and depressing as the next, eventually stumbling across Murrigal's mother toiling in the kitchen cleaning dishes. Tom clutched at the dark eyes in his pocket. The draughoul froze and hissed under her breath before returning to her chores.

"I don't know your name," said Tom.

"Call me Fullō." The draughoul sniggered as if she'd made a clever joke.

"Where's Murrigal?"

"Outside. Keep going. Back." Fullō waved her bony hand at another door.

Tom pushed through it and gasped as he stepped into an immaculate, manicured garden, bathed in blazing sunshine, that stretched to the horizon. Flowers bloomed in every colour like an organic, growing rainbow. A bumblebee as big as his nose buzzed past, and he followed its flight path to a hedge of brilliant emerald green. Murrigal stood there, trimming the growth and dressed in the same dowdy rags of hessian as before, crudely stitched into a tunic and pants, with a straw boater teetering on his unruly black mane.

"Good morning," said Tom, wondering if it was morning.

"Ah, Tom Anderson. Here you are." Murrigal beamed, dropped his shears, strode over to Tom and wrapped his arm around Tom's shoulder, pulling him close like a long-lost friend. Tom stood stiff, his mouth ajar and his nostrils flaring at the pungent smell of a man who likely hadn't washed in days.

"Let me show you the garden." Murrigal took Tom's hand and led him along a gravelled path into a sea of green.

"This is beautiful," said Tom, overwhelmed by everything and trying to process the transformation in Murrigal's personality — the ebullient phoenix arising from the ashes of malcontent.

Murrigal led him through a narrow ravine full of bright and growing things. Rows of trees, shrubs and creepers, bordered by trimmed hedges, grew in tiered collections with grassy paths meandering among them.

"This is my life's work," said Murrigal. "Look over here." He dragged Tom to another part of the garden lined with fruit trees. "It's the storm season, so nothing much is growing now. Only the last apfels clinging to the branches." Murrigal pulled off a fruit and gave it to Tom, who bit into the sweetest and juiciest apple he'd ever tasted.

"I have to keep Mr Prickles away from these and other fruits. Here..." Murrigal tugged on Tom's hand. "Here's a shrub that grows wild in the Scaur Hills. The werps introduced me to its *medicinal properties*. I chew the leaves every morning. It gives me a lift." Murrigal plucked a leathery green leaf from the shrub and handed it to Tom. "Fold it up, pop it in your mouth and chew. It's not poisonous. I promise."

Tom traced the branching white veins on the leaf with his eyes, then scrunched the foliage in his fist and placed it in his mouth. A peppery flavour mixed with mint and lemon burst onto his tongue.

"Chew it. It works almost immediately."

Tom chewed, squeezing juice onto his tastebuds until his head started to feel light. Slightly dizzy. Happy. He smiled at Murrigal.

Caeli's father smiled back and led Tom through more of the garden until they reached a rock ledge overlooking the ocean. They sat on a stone bench and listened to the waves crashing on the jagged shore far below them. Mr Prickles trotted over, and Murrigal pulled an apple from his coat pocket, handing it to his pet.

Tom couldn't resist patting the tame dodo. "I asked a lot of questions before."

"A fool asks no questions. Did you sleep?"

"Yes."

"Good. Then you must feel comfortable here. You had a long journey. It will be nice to sit in the garden for a while. Over there..." Murrigal pointed into the distance, "I'll build a fountain. Mother would like that. She loves the sound of falling water. It will have..."

Tom interrupted. "You said before, there might be another way to defeat Malphas."

"Did I?"

"At the dinner table. Last night or whenever it was. I can't tell if it's day or night in that house."

"It's not a house. It's a prison. It would be more than I could bear to mark the passing of time so I keep it dark, not knowing when is day or night."

"What are you hiding from?"

"Two worlds."

Tom's eyes pleaded with Murrigal.

"I can see your hurt, Tom. Another way...another way..." Murrigal rolled a white-veined leaf in his hand and popped it into his mouth. "You know, Malphas thought he was the only one who could read the First Scripture. He became careless. Left it out in plain sight. Mother, she copied passages from it. Brought them to me. I learned the ancient language. I learned some of the secrets of the scripture." Murrigal tapped his nose and smiled, then turned and buried his nostrils in the tubular petals of a bright pink flower, seemingly enamoured with its bouquet.

Tom had never heard of the First Scripture, and he became impatient with Murrigal's storytelling. "What did you learn?"

"There is another way. To get home and thwart Malphas. All you have to do is..." Murrigal paused and theatrically swallowed the chewed leaf in his mouth.

Tom leaned towards him.

"All you have to do, Tom, is click your heels together three times and say there's no place like home, there's no place like home." Murrigal doubled over with laughter. Not cruel laughter, but manic and crazed nonetheless.

Instead of pounding Murrigal with fists of rage, Tom smiled at the complete madness of it all.

Murrigal composed himself, squeezed Tom's hand and fixed a severe gaze on his face. "I'll search the passages from the scripture. If there's another way for you to get home, it will be written there. But be prepared. Likely the attempt will put your life in grave danger."

Tom shrugged. "What else is new? Will that stop Malphas? Me going home."

"Yes and no. He may pursue you again, or he may pursue others. It will be a major setback, though. I think Malphas believes that sometime during this yarle is when the immortal sacrifice must occur. That darkness will descend in the coming days. Who knows exactly when? Maybe he does? Or maybe not. And who knows when the time will be right again? It could be in many, many yarles."

Tom bowed his head.

"I'm sure you've thought about the other option. You're a smart young man. You've worked out if you kill Adalwolf, you can go home. You've worked out if you become immortal, you can kill Malphas and avenge your grandmother. However, do you want to be responsible for taking two lives? Is that a burden you want to bear?"

No, thought Tom. He never wanted to relive the sickness that bubbled in the pit of his stomach after killing Captain Adcock. And he had no desire for immortality, even if that was the price to pay for finding justice for his grandmother. But what other revelations might Murrigal be concealing?

"The combination that opened your door came from the blue book, and there are lemniscates drawn on one of the pages in that stuffy room with the paisley chair," said Tom. "You know things you're not telling me."

Murrigal turned away and stared at the ocean. "Mother goes into that room and doodles all the time. I can't be answerable for her scrawls. You're looking for meaning in coincidence, Tom. Don't torture your mind so. Trust me, it won't end well."

Tom wasn't convinced. It seemed that Murrigal's answers were the ones the man wanted to give, not necessarily the ones Tom needed to hear.

Murrigal stood. "I will begin my search for your path home. Be patient; it might take a while to find it."

He disappeared back into the garden, and Tom sat in silence, listening to the waves crashing below him and thinking about Grin and Thaly and how he would feel leaving Enthilen behind.

~ Chapter 35 ~

Where Babir Birramal met the Dambay Plains, wild grells gathered at the ngulubul to prepare for the march to Malang Gunya. Thaly sat on the grass with them as they sharpened stone-tipped spears, carved designs in daggers made from the leg bones of deer, strung supple bows with tightly bound plant fibre and filled quivers with arrows made from the cured wood of the bilawi tree. The grells went about their work with sombre determination, Thaly wondering if it was all for nothing. While there were over six hundred grells in the camp, this wasn't an army. The Dobunni army of five thousand had been easily defeated at Laodicea. Who knew what the Erstürmen had waiting for the grells in Malang Gunya?

Grin had told Thaly that grells rarely fought in large groups and had no leadership hierarchy suited to significant battles. Nevertheless, veterans of past skirmishes moved about the gathering, dispensing what knowledge they had to the inexperienced. Thaly contributed by training the younger grells in the basics of hand-to-hand combat. Although she tried to instil confidence in the fighters, their eyes betrayed the fear of defeat. Yet, nobody wanted to be the first to turn their back on the group.

Thaly ran a sharpening stone along the blade of the short sword she'd taken from the pile of spare weapons carried by the Laodicea refugees.

The sword had seen numerous battles, the blade's edges notched and chipped, but it would see out a few more. As she checked the keenness of the edge, Mirrian approached wearing a comforting smile that split her facial tattoo of panalope flowers. With Dwarrow and Caeli gone, and Grin yet to return from his initiation, Thaly had latched onto the motherly stone-grell, yearning for the promise of familial affection even if it came from a virtual stranger.

"You have such beautiful long hair, Thaly," said Mirrian. "Are you sure you want to do this?"

Thaly nodded. "All the females are shaving their heads. I don't want to be treated any differently."

"Next, you will be asking for a facial crest," said Mirrian, kneeling behind Thaly.

"I don't think I'll go that far."

Mirrian ran her thick, calloused fingers through Thaly's straight black hair. Thaly hated her hair anyway, flat and lifeless, and always having to be tied back to stop getting in the way of more important things.

"It is such a pity," said Mirrian. "Even bald, the Erstürmen will know you are not a grell."

"And they'll know the female grells are not males no matter how much they try to look like them."

"It is a small thing we do to try to stop the Erstürmen targeting us. To confuse them. Always they have hunted our females, to breed more slaves or to stop us from breeding wild grells." Mirrian tied Thaly's hair into a ponytail. "The knife is getting blunt. We have only a couple of metal knives, and this one has already shaved many heads."

Thaly held up the sharpening stone. Mirrian took the stone and ran it along the blade while humming to herself. Thaly sat in silence, drifting with Mirrian's melody and trying not to think about the uncertainty of her future. Instead, she thought about the door to Grin's milbi and focussed all her attention on being in this moment. The midday sun warmed the edge of the forest, and tiny, twitchy birds with feathers like spotted waist-coats, and fiery red rumps, hopped around in the grass looking for seeds.

Gubadhang, she thought to herself. Grin would call those birds gubadhang.

Mirrian stopped humming. "I think this is as sharp as it will get."

"Hack it off," said Thaly.

Mirrian sighed and began cutting. "We do not know much about you, Athalee Wallace of Bagendon. My son cannot tell me much. Where is your blood family?"

"Dead probably."

"All of them?"

"My birth family abandoned me when I was a baby. Gave me to the Dobunni rebels."

"A mother does not abandon her child without good reason. She must have been in a desperate situation."

"I never found out. Emelin and Thane Wallace adopted me. It was only the three of us until my younger sister came along. Dayna. I could tell Thane loved her more than anything. His blood flowed in her veins. She even grew to look like him. After he was killed by the Erstürmen, Emelin shared her love equally between Dayna and me, but it's not the same. Do you understand?"

The knife grazed Thaly's scalp as Mirrian scraped the blade gently across her skull. Locks of black hair fell down the front of her tunic. She thought nothing of it. An old life had gone now. Here marked the begin-ning of a new one.

"Yes," said Mirrian, "I understand. The love of kin is a sacred and precious thing. Life must have been hard for you, not knowing your birth family."

"I know who they are," said Thaly.

"And you did not seek them out?"

"They never came looking for me. Why should I go and beg for them to take me back? Emelin was...*is* the only mother I've known, and when Thane died, Jacob became like a father to me."

"Grin told me about Jacob. I am sorry he fell."

"We've all lost so much in recent times."

Mirrian stopped shaving and sat quietly behind Thaly. The old grell's deep breaths suggested she wrestled with burdensome thoughts. Thaly's mouth turned dry, her mind stolen away from the forest and taken to another terrible place she wanted to forget.

"What happened to my son?" whispered Mirrian. "On that ship."

No, thought Thaly. No. She couldn't do this. Rape was such a foreign concept to Grin; how could she be expected to explain it to his mother? Grin should have dealt with this.

"I know something happened to both of you," said Mirrian. "Grin will not tell me all of it. I am left to guess the cause of the awful suffering that dulls his eyes."

Thaly steeled herself, turned and faced Mirrian. She felt like crying. Breaking down and collapsing into Mirrian's arms, but she fought against it. She'd grown tired of being a victim. She wanted to be stronger. To begin the healing. Confronting the terror head-on could be the first step.

Thaly clenched her jaw. "We were raped. Assaulted by men who used sex to punish us. They were disgusting, vile creatures. We tried to fight them. I tried to help Grin, but..."

Mirrian placed her finger on Thaly's lips and shook her head. "There is no need for you the explain further." Mirrian leaned forward and kissed Thaly on the forehead. "Thank you, Thaly, for being there when Grin needed you. I am so sorry you had to endure such a terrible thing."

"I'm worried about Grin," said Thaly. "I'm worried he's locking away all the suffering. All the emotions. He tried to talk to me about it. I wasn't ready to deal with it then. I was doing the same thing he's doing now — trying to shut out the world. But I found someone to talk to. An Erstürmen princess no less. Grin needs someone too, before the agony becomes unbearable."

Mirrian nodded. "I will speak with him."

A commotion rippled through the crowd when Grin and the other initiates walked into camp. Mirrian jumped to her feet and went to her son, embracing him in a formal greeting. Thaly ran her hand over the rough stubble on her scalp, keeping her distance from another family reunion. Although the initiated Grin didn't look any different, he carried himself with more confidence and maturity. It seemed his youthful innocence had disappeared, which saddened Thaly until she realised Grin also had marked an important change in his life. She hoped he had gained the courage to deal with the demons inside him.

Thaly stood, brushing hair from her clothes. Grin walked over to her, and they embraced in a formal greeting.

"I almost did not recognise you," said Grin.

Thaly laughed. "I'm the short one."

Grin's smile broadened. "Yes. An honorary grell. Are you sure you want to do this? Join us on the homage march. It may be our last."

"Whatever end awaits, we're going to face it together. We could be the ones to bring down the Erstürmen Kingdom."

Grin's expression turned sombre. "I have been thinking about what Dwarrow said during the meeting of the Mulugan. If Adalwolf and Tom are birth twins, then it seems we must protect Adalwolf also."

"I almost killed Adalwolf on Hansen's Bluff," said Thaly. "I didn't know Tom would die too."

"None of us did. My father told me some of the grells want to assassinate the new king. End the reign of the Heine Empire once and for all."

"We can't let that happen, Grin."

"I will talk to my father. I hope he will understand, though I fear he will not be able to convince everyone to let the king live."

"We could kidnap Adalwolf. Lock him up to keep Tom safe."

"Even if we reach the king, we cannot isolate him forever. There must be another way out of this predicament."

A further complication involving Tom Anderson, thought Thaly. The young man had exposed a world she never knew existed — a strange world of dark eyes, birth twins and immortality. Thaly guessed it didn't end there either. She wondered what other secrets would be revealed in days to come.

* * * *

In the late afternoon, at the edge of the grell camp, Grin paced around giagan, an enormous, sacred panalope tree, its trunk six times as thick as his body. The tree's long, cascading branches swept the ground clear of moss and lichen, exposing the rich black humus of Babir Birramal. He touched every one of the thousands of flower buds growing in the nodes between the leaves and stems, examining the glimpses of pink petals that struggled hard to push through the green sepals, looking for a sign that a flower may soon burst into life. As a new initiate, he had the honour of searching for the first panalope blossom that would mark the beginning of ngurung-ginya, the season of short days and long, bitter nights. The first flower would signal that the time had come for grell pilgrims to begin the homage march to Malang Gunya.

His ground search exhausted, Grin climbed among the branches, lifting himself into the canopy of the tree until the earth below fell away and his entire being became immersed in a synthesis of life. There, near the tip of a branch, a delicate, tubular blossom with fringed petals striped pink and white, had burst open. Its golden stamens waited for the first visit from a nectar-hungry pollinator.

Grin sat and shimmied along the smooth branch until reaching the flower, then bent over to breathe in its tempting, sweet aroma. In the season others called the long dark, the flowering of the panalope tree reminded grells that life, light and hope would always pierce the darkness.

After sitting in the tree for a moment to bathe one last time in the beauty of the forest, Grin climbed back down to the ground and went to spread the news. The homage march could begin.

~ Chapter 36 ~

Days passed, and Tom filled his time by exploring Murrigal's garden, feeding Mr Prickles, reading some of the books scattered around the house, eating and sleeping. Fullō prepared him meals but spoke little, Tom hiding the dark eyes in his bedroom rather than bringing them to the dinner table, hoping that would alleviate the draughoul's suffering. He rarely saw Murrigal, the disordered man occasionally appearing at mealtimes to wash down food with copious amounts of meduz. Inside the house, Murrigal's ill-temper returned despite his constant chewing of the white-veined leaves. Once, while exploring the dwelling, Tom had passed a cavernous, unfurnished room where Murrigal squatted on the floor beside a barrel of meduz, surrounded by parchments and books strewn across the flagstones. When he saw Tom, he got to his feet and slammed the door shut.

Another morning dawned, and Tom took his regular walk in the garden under a grey sky, wondering how long he would have to wait until Murrigal came to him with an answer. Stopping at the stone bench overlooking the ocean, he sat and began counting the blue, yellow and white flowers. Murrigal appeared, ambling along the path, then sat with Tom, a repugnant odour wafting from Murrigal's hessian tunic. Tom slid further along the bench, away from the graveolent man, and waited while the ocean swell crashed on the rocks below.

Murrigal rolled another white-veined leaf between his gloved fingers and popped it into his mouth, chewing until frothy, green spit dribbled from the corners of his lips. Mr Prickles waddled over and pecked at Murrigal's pants. He swatted the bird away.

"I don't have anything for you," he said. "Pest of a bird."

The clouds parted. Murrigal swallowed and faced Tom, speaking in a lilting, almost musical voice,

"Return the eyes

From whence they came

Briefly

The ingress will reveal."

Tom sat, silent, waiting for more information.

"That is the sum total of my study, Tom Anderson."

"I don't understand what you mean."

"Come closer. Together we can uncover more."

Tom took a depth breath and shuffled towards Murrigal. Through tired, disjointed thoughts, he told Tom about the throne of the dead, the original resting place of the eyes of lost souls. He spoke of the beast crowning the backrest of the throne and the eye sockets that now sat empty, blind to the world. Murrigal believed that as soon as the dark eyes were placed back into the sockets, a portal would open, linking this world with Tom's. The ingress would reveal only briefly before the opportunity was lost for Tom to travel home and thwart Malphas' plans to sacrifice Adalwolf and bring forth an endless reign with Volerdie and Malphas as its monarchs.

"I can't guarantee what I say is true," continued Murrigal. "I don't know how the ingress will manifest or how you can access it. My guess is the throne itself will be the point of transfer. I've searched all my notes for evidence this method of travel has been used in the past. I can't find any. If you succeed, you may well be the first to travel this way since Volerdie himself."

Tom shivered at the thought of following in Volerdie's footsteps. *Do I have another choice?*

"Die here," said Murrigal, as if reading Tom's mind. "By Adalwolf's hand or another misadventure. Or from old age if you're prepared to hide for the rest of your life, like me. I don't know which is worse. You asked me to help you, and this is all I have to give."

"Where would I find the throne of the dead?"

"I've never seen it, though I've read the passages in the First Scripture describing its making. Carved from wretched souls sacrificed to feed Volerdie's power. It's impossible to tell where one body ends, and the other begins, melted together and set like stone. Atop the backrest is the horned beast, mouth agape, eyes wild and consuming, perched over the wreckage of Volerdie's offerings. From this throne, the Divine Creator delivered judgement and punishment. I'm convinced Malphas has the throne. He probably sits on it now, surveying the madness surrounding him. Find Malphas, and you'll find the throne."

*   *   *   *

That evening, Murrigal, Tom and Fullō sat at the dinner table, picking at plates of pickled cabbage and boiled potatoes. Through the entire meal, a gloomy Murrigal toyed with a folded piece of paper.

His appetite for food satiated, Tom's curiosity hungered. "What's that?" he asked, pointing at the paper.

Murrigal leaned back in his chair. "A note from the outside world, left in my message box. A note from a sick, vile person playing a cruel game."

"What does it say?"

"It claims Caeli, my beautiful Caeli, waits for me outside. I don't believe a word of it. She would never have survived the overthrow of Ewald. Yes, he was her gaoler, but he protected her also. From others who might do worse. Malphas would love nothing more than to teach me a lesson by taking her life or use her to find me."

"Why not open the door to check?"

Murrigal scowled. "No. We can't open the door now we know some-one is there. Mother wanted to, and I forbade her. This is nothing more than a trick — a ruse to get me into that horrid gorge where I'm exposed and vulnerable. That's what my enemy would do, use the promise of my daughter to lure me out. Don't you see? Demons have eternal patience. They sit and wait for me to make one false move."

"Who are these demons?"

"Those who seek to end my life." Murrigal emptied his tankard of meduz. "Forget everything you know about the outside world. Forget what I said about the throne. You're trapped in here with me now — with mother and me. If you leave, I can't protect you anymore. They will come for you. Hunt you endlessly as they hunt me. Better to stay here with us. Safer that way. At least, eventually, you'll die. Even the blood compass can't find you down here in this desolate hole."

"The what compass?"

"Forget it!" cried Murrigal before storming from the room.

After the meal, Tom sat in his bedroom, pondering Murrigal's words and twisting the bed sheet around in his hand. Twist. Untwist. Twist. Untwist. He stopped and tossed the sheet away, refusing to let the claus-trophobic dark of the room and this underground house defeat him. Jumping from the bed, he marched along the hall to the door leading to the damp, mist-filled gorge of Bindari. He turned the handle and pulled. The door didn't budge.

If Caeli's on the other side, she'll be sitting in that dismal gorge wonder-ing how to open the door. Should I call out to her? Murrigal would hear. Murrigal or Fullō. They'd come running for sure. I need to do this in secret.

In the room with the paisley chair and scattered books, Tom found a piece of carbon filed to a point that could be used as a pencil, and a sheet of blank parchment. He wrote a note in English, folded the paper in half and placed it and the pencil inside the narrow metal drawer of the message box embedded in the wall beside the door. After he pushed the drawer into the wall and through to the outside world, he tapped on the backend with Dwarrow's key, as if transmitting Morse code, then fell silent.

A creak announced the raising of the message box lid outside. Tom rested on his haunches and waited. The lid creaked again, and the drawer returned back inside, his piece of paper and pencil sitting in the message box. He retrieved the parchment, reading the question he'd scrawled on its surface.

What book did you show Tom Anderson in your room?

Below his question was an answer written in English.

Through the Looking Glass and What Alice Found There.

It had to be Princess Caeli. Now Tom needed to work out how to open the door. Fullō may have reset the combination. Tom had noticed she disappeared sometimes, not to be found inside or in Murrigal's garden. He scribbled instructions, placed the paper inside the message box and waited, resting his back against the clay render lining either side of the shadowy hall, and scratching his fingernails into one of the cracks.

In the murkiness, he panicked. *What if Caeli told someone else about the book? They'd have to be able to read English. Malphas can read English.*

Time moved with aching slowness until the door lock clicked. He sprang to his feet and retreated into the dark. The door swung open, stiff and slow, and a short figure dressed in a cloak and fur hood stepped into the doorway. Tom drew a sharp breath as the person removed their cowl.

"Caeli," he said. The princess' face looked haggard and tired, not the round, rosy cheeks he remembered from Sardis. But her smile was still as beautiful.

"Tom Anderson, how lovely it is to see you again." She reached out and embraced him. "I'm so glad you made it here. You must have had an astonishing adventure."

"And you," said Tom, noticing how much weight Caeli had lost as he wrapped his arms around her back.

"What's this?" Down the hall marched Murrigal in a violent fury. "Lock the door. Now! Who is this intruder?"

"Papa? Don't you recognise me?"

Murrigal stopped and peered at the pale-skinned woman, her flat, auburn hair glinting in the moonlight coming through the door.

"Caeli...is that...no, no, it can't be. This is an aberration. A barbaric, twisted ploy." Murrigal wrapped his arms across his chest as if to mend a broken heart, leaned against the wall and slid to the floor in a sobbing mess.

Caeli ran to her father, dropped to her knees and hugged his bony frame. "It *is* me, Papa."

Tom flinched at the brutally painful cries flowing from Murrigal's mouth. Father and daughter crouched in the half-light, hugging and caressing, and whispering long unspoken thoughts of love and regret.

Murrigal finally composed himself enough to speak clearly, stroking Caeli's hair with every word. "My little girl. My little girl. All grown. Did Ewald hurt you? Let me see."

"I'm alright, Papa. Don't worry."

"You must be cold and hungry. Come, we'll light a fire in the dining room. Granny is here. She can make us a meal."

Murrigal led Caeli down the hall, and Tom followed. She removed her cloak, exposing a soiled dress of faded floral prints that made her look like the little girl her father seemed to think she was. Fullō entered the room, but showed no emotion that Tom could discern.

The draughoul drifted over to Caeli and brushed her wasted hand across her granddaughter's face. "I remember you," she said before turning away and scraping leftover cabbage and potatoes onto a single plate, then placing it in front of Caeli.

The princess ate in silence, cleaning every scrap of food from the dish, then faced her father. "Why didn't you visit me? You knew I couldn't leave the keep, but you could have visited. I longed to see you."

Murrigal bowed his head. "I'm a coward, Caeli. If Uncle Oldaric found out..."

Uncle Oldaric, thought Tom. *If Oldaric is Caeli's uncle, then Murrigal is...* "You're his brother. Malphas' brother."

Murrigal nodded. "Yes, I'm Oldaric's brother. The only sibling still alive. My real name is Widukind."

"Why did Uncle Oldaric become Malphas?" asked Caeli. "What happened to him?"

"He's spent so long buried in the text of the First Scripture, he's instilled utter truth in every phrase, completely unable to look past a literal meaning. His entire will is bent on the return of a prophesied god, Malphas to rule by his side for all time."

"What do you believe, Papa? You've read the scripture."

"I don't know what to believe, sweetness. Part of me says the text the Erstürmen revere is nothing more than a fairy tale. Like a young girl disappearing down a rabbit hole and finding a magical world. But is it all fantasy? The writer of the First Scripture could have mastered an elaborate subterfuge, embedding real steps to enlightenment within a larger story so fanciful it could never be completely believed, except by someone like Malphas."

"You told me the throne of the dead is real," said Tom. "I'm not risking my life on fairy tales."

"It is real," said Caeli. "King Adalwolf sat on the throne as he led the people to Pergamos."

"Pergamos?" asked Widukind.

"It's going to be the new royal city. The old grell city of Malang Gunya will be destroyed." Caeli's face lit up. "Oh, goodness. Silly me, I'm so tired from my journey I almost forgot. Your friends, Tom, your friends Grin and Thaly, they're with the grells. They plan to march to Malang Gunya to honour those who fell during its invasion."

Tom's thoughts began spinning out of control. "Grin and Thaly are alive?"

"Yes."

They're alive! Thank goodness. They survived the shipwreck. Made it back home. I can't believe it.

Widukind sighed. "Malphas found the throne of the dead as I expected, and he's returning it to Pergamos. To Volerdie's seat of power."

"Then that's where I have to go," said Tom. "My friends are marching there. I need to stop them before they reach Malphas. I need to place the dark eyes into the throne of the dead and end this madness." He jumped to his feet and stormed to the bedroom, planning to leave immediately.

Caeli followed him and leaned against the door jamb, watching him shove supplies into his backpack. "I'll go with you," she said.

"You should stay here with your father. You've only just arrived."

"How will you find Malang Gunya? How will you travel there?"

"It's in the Dambay Plains, right? Someone will know the way. I'll buy a horse." Tom put his hands in his pockets. No coins magically appeared.

Caeli reached into her dress. "I still have the coin you gave me back in the Sunrise Keep. The silver tausen. On the black market, it would buy a dozen horses. I should show Papa the coin. He was the Master of the King's Quarter once."

As Caeli spoke, Widukind loomed up behind her. "Let Tom Anderson go where he needs to."

"I have to go with him," she said, not turning to face her father. "He won't make it alone. My horse is at a stable in the town of Rufous on the edge of the forest. We can buy another horse for Tom with this coin."

She held the silver tausen up to Widukind's face. He slapped it out of her hand and grabbed her wrist. "You can't leave."

"You're hurting me, Papa. I'll come back. I promise I will."

"No. Now I've found you again, I can't let you leave. It's too dangerous." Widukind released Caeli's arm and spread himself across the hall, blocking the exit.

"I can't hide here for the rest of my life. I'm not like you. I'm all grown up now."

Widukind doubled over like he'd been kicked in the stomach. He dropped to his hands and knees, searching for the silver tausen, and began to sob again.

Tom pitied the lost father. Pitied what he'd become.

Fullō glided into the hall. "Poor Widukind. Always the one needing my protection. He idolised his older brother, but his brother used him, destroying many lives in the process. I have a solution. Stay for a while, Caeli, then I will lead you and Tom Anderson to the edge of the forest. I know a secret path that will take no more than a moment. You're stronger than your father, Caeli. Stay for another day and share that strength with him."

* * * *

Tom sat with Caeli on the bench seat in Widukind's garden, enjoying the warmth of sunrise. They planned to leave for Malang Gunya the next day, Fullō having convinced Widukind it was the right thing to do.

"These were my mother's clothes," said Caeli, holding out the hem of a blue silk top that reached almost to her knees, over a pair of brown leather riding pants. "She died soon after I was born."

"Did Jürgen...?" asked Tom.

"Yes, he died too. Right outside my door."

"I'm sorry."

"You have nothing to be sorry for. If anyone's responsible for Jürgen's death, it's me. I used him to save you. That's a burden I must bear."

"I'm thankful you saved me."

"Are you?" said Caeli, wistfully, as she stroked Mr Prickles' feathers, the dodo sitting at her feet as if he'd spent his whole life there. "I miss my books."

"What happened to them?"

"They burned most of them. Right in the middle of the inner circle." Caeli winced and rubbed her legs. "My body's still sore from the riding. It's been such a long time since I rode a horse, and being trapped inside that small room in the Sunrise Keep, well, walking isn't so easy for me anymore either."

"Did your father teach you how to ride?"

"Yes, he bought my first pony — a spotted-grey gelding I called Alfie. Back in those days, people could move easily between the circles of Sardis. King Oldaric wasn't as paranoid as King Ewald. With my cousin, Genevea, we'd ride across the Anchep River, out through Slumstadt and onto the Dambay Plains and back without being challenged."

"What was Oldaric like?"

"Distant, but not brutal. He was devoted to the Erstürmen Kingdom, and I was part of that kingdom. Royal blood flowed through our veins. On occasion, he would instruct my riding or sit with me in the kirika to pray to Volerdie. Those were more innocent times. I guess King Oldaric showed his true nature when he refused to cede the throne to Ewald. Demanded his reign continue. Ewald won the battle, killed most of

Oldaric's supporters and banished the old king. Then Ewald imprisoned me at the top of the Sunrise Keep so that one day I might bear him a son. In case Romilda couldn't fulfil her duties. My father was furious with Ewald. I remember him pacing around the prison cell. 'I'll make him pay,' he said. 'Ewald will get what's coming to him.' The next day, Ewald banished my father from Sardis, and I never saw him after that."

"Without a mother or father, without siblings, you must have been lonely," said Tom.

"The isolation became unbearable. Then, one night, deep in the dark middle, yarles after I'd been imprisoned, I woke to the sound of scratching coming from inside my room. Nothing more than a mouse or rat, I thought, trapped inside the wall. However, the scratching turned into a knock. Not like a bump from a wayward animal or the rattle caused by a stiff breeze, but a knock like someone was at the front door. I got out of bed and checked on my guard. He was slumped against the wall, snoring. The knock came again, and I spun around.

"It sounded like it came from behind the tall mirror fixed to my wall. I pressed my ear up against the cold, reflective glass, and another knock reverberated in my eardrum. I tapped back, mimicking the pattern of the knocking until a note slid out from the gap at the base of the mirror. *Find the latches and push across.*

"What could that possibly mean? I searched all around the mirror for ages until, on the side of the frame near the back, camouflaged into the grain of the wood, I found two latches no bigger than my thumbnail. I flipped the latches outwards and turned them a half-circle until I heard a faint click, then pushed on the frame bracing my feet against one of the bookcases. The mirror freed and slid across the floor with a scrape. I couldn't believe it, behind the mirror hid a dark, endless hole. And standing right in the middle, a small, furry creature with a pink face and a dozen pouches hanging from a belt cinched around a pudgy waist, twitched its long, glistening black nose in my direction. 'You must be Princess Caeli,' the creature said. 'I'm Dwarrow. I have news from your father.'

"Dwarrow handed me a sealed letter he'd received from a draughoul messenger. The werp swore he hadn't read it. I broke the seal to find the letter was indeed written by my father. He'd hidden away in a place called Bindari and would remain there forever. Someone hunted him. He asked me never to divulge his whereabouts to anyone.

"My heart broke a second time when Dwarrow delivered that letter. It felt like I'd been abandoned all over again."

"You could have escaped, Caeli," said Tom. "Down the secret passage."

"I needed permission to forgo my duty to the kingdom and to risk my father's life. I needed *his* permission. As the seasons passed, Dwarrow became a regular visitor, often bringing letters, books and other presents. Funny, Ewald never asked about the books, not once. He must have thought the guards brought them. Dwarrow claimed never to have met my father, and he remained ignorant of his whereabouts, the letters always being passed on by the same draughoul. Now I understand; she would have been my grandmother. Father would never have let her enter Sardis, even via a secret passage. If she got caught..."

"Will he try and stop us from leaving Bindari?" asked Tom.

"No. My father understands what needs to be done. He knows he lost his daughter a long time ago."

"Have you seen Dwarrow recently?"

Caeli beamed. "Oh, yes. He rescued me from Sardis. If we make it to Malang Gunya in time, you will see him there."

*   *   *   *

Seaweed-like tassels of algae clung to the wall of jagged grey stone that loomed over Tom and Caeli, water dripping down the wall's face from condensing mist that never seemed to completely dissipate from the gorge outside Widukind's front door. Tom wrapped his coat around himself to ward off the cold and pulled a woollen hat he'd found in the house down over his ears. Standing right beside him, Caeli was barely visible in the mist. They'd said goodbye to Widukind, who had refused to take one step outside the door, but had weakened in his resolve to convince Caeli to stay.

Fullō emerged through the fog, looking more like a ghost than any draughoul Tom had seen so far. She would lead them out of Bindari and to the edge of Babir Birramal near where Caeli had stabled her horse. Tom dreaded the climb back up the treacherous stairs cut into the side of the gorge, and the trudge down muddy paths, past the reverent miyans and the stone monuments marking each grell gravesite. He wondered if he had the strength for one last journey before the end, whatever form that end may take.

Fullō pulled Tom close, and the dark eyes clinked together inside the pocket of his coat. A feeble, painful whimper escaped her lips. "Give one to me."

"What?" asked Tom.

"Give me one of the eyes of lost souls. For Caeli."

"I don't understand."

"To hold in her hand. Otherwise, she cannot follow."

Tom pulled a dark eye from his pocket. Fullō snatched it from his palm, turned from Tom, reached out and placed the eye in Caeli's hand. Grasping the princess' free hand, she whispered something into her ear, and together they walked towards the wall. Fullō disappeared first, stepping into the rock like it was thin air. Caeli followed without a flinch. Tom's mind drifted back to his first days in Enthilen when Frennan taught him how to find the door of the milbi.

Focus on the now.

He stepped up to the wall and ran his hand over the slippery rock; nothing except wet, icy-cold stone. No plants or animals danced before his eyes to form a doorway, no matter how much he tried to clear his mind of doubt and worry.

As the morning dragged on, it seemed he may be left behind until Fullō reappeared and took his hand. "Dispel the memories of the past and the hopes and fears of the future. Draughouls have none of these things. They think only of this moment."

Focus on the now.

Tom placed his other hand in his pocket, wrapping his fingers around the remaining dark eye, and followed Fullō into the wall.

Something bizarre and wonderful happened he had trouble comprehending. He didn't walk through a doorway in the stone. He *was* the stone. He was the soil and roots, the worms and detritus. As he moved forward, still clutching onto Fullō's hand and the dark eye in his pocket, he became the peat and mud and dirty snow of Bindari, the etched stone of the monoliths, and the blood of the miyans. He cried when Annian's resting body passed through him, then rejoiced at the connection formed with the living, breathing creatures of the forest. He became the thylacine, the deer, the panalope tree, the yurali bushes.

Tom had become Enthilen and the land him, a magical, terrifying, unbreakable bond. He wondered if the sad, desperate draughouls also felt this way, then understood almost immediately. Their souls were already bound to one of the land's treasures, the dark eye sitting in his pocket. The eyes connected the draughouls to Enthilen in a way few would ever understand, and now Fullō had shared this gift with Tom and Caeli.

Empathy replaced the fear and pity Tom once had for the soulless. He understood their desire to be close to the dark eyes or that which spawned them. And he understood the power resting within the eyes beyond stealing souls and granting immortality. There was so much more to these obsidian baubles with the flaming pupils.

In what seemed like a moment, but could well have been half a day, Tom stepped out of another rock face and into a cathedral of panalope trees. Caeli stood there, smiling, with Fullō at her side.

"Can everyone do that?" said Tom, his mind still reeling.

"Draughouls, yes," said Fullō. "People, no, unless they hold the eyes and we lead them. I can still show you secret paths, but it will take much longer to travel them, and you will not become one with the land as you did during this journey." Fullō ran her osseous fingers through Caeli's hair, "Goodbye, Caeli," then turned and stepped back into the rock.

"She's returned to my father," said Caeli, handing the other dark eye back to Tom. "It's only a short walk to the stables."

"Then let's hurry," said Tom.

~ Chapter 37 ~

Grin bore an immense responsibility, more monumental than any so far in his young life. The elders had taught him the most sacred of stone-grell lore. Such a privilege came with expectations and duties he must fulfil, to teach others the ways of grell culture and to protect all that grells revered. He also wore a new tattoo made from an ink mixed with the blood of muwin, the ground spider; a circle of scarlet dots on the back of his right hand representing the marble columns of the calendar of life in Malang Gunya. The tattoo served to remind him of the cycle of life and his place within that cycle.

Though the pride and honour of initiation filled his soul, his legs weighed heavy as he trudged, head bowed, across the Dambay Plains to Malang Gunya. He carried a spear, and on his shoulders rested a pack of food and bedding, and a bow and quiver full of arrows. He also laboured with the emotional scars from the attack on the *Vulking*, the anger inside him refusing to abate. Although his mother had tried to speak to him about it, he pushed her away, choosing to suppress the hurt rather than relive it. At the back of his mind, he worried where such a choice may lead.

Other worries played on his thoughts. The settling of Malang Gunya by the Erstürmen, and how they would receive the grell pilgrims. The re-emergence of Tom Anderson, the birraman. Only days ago, Grin had accepted his friend had died in the ocean. Yet, Dwarrow appeared confident Tom was alive, and Grin had no reason to doubt the little werp. Frennan had spoken to the other grells about Tom and Adalwolf being birth twins and the need to let Adalwolf live. Grin's father told him not all of them would agree to such a demand. The fall of the Erstürmen Kingdom held priority over the life of a traveller from a distant land. Once again, the responsibility of protecting Tom had fallen at Grin's feet.

He used those huge, bare feet now to flatten the grass of the Dambay Plains, leaving a faint trail for others to follow in seasons to come. Thaly trotted beside him, trying to keep pace with the giant strides of the grells, dressed in the same patch-work, animal-skin tunic that all her travelling companions wore. They'd been walking for six days since leaving Babir Birramal, always lagging behind most of the six hundred who marched to Malang Gunya. Grin expected Thaly to give up, yet her resilience appeared unbreakable. A new resolve had set in her eyes, their resolute gleam shining even more brightly under a shaved scalp.

As they breached the crest of a hill, Grin stopped and caught his breath. The expanse of Malang Gunya spread out before him, and for the first time in his life, he stood on the doorstep of his ancestral home. Thaly joined him, gazing at the horizon where the midday sun shone brightly onto the peak of the stepped pyramid marking the centre of the grell city.

"We will travel until sunset, then camp on the outskirts of the city," said Grin.

"When is the homage march?" asked Thaly.

"The final preparations will be made tonight. Then, at sunrise, we walk into Malang Gunya."

A nervous smile passed across Thaly's face, reflecting the mood of all the marchers. Grin sensed the blend of joy and apprehension rippling through the company. Like all those around him, he wondered how this journey would end.

* * * *

In the throne hall of Pergamos, Adalwolf sat on the throne of the dead at the head of a rectangular table, a feast laid out before him from the supplies carried from Laodicea. Malphas had called for a banquet to celebrate the renovation of the throne hall, and, with the room full of Erstürmen, the pantomime of Adalwolf's rule needed to be on display.

At the king's table with Adalwolf sat Malphas, Romilda, Lothar, Krieg and Ende. The sad, hideous concoction of the king's court. Malphas appeared bold tonight, sitting tall and proud with no cowl hiding his face.

Some in the room would remember him as the exiled King Oldaric, thought Adalwolf. Maybe it didn't matter anymore? With the rise of the tainted grells and the Rephaim, it seemed nothing could challenge the entrenchment of Malphas' power. Almost nothing.

In addition to the king's table, another twelve round tables filled the hall, each one seating twenty-four guests, mostly military men from the King's Shield and their wives, or residents from the inner circle of Sardis who had journeyed to Pergamos. At one table sat Lothar's Heilig-jün, the twenty-four old men who hung on every word from the Hoch-Vater's mouth. Lothar called them his disciples in honour of the twenty-four devotees Volerdie had chosen as his closest confidants. Adalwolf wondered at the blasphemy of such an audacious act, but it appeared Malphas didn't share his concerns.

Around the perimeter of the hall stood over one hundred Rephaim, still and silent like colossal armoured statues. The grell army grew in size with each passing day. Soon, thought Adalwolf, the Rephaim would

491

be unassailable, and whoever commanded them would be the true ruler of Enthilen.

The murmurs in the hall grew louder when grell slaves wheeled in spits of roasted pig and horse, signalling the meal would soon begin. Fat from the meat spat into the trays of flaming coals that sat underneath the rotating metal skewers, sending aromatic plumes out into the crowd of salivating mouths. The slaves brought the spits to the king's table and stepped back. Adalwolf knew what came next, having endured Ewald's banquets in the inner circle of Sardis. He stood, pulled his royal-blue robes together in front and grasped a golden goblet from the table. All the eyes in the room turned to him as he raised the goblet into the air. Murmurs subsided to an awkward silence.

"Welcome, friends, to Pergamos," said Adalwolf, his voice echoing around the enormous room.

"Hail, King Adalwolf!" came shouts from the crowd.

Adalwolf couldn't help but smile. "This is our first banquet in Volerdie's grand hall. It will not be our last."

"Hurray! Praise Volerdie!"

"Tonight, we celebrate many things. The return of the Erstürmen to Pergamos, the home of our first ancestors. The dawn of a new and glorious kingdom. The defeat of our enemies at Laodicea and in the Scaur Hills."

"Death to the rebels!"

Adalwolf raised his free hand to still the crowd. "And...and, my friends, the yarle in which darkness will descend..."

"Hurray!"

"...Volerdie will return to Enthilen..."

"Volerdie's mercy!"

"...and the road to paradise will be revealed!"

The crowd roared and cheered, thumping tankards and cutlery on the tables and stamping their feet. Adalwolf puffed out his chest and stepped over to the first of the six spits, waiting for the din in the room to diminish. As silence descended on the throne hall, he raised the golden goblet higher and, with a theatrical flourish of his wrist, tossed the contents of the goblet into the coals of the spit. Flames burst from the tray, licking up the sides of the roasted pig. Some in the crowd gasped, likely having never been to a royal banquet and unaware of the protocol. Adalwolf's goblet contained serpent oil, not meduz, the highly combustible liquid exploding in flames as soon as it hit the fiery embers.

The crowd settled, Adalwolf resumed his seat, and the grell slaves began to carve the roasted meat, the first slivers placed on the king's plate. Adalwolf was so hungry he took a slice of meat in his hands and threw it into his mouth, thinking only after the succulent fat burst onto his tongue about the possibility of poison. But he wasn't Ewald, refusing to let paranoia cripple his rule. *Nothing* would cripple his rule.

A slave cleaned his goblet and poured meduz as a King's Shield in full armour approached the throne and bowed his head. "The wild grells have reached the outskirts of the city, your majesty. They're setting up camp on its southern border."

Adalwolf sipped his meduz, contemplating a response.

"Shall we prepare to attack, majesty?" asked Lothar.

Adalwolf squirmed atop the throne of the dead, the mash of contorted bodies offering little comfort for a new king, then placed his goblet on the table. To his right, Malphas sat quietly, rubbing his thighs as if he could never entirely rid them of the aches of old age. Adalwolf knew his father's silence was another test. An opportunity for the young king to conjure a strategy to please the Worshipful Master.

Adalwolf turned to Lothar. "We will hold steady for now, Hoch-Vater. The wild grells seek to honour those who fell defending their settlement. Folcher's men have advised me that the grell ceremony always takes place in the open temple at the pyramid's base. I assume it still stands?"

"Yes, majesty," said Lothar.

"Good. The grells are feeble in some ways and tenacious in others. I'm confident they'll want to conduct their ceremony as normal, and we should let them try. Allow them to walk into the city unhindered, right to the base of the pyramid. Then our soldiers can encircle them. There will be no escape from Pergamos for the grell heathens."

"Who will greet them, majesty?" asked Malphas.

Adalwolf flinched. That's not a question, he thought; it's a statement. Malphas was ordering him to meet the grells.

"I will, Worshipful Master," said Adalwolf. "I will receive them on the steps of the pyramid, and because I'm a virtuous king, I'll give them a choice. Pledge fealty and service to our kingdom or suffer the consequences."

"An excellent idea, majesty."

"Yes, Worshipful Master." Adalwolf turned to the soldier, who still stood to attention at the side of the table. "Prepare the men to meet the wild grells when they march into the city. Make sure the grells aren't touched until they gather in...what is that temple called?"

"The calendar of life," said Malphas.

"Yes, the calendar of life. Let them gather, and we'll snare them in a trap. One of my advisors will provide further orders in due course. You're dismissed."

The soldier bowed his head again and left the hall.

"I've been thinking, majesty," said Malphas, "on a task we might complete before the grells march into our city. May I interrupt your meal and speak with you in private?"

Adalwolf nodded. Both men stood at once, and Adalwolf followed his father to a dark, empty corner of the cavernous hall where Malphas had chained his draughoul servants.

Malphas leaned in close and whispered, "My spies have confirmed the wild grell and rebel girl from Hansen's Bluff are among the marchers. It seems the weregrims failed in their task. Tom Anderson's friends still live."

Adalwolf remembered the beautiful, terrifying rebel woman who had attacked him. His face flushed with shame and anger, recalling his failure at her hands — the thief who stole the eyes of lost souls.

"The wild grell is called Grin, and the rebel girl is Athalee. I have plans for both of them. To exploit the weakness of loyalty that exists among friends."

"What might these plans be?" asked Adalwolf.

"Nothing you need to worry about. I will entrust Krieg and the Rephaim with this task."

"What about Tom Anderson? What does the blood compass say?"

"It didn't spin for days, and I thought the magic had failed. However, today, it's spinning again, more slowly than before, and when it stops, it points south-east. The boy is getting closer with each passing moment. We have little time to lose. Krieg must complete his mission tonight before Tom Anderson comes to Pergamos. And you must prepare yourself for another confrontation."

Yes, thought Adalwolf, he would be ready. To wrest the kingdom from those who would deny him.

* * * *

After the banquet, when the crowd had filed out of the throne hall, Romilda made her way to Adalwolf's private quarters off the central passageway connecting the royal rooms with the hall and the stairs that led above ground. Two Rephaim guarded her son's door, the grell soldiers having replaced the King's Shield at Malphas' command. She'd never spoken to one of the armoured grells. Most of them were slaves once. Deferring to someone of higher authority should come naturally to them.

"I wish to speak with my son," said Romilda.

A Rephaim stepped in front of the door and placed his hand on the hilt of a notched broadsword. "Is the king expecting you?" he asked.

"I'm his mother. I don't need an invitation."

The soldier looked sideways to his companion, who stood in silence and stared at the opposing wall of the passageway.

"I will ask the king." The soldier turned and tapped on the door.

"What?" Adalwolf called from inside.

"Your mother is here, your majesty."

"What does she want?"

"I want to speak with you, Adalwolf," said Romilda, feeling small and indignant it had come to this.

"Alright," said Adalwolf.

The soldier nodded and opened the door, closing it behind Romilda as she stepped into her son's quarters.

"What do you want?" asked Adalwolf, standing beside his bed, already dressed in his chiffon bedclothes. "I'm about to retire."

Romilda stepped from the door and over to her son. "The servants have done a fine job at decorating your room. All these tapestries and paintings, and that beautiful chest of drawers Ewald and I had in Sardis."

"You didn't come here to admire the decorations."

Romilda sighed and sat on the edge of the bed, facing her son. "It wasn't so long ago you would come into my chambers and sit with me, talking into the night about all your hopes and fears. When Ewald shunned you, when he called you worthless and threatened to keep the throne, you always came to me for consolation, and I was always there for you. To remake the vessel of your confidence, smashed by the man who thought he was your father. Do you remember, Adalwolf?"

"I can't show such weakness now. I can't be clutching your dress every time my rule is challenged."

"No, you can't. Those days are gone forever. You are king now. The ruler of all Enthilen. But how long do you think your reign will last?"

"Malphas believes it can last an eternity."

"Does he? What if I had information painting a different picture? Proof your rule could end before the onset of the next harvest season."

"Where did you get this information? Who threatens my reign?"

"The man who placed you on that repulsive throne. Malphas has a plan for you, my son. A plan never spoken, taken straight from the pages of the First Scripture."

"How can you know such things? You have no right to read the scripture."

"I have no need to read it. Someone has done that for me. And from the First Scripture, Malphas has hatched a scheme that will lead to your death. If you wish to see another harvest season, King Adalwolf, we must make our own plans to thwart the Worshipful Master."

*   *   *   *

Exhausted from a night of serving food to guests at the king's banquet, Seronan stumbled into the cramped, roofless shelter being used to house Henruld's cohort of grell slaves, searching for her friend, Myan. She found him asleep on the dirt floor in a back corner of the building.

Seronan sat and shook Myan's shoulder, whispering in his ear, "Wake up. Wake up."

Myan stirred, wiped the sleep from his eyes and sat up, resting his back against the cold stone wall. "What is it?"

"I have news from the banquet. The wild grells have made camp on the edge of Malang Gunya. They will soon march into the city. Are you ready?"

"No more than ten Rephaim would commit to protecting the grells. The rest are too frightened of what Krieg might do to them."

"It will have to be enough," said Seronan. "The Queen Mother is with us. I have delivered to her something of substantial importance. She will convince her son to let the wild grells honour in peace."

"Be careful, Wortle. Misplaced trust could end..."

"Hoi! Wake up y'scum!" yelled Henruld from outside the front door. "All slaves trainin' with da Rephaim need t'meet outside. Now. Da red grell's called for ya."

Myan went to stand, and Seronan grabbed his forearm. "Remember to protect your kin. Seek pride in the sanctity of their lives, not the shame of treachery."

Myan nodded, then lumbered off. Seronan curled up on the floor and tried to find rest among a calamity of troubled thoughts.

*   *   *   *

Late in the night, only the quarter moon of Seena floating in the sky, Thaly stood guard on the fringe of the camp the grells had established near Malang Gunya. She couldn't sleep, despite her muscles aching from the long walk from Babir Birramal, her thoughts turning to her departed trainer and friend, Jacob. If he was here, he'd be on watch, keeping his eyes peeled for any trouble, expecting it would come, yet hoping it wouldn't. Although the Dobunni rebels may be no more, the stone- and weald-grells needed protecting.

Next to Thaly, a young female weald-grell named Yulan leaned on a spear with one leg folded up, her foot resting against the inside of her knee. Before them, a myriad of flaming torches lit up the grell city. To Thaly, it resembled a fire seeping its way across the Dambay Plains. Her eyes blurred the firelight until the face of a beast appeared with its tongue a flaming whip, and its expression cruel and mocking.

What awaited them in Malang Gunya? she wondered. What reward would the grells receive for a folly such as this?

Exhaustion must have dulled Thaly's vigilance. She failed to notice the shadows creeping across the Dambay Plains towards the camp before it was too late. Stalking the wild grells came dark giants hunched low, only their arched backs showing above the tall, dry grass. As she went to raise the alarm, an arrow pierced Yulan's throat, and the weald-grell crumpled onto the grey soil like a discarded coat.

Thaly screamed, "Attack!"

Another yell came from the opposite side of the camp. "Traitor grells!"

The shadows stood tall, growing out of the plains like the trunks of blackened trees silhouetted in the pale moonlight.

Grell soldiers, thought Thaly. They didn't lumber as she expected, but moved fast and silent like a wolf hunting its prey, enveloping the camp before a further alarm could be raised. Thaly drew her short sword and confronted the first soldier crossing her path. This is now the enemy, she thought, armoured grells with black souls.

The soldier reared up, raising a broadsword above his head while arrows whistled into the camp. Bracing her legs shoulder-width apart, she raised her sword, preparing to deflect the blow from the grell soldier, when a bark exploded from behind him — a fierce, guttural yelp to withdraw. The soldier lowered his sword and marched straight past her. She was about to pursue him when something more terrifying appeared, tainted red skin glimmering in the moonlight. Instinctively, she reached for her wrist, still bound with Tom's white handkerchief. The wound ached with the memory of what happened on Hansen's Bluff. Now Krieg had returned to finish the job.

In a furious panic, Thaly forgot all her training, screamed and raced at the demon, lifting her sword above her shoulder, preparing to cut him in half. As she flailed the blade with a weary arm, the weapon twisted in her hand, nicking the grell's thigh. Seemingly steeled by the wound, he smashed his mace into Thaly's sword, wrenching it from her grasp and dislocating her thumb. In agony, she clutched her hand, refusing to utter a cry of pain.

Krieg bent down and lifted her from the ground by her throat. She grappled with his giant, clutching hand, trying to pull the fingers away, but they'd latched onto her skin like gorging leeches. The darkening night spiralled around her, silhouettes of grell battling grell fusing into a single chaotic mess. Saliva caught in her throat, and she gagged, gasping for space for the air to pass through.

Krieg yelled to his companions, "I have the rebel woman. Find the grell called Grin."

Then, Thaly blacked out.

* * * *

Inside a dangal with Frennan and Mirrian, the clamour of battle woke Grin from his slumber. He grabbed a spear from beside his sleeping mat, roused his parents, threw back the flap of the shelter, then froze at the entrance. An armoured grell soldier pushed the tip of a broadsword into Grin's face, forcing him back inside. Grin simmered with anger as he clutched the spear shaft tighter and prepared to thrust the blade into the soldier's chest. Then the soldier did something unexpected, lowering his weapon and raising a hand in deference.

"We're searching for the one called Grin," said the soldier in fluent

Erstürmen. "With the facial crest of a spider."

"We do not know anyone…" Frennan started.

Grin interrupted. "Why do you seek him?" He knew he couldn't hide for long. The tattoo on his face announced to the world who he was.

The soldier lifted the face-grill of his helmet. "Our master didn't say, but he wants him taken alive. If you…" He paused, staring at the crest on Grin's face.

Grin lowered his spear, resigned to the inevitable. "I am Grin."

"Please, no," said Mirrian.

"Krieg hunts you," said the soldier. "Him and his Rephaim. You must flee. Otherwise, you'll be a slave to the Erstürmen like the rest of us."

"I will not flee," said Grin. "I will stay to fight beside my family and kin."

"If they capture you, endless torment awaits."

"Go," said Frennan to Grin. "We will fight them off."

"No," snapped Grin.

Mirrian begged, "Please, son. I cannot bear your end."

Grin looked to his parents. He wanted to fight like the rest of them. To have the honour of protecting his ancestral home. Outside, the clang of battle grew louder. It wouldn't be long before a Rephaim loyal to the Erstürmen masters burst into the dangal.

The soldier grabbed Grin's arm and pulled him close. "Go now and fight another day. There are those of us who will stand by your side when the time comes."

Before Grin could protest further, a strange noise rumbled across the plains and shook the walls of the dangal. He pushed past the soldier and peered through the animal-hide flap. At the edge of the camp, Krieg stood defiant with a limp body slung over his shoulder.

Thaly, thought Grin, trying to brush aside his indecision and gather the courage to save his friend. But something stopped him; a throng of tiny creatures that scampered across the plains and swamped Krieg like locusts in a plague. Dwarrow had arrived with the mouldewerps, primed for war.

Krieg screamed in agony when a mouldewerp spear punctured his calf. He lashed out with a foot and impaled a werp on the end of his sabaton, still balancing Thaly on his shoulder. "Return to the city!" he yelled, swinging his mace with his free hand to keep the werps at bay. The Rephaim began to retreat, overwhelmed by the arriving horde of werps.

The soldier pushed past Grin to join his retreating companions. "I have to go. Otherwise, my treachery may be exposed."

"What is your name?" asked Grin.

"Flea...I mean, Myan. My grell name is Myan."

"Thank you for warning me, Myan."

"If you march to Malang Gunya, some of us will try to protect you."

Grin nodded and let the soldier leave, hoping he wouldn't regret it. He rushed outside and ran to where he last saw Krieg and Thaly. However, the red grell had disappeared into the night like a tendril of smoke caught by a howling wind.

Dwarrow ran up to Grin, trying to catch his breath. "It appears...it appears I've saved your life a second time, Grinnian stone-grell."

"They took Thaly," said Grin. "We have to go after her."

"The traitor grells have fled back to their city."

"It is not their city."

"No. Of course. Nevertheless, a mindless pursuit may well see us run straight into a trap. If we wish to defeat tainted grells and their perfidious followers, we'll need all the guile we can muster. It's time for us to regather our wits and consider a new plan."

Grin wanted to dismiss Dwarrow's advice. Save Thaly's life like she'd saved him on the *Vulking*. But as the Rephaim disappeared into the breaking dawn, he knew the little werp was right.

The sun breached the horizon, and injured or exhausted wild grells wandered among the dangals in a trance while others knelt beside the bodies of the dead and mourned. Dozens of corpses lay in the grass, unmoving bodies offering their last bloody sacrifice to the land that spawned all life.

Frennan and Mirrian attended to the wounded while Grin slumped down next to a cold campfire thinking only of his lost friend. Dwarrow sat with him.

"Someone has to rescue Thaly," said Grin.

"And we will," said Dwarrow. "In time."

"We do not have time."

"Now, now. No need to get uppity. Fools rush in when the wise hold back."

"Why did they take her?"

Dwarrow sighed. "Malphas will likely use Thaly as part of his plan to capture Tom."

"I still do not understand what we are trying to protect Tom Anderson from."

"Even I, with all my undoubted wisdom and worldliness, haven't uncovered every detail of Malphas' plan. From what you told me about the encounter on Hansen's Bluff, it seems we must keep Tom away from Adalwolf. If the king kills his birth twin with the dark eyes, eternal life will be his gift. How that benefits Malphas, well, I simply don't know, and neither do the elders. It's an awfully complex calamity. Awful indeed."

The day wore on. The Mulugan called a meeting to discuss their next step. Many of the wild grells wanted to return to the welcome safety of Babir Birramal or Giigal, the bravado evident at the ngulubul now gone. More than half of the marchers had already packed up their shelters, refusing to go any further regardless of what the leaders decided.

Others vowed to carry the dead to Bindari rather than march into Malang Gunya.

Grin had long dreamed of his first homage march. He didn't know what to expect, but he never expected this. Hopes of seeing the grell city and paying his respects to his ancestors in peace shimmered like a mirage on the horizon that would never materialise.

What would he do now? What *could* he do now?

Dwarrow had sat with him all morning. He'd led a troupe of nearly one hundred mouldewerps, enough to thwart the Rephaim attack on the grell camp, but not enough to protect the marchers travelling into Malang Gunya or to launch a raid to rescue Thaly. The werp fighters had disappeared, for now, sheltering in secret underground dwells, according to Dwarrow.

Tired of the indecisive silence, Grin faced his werp friend. "Regardless of what the Mulugan decide, I am going to march."

"That initiation thingy of yours seems to have dulled your senses," said Dwarrow. "What did I say about being hasty? Thaly needs you. Tom Anderson will need you again before the end. We must take a different path."

"Are you asking me to abandon my kin?"

Dwarrow softened his voice. "I understand you're faced with a difficult decision. Nobody doubts your loyalty to your family or to wild grells, but if you join the homage march, I see only two outcomes for you — death or enslavement. Neither will serve the greater good. One thing I do know is the future of Enthilen is tied completely and utterly to the fate of Tom Anderson. And the more I meditate, the more I realise Thaly also has a most critical role in shaping that future. If we can save them both, we may well save all of us from generations of despair."

The debate among the Mulugan ended that evening. More marchers returned to Babir Birramal, leaving about two hundred who would honour their ancestors in Malang Gunya, including Frennan and Mirrian, Grin's parents. Grin had spent a restless afternoon pondering Dwarrow's advice. He changed his mind more than once, before finally deciding not to join the march. Although the schism cut at his soul, Dwarrow's words rang inside his head, *save all of us from generations of despair.* The needs of the many, the needs of the land, outweighed everything else.

The following morning, Grin bade his parents farewell in the formal way, resting his fingers across Mirrian's facial crest of panalope flowers with fringed petals, then Frennan's crest of the wings of walga, the sparrowhawk.

Frennan turned away without speaking. Mirrian stayed with her son a while longer. "We understand your decision," she said, "and we are proud of you. We have always been proud. There are other ways to honour the legacy of our ancestors. I can think of no better one than trying to protect Enthilen from a dismal future."

She smiled and walked off, trotting to the front of the line to lead the marchers into Malang Gunya. Grin tried to shake the thought from his mind, but something told him this may be the last time he saw his parents.

Dwarrow tapped him on the knee with his walking stick. "No time for feeling sorry for yourself. I've been working on a plan. I need you to watch the south road."

"Watch the road?" said Grin. "How is that such a contribution to the future of our land?"

"Too many questions, Grinnian stone-grell. My nose gets all twitchy from too many questions. Princess Caeli told me she sent Tom Anderson to Bindari."

"Yes. Tom wanted me to tell him the location of the grell graveyard. But I did not know the location until my initiation. And I am unsure if I would have told him anyway."

505

"Tom's resourceful. More than he gives himself credit for. I'm going to assume that he reached Bindari. That means, if he comes to Malang Gunya, he'll come from the south."

"Why did Caeli send Tom to the grell graveyard?"

"*Hmph*, well, that was a secret she wouldn't reveal even to me. Nevertheless, I've put my nose to the ground and come up with some important conclusions. Very important, indeed. Caeli has also gone to Bindari to find her father. I'm sure of it. If she crosses paths with Tom Anderson, she'll tell him about you and Thaly, and the march to Malang Gunya. Tom will want to return to his friends. To do something to protect them."

"I do not understand how you know all these things."

"Never you mind. I'll tell you what you need to know and nothing more. Don't forget, you're in my service. I could return you to the mouldewerp elders and let them decide on a less desirable fate."

Grin half-smiled. "*Is there a less desirable fate?*"

"Very amusing. Trust me, Grin, I know what I'm doing. I need you to watch the south road and intercept Tom before he reaches Malang Gunya. We can't have the young fool bumbling into the city without knowing what might be waiting for him."

"Are we not supposed to be keeping him *away* from Adalwolf?"

"Well, yes...and no. Oh, I don't know. Despite my unfathomable intellect, parts of the puzzle still elude me."

"What about Thaly?"

"I'll find out where they're holding her. Trust my nose. It's never let me down before. Well, almost never. There are numerous dwells under these plains, and some lead right into Malang Gunya. I can smell my way there. I want you to wait here until I return. Should Tom arrive before then, don't let him go any further. He must not enter the city alone."

Dwarrow scampered off into the tall grass of the Dambay Plains, and Grin sat beside the south road to begin his vigil.

*   *   *   *

At the northern edge of Babir Birramal, a lone masked rider with a broad-brimmed hat sat on his horse, conversing with one of the few wild grells left to watch over the forest. The wild grell pointed north to Malang Gunya. The rider tipped his hat and yanked on the reins of his horse, urging it towards the city.

~ Chapter 38 ~

Lying on her side, curled up in the foetal position and facing the back wall of a prison cell, Thaly heard something being dragged across the stone floor and then a clunk. Behind her, somebody groaned as if lowering aching bones onto a seat.

"Are you thirsty?"

Thaly recognised the voice. Raspy and adenoidal. The old man from Hansen's Bluff. The master of the tainted grells. Malphas. She didn't answer, despite her swollen tongue searching a parched mouth for an elusive drop of moisture.

"That was a stupid question," said Malphas. "Of course, you're thirsty. And hungry. My slave tells me you haven't eaten or drunk anything since you arrived."

Thaly heard water being poured and then the clap of wood on stone.

"Here, take this."

She remained still, focussing on her breathing and trying to conserve her energy for an escape. The opportunity would come, and she'd be ready when it did. She wriggled the thumb that had been dislocated by Krieg's blow. Someone had set it back in place. Their mistake, thought Thaly. Now she could wield a sword equally well in either hand.

The disembodied whine continued behind her, "It may surprise you to learn, I didn't bring you here to die."

Thirst overcame Thaly's resolve to give nothing away. She rolled over to face a wooden cup sitting on the floor of her cell, placed inside steel bars as thick as an arm. Dressed in white robes cinched with a black belt, Malphas squatted on a small stool outside the cell, smiled at her, and then shivered.

"It gives me the chills to think about the creatures Volerdie must have kept in this bleak prison," he said. "Move closer, child. Take the water."

Thaly muttered through gritted teeth, "I'm not a child."

"How wonderful. Your fortitude isn't completely broken. I would have been most disappointed if we'd already crushed your spirit."

As she glared at Malphas, something caught in the back of her throat, causing her to cough.

"Oh, come now," said Malphas, "you need this water."

Still coughing, Thaly shuffled her bottom across the cell floor to within reach of the cup and stretched her arm towards it. She must have briefly taken her eyes off Malphas because she didn't see him move. Like the strike of a venomous snake, he thrust his hand through the bars and grabbed her forearm, right at the point where Krieg's arrow had inflicted its wound.

"Even a grimace cannot despoil such a pretty face. I wager that stupid boy fell for your doleful eyes. They herald so much suffering. But what have you done with your beautiful long hair?" Malphas twisted her arm. "And what's this white cloth wrapped around your arm? It seems someone has embroidered two letters into the fabric: T. A. What could they ever stand for?"

Thaly snarled and tried to wrench her arm free, but Malphas' fingers tightened, stained nails digging through Tom's handkerchief and reopening the wound on her arm.

"Strong for an old man, is that what you're thinking?" He released his grip, and she slunk to the back corner of the prison cell with the cup of water, sniffing the liquid.

"It's not poison," said Malphas. "Why is there no trust in this world anymore?"

Thaly's thirst overwhelmed her suspicion, and she downed the water in a single gulp, tossing the cup back through the bars. If he'd poisoned her, better to get it over with quickly than let the pain linger.

"Feeling ill? No, of course not. I hope the water has lubricated your vocal cords because we have so much to talk about, Athalee of Bagendon."

She flinched at the title. How much did Malphas already know about her?

"Where do I start?" he asked. "Ah, yes, you probably didn't hear. Krieg has destroyed Bagendon and slaughtered every rebel cowering behind its walls. I guess that makes you Athalee the Homeless. With the fall also of Laodicea, the Dobunni are no more. The cowards that fled to Gestade will soon be dealt with. Here marks the end of your people. What future awaits you now? I can always use another good fighter in my ranks. Why not pledge allegiance to King Adalwolf? Such an act of apostasy is not foreign to the likes of you."

Thaly growled, "I'll never fight for you. I'm going to kill you."

Malphas' body shook with laughter so much he almost toppled from his stool. "Child...child, you don't realise how ridiculous you are." He stumbled to his feet, yelling for a guard. An involuntary gasp escaped Thaly's lips when an armoured grell marched into the room, the soldier looking much more ominous when not hidden under the veil of night.

Malphas stood side-on to the cell bars, opened his robes and raised his undershirt, revealing a flat, wrinkled stomach. "Take your sword and slash it across my flesh."

The soldier froze.

Malphas raised his voice. "I command you to slash your sword across my flesh."

"Yes, Worshipful Master," came the reply from behind the slits of a grilled black helmet masking the grell's face and head. With a hand covered in a studded leather gauntlet, the soldier drew his broadsword, hooked along the top edge, and swept the blade across Malphas' stomach. The wound opened and immediately healed itself before the blade had been withdrawn. The grell removed and examined his bloodless sword as if he'd discovered the skull of a mythical beast. Thaly sat at the back of the cell, mouth agape.

"Return to your post," ordered Malphas.

The grell stumbled from the room, and Malphas resumed his seat. "Now, Athalee, where were we? Ah yes, that's right. The end of the Dobunni. Forever. And the wild grells will soon follow. Clumsy, oafish brutes, staggering blindly to their demise. My spies say mouldewerps march with them. Who would believe it? I thought they'd vanished long ago. It seems adversity makes strange bedfellows. There could be hope yet for you and I."

Thaly fought to keep in place a mask of resistance, but inside she felt helpless, lost and confused.

Malphas leaned forward on his stool. "What was the name of that poor soul we cut down on Hansen's Bluff? The feeble man with dark skin, grey hair and a scar across his face. Was he someone you admired? He didn't die right away, you know. Ende is clever like that. She likes to make the anguish linger. Says it gives her victims time to reflect on their missteps. Your friend lasted for quite a while. In the end, we skinned him alive. The screams were deafening."

Against all her will, Jacob's face flashed before Thaly's eyes, and her mind pleaded for his help. He offered none, and the vision faded into emptiness. She snarled like a mother bear protecting her only cub, sprang to her feet and rushed at the gloating old hound, smashing her fists against the cell bars.

"Monster!" yelled Thaly.

He didn't flinch. Not one bit. "Sit, child. Your precociousness has landed you in trouble more than once already. Use your mind to guide your actions, not your emotions."

She remained standing, sneering at Malphas and clutching the cold steel bars with numb hands. "I don't know how, but I *will* kill you. I will end your life and the lives of all who serve you. Bringing me here was your first mistake."

Malphas ignored the threat and fossicked around in the shirt under his robe. He withdrew a shiny, gold pentagram, one of its points stained with blood, and placed it on the palm of his hand. "Now, we should talk about the boy. Tom Anderson."

"He's dead."

"We both know that isn't true. I am, however, having trouble locating him. You wouldn't happen to know his whereabouts? And the eyes of lost souls, Athalee. The ones you stole from King Adalwolf. What happened to those?"

"I should have thrown them into the ocean."

"A wistful life is full of should haves." He twirled the pentagram between his thumb and forefinger, then doubled over and balanced the golden star on the floor. It spun immediately, but the spinning ended almost as soon as it had begun, and Malphas cried out, "Well, well, it seems our saviour is on the move directly south of here, and it looks like he's coming this way. The compass hardly spun at all. That *is* excellent news." He stood and placed the compass back in his pocket as a grell slave entered the room with a plate of food. "I must go now, Athalee," said Malphas. "There's much to prepare for Tom Anderson's arrival. I'll leave you with...with Wortle. I think that's her name. These slaves all look the same to me. Try to eat something. Keep your strength up. I can't have you dying before the boy arrives."

Malphas left the room, and the grell slave, who Thaly recognised as a weald-grell, placed the plate of bread and potato outside the cell and went to leave.

"Wait," said Thaly. "Have the wild grells marched yet?"

The slave, Wortle, stopped but didn't speak, her nervous turquoise eyes darting between the door and Thaly's prison cell.

"I was going to march with them," said Thaly. "I only want to know if they're safe."

Wortle stepped towards the cell and whispered, "It is still night. If they march, it will not be until the daylight."

"Can you help me get out of here?"

Wortle flinched at the question.

"Please," said Thaly. "The grells and the Dobunni have always been friends."

Wortle nodded. "I will try." Then scurried from the room.

* * * *

At midday, nearly two hundred wild grell pilgrims entered Malang Gunya. Seronan stood near the calendar of life to watch them approach. Although she had duties to complete, they could wait. This may be the one and only time she witnessed a homage march. What struck her first were the crests, black, bold and proud, tattooed onto every face. She couldn't remember the last time she'd seen a facial crest that wasn't worn and faded from long neglect. The shaved heads of the female marchers meant their crests stood out even more.

Dressed in tunics of stitched animal skins, the pilgrims came armed with spears, bows and daggers, and Seronan worried the Erstürmen may consider this a provocation. Yet, the citizens lining the route stood like silent mourners at a funeral procession and simply watched the grells file past. Queen Romilda had promised Seronan she would convince her son, the king, to spare the pilgrims' lives. To let them pay their respects in peace, then return to Babir Birramal. So far, it seemed Romilda had kept her word.

At the base of the stepped pyramid, a male stone-grell with the facial crest of walga led the marchers into the calendar of life, its white marble columns fashioned as tree trunks and a polished stone floor open to the sky and painted with a pictorial history of grell culture. The slaves around Seronan dropped to one knee and bowed their heads to honour the sacrifices of those who lost their lives trying to protect Malang Gunya. She did the same, yet held her eyes on the wild grells who packed into the calendar of life, standing shoulder-to-shoulder in sombre reverence.

A female stone-grell with a facial crest of panalope flowers began a hushed, mournful chant that spread through the crowd of pilgrims. Sunlight bounced off the marble columns, creating a soothing, radiant aura filling Seronan's thoughts with hope. She almost smiled, dreaming of another life far away in a lush forest, living wild and free, smothered by the love of her family and tribe. But something shattered the dream: a threatening *thump, thump, thump* of marching boots.

From the other side of the stepped pyramid filed Erstürmen soldiers, the King's Shield, dressed head-to-toe in silver and black armour glinting with a menace that forced Seronan to shield her eyes. Halberds held out front, the Shield slithered towards the wild grells like an armoured serpent then encircled the calendar of life, clacking the blades of their weapons against their breastplates before standing still and ready.

Now trapped inside the rotunda, dozens of wild grells ended their chant and turned to face the soldiers. Others dropped to one knee to continue their tribute to the fallen protectors of Malang Gunya. The crowd around Seronan fell silent. She stood and waited, a restless heart pounding in her ears.

Partway up the stepped pyramid, out of an archway, strolled King Adalwolf outfitted in robes of blue and black, and a bone-white crown resembling the skeleton of a curled snake teetering on his black, curly hair. The king stood to one side as Lothar stepped forward, robed in flowing sangria, and raised his arms to the sky.

"Welcome, grell friends, to the Kingdom of Adalwolf the Redeemer," said Lothar. "Welcome to Pergamos!"

A handful of wild grells raised their spears or unshouldered bows, and Seronan tensed, expecting a battle to begin.

Lothar faded into the shadows, and King Adalwolf stepped forward. "Welcome, my dear grells. There's no need for you to brandish weapons. You've entered an ancient and sacred place; it would be tragic to defile it with your own blood. The antiquity of Pergamos stretches further back than you could imagine. Long before grells arrived in Enthilen, there stood here the eternal palace of Volerdie, the Divine Creator. And we will rebuild this palace in preparation for the Creator's return. On such a momentous day, I offer you the opportunity to share in this undertaking. To replace your aimless meandering through tree and grass with glorious purpose. Lay down your weapons and join us. Pledge allegiance to my kingdom and find nobility in the service of your king."

An unnerving twitch began in Seronan's arm, and her fingers trembled as the male stone-grell with the crest of walga stepped between the ring of soldiers and climbed onto the lower steps of the pyramid to face Adalwolf.

"Your Divine Creator did not create us," said the grell, his voice booming across the menacing silence. "We come from the soil and water; the plants and animals. We come from the land itself. We belong to our country and do not worship false gods or fiends."

"Your words are blasphemous," said Adalwolf. "It is a heinous violation to denounce Volerdie, Creator of all. You are indeed one of his creations, albeit one he remains ashamed of. However, I offer you a chance at redemption. Paradise will never be found by the sinful."

"We have already found paradise," said the wild grell. "Right under our feet and in the joyful surrounds filling all our senses. This land *is* our paradise. We want for no other. The Erstürmen do not respect the land. The time will come when it consumes you, and not even your beloved Volerdie can offer salvation."

"Your ungratefulness disappoints me, but I was told to expect as much. I sought to offer you a choice because I'm an honourable king. Let me give you one more chance to choose between redemption in my service or death in your denial."

Please, thought Seronan, there must be another way out of this. Where is Romilda? Did she not ask her son to let the pilgrims be? Has she betrayed all of us?

The wings of walga, the sparrowhawk, appeared to take flight as the stone-grell bellowed at the king, "We will never serve the Erstürmen!"

"Then the end is upon you," said Adalwolf. He raised his hand, and from inside the pyramid spewed forth dozens of grell soldiers led by the red demon, Krieg. Myan was among them, following his new master as they bounded down the steps of the pyramid and encircled the calendar of life, towering above the King's Shield already there.

More wild grells nocked arrows and raised spears, ready to throw, while others remained kneeling, continuing their remembrance at whatever cost. Sweat beaded on Seronan's brow and dripped into her eyes. She clenched and unclenched her fists, wondering what she could do to stop a confrontation.

The stone-grell standing on the lower steps of the pyramid appeared to plead for calm, but Seronan couldn't hear what he said, the murmur of the crowd drowning out any other sound. From the middle of the wild grells, a spear exploded into the air, hurtling straight at King Adalwolf. Seronan's mouth dropped open as the stone-grell with the facial crest of walga threw his body in front of the projectile. The spear cannoned into his chest, and he collapsed onto the pyramid steps. The female stone-grell with the facial crest of panalope flowers raced up the steps and clutched at the limp body of the male grell. She sat and cradled his head in her lap, rocking back and forth as blood trickled down the steps.

Although she had wished for another outcome, although Queen Romilda had promised as much, resignation crushed Seronan's faith. The battle had begun. She searched the crowd of onlookers for the slaves she'd spoken to, the ones who'd promised to help the pilgrims, but they had slunk away from the danger. Her last hope rested with Myan and his resistance. The Rephaim who would fight alongside the wild grells.

A handful of wild grells burst through the ring of King's Shield and Rephaim and raced up the steps in pursuit of King Adalwolf, who had escaped into the bowels of the pyramid. More Erstürmen soldiers appeared on the balcony and fired crossbows at the grells, sending their giant bodies tumbling and sliding down the pyramid steps with bolts embedded in their flesh. At the same time, the King's Shield advanced on the grell pilgrims trapped inside the calendar of life. Stone-tipped spears, whittled arrows and bone daggers were no match for armour, shields, swords and halberds. The Shield cut down the wild grells like a farmer scything through a crop, paying no heed to whether a pilgrim brandished a weapon or remained in defenceless, sombre prayer. Blood, flesh and bone spattered over the faded paintings of grell history.

The citizens standing near Seronan turned away from the unfolding slaughter. The battle appeared lost until a bloodcurdling scream exploded from the depths of Malang Gunya. Like ravenous moles, fervent, furry creatures poured out from hidden holes and secret passageways underneath the city and pounced on the Erstürmen. Seronan had never seen the creatures before, but she'd heard the stories. She recognised them. Mouldewerps had come to fight with the wild grells.

The surprise attack caught the King's Shield off guard, the mouldewerps smothering the soldiers like ants over the hand of an intruder at their nest. The werps fought their way into the calendar of life to stand together with the remaining grells. Their advance spurred the Rephaim into action, the armoured traitors bursting through the stone columns of the rotunda and crashing down upon the wild grells and werps like an avalanche.

Even among the clang and screams of battle, the calamity of flailing swords and spears, and the cascade of bloodied corpses, Seronan heard Myan yell his command.

"Now!"

A handful of Rephaim turned on their companions to fight alongside the pilgrims. But it was a pitiful handful, thought Seronan. They would never defeat Krieg. Yet, the Rephaim defectors forged a pathway between the Erstürmen attackers, and Seronan watched Myan urge his wild kin to flee.

They needed little encouragement. Around a dozen pilgrims ran from the calendar of life and into the streets of Malang Gunya towards safety. About twenty mouldewerps followed, retreating back into the underground passages beneath the city. Seronan turned her attention to the female grell with the panalope-flower facial crest, who still sat on the steps of the pyramid cradling her dead companion.

Go now! thought Seronan. While you have the chance.

However, the chance faded like a star at dawn. Erstürmen soldiers set upon the wild grell and dragged her off — another slave for the masters.

Inside the calendar of life, Krieg rose among the warring grells like a burning pyre, the top of his black helmet almost protruding above the

marble columns, and his blood-red skin boiling with rage at the treachery of his Rephaim. He stalked the rotunda with startling anger, using
his mace to cut down each and every grell soldier that failed to flee,
even those appearing to remain loyal to the Erstürmen. Seronan should
have felt sickened by the senseless slaughter, but the whole surreal event
looked more like the tantrum of a child knocking over annoying toys.

At the end of Krieg's onslaught, Myan stood alone in a sea of corpses,
facing an enemy he had no hope of defeating. He dropped his sword,
removed his helmet and planted his feet in the centre of the calendar of
life, turning his eyes to Seronan. With Krieg almost upon him, Myan
dropped to his knees and kissed the ground beneath his feet.

Seronan's hopeful defiance crumbled, her tears pooling on the flagstone pavers of Malang Gunya.

*   *   *   *

Seronan picked her way through the bodies of grells and mouldewerps
littering the calendar of life, unsure what to feel at the odd sight of the
giants and imps of this world lying side-by-side in death. She didn't
mourn or wail, instead retreating into her integument, refusing to let the
abandonment of hope torture her.

Beside Seronan, Henruld barked orders, demanding that his slaves
stack and burn the corpses. Even if it meant her death, she refused
to follow his order, instead dropping to her knees to collect the items
strewn across the ground: carved bone knives, pouches with dried
herbs, family totems. As she crawled over the dead bodies, she stumbled on a battered face, an unrecognisable collection of flesh and bone.
On the corpse's left forearm, a scar ran from the wrist to the elbow.
Myan had a scar just like it.

Romilda emerged from the underground chambers dressed all in black with the ever-present veil masking her face. The woman who'd promised Seronan she would convince the king to let the grell pilgrims remember in peace. The woman who lied. Seronan wanted to take a bone dagger and plunge it into Romilda's chest, but she wouldn't. She was only a slave, and Romilda was the Queen Mother.

Adalwolf, the murderer, trotted down the stairs of the pyramid and called out, "Mother! Did you see? We've routed the grells."

"You are brave, my son," said Romilda.

"They'll never threaten us again."

Lothar approached the king and whispered in his ear. The two of them disappeared down the stairs to the underground kingdom as the Queen Mother walked across to Seronan.

"I know you won't believe me, but I tried to stop him," Romilda said.

Seronan responded with a silent glare, setting a fire in her eyes in hopes of burning the veil from the liar's face.

Romilda didn't seem to notice or care, bending down and picking up a totem. "What is this?"

Seronan gritted her teeth. "A sacred item telling the life story of its owner."

Romilda turned the totem over in her hand. "It's beautiful. Take it to my room." She held it towards Seronan.

On her knees amid the barren flesh of her kin, amid the smothering of blood and the acrid smoke that billowed from a pile of corpses set aflame, Seronan didn't move.

"Did you hear me, Wortle?" asked Romilda. "Take this to my room."

"The totem does not belong to you, Queen Mother. It should be passed on to the next of kin or buried alongside the grell whose life story is etched on its surface."

Romilda glanced over her shoulder at the burning corpses. "It seems there won't be any burials. And do you think any of this grell's kin still live?"

Seronan sat still and quiet, but her insides churned and twisted in a raging knot.

The Queen Mother grew more impatient. "Stand, Wortle. Get to your feet and take this trinket to my room."

A chance will come, thought Seronan. An opportunity to seek revenge. She stood and took the totem, then bowed her head and walked into the halls underneath Malang Gunya.

Seronan found herself alone in the shadows of the central passage-way that ran past the throne hall and royal residences, and then onto an awful room full of prison cells that made her skin crawl. She'd never seen the room until the Worshipful Master locked a prisoner in one of the cells, a young woman with a shaved head. Now, Seronan had to feed the prisoner once a day, though so far, she'd refused to eat anything. The prisoner had asked for help, but Seronan didn't know if she had the strength to shoulder another burden to bring freedom to the enslaved.

Passing a Rephaim guard posted outside King Adalwolf's quarters, she turned a corner into the darkest section of the passageway and a noise burst from the shadows.

"*Psst.*"

She stopped, still clutching the totem to her breast, and listened. Nothing there. Keep moving. But the voice came again, more urgent.

"*Pssst!*"

"Who is there?" she asked.

"Come into the dark," whispered the shadow. "I need your help."

"Why should I help you?"

"Grells and werps are allies now. You're a grell. I'm a werp. You are bound to help me."

Seronan crept towards the voice, stumbling upon a mouldewerp hiding in the dark. "Who are you?"

"My name is Dwarrow. I'm looking for a young woman. A Dobunni rebel called Athalee. Might you have seen her?"

"I have been serving a woman prisoner. She has olive skin, and her head is shaved."

"That's Thaly."

"She asked me to help her, but now I cannot." Seronan turned to walk off. The creature reached up and grabbed onto the hem of her slave dress.

"Wait," said Dwarrow. "Our kin have been slaughtered. I saw you picking your way through the bodies. That's where you got that totem from, isn't it?"

"What do you know of grell totems?"

"Sacred objects. Very sacred. I have another sacred treasure." Dwarrow searched inside the satchel slung over his shoulder and pulled out a stone, holding it towards Seronan. "This is a flake of stone from Marradir, given to me by the Mulugan. It's called gulba, the peace stone, and signifies the truce between grells and werps."

"That could be any rock," said Seronan.

"Look at the symbol etched onto its surface."

"I cannot see anything in this poor light."

Dwarrow huffed, "Hold this," and handed Seronan the gulba. He fished inside one of the many pouches hanging from his twine belt and pulled out a giba stone that lit up the hallway like a hundred candles.

"Put that away," hissed Seronan. "You will attract the guards."

"I took it out so you can see the symbol."

She glanced at the gulba nestled in the palm of her hand and nodded. "Yes, I know this symbol. It means a treaty has been forged."

"Between grells and werps." Dwarrow snatched the gulba from

Seronan and dropped it and the giba back into his satchel. "I've been a friend of the grells for a long time. They don't hand out magic, sacred rocks to just anybody, you know."

"I believe you. I still cannot help."

"You must. Neither of us has a choice. We are bound by the treaty."

She scanned the hallway. Guards waited around every corner, standing outside each door, ready for her to make a mistake. But what did she have left to lose? The wild grells were slaughtered, and her friend Myan was dead. The werp offered her an opportunity for one last chance at restitution. A chance for the revenge she sought. So Seronan listened closely to Dwarrow as he laid out his plans, the werp's voice chattering nervously and quickly. Although he wanted her to risk her life, such a sacrifice was immaterial now.

Fixated on this strange creature, Seronan noticed the footsteps coming down the passageway too late.

"Who are you talking to?" asked Romilda.

Seronan spun around, trying to mask Dwarrow's presence with her giant frame. "No-one, Queen Mother. I was mourning the loss of my kin."

"No time for that. Bring the totem to my room. We have more things to discuss."

Seronan glanced over her shoulder. Dwarrow had already disappeared.

"Now, Wortle," said Romilda, with an authority that made Seronan feel like a child.

* * * *

Adalwolf strode into the throne hall of Pergamos, buoyed by his victory at the calendar of life. Malphas paced across the platform that supported the throne of the dead, projecting the power Adalwolf began to crave. He'd orchestrated the routing of the wild grells and proven himself a skilful king, but he now understood that while Malphas lived, he'd never truly be the ruler of the Erstürmen.

Krieg knelt before the bottom stair; the behemoth reduced to a quivering child in his master's presence.

How can Malphas wield such power over these tainted grells? thought Adalwolf. He stood behind Krieg, wincing at the blood pouring from wounds lashed into the grell's bare back. Malphas didn't seem to notice the arrival of the king.

"Explain again, Krieg, how the Rephaim turned on us," said Malphas.

"I could not foresee it, Worshipful Master. My training has been calculated and thorough. Their loyalty should not have wavered. I will take a stronger hand to my grell army…"

Malphas interrupted, "Your grell army?" He walked down the steps of the dais, stood in front of Krieg and lifted the grell's chin with a single finger. "*Your* grell army? Maybe that's the problem? You've forgotten who the Rephaim serve. You've forgotten the consequences of treachery. It's time I reminded you. Then you can pass the lesson on to *your* grell army." He signalled to Ende, who stepped from behind the throne, tottered down the stairs and led Krieg from the throne room, leaving Adalwolf alone with his father.

"The wild grells and mouldewerps are no longer a threat," said Adalwolf.

Malphas turned a blank face to him. "No. It seems most of them are dead. Did you not think to capture some of the grells? For slaves or soldiers?"

Adalwolf stammered, "I…we…I thought…"

"Don't think," spat Malphas. "Just do as I tell you. The opportunity is lost, and we have other pressing matters. Come closer."

Adalwolf stepped around the pool of fresh blood on the floor and stood beside Malphas as he took the blood compass from his robe, placing it on the bottom step of the throne platform. It spun twice only before stopping.

"See, my son. He is almost here. You're prepared this time, aren't you? You understand what to do?"

Yes, thought Adalwolf, he was prepared. More prepared than he'd ever been to secure the kingdom that was rightfully his. Adalwolf locked eyes with Malphas in an act of defiance, though his heart pounded so much an echo seemed to bounce from the walls of the throne room.

"Clench both eyes in my right fist and thrust it onto his chest," said Adalwolf. "Hold it there no matter the pain. Until he's dead. I won't fail this time, Worshipful Master."

~ Chapter 39 ~

Tom and Caeli raced their steeds at breakneck speed across the Dambay Plains to Malang Gunya. From the stables in the town of Rufous on the edge of Babir Birramal, they'd been riding day and night with little rest, the urgency to reach the grell city consuming Tom's attention. As the sun dropped below the ridgeline of the Scaur Hills, the outline of Malang Gunya came into view and set his mind racing. He steeled his nerves, knowing precisely what he had to do to protect his friends and Enthilen from the threat of Malphas and Adalwolf.

In the dusk light, a stone-grell stood alone beside the south road leading into the city. Tom was almost upon the giant when it raised its hands, causing his horse to rear in fright. He fell backwards and landed on a clump of tussock grass, briefly losing consciousness. When he opened his eyes, Grin's sombre face and the crest of muwin looked down at him.

"Am I back in your milbi?" asked Tom.

"I wish it were so, Tom Anderson. I would like nothing better. Are you hurt?"

Tom shook his head and stood up. He reached towards Grin's face, preparing for a formal greeting, but Grin pushed his hands away.

"I am not...it is not necessary," said Grin.

The hurt on Grin's face made Tom wonder if he'd done something wrong. Princess Caeli dismounted, drove pegs into the ground and tethered Casfern and Tom's horse, Raken, before walking across to the reunited friends.

"Is Thaly here?" asked Tom.

Grin's jaw clenched. "Krieg and his soldiers raided our camp and took her hostage. Dwarrow says it is a trap set for you. To lure you into Malang Gunya."

"I'm going there, anyway. To find the throne of the dead. It's the only way to stop Malphas. Thaly's in danger because of me. Sardis, Hansen's Bluff, the Vulking, and now this. I've put you all in danger, time and again. But I'm going to fix it. I'm going to fix everything."

"We thought you had died at sea," said Grin. "We searched...but I had to return home to my family and for my initiation."

"I understand," said Tom. "You've done so much for me already."

"Dwarrow plans to rescue Thaly. He has disappeared for now, as he tends to do, but he may return with her soon."

"What of the grell pilgrims?" asked Caeli.

"Most refused to march and returned to Babir Birramal. My father and mother led the remaining into the city. I have been sitting here in the hope they will return. As the sun wanes, my hope fades."

"You didn't want to march with them?" Tom asked Grin.

Something flashed across Grin's face that Tom had never seen before. An aggrieved contortion laced with anger.

"Yes, I wanted to march," snapped Grin. "More than anything. But Dwarrow told me I have a more important responsibility. To keep you here until we decide on our next action. To protect the land we love."

Tom ached with Grin's pain. "I'm so sorry, Grin. You've made another sacrifice for my sake."

"It is for Enthilen's sake, not yours. All of us have made sacrifices."

Grin led Tom and Caeli to the remnants of the grell camp, where they sat around a campfire and talked into the night, Grin recalling his journey to Gestade with Thaly and Whibly, and the deliberations at the garrabari. When Tom asked how they had survived the wreck of the *Vulking*, Grin went quiet and turned away. His friend hid something from him, but Tom didn't press, instead changing the subject and telling Grin about his time with Jameus and Melinda, the long walk to Bindari with Annian, and Widukind's plans to thwart the rise of Malphas.

"I'm going to try to return home, Grin. Widukind believes it's the only way to end this."

"What if he is wrong?"

"Then it's all over. I'll be trapped, Adalwolf will steal my soul, and Malphas will use Adalwolf to try and bring forth Volerdie."

"So much to risk," said Grin.

"There could be another way," whispered Caeli.

"What other way?" asked Tom.

Caeli smiled and shook her head. "Oh, nothing. We don't need more silly schemes filling our heads with false hopes. I know my father is... unbalanced, but he's studied the First Scripture for yarles. We should trust his judgement."

"You will not seek justice for your grandmother?" Grin asked Tom.

"Malphas can't be killed. Not by me. He's immortal. The only way to keep everyone safe is for me to disappear. Back in my own world, I'll be out of Malphas and Adalwolf's reach, and they'll have no reason to harm you."

"Do you think Malphas will give up that easily?"

"Probably not, but what choice is there? I feel so guilty about it. I've played it over in my head constantly, debating if it's the right decision. If I succeed, I'll never see you, Thaly or Enthilen again. If I fail, Enthilen will never be the same. Either way, our friendship ends."

Grin sighed. "We have all been faced with difficult decisions, and we have faced them with honest hearts. You are not the cause of our suffering, Tom. I am proud to call you friend." He reached inside a pack and brought out a totem, handing it to Tom.

Tom rolled the length of softstone around on his palm. "There's no writing on this."

"That is because you are yet to begin."

"What?"

"This is your family totem, Tom Anderson. Etch your life story into the stone. I hope one day I will get to read it."

Tom wanted to hold back the hurt, but he couldn't. Exhaustion, fear and confusion melded into one despairing emotion until the tears rolled down his cheeks and dropped from his chin onto the green-white surface of the totem. "Thank you. I don't know..."

"Tom Anderson and Princess Caeli."

"Dwarrow!" Caeli jumped up and raced over to the diminutive werp, lifting him from the ground and swinging him around in a circle.

"Oh, Princess. Getting dizzy. Dizzy. *Dis-com-bob-ulated.*"

Caeli laughed and placed Dwarrow back on solid ground.

Tom wiped the tears from his face. "Did you find Thaly?"

"It's lovely to see you again, too, Tom Anderson," said Dwarrow.

"Sorry. Yes. I'm glad to see you. Where's Thaly?"

"My nose found her. Never any doubt about that. No doubt at all. She's alive, held prisoner in a cage with a guard at her door. One of those horrid Rephaim no less."

"We have to save her," said Tom.

"We will — no need to worry. I've contacted someone inside, and I have a plan, but I'll need help. I couldn't do it myself, this time."

"What of the pilgrims, Dwarrow? Did you see my parents?" asked Grin.

Dwarrow cast his face to the ground. "I came across seven werps in a dwell beneath the city. The Erstürmen attacked as the grells gathered in the calendar of life. Few escaped. I haven't seen your parents or any other wild grells. I'm sorry, Grin."

Grin's lilac eyes burned red as he glared at Dwarrow. "You could not save them? With all your cunning and secrets. All your conspiring and scheming. You have a plan to save Thaly, but you left my parents to die?"

"Grin, please..." started Tom, then shrunk away as Grin rose to his feet and loomed over Dwarrow.

"I waited here because you asked, little mouldewerp," growled Grin. "I put the fate of Enthilen before my own blood because you demanded it. What advantage has that gained? I could have protected my parents. I could have guided them from Malang Gunya."

Dwarrow lifted his head, his nose twitching warily as it searched for the threat of Grin's anger. "There were hundreds of soldiers. No-one could have..."

Grin lashed a giant hand down and picked Dwarrow up by the strap of his satchel.

"No!" yelled Caeli, yanking on Grin's forearm. "Put him down."

With his free hand, Grin pushed Caeli away and raised Dwarrow even higher. The werp flailed his arms about like a fledgling learning to fly.

"No, Grin," said Tom, standing and reaching for the handle of his knife. "This is not Dwarrow's fault."

Grin glared at Tom, and at that moment, Tom saw how lost his friend had become.

"*Arrgh!*" Grin screamed and flung Dwarrow to the ground like a sack of grain, then stormed off into the long grass of the Dambay Plains.

Tom went to follow.

Dwarrow stopped him. "Leave him be," said the werp, brushing himself off.

"Are you alright, Dwarrow?" asked Caeli.

"Yes, Princess. I'm fine."

But he wasn't. The little werp's body trembled like a mouse trapped under a lion's paw.

As Grin disappeared from view, the three companions sat around the campfire in silence until the fear subsided enough to turn thoughts elsewhere. Tom fought to dismiss every voice inside his head telling him to give up. He'd come this far. There was no turning back.

After Dwarrow recovered from his shock, he described all that he knew about the residences and halls below Malang Gunya.

"I need to find the throne of the dead," said Tom.

"Whatever for?" asked Dwarrow.

Tom explained his plan to Dwarrow, who became upset at the revelation. "You have a terrible habit of making my life more complicated, Tom Anderson. A most awful habit. I'm going to have to change my strategy."

"Do you know where the throne is?"

"I passed two large doors leading to a room that smelled particularly sinister. I dared not go inside. If my nose is right, I expect the throne is in that room."

"How can I get inside?" asked Tom.

"I haven't worked it out yet," said Dwarrow. "My plan is to save Thaly, not place a fool on the throne of the dead. I'm going to have to make new arrangements, but that can wait until tomorrow. I need to rest."

"What am I to do?" asked Caeli.

"You should stay here, Princess," said Dwarrow. "It's the safest place for you."

* * * *

Despite Fullō's help, Caeli found the journey from Bindari to the edge of

Malang Gunya exhausting. Once Dwarrow and Tom retired, she should have fallen asleep straight away, but her thoughts kept her awake. Grin hadn't returned, and she worried about where he may have gone and what he might do. She worried about Thaly, trapped in a prison cell at Malphas' mercy, and about Tom's chances of reaching the throne of the dead, let alone using it to travel to another world.

Whatever plan Dwarrow concocted, she convinced herself there would be too many risks. Too many chances for things to go wrong. There had to be another way to keep Tom, Grin and Dwarrow out of danger and save Thaly at the same time.

When she had decided on it, she rose from her bed before sunrise, untethered Casfern, straddled her faithful horse and galloped to Malang Gunya.

~ Chapter 40 ~

"I apologise for the interruption, majesty," said the soldier from the King's Shield. "We've been approached by a woman who claims to be your cousin, Princess Caeli. She's requesting an audience."

Sitting at the head of the breakfast table in Pergamos' dining room, Adalwolf glanced at Malphas, who sat on his right, then up at the King's Shield who'd interrupted his meal.

"We should see her," Malphas whispered.

"Bring her to me," said Adalwolf to the soldier.

"Yes, sire."

The King's Shield left, and Adalwolf conjured memories of his furtive visits to the princess' room atop the Sunrise Keep in Sardis to watch her sleep and dream of sharing her bed. To lust for a temptation he could never have. He knew Ewald had treated her poorly. She deserved so much more.

The Shield returned escorting Princess Caeli, and Adalwolf's heart beat faster as he sat up straight and puffed out his chest. "Leave us," he commanded the soldier.

Malphas grinned like a man possessed. "Well, this is a pleasant surprise. How lovely of you to come and visit your cousin, the king."

Caeli stood at the far end of the table. "It's you I came to see, Uncle Oldaric."

Malphas frowned momentarily before his smile returned. "That's even more delightful. Sit, child, and share our bounty. There's plenty of food here. We're having roast mouldewerp this morning. It's been so long since I tasted the flesh of those little beasts."

Malphas pointed to two werps on silver platters, skinned and burned such that Adalwolf had to peel flakes of charcoal from the flesh before tasting it. An unsteady Caeli clutched the chair, and Adalwolf almost sprang from his seat to comfort her. He'd never seen her outside the keep prison of Sardis, and now she stood right in front of him.

Adalwolf simmered as Malphas continued to toy with the princess. "Oh, that's right," said Malphas, "I heard it was the mouldewerps that saved you from the dastardly Hunfrid. I hope we aren't eating any of your friends. Sit now."

Caeli slumped into a chair at the end of the table.

"What is the purpose of your visit? I assume you're not here out of loneliness."

"Uncle Oldaric, you were…"

"*Malphas*. Address me by my proper name."

"You were kind, once," said Caeli. "You used to read me stories about the brave and honourable Erstürmen kings of old. Why are you bringing so much death to Enthilen? Why not help Adalwolf be a glorious king like those from our past?"

"Where did you go when you fled Sardis?" asked Malphas.

"What?"

"Where did you go, child? You haven't been skulking in the shadows all this time, waiting for the chance to meet with me. You must have gone somewhere."

"I stayed with my werp friends like you said."

"You didn't seek out your father? The long, lost Widukind. It's been nearly half a generation since he showed his face in the kingdom. You must wonder where he went? Why he never came to rescue you?"

"It was a long time ago when I last saw my father."

"I think you're lying. What do you say, Adalwolf? Is your cousin a liar?"

Adalwolf didn't know what to say to Caeli. Although he'd spoken with her inside his head numerous times, now he was dumbstruck.

Malphas groaned. "Steel your weak heart, boy. Is she a liar or not?"

"I-I-I don't know. She's always been loyal to the kingdom."

"The appendage between your legs has kidnapped your brain. Am I the only one who sees past the veil of innocence in this temptress?"

"Uncle Oldaric, please..." said Caeli.

"Silence! Never use that name again. Oldaric is dead." Malphas sliced off a portion of werp flesh, folded it in half and shoved it in his mouth as if chewing the gamy meat would calm his anger. "But your father is definitely alive. I think you sought him out. In fact, I'm sure of it. My spies saw you riding a horse, south-east into the forest. Deep into the forest. Is Widukind down there? In that place where the grells go to die?"

"I don't know what you're talking about," whispered Caeli. "I didn't ride anywhere."

"Now I know you're a liar."

You're not going to kill her, thought Adalwolf. I won't let you.

Caeli turned pleading eyes to him. "Adalwolf, please," she said. "We're second cousins."

"First cousins," Adalwolf interrupted, then scolded himself for revealing a secret he shouldn't have.

Caeli's mouth twisted. "What?"

Adalwolf glanced at Malphas, who gave a dismissive nod of the head, then continued the revelation. "Malphas is my father, not Ewald."

"Don't look so surprised, my dear," said Malphas. "You of all people should know Ewald could never have sired an heir."

"I should have an heir," said Adalwolf.

"You won't need an heir after we're done with the boy," said Malphas.

"Leave Tom alone," pleaded Caeli. "Leave them all alone. I know Thaly is your prisoner. I've come to beg for her release. Take me instead. Keep me prisoner. Kill me. Do whatever you want. I'll give birth to an heir for you, King Adalwolf. I would do it gladly. Don't listen to Malphas. You're the true ruler of Enthilen. You're the king. You can have me every night. Whenever you want."

Yes, thought Adalwolf, he wanted that.

Malphas crushed the hope as soon as it appeared. "You're of little worth to King Adalwolf. He can have any woman he chooses."

Adalwolf fumed. Malphas threatened to take something else from him. "She's an Erstürmen princess," said Adalwolf. "She deserves to be treated with respect."

Malphas bristled. "I'll decide her fate. For now, I want to keep her alive. She knows where her father is. If we can find the lost Widukind, that changes everything." He held a piece of meat towards Caeli. "Now, child, do you want breakfast? You must be starving."

Caeli turned away, her eyes welling. Adalwolf pictured himself consoling her. Holding her close and whispering that everything would be alright. He would fix things. He was king after all, and only he could turn dreams into reality.

* * * *

"Dwarrow, wake up." In the grell camp outside Malang Gunya, Tom shook the mouldewerp from his sleep. "Caeli's gone. She's taken her horse."

"What?" said Dwarrow, rubbing his tired face.

"Caeli's disappeared," repeated Tom.

Dwarrow sat up, yawned and then sniffed the air. "I expected as much. My nose tells me she's gone to negotiate with our enemy. To try to rescue Thaly and avoid any more bloodshed."

"How?" asked Tom.

"She'll offer herself to Malphas and Adalwolf in exchange for Thaly's freedom and beg them to leave you alone. If I know the princess, and I know her well, that's exactly what she'll do."

"Will she succeed?" asked Tom.

"No. It was a silly idea."

"Then we have to save her."

Dwarrow stood and tramped around the dying campfire. "Now we have someone else to save. Is it the sole desire of you people to make my life a tortuous labyrinth from which I can never escape?"

Dwarrow stopped in his tracks as Grin appeared at the camp's edge and lumbered over to them. Tom stood and reached for his knife again. He couldn't believe it had come to this, but if he had to stab Grin to protect Dwarrow, he would.

Grin ignored both of them and slumped down beside the smouldering coals, his face still wracked with sorrow. Tom relaxed, yet kept his hand near his knife. Dwarrow moved to the other side of the campfire, as far from Grin as he could.

"I will not attack you again," said Grin, staring into the failing embers.

"Well," said Dwarrow, "at least that's one less thing I have to worry about."

"Caeli's gone to Pergamos," Tom said to Grin.

The giant grell turned to Tom. "That is where I am going. To avenge the death of my parents."

"Yes, yes, yes," muttered Dwarrow, "we're all going to Pergamos. All we have to do is enter the city without being spotted, rescue Thaly and Caeli, help Tom find the throne of the dead and make sure he returns home without Malphas or Adalwolf getting anywhere near him, avenge the sacrifice made by the grell pilgrims, and then escape Pergamos with our lives intact. Simple."

Dwarrow gathered his walking stick and satchel and crept over to Grin. "I am sorry, Grin. I truly am. I wish I could have brought more mouldewerps to fight alongside the grells. Then, things may have turned out differently."

"I should not have blamed you," said Grin. "I accept my parents have perished, but now someone must pay."

Dwarrow sighed. "Yes, I guess they must. Whatever hurt you're feeling, Grin, do not hide it away and let it fester. Bad things grow in the dark. Bring the pain into the light so we can help you deal with it."

Grin bowed his head and fell silent. Dwarrow rested his hand on Grin's shoulder for a moment of comfort, then withdrew.

"I'm off to make new arrangements," said Dwarrow. "My contact in Pergamos is a grell slave called Seronan. She has promised to help me."

"What do you want us to do?" asked Tom.

"Wait here until the afternoon is late before following the south road to Malang Gunya. I'll leave my walking stick by the side of the road, pointing in the direction you must take. North-west of the road, there's a dwell on the city's outskirts where we'll meet. Don't approach until nightfall. I'll signal with my giba like a blinking star. Come to the light and don't let anyone see you, and don't forget to bring my walking stick."

As Dwarrow trotted off to Malang Gunya, Grin sat in silence while emotions ripped at Tom's chest. He wondered if Grin would recover from the loss of his parents. If Tom would again see the buoyant, compassionate, ardent young grell he'd met in Babir Birramal. The one who had saved him from drowning in the stream and agreed to guide Tom to Laodicea to find his grandmother's killer. The one who had rescued him from Malphas.

Grinnian stone-grell. His friend.

I know how to make things better, thought Tom. *I know how to help Grin, Thaly and Caeli, and to end the tyranny of Malphas. I have to leave Enthilen forever. Leave Enthilen or take my own life so that Adalwolf dies too and Malphas' plans fall apart. They're the only two options. I'll accept nothing else.*

* * * *

Thaly rolled over, sat up and rubbed the sleep from her eyes. Outside the bars of her cell, a person sat tied to a chair with a sack covering their head.

Had a new trick been devised by her tormentor? she wondered. More theatre to accentuate the misery of her imprisonment.

"Hello?" Thaly said.

The head inside the sack tilted to the side, and a feeble, pleading voice came through the canvas, "I know someone's there. I can hear you shuffling about. Please, let me go or end it now."

"Caeli?" Thaly whispered.

"Hello?"

"Princess Caeli, is that you?"

"Yes...Thaly?"

"It's me. I imagine I sound terrible."

"Where are you? Where are we?"

"I'm locked in a cell. I don't know where exactly. You're outside the bars. Malphas is here, somewhere."

"I came to try to talk reason with him. It was a stupid thing to do. He's my uncle. I hoped that would count for something."

Thaly crawled to the front of the cell and crouched beside the princess. "Can you get your arms free?"

"I've been trying. They're tied fast."

"Keep trying. There's a guard outside the cells. We'll need to be quiet."

"Even if I free myself, then what?"

"Let's take one thing at a time. See if you can loosen your arms. Then we can..." Thaly stopped and slinked to the rear of the cell when Malphas entered the room.

"Ah, I see you two are getting acquainted. How wonderful." Malphas yanked the sack from Caeli's head, and she blinked to ward off the torchlight, her face afflicted with fear and confusion.

"What are you doing?" asked Thaly. "Why are you keeping your niece prisoner?"

"So many questions, Athalee. Your world is a tangled web, and everyone you encounter is a venomous spider. I'm surprised you've survived so long. Lucky for the princess, she was safely locked in a tower. No spiders up there. Plenty of snakes, though." Malphas chuckled and sat on a stool next to Caeli. From a bag, he pulled out a copper burner and a frying pan the size of two hands. He struck a flint and lit the oil in the burner, balancing the frying pan on a rack over the open flame.

"Please, Uncle, you don't have to do this. Lock me in the cell and let Thaly go."

"I'm afraid I have no choice in the matter. Everything was put in motion yarles ago. If you're looking for someone to blame, look to your father. If he hadn't betrayed me, none of this would be necessary. If Widukind was in Pergamos, instead of cowering in a hole with the worms, I wouldn't need Tom Anderson or Adalwolf. I wouldn't need Thaly, either. She thinks I'm a monster, yet I have a gentler side. Let me prove it by giving you one last chance, Princess. Tell me where your father is, and I'll set Thaly free."

"Don't do it," said Thaly. "Don't do anything he wants. Damn the consequences."

Caeli sobbed, eyes welling, face puffy and red. But she didn't speak.

Malphas reached into his robe and withdrew a petite, silver object with two wheels of sharpened metal on either side of a drum adorned with hooked nails. The wheels and drum rotated around an axle attached to a handle carved from bone. Malphas held the object aloft like someone admiring a precious gemstone.

"A flesh renderer," he said. "Have you seen one before?"

Thaly's mind reeled in curious horror. "No."

Malphas took a knife and cut a hole in Caeli's leather pants above the knee, then caressed her bare, pale thigh. "You put on good condition while locked in that tower, little princess. Good condition. I imagine the flesh has a nice marbling to it." Malphas spat in his hand and rubbed the spittle across Caeli's skin, washing away the dirt. His eyes lingered over her thigh, then he thrust the renderer into her skin and wheeled the device along the top of her leg. The princess screamed, the most torturous scream Thaly had ever heard. She jerked her head away from the spectacle as Malphas began humming to himself, fighting to be heard over Caeli's cries.

Don't look, thought Thaly. Don't show him any weakness.

Caeli went quiet, and Malphas stopped humming. The momentary silence was broken by the spit and sizzle of something frying in the pan. The horrifying smell of burning flesh filled Thaly's nostrils, and she dry-retched.

Caeli groaned.

Malphas sighed. "Oh, she's passed out. How unfortunate. I always believed that unconsciousness taints the meat. Never mind. I thought she would hold out a little longer."

Save her, Thaly's mind screamed. *Save her!* She turned as Malphas skewered a morsel of cooked flesh on the tip of his knife and held it near his face before plunging his teeth into the tissue. Thaly slammed her body against the back wall of the cell and vomited bile.

"*Mmmm*," said Malphas. "I knew it would be tasty. I can't wait to try more."

"Stop it!" screamed Thaly. "What do you want? I'll give you Tom Anderson. I'll help you capture him. Then you can do whatever you want. Just let her go."

"You'll give me Tom Anderson regardless. You're in no position to bargain."

~ Chapter 41 ~

At sunset, Tom and Grin found Dwarrow's walking stick by the side of the south road leading to Malang Gunya. Since travelling from the grell camp, they hadn't seen anyone on the road, the only movement coming from the sweep of long grass along the verge that swayed back and forth with a whirling breeze. Grin had hardly spoken, and Tom worried about how his friend was coping with the loss of his parents and everything else that had happened. The massacre of the wild grells. The further desecration of Grin's homeland. He sensed Grin had reached a breaking point and wondered where that would lead.

They travelled north-west, following Dwarrow's directions, with the silhouette of the city looming before them. A light flickered in the distance like a winking star, and Tom quickened his pace, Grin following close behind. They soon found Dwarrow, waiting near a tiny hole on the edge of Malang Gunya. The entrance to the dwell was much smaller than Tom had imagined; even Dwarrow would have to crawl on his stomach to get inside.

The sounds of the city drifted on the breeze. People talking. Dogs barking. Metal pinging on stone and rock falling to the ground. Masters yelling orders.

"Have you devised another plan?" Tom asked Dwarrow.

"Most certainly. Seronan should be here soon with the armour."

"Armour?"

"Neither of you will squeeze into this dwell, so you'll have to enter Pergamos in disguise. Grin will be dressed as a Rephaim, one of those armoured grells, and you, Tom, as an Erstürmen soldier. Seronan will bring the necessary attire and weapons to make it look convincing, and you will escort her into Pergamos, a slave you've captured trying to escape the city."

"Once there, I'll seek the throne of the dead by myself," said Tom. "After we know Thaly and Caeli are safe. I don't want anyone risking their life on my behalf."

"It appears to be too late for that," said Dwarrow.

"Is there a way out?" asked Grin.

"Yes, I've thought of that. You and Thaly will march out as Erstürmen soldiers, escorting Princess Caeli on an evening stroll. Thaly can use Tom's armour. He won't need it once he finds the throne."

"The Erstürmen don't have female soldiers," said Tom.

"Yes, yes, yes. I know that. Don't you think I know that? But Thaly's head is shaved, and Grin can do the talking. Oh, now I'm starting to have doubts. See what you've done."

Tom placed his arm on Dwarrow's shoulder. "It'll work out."

Dwarrow raised his nose to the night sky and pulled away. "Wait, I smell someone coming. However, their aroma isn't right. Where's my walking stick?"

Tom gave Dwarrow his stick, and the werp held it above his head, preparing to strike. Grin pulled a bone dagger from his belt.

A rustle of grass announced the new arrival, a veiled figure dressed all in black, carrying a wicker basket and struggling over the lip of the swale that hid the entrance to the dwell.

Dwarrow sniffed. "You're not who I was expecting. Name yourself."

The person stopped and, with a groan, placed the basket on the ground. "I'm much too old for this."

"Where's Seronan?" asked Dwarrow.

"I've come in her stead. It's safer this way. I'm Romilda, the mother of King Adalwolf. You can lower your weapons. I'm no threat."

Tom drew his knife. "We can't trust her."

"If I was going to spring a trap, wouldn't I do it now?" asked Romilda. "I've brought armour and swords, but I couldn't carry everything. It'll be enough to convince the guards, and I'll be with you. Returning an escaped slave to her master would raise numerous concerns. Seronan and I decided it would be better if you act as my guards. The Queen Mother coming home from her evening walk around the city with the necessary and prudent escort will attract much less attention, and I can more easily deflect any challenging questions. I'll lead you into Pergamos so you can save the rebel girl."

"Do you know where the throne of the dead is?" Tom blurted out.

Romilda looked at him through her veil. "You must be Tom Anderson."

"How do you know my name?"

"A mother knows her own son, and his fate is bound to yours. You can trust me, Tom. Malphas wants to murder my son after Adalwolf's captured your soul. Sacrifice him on the throne of the dead when darkness descends in hope of bringing forth Volerdie. Am I right?"

She knows, thought Tom, exactly as Widukind described. "Yes."

"Do you think a loving mother would consent to the murder of her own son? All of us want to see Malphas fail. He thinks his most devious plans are secret. I've discovered his confidants are not so resolute."

"No doubt you know all of Malphas' desires, but we don't have time to dally further," said Dwarrow. "We're going to have to trust you."

"The throne of the dead is in the throne hall of Pergamos," said Romilda. "I can lead you there and to your friend."

"Then we need to prepare," said Dwarrow.

Tom nodded in agreement. He slipped Hadufuns' knife into a sheath he'd found at Widukind's house and placed the carefully crafted blade onto the ground. It didn't feel right to take the knife into Pergamos, and there was an Erstürmen sword in the wicker basket that he could use as a weapon. He removed the thick, fur-lined coat Jameus had made, folded it and laid it on the grass as if he would come and collect it again soon. He smiled, thinking about Melinda and fuzzy sugar nuts, then unbuttoned the leather waistcoat Whibly had given him on the *Vulking* and placed it beside the coat. Although soiled and fusty, he kept his white shirt on, not wanting to reveal his Dobunni pledge scars to the Queen Mother of Enthilen.

At that moment, a stone of recognition lodged in the pit of his stomach. He wouldn't be back to collect the knife or the waistcoat or anything else. If everything went as planned, he was leaving Enthilen forever. Leaving Grin, Thaly, Dwarrow and Caeli. Everything and everyone. Leaving them all behind.

Tom tried to shake the thought from his mind. *Focus on the now.* The eyes of lost souls nestled inside the front pocket of his pants where he could easily reach them, and he'd strapped the totem Grin gave him to his stomach with a strip of hessian. Romilda handed him a blue and black tunic and helped him into the metal cuirass with the two-headed snake embossed on the front. Although the armour was lighter than he expected, it still weighed on his thin shoulders, and he doubted he'd make it to the throne hall. He wondered how the Queen Mother had managed to carry the armour so far, or if somebody had helped her.

Romilda cinched the side straps of the cuirass and plonked a span-genhelm on Tom's head. "It's the King's Shield breastplate," she said, handing Tom a belt, scabbard and short sword. "I hope it's enough. It's all the armour and weapons I could manage."

King's Shield, thought Tom. *Now I'm a King's Shield.*

* * * *

Grin trudged behind Romilda and Tom through the centre of Malang Gunya, the black plackart covering his stomach pinching his skin, reminding him the first-ever visit to his ancestral home came not as expected. He clutched the strange-looking broadsword in his right hand as they walked around the base of the stepped pyramid, thinking he might cut down each and every Erstürmen crossing his path. A rancid, deathly smell polluted the night as a charred pile that resembled a single, colossal creature with hundreds of blackened limbs twisted and contorted into grotesque angles, smouldered inside the calendar of life.

This is where the slaughter happened, Grin thought. He walked to the smouldering pile and peered through the slits of the grilled helmet covering his face for a sign his parents were among the dead. But the bodies were unrecognisable. In his heart, he knew Frennan and Mirrian had perished. They would have returned to the grell camp otherwise. No tears washed the tattooed ink of muwin, but Grin's head throbbed with a resolute fury that wouldn't abate.

"Grin," whispered Tom behind him. "This way."

Grin turned and focussed on Romilda's back, following her and Tom to a hole in the ground leading to a wooden staircase.

"Halt!" said one of the guards watching the hole. "What business have you here?"

"Stand aside," ordered Romilda. "I'm the Queen Mother."

"Remove your veil."

Romilda lifted her veil, and the guard searched her face then averted his eyes. "My apologies, your majesty."

"Accepted. My evening walk is over, but I still require the services of my escort. Let us pass."

The guard hesitated. "Your soldiers are not in full armour."

"Some of it was damaged during the famous victory over the wild grells. There's no smithy in Pergamos yet to mend it," said Romilda.

The guard stood in front of Tom. "You're young to be a Shield. Too young by the looks of you."

"King Adalwolf himself appointed this fine young man to the King's Shield. They're the same age. Would you also claim that my son is too young to be king?" Romilda shivered. "Should I fetch King Adalwolf so you can explain why you've delayed his elderly mother in this bitter cold?"

"No need, majesty." The guard stepped aside.

Grin and Tom followed Romilda down the staircase and into a hall full of tables and chairs. They stepped through a side doorway into a dim passage that appeared to lead to other rooms. Romilda quickened her pace into a darkness breached only by the occasional lit torch hanging from the wall.

"This way," she whispered.

When they reached a junction, Romilda stopped. "I must leave you now. I risk my life if I'm found in your presence. Follow this passage. The next doorway you come to on the left leads to the prison cells where you'll find your friend. There's one guard outside the door — a Rephaim. He has the keys to the cell."

"What about Princess Caeli?" asked Tom.

Romilda shook her head. "I've not seen her since Sardis."

"And the throne room?"

"We've passed it already," said Romilda, pointing back down the passage. "Behind the oak doors taller than a grell and arched at the top." She scuttled off down another aisle that branched to the right, leaving Grin and Tom alone.

"I hope Dwarrow made it," said Tom.

On cue, a snuffle emerged from a dark corner. "There you are," said Dwarrow. "And about time. I've been waiting for ages."

"Let's find Thaly," said Tom. "Caeli might be with her."

The three friends raced along the passageway, Dwarrow leading the way in the half-light. As they turned another corner, they came upon a Rephaim standing guard outside a door. Grin raised his sword, but Dwarrow tapped his walking stick on Grin's knee.

"I'll deal with the guard," said the werp. "You stay here."

Dwarrow crept ahead, then surprised the Rephaim, who doubled over from a sharp jab to the stomach. The monstrous grell soldier collapsed to the ground when the little werp thumped him on the back of the neck with his walking stick. Dwarrow retrieved the guard's keys, reached above his head and unlocked the prison door, then beckoned to Grin and Tom. All three ran into the prison where a lone body lay on the floor of a cell, curled up under a blanket and facing the back wall.

"We're here, Athalee," said Dwarrow as he fumbled with the keys.

"Thaly?" whispered Tom, his voice breaking.

The body didn't move when Dwarrow opened the cell door. Tom ran in and placed a hand on a cold shoulder, turning the prisoner over. A blank and unfamiliar face, eyes closed, greeted him.

"It's not her. Dammit. It's not Thaly."

"It is a grell," snarled Grin, removing his Rephaim helmet and flinging it into the wall.

Dwarrow sniffed the body. "It's Seronan, the slave who was supposed to meet us at the dwell."

Seronan moaned.

"She's still alive," said Tom, cradling her head.

"Seronan. Can you hear me?" asked Dwarrow.

The grell slave opened her eyes and moved her arm. The blanket fell away, revealing a naked body vandalised with wounds weeping blood. Seronan whispered a single word, "Trap," then died in Tom's arms.

Boots; loud, slapping, marching boots, bounded along the passageway, their approaching threat bouncing off the stone walls. Grin winced at the fear in Tom's eyes.

"What do we do?" said Tom.

"Run!" hissed Dwarrow.

They bolted from the prison and into the passageway. Rephaim blocked one of the exits, so they ran back the way they came, towards the massive oak doors. As they neared the doors, a dozen King's Shield appeared, blocking any escape back up the wooden staircase and outside to freedom. The Rephaim and the King's Shield moved in from either end of the passageway, squeezing the three friends like a vice such that there was only one place they could go.

Tom and Grin nodded to each other, braced their shoulders against one of the oak doors, turned the black metal handle, cast as a serpent's head, and pushed.

*   *   *   *

Tom blinked hard at the blinding light inside the massive hall, lit up in grand celebration. Dozens of tiered chandeliers hung from the ceiling, sprouting candles like flowers, wax dripping to the floor like shed petals. Rows of flaming torches clung to every wall, illuminating pedestals decorated with busts of men, and vases painted with Enthilen landscapes full of virtuous citizens.

As Tom's eyes adjusted to the light, Dwarrow and Grin pushed in close behind him, and the doors to the throne room slammed shut, the Rephaim blocking the exit. A waft of cold air raised the hairs on the back of Tom's neck, suspended in a moment of silence.

"My friends!" came a shout from the far end of the hall. "Finally. Finally, we meet again. All good things come to those who wait."

Raised on a platform, Malphas sat on a throne that resembled a single, contorted body. Tom had no doubt he'd found the throne of the dead. Behind the throne, the pale grell stood still and expressionless. *Ende.* Tom remembered her from Hansen's Bluff.

"That armour suits you, Tom," said Malphas. "How different this all would have been if you were Erstürmen. And look at Grin! A Rephaim no less. I wonder if this is an omen? And you've brought with you another one of those werps. This world truly amazes me. I don't see a mouldewerp for countless seasons, and now Pergamos is riddled with the things."

Malphas stood and ambled down the stairs, drawing Tom's attention to two fluted, stone columns on either side of the platform. There, bound to the columns, Thaly and Caeli framed the throne of the dead with a desperate misery barely clinging to life.

On the left of the hall, fidgeting with his robes, stood King Adalwolf flanked by the red grell, Krieg, and the man in sangria robes. *Sangria man.* Tom hadn't seen him since Süden Forst. Since the sacrifice of children to appease Volerdie. Behind the king lurked the veiled Romilda.

Malphas drew a knife and poked it into Thaly's side until she winced.

"Leave her alone," said Tom, striding further into the hall, drawing his sword and stopping at the end of a table long enough to seat more than twenty. Focussed on Thaly, he momentarily forgot about Grin and Dwarrow until a shriek of brutal hatred exploded from behind him. Sword raised, Grin stormed past Tom and rushed at Malphas. At the same time, Krieg, his red torso covered in wounds, leapt forward and swung his mace at Grin's head. The young grell ducked the strike, but it put him off balance. Krieg swung again, cannoning the spiked ball into the plackart covering Grin's stomach.

Tom cried out as his friend crumpled to the floor, and Grin's sword dropped to the flagstones with a resigned clatter.

"Act in haste, repent at...repent at...at... Do you remember how the saying goes, Tom?" asked Malphas.

"*Fuck you!*" Tom screamed in English, clutching the back of a chair with his right hand and digging his fingernails into the wood.

"*Tsk. Tsk.* It's rude to speak in a language only some of us understand." Malphas tottered over to Caeli and traced the knife across her cheek. The princess prised open swollen eyes, her head lolling to the side, spit dribbling down her shoulder.

"What's going to happen now, Tom?" asked Malphas. "I have three of your friends on the brink of death, and you have no escape."

Tom squeezed his fingers around the hilt of the sword that still dangled in his left hand. *Adalwolf's scared. Look at him. He knows I can end this. Malphas knows it too. Use the sword to cut my throat. If I kill myself, Adalwolf dies. But that won't help my friends.* He scratched his fingernails on the chair and searched every face waiting on him for an answer.

"I'll give you the eyes," he whispered.

"What was that?" asked Malphas.

"I'll give you the dark eyes. But you have to let my friends go first. Otherwise, I'll kill myself." Tom placed the edge of the sword across his neck to make the point.

Adalwolf's mouth fell open, and Tom thought he heard the king whimper.

Malphas shot a vicious glare at Adalwolf. "That won't be necessary, Tom. I'll release your friends. But first, put the eyes of lost souls on the table. Let me see them."

Slowly, Tom rested his sword on the table, lifted his breastplate and reached inside the front pocket of his pants, retrieving the dark eyes. Clenching them in his right hand, he glanced at Adalwolf again. *How quickly can I reach him? Thrust my fist into the bastard's chest and steal his fucking soul.*

"Place them on the table, Tom," said Malphas.

Tom relaxed his hand, put the dark eyes together on the polished tabletop, and then picked up his sword. Malphas stepped behind Caeli and cut the bonds around her hands. Her arms unwrapped from the column, and she fell to the floor.

"She's alive," said Malphas. "Don't worry."

"Now, Thaly," demanded Tom.

Malphas cut Thaly free, and she stood on quivering legs.

"You see," said Malphas, "I'm a reasonable man."

"My friends need to leave Pergamos."

"I can have Romilda escort them to safety."

Tom flashed a burning gaze at the veiled traitor.

Malphas chuckled. "Or maybe not. I'm sure we can come to an arrangement. Now roll the eyes to me."

"What?"

"Roll the dark eyes along the table to me, and I'll let your friends go. You still have the sword, Tom. You can still threaten suicide and end the life of King Adalwolf in the process. It would disrupt my plans, no doubt. As an act of good faith, roll the eyes to me, and your friends can go, including the grell and the werp."

Dwarrow moved in close to Tom and said, "Follow your instincts."

Tom sighed. With a heavy right hand, stiff and brittle like set plaster, he rolled the eyes of lost souls across the table towards Malphas, their obsidian depths devouring the light as they inched closer to the grasp of the crooked old man. At the same time, Romilda whispered into her son's ear. As if the king had woken from a trance, Adalwolf sprinted from the side of the hall and threw himself onto the table, scooping up the dark eyes.

Malphas' expression went blank. "What are you doing?"

Romilda stepped forward and yanked the veil from her face. "Kill the boy, Adalwolf. Become an immortal. Become the one thing that can rid this world of your twisted father."

"What nonsense is this?"

Romilda turned to Malphas and sneered. "You've always thought yourself smarter than everyone else. The rest of us are nothing more than fools, here to complete your bidding. However, your arrogance is your weakness. I uncovered your plans for our son. Once he's immortal, you'll sacrifice him on the throne of the dead. Use his body of eternal youth to tempt Volerdie to return to our world. Your plan, though, has one major flaw. If Adalwolf becomes immortal, he'll be the only person in Ostamp who can take your life. One immortal can kill another. You're not the only person to have studied scripture, *old man*. Adalwolf is the rightful king of Enthilen, and his eternal rule will be a glory that others only dream of. My son refuses to be a sacrificial doll to serve the conceited ambitions of a madman."

Malphas' face burned so crimson red, Tom thought it might explode. The old man opened his mouth, but no words came out, only froth and bubble. Eventually, he found his voice, a screeching, vile, furious wail that rattled the walls.

"Don't you understand what I'm doing here?" cried Malphas. "Don't any of you understand!? I'm the only person alive who can bring back our one true god. That can lure Volerdie from his failed kingdom in the world of this fool boy." Malphas flailed his arm at Tom before continuing his tirade, "I've seen that world. It's a monstrosity. I'm sure Volerdie longs to abandon it, but he won't unless his soul can enter an eternal vessel. Have you all forgotten the generational desire of the Erstürmen? Since our beginning, we've longed to be led into paradise. Desired it beyond all else. And I'm the one who can do it. I'm the one who can lead our people into paradise!"

"Only Volerdie can open the door to paradise," said Sangria man.

Malphas snarled, marched across the room, clutched the front of the man's robes and pushed a fist up under his bearded chin. "I've done more than any man in history to find that door, Lothar. For fifty yarles, all my thought has been bent on it. For fifty yarles, I've risked every-thing to discover the path to paradise. Focussed every ounce of my will on bringing forth this glorious time."

Malphas released Lothar and stepped in front of Romilda. "How could you ever believe, Queen Mother, I would let you foil my plans? That I would let someone as weak and as pitiful as you snatch away the Erstürmen dream of paradise?" Malphas lashed out at Romilda with his knife, slashing it across her stomach. She clutched her black dress and fell to her knees.

"Leave her!" yelled Adalwolf.

"Kill the boy," Romilda urged in a weakening voice. "The King's Shield are with us, Adalwolf. They'll protect you from Malphas. Take the first step towards your eternal reign."

Malphas turned from Romilda as Adalwolf moved nearer to Tom, seemingly torn between helping his mother or rushing his birth twin. Tom raised the sword to his throat again, thinking his death a small sacrifice to stop this madness. Briefly, the room stilled, everyone fixed in place like porcelain figurines in a macabre diorama.

Then Adalwolf took another step closer to Tom and raised his right fist. Princess Caeli staggered to her feet and screamed, rushing at the king. She wrapped her arms around him from behind, trying to pull him away from Tom.

"Don't do this, Adalwolf," said Caeli. "Please."

Adalwolf turned his body and met the princess face-to-face. Still hold-ing the dark eyes, his right fist became jammed between his chest and hers, pressed close to her heart. Tom grimaced at the agony etched on Caeli's face. He'd seen it before, on Nanna's face in his bedroom eleven

555

years ago. He'd *felt* it before, on Hansen's Bluff. Caeli's body quaked and convulsed, foam spraying from her mouth and splashing across Adalwolf's face. As her spine bent backwards, it pulled Adalwolf tighter into her arms. Although he looked to be fighting to break free, the theft of her soul held him in place like a vice. An agonizing shriek erupted from his mouth as Caeli went limp in his arms and dropped to the floor.

Tom clutched at his chest, feeling Adalwolf's pain coursing through his own body. Then a flash of movement caught his eye. Thaly raced towards Adalwolf, swooped down to retrieve Grin's fallen sword, and with the balance and ferocity of a boulder lion, swung at the king, severing his right hand from his forearm. Adalwolf and Tom screamed simultaneously.

Adalwolf's severed hand plonked on the floor, the dark eyes rolling out from the lifeless palm.

"Now!" cried Dwarrow. "Now's the time!"

Tom dropped his sword, reached for Thaly's hand and bleated, "I'm sorry." He released her, bent down, gathered the dark eyes, and sprinted towards the throne of the dead. Malphas stepped in front of the platform, waiting for Tom to arrive, and Krieg closed in from the side of the room. The red grell had almost intercepted Tom when Dwarrow thrust his walking stick between the grell's legs, sending the giant crashing to the flagstones.

Still lying on the floor, Grin lifted his hand and wrapped it around the end of Krieg's mace, taking the spiked ball and smashing it into the grill of the red grell's helmet. At the same time, the ground beneath the throne hall started to shake. Busts and vases toppled from pedestals, chandeliers swayed and trembled, and cracks appeared in the walls and ceiling.

"We've roused Volerdie's Wrath!" yelled Lothar. He went to help Romilda when a chunk of the ceiling the size of a dining table crashed down on top of him and pinned him to the floor.

Romilda dragged herself to her feet, still clutching her bleeding stomach, and staggered to the double doors. In a pitiful action, Adalwolf collected his severed hand and followed his mother as they both escaped with the fleeing soldiers into the passageway.

A chandelier crashed onto the floor right at Tom's feet. Above him, a hole in the ceiling opened to the night sky, stars shining down on the throne of the dead. He fought to maintain his balance, careering into the table and knocking over chairs as he ran to the throne. Malphas lunged at him, but Grin had regained his feet, throwing his giant frame onto the old man, both of them collapsing to the floor. Tom bounded up the platform's steps and faced the hideous beast crowning the backrest of the throne of the dead, its eye sockets glowing bright crimson. As he reached up to place the dark eyes in the empty sockets, Ende glided out from behind the throne, unmoved by the chaos around her. She raised her sparth, a glint from the razor-sharp metal catching Tom's eye.

"No!" Thaly screamed from behind Tom, sprang onto the platform and flailed her sword, cutting into the pale grell's side.

Thaly faced Tom. "Do what you came here to do. I trust you. I trust you're doing what you believe is right."

Tom relaxed at the surety in Thaly's voice. He would have done whatever she wanted. Clutching the eyes, he reached up to the face of the beast and placed one eye into a socket of crimson, then the other. As soon as the eyes were in position, the throne transformed. Petrified, contorted bodies came alive. A hand from the throne's armrest dropped a stone sphere and reached out to grab Tom's arm, pulling him into the chair. Another arm wrapped around his waist, trapping him in place. Once ossified legs intertwined with his.

"Thaly," he cried. "Help."

Thaly grasped Tom's hand as Malphas loomed behind her with his knife raised. Thaly's grip wavered when the blade plunged into her body.

Another level of chaos ensued, the whole room lurching from side to side, like a boat being tossed by monstrous, foaming waves. A giant mass of marble broke from the ceiling and knocked Malphas off the platform. Thaly clutched at her ribs, blood pouring through trembling fingers.

Then, it all stopped. Everything. Frozen in place. And in the unsettling calm, something entered Tom's mind. A thought of the most distressing and pitiless evil. He smiled — the briefest flicker of triumph. Then the thought vanished.

* * * *

The tremor had subsided, but the damage to Pergamos was complete, its grandiose halls and passages nothing more than rubble. Another wave of Volerdie's Wrath had claimed many victims. Inside the collapsed throne hall, Dwarrow stumbled about the piles of debris, looking for Caeli. Sitting beside an empty throne untouched by the destruction, Grin cradled a dying Thaly, using his desperate, giant hands to try to stem the bleeding from her flank. Behind him, a masked man with a broad-brimmed hat crawled over the rubble.

He removed his face mask and placed his hand on Grin's shoulder. "I will look after her now," said the man.

At the sound of the warm, comforting voice, Thaly turned to the man and saw her own eyes looking back at her.

~ Epilogue ~

Hál gasped for breath and opened her eyes. Draughouls floated to her with pained expressions on their faces.

"Are you alright?" asked Pida.

Hál steadied her breathing. "Yes, thank you, Pida. Water would help."

Pida reached for a cup on a side table next to Hál's bed. "What troubles you?"

"He's gone. The young man. He's left this world for his own."

"Maybe he wasn't the one to release you from your burden?"

"After the failure of Widukind, I was so sure. It appears I was wrong." Propped up on pillows, Hál took a sip from the cup as Pida held it to her lips.

"You once told me the threat of Malphas cannot end by the hand of the young man alone."

"Yes, Pida, you're right. Others must help."

"How does the verse go again?"

Hál nestled her back into the feather pillows and faced her draughoul friend.

"*Blood and bone*
Destroy the throne
Naevus and twin
Blood flows thin

Kindred lost souls
Here and there
Bones to crush
Dust laid bare."

To Be Continued In
Book III:
She Will Rise

Dramatis Personae (Book I and II)

Character	Culture ∞ First appearance	Relations/Notes
Adalwolf Heine	Erstürmen ∞ Sardis	Son of Ewald [disputed] and Romilda
Adcock	Nordmen ∞ Laodicea	Captain of the Vulking
Adela Heine	Erstürmen ∞ Laodicea	Wife of Widald, mother of Helmut, Amelia and Brunhilde
Alaric Heine	Erstürmen ∞ Malang Gunya	Father of Oldaric and Widukind
Alfred Harrington	Dobunni ∞ Bagendon	Member of leadership council
Allum Barron	Erstürmen ∞ Sardis	Son of Yonna and Heady, brother of Rosalie, Petas and Nettie
Alvena Myerscough	Dobunni ∞ Bagendon	Dobunni rebel
Amelia Heine	Erstürmen ∞ Laodicea	Daughter of Widald and Adela, sister of Helmut and Brunhilde
Annian	Weald-grell ∞ Dorfisch	Servant of Jameus and Melinda
Anselm	Erstürmen ∞ Sardis	Inner circle's curate
Athalee [Thaly]	Dobunni ∞ Süden Forst	Adopted daughter of Emelin and Thane, adopted sister of Dayna
Audie	Morundanian ∞ Laodicea	Healer to Lily LáDown

Character	Culture ∞ First appearance	Relations/Notes
Badulf Wolfhart	Erstürmen ∞ Riverlands	Field Commander
Balack	Erstürmen ∞ Sardis	King's Shield
Bert Anderson	Australian ∞ Littlehampton	Father of Tom, husband of Elaine
Brennian	Stone-grell ∞ Malang Gunya	Father of Frennan, grandfather of Grin and Hanni
Bron	Erstürmen ∞ Süden Forst	Soldier
Brunhilde Heine	Erstürmen ∞ Laodicea	Daughter of Widald and Adela, sister of Helmut and Amelia
Brynlee	Unknown ∞ Bagendon	Born in Slumstadt
Caeli Heine	Erstürmen ∞ Sardis	Cousin of Adalwolf, Ewald and Genevea and siblings
Cedrald	Docklander ∞ Laodicea	Dealhia's lieutenant
Conrad	Erstürmen ∞ Sardis	King's Shield, Hunfrid's nephew
Crick	Erstürmen ∞ Sardis	King's Shield
Dalton	Dobunni ∞ Bagendon	Dobunni rebel
Darius Roebolt	Unknown ∞ Sardis	Husband of Ella, father of Tilly
Dayna Wallace	Dobunni ∞ Bagendon	Daughter of Emelin and Thane, adoptive sister of Thaly
Dealhia Rossingbird	Docklander ∞ Laodicea	Mother of Yannus, Master of the Docklands
Dwarrow	Mouldewerp ∞ Scaur Hills	Parent of Wirrikow
Edith	Dobunni ∞ Bagendon	Member of leadership council
Elaine Anderson	Australian ∞ Littlehampton	Mother of Tom, wife of Bert
Ella Roebolt	Unknown ∞ Sardis	Wife of Darius, mother of Tilly, daughter of Zaria
Elmbray	Unknown ∞ Slumstadt	Possible mage

Character	Culture ∞ First appearance	Relations/Notes
Emelin Wallace	Dobunni ∞ Bagendon	Wife of Thane, mother of Dayna, adoptive mother of Thaly
Ende [the pale grell]	Tainted grell ∞ Breadelbane	Servant of Malphas
Eroberung [the white grell]	Tainted grell ∞ Süden Forst	Servant of Malphas
Essiah	Unknown ∞ Sardis	Peasant from Slumstadt
Eutropia	Germalian ∞ Riverlands	Senator in Germalian Conventus
Ewald Heine	Erstürmen ∞ Sardis	Son of Oldaric, father of Adalwolf [disputed], husband of Romilda, brother of Hadufuns, Widald, Gerulf and Genevea
Folcher	Erstürmen ∞ Malang Gunya	Field Commander
Frennan	Stone-grell ∞ Babir Birramal	Husband of Mirrian, father of Grin and Hanni
Fullō	Draughoul ∞ Rārian Falls	Mother of Oldaric and Widukind
Genevea Stansfield [née Heine]	Erstürmen ∞ Sardis	Wife of Jurelle, mother of Jürgen and Saskia, sister of Ewald, Hadufuns, Widald and Gerulf, daughter of Oldaric
Gerulf Heine	Erstürmen ∞ Sardis	Brother of Ewald, Hadufuns, Widald and Genevea, son of Oldaric
Grinnian [Grin]	Stone-grell ∞ Babir Birramal	Son of Frennan and Mirrian, brother of Hanni
Hadufuns Heine	Erstürmen ∞ Süden Forst	Brother of Ewald, Widald, Gerulf and Genevea, son of Oldaric
Hál	Unknown ∞ Revelé	'Sage'

Character	Culture ∞ First appearance	Relations/Notes
Hannian [Hanni]	Stone-grell ∞ Dalman	Daughter of Frennan and Mirrian, sister of Grin
Harris Snape	Unknown ∞ Slumstadt	Son of Wesley
Hartmut Adelmund	Erstürmen ∞ Gestade	Field Commander
Heady Barron	Erstürmen ∞ Sardis	Wife of Yonna, mother of Rosalie, Petas, Nettie and Allum
Helmut Heine	Erstürmen ∞ Laodicea	Son of Widald and Adela, brother of Amelia and Brunhilde
Henruld	Erstürmen ∞ Laodicea	Slave overseer to Myan and Seronan
Hul	Erstürmen ∞ Süden Forst	Soldier
Hunfrid	Erstürmen ∞ Sardis	Master of Executions, Steward of Sardis
Hunger [the black grell]	Tainted grell ∞ Laodicea	Servant of Malphas
Jacob Seamaster	Dobunni ∞ Süden Forst	Dobunni rebel, Field Commander
Jameus	Non-aligned ∞ Bramble Island	Father of Melinda, employer of Annian
Jean Anderson	Australian ∞ Littlehampton	Mother of Bert, grandmother of Tom
Jenrik	Erstürmen ∞ Süden Forst	Stable-keeper
Jurelle Stansfield	Erstürmen ∞ Sardis	Husband of Genevea, father of Jürgen and Saskia, once leader of the Dobunni rebels in Bagendon
Jürgen Stansfield	Erstürmen ∞ Sardis	Son of Jurelle and Genevea, brother of Saskia
Kenelm	Dobunni ∞ Laodicea	Field Commander of the Southern Vale
Krieg [the red grell]	Tainted grell ∞ Laodicea	Servant of Malphas

Character	Culture ∞ First appearance	Relations/Notes
Lily LáDown	Dobunni ∞ Laodicea	Master of the Southern Vale
Lothar [Sangria man]	Erstürmen ∞ Süden Forst	Hoch-Vater of Enthilen
Maida Astley	Dobunni ∞ Bagendon	Member of the leadership council
Maxton Nash	Dobunni ∞ Bagendon	Member of the leadership council, prime lieutenant to Jacob Seamaster
Melinda	Non-aligned ∞ Bramble Island	Daughter of Jameus
Mirrian	Stone-grell ∞ Dalman	Mother of Grin and Hanni, wife of Frennan
Myan [Flea]	Stone-grell ∞ Laodicea	Slave
Nannian	Stone-grell ∞ Dalman	Member of the Mulugan
Nettie Barron	Erstürmen ∞ Sardis	Daughter of Yonna and Heady, sister of Rosalie, Petas and Allum
Oldaric Heine [Malphas]	Erstürmen ∞ Malang Gunya	Son of Alaric, father of Ewald and siblings, brother of Widukind, claimed father of Adalwolf
Payton	Dobunni ∞ Bagendon	Lufu of Jacob
Pelagia	Germalian ∞ Riverlands	Senator in Germalian Conventus
Petas Barron	Erstürmen ∞ Sardis	Son of Yonna and Heady, brother of Rosalie, Nettie and Allum
Pida	Draughoul ∞ Revelé	Servant of Hál
Plunan	Stone-grell ∞ Bindari	Miyan (guardian of the graves)
Quenan	Weald-grell ∞ Dalman	Member of the Mulugan
Randel Beckwith	Dobunni ∞ Bagendon	Dobunni rebel
Roben	Erstürmen ∞ Gestade	Lieutenant to Field Commander Hartmut

Character	Culture ∞ First appearance	Relations/Notes
Rohesia	Dobunni ∞ Bagendon	Dobunni rebel
Rolph	Dobunni ∞ Bagendon	Dobunni rebel
Romilda Heine	Erstürmen ∞ Sardis	Wife of Ewald, mother of Adalwolf
Rosalie Barron	Erstürmen ∞ Sardis	Daughter of Yonna and Heady, sister of Petas, Nettie and Allum
Rostard	Erstürmen ∞ Sardis	King's soothsayer
Ryder	Dobunni ∞ Bagendon	Leader of the Dobunni rebels
Saskia Stansfield	Erstürmen ∞ Sardis	Daughter of Jurelle and Genevea, sister of Jürgen
Scootle	Unknown ∞ Laodicea	Deckhand on the Vulking
Segie	Erstürmen ∞ Sardis	Sergeant-at-arms to General Jurelle
Seronan [Wortle]	Weald-grell ∞ Laodicea	Slave
Sleame Excelis	Terrace-dweller ∞ Laodicea	Master of the Terraces
Snick	Unknown ∞ Slumstadt	Assistant to Elmbray
Strentan	Erstürmen ∞ Malang Gunya	Lieutenant to Field Commander Folcher
Sunan	Stone-grell ∞ Dalman	Member of the Mulugan
Theodoar	Erstürmen ∞ Süden Forst	Field Commander of Süden Forst
Tilly Roebolt	Unknown ∞ Sardis	Daughter of Ella and Darius, granddaughter of Zaria
Tom Anderson	Australian ∞ Littlehampton	Son of Elaine and Bert
Veremund	Erstürmen ∞ Desolate Mountains	General in the King's Shield
Wesley Snape	Unknown ∞ Slumstadt	Father of Harris
Whibly	Unknown ∞ Laodicea	Skullard of the Vulking

Character	Culture ∞ First appearance	Relations/Notes
Widald Heine	Erstürmen ∞ Laodicea	Husband of Adela, father of Helmut, Amelia and Brunhilde, son of Oldaric, brother of Ewald, Hadufuns, Gerulf and Genevea, Master of the King's Quarter
Widukind Heine	Erstürmen ∞ Desolate Mountains	Son of Alaric, brother of Oldaric
Willem	Erstürmen ∞ Riverlands	Lieutenant to General Badulf
Wirrikow	Mouldewerp ∞ Bagendon	Son of Dwarrow
Wyan	Weald-grell ∞ Dalman	Member of the Mulugan
Yannus Rossingbird	Docklander ∞ Laodicea	Son of Dealhia
Yonna Barron	Erstürmen ∞ Sardis	Husband of Heady, father of Rosalie, Petas, Allum and Nettie
Yulan	Weald-grell ∞ Malang Gunya	
Zaria	Unknown ∞ Slumstadt	Father of Ella, grandfather of Tilly
Zenais	Germalian ∞ Riverlands	Senator in Germalian Conventus

Appendix (Book I and II)

A Guide to Ostamp

Abrolous Isles — a group of sparsely populated islands off the east coast of Enthilen.

Al Mōr Sŭrl — watchtower built by the Dobunni in the old settlement of Iglund (an island in the middle of the Anchep River). The watchtower was renamed the Sunrise Keep by the Erstürmen and incorporated into the inner circle of Sardis.

Anchep River — major river running through the north-west of Enthilen and surrounding Sardis.

Babir Birramal — expansive forest covering the southern region of Enthilen, occupied by stone- and weald-grells.

Bagendon — a town built in the Scaur Hills by Dobunni rebels pledged to overthrow the Erstürmen Kingdom.

Barbarians — invaders/marauders from the lands of Morund, Oder and Sexton.

Bargan — the name of one of the two moons in the sky above Ostamp.

Bay of Deception — a bay in Nordland where King Giltbert made his last stand against barbarians.

Bay of Fires — a deep, protected bay surrounded by the Abrolous Isles and often used by barbarian ships for anchorage.

Bethesda — the Dobunni name for Laodicea.

Bilawi tree — a tree with needle-like foliage found in Enthilen.

Bindari — secret location of the graveyard for stone- and weald-grells.

Birraman — stone-grell name for travellers from far-away lands.

Birth twins — two individuals born at precisely the same time, one of them on Earth and the other in Ostamp. Birth twins usually don't look alike and can be of different genders. However, they will always have the same birthmark, which persists until death.

Blood compass — gold pentagram that spins of its own accord after a single point of the star is dipped in the blood of a birth twin when their twin occupies the same world. There were once five compasses; only one remains.

Blue book — a book left for Tom Anderson that translates the Erstürmen language to English, and tells stories of Erstürmen culture.

Bramble Island — a popular fishing destination off the east coast of Enthilen.

Breadelbane — abandoned village on the western edge of the Dambay Plains near the Scaur Hills.

Bullroarer — implement used by Dwarrow to call up his steed, Xaviary, the giant lizard.

Bunbili weed — tobacco-like plant smoked by the Erstürmen.

Calendar of life — the most sacred place in Malang Gunya. An open, circular temple surrounded by marble pillars with paintings decorating the tiled floor depicting essential aspects of grell culture.

Crest — facial tattoo worn by all free grells. Each crest is unique, representing a plant or animal that the grell is responsible for protecting.

Curate — a holy man [priest] in the Erstürmen culture.

Dalman — a secret location in Babir Birramal where stone- and weald-grells hold the sacred ceremony called garrabari.

Dambay Plains — vast grassland region in the centre of Enthilen once occupied by mouldewerps and stone-grells.

Dangal — shelter made by grells from branches, sedges, sticks and leaves.

Da Und Sepcarture — ancient name for the First Scripture.

Deeping pits — Erstürmen gaol adjacent to the outer wall of Sardis.

Desolate Mountains — an extensive mountain range in the north of Enthilen, marking the border between Enthilen and Nordland.

Detranté — narrow pass through the Desolate Mountains connecting Nordland with Enthilen.

Dhawura — grell name for the season of strong winds.

Divine Creator — another name for Volerdie.

Dobunni — settled Enthilen after the stone-grells and built Bethesda, Iglund (a village on an island in the middle of the Anchep River, now the location of Sardis) and the watchtower of Al Mōr Sürl. Came as peaceful settlers rather than invaders. Ousted from much of Enthilen by the Erstürmen and now mostly confined to Bagendon and the Southern Vale in Laodicea.

Dobunni rebels — those Dobunni pledged to overthrow the Erstürmen Kingdom. Most live in Bagendon, but some secretly occupy the Southern Vale.

Docklands — one of the four quarters in Laodicea. Wharf area next to Traders Bay.

Docklands Guard — soldiers tasked with keeping the peace and defending the Docklands from enemies.

Dorfisch — fishing town on the east coast of Enthilen near Gestade.

Draughoul — a creature that has had its soul captured by the eyes of lost souls. They exist in a state of almost suspended animation but aren't 'undead' as such. They can be killed or, over time, their body will wither away to nothing. However, a natural demise can take hundreds to thousands of yarles. Only human-like creatures can become draughouls.

Dwell — name for both a specific hole in the ground where a mould-ewerp lives and the collection of holes in a given location. Akin to 'home'.

Elagear — person in charge of supervising the election of the Dobunni rebel leader.

Embruisia — also called **cerulean honey**. Mind-altering substance used by the Erstürmen.

Enthilen — land in the eastern half of Ostamp occupied by Erstürmen, Dobunni, stone- and weald-grells, mouldewerps and others.

Erstürmen — settled Enthilen after being ousted by barbarians (the ancestors of Nordmen) from what is now called Nordland. Came as invaders and conquerors, claiming Enthilen for themselves regardless of other inhabitants.

Eyes of lost souls — two obsidian glass eyes with flaming pupils. One of the seven treasures from the throne of the dead.

Felsie — also called the pool of reflection. A lake in Laodicea located at the bottom of Hansen's Bluff.

Field Commander — rank in the Erstürmen army usually bestowed on those commanding one of the Erstürmen outposts or significant battles. This rank is immediately above that of lieutenant and below that of General, although many in the military view General and Field Commander as equivalent ranks. The Dobunni have also adopted the rank of Field Commander.

First Scripture — also known as *Da Und Sepcarture* in the old language of Pergamos. Ancient parchment believed to be written by Volerdie in his own blood, documenting his lore and secrets.

Flüsse — the central, most fertile and densely populated region of the Riverlands.

Gadhang — vast ocean to the south of Enthilen. Crossed by the first stone-grell settlers.

Gaping hollow — deep chasm that breaches the floor of the cave leading to the secret passage into Sardis.

Garderobe — small room off the throne hall in Sardis that houses the royal robes.

Gari yala — the speaking stone used to denote permission to speak during grell meetings.

Garrabari — ancient stone- and weald-grell celebration involving dancing and singing, telling stories and sacred ceremony. It happens in Dalman when both Seena and Bargan, the two moons, are full.

Gawimarra — grell name for the harvest season.

Germalia — region in the western half of Ostamp occupied by the Germalians. Main city, Portum.

Gestade — Erstürmen outpost on the central east coast of Enthilen.

Giagan — the sacred panalope tree on the edge of Babir Birramal.

Giba — a stone sacred to stone- and weald-grells that casts its own light.

Giigal — weald-grell city on the south coast of Enthilen.

Grōz Forst — Erstürmen name for Babir Birramal.

Grōz Wüste — large desert in the western half of Ostamp claimed by Germalians (who call it Magna Avium), but includes disputed territory claimed by both Germalians and the Pordillo.

Guma — grell name for the storm season.

Hansen's Bluff — limestone cliff to the north of Laodicea and overlooking the city.

Heilig-jün — twenty-four disciples that follow the teachings of Lothar.

Heine Empire — name for the unbroken reign of kings from the Heine family, beginning with King Giltbert Heine.

Hoch-Vater — one of the titles used by Lothar, meaning 'high father'. The title is permitted to be used only by the most respected curate in Erstürmen culture.

Homage march — march from Babir Birramal to Malang Gunya undertaken every yarle during the long dark by stone- and weald-grell pilgrims to honour the grells who died trying to protect Malang Gunya from the Erstürmen invasion.

Hurna — a horn used to rally troops in battle.

Hurst — tall pinnacle of rock in the Nordargen Sea where Erstürmen kings of old would hide treasures and jewels, and where legend has it, griffins used to nest.

Iglund — Dobunni village, built on the island in the Anchep River that is now home to Sardis.

King's Quarter — one of the four quarters of Laodicea occupied by the Erstürmen.

King's Shield — elite Erstürmen soldiers who have vowed to protect the king with their life.

Kirika — building in most Erstürmen settlements containing a chapel for worshipping Volerdie, and other rooms. Often built underground and above the dungeon.

Laodicea (Bethesda) — port city on the north-east coast of Enthilen at Traders Bay. Divided into four quarters (King's Quarter, Southern Vale, Docklands and The Terraces) and occupied by Erstürmen, Dobunni, and others. Dobunni settlers built the city and named it Bethesda.

Leichenhalle — room where the Erstürmen keep corpses before burning or burial.

Leviathan — enormous statue of a monstrous and mythical sea creature, spanning the heads of Traders Bay.

Levit — young boy or girl tasked with assisting curates.

Lieutenant — rank in the Erstürmen army immediately above that of sergeant-at-arms and below that of Field Commander. Some armies also use **Prime Lieutenant** to denote a rank above Lieutenant.

Lufu — Dobunni word for 'lover'.

Magna Avium — Germalian name for Grōz Wüste.

Malang Gunya — ruined stone-grell city in the middle of the Dambay Plains in Enthilen. The Erstürmen maintain an outpost among the ruins.

Marduk — life-size statue of an ancient man believed to have travelled between worlds and become a god.

Marradir — a boulder in the middle of Dalman on which the stone- and weald-grells wrote and signed the truce that marked the end of tribal conflict between the groups.

Master's Hall — largest building in each quarter of Laodicea used by the quarter's master to conduct various business.

Meduz — grainy, milky alcoholic beverage found throughout Ostamp.

Meladoor tree — barbarians use the timber from this tree to make their ships.

Mendeal herbs — herbs found throughout Enthilen and used for medicinal purposes.

Milbi — small stone shelter used by stone-grells.

Miyan — the name for the grell custodians that tend the graveyards in Bindari.

Morund — a landmass situated east of Ostamp, across the Veiled Occyan, and home to people the Erstürmen and Dobunni call barbarians.

Mouldewerp — long-time inhabitants of Enthilen. Previously lived in the Dambay Plains until ousted by stone-grell settlers who used to hunt mouldewerps for food and sport. Now live in small and secretive groups, mostly in the Scaur Hills.

Mulugan — the group of stone- and weald-grells tasked with decision-making and guiding the two tribes.

Mumbal — grell name for the season of blossoms.

Muwin — a ground spider. Grin's facial crest [tattoo].

Needle — a narrow passage connecting the inner circle of Sardis with the second circle. The only [widely known] way to gain access to the inner courtyard.

Ngulubul — meeting place on the edge of Babir Birramal where grells gather before undertaking the homage march.

Ngurung-ginya — grell name for the season of the long dark.

Nordargen Sea — sea to the north of Nordland.

Nordland — land to the north of Enthilen occupied by Nordmen (descendants of barbarians).

Oder — a landmass situated east of Ostamp, across the Veiled Occyan, and home to people the Erstürmen and Dobunni call barbarians.

Ostamp — landmass that includes Enthilen, Germalia, Nordland, Pordillo Territory, Grōz Wüste and Babir Birramal.

Overseer — leader of a group of twenty grell slaves.

Panalope tree — a favourite tree of stone- and weald-grells used for various purposes. The largest tree species in Babir Birramal.

Pergamos — a lost and ruined city, lying underneath the foundations of Malang Gunya. Believed by some Erstürmen to once be occupied by their ancestors. Also believed to be Volerdie's seat of power when he ruled over Ostamp and other lands.

Pledge Feste — name of the ceremony in which the Dobunni ask for citizens to pledge allegiance to the Dobunni rebels and their cause.

Pordillo Territory — land in the south-west of Ostamp occupied by Pordillo nomads.

Proclaimant of the King — title bestowed on Lothar by Malphas.

Rārian Falls — where the Anchep River tumbles over the Riverlands Escarpment, west of Sardis. The Erstürmen maintain guardhouses at the top and bottom of the road that zig-zags down the escarpment face next to the falls.

Rephaim — the grell soldiers, trained by Krieg and loyal to Malphas.

Revelé — small town in the northern foothills of the Desolate Mountains.

Riverlands — fertile farmland wedged between the Scaur Hills and Groz Wüste. Occupied by unaligned farmers and villagers.

Riverlands Escarpment — steep, sheer cliff running along the western edge of the Scaur Hills.

River Milawa — river in the Dambay Plains and closest river to Malang Gunya.

Rufous — small town on the outskirts of eastern Babir Birramal.

Sardis — royal city of Enthilen, occupied and built by the Erstürmen, comprised of seven concentric circles. Each circle of the city is occupied by Erstürmen of different status; the closer to the inner circle, the higher the status. The inner circle is occupied by the royal family and trusted court.

Scaur Hills — a rocky range running along the western edge of Enthilen marking the border between Enthilen and the Riverlands and eventually Grōz Wüste.

Scripture verses — also called *Polus Sepcarture* in the old language of Pergamos. A black book believed to be an interpretation of the First Scripture. Only curates are typically permitted to read and interpret the scripture verses.

Seena — the name of one of the two moons in the sky above Ostamp.

Sergeant-at-arms — rank in the Erstürmen army immediately above that of soldier and below that of lieutenant.

Serpent oil — highly combustible liquid.

Sexton — a landmass situated east of Ostamp, across the Veiled Occyan, and home to people the Erstürmen and Dobunni call barbarians.

Silver tausen — very rare and valuable coin.

Skullard — the title of a first-mate on a merchant ship.

Slumstadt — shantytown/ghetto on the fringes of Sardis.

Softstone — stone used for grell totems.

Southern Vale — one of the four quarters of Laodicea occupied mostly by Dobunni.

Steward's Shield — soldiers sworn to protect Hunfrid, Steward of Sardis.

Stone-grell — [grell] early inhabitants of the land now known as Enthilen. Built Malang Gunya and occupied the city until being ousted by the Erstürmen. Currently living in isolated shelters known as 'milbis' along the northern edge of Babir Birramal (males only), or as guests of the weald-grells in Giigal (women and children only).

Süden Forst — Erstürmen outpost in the south of Enthilen on the edge of Babir Birramal.

Sunrise Keep — Erstürmen name for Al Mōr Sŭrl; one of the two keeps in the inner circle of Sardis.

Sunset Keep — one of the two keeps in the inner circle of Sardis.

Tainted grell — a stone-grell whose skin has been tainted by Malphas using arcane, evil arts. There are four tainted grells with four different skin colours: Eroberung (white), Krieg (red), Hunger (black), and Ende (pale).

Terraces — one of the four quarters of Laodicea occupied by wealthier residents.

Testament of Fire — a ceremony used by the Dobunni to select rebel soldiers for critically important missions.

The Feign — the southern foothills of the Desolate Mountains.

The Ravage — a fatal disease that spread through Enthilen (mostly Sardis) during the final days of King Ewald's reign and the rise of King Adalwolf.

Throne of the dead — believed to be Volerdie's throne. Made from desiccated, ossified bodies.

Thyatira — ruined city in Nordland, once occupied by the Erstürmen before they were expelled from the north of Ostamp by barbarians.

Totem — softstone about the size of a taper candle. Grells etch the story of their life on its surface and totems are handed down to next-of-kin or buried with the grell.

Traders Bay — bay neighbouring Laodicea, where the city port and docklands are located.

Umbo — title bestowed on the figurehead/commander of the King's Shield. Rarely participates in actual battle.

Undred — giant, horse-like creature with a single, curved horn protruding from its forehead.

Vater — a title given to the tainted grells, meaning 'Father.'

Veiled Occyan — ocean to the east of Enthilen.

Vertraúlich — dressing room for curates.

Volerdie — a god worshipped by the Erstürmen. Also known as the Divine Creator.

Volerdie's Lore — another name for the scripture verses.

Volerdie's Wrath — seismic events that can occur in Enthilen from time to time.

Vulking — merchant ship owned by Captain Adcock.

Weald-grell — [grell] once identified as stone-grells until the tribal war that saw them abandon Malang Gunya and settle on the south coast of Babir Birramal at Giigal.

Weregrim — large, blind hound residing underground in the tunnels connecting to Pergamos.

Whale-master — person in charge of guiding the whales that pull ships.

Wilay — furry, arboreal, cat-sized animal eaten by grells; skin used for clothing.

Worshipful Master — preferred title of Malphas [Oldaric].

Yarle — Erstürmen word for a time-period covering six seasons/three hundred and sixty days.

Yirany — yellow tuber eaten by grells.

Yirra — grell name for the growing season.
Yurali bush — common shrub in Babir Birramal.

Acknowledgements

I don't know about you, but I found *At the End of Everything* quite intense. We descended into some dark places, and I apologise if anything caused you distress. I hope the end justifies the means, as *She Will Rise* attempts to pull us all back from the edge of the abyss.

As usual, many people helped along this journey. Thanks to my wonderful beta readers: Margrit Beemster, Raf Freire, Tansy Roberts and Ashlea Zivanovic. Special thanks to my brother in words, Ian Boyd, for pushing and challenging me all the way with this story. And the biggest thanks to Gayle, who read multiple drafts, proof-read the final draft and tolerated another year of animated discussions about plots and characters.

During the last year, I've had great fun collaborating with fantasy artist Jessie S. A'Bell who has done a brilliant job of bringing some of the characters to life (see my blog: https://relevationtrilogy.com/ for examples). Luke Harris from WorkingType Studio did another professional job of the cover and typesetting. Thanks to Katrin Küker for advice on the interpretation and use of German words.

And thanks to you, my readers, for sticking with the journey. The grand finale awaits us. It's time for the downtrodden to rise up.

About the Author

G. W. Lücke shares a small part of Tasmania with his partner, a mischievous border collie and a menagerie of animals and plants. He has no spare time, but when not writing, he fills the days with gardening, growing food, forest and beach walks, and being healed by nature.

www.ingramcontent.com/pod-product-compliance
Lightning Source LLC
Chambersburg PA
CBHW022358110726
47903CB00004B/1044